Time to Kill

Time to Kill
Book One of The Chivalrous Welshman
The Timekeeper Chronicles

Brooke Shaffer

Black Bear Publishing

Published in Michigan by Black Bear Publishing.

This novel contains an excerpt of *Tick Tock* by Brooke Shaffer. The excerpt is provided for this novel only and may not reflect final published content.

ISBN:
    Hardcover: 978-0-9991392-0-2
    Softcover: 978-0-9991392-1-9
    eBook: 978-0-9991392-2-6

Prologue
April 6, 1855

It was April 6, 1855, when eight year old Tommen Forbes sneaked away from the farm and set to climbing Frost Mountain. It wasn't the actual name of the mountain, just the one he'd given it because, even in the middle of summer, it always seemed to have a layer of frost on it. As he got closer, he saw it was more likely from the salt encrusted on each rock, ground in every tree, and crunching irritably under his feet.

The Appalachian Mountains were famous for the salt and copper buried beneath them, though making his way through secret trails that only a child knows and can access, Tommen wondered why they bothered digging underground to get to the salt and copper when they could just as easily scrape it off the rock face.

Then he saw it. A sort of reflection off salt crystals or water, he didn't know, but it drew his attention to a gaping hole in the side of the mountain, not far from where he climbed. He picked his way there.

It was indeed a hole, most likely a closed-off mine, though poorly closed off at best. A few boulders had been messily rolled near the entrance and then abandoned, as if they were just too heavy to go even the last little distance. Two large trees had been felled in front of the mouth instead but even those were now rotting. As he got closer, he saw one of the boulders had something etched into it. Tommen could not read well, but he knew his letters from the Bible his pa read from each night. The letters read K-E-E-P O-U-T B-E-W-A-R-E.

Such letters meant as much an invitation as a warning as Tommen scrambled over the rotting trees to get to the cave. When he

1

stood fully in the cave, the boulders and the trees blocked most of the light, but it didn't scare him, even as he felt a chill creep over him. The light flickered and wavered, probably as clouds passed over the sun.

Tommen went into the cave, constantly daring himself to take just one more step, trying to focus more on how much the salt irritated him rather than the darkness or the cold or how his vision seemed to waver and change. Just a trick of the dark, he told himself. His brother Teo talked about it sometimes when he came home from the mines. "The darkness will play tricks on you. Best you can do is try to play a few tricks yourself."

The little boy didn't know too many tricks, but he knew that the best way to combat silence was to make noise. So he did. He yelled into the darkness.

"Hello!"

And the darkness answered. "Hello! Hello!"

"I'm Tommen!" he yelled.

And the darkness yelled back. "Tommen! Tommen!"

Tommen grinned stupidly, his fear gone, and rather excited by his find. He pulled his arms close and jumped into the air. "Yeah!"

But the darkness did not share his glee this time, and the sound that returned to the little boy was one that he would swear until the day he died was the shrill shriek of a tortured soul or even a demon. Tommen felt wet run down his leg even as he burst into tears, turned, and ran screaming back the way he came.

He wasn't sure if he had taken a wrong turn or what, but he tripped over something in the darkness. He didn't remember anything being in his way when he entered the cave, and it didn't clatter like rocks. Either way, it threw Tommen flat on his face, scraping his cheeks, his hands, tearing his pants. Sniffling but too shocked and too tired to cry, Tommen got to his hands and knees. He felt something under one hand, leather or some such thing.

His eyes slowly cleared of tears and adjusted to a faint gloom, and he could see that he held a leather-bound book. Then he looked up and screamed again as the grin of a rotted skeleton looked down upon him. Tommen had scattered the legs when he tripped over them, but moss and lichens held the torso upright to sit in judgment of any who disturbed the mine.

Tommen stood and started running. He didn't care where as long as he followed the light and made it out.

The mouth of the cave loomed wide before him, the moon just starting to peek over the horizon. Tommen burst from between the boulders and ran full-speed down the slope, fighting for balance and struggling to locate his little secret trails but finding none. Where once he had a sure step, his foot met rock or tree and he fell several times, once losing the book for a minute until he found it a short distance away.

At last the tree line cleared, and he broke into the open, running across a flat, rocky surface to the crest of a steep slope. Spread out before him was a sea of lights and unfamiliar sounds, like thousands of fireflies flickering and bears growling. He stepped back onto the rocky surface, looking around and seeing that the surface had white and yellow lines painted on it. Suddenly, his shadow appeared. He turned just in time to see the bright glowing eyes and roar of a demon. Then he was flying.

The date was August 12, 2005.

Chapter One
Birthday

Tommen gripped his backpack strap harder, pretending it was Tyler's throat, pretending he could crush it, even though he knew that in real life, he wouldn't do it. The old Cadillac squealed to a stop in front of him. He tossed the backpack in the backseat and slid guiltily into the front, turning his body toward the outside, holding the bloody napkins under his nose as discreetly as he could, even as he wore down the clean ones in his pocket.

"What happened?" Walter demanded, his bushy blond mustache twitching irritably, fingers tapping on the steering wheel as he pulled out of the school parking lot in the middle of the day. A few seniors returning from open-campus lunch saw the car. They pointed and snickered and hurried away, as if afraid Detective Forbes would suddenly pull over and arrest them for mockery.

"Tyler Freeman happened," Tommen mumbled, trading his soaked napkins for a couple clean ones, seeing a new tear in his coat. Well, one more to add to all the others.

"What about him?"

Only that he'd been the class bully since fourth grade and Tommen had always been his go-to target when he needed someone easily-provoked to fight. And Tommen knew it. And still he gave in. Like calling Marty McFly a chicken, he just couldn't back down.

"He started the fight," Tommen began.

"So he just came up and punched you point-blank?"

"No." Tommen shifted in his seat. "He interrupted me when I was talking to Emily."

"The crime of the century I'm sure."

"You know, this is why I don't talk to you. You don't care about what happened; you just like making sarcastic remarks."

"No, I make the sarcastic remarks because I know you are a young man trying to carve out his place in the universe, and you feel the need to defend yourself. Now, what—happened?"

Tommen hated it when Walter was right. "He said I would never have a chance at asking Emily to the homecoming dance and I should just give up. He called me weak, and then he shoved Emily, kind of got between me and her. I tried to get around him, he shoved me back into my locker. I told him if he wanted to go with her to the dance, he would have to challenge me and go through me. I try to kind of force my way around him, he grabs me and punches me."

Walter sighed, a few loose mustache hairs fluttering in the breeze. "Tommen, you know things just aren't done that way anymore. You've been here for eight years now."

Tommen shifted to face him, wincing at the pain in his face. "Which puts me almost exactly half my life at my old home and half my life in my new home. My pa always taught me to be respectful. I guess I'm more offended that basic respect and human decency from back then is considered some sort of chivalrous superpower today."

"Hardly a superpower."

"Why? I've never seen anyone hold open a door for a girl because she's a girl, or seat her at a table. It's cause for gossip and whispering and rumors. I'm a target for bullies like Tyler because I'm a nice guy." He looked out the window where thick city life gave way to less-dense outskirts.

"Fair enough. So tell me this: why keep doing it? Either you enjoy fighting, or you still believe in that chivalry regardless of what may come."

Tommen chuckled. "I have to live up to my name somehow. Where would I be if The Chivalrous Welshman stopped being chivalrous?"

He removed the bloody napkins and flipped down the visor to see the mirror. The left side of his face was turning all sorts of pretty colors; the main swelling was around his cheek but it didn't make the pressure on his eye any less uncomfortable. He replaced the napkins again and noted that the bleeding had largely subsided.

"Tommen, you don't have to live up to a name that someone else gave you," Walter was saying, "especially when that name was given to you out of spite and mockery. I may be old, but I believe we call that a label."

Tommen scoffed as he flipped the visor back up. "Yeah, and there was this big movement back in the 00's to get rid of the shame and embarrassment of labels." He shook his head. "Movements started by students only last as long as those students are in school. Movements started by adults never catch on because your ideas of what needs to change and how, are different than what we think needs to change and how."

Walter gave Tommen a sideways glance. For all intents and purposes, Walter was a funny-looking guy. About six feet two inches, 200 pounds, and, despite his blond mustache, he had brown hair and piercing blue eyes. "All right then," he said matter-of-factly, "what do you think needs to change, and how is that going to be effectively accomplished?"

"I think more respect needs to be given to chivalry. And Welshmen, but mostly chivalry."

Walter grinned. "Tommen, you're made fun of for it now, but once you get out of high school, women will be flocking to you just to hear you speak."

"Oh, good, I always wanted to be surrounded by crass, shallow, petty women."

Walter rolled his eyes. "Quite frankly, what I think needs to happen is to make a bigger deal out of being intelligent and less of a deal out of drama."

Tommen shook his head. "Good luck on that."

"Which also includes respecting chivalry so that it's no longer a cause for gossip and rumors; it's just simply basic respect and human decency."

Tommen caught Walter's gaze and managed a swollen half-smile. "Thanks."

"Make no mistake; I do not approve of the fighting. But as long as you don't throw the first punch, I guess I can't fault you too much."

They pulled into the driveway then, sitting in front of a single-story ranch-style home. Technically there was an attached garage, but it was rather full of tools and other assorted items and projects that Walter barely got around to. The thought gnawed at Tommen's gut and he felt guilt creep in there, too, that he'd interrupted Walter's day off. As he walked in the kitchen, he saw lunch still set out on the table — leftover chili long since cold.

"Did you get lunch?" Walter asked, walking in behind him.

"Huh? Oh, yeah."

Tommen moved out of Walter's way as best he could, pressing himself into a tiny alcove that housed the washer and dryer. The house wasn't tiny, but a mish-mash of thrown-together rooms and poor taste in interior design, a leftover relic from World War II — or maybe World War I — whose last major renovation had been the 1960's. Stainless steel appliances clashed atrociously with faded yellow wallpaper and peeling vinyl in the kitchen. The countertops were cut and hacked from years of knife abuse. Someone had once tried to paint the cabinets black, but that layer had largely flaked and peeled off to reveal several more layers of paint — gray, yellow, blue, even a glimpse of the original wood below. Perhaps the only thing that tempered such a decorating disaster was the curiosity of how the oversized appliances even fit in the kitchen at all. They might not have except for the tiny wooden table with chewed up legs huddled like a mouse in the center of the room, more TV tray than table. Tommen and Walter rarely ate together, but they couldn't anyway even if they wanted to; the table was barely big enough for Walter, his food, and the morning newspaper folded up.

"Get yourself cleaned up, then start on your homework," Walter said, throwing the chili in the microwave before easing back into his chair and opening the newspaper.

"Is there still leftover pizza?" Tommen wondered diplomatically. He might have checked himself except the fridge wouldn't open as long as someone was occupying the seat at the table.

"I haven't eaten any," Walter replied, his expression telling Tommen that despite their friendly chat in the car, he was still in trouble, and Tommen hurried off.

The living room wasn't much better than the kitchen as far as interior design. The shag carpet had certainly seen better days, despite being hidden under multiple layers of equally shaggy rugs whose patterns varied from true 60's hippie paisley and flower power, to equally true 60's hippie earth-tones and Indian-pattern. Part of the walls were wood paneling in remarkably good shape. The wallpaper in the rest of the living room was some metallic pattern but the metallic had faded decades ago, leaving just a single, bland color. This was saved, thankfully, by a number of old posters to break up the boredom, though Tommen questioned whether Elvis and retro UFO posters were really much of an improvement. The sofa would have been a screaming testament to flower power, but years of wear and tear and probably some animal urine had reduced neon flowers to wilted Valentine's leftovers. The TV was an odd antique from the days when flatscreens were just coming out. Still enormous box TVs that weighed a bajillion pounds, but the screen was flat. Perhaps the only furniture in the living room that had been replaced in the last decade was Walter's recliner, an oversized LaZboy perfectly contoured to his napping form.

Tommen's bedroom was probably the most updated-looking room in the whole house, though if Walter was right, his bedroom was the original house, barely more than a shed for some miner. Ever since, occupants of the house had seen fit to just continue adding as needed. When Tommen had taken up residence when he was eight, the room had been little more than a storage room, and not well-insulated at that, and it had been a long first winter.

These days, Tommen's room had carpet—thankfully not

shag—and drywall with insulation. It hadn't been painted since he moved in. It was still the same dull gray—well, technically green—he'd picked out years ago and still bore the patch that Walter had done after a fight in which Tommen had punched the wall, nearly electrocuting himself when he came within a hair of the switch (the wiring in the house was not exactly up to snuff). He saw that patch every time he walked out of the room, and truthfully wished he could either undo it or cover it up. Elsewhere around the room, Tommen chose to decorate with bookcases overflowing with books, trinkets, and doo-dads. His most prized possession was his stereo, an impressive rig set-up for vinyl, cassette, compact disc, and a variety of mp3 players. Posters also littered his walls, depicting various bands, events, even a few plays.

Tommen's bed was easily the newest piece of furniture in the entire house, bought just three years ago when he finally had his growth spurt and seemed to outgrow his old bed overnight. He still wasn't convinced that he was done growing, though. There was no way he could stop at only five foot ten. No, he had to make it to six foot before he would be happy.

He dropped his backpack among the mess of tangled blankets on the bed and headed to the bathroom. It, too, was a tragic mess of 60's decor, perhaps the worst offender in the house. It was like some sort of sick 60's paint beast had gotten high on psychedelics, gotten sick afterwards, vomited yellow, then had some kind of gray diarrhea to try and cover it up, then misted it with blue to try and make it all better. Tommen could think of no possible reality where a solid yellow sink, a blue and gray tub, a yellow toilet, and blue, yellow, and gray tile made any kind of sense. It was probably even worse in full color.

Tommen looked at himself in the mirror and almost wished he hadn't. He almost couldn't for the swelling around his left eye. Pretty much the entire left side of his face was black and blue and swollen like a balloon. He ran his tongue over his teeth; none of them felt loose. Maybe it was that which helped take away some of pain that came simply from stress. He'd already lost two permanent teeth because of fighting; he didn't need to lose their porcelain replacements, nor add any more to the ranks.

He shook his head. Some days he felt the idiot. Some days he had the presence of mind to actually think more than a day ahead and consider what his life's story would be. If, on the extremely off-chance, one day he had kids, what would he tell them? "I got in fights, got my brains beat in and my teeth knocked out"?

But for all his resolve to be the bigger man, it truly was just like calling Marty McFly chicken. Call him that and he'll do anything. Challenge Tommen's code of honor and chivalry, and watch him fight to the death to defend his honor or the honor of others. As if honor meant anything these days.

Tommen took a breath and put his hands out on the tiny countertop. He could do it. He could heal himself. All he had to do was Band himself into a faster Time, reduce three days of healing into three minutes. There was just one problem—two if he wanted to get technical. First, he couldn't double Band. He would literally experience three full days. He could do anything in that time, three days all to himself while he waited for his face to heal. But then he would only come back to the same day it had been. It was like taking a detour on a Monday, going through Tuesday, Wednesday, and Thursday all by himself, then returning to Monday, and as far as the rest of the world was concerned, only three minutes had passed. Double Banding would allow his body to heal over three days while his mind perceived the same three minutes everyone else did.

And second to that point, he couldn't pinpoint Band. If he'd broken his finger and could pinpoint Band—and double Band for that matter, he could heal his finger extremely quickly with virtually no side effects. As it was, he would have to Band his entire body. Generally speaking, metabolic processes were moderately suspended within Bands so he wouldn't feel hunger, thirst, or the need to relive himself. Until he ended the Band. Then all that would catch up to him. Pinpoint Banding would allow him to focus on only his wounds.

The worst side effect would be a tingling sensation and possible temporary drop in body temperature and blood pressure because of the nerves and blood vessels trying to get back on the same page with the rest of the body.

"So, how many days will you be gone?" Walter asked, leaning on the wall opposite the bathroom door, chili in hand.

Tommen sighed. "I don't even mind the colors; I just hate the swelling."

Walter gave him a cheeky grin. "Aren't you the one who likes to quote your pa? And didn't you say he once told you that, 'If the fist comes first, don't be surprised by what comes next'?"

"To which Teo would add, 'If it's not another fist, it's probably the sheriff,' " Tommen grumbled.

"In this case, it's swelling, discomfort and discoloration," Walter concluded.

"True, but I do have my review coming up. I have to practice for that."

"Tommen, I have little doubt that you are more than proficient in Banding to satisfy the Hands. Unless you haven't been Banding in these fights of yours?"

Tommen grumbled under his breath but couldn't deny it as he turned to look at Walter. "If I don't, you know what will happen. It's why you decided to teach me early in the first place."

Walter nodded around a mouthful of chili. "Very true. And believe me when I say that I am very glad that you use it with such restraint, rather than playing it up and truly hurting Tyler."

Tommen shrugged. "I already have a reputation for fighting. I don't need to get arrested by my own dad. And you don't need to try to explain that one to the guys at the precinct."

"And it works well for you on your review."

"What, that I'm a probationary Timekeeper who gets his ass kicked all the time?"

"Watch your language, Tommen. I'm talking about using restraint so as not to introduce Time to a greater society that isn't ready for it. And in that restraint, you have great control over your abilities, more so than some other probies I've seen. You'll have no trouble in the skill test."

"Yay for me." Tommen looked back in the mirror. He took a breath and Banded.

Banding wasn't difficult. It didn't hurt. There was no noise to indicate the start or end. Depending on the strength of the Band, there wasn't even much of a feel to slipping into one except maybe like the feeling of a tug of wind on the hair. In Tommen's mind, his very being, he could feel the Band, in the same way that one might hear the hum of a refrigerator; it was always there to remind him that he was in a Band, but he could choose to listen to it or not. He could choose to adjust the Band or step out of it.

He'd barely had the thought before he felt a "push" on his Band, like someone else had slipped into it. But as he looked in the mirror, he watched the swelling on his face go down in only seconds, before the Band was broken completely, arbitrarily, sucking the breath from his lungs and making him cough violently. He looked at Walter, eyes watering, ears ringing, throat burning.

"You could have warned me," Tommen rasped.

"I only took down the swelling," Walter told him. "The colors will have to stay, otherwise it'll be mighty suspicious at school tomorrow."

Tommen sighed and spit in the sink. "Thanks."

"You're welcome," Walter replied amiably, scraping the rest of his chili. "Now, get your homework done. What time do you have to be to work?"

"Three."

"Plenty of time then."

He might have been talking about time for Tommen to do his homework, but more likely he was talking about having enough time to take a nap. It was impossible to Band while unconscious, else either of them would gladly stay up to the wee hours of the morning doing work or pursuing hobbies, take an eight-hour nap in only a few seconds, and carry on like normal.

Even so, Tommen retreated to his room to start his homework—door open, music low.

Normally, Tommen rode the bus from school straight to work, and Walter would pick him up when he got off. Or he might walk home if Walter was busy or the weather was nice, or if he just felt like it. But today was an odd day. Walter initially seemed confused when Tommen woke him up from his nap, but soon they were out the door, heading back toward the city.

"Finish your homework?" Walter asked.

"Yeah," Tommen lied, looking out the window.

Tommen was ready for his driver's training to start; the first class was in a week. He'd had to pay for it himself with his own money, but he knew it would be well worth it. To not have to ride the bus, to be able to go out for lunch, to be able to go somewhere after work like a movie or something. Car meant freedom. He'd already set aside for the second segment of driver's training and was already saving for his first vehicle. He wasn't about to get stuck in the trap of having his license but still having to borrow a car.

They pulled up into the parking lot of Bakery na hÉireann just as Tommen's bus made the turn at the light. Tommen got out, confused for just a second until he realized he didn't have to lug his backpack in with him. He paused as Walter got out also.

"I can go to work by myself," Tommen told him.

"And I can buy a pastry by myself, thank you," Walter replied.

Tommen felt his cheeks burn hot as he turned and hurried into the store.

The bakery wasn't a huge place; the dining room could hold thirty-seven people according to the fire marshall—four booths, a couple tables, the rest barstools lining the large bay windows and part of the counter which ran two-thirds the length of the store, half of which was a dedicated display case showing off any number and variety of baked goodies throughout the day. The floor of the dining room was concrete like the rest of the shop, but painted and lacquered so it resembled the countertops — black granite flecked with silver and gray, slightly marked and scuffed from use. The walls were tasteful, calming earth tones, grays and browns accented with blue and beige.

Perhaps the most unique thing about the store, however, was its choice of decor. The owners of the bakery, and by default Tommen's bosses, were Micaiah and Micah Durvin, identical Irish twins and proud of it. They put their heritage on display with everything but the neon sign. The signs they did have were bilingual, as were the menus and the website. Little decorative knick-knacks around the store all had some sort of Irish or Celtic theme — decorated Celtic knots, four-leaf clovers, a beautifully illustrated Gaelic poem which Micah had explained was a traditional Irish blessing.

But in spite of the explosion of Ireland that went on in the store's decor, the twins themselves were rather plain. Both stood roughly six foot with dark brown hair. Micaiah, the elder twin, elected to work out and had a general bulk to him that Micah did not care to emulate, and so remained lanky and awkward. Micaiah also kept a general stubble about his face and chin, though he dared not grow his beard more than that as, according to him, it was an atrocious conglomeration of brown, blond, and red. Micah avoided the whole thing by just keeping a smooth face.

It was the bearded twin who met them as the little bell jingled on the door when they walked in.

"Dia daoibh," Tommen muttered hastily as he went to the back to punch in and find an apron.

"Bhí muid buartha nuair a chuaigh an bus thart agus níor tháinig tú amach," Micah said, meeting him in the kitchen. (We were worried when the bus passed by and you didn't get off.)

"Tá a fhios agam, tá brón orm," Tommen told him. (I know, I'm sorry.)

"Another fight?" Micaiah asked Walter up front even as Tommen heard the door on the display case slide open.

"Yes," Walter sighed. He said more that Tommen couldn't catch.

"Tyler aris?" Micah asked from across the table where he beat on some dough. (Tyler again?)

Tommen nodded.

"An chabhraigh Walter leat?" (Did Walter help you?)

Another nod.

That was the other thing about the twins: they were Timekeepers just like Walter. Well, not exactly like. They were Lieutenants where Walter was the District Captain. They answered to him. It was probably the only reason why they hadn't fired him for being to work late because of detention on multiple occasions.

Technically, he'd been "working" at the bakery since he was about ten, but officially he'd only been there about two years. Mostly, he was there so the twins could get the behind-the-scenes work done without having to worry about the counter. Usually that meant Micah in the kitchen baking while Micaiah manned the office working on invoices and billing. Between the three of them, and with a lot of help from Time and their Banding abilities, the little bakery cranked out three times their estimated baking capacity, and no one could figure out how.

Tommen tried to put on a good face as he walked back up to the counter.

"S'mae, p'nawn da," he greeted coyly. (Hi, good afternoon.)

"Hey now, none of that foreign stuff in here," Micaiah said, jabbing him in the ribs.

"Mae'n ddrwg gen i," Tommen continued. He looked at Walter. *"Mwynhewch eich bwyd. Da boch chi."* (Sorry. Enjoy your food. See you later.)

Even Walter had to smile. *"Hwyl, Tommen."* (Bye, Tommen.)

He took his little wax paper bag and headed out the door, leaving Tommen to fend for himself for the next four hours.

"So, we've got a birthday party coming in sometime in the next half hour," Micaiah told him and opened the cold case in the front of the store behind the counter. "Here's the cake. Mom says they're just doing cake and ice cream, and they're heading elsewhere for presents and stuff. Think you can handle it?"

"Not my first birthday party," Tommen told him.

Micaiah patted him on the shoulder. "Good man."

Tommen went to the cold case and looked at the cake within. Rectangular cake decorated with orange, yellow, and white icing, wishing Amanda a happy seventh birthday, and littered with little crunchy edible flowers.

Bakery na hÉireann serviced most all baking needs—donuts, cookies, cake, bread, cinnamon rolls, brownies. If it was baked, it was probably available. As such, they stayed fairly busy, even through winter. Tommen rang up eight cookies, a dozen cinnamon rolls, four donuts, and two loaves of bread before the birthday party entourage crashed through the front door.

Suddenly, little girls were everywhere. A couple of them made for a booth where they huddled secretively under the table. A few picked a table and scraped the chairs noisily across the floor before clambering into the seats. Most of the girls, though, made for the barstools, all them enamored with the height like they could never imagine being—gasp—five feet tall.

A few of them chose the barstools at the counter, almost climbing on the counter itself as they watched the TV mounted on the wall. It was only the weather channel. Out of the corner of his eye, Tommen saw Micaiah in the office—one wall of which served as the other half of the equation of the wall on which the TV was mounted. The other interior office wall was actually a huge window, split between the front and the kitchen with separate blinds for both. Micaiah met Tommen's gaze and gave him the "If the parents don't wrangle these kids, you'll have to, because they won't like it if I have to" look before yanking on the cord and dropping the blinds.

Tommen sighed and retrieved the TV remote, finding some cartoons just as the parent—yes, one single adult—showed up and managed to get the children in some semblance of order before approaching the counter.

"Birthday party for Amanda," she said breathlessly, bouncing on her toes while a very pissed baby squirmed and whined in a little front baby holder thing.

Tommen nodded, figuring that saying nothing was safer than trying to be polite when he didn't feel like it. He retrieved the cake while the woman gathered all the little girls from all corners of the store and herded them to a couple tables within sight line of the TV.

While he walked across the floor with the cake, Tommen reflected on places that made their employees do some kind of birthday song and dance. Why did they bother? Why did they do it? Why did people celebrate their birthdays so lavishly? What was the purpose of it all? Tommen had never cared for his birthday that much when he was little. In truth, he wasn't sure how old he was. Yeah, sixteen, a little hard to go wrong, especially when he'd spent eight years in a society that placed so much emphasis on birthdays, age, driving age, smoking age, drinking age, anti-aging. But prior to stepping in that cave, he actually hadn't been sure if he'd been six or seven or eight. According to Walter, it was the emergency room doctor who'd decided he was eight, and that's what they went with.

"I'm this many!" one little girl, presumably the birthday girl judging by her tutu and blue birthday hat, squealed, holding up seven tiny fingers.

"Really?" Tommen said with mock interest.

"How many are you?"

"I'm afraid that would take a lot more fingers and toes." He smiled smugly and squatted down to the children's eye level. "I am one hundred and sixty-six years old."

The girls erupted in squeals of laughter that literally hurt Tommen's ears and probably made him a little deaf.

"You can't be that old!" another girl said. "That's impossible!"

"And how did you get to be that old?" the mom wondered, going along with what she assumed to be a game. The girls abruptly fell silent and waited for his answer.

"I stepped into a magical cave and was transported a hundred and fifty years into the future," Tommen told them mysteriously.

Again, squeals of laughter. Again, going deaf.

Tommen laughed along hollowly and gave the mom the speech about "if they needed anything." She thanked him and he retreated behind the counter and, after serving up a couple brownies and another pre-ordered cake, headed back to the kitchen.

To those who could see them, different types of Bands were different colors. Fast Bands were blue and Slow Bands were orange. The stronger the Band, the more intense the color. And the kitchen was crawling with color. Micah was a master of Band-baking as he called it, moving with fluid grace like some sort of baking ballerina.

"An bhfuil cabhrú de dhíth ort?" he asked, pausing in his work and slipping out of his Band. (Need help?)

"Ó, níl," Tommen answered. (Oh, no.)

"An bhfuil rud éigin cearr?" (Something wrong?)

"Níl. Táim ag briseadh ón gcóisir lá breithe agus ó fiche cailín." (No. Just taking a breather from the birthday party and twenty little girls.)

"Ní féidir liom an milleán a chur ort." Micah pointed. *"Tabhair dom an spadal seo."* (I don't blame you. Hand me that spatula.)

Tommen handed over the utensil. *"Cén chaoi a fhásann nithe beaga bearránacha den tsórt sin suas le bheith ina gcailíní téisiúla ar aon nós?"* (How do such annoying little things turn into hot chicks, anyway?)

Micah chuckled. *"An bealach céanna agus a fhásann dailtíní béalscaoilte suas le bheith ina bhfir óga dathúla."* (The same way big-mouthed little brats turn into handsome teenage boys.)

Tommen had a smart reply to that but was interrupted by the little service bell. When he returned to the counter, he found the mom. He got her some more napkins, and was too grateful to have to service someone who just couldn't make up their mind on what they wanted for an afternoon sweet.

Thankfully, with just cake and ice cream, the birthday party wrapped up pretty quickly, the little girls running outside like a pack of laughing hyenas while the mom was torn between trying to clean up the mess and chase after them before one of them got hit by a car. Finally, wanting nothing more than to just see them all gone, Tommen went over to her.

"I got it," he told her, hoping he sounded caring instead of cranky.

She straightened, the baby still fussing. "Oh, no, I mean, we made the mess. It's only right that—"

"I got it."

She still seemed uncertain but took the hint, grabbed her purse, and left. The store empty, Tommen dragged a trash to the table and did a massive sweep of cups, plates, and napkins into the bin. He stopped when he got to a perfectly preserved piece of cake with a single crunchy edible flower on it and a sticky note on the paper plate: Happy 166th Birthday.

Tommen stared at the note for a minute, almost oblivious to a customer walking in. He wasn't sure what they ordered. Then he was back staring at the piece of cake. Finally he sighed and swept the cake into the trash with the rest. Birthdays were for children of the twenty-first century.

Tommen tied off the trash bag, took it out to the dumpster, then returned to wipe down the tables and put them back in their proper spots. Lastly, he turned the TV back to the weather channel before telling Micah he was taking a quick break. He didn't smoke, and Banding allowed him to take as many breaks as he wanted. But sometimes he just needed to be alone. Sometimes he just wanted to tell his story to someone normal and not have them think he was crazy.

Chapter Two
School Daze

Tommen had been getting in fights since he was ten years old. His first fight had landed him in the hospital, which had prompted Walter to teach him to Band three years earlier than was normal for a human Timekeeper.

Banding managed to keep him out of the hospital, but that didn't mean it kept him out of trouble entirely, and any time he got in a fight, the news flew through school like a new drug. Somehow, it was never boring, never, "Oh, Tommen got in a fight? Gee, that's new."

He knew why. He could hear them whispering behind him on the bus, snickering as he walked into the school and meandered his way through the halls until he found his locker.

There goes The Chivalrous Welshman, defender of women, the weak, the poor and destitute, the honor of others and himself. See how he kneels to those in authority and vows his life and sword to their cause and whims. Behold as he fights fair and clean, waits for his opponent to be ready before engaging, and never even considers a sucker punch. Watch as he slays dragons and protects the fair maiden, but never lets it cross his mind to compromise her honor. Such a noble man and a gentleman, the epitome of human greatness and potential. Behold, brethren, for we shall never see another like him.

It was a lovely, bittersweet monologue he'd cooked up himself from the bits and pieces of mocking gossip that floated around about him. Not all of it was true, of course. He had plenty of problems with authority; he was just smart enough not to challenge them unless he could destroy them. Since he couldn't do that, he had to play by their rules, which meant waiting for Tyler to throw the first punch. And he was never opposed to taking a sucker punch opportunity. There just never were any. Tyler wasn't an elementary school bully looking for lunch money; he was, for all intents and purposes, a street thug who had fights under his belt, which happened to be black in a number of martial arts.

And that whole bit about not compromising fair maidens? True, only in that he'd never had a girlfriend long enough to get into bed with. He didn't believe in sex on a first date, but he wasn't entirely his father's son anymore. Maybe if the girl was noble enough and had enough of a spine to want to wait, that much he could honor. But as it was, playing the shy maiden while wearing short shorts and a low-cut top, that was too much of an ignoble tease to be taken seriously on any stance other than "sleep with me."

"Good morning, Tommen," Mr. Layman said, walking up. He leaned against a locker two down from Tommen's. Layman was the poster child for the "big and tall" section in the men's department, six-foot-six, 250 pounds of mostly muscle, hair buzzed like a Marine, gaze as condemning as a priest. But, in a school of over a thousand students, little Miss Johnson from elementary school would command no respect, and as evidenced from the fight yesterday, Layman had gotten in the middle of a number of fights to separate students. He commanded respect.

"Good morning, sir," Tommen mumbled, not looking at him, fiddling in his backpack like he'd lost something.

"You're looking better this morning," Layman observed casually.

"A hot shower does wonders."

"Indeed it does. I expect we won't have any trouble today?"

"I never plan on it," Tommen told him, shutting his locker and looking at him. "Some days it just finds me."

But it wouldn't today because Tyler had been suspended for three days.

Layman nodded slowly. "Have a good day, Mr. Forbes."

It was his way of telling Tommen that he would be watching him. Tommen never understood why he was the victim of the bullying *and* the scrutiny. Tyler was always the instigator. Tommen was just his unlucky victim, had been for the last six years.

"Hey, Tommen."

He stopped and whirled as Emily approached him. His breath caught in his throat. Her hair was dyed blond this week, styled so as to look windswept, but with grace. Her makeup reminded him of the lonely girl on a street corner in the rain, waiting for a bus in order to run from it all, whatever "it" was. She wore flat sandals revealing pink-painted toenails peeping out from under ripped jeans, and a yellow top cut so low that her purple bra peeked through at the "V." Unless she was sleeping with the Powers That Be, there was no way she wasn't in violation of the school dress code. Not that Tommen was complaining.

"Emily," he stated dumbly.

"You're looking better," she said meekly, her cool breath wafting with the smell of fresh gum.

"Yeah, um, it really wasn't all that bad."

"That's good. Yeah." She nodded and looked away briefly. "Yeah, so, Mariah was saying that you were trying to ask me to the homecoming dance before Tyler interrupted us."

"Yes!" His sharp word made her take a step back. He felt his cheeks burn. "Um, yeah. I was. Trying to ask you. To the dance, I mean. Trying to ask you to the dance. I was. Will you?"

Emily managed a lopsided smile that Tommen knew belonged on some vintage collector's edition of a magazine. Or maybe first prize of some photography competition. God, she was gorgeous. And oh, how he wanted her.

"It's really sweet," she said, and Tommen felt his hopes plummet. "I mean, the chivalry thing. It's really nice and all, you know, 'defend your woman' and stuff. But..." She shrugged. "It's just...not for me. And I don't think it would work between us." She took a few steps back, clasping her hands in front of her and leaning just slightly forward, exposing just a little more cleavage. "Anyway, I've decided to go with Luke. But I mean, I'll see you at the dance, so it's not all bad. So, yeah, I guess I'll see you around."

She took another awkward step back before turning and walking away, meeting up with her friends a little farther down the hall. Immediately, they broke into grins and giggles and girl hugs.

Tommen sighed, feeling his hopes flying out the window, but not before mocking him that he'd ever had any hope to begin with. He also felt something else and Banded before heading to the bathroom to deal with it.

There were days when he would have given anything to have his brother with him, to see Teo's soot-covered face from a long day at the mines, to hear his laughter as even the worst of days could be combated with humor. Teo had been almost ten years older than Tommen, but they were their mother's only surviving children; the rest had perished from sickness. Vaguely he could recall a couple sisters but, to his shame, couldn't remember their names.

Once, Tommen had decided to research what had happened to his brother. The Forbes were not a particularly well-known family and the most he ever found was a brief obituary from 1901, stating only his birth year, death date, and that he'd been married twice with seven children total. Tommen never found Teo's wife's names, or why he'd been married twice—death or divorce. Tommen didn't know if his brother had named one of his children after his long-lost brother as he'd only found the names of three of his children because their children had fought in World War I.

But to have Teo beside him just one more time. Just to talk. Give brotherly advice. How to handle bullies, how to handle girls. And, damn it all, how to handle unwanted and rather embarrassing boners. Being able to Band and escape to deal with them certainly helped, but Tommen would have gladly given it up to talk to his brother.

Tommen went to the sink to wash his hands. Of course, what

advice would Teo give that Tommen didn't know already? Teo would only give advice as it applied to the 19ᵗʰ century. Tommen had been in the 21ˢᵗ century for almost a decade and he still didn't quite understand the rules.

He looked in the mirror. The left side of his face was a pretty palette of colors ranging from jaundice yellow to blueberry. He thought about Banding, taking a couple days to himself, and healing his wounds. Wouldn't that mess with them? Walk into school with a battered face, walk to first period perfectly fine.

Fuck, first period Chemistry. He sat right behind Emily. He was going to have to look at her for seventy minutes and somehow either not think about her good looks and low-cut top and purple bra, or try to not feel hurt by her rejection and not be subsequently enraged that Tyler had been the one to cause it. If he hadn't interfered, Tommen would be going with Emily to the dance; he was sure of that.

The bell rang to signal the start of the school day. Reluctantly, Tommen returned to his locker, grabbed his books, and moseyed his way to first period. Even worse, Mr. Gillingham was the teacher and another one of those who'd stepped in to break up the fight yesterday. As expected, he gave Tommen an elongated regard, complete with a raised eyebrow, but thankfully he said nothing.

Tommen took his seat and fished out his homework. Sure, he had all the time in the world to get his work done, but he hardly saw a point to it. He wasn't even sure he wanted to go to college. Ultimately, all he was doing was biding his time because the United States government told him he had to. Once he was finally done and gone, he would most likely become a Time Scout and just finally leave. Leave and not look back. Get away from a place that was so similar and yet a century and a half removed from his real home. If he was going to be taken away, he would go all in.

"All right, class, please pass your homework forward and we'll get started," Mr. Gillingham said.

Immediately, there was a whirlwind of papers as some passed

papers and others dug frantically for them in cluttered folders. Tommen turned to grab papers from those behind him, then held them out for Emily to take. She twisted in her seat. Tommen didn't want to meet her eye as if he was accusing of her of something, but the only other place to look was down her shirt where he saw that the only solid part of her purple bra was the connector between cups which were basically just lace.

Tommen swallowed and Fast Banded. He closed his eyes, tried to clear his head. In his Fast Band, there were any number of things he could feasibly do. His Band was so strong and so tight, essentially it looked like everyone around him had stopped. He was like Quicksilver, man. If he wanted to, he could go up and doodle on Mr. Gillingham's whiteboard. He could walk down to the ice cream shop, grab an ice cream cone, not have to pay for it, come back, and no one would be the wiser. He could stand up, go over to Emily, and get a better feel of that lacey purple bra and what it hid — or didn't hide.

When Walter had first taught him to Band, he'd made Tommen promise not to use the Bands to do anything bad like steal candy. Then, when Tommen hit puberty, Walter made him promise not to use the Bands to do anything "inappropriate." Such as reaching down girls' bras or pants or anything of that nature. So far, he'd made good on both promises, even when he'd had a girlfriend.

But...damn. He wanted her. And she was basically screaming "touch me."

He released the Band and handed over the papers to her. Then she turned away, and he was left to stare at blond hair and the back of a yellow shirt.

For all his fighting, Tommen was amazed at how much self-control he exhibited when it came to not touching girls when he clearly had the ability to not only do so, but completely get away with it. Maybe it was the little promise he made to Walter, maybe it was some residue honor leftover from his pa's teachings. After all, how would it look if The Chivalrous Welshman went around touching girls like that?

That wasn't to say he didn't still look. Chemistry, like the rest of school, was boring. Tommen enjoyed science, especially applied science, like physics. Time, for example. Being able to bend the physical laws of Time to move faster or slower than the Base Time going on around him. Sitting in Gillingham's class learning the properties of protons and neutrons and electrons and atoms was hardly thrilling. Tommen would have taken the staple baking soda and vinegar volcano over book work.

But his options were limited. On the one hand, he could sit and give Gillingham the same blank stare as all the other students—well, except that one kid who was as great at chemistry as Tommen was at physics. On the other hand, he could lean back in his seat and keep one eye on his table partner who spent pretty much the entire class period every day sending inappropriate photos to his significant other. On a third hand, he could Slow Band, move himself into a slower Band of Time and watch the whole class go by like a sped up VHS tape.

The problem with that was that he was likely to miss something important. Not in the lecture or the book, mind you, but it would be his luck that he would Slow Band and Gillingham would call for some kind of group work. Tommen would completely miss the assignment and where he was supposed to be, and he would end up getting marked down for lack of participation. Or Gillingham might call on him randomly to answer some question that he would miss. He was good at controlling his Bands, but just like VHS tapes of old, you had to pay attention in order to stop in time to get to the spot you wanted, and Tommen couldn't predict when Gillingham would call for group work or the answer to a question.

Ultimately, both things happened. First, Gillingham called on him randomly to answer a question, which he did with about as much enthusiasm as Eeyore, but with a Welsh accent. Then the class was divided into groups to do some group work assignment in the book. Something about using everyday objects to model an atom and labeling the different parts, and there was some part that Gillingham threw in there about the group giving a brief presentation of their model. Because one eraser being orbited by several smaller erasers was any kind of exciting atomic model. And because no one would understand the parts of an atom except if it was repeated six times by six different groups.

Because ninety percent of the people in the room would give a rat's ass about the structure of an atom once they graduated.

Tommen enjoyed science. He really did. He enjoyed learning. He just wished it could be more focused and directed and useful. His ma and pa had gone their whole lives without needing to know the structure of an atom. Teo had never cared to know the chemical make-up of salt and copper. Tommen's interest was purely in the realm of physics and time. Atomic models meant next to nothing.

Still, he danced to the same fife everyone else did, his group being chosen to go first where he delivered two whole sentences about the atomic nucleus as his part of the group work before sitting down and watching the same song and dance repeat five more times. The most exciting part came when Emily went up with her group and he could stare at her some more. Then the presentation was over and she sat down, and Tommen was left with only the back of her shirt.

"Very good on your models," Gillingham was saying as he stood and returned to his spot at the front of the class. "I realize it was a bit of a surprise and many of you said you didn't have much to use, but you all came through and improvised and worked together to make it work."

Because all scientists sit together and sing kum-ba-yah, and don't try to climb over each other for precious funds and resources.

"For homework, I want you all to do the section review, the multiple choice and the short answer. Tomorrow will be similar but we'll have to kind of rush through the last two sections. Then Thursday we'll be reviewing for the chapter test on Friday that way you won't have any homework the night of homecoming."

Any groans about the chapter test quickly turned to exciting whispering about the homecoming dance and the football game.

Emily leaned over to her table partner and whispered something, but Tommen didn't miss the glances she stole in his direction.

Tommen felt his cheeks turn red as he was sure she was gossiping about him, but he was saved by the bell. He should have suspected something was amiss when Gillingham went to the door and kept the incoming class at bay. Normally there was a confused mingling of first period students trying to get out and second period students trying to get in.

Tommen wasn't the fastest person, never the first one to bolt for the door, though he usually felt like it. He preferred a leisurely stroll, getting in the back of the line of students filing out the door.

"Hang on, Tommen," Gillingham said, putting a hand to his chest and guiding him back into the classroom, closing the door behind them. "I want to talk to you for a minute."

Tommen sighed. "I'm fine. I'm better. I know I shouldn't fight so much."

"Glad to hear it." Gillingham leaned against his desk and folded his arms. "In all reality, I've never blamed you for the fights; I know how Tyler can be. And I'm glad to see someone willing to stand up for themselves and others against such odds."

Tommen eyed Mr. Gillingham suspiciously. The man wasn't exactly a portrait of sinister intentions or hidden agendas. Five-foot-ten, 220 pounds with the tubby belly of a middle-aged man, the top of his head was bright and shiny but he kept the ring around his head well-groomed. He was pretty much just an average guy. Never had Tommen heard him say much outside of school or teaching. Except for the ring on his finger, Tommen never would have known the guy was married, didn't know if he had kids or pets or anything. Even when he'd pulled Tommen away from the fight, he'd left all the talking to Layman.

"But that's not what I want to talk to you about," he went on. "I want to talk about your academics."

There it was. Good old Gillingham.

"My academics?" Tommen echoed.

"Tommen, you're a smart kid. I can see that. I saw it last year when you took my Physics class. You have a mind for mathematics, analytics, taking pieces of a puzzle, solving it, and, most importantly, applying it."

Tommen shrugged. "Why me? I don't have the highest grade in the class. Why not talk to—?"

"Because I see what you're doing. You're intentionally holding yourself back. I've seen it before. Students who don't want to get singled out try to fly under the radar. You...I think you're just trying to cut your losses, trying not to give Tyler and other bullies an excuse to pick on you."

"My scores are consistent," Tommen protested, feeling like Gillingham was looking right through him.

Gillingham shook his head. "They're too consistent. I think they're planned. What I know you're able to do and what you do in class are too different from each other."

"So you think I should do my best and take what comes?"

Again he shook his head. "You make it sound worse than it is. What I'm suggesting is simply rising above it. Stop worrying about those who would bully you because of your intelligence. Clearly you have more of it in more than one department." Tommen couldn't help but smile. "Don't let yourself get held down by them. You can't beat them physically. But you can do something better than that. Beat them intellectually. One day, you'll be the guy who discovers a cure for cancer or invents cold fusion, and they'll be the ones delivering the pizza to your Nobel Prize acceptance party."

Tommen had to admit that he was more stunned by Gillingham's surprise faith in him than anything else. Yesterday he'd been just a teacher who'd picked him up off the floor, gotten him to a chair, and gave him a cold pack and glass of water. Suddenly he was like the coach in his corner of the ring. "Ya got 'im right where ya want 'im."

"What I'm offering you, Tommen," Gillingham continued, "I don't offer lightly. And I only offer it once. There is a test that you can take. It's 200 questions, about three hours long. It is a science placement test, one they use in college and career studies. It covers five major scientific disciplines: chemistry, physics, astronomy, geology, and medicine. There are no straight equation questions; it's all story problems and critical thinking.

"The purpose of this test, as it applies to you, is to try to get you in classes that not only interest you but are beneficial to your college class placement, as well as get you started on a career path. I know the biggest complaint in school is, 'When am I ever going to use this?' Well, this test, combined with the right classes, will hopefully answer that and get you where you need and want to be. How does that sound?"

It sounded like a dream come true, and Tommen's heart leapt at the thought of getting out of his boring class into something that was challenging and worthwhile.

"So, if I take this test...what happens if I pass? How will I know?"

"Unless you completely fail it—which if I thought that would happen, I wouldn't even offer it in the first place—there is no right or wrong per se. You could completely 'fail' the geology portion but still 'pass' the test in medicine. It's evaluation and placement.

"But to answer your question, if you 'passed' the test, then I would take the results to Mrs. Wendell and three colleges or universities of your choice. Then we would work with them to determine the best course of action for you. Most likely it would mean advanced placement courses starting next semester and through your junior year. Then, your senior year, you could dual-enroll. It not only saves you a lot of money in tuition, but it jump starts your college career and your working career."

"Would I still have to finish out the semester in this class?"

Gillingham shrugged casually like, "What can you do?" and nodded. "I know it's only the second week of October, but it's too late in the semester to switch you. This class may be a cakewalk for you, but there is no feasible way you could catch up in the AP courses. It's just the way it is. But at least you would have something to look forward to."

That was for darn sure because taking Chemistry 10B with Miss Perdue next semester was guaranteed to be as boring academically, but with twice the drama. No, thank you.

Tommen was suddenly very aware of all the eyes staring at him, crowding around the tiny window in the door. He shifted his stance. "When would the test be? How does that work?"

"Like I said, it's three hours long, timed, so it would have to be after school. I don't know your work schedule, but it's available whenever you are. It would be done either in here or in Mrs. Wendell's office. You take the test, I grade the numbered results, I send in for the analytical results, and then we meet and discuss. The whole process would take about a week or so. You would know before Thanksgiving what the results are."

"What do you mean, sending in for analytical results?"

"Medicine itself is an enormous field. The analytical results simply narrow down potential career fields. It's based on the test, but it's still only a suggestion."

"But how — ?"

"Tommen," Mr. Gillingham cut in, "I'm not telling you anymore about the test unless you agree to take it. We could spend all day here discussing it. But I have a class to teach, and you have a class to be in. Now I'll give you until first period tomorrow to think it over, talk it over with your dad, and — "

"I'll do it," Tommen said. "I have Friday off if that's okay. With the dance and everything."

Mr. Gillingham nodded once slowly. "Friday it is then. Be here right after class. Two pencils and a calculator, nothing more. And if you are planning on going to the dance, I suggest you bring a bag packed with your clothes."

With that, Gillingham wrote him a note to his next class and dismissed him. Tommen grabbed his things and burst out of the room to the surprise and amusement of the class standing there forlornly in the hall. Let them stare, let them whisper. One day, he would discover a cure for cancer or invent cold fusion, and they would be delivering the pizza to his Nobel Prize acceptance party.

More realistically, though, his career path wouldn't lead him to either of those things. More likely he would end up like Doc Brown, a batty old failed inventor who finally masters time travel, and even then, he still doesn't get taken seriously. Tommen pondered this as he swapped his books in his locker and headed off to second period history.

Earth wasn't ready to be exposed to the Time industry just yet, according to the Powers That Be. What would happen if Tommen introduced them to it? Initially, he would probably get carted off to a government asylum where he would be experimented on. Then they'd probably fake his death, rule it a crazy man's suicide, and then move from experiments to torture because, after all, who was going to know, right?

And, as Walter pointed out many times: People already had access to tools and weapons of far less consequence than the ability to Band or Harvest Time. A majority of the people used these tools and weapons responsibly within the scope of the law. Unfortunately those who did not understand how to use such tools tried to demonize them, paving the way for those who would use them maliciously. Thus, crime. Thus, a vicious circle of crime, punishment, and laws. Thus, keeping Walter busy in the Homicide Department. If people had access to Time, it would be like giving everyone access to a nuclear bomb and told to be good. It wasn't just America and the First World that they had to think about.

Tommen arrived in history and handed Mr. Morris his excused note from Gillingham. Morris, all five-foot-six, 150 pounds of him, simply nodded and Tommen took his seat, ready to spend another sixty minutes pondering what history would have been like if people had access to Time.

Presently they were studying the French Revolution. How different would the world be if Napoleon had been able to Band? For as much as people made fun of him and based their judgments on simple win or lose, Napoleon had been a brilliant tactician. Would he have been victorious if he could manipulate Time?

Well, why not? What army wouldn't be victorious if they could Band and their opponents could not? To move through the advancing enemy ranks, slicing down adversaries left and right, slaughtering them in only the blink of an eye. Imagine how many sieges could have been avoided if the men simply had the time to stand at the wall and chip away at it without having to worry about rocks or boiling oil or pitch? Imagine naval battles, as enemy ships were turned to swiss cheese and sunk before they even had time to get mustered.

Even more perplexing and exciting to imagine were battles in which both sides could Band.

Tommen had never actually seen such a fight. He'd never seen Walter have to fight anyone with the same abilities, never seen the twins fight, even each other. The most he'd ever witnessed was Walter apprehending a Runner whose Banding abilities were almost nonexistent. It had been nothing for Walter to break the Band and arrest the Runner, taking him to the Wheel so the Grandfathers could dispense justice for Time theft.

But according to Micah and Micaiah, to witness such a fight was a rare thing. Not only in that it didn't happen often where such abilities were matched, but that the overlapping of Bands and the sheer willpower to continuously build and break them usually meant that the Bands were extremely strong and thus emitted light and color that was almost impossible to look at.

And according to Micah, off the record, Walter had once been in such a fight, about eleven years before Tommen's arrival. The way he told it, it put such a strain on Walter that it nearly killed him. Micah did not go into detail, only using the abbreviated story as a warning, first to not get into such fights, and second to have more appreciation for just how much strength Walter really had. Tommen immediately thought of how deftly Walter had broken his Band in the bathroom and then effortlessly double-Banded him in order to take down the swelling on his face. And Tommen had to focus just to build any Band.

Like Gillingham in Chemistry, Morris warned the class of an upcoming test on Friday, hurrying to finish his sentence as the bell rang and they began pouring out of the room.

"Tommen! Hey, Tommen!"

Tommen turned as Varad hurried out of the classroom and caught up to him in the hall. Varad was Indian. Like Tommen, he was bullied, but not because they shared the same code of chivalry. Varad was made fun of for not being the stereotypical Indian who worked tech support for American companies and was secretly a super engineering genius on the side. Actually, he was a very astute history buff, his dream to travel back to India to record oral histories from remote villages and preserve them for future generations.

"You in trouble already this morning?" Varad asked, following Tommen to his locker.

"No," Tommen told him. "Actually, just the opposite. You might say I'm getting promoted."

"Aw, man, don't let Layman fool you. Being in charge of detention isn't nearly as fun as just participating in it."

Tommen grinned and shook his head. "No, dude, I'm getting moved to AP science classes."

"Really? Dude, that's totally awesome. Hey, tell me about it at lunch."

Varad hurried off to his locker while Tommen again swapped books and headed the opposite direction to Spanish class.

Spanish might have been his most miserable class except it was fun to banter with Mrs. Perez, barely five feet tall and probably 200 pounds of curves in all the wrong places. And it wasn't like friendly banter, but Tommen poking fun at her and being insubordinate just because he knew he could get her riled up.

He didn't care for Spanish, much to her dismay. He did just enough to keep a passing grade, but most of the time, if an assignment called for answers in Spanish, he would answer in Irish. And if the answers were to be in English, he chose Welsh instead.

"And what would you say if I told you that because you already know two foreign languages, picking up a third ought to be as easy as cat hair to a black dress?" she asked him once.

Tommen nodded thoughtfully to that as if seriously considering her words. Then he just smiled and said, *"Tá, a bhean Perez."* (Yes, Mrs. Perez.)

So it was to his dismay that he walked in and found a substitute sitting behind Mrs. Perez's desk. Tommen generally tried not to judge based on appearance, but if this woman's demeanor said anything, it was that she couldn't talk to Dora the Explorer if she tried.

His assumption turned out to be mostly correct. She was able to go over their homework assignment well enough, but there was no way she could teach a lesson. Instead, the class was dubbed a "review day." Per the notes that Mrs. Perez had given the sub, she suggested they, the students, take the review seriously because their test was Thursday, not Friday like everyone else.

But other than a few truly studious students, little studying and reviewing actually got done. What little Spanish was spoken was mostly profanity and lewd comments, all of which went right over the sub's head as she looked out over the class and spoke up only if they got too loud.

Tommen didn't have any friends to socialize with in his Spanish class and instead opted to open his notebook and start writing in Welsh. He wasn't a journal person—God only knew what would happen if Tyler ever got even a whiff that Tommen might—gasp—journal—but sometimes he found it helpful just to write. It wasn't inner feelings or girly stuff like that, but accounts of his day or short stories that usually ran along the lines of life in the Appalachian Mountains in the 1800's. Historical fiction, some would say. Some was fiction, true, but most of them were rooted in his childhood experiences.

It helped. On days when he wondered if he hadn't just

imagined the little cottage on the hillside or the scary salt cave, when he questioned whether Teo actually existed or if he'd just been some imaginary big brother. The stories helped to not only keep alive the memories, but keep them separate from his present life so he could function without going insane.

"So, are you the Welsh student Mrs. Perez told me to watch out for?"

Tommen reflexively threw an arm over his writing and looked up as the substitute pulled up a chair close to his front row desk and sat down.

"She told you to watch out for me?" Tommen wondered dumbly.

The sub looked at her notes. "Third period, Spanish IIA. There is a Welsh student named Tommen who loves to banter and make jokes, usually in Welsh or Irish and not in Spanish. It can be fun, but try not to encourage him too much."

"How did you figure it was me?"

"Because that's not English." She indicated his notebook. "Figured I'd take a guess."

"Oh. Well, yeah, I guess that's me."

"Are you an exchange student?"

"No, not even. Immigrant, you might say."

"I might say?" She raised a brow but did not pursue. "Very cool. What do you write? Letters to family?"

"Kind of. Sometimes. Short stories mostly. About home."

The sub nodded. "I'm actually an English sub, but in a pinch, they pulled me for Spanish duty. You know, if you chose to write your stories in English, I have contacts in a couple newspapers around the state that might be interested in running them as a student editorial."

Tommen blinked, then shook his head and closed his notebook. "Oh, no. Thanks, but...these stories...they aren't going to see the light of day. My eyes only and all that."

The sub nodded. "Too bad, but I understand." She stood and

smoothed her skirt. "Still, if you see me around subbing and change your mind..."

He merely nodded and packed up his stuff as she called a warning for the end of class. Bad enough someone suggested writing his stories in English. At least in Welsh, even if someone did find it, they'd never be able to read it. Publish? Not even an option.

Tommen left Spanish with a mixed bag of emotions. His day had started out getting rejected by a hot girl, then told that he could get out of the boring science classes into some that actually mattered, then slogging through another mental session of "What Would History Be Like If...?", and finally coming to a point where someone had not only seen his short stories but told him that he should put them in front of people. And he still had two classes to go. Today was just...weird.

Thankfully, lunch not only broke up the mundane boredom of school, but it helped him to reset and process the events of the day thus far. Not that the options in the cafeteria were particularly appetizing since the Powers That Be decided to jump on the bandwagon of, "Healthy food for all!" effectively doing away with pizza and chicken nuggets in favor of tossed salad and whole grain rice and lentil stew.

Of course, this opened up a brilliant opportunity for the seniors who were able to leave campus for open-lunch. They charged a fee for taking orders, but unless you wanted to get stuck with kale and spinach with a healthy drizzle of olive oil, you paid or you starved.

Or there was brown-bagging from home, which Tommen did most of the time. Ham sandwich on rye with a healthy dose of mustard. He sat with Varad at the table where outcasts banded together in order to avoid being picked on by the in-crowd. A moment after they sat down, Eric joined them. He was a senior who could technically leave campus, but the reason for him not going was as obvious as the second-hand clothes he wore.

Like Tommen for his chivalry and Varad for not being a

stereotype, Eric was also bullied, him because his family was poor. They hadn't had electricity or running water until about three years ago. But even so, he was a smart kid, with a better knowledge and understanding of nutrition and cooking than a love child between Martha Stewart and George Foreman. His family didn't have much, but when Eric worked every day, he made sure they didn't go hungry and that they weren't forced to survive on junk food.

"So, what were you saying about getting moved to AP classes?" Varad asked.

"You're getting moved to AP classes?" Eric wondered. "In what?"

So Tommen explained the test that Mr. Gillingham had offered, how it worked to test different areas so he could take the classes he needed to jump start his career instead of piddling around with table partners who spent the time texting inappropriate photos to their significant others.

"Good for you, dude," Eric said once he'd finished. "I wish I could have done something like that, but we don't have anything like that for nutrition. No offense, Tommen, but the world focuses too much on science and the 'new' when we should be focusing on the 'old' and getting back to basics. Farming worked just fine for thousands of years; there's no need to go mucking it up. I mean, look at my family. Dirt poor and we eat better than some of the richest snobs in here."

"I'll be sure to mention that in my next history paper," Tommen told him. "Maybe the one on yellow fever or Black Death or something."

"Apathy is no excuse for poor hygiene."

Tommen shook his head even as Varad rolled his eyes and sighed dramatically before lowering his voice conspiratorially. "So, I got a hit from a couple of the guys."

Eric and Tommen glanced at each other briefly.

"How much?" Tommen asked cautiously.

Varad waved his hand. "No worries; I paid for it this time.

Next time is on you two."

"How much did you get, you dolt?" Eric said.

"Oh. Three different shots, one each, and one roll each."

"So what's the plan then?"

"Friday night, we all come to the dance, make sure people see us so we have a good alibi. Then we leave, head to the soccer fields—because everyone is going to be focused on the football field—have a quickie, sneak over to the football field, make sure we get seen there, have a hot dog and a soda, then boom, we've got an alibi and we're home and in bed before any of our parents know something's up."

Tommen scoffed and nodded. "Yeah, no kidding."

"Dude, it takes an hour for your body to metabolize an eight ounce glass of beer," Eric stated. "Three cheap little shots, and if we stay at the game long enough, your dad will never find out. Drink enough soda at the game and you'll piss out the weed before you can say 'urine test.'"

It wasn't like this was their first illegal venture, but they weren't exactly hardened criminals dealing weed to little kids and stealing alcohol from the party store. They were opportunists who did a little binge here and there. And yet there was always the terrifying fear that one day Walter would find out. Eric and Varad would be in the standard run of trouble. But Tommen? Oh, there would be a whole new level of punishment invented especially for him.

"So what do you say?" Varad pressed.

"I'm in," Eric said.

Tommen sighed. "Me too."

"Great. So, Eric, you'll pick me up at six. Tommen, you'll already be here so we're good there. Just remember that we have to be seen at both places: the dance and the football field."

Tommen finished off his sandwich and returned to his locker. Well, none of them had dates for the dance, so none of them would be sneaking off to have sex under the bleachers. A little alcohol and marijuana among friends was probably the best they were going to get that night.

After lunch, Tommen headed to math, specifically Geometry. He'd heard that a person was either really good at analytical reasoning—equations, symbols, algebraic math—or spatial reasoning—shapes, distance, measurements, geometry. Tommen figured he was more analytical since he excelled in physics, writing and solving equations within equations, turning letters and symbols into numbers, and then sometimes back into letters. Yes, the public school system saw him as being only in geometry, but he was far beyond that. He had lots of time to study.

Not that there was much to look at in the classroom. The math posters around the room were not only old, but extremely outdated. Seriously, who did logarithms on paper anymore? Oh, and the one about the all new calculator, now with graphing capabilities. His favorite was the one detailing all the cool features of the new math textbooks—from 1993.

So to say that Mrs. Cheerheart—yes, Cheerheart—was a little outdated herself was an understatement. A lot of older women might have retired to travel or be with the grandkids, and Tommen knew of a half a dozen who were retired but elected to continue substitute teaching as a way to stay active in their retirement. Mrs. Cheerheart not only should have been retired, but in a nursing home, if not already dead and buried. She was eighty-something years old—maybe ninety-something—and looked every day her age and more. To her credit, the only thing that hadn't aged since her sixtieth birthday was her voice which Tommen could easily believe had kept all nine of her children in line and probably still scared the piss out of them—the grandkids, too. He could also easily imagine her being a woman who might have disguised herself as a man and gone to fight Nazis or some such thing.

That didn't mean she was an able teacher, though. Tommen learned more from looking through the book than listening to her talk. And he, like most of the students, simply looked at the day's assignment and homework written on the board as they walked in, and started on it while she lectured. He could get away with it because he sat in the back corner.

Tommen normally shared this class with Tyler who also sat in the back row, only three seats between them. Oddly enough, class normally passed without incident, probably for the simple reason that it was after lunch which generally meant nap time which Mrs. Cheerheart almost never failed to oblige them. Where her voice was incredible, her vision was not.

That wasn't to say there were no problems between Tommen and Tyler during class. Being in the back row also meant that note-passing generally went unnoticed in Cheerheart's failing eyesight. Tommen always told himself to just leave the notes alone, don't read them, but damn his curiosity. Sometimes they were attacks on his character, other times blatant threats. And every day, Tyler never missed an opportunity to throw Tommen into a locker or against a wall when he left the room.

Except today, of course. It was a strange sensation, being able to walk out of the room and not have to spend an extra minute or two recovering his papers and his cognition. He made it to his locker unmolested to trade his math books for his English books and head off to his last class of the day.

If there was any teacher in the school Tommen might have called a friend, it would probably be Mrs. Reisig. She taught college classes on nights and weekends and was always losing things, but she was perhaps the most tolerant of his oddness and the least tolerant of those who bullied him, stepping in more than once, not just as a teacher trying to stop a fight, but as someone who willingly intervened on his behalf.

More than that, she was more willing than most to let his writing talents fly solo under the radar. Others thought her "special assignments" for him meant that he ought to have been in some sort of special needs English class, when really, she kept a store of such assignments for students who could never make it in the government-mandated academic world, but had just as much, if not more, to offer. Class had to write a paper on the themes of the novel they just finished? He wrote a paper on the characters of the novel and how the story might have changed as told from the point of view from each character. Class had to write a short story about some aspect of a novel that was never explained in book so they wrote it themselves? Tommen had once—and only once—translated one of his Welsh stories of which Reisig was the only teacher to know just what they were and how many he had.

Not that he didn't do any of the work the rest of the class was doing, but Reisig had been around the block a few times and understood the needs of her students.

Maybe that was why he didn't mind his English class, and sometimes even looked forward to it. He also enjoyed the free reading time they took at the beginning and end of each class. Just five minutes to read a book of their choice and just share what it was about and anything they had learned from it—about character development, plot development, writing style, vocabulary. Tommen had more than once read a Welsh- or Irish-language novel and so educated his teacher and his class on such languages. It earned him sneers and leers and jeers and fuel for Tyler's fire, but if there was any class that felt safe, it was Reisig's class. And he almost didn't care about what followed.

So it was more than a little annoying when the start of their end-of-day free reading time was interrupted by announcements from the office, as it had been and would be every day this week.

"Good Tuesday afternoon, everyone!" the secretary, Mrs. Puifall, greeted. "We have the results from today's spirit competition!" Because dressing up like a different moron every day of the week to show school pride was a competition anyone would be proud to win. "In first place, juniors with 87% participation, so they get five points. Second place, seniors with 85% participation and three points. Third place, freshmen with 77% participation and two points. And last, sophomores with only 43% participation and earning just one point.

Remember, tomorrow is Twin Day!

"Also don't forget to find that special date for the dance on Friday night. The theme is Alice in Wonderland, so get creative, all you Cheshire Cats out there!"

Tommen really couldn't care less at that point. First, it was a fact of life that his class was known for their lack of enthusiasm and participation in spirit days, so they would never win that competition. At least until their senior year because the seniors always won regardless of actual participation. And second, he had no one to go to the dance with, and it wouldn't matter since whatever he wore, he was going to have to ditch quick in case he got alcohol or ash on it or it somehow got imbued with the smell of drink or weed.

The day over, Tommen slogged back to his locker. Another day done. Just a few thousand more to go before he was finally free of the government-run daycare known as the public school system.

"Hey!" Eric called, jogging up beside him on his way out to his car while Tommen headed for the buses. "So we still good for Friday night?"

Tommen shrugged. "I guess. Nothing's changed since lunch."

"Well, Tommen, I might say I'm surprised, but...I'm really not."

Tommen cringed as he turned and looked for the owner of the voice. Tyler Freeman sat in his car, pulled up to the curb. He was only suspended from classes, but he still had to pick up his little brother who was, ironically, also a sophomore.

"So is this why you're so chivalrous towards women. Not because you can't get laid by them but because you don't want to?" Tyler taunted. "So you and Eric are going instead? How cute."

"Come off it, Tyler," Eric told him.

"Oh, you're telling me to 'come' off it? How cute. How quaint. How chivalrous yourself." Tyler laughed unabashedly. "You two are made for each other."

Ricky, Tyler's younger brother, walked out of the school then and toward the car. He tossed his pack in the backseat before taking his place beside his brother in the front seat. He looked at his brother, looked out the window, and gave Tommen an all-too-familiar expression followed by a very familiar obscene gesture before they drove away, laughing as they did so.

"Don't listen to them, man," Eric said. "Most of the students here are intelligent enough to—"

"No, Eric, they're not intelligent enough," Tommen cut in. "If they were, bullying would never make it past elementary school."

Tommen got on the bus feeling bitter and dejected. No, people were not "intelligent enough." Intelligent enough for school maybe. Intelligent enough to get into prestigious colleges and universities. Intelligent enough to impress adults and those in power, to convince them that they were against bullying while secretly cheering on the fight, in the same way that a girl might tell her pastor that she didn't believe in sex before marriage but went home every night to masturbate and watch porn. Was there really a difference? Were two people really needed for it to be sex? Did they have to be the one to pass the note in order to bully someone?

No, his classmates were not "intelligent enough" to know that he and Eric were not a gay couple without stepping in to stop Tyler from insinuating such things, embarrass both of them, and driving away laughing. Didn't matter if everyone knew he was a bully and a thug. It was damn funny and they were going to laugh, too. They would also probably lightly assure Tommen that they knew Tyler was lying, even as they joked about the encounter and perpetuated such lies. The previous fight and being rejected by Emily would only add fuel to that fire.

Not that Tommen expected it to get to be that big of a rumor or an issue—it was hardly the first blatant lie about him to run the rumor mill—but there were some things through the years that had taken months or years to completely stamp out. Some of them were sexual in nature, others physical, some psychological, and some rumors had tried to drag Walter through the mud by saying that he was abusing Tommen.

So to say that Tommen arrived at work in a less-than-cheery mood would have been an understatement. He wasn't sure if he wanted to be relieved or even angrier when he saw how busy the bakery was. God only knew why; it was a Tuesday. Sure, they were usually pretty steady, and they had in the occasional party, but to have every seat filled plus a line at the counter, plus people milling about more waiting to get in line, it was insanity like they wouldn't normally see except around Thanksgiving or Christmas.

Tommen had to push his way through the mob. Micah noticed him first.

"Oh, Tommen, there you are," Micah said, barely looking at him. "Hurry up and punch in. There's some stuff in the ovens ready to come out. Take them out, do what they need, and then trade me places."

Translation: I'm busy and I'm sweating my brains out because I'm trying to hold Bands in place while not being in them, and if I let them go, we're going to lose a hell of a lot of product.

But Tommen did as he was bid, shrugging off his backpack into a tiny closet, punching in, grabbing an apron, and washing his hands before heading to the kitchen which was an explosion of Fast and Slow Bands.

The difference between holding a Band from the inside and holding one from the outside was kind of like running a giant hamster wheel. When the hamster's inside, both the hamster and the wheel move and it's like a symbiotic being, and all is right with the world. Trying to spin it from the outside requires much more work as halting movements make the wheel spin clunkily or else it tries to drag you along with it and can be very tiring.

That wasn't quite how it had been originally explained to Tommen, but it was what worked for him. Still, Micah's Bands were incredibly powerful, and trying to break into them and control them was like running into a wild horse stampede, singling out a single horse, and trying to rein it in. He took a breath, singled out the Band, then dove into the stampede.

It was like being throttled by Tyler all over again as the wind was driven from his lungs, and he felt like a piece of paper being tossed around in the wake of speeding cars on the interstate. He coughed and almost fell forward on the table, putting his arms out at the last minute. After a moment of mentally and temporally tumbling around in Micah's Band, he found his feet and found the reins. He felt a snap of tension, like a broken rubber band, as Micah gratefully released the Band to him. A headache sprouted somewhere in the back of his mind as he fought to control the Band and ease it into Base Time.

Tommen blacked out momentarily and soon found himself standing over six dozen cupcakes. Very slowly, sound came back to him, and reason. He shook his head and set to icing and decorating.

Tommen could create Fast Bands with a ratio of days to seconds, or day:second, one day in the Band was like one second in Base Time. On the whole, they were not nearly as traumatizing as Micah's Band which was, for all intents and purposes, very mild, only hour:minute. The difference came not only in that Micah had been controlling it from the outside, but that it had been extremely tight, pin-pointed to a specific oven with specific foods, and it was battling half a dozen other Bands in the room, like magnets of the same polarity fighting each other. A Fast Band and a Slow Band could coexist relatively peacefully, but with the volume of baking going on, these were almost exclusively Fast Bands, and they didn't play nice with each other.

He delivered the cupcakes, Micah and Micaiah distributing them almost as fast as he set them out on the tray. Then he took a breath and dived back in, wrestling a slightly less wild Band and bringing it to heel in Base Time. Now his head was throbbing. Still, he cut the brownies masterfully and delivered those, too.

"How many did you say you had back there?" Tommen wondered. The Bands were all the same color, but they ebbed and flowed like water. But in such close proximity, it was tough to tell one from another.

"Nine," Micah replied shortly. "Seven more to go."

The younger twin's shirt was plastered to his back and sweat dripped from the end of his nose. Tommen simply nodded and returned to the kitchen.

Tommen managed to get three more Bands done before Micah returned, reaching into one Band after another and breaking them. Tommen stumbled to a chair and put his head down on the table. He looked up, eyes feeling like they were bleeding from an overabundance of light, as Micah handed him a glass of water.

"Why couldn't you do that and I take your place up front?" Tommen asked wearily, acutely aware that this was probably how he'd feel Saturday morning after binging with Eric and Varad, regardless of sticking around to 'metabolize' the alcohol.

"We had a system going," Micah said, sitting down across from him with his own cup. Experience told Tommen it was most likely Coke. He took a drink. "And anyway, Walter asked us to."

"To what?"

"Challenge you with things you're going to be learning as an Apprentice. Granted, this was probably on the extreme end of what he had in mind, at least to start out with, but you might as well learn what it feels like now."

"So would Micaiah feel as miserable if he were the one to break into your Bands?"

Micah shook his head. "Nah. You're a child from the kiddie pool thrown into rushing rapids."

"Gee, thanks."

"Like I said. We had a system going, and Walter asked us to do it." He stood up, leaving his cup on the table. "Cai's got the front pretty well handled. You chill here for a few minutes."

Tommen wasn't going to argue. He kept his head down, eyes closed, and tried not to fall asleep. A child in the kiddie pool thrown into rushing rapids, yeah, that was probably an accurate description of how it had felt and only served to remind Tommen of how puny his abilities were, comparatively speaking. He could make Fast and

Slow Bands. Micah could create and hold nine Fast Bands, and who knew how long he'd had to hold them before Tommen arrived to take them? The amount of energy that would take was beyond comprehension.

"Where did all the people come from, anyway?" Tommen asked, turning to try and look at Micah who was busy with some cookies.

"Huh?" Micah looked up. "Oh, heck if I know. We had nothing until about two o'clock. Then it got a little busy. And then at like two-thirty on the nose, wham! People! They just kept coming and we really weren't sure where they came from either."

Even as he spoke, there came the ding of the service bell. Tommen made to get up but Micah shook his head. "You stay back here and work on these cookies; I'll get the customer."

Tommen's head felt like it weighed a couple tons as he dragged himself from the break area table to the baking table where several dozen cookies sprawled out before him. For a second he couldn't remember what to do with them. Then he blinked, shook his head, and started sorting them onto trays: Chocolate Chip, Peanut Butter, Oatmeal Raisin, Sugar.

"Are we in for another rush?" Tommen asked when Micah returned.

Micah shook his head. "Nah."

"Where'd Micaiah go?"

"Sunshine?" Micah sneered and jerked his thumb back in the general direction of the office where both sets of blinds were closed.

"Something wrong?"

"Nothing you need to worry about. Another satisfied customer is all."

"It wasn't the birthday party, was it?"

Micah shook his head. "No, just some hotshot executive party we did a catering package for. *Gamail.*"

Tommen grinned.

"Now then, if you're feeling up to it, we're going to make our last batch for the day. Thankfully, since the rush died down, most of it actually already got done. We just need some rolls and a few pastries."

They did it in Base Time, both of them exhausted from so much Banding. Tommen pulled the ingredients and read the recipes, while Micah rummaged through the pots and pans, pulling out this and that as needed. They traded off on helping customers as the need arose, and generally they worked in silence.

When Micah had put in the last pan and set the last timer, he turned to Tommen and mentioned being in the office and to man the front.

Not usually a problem, although given what he'd walked into, Tommen expected a lot worse once the five o'clock crowd came running in.

The tidal wave of angry, impatient well-to-do's never came. Instead, Tommen managed the more commonplace tidal wave of passive, indifferent well-to-do's who were glad to get something to eat and get off their feet for a bit. A few greeted Tommen by name. A few Tommen actually knew. He caught snippets of office gossip here and there, but it was the usual stuff: Bosses were horrible, pay was horrible, benefits were horrible, he was sleeping with her, she was cheating on him, and as always, she had to be sleeping with him because how else could she have gotten that promotion?

It made Tommen want to never work in a corporate setting, or any workplace with more than just a few people. People always said that work was so much different and so much better than school. Was it really? Or was it just that the competitors and the prize to be won were different?

The five o'clock crowd cleared out almost as quickly as it came in, all of them eager and wanting to get home to a nagging wife, cheating husband, bratty kids, and a neglected dog that pissed on the couch again. This left Tommen alone to start on clean-up chores, and with two huge waves of people having rolled through, said chores would probably take longer than usual.

So Tommen picked up napkins and wax paper covered in chocolate icing, gathered the trashes, replaced the bags, and huffed them out the back door one by one, occasionally having to run back in at the sound of the service bell. He'd just gotten the last trash into the dumpster when he heard the bell again.

"Can I help you with something?" he asked as an egregiously busty middle-aged woman walked in and surveyed the display case.

She blinked as if confused, then looked up. "My God, what is that smell? I hope your kitchen is sanitary. I have very specific dietary needs. No other bakery in this city can give me what I want, so I hope you can, and I hope I don't get sick from it."

"Just cleaning up ma'am, taking out the trash," Tommen told her stiffly.

"And you're not wearing gloves?" She wore an expression like Tommen just drop-kicked her dog. "Have you at least washed your hands?"

"I have washed my hands and I use tongs or wax paper to go after what you want as soon as you tell me what that is."

She shook her head and squinted her eyes to read his makeshift nametag. "I have very specific needs, erm, Tommen. Go wash your hands and put on some gloves. Maybe in that time, I will have made up my mind."

He would have rather throttled her, but instead gritted his teeth, turned, and went to wash his hands. He stole a glance toward the office, but the blinds were still closed. Good grief, how upset was that catering party? As he walked into the kitchen, however, he smelled something, like something burning. He looked up at the lights; smoke was misting in the beams.

Hand-washing forgotten, Tommen ran through the kitchen and rounded the corner to the ovens.

"Shit," he whispered.

Sneakers squeaking on the floor, Tommen ran back through the kitchen to the office window and beat on it as hard as he could until the door swung open and a very irate Micaiah looked out.

"What?" he demanded.

"Sir? Young man, I am waiting," the woman said impatiently at the counter. "I know what I would like to buy."

"The kitchen's on fire!" Tommen blurted.

"*Cac!*" Micaiah swore, reaching back long enough to grab Micah out of the office and the three of them crossed through the kitchen once more where fire was jumping from oven to oven, feeding as much on electrical wires as the structure of the building.

"*A Thommen, glaoch 9-1-1,*" Micaiah ordered. "*A Mhicah, múch chumhacht chun an seomra! Táimid ag dúnta go luath!*" (Tommen, call 9-1-1! Micah, kill power to the suite! We're closing early!)

Despite the fire, there was a calm certainty with which Micaiah commanded them, and it was a bit contagious. Tommen hurried to the office to find the phone, but he did not rush, and he found that he was far less nervous than he thought he would be, having to call 9-1-1.

"9-1-1, what's your emergency?" the dispatcher answered.

Tommen gave them the address of the bakery. "The kitchen is on fire. We're evacuating our suite first. No one's injured. Then I think my boss is going to sound the alarm in the neighboring suites."

The dispatcher asked him to hold, probably so the fire department could be dispatched, and took some more information. Even as the call was ended, Tommen heard sirens and air horns, and by the time he ran outside with Micah and Micaiah, big red trucks pulled into the tiny parking lot, their flashing lights only reminding Tommen of the headache still assaulting his brain.

Not far behind the fire trucks, police cruisers also pulled in, and then the ambulances. Micaiah went to talk to the authorities.

"Should I go with him since I, I don't know, saw the fire? Discovered it?" Tommen asked Micah.

Micah shook his head. "If they need you, they'll ask for you. For now, just sit tight; I already called your dad to come get you."

"Okay."

After that, it was a lot of sitting and waiting. The police, seeing that there was no apparent criminal activity, packed up and moved on to their next disturbance. The paramedics, seeing that there were no apparent injuries, packed up and moved on to their next victim.

That just left the firemen as they meandered from here to there, from inside the building to the trucks and back with various tools and gadgets. From what conversation snippets Tommen could catch, the fire had stayed relatively contained to the oven area and was out, but looks could be deceiving and they were going to hose down the area until the drywall was no better than a sponge, followed by a lot of fans to drive the smoke out of the building.

A familiar brake squeal brought Tommen out of his trance and he turned to see Walter's old Cadillac pulling into the parking lot. When he got out, he was still in uniform. He didn't see Tommen right away, instead approaching Micaiah and Micah who were with one of the firemen. They exchanged words and Micah pointed toward Tommen.

Tommen was not a huggy person. He was not a particularly touchy-feely person. And in pretty much any other circumstances that didn't involve potentially life-and-death situations, he might have pushed and forced his way out of the embrace that Walter pulled him into. But as it was, there had been a fire and Tommen had been in dangerous proximity to it. Let the man have his moment.

"Are you okay?" he demanded, finally letting Tommen go. "You're not hurt, are you?"

"The paramedics already checked me out," Tommen told him. "I'm fine."

"Are you sure? I'll take you in."

"Are you kidding me?" Tommen grinned. "If I got hurt, it would be way cooler to go in to the hospital by ambulance instead of a beat-up old Cadillac driven by my police officer dad who is still in full uniform. I mean, seriously, how do you expect to catch bad guys when you can't even get a speeding ticket in that thing?"

The look of relief on Walter's face made Tommen feel pretty good. "All right, fair enough. But don't diss the car; that thing's going to you once you get your license."

Tommen waved a hand. "Pft. As if. I'm already saving up on my own. That Cadillac is going to the junkyard before I have need of it."

Walter raised a brow. "We'll see about that. Listen, I'm going to check in with Micaiah and Micah for a minute, make sure they're good. If you want to, wait in the car."

A thought occured to him then and Tommen groaned. "Oh no."

"What?"

"My backpack was in there. If it's not burned, it's probably soaking wet."

"I'll see if someone can't bring it out for you." Walter patted his shoulder. "Go wait in the car."

Tommen did as he was told, not realizing until after he'd gotten his seatbelt on that he was also still wearing his apron, and somewhere along the way the backing to his nametag had gotten lost and the pin poked him in the chest. He was wiggling out of the apron just as the backseat door opened and a backpack was tossed onto the seat. It looked like his, but with a few more black marks.

"Not burned, not soggy," Walter reported as he climbed in the driver's seat. "A little smoky, maybe, but no worse for wear."

"Okay. What did the twins have to say? Are they okay?"

"They're fine, a little shaken, a little anrgy. And you're not out of work yet. They're going to call it a night once the crews leave, go home and take a break, then start on clean-up tomorrow. Whatever hours you work in the next day or two to help clean up, they'll pay you for. At least until they have to call in professional contractors."

"Cool."

"Sounds like they won't actually be open for a week or two. I didn't go in, but the fire chief says the damage is minimal."

"So that means that one of them probably Banded the fire so it wouldn't spread, right?"

Walter shook his head severely. "No. There are limitations to

Banding, Tommen. You know a few of them, like some technologies. Fire is another thing that Banding does not control well. It's like air. Air is not affected by Bands. If it were, you would use up all the oxygen in a Fast Band in a matter of minutes. Fire works the same way because of the properties of fire. It's not air, but it's not a solid. It's a chemical reaction that supersedes—"

"I know what fire is. Why can't it be controlled in a Band?"

"Ignition makes fire. Oxygen, heat, and fuel sustain it. In a case like today, the fire had oxygen, per the atmosphere. Because air is not controlled by Bands, the fire will always have oxygen. Heat is part of air, the excitement of the molecules. Therefore, uncontrollable by Bands. The same way that even if you Fast Banded in order to walk home quickly in the middle of winter, you could still freeze to death, because the cold still affects you."

"And the fuel?"

"The fuel may start inside a Band, but because the oxygen and heat can pass in and out of the Band freely, it only needs to find a fuel source and the fire jumps, essentially self-combusting out of the Band. It can actually pose a real threat to someone trying to Band the fire. Firefighters call it a flashover.

"Now, smaller instances like, say, a match or a lighter, those can be better controlled."

"Gas stoves?" Tommen wondered.

Walter shook his head. "Gas is a gas, it doesn't Band well and that's what supplies the fuel."

"Campfires?"

Walter's mustache twitched thoughtfully. "Possibly. Depends on the size, I suppose."

They rode in silence for a time after that, leaving the city and plunging into the growing darkness of the outer suburbs.

"And how was school?" Walter finally asked.

Tommen shrugged. "Okay."

"What happened?"

"Emily said she didn't want to go to the dance with me. Said that chivalry just wasn't her style."

"I'm sorry to hear that. But tomorrow's only Wednesday. Are there any other girls you can ask?"

Tommen shook his head. "Pa always told us, 'Never make a girl feel like second best.' "

Walter nodded once, carefully. "Good advice."

Sometimes Tommen wondered how Walter felt, when he invoked his pa's advice. Was he jealous of Tommen's pa? Was he mad at himself for not imparting similar advice? Did he want Tommen to shut up about him and stop living in the past? Or was he proud of Tommen for not abandoning his pa?

When they arrived home, Tommen changed clothes and dumped out his backpack. His books and papers smelled a little smoky and a few had singed edges. He briefly wondered if he was going to be charged for that. He gathered his pack and smoky work clothes and tossed them in the laundry before sorting through his backpack, immediately concluding that he should have done this a long time ago. And it was only six weeks into the school year.

"So what do you think?" Walter asked from his bedroom across the hall, unbuttoning his blues.

"About what?" Tommen wondered, moving his trash can beside the bed and sorting through his papers.

"Are you riding the bus to the bakery tomorrow or coming home?"

"Bakery."

"All right, but know that you're going to stay as long as they need you, and that'll be your punishment for fighting. In full."

"I can't stay past nine o'clock, though," Tommen said smartly, tying off the trash bag.

Walter shrugged. "What's a few more hours gained in the last five minutes before closing?"

The bakery fire didn't make the evening news, but for those whose buses went past the bakery, news of the fire still made it to school in time for first period, and Tommen spent pretty much his entire day being harassed by one person or another about the fire. What happened? Was everyone okay? Was it a complete loss? Was he the one who started it?

It almost made him not want to go and help clean up, but there he was, on the bus, getting dropped off in a parking lot that serviced a small line of suite businesses, one of which was still officially taped off with a handwritten sign on the door explaining what happened. More or less.

But when Tommen entered the building, shifting his bundle of dirty work clothes under his arm, he was surprised to hear a female voice among those in the kitchen. Cautiously, he peeked around the corner into the kitchen.

First, he noticed that the kitchen wasn't as badly destroyed as he had feared, else Micah and Micaiah had done a hell of a lot of cleanup already. The ovens had been pulled out and sorted by either salvageable or sell for scrap; the tables had been moved, making the kitchen feel easily two or three times its size. All the racks of product, pots, pans, anything that could be moved was moved.

The woman who was standing in the kitchen with the twins, her back to Tommen, was hardly dressed for clean-up work. She wore flat sandals despite the chill in the air, dark jeans that looked like they'd been bedazzled by a twelve year old, and a formal blouse that had probably cost a pretty penny for whosever name was on the label sticking up off the collar, just barely visible under black hair done up in a deliberately messy bun. She spoke in a way that reminded Tommen of really snobby middle schoolers who thought they were all that. She alternated between folded arms and hands on hips, either way standing like she was posing for a magazine.

Eventually, Tommen figured she must have sensed that she was being stared at because her talking finally ceased and she turned around.

"Ah, so this is Walter's little pet, I mean, son," she said, her tone suggesting there had been no slip of the tongue whatsoever. "Tiny thing; has he had his growth spurt yet?"

"I'm five-ten," Tommen blurted in his defense, immediately feeling his cheeks grow warm.

"Aw, so cute." Her lip went pouty. On Emily it was adorable. On this lady, and especially when she was mocking him, Tommen wanted to deck her. She looked back at the twins. "I see why you keep him around."

"We keep him around to help," Micah told her acidly. "Unlike you."

She sighed dramatically and walked over to Tommen, hips swaying so he thought they were in danger of somehow falling off. "Not even a proper introduction. Well, you may as well know my name is Lily. Lily Guile. Obviously Micah hasn't mentioned me. Has dear Walter?"

"I know the name," Tommen said, cautiously extending a hand. "You're a Harvester."

She grinned, her teeth glinting like something out of a toothpaste commercial. "That's right. I work in NICU—that's the Neonatal Intensive Care Unit—at the children's hospital. And you are?"

"Tommen."

She clicked her teeth dismissively, like she'd merely forgotten his name. "Of course."

Tommen wondered if Walter had ever mentioned him to this woman. He couldn't decide if it might have been a good thing. Still, she looked back at Micah and Micaiah. "I'll let you three hard-working men get back to your job."

And she strode out like the universe itself was her doormat, to say nothing of the Porsche she drove away in.

Tommen looked at the twins. "Who was that?"

Micaiah shrugged. "Well, she introduced herself, didn't she? Lily Guile, nurse at NICU. Actually, she's the director."

"But who is she? Why was she here? She mentioned Micah specifically."

Micah ripped his gloves off a little harder than Tommen

thought necessary. "We dated for a while. Eventually, she decided that me being a Timekeeper was not in her best interests as a Harvester."

"Why?" Tommen pulled on his work clothes over his regular clothes. "Wouldn't that be like having her own personal bodyguard? I mean, I don't know a lot about Harvesting, but she probably gets some pretty good Time Capsules out of NICU."

"She does," Micaiah said. "It also makes her one of the richest and most corrupt Harvesters. If a Time Capsule goes for ten million turns at regular auction, it'll go for twenty million on the black market, and she gets a bigger cut of the profits."

Tommen crossed the kitchen to the burned oven alcove and started helping Micaiah to tear out drywall. "So turn her in."

"Problem is, everything she does is legal. She's no fool, Tommen, however much her outward appearance may say otherwise. She gets others to do the dirty work." Micaiah tossed the drywall sheets and pieces into a pile. "Believe me, if we could get the proof we need, she'd already be out of business."

"Not that it would matter even if we got the proof," Micah grumbled. "For a Harvester, she has an awfully big hand in the elections."

"What, like buying votes?"

Micaiah paused in his work. "Another time, when we're not already busy, we'll explain it to you. And it'll be a little easier after your review because the Hands and the politics will be more fresh in your mind. Until then, grab that and help pull this out."

Tommen did as he was told and together the three of them managed to completely gut the burned-out alcove, effectively tearing out one wall, stripping another, and exposing the brick of the outer wall. By the time they got all the debris out to the dumpster and the ovens sorted and moved, it was long since dark.

"But, seriously," Tommen said, taking his gloves off and wiping his forehead with a towel while Micaiah got a drink of water, "what did happen between Micah and Lily? I mean, job disagreements aren't uncommon."

Micaiah shook his head. "Lily's got a bit of a God Complex, seeing her role as a Harvester like some sort of demented Grim Reaper or Angel of Death."

"Oh. But still..."

"Tommen, you don't understand now, but you will once you become an Apprentice, how Timekeeping affects us as we age."

In truth, Micah and Micaiah were about ninety years old. Walter? He refused to say. About fifteen to twenty percent of Timekeepers experienced an accelerated aging process, the rest, a slower aging process. The degree of either was determined usually by how much they used their abilities. Tommen would currently only experience residual effects, maybe living to be ninety or a hundred and still in relative good health if he stopped cold turkey.

Micaiah continued, "Harvesters experience something similar, leeching off a few seconds or minutes or years from their victims. But they also seem to acquire some physical aspects over a long period of time. A change in hair color, change in skin tone. It wouldn't surprise me if Lily has managed to acquire a more child-like mentality."

"So, theoretically, a Timekeeper and a Harvester could get together," Tommen stated.

"Oh, yes. And when he said they dated for 'a little while' it was actually about five years give or take." He sighed and looked around suspiciously for his younger brother. "The night he was going to ask her to marry him, he took her to a magnificent restaurant, the kind where you have to learn proper etiquette and wear a tux and stuff? Well, he had it all planned out, the ring, the music, the wine, it was like something out of a storybook. He got down on one knee and asked."

"Obviously she said no."

Micaiah nodded sadly. "She dumped the entire wine bottle on his head, flipped the table, and stormed out. Never had he been so humiliated." He folded his arms. "Of course, seeing her now, he's glad things didn't work out. But still..." He shook his head and fixed

Tommen in a serious stare. "I know you have your own code of chivalry about being kind to women. And that's good. But that doesn't mean you have to take shit from them either. You deserve respect as much as they do."

Tommen nodded and moved to head off elsewhere in the store. Micaiah grabbed his shoulder and spun him around. "You heard nothing, at least not from me. You got that? I'm telling you this only to warn you about her. But I'll be telling you something else if you use it to hurt Micah. Got it?"

"Yes, sir."

Chapter Four
The Dance

Friday rolled around like a surprise punch to the face while walking around a corner. Tommen was not overly fond of the idea of spirit days and dressing up in school colors and going to the homecoming pep rally, nor was he looking forward to the dance later that night. Truth be told, he wasn't too thrilled about sneaking off to the soccer fields with Eric and Varad except that he had little else to do that night, and he needed some kind of a thrill. Sitting at home on the computer while Walter fell asleep watching TV was not his idea of thrilling.

Perhaps the only thing that made the day bearable was the science test. He'd confirmed it with Gillingham that morning. Yup, show up after the buses left with two Number 2 pencils and a calculator, nothing more. Well, what Gillingham didn't know wouldn't hurt him. After all, the man couldn't even see Bands. And even if he could, how would he be able to rightly disqualify the test?

It put a smug smile on Tommen's face as he walked in the classroom armed with his pencils and calculator.

"So it seems I couldn't scare you off," Gillingham said from behind his desk.

"You'd have to do a lot better than that," Tommen told him.

"Of course. Pick any seat you like and we'll get rolling."

There was an art to picking the seat with the best vantage point. He might have chosen his normal seat next to the wall, except lab equipment blocked his view of some of the posters in the room which detailed a number of equations, conversions, and other tidbits to know. He could have chosen the back, except he'd learned from experience that despite teachers putting troublesome kids in the front row, they actually watched the back row more. No need to draw suspicion, even if he could just create a Fast Band, cheat however he wanted, and Gillingham would see no more than a twitch or a shuffle of movement.

But Tommen was determined to win on his own merit, even if that meant bending and stretching Time as he needed to. Ultimately, he didn't believe in arbitrarily timed tests, especially in science. The crunch meant that shortcuts would be taken and possibly bad or false results given. And that was just bad science.

All this went through his mind in hardly ten seconds as he chose a seat in the middle row close to the lab where he could easily view all the posters and equipment. He set out his pencils and calculator.

Gillingham handed him a blank paper and a test booklet, then returned to the front of the room to open the proctor's book.

"The blank sheet you have been given is for scrap use and is yours to use however you wish," he read, with about as much enthusiasm as reading the ingredients list on a sack of flour. "This sheet will not be turned in. If you require more paper, raise your hand and another will be given to you."

And so it went on for pencils, erasers, calculator troubles, and on and on. No food or drink was allowed during the test although a short snack and bathroom break would be given halfway through the test. Exactly four minutes, any later and the test would be forfeit. Then it went into properly marking the answers, how to change an answer, and so on and so forth. Tommen thought he might have dozed. It was like watching Bob Ross reruns.

"And now, finally, without further ado, you may break the seal and begin the test," Gillingham said with a relieved sigh.

Tommen did so. His first thought was to immediately plunge headfirst into a Fast Band, then he determined that to be rather unwise. Aside from how obvious it would look if he finished the test before Gillingham even got back to his seat, the physical toll it would take on him wasn't worth it. He'd never recover in time to be able to make it through three drinks and a smoke.

And as he read through the first story problem and the ensuing questions, he figured he might not need to Band at all. True, he was no doctor, but everything was laid out so plainly he almost forgot he needed an equation to solve it.

It wasn't the first time his confidence had landed him headlong into trouble as the stories became more complex and the questions more confusing. He had to go back and reread entire passages to gain a single detail in order to get one variable for an equation that only fed a larger equation. And then, surprise, the answer he got wasn't one of the multiple choice options.

Even better were the questions that didn't necessarily use straight equations to get the answer, but instead asked, "What would happen if X were increased?" or "What could you conclude if the results had come out like this?"

"Pencil down," Gillingham said suddenly.

"It hasn't been three hours!" Tommen protested, looking at the clock.

"No, but it is time for the four minute break. Starting...now."

Tommen headed for the bathroom even though he really didn't have to go. He just had to get up, get out of the room, stretch his legs, walk a little. He got a drink from the fountain.

Maybe he'd been overestimating his abilities. Sure, chemistry was boring as hell, but still...he was in the middle of a college-level test. College. He had all of two and a half high school science classes and a bunch of TV documentaries under his belt. Where had he come off thinking he could just ace this test and waltz into AP Physics like the new bad ass on the block?

Still, he had come this far and he wasn't about to chicken out now. If nothing else, at least he would have the bragging rights to say he'd been offered and taken such a test, one which Gillingham said he didn't offer lightly. It was small comfort as he returned to the room, did one final stretch, and sat down. He had to endure a brief reprisal of the rules, but was on his way once more in no time.

This time he did dive into a Fast Band, consequences be damned. He needed AP Physics more than he needed a couple drinks. And even so, what was the difference between a Time hangover and an alcohol hangover? At least a Time hangover he could explain to Walter.

The questions only continued to get harder, more complex. The test had started out with a medical scenario, then a physics scenario, then geology, and so on. Now the lines were no so clear-cut. Chemistry mixed with medicine; geology mixed with physics.

In a way, it was a glorious thing to behold, all the sciences melting together in real-world situations. At the same time, Tommen was also acutely aware that maybe the timed tests weren't so awful after all. Sure, scientists that poked around in a lab needed time and had the luxury of pencils and paper. A paramedic who needed to give an emergency injection didn't have time to work out chemical compounds and figure out reactions; he needed to know that on the spot, or at least have a guess that was good enough to risk his job and his patient's life.

It wasn't enough to make Tommen drop his Band. His pa always said, "When yer fightin' a bear, ya don't throw yer gun away 'acause the bear don't 'ave one. You use every weapon ya got."

And damn was he fighting a bear. This was like the grizzly bear of science tests. A starving grizzly bear, here to chew up his science career and spit it out in some elementary school science fair with the baking soda and vinegar volcanoes.

He kept up his Band until he'd finished everything once, marked an answer for every question. Then he moved back into Base Time to look over his work and double-check his answers. He redid a problem here and there, changed an answer, changed his mind, changed the answer again. He stole a glance at the clock; technically he still had an hour or more.

He had to admit, when he walked into the room, he was surprised Gillingham hadn't covered up the posters with all the equations like most high-stakes tests did. Now he realized that he really hadn't needed to look at them because none of it mattered. He didn't need to know x + y = z. He needed to know why. And that was why the test had been so damn hard.

Eventually, Tommen called it. He was going to go crazy if he had to look back over his answers one more time. Finally he just stood up, grabbed his booklet, and went to Gillingham who was grading tests at his desk.

"Done?" he wondered.

"I suppose," Tommen said.

"You don't sound too confident."

"I'm as confident as I can be at this point."

"More difficult than you anticipated?"

Tommen shrugged. "Different."

"More real-world stuff, huh? More of what you'll actually need to know to get anywhere in the scientific community. But that's not to say that all of this—" He swept his arm around the room full of useless posters. "—is for nothing. No matter what you study, you always need a good foundation. You've just surpassed that stage." He took the booklet. "I'll get this graded and sent in. Then me and you and your dad and Mrs. Wendell will sit down and talk about where you can go from here. How does that sound?"

"Sounds fine to me."

"Good man. Now then, I think they're still decorating the gym for the dance. Why don't you go help them?"

It was the last thing Tommen wanted to do. Decorating was overseen by the student councils from each grade, the National Honor Society, and a host of snobby preps, jocks, and overly-exalted studious students. Low-lifes like him just didn't get involved.

Instead he found his clothes and changed into them, telling himself it was just long enough to get an alibi. Fruitlessly hit on girls, make small talk with a bunch of teachers, make sure as many people as possible saw them at the dance. Go get a little tipsy, a little high, then make an appearance at the football game. Some concessions to ward off any unpleasant odor, more small talk with teachers, and home they went. No muss, no fuss, and no questions asked.

It was a simple enough plan, certainly far simpler than whatever monster had unfurled itself in the gymnasium. The theme was supposed to be Alice in Wonderland. Tommen had an appreciation for Alice in Wonderland and all its creative complexities and nuances. What lay before him was anybody's guess.

Twirled and gnarled old maple trees more resembled brightly-colored palm trees with swirls painted on in cheap acrylic, the fake wood faces one might find at the hardware store poorly glued on; Tommen picked up an eye and a mouth that had fallen. The Cheshire Cat had apparently had an affair with Waldo because he was hiding everywhere, around every corner, in every nook and cranny, from every height, all in a variety of cat poses. It took a moment for Tommen to also realize that the striped bananas littering the walls were supposed to be the smile of the Cheshire Cat.

The Jabberwocky was the most egregious bumbling of theme, looking like some paper mache Chinese dragon thrown together by kindergarteners asked to create the headpiece of a Viking war ship. It sprawled confusingly along one wall, over the mats beneath the basketball hoop, and somehow looped back around, the hoop poorly converted into the head and looking almost ready to fall from the ceiling.

And through and over and around it all, gray and blue streamers, confetti, origami creatures, tissue paper, and other assorted cheap, quick, decorations littered the walls and floor like Christmastime in an orphanage. Glitter was also very noticeable and Tommen suspected that he wasn't going to be able to cross the floor before he was covered in the stuff.

"Hey, Tommen! Come help out, would you?"

It was Eric who had called, standing on a ladder, trying to hang something from the basketball hoop not currently being used as the head of a Chinese Viking dragon. Despite being an outcast like Tommen, Eric was part of NHS and expected to help with all manner of activities.

"Hand me those one at a time, would you?" Eric pointed to a box.

Tommen went to the box and fished out a fake rose that had been modified so that in the center was a single Christmas light, probably red, a tiny battery hidden in the stem. He flicked it on and off a couple times before handing it to Eric.

"I think these are the best decorations I've seen so far," he commented.

Eric shrugged. "What do you expect given who's in charge?"

Tommen faked a gasp of surprise. "You mean you were ousted?!"

"I was told to be in charge of the roses, so I made the best damn roses I could."

"They didn't put you in charge of food?"

Eric barked a laugh. "Are you kidding? Lindsey." He put one hand to his chest and held one out in a mock snobby gesture. Then, in an equally mocking voice, "My daddy's a master chef; he can get us whatever we want to have. After all, I am a senior and this is the last time he'll be able to do such a thing for me."

They laughed at his impression, mostly because it was basically accurate. Tommen shook his head and handed up another rose. "Oh well. It would have meant 'missing the football game.' "

Eric only grinned but said nothing.

"Aw, how cute. Look, guys, they're sharing a moment. And the flowers, how precious."

It didn't take an NHS member to know who stalked toward them. Tommen deliberately turned his back and handed up another rose, determined to ignore Tyler and his cronies. As he was reaching down for another rose, he felt a very familiar boot in his backside and he went sprawling. Giggles and snickers came from elsewhere in the gym. Tommen rolled his neck and got up just as Eric got off the ladder.

"You all right?" he asked.

"Fine!" Tommen snapped, fixing Tyler in his best death stare. He might as well have tried to stare down a cat. A cat who'd caught his prey and was now toying with it, waiting to deliver the killing blow.

"Aw, the concern of a lover," Tyler went on. "You know, I've seen this thing before, like in chick flicks, where the girl always passes up the nice guy and goes after the jerk. You seem to be passing up the nice guy, too, Tommen, and going after a girl who doesn't even care about your chivalry."

Tommen grinned. "You seem to be well-acquainted with chick flicks to know that one, Tyler."

The bully had walked right into that one, and his expression said he knew it. He took a step forward and kicked Eric's box across the floor. "If you've got something to say, I might have something to say as well."

"You approached me. Are you going to fight Eric now to be able to take me to the dance? I'm flattered. I've never been the girl someone's fighting over."

The thing about Banding was that, at least for Tommen, it wasn't necessarily reflexive. It was a conscious effort. So when Tyler's fist came flying through the air, Tommen had to consciously build his Band in order to be able to move out of the way in time. Suffice to say, this did not happen, and instantly Tommen knew that now the right side of his face was going to be swollen and discolored for the dance. And just after the left side had returned to normal.

The strange thing was, even for Tommen's relatively simple training and lack of experience, building a Band was not that hard, nor did it take that long, especially since he was a little more attuned to the passing of time than most. Heck, he'd just done it in order to get around the rules of his science test.

So when Tyler's foot flashed out to catch him in the ribs while he was down, Tommen was able to perceive the seconds as they ticked by so he could Band and roll out of the way, feeling the steel of the toe just brush his coat. He rolled and stood up, keenly aware that Tyler's goons were starting to surround them; they would be no help but to their master, like a pack of trained hounds.

Banding made Tommen's reflexes appear quick as he dodged and ducked and skirted around his opponent, but Tyler had the natural speed and aggression to negate it, pushing Tommen to a point where his pithy little party tricks would do nothing but delay the inevitable; he would have to go all in if he actually wanted to do any damage.

He managed to land one good blow before the corner of his eye caught sight of Eric and Gillingham entering the gym. In that split-second of hesitation, his vision blacked out and then he was on the ground, groaning like an idiot, Gillingham over him.

"Tommen? Tommen, can you hear me?" Gillingham was saying.

"Huh?" Tommen blinked, tried to clear the spots from his vision, wondering why his face felt wet. "What?"

Slowly he got to a sitting position. Someone brought him a chair and he got into it, wordlessly accepting a box of tissues. Bloody hell, twice in one week. Decorating. Always a bad idea.

"Tommen, do you understand what I'm saying?" Gillingham asked.

"Yeah," Tommen mumbled, not looking at him, wiping the tears from his eyes and the blood from his nose. He ran his tongue over his teeth. Nothing loose. Good. Lucky again, but how long would that last at this rate?

"How do you feel?" Eric demanded. "Did you black out at all?"

Tommen shook his head, nausea swimming over him. "No," he lied. "Just a little confused was all."

"Are you sure?" Gillingham wondered. "If you blacked out, we need to call an ambulance."

"Call the fucking police," Tommen growled, continuing before Gillingham could protest his language. "Where'd Tyler go?"

"Layman took him and his cronies," Eric reported. "I don't

think we'll have to worry about them tonight."

Tommen scoffed. "Who cares about tonight?" He stood up, wobbled, wasn't about to go back down, forced himself to walk. "I'm going out for a bit."

He left the gym before either of them could protest. The cold air outside hit him with all the friendliness of a metal flyswatter left to chill in a freezer for a couple hours. Still, he made a couple loops of the parking lot, enough for his nose to stop bleeding, and the cold helped to ease the pain and soften the swelling in his face. He didn't dare look in a mirror even though he knew it probably wasn't as bad as earlier in the week. This time he'd only taken two blows instead of five. Or maybe six. He couldn't remember.

Some people had never gone home for the dance, like Eric and those who had spent the afternoon decorating. But as Tommen made his final loop of the parking lot, more and more people started showing up. Some were chaperones, parents and teachers coming to have a good time and make sure the students didn't.

Most of those arriving, however, were students. Homecoming wasn't as fancy as prom, but still, some made as much effort to look good for their date as any bride or groom on their wedding day. Tommen wouldn't doubt that some probably spent just as much, too, on the dress or the tux, the hair and makeup, the shoes and jewelry. For goodness' sake, guys, it was only the homecoming dance.

He made it back to the front doors just as Eric was leaving.

"Where are you going?" Tommen wondered.

"Pick up Varad," Eric said, brandishing his keys. "Wanna come?"

It was better than sticking around the dance, Tommen figured, following Eric to his little silver Subaru and climbing in.

"You feeling any better?" Eric asked as they pulled out of the parking lot.

Tommen shrugged. "The bleeding stopped."

"Well, you know what, we don't have to be at the dance very long. We get in, we make small talk with a couple key figures, we get out, and then you can forget the rest of your problems. At least for tonight. Then you can put them on hold for a while this weekend. Good?"

"Sure. Seeing how I'm currently out of a job."

"You said the damage wasn't that bad. They'll be back in business in no time. Unless you don't want to go back?"

"No, I like the work. That's not the problem."

"Then what is the problem?"

Tommen gingerly touched the side of his face. Not nearly as bad as Monday. "Nothing. At least nothing that a couple shots can't fix."

"Amen to that, brotha."

Even as he said it, they pulled into the driveway at Varad's house where the young man waited like he expected a princess to greet him. He piled in the back seat, all smiles, situating a black backpack as far underneath the driver's seat as he could until Eric complained.

"Hey, guys, I—oh. Shit. What happened?" Varad asked.

"Tyler," was all Tommen said.

"Already? Weird. Normally he waits a couple days."

"What do you got, Varad?" Eric cut in.

"Right! So, as far as anyone is concerned, this backpack has some street clothes because obviously I don't want to mess up the tux with ketchup or relish. But tucked inside those clothes are the objects of our affection tonight."

"Because we're driving to the soccer fields?" Tommen wondered. Everything was within walking distance.

Varad sighed dramatically. "No, you dolt. When we decide to leave, I make a well-heard comment that I want to change clothes. I come out, grab the stuff, change my clothes, stash the dope, and we're on our way."

"Sounds pretty fool-proof to me," Eric said.

They made it back to the school not long after the dance had officially started. The senior class president was stamping hands. She said it had to do with keeping a number count. Tommen suspected it was just because she liked the smilies.

"Doing better, Tommen?" Gillingham asked as they entered the gym.

"As better as can be expected of the last half hour or so," Tommen replied. "How long does that test take to grade?"

"It'll be a week or two. Don't worry about it. Especially not here. Go have fun and enjoy yourself."

"And Tyler?"

"Not here."

"Where?"

Gillingham gave him a severe look. "Not here."

Tommen might not have pressed except for the need to be slightly conspicuous. Even so, he found himself at the same spot he ended up at most dances. The punch bowl. With the rest of the bachelors.

He saw Emily a short distance away, laughing and hanging out with her girlfriends. She looked stunning in a deep blue dress with straps as thin as the dress code would allow. Her hair was up in some outlandish style, but then, she could pull off anything. Bedhead probably looked sexy on her.

One of her friends said something and pointed. She looked at him and he looked away, at the Chinese Viking dragon. Given the dimness of the room and the scant blue, gray, and yellow lights, the decorations didn't look all that bad. Still atrocious and having no real respect for Alice in Wonderland save ripping off the name, but not any worse than any other dance, Tommen supposed.

He didn't really pay attention to the music and when the songs started and ended, but he did notice when Luke appeared from somewhere and approached Emily. They talked for a just a minute, Emily giving him cute looks and playful swats before finally following him out onto the dance floor.

Jealousy burned in Tommen's stomach. How was it that such a beautiful girl had no respect for chivalry, no desire to see it implemented? How could such a girl just brush it off like it was a choice and not a special gift? Yes, chivalry protected all women, but there were still ways to make a special girl feel special. So why in the world would she not accept the specialness Tommen wanted to bestow upon her? What kind of girl was she?

Perhaps it was that line of thought that finally broke both the jealousy and the desire within Tommen. He had his answer. How could such a girl reject chivalry? Because she was just a girl. Chivalry was reserved for women, those who understood and appreciated it, not because they were weak, but because it was necessary, because it was special. And Emily...she was not special.

Tommen milled around the punch bowl for a moment longer, oblivious to the action around him. All these people, all these girls, he wouldn't see them again after graduation, so why did he try to hard to win their affections? They called him The Chivalrous Welshman because it amused them, because he amused them. But it was all meaningless.

His resolve lasted only until he turned and found himself face-to-face with Emily. His mind was suddenly torn between wanting to rip that dress off her and take her there—or maybe under the bleachers, public decency and all that—and simply step aside and let a girl get herself some punch.

"Emily," he said lamely. "Is there...can I get you some punch?"

She gave him that lopsided smile. "Thanks, Tommen, but I think I can get it myself. I don't need to trouble you, all that chivalry and stuff."

And there was the girl. His lingering affections vanished even as she continued to speak.

"I know I probably embarrassed you the other day by not really coming with you to the dance. So if you want, I'll let you have the next dance."

"What about Luke?" Tommen wondered.

She shrugged. "He's in the bathroom. He'll never know." She rolled her eyes playfully. "He takes forever."

Even his respect for her was beginning to wane. She was beautiful, but vain, and he no longer wanted her. Instead, he just set down his punch. But rather than offer his arm to her, he simply said, "I'm sorry, my lady, but I will have to decline. After all, how would it look for The Chivalrous Welshman to be seen not only dancing with another man's girl, but doing so entirely without his knowledge at his lady's behest?"

Emily could only open her mouth, but no words came out as he did a sweeping mock bow and walked away. He'd had enough of this scene. He found Eric and Varad on the staircase to the storage area, eating.

"I'm ready to head out," Tommen announced.

"We just sat down to eat," Eric told him. "You should, too. Matt just told me they've raised concession prices just for this game. Frickin' communists."

"I think the word you're looking for is capitalist," Varad corrected. He looked at Tommen. "Besides, the DJ is going to play some awesome songs here in a minute. Stay, have fun. The game will always be there."

Tommen sighed. "Eric, can I have your keys?"

Eric raised a brow but tossed him the keys. "What do you plan to do?"

"I'm going out to sit."

He left the gym, trying not to seem upset or in any kind of real hurry as he crossed the parking lot to Eric's car, meticulously parked to allow them the best cover for getting to the soccer fields. Naturally, there were also cameras pointed every which way, but no one actually sat watching them. If something bad happened, like vandalism or something, then the tapes could be reviewed. But so long as nothing stupid happened tonight, they should get off free and clear. Of course, this depended not only on them being good, but everyone else being good, too. Layman could easily watch the tapes looking for someone else spraying graffiti and catch them in their little stint, a two-for-one as it were.

Tommen sat in the backseat for a few minutes, not really thinking about a whole lot. He glanced at the black backpack stuffed behind the driver's seat. Varad had said he had three drinks for each of them. Would anyone care if he broke in and started a little early?

Eventually he pulled out his phone and tried to connect to the school's public wifi. Of course, everyone else was also connected to the wifi, rendering it all but useless for as slow as it became as they took tons of pictures and videos, uploading and downloading, as if anyone would care in five years—or by the end of the year for that matter—who went with who and what dress she was wearing, and on and on it went. Later on, they'd all look back and wonder, "What was I thinking?"

Tommen wondered that sometimes, too, as he perused his social media sites, each one pretty much the same as the last. Walter tolerated his use of social media but always warned against it, citing the inevitability that his Banding would only slow his aging and eventually he would have to leave, lest someone grow suspicious. But for the meantime, while he was a teenager, highly visible in a technologically-dependent society, Walter allowed him to keep a few profiles.

Not that he didn't consider deleting them all and just walking away. Social media was nothing but fighting, drama, and passive aggressive comments aimed at everyone and no one.

And where were Eric and Varad anyway? They weren't supposed to stay for very long, just long enough to get noticed. The game would be in half-time before they even got started in the soccer fields.

Grumpily, Tommen started viewing Internet videos. He'd tried to Band them once, trying to watch a couple pirated movies before class, and found he couldn't. Micaiah had explained that it had to do with the Band having nothing to "grab" so to speak. The phone was an object, true, but ultimately the video was simply encoded data sent to his phone through the air from a remote server. Essentially, he was trying to Band air, and it just didn't work.

He wasn't sure how many videos he watched, but he jumped when the door suddenly opened and Varad was making a grab for his backpack.

"What the hell took so long?" Tommen demanded. "Do you know what time it is?"

"Chill out, dude," Varad said, giving him a look. "Eric and I were in there trying to get laid. Not our fault you didn't stick around."

"So did you?"

"What?"

"Have a second glass of punch. Get laid!"

"Dude, if we had, we'd all be going to the soccer fields. You think we're dumb enough to try it in the school? Layman's got this thing run like a prison tonight. When we go, we'll have to move pretty fast, okay?"

"Whatever. Is Eric coming?"

"Poor soul is still trying." Varad hoisted his backpack on his shoulder. "I'm going to change, grab Eric, then we'll be out. Okay?"

"Yeah, fine."

Varad rolled his eyes and started back toward the school; Tommen watched him go. There were times he wished Varad was the stereotypical Indian kid so he could help him get into the school's private network that the teachers used. But he was pretty much like every other student, maybe a little more networking knowledge than most, enough to get into a few not-so-hidden files and play pranks, but nothing serious.

Tommen would have given Varad five minutes to change, then maybe a few more minutes to pull Eric away from whatever girl he was foolishly attempting to woo. But when ten minutes passed, then twenty, Tommen was pretty sure they'd been caught. If Layman was keeping things as tight as Varad said, there was every chance he'd also checked the backpack and found the goods. Question was, had only Varad been found, or had he implicated Eric and Tommen also? It was likely, given that there were three of everything and it was no secret they hung out together. Maybe Tommen could make a break for it and make it to the football field and establish an alibi before Layman came out looking for him.

Then he spotted the two bachelors heading in the direction of the car, laughing as only a couple of rejected bachelors can. Varad opened the door and swung his backpack in the backseat just as Tommen was getting out on his side.

"So what happened?" Tommen wondered, hoping he sounded a little less cranky and itching to get going. The last thing he needed was Walter showing up tonight.

"He did it," Varad said, grinning. "The bastard did it."

"Did what? I'm confused."

"Did Michelle," Eric told him.

"Dude," Tommen said, then lowered his voice. "You got laid? How, with Layman around?"

Eric shook his head. "Storage closet between the locker rooms."

Tommen raised a brow. "Really? That was the best you could do? Why not bring her with us?"

"She was looking for a thrill, said that a small room with the music hammering through the walls and the threat of getting caught was enough for her."

"And...that's it?"

"That's it. No muss, no fuss, no looking back."

Tommen just shook his head. He wasn't really his father's son anymore, didn't particularly believe sex was much of anything special, but damn...at least do it in a clean room, not a room full of cleaners.

"All right," Varad said, "are we going out or what?"

Chapter Five
Under the Bleachers

There were three different soccer fields scattered about the grass; Tommen, Eric, and Varad elected for the one farthest from the school. Only when they were as far as they could possibly get before hitting the treeline that separated the fields from the tiny parking lot and the busy road beyond did Varad fish in his pockets and bring out a bag containing a number of shot-sized drinks.

"Now then, as this is a formal event — less the Indian's servant garb — let us welcome our keynote speaker tonight, Admiral Nelson, with his good friend Captain Morgan, and their mutual acquaintance, Jack Daniels." Varad distributed one of each to each of them. He then produced a second bag containing three weed rolls. "And for the formal occasion, we shall also require proper rolls for the eloquent smoking man."

Again, he distributed them, one to each, and also produced a lighter to light them. First, a drag. Tommen coughed. He'd never actually been particularly fond of the smoking portion of their outings, preferring to get straight to the drinking part, but the two always seemed to go hand-in-hand, so he put up with it.

"Cheers, gentlemen," Eric said, cracking his first drink.

Tommen and Varad raised their first drinks in return, toasting and drinking, and taking yet another drag. Then Varad raised his second drink.

"And a job well done this evening, Sir Eric. May the maidens forever covet your name. And your dick."

"Here, here," Eric joked as he and Tommen raised their drinks, and together they drank again. Eric went on, "She wasn't even

79

wearing anything under her dress. She was looking to get laid tonight."

"Glad you could oblige," Tommen said. "I'm just sorry it wasn't me."

"Why?" Varad said, grinning. "You were swooning over Emily all week."

Eric shook his head. "Dude, when their back is to you, they all look the same."

"Probably dark, too," Tommen pointed out.

"No, the maintenance guy has a little like night light in there."

"For just such an occasion, I'm sure."

And they took another drag. Tommen coughed again.

"Good grief, Tommen, it doesn't take that much effort," Eric said, patting him on the back. "And remember you exhale after inhaling. You don't swallow."

"Spit, don't swallow," Varad chortled.

"Ha ha ha," Tommen said sourly. "I've never liked the smoking."

"No, but it makes you much more fun."

Yeah, because Tommen had been having just a ton of fun today. Because life just couldn't get any better than constantly being the low man on the totem pole, always getting targeted by Tyler. Guaranteed if Tyler hadn't interrupted him while he was talking to Emily, that's what he would be doing right now. That's what they would both be doing right now. Each other. And it would be more than just a quick fling in some storage room with a night light. Nope, they would have been on a bench in the locker room at the very least, maybe in the back of Eric's car. And her legs would be wrapped tight around him and —

"Are you sure you're a virgin?"

Tommen blinked back to reality and realized that he'd somehow gotten up into the bleachers, about seven rows up, near the top. His last drink was in one hand, half-burned roll in the other. He also realized that he'd been voicing some very private fantasies aloud.

Eric and Varad were at the bottom of the bleachers, staring up at him, eyes huge, mouths open.

Inwardly grimacing, Tommen took a last drag and flicked his roll away. Varad scrambled after it to see if it could be saved while Tommen descended the bleachers, popping the lid on his drink, downing it, then throwing the bottle away into the grass.

"You shouldn't do that," Eric said severely.

"What? Litter?" Tommen scoffed.

"What if someone found that, turned it in, and they pulled your prints off it?"

Tommen barked a laugh. "Oh, please. It doesn't work like that. If someone found that, they'd probably think some stupid high schoolers—or maybe some homeless guy—had a little drink out here. They wouldn't know who it was, and they'd throw it in the trash."

"If you're sure. I mean, I don't want that to happen to me. Last thing I need is to ruin my college prospects."

"College prospects? How are you going to afford a thing like college?"

"I've got some scholarships lined up. I can make it through my first year. Hopefully by then I'll be able to work more to save up more money for the second year."

"What are you going for anyway?"

"Registered Dietitian, what else? Failing that, I could always become a professional chef. Open my own restaurant."

"Do the restaurant, dude. No one gives a rip about a registered 'dietitian.' They don't even like the nutrition facts on the cereal box telling them what to eat."

"You might not care, but some people pay big bucks for an RD's advice."

"Well, those people don't live around here, so." Tommen shrugged.

Eric shrugged in return. "So, I'll move. There are colleges all around the country."

"You're moving?" Varad said, walking back up to them,

tucking Tommen's salvaged roll in his pocket. "So am I. Where are you going?"

"Nowhere yet," Eric told him. "Not until college."

"When are you moving?" Tommen asked. "More importantly, when were you going to tell us?"

"Oh, well, nothing's official yet. It probably won't be until the end of the school year, for the sake of all the kids. My parents want to return to India to reunite with their separated families. At least, that's the excuse they're using. I asked why they couldn't bring them here. My dad told me it is important for families to be together in their home country. I thought he was talking about a visit. Then I heard him say later that it was time to leave before the racists target us next."

"That's bullshit," Tommen cut in. "Everyone loves your parents."

Varad shrugged. "I don't know what to say. I am an American citizen. The last time I was in India, I was still in my mother's belly, and she didn't even know it yet. When they did find out, they were staying here in Charleston, and my father declared it a sign from Vishnu that this was where they were meant to be. America is all I have known, yet now my father tries to teach us the language of his village. Every night, all seven of us speak together in that language. The little ones pick it up better than I do."

"What are you going to do?" Eric asked.

"I'm only seventeen; I can't just say no. So I work. I'm saving up so that when I turn eighteen, I can buy a plane ticket back to the United States. I don't know where I will go or what I will do, but I will find a way."

"Dude, you can stay with me if you have to," Eric told him. "I will seriously smuggle you into my dorm room and you can hide under the bed."

"What makes you think you won't enjoy it?" Tommen wondered.

Varad sighed. "I'm sure I will. I will be very glad to finally meet my relatives. But it is not my home. Let the racists come, if indeed they will. America is my home just as much as theirs."

It was a sobering thought as they continued their trek around the soccer field, the drinks being tossed, rolls smoked to ash and discarded. None of them wanted to intrude on the others' thoughts, yet each wanted anything else to think about, Tommen especially. Eric leaving for college was inevitable, but if Varad left, too, he would be left alone in school, an even bigger target for Tyler and those like him.

"We should probably head over to the football game," Eric said at last. "They were just starting half-time when we left the dance. It'll be fourth quarter probably by the time we get over there."

"True," Tommen conceded. "But let's get there by way of the outer lines."

And so they made another lap of the soccer field. Tommen noted that the grass needed to be mowed and repainted. The weeds had grown up and the stripes were almost gone. He looked around the field in the darkness, only dimly lit by the city lights on the other side of the pine trees. He could hear something in the distance, on another field. He was hardly an expert, but it sounded like someone else had a similar idea to sneak off to the soccer fields. Except their intentions sounded more...interactive.

"You never did answer my question earlier," Eric said suddenly, grinning and looking at Tommen.

"What question?" Tommen wondered.

"Are you a virgin?"

Tommen stopped and grinned as he unzipped his pants. "You want to find out?"

"No, dude, put that thing away." Eric shook his head and rolled his eyes. "God, you're a dolt. But did you seriously have plans to fuck Emily tonight?"

"Assuming we'd gone to the dance, yes."

"You still want to fuck her?"

Tommen frowned and shook his head. "No. Not really."

"What about her?" Varad said, pointing to a figure that, in the dim light, appeared to be a girl sitting against one of the bleacher supports. "She's out here alone."

Tommen slapped Varad's hand away from his shoulder. "If she's out here alone, she's probably not waiting for three random guys to just walk up and fuck her. Chances are, that's what she's trying to get away from."

Rape was not in Tommen's fantasy repertoire, having heard several stories from the police department, never mind his chivalrous nature. Cautiously, he approached the girl. Blond hair tumbled past her shoulders to about mid-back level. He couldn't tell what kind of clothes she was wearing, but it wasn't a dress.

"Hello? Excuse me?" he ventured.

She didn't answer.

"Are you okay?" Tommen pressed. "We're not here to hurt you."

"We came out here to drink; why are you here?" Eric asked.

"Are you an idiot?" Varad said.

"What?"

"If she's out here alone and three guys say they just came out here to drink, what do you think she's going to think about us walking up to her? She's going to think—"

"Nothing," Tommen cut in, walking around to stand in front of the girl. "She's not going to think anything at all."

He could see Eric had gone pale as he and Varad walked up beside him.

Eric was sick immediately, vomiting almost on Tommen's shoes.

Perhaps the first and most obvious thing was her face, sliced with surgical precision into little half-inch squares, like someone had taken wire mesh and imprinted it on her face from ear to ear, under her jaw to her hairline. The next obvious thing was her throat, or lack thereof, as it had both been cut, evidenced by the huge gouge that had nearly decapitated her, and then removed, a gaping hole running from under the jaw where the cut marks ended to the nape of her neck. Her entire trachea had been removed. Looking down, her hands were pierced, an eight-inch railroad spike holding them together and then placed in her lap with care.

And yet the oddest thing, once Tommen thought about it, was the surprising lack of blood. She should have been completely drenched in it—her hair, her clothes, the rest of her body. But she wasn't. There was no blood outside the wounds which were clotted normally, and there was no evidence that the clothes had been scrubbed clean or her hair recently washed.

"Oh, sh-sh-shit," Eric stammered weakly, finally finding his voice even as he vomited again. "Oh shit. Oh shit oh shit oh shit. Shit." He stumbled a few steps back, hands on his knees like he was going to be sick again. "Shit."

Varad backed up a couple steps and tapped Eric on the shoulder. "Dude, we have to fucking run, get the fuck out of here."

Tommen turned. "What? No we can't!"

Varad shook his head, turned, and started to run. Eric held up a hand. "I'll be right there!"

Tommen took off after Varad, easily overtaking him and catching him by the shoulders, not slowing until they were both rolling on the ground. It was one fight that Tommen knew he could win, and he pinned Varad.

"We can't run," Tommen said sternly.

"There's a fucking body, dude," Varad whimpered. Tommen saw he was crying. Probably pissed himself, too. "I'm not going to prison for murder."

"We run, we're the first people the cops are going to suspect."

"We stay, we're still the first people the cops are going to suspect."

"Running looks guilty. Yeah, we're out here drinking and smoking. Cops are going to have bigger fish to fry. And it's the perfect alibi anyway."

"There's a fucking body, dude. Doesn't that scare the fuck out of you? What if the killer's still around? What if he's watching us?"

Tommen shook his head. "She wasn't killed here."

"How do you know?" Eric asked, walking up, still quite pale.

"She's wearing scrubs; she works at the hospital. There's no reason for her to be out here. And she's clean, no blood on her."

Carefully, he got off Varad and helped him up. "Listen, I'll call 9-1-1. But we have to stay here. Weather the storm today and get it over with, or run and always have that storm following us. Okay?"

"There's a fucking body over there, dude," Eric echoed. "I'm not going anywhere near that thing."

Tommen nodded. "Good. Find a stick and draw a huge circle around the body. Huge, enormous, as big as possible. Then we stay outside that circle." He dug his phone out of his pocket. Almost dead, but there was always that small reserve for emergency calls.

"So you're talking like a crime scene boundary," Varad said.

Tommen nodded and Varad bounded off to help Eric.

"9-1-1, what's your emergency?" It even sounded like the same dispatcher from when Tommen called in the fire. He briefly wondered if she would recognize his voice, too.

"I need to report a body," Tommen told her, walking back toward where Eric and Varad were busy drawing a boundary line, good and thick, around a large area. As he walked, he suddenly felt the weight of his words and the reality of the scene. There was a body. As in, dead. Like, not alive. And not just dead, but murdered. With not even any blood to show for it. His stomach jumped.

"Sir, did you say a body? Sir?" the dispatcher asked.

"Huh? Oh, yes. Yes, a body. Here at...at..." He felt woozy.

"Sir, are you all right?"

"Just...a bit...sick." Even as he said it, his glass of punch and all three drinks resurfaced. He gasped for breath. "South Charleston High School, the soccer fields, the farthest one from the school, by the road."

"Sir, can you remain on the line?"

He nodded uselessly. "Yeah."

He was put on hold briefly while police were dispatched, which gave him enough time to be sick once more and, hopefully, end that so he could regain his composure. Then the line clicked and the dispatcher came back through.

"All right, sir, I'm dispatching units to that location. I am going to ask you to remain calm and to please stay in the area, but do not disturb the body or the area around it. Are you the only one present?"

"No, it's me and a couple friends, but we're staying well away, believe me."

"All right, sir, do you have a phone number to call back on?"

Tommen gave it to her.

"And what is your name, sir?"

Oh, he knew she was going to ask that. Just standard protocol with major cases like these. Well, either way, Walter was going to find out. He took a breath and answered, "Tommen Forbes."

"Tommen...Forbes?" She sounded almost disbelieving.

He sighed. "Yes, my dad is Homicide Detective Walter Forbes."

The dispatcher seemed to remember herself then. "Mr. Forbes, units are en route to your location."

Tommen got off the phone with dispatch even as he heard sirens wailing in the distance. He wasn't sure what their hurry was. He wasn't going anywhere. Eric and Varad weren't going anywhere. The girl, whoever she was, was definitely not going anywhere.

"Is that a big enough circle?" Varad asked as he and Eric finished up their digging in the dirt with their sticks and met Tommen outside the line, facing the body.

"Well, it looks more like a demented oval," Tommen observed, "but it certainly looks big enough."

They'd scratched from the dirt lot and the pine trees, gave the bleachers and the body a wide, wide berth, and then continued into the playing field before splitting it up the middle. Tommen had a brief thought that digging that boundary probably wasn't the brightest idea he'd had today, but if anyone asked, he'd done his part to try to keep the scene clear. Yes, he engaged in little illegal binges, but he'd picked up a thing or two from Walter, and he more than respected the men in blue.

One cruiser pulled up in the dirt lot while another parked in the school parking lot.

"Stay here," Tommen told Eric and Varad. "And if possible, stay a short distance apart, otherwise they're going to think that you're trying to collaborate a story."

"Why shouldn't we?" Varad asked.

"Just do it."

He headed off in the direction of the officer who'd parked in the school parking lot. It wasn't unusual for the cops to "check up" on some school activities, but as soon as the words "dead body" were uttered, all hell would break loose. And if the officer brought that up to Layman first, who had no idea about any of this, then Tommen and his crew were all in serious trouble immediately. Guilty until proven innocent and all that.

And that was exactly how Tommen found them, in the front entry way, speaking in hushed voices despite the severity with which Layman whispered.

"I don't know anything about—" He stopped as Tommen walked in and approached them. "Please, Tommen, not now."

"Tommen?" The officer turned.

"Evening, Gary," Tommen greeted. "I think I'm the one you're looking for."

"I think you're the one who ought to explain this to me," Layman said sternly.

So the three of them walked out across the fields where the second road officer had already begun rolling tape. Tommen looked around and saw Eric seated at one end of the tree line and Varad at the other end. More flashing lights pulled into the dirt lot.

"What is going on out here, Tommen?" Layman demanded.

"Eric, Varad, and I found a body and we called it in," Tommen told him.

"And when were you going to tell me? This is my school, after all."

"By the time I hung up with dispatch, the cops were already here."

"You should have come to me first."

"We didn't have time. Every minute wasted is a minute the killer can get away."

Layman couldn't argue with that one; he had too much respect for Walter and knew that Tommen knew a few things about homicide investigation. Of course that would only make Tommen more suspicious in his eyes, despite most adult figures agreeing that while, yes, he was guilty of a few binges, murder wasn't his thing.

By now, more officers were pouring in, scene safety crews, evidence teams of a variety of specialties, photographers, and good old-fashioned homicide detectives, or at least the ones who got the preliminary information from the scene and relayed it to the detective who would ultimately be assigned the case.

Tommen knew the detectives well enough as Walter worked with one or another on cases. The one who stood about six-foot-four with brown-blond hair and a full beard was Standish-Something or Something-Standish. He was a friendly enough guy, good at his job, but Tommen always thought he was more suited to computer work—not administrative secretary or anything, but cyber crime.

The shorter one whom Tommen had surpassed by way of height recently was Percy-Something or Something-Percy. Walter spoke well of him, but Tommen just found him annoying, more actor than detective, who fancied himself the star of a *Law & Order* rerun, and dressed for the occasion, trenchcoat and all.

About five minutes into the scene, EMS arrived with the coroner in tow. He was a short man, slender, dark skin, dark hair, dark eyes, and bright blue surgical gloves. He carried a clipboard with several papers fluttering in the breeze. The evidence teams directed him where to step to disturb the scene as little as possible until he reached the body and could officially declare it dead.

And no party was complete without the news crew. The scene safety crew intercepted them before they could waltz about in the scene, and then the two parties engaged in the age-old debate of crime scene vs. news story. Mostly it was Officer Davis arguing with Roxanne Hart, the reporter. They argued constantly at scenes, and Tommen speculated that one day they'd end up married. Her cameraguy, Paul, simply stood back, waiting for his master's lead.

This wasn't to say Tommen spent a lot of time at crime scenes, only that he had more general exposure to them, and because he did listen to Walter when he vented about his day. If Walter knew just how much he listened, though, Tommen was more afraid that he'd try to get him to either become a police officer or a Timekeeper officer.

Through it all, people had come from near and far, drawn to the spectacle. They came from the school, across the fields, across the road, through the tree line, like they'd all just suddenly appeared. More officers were called to assist with keeping people out and soon the only people left inside the scene were the evidence teams, working swiftly and with unbelievable efficiency.

"And what were you doing out here, Tommen?" Layman asked.

"Going for a jaunt down to the burger joint," Tommen told him firmly.

"A joint, maybe, but not a burger. Your breath gives you away."

"Tommen!"

Walter pushed his way through the treeline. Tommen knew he would have been at home when the call came in. He also knew that if he'd just been called to get Tommen, he wouldn't have taken the time to get in uniform. More than likely, he'd been assigned to the case.

He made a beeline for Tommen, remembering himself at the last minute and skirting the scene, following the tape until he faced his son.

"Are you all right?" Walter demanded.

"He's fine," Layman assured him genially. "He did a brave thing, keeping his head together when him and his friends stumbled on this little...discovery."

Tommen wished he could have decked Layman, but Walter's expression said he wasn't fooled. By either of them. Suddenly Tommen was sucked into a Fast Band of Walter's making.

"And what were you doing out here?" Walter asked.

"Nothing," Tommen answered.

"I'm not asking if you had anything to do with this, I'm asking what you were doing out here. The dance is at the school and the football field is the other direction."

"Nothing!" he insisted. "Just...hanging out."

"Uh-huh. And the booze and smoke on your breath?"

Tommen looked away.

"We'll talk about this later," Walter promised. "But don't you go lying to the officer who formally interrogates you, because that could be considered impeding an investigation."

"It's not relevant to the murder, though."

"You let us decide that."

Then Walter dropped the Band and nodded slowly. "So who were your friends with you?"

Tommen pointed to Eric and Varad, seemingly forgotten as they sat by their respective trees. Their terror from earlier seemed to have subsided as they just soaked up everything that was happening—the officers, the people, the crime scene, the investigation, all of it new and exciting for them.

"Are you assigned to the case?" Tommen wondered.

Walter nodded. "I am. In any event, I cannot interrogate you. Detective Standish will do that. Mr. Layman."

Tommen inwardly snickered. Layman stood at attention, always ready to be of service to Charleston's finest. Walter still wasn't fooled. "This happened on your school grounds. You know the protocol. Give the morning news something to chew on for a bit so we can get our work done."

"Not a problem." Layman nodded and headed off to speak to Roxanne who was still arguing—well, at this point, amiably conversing—with Davis.

"Just stay here, Tommen," Walter said, cutting into his thoughts. "I know you know how this goes. And remember what I taught you about witness testimonies."

Tommen sighed. "I know." And he sat on the ground.

Walter was no rookie when it came to interrogations. He knew what questions to ask and how to ask them, but he also knew how to answer questions as well, having had to testify in court and defend some of his decisions on the job. He'd trained a number of detectives on such techniques and the success rate of positive ID's on criminals almost tripled. It wasn't about beating the system; it was about telling a well-constructed story containing only the facts so that they could not be called into question later.

For example, asking if a suspect was short or tall subconsciously imprinted those thoughts on the witness' mind that the suspect was either short or tall, and their personal perceptions about what constituted short and tall could skew the results. Instead, asking how tall the suspect was forces the witnesses to consider height relative to the environment, such as "he had to duck to get out the door" or "he had trouble climbing over the low wall."

Similarly, asking if the suspect was black or white subconsciously limited the narrative to those two skin tones—thus excluding the possibility of it being Latino, Arab, Native, etc. On the other hand, simply asking what color the suspect's skin was could even tap into unseen prejudices of the witnesses. If the suspect was white, and the witness only saw him in dim light, but that witness was also prejudiced against Hispanics, he might justify to himself that the suspect could have only been Hispanic because, well, crime.

"The best way to get a suspect description," Walter had once said, "is to simply separate the witness from the scene, from all the excitement, and simply try to recall what happened, and what the suspect looked like. Don't give any suggestive, subjective conditions. At the same time, don't leave them alone too long or else they'll talk themselves into a completely different story."

The same went for non-suspect-viable stories, like the one Tommen was considering right now. There was no suspect to describe, only a story to give. He could hear Walter's voice now. "Don't worry about Eric and Varad; only tell what you know. Let them hang themselves. You can't be punished for guilt by association if your story is true."

Tommen wanted to ask how conspiracy charges ever flew, then, but that was a conversation for another day, when there wasn't a dead body sitting only twenty yards from him, the coroner still examining her and taking down notes on his clipboard. Walter approached him. They conversed.

Tommen could only see Walter's profile, but the man got a certain look when there was more to the story than what met the eye. And Tommen figured he could see it, too. A murder was a murder, but the way the face was cut so precisely and the hands pierced, he smelled a serial killer. Maybe he watched too much TV, but grudges were carried out with passion. Need was carried out with cold precision. And if those little squares on her face were any indication, someone had a serious need to be fulfilled by it.

"Tommen?"

He looked up to see Detective Standish standing over him. Slowly, Tommen got to his feet, his head starting to ache, whether from the excitement or the alcohol was anyone's guess.

"You were the one who found the body?" Standish asked, always straightforward.

Tommen shrugged. "Well, we all found her; I was the first one to go up to her, and I guess you could say I was the one who found her dead."

"How did you approach her? What were your intentions?"

"It's the night of a dance. Girls, guys, not hard to draw some conclusions. We wanted to make sure she was all right, that nothing bad had happened to her."

"Uh-huh. And what were you three doing out here? Looking for lonely women?"

"No! We were just..hanging out."

Standish raised a brow and jotted down more notes than just Tommen's response. "And do you know the identity of the woman?"

Tommen shook his head honestly. "No. If I had to hazard a guess, I'd say she works in a hospital because of the scrubs and non-mark tennis shoes."

"What did you do after you found her?"

"Well, Eric got sick. Varad tried to run. I tackled him. I told them we couldn't run, that we had to call the cops. Then I told them to..." Suddenly he felt the idiot. Again.

"Told them to...?" Standish prompted.

Tommen sighed. "I told them to take sticks and mark out a wide area around the scene and then get out of it, mark the crime scene and keep people from coming in. No one here, but...it just came to mind. While they were doing that, I called 9-1-1."

Standish jotted down some more notes, shook his pen, scribbled a bit on his paper, then continued writing.

"Out of ink?" Tommen wondered casually.

"Almost," Standish grumbled. "Tommen, what time would you say you left the dance?"

"I left the dance earlier than Eric and Varad."

Standish's eyebrows shot into the air. "Why is that?"

"Bad night for me. No date. I wanted to leave, but Eric and Varad were still enjoying themselves. So I went and sat in Eric's car for a while. I don't know what time or how long, but Eric said that when they left the dance, the game had just gone into half-time."

The detective wrote some more, fumbled with his pen, got frustrated, fished around in his coat until he found another one, continued writing. Tommen stifled a sigh. The man was good enough at his job, but he really was better suited to something in cyber crime.

"And do you remember anything suspicious going on in the soccer fields while you were out here? People who looked out of place, equipment that had been moved...anything at all?"

Tommen paused, and then the funny feeling he'd had about the whole thing suddenly came into focus. "Yeah, actually. We'd been doing laps of the field for probably half an hour. Not fast laps necessarily, but we never saw anything. She didn't appear until our last lap; we were going to head to the game. But...either we just kept missing her in...I don't know, half a dozen laps...or...shit, we totally missed the guy." He took a bewildered step back and looked around, hands on his head. "Fuck, we missed the guy. Totally missed him. Shit."

"It's dark out, and with the trees so close, the guy really could have slipped in, dumped her, and slipped out." Standish's tone was halfway to reassuring, but his expression said he thought Tommen was lying about something somewhere.

"Shit," Tommen said again. He looked around. Statistically, something like that, the killer would probably return to survey his handiwork and see how the investigation was proceeding. He might try to get involved, offering whatever assistance he could. Tommen couldn't pick anyone out in the crowd which was finally beginning to disperse.

"Is there anything else you'd like to add?" Standish inquired.

He stopped, closed his eyes, tried to remember anything and everything. The whole thing was creepy as shit, but leave the deeper investigation to the detectives. What did he know? Was there anything else about it that felt funny? He stole a glance at Eric and Varad, both under the guns of different detectives. Percy-Something interrogated Varad while Walter spoke to Eric. Neither of them looked at him. Neither of them looked particularly thrilled either, more like whipped puppies.

Finally Tommen shook his head. "No. I can't think of anything."

"And you're sure you'd like to stick to your story about 'just hanging out' out here?"

"Yes, sir."

Standish raised a brow and Tommen almost expected him to break out the handcuffs. Instead, he only took a business card out of his wallet. "Not that I expect you'll need it since your dad is going to be leading this case, but if you don't feel like talking to daddy about something, here's my number."

Tommen took the card, hoping his sigh of relief wasn't too obvious. "Thanks."

"Do you have a ride home tonight?"

"Yeah, Eric can take me."

"Eric isn't taking you anywhere," Walter said gruffly, walking up. "I will be taking you home."

Tommen felt his cheeks turn red and his stomach turn to lead. Walter went on, "You go to the game. You stay there. I'll be by."

Tommen slunk off to the football game, feeling very much like he was tiptoeing through the calm before the storm, and yet relieved that the hard part was over with. But still, he just couldn't get over it. Fuck, they'd found a dead body on school property. Like, that was the stuff of nightmares. That was the kind of stuff where parents would be calling the school for weeks demanding to know what actions were being taken to ensure their child's safety and what measures were already in place to keep them safe from wackos and crazies. Yeesh, the murder hadn't even happened on school property and the woman wasn't even a student. It was a convenience thing, a short distance from a blocking treeline on a dark soccer field that wouldn't be mowed until Monday probably.

When he reached the football field, some of the fans had departed, meaning it wasn't shoulder-to-shoulder cramped and packed with sardine people. Surprisingly, the third quarter wasn't even over yet; it still had two minutes or so left on the clock. Judging from general chatter, the home team couldn't stop getting penalized and calling time outs, and the visitors were down five guys just that night from injuries ranging from a blown knee to a concussion that ended up sending the kid to the hospital. Hardly the ferocious, school spirit touting football game they'd all come expecting to see.

Still, Tommen bought a hot dog with all the fixings, forking over the money to accommodate the jacked-up price, and raised it in a mock toast. "To you, Eric and Varad. May our friendship never cease to amaze."

Despite the penalties, the time outs, and the injuries, the game itself—when it was going on—stayed pretty close in score. Home would score, pull ahead. Visitor would score, close the gap. Visitor would score and overtake. Home would score twice and pull away again. And so it went from the end of the third quarter into the start of the fourth quarter.

About halfway through the fourth quarter, there was yet another injury, but this time it was for the home team. At first, it started out as a kid just getting tackled a little too hard and getting the wind knocked out of him. Then it turned into a concussion when the kid proved to be extremely disoriented and confused. Things got really exciting when whispers started floating around about a possible broken neck because he couldn't get off the field by himself and really couldn't move at all. Tommen figured that at most the kid probably had a concussion and a strained neck. If his neck was broken and he didn't die, he still wouldn't be breathing because of the part of the spinal cord that controlled the lungs. Right?

But what did he know? Tommen occasionally glanced through Walter's medical books. He had to keep an Emergency Medical Responder license for those special occasions when he got on scene and the suspect was dying and he hadn't been the one to shoot him. But Tommen didn't know squat.

The player was carried off the field on a backboard, but Tommen could see he was trying to make a fist and flex his feet. No broken neck here. At least, no spinal cord injury.

Tommen heard the crowd parting before he heard him speak.

"Well, it's just a night for all the injuries to come out," Walter observed. "Must be a full moon."

"No kidding," Tommen replied, not looking at him. "Sixth one tonight, or so I hear."

"Are you intent on keeping a tally?"

Tommen sighed. "No."

He followed Walter out to the cruiser and got in the front seat. As a kid, he'd always loved playing with the buttons and switches, making lights flash and the sirens do all sorts of tones and patterns. Now it just felt like a big clumsy center console.

They rode in silence back to the precinct. Most of the cars had returned and the big ugly Cadillac awaited them on the other side of the parking lot. Tommen climbed into it while Walter went in for a few minutes. Probably to start some paperwork and trade a little gossip with the night staff before returning and trade his epic, Hollywood-style Dodge Charger police cruiser for an embarrassing, beat-up old Cadillac.

This time, they did not ride in silence.

"Alcohol and weed," Walter stated. "Explain."

"It was just a little fun," Tommen mumbled.

"Tommen, if that body hadn't been there to take precedence, and especially if you all hadn't been so forthcoming about everything else, you would all be spending the night in jail and hit with an MIP." Tommen opened his mouth, but Walter cut him off. "I'm not an idiot, Tommen, I know you sneak out sometimes. I keep my mouth shut because I want you to do stupid stuff now while it's more or less harmless, get the little rebellions out of your system before it becomes a real issue later in life. But not anymore. Tonight ends it. No more binges, no more sneaking out. For now, I will hold you to this on an honor system. You break it, I go from being lenient dad to jailer and warden. I don't want to do that. Do you?"

"No."

"I didn't think so. Now then, since we've established that you lied through your teeth about that one, tell me what happened tonight, starting with your face."

So Tommen told him everything, starting from the decorating, to Tyler once again beating him up.

"If I thought it would do any good, I would go after him for assault," Walter growled. "You shouldn't have to take that and live in fear of him."

"I don't fear him," Tommen protested.

"And he doesn't fear the law, which puts me and him in the same circle as him and you. Difference is, my circle is the court system, a lot more complex than a simple fight club ring. Difference is, even if he can't win, he'll keep fighting." Walter sighed. "Continue."

So Tommen told him a more honest version of events from the evening, making the story more complete by including the drinking and smoking, trying to soften it up by mentioning Eric's college prospects, and trying for some emotion by mentioning Varad's potential move.

Walter frowned. "So then maybe next year is the year you switch to a different school. Make new friends and get out of dodge with Tyler."

They'd been over this before, Tommen always wanting to stay with Eric and Varad and stick with the familiarity. But if they were both gone, Tyler was one familiarity with which he would have no trouble parting. Finally he just shrugged. "Maybe."

He sucked in a breath as his vision popped with color and in the space of a few seconds, the swelling on his face went down. He flipped the visor down and opened the mirror. Even the color was normal again. He looked at Walter.

"Less traumatic than the first one," Walter said. "And over the weekend, I doubt too many people are going to see you, or remember that you got in a fight. Right now, you're the kid who discovered a dead body on school property."

"Yeah." Tommen's mouth felt numb as he said it, trying to work through the pins and needles of his nerves and blood flow all coming back into alignment in Base Time. "But...about that. I don't know, when you were talking to the coroner, you just got this look, like something about it wasn't right. I mean, it's a dead body, but like something about it, I don't know what, but something about it was off."

Walter grew gravely silent for a long moment and Tommen almost feared his answer. Walter bought himself time by pretending to intensely focus on pulling in the driveway. But even as he pulled in, parked, and turned off the car, he did not get out of the car right away. Instead, he looked at Tommen. Not as a police officer or even as a father, but as the Captain of the Fourth District of the Fourth Region of the Thirty-Eighth Planet of the Fourth System of the Fifth Sector of the Eleventh Parsec of the First Quadrant of Timekeepers. And his mentor, the one who would see him from probationary to Master.

"Tommen, you are a probationary Timekeeper. Right now, you only understand Fast and Slow Bands, and you have a very base knowledge of the Time industry. After your review, you will be an Apprentice, and you will learn many more abilities to further manipulate Time. But for tonight, we're going to have a little discussion about Harvesting."

Tommen followed him inside the house. "Wait, like, you're going to teach me to Harvest?"

Walter glanced back at him. "No, not quite. I am going to teach you a bit about it, though, what it is, what to look for."

"It's the, well, Harvesting of the remaining Potential Time of someone who is dying, isn't it?" Tommen wondered, stopping in the doorway of Walter's bedroom while he took off his blues. "Someone's eighty years old, no one's going to notice if they die a day early because no one could predict it anyway, right?"

"Very true," Walter conceded. He took a step back to see where Tommen was, then resumed hiding, as if he hadn't seen him in his underwear before. "You and I see Time in motion, in Bands. Essentially, Base Time in any given area, is invisible to us. A Fast Band emits red light, Slow Band emits blue light. Basic principles." He pulled his shirt down and headed out the door, past Tommen, shutting off the light and going out to his recliner.

"What do Harvesters see?" Tommen dared ask.

"Harvesters see our natural biological clock," Walter explained. "From what I'm told, any given healthy human—or whatever being—is as invisible to them as Base Time is to us. You remember I told you about Lily, right?"

"Yeah." Tommen elected to omit the part about her visiting the bakery.

"From what she has told me, the more Time a being has to give, relative to the average life span of that being as well as the individual itself—these are her words, I don't know the details—their color changes when they are within capacity to be Harvested. The neonates that she works with, she describes as being a gold color because they have entire lifetimes to give. Older people at the end of their natural life span she says are black in color. And there is apparently a broad spectrum of silver, white, and gray in between."

"So she could Harvest any one of those neonates, effectively murdering that child, and no one would know or care?" Tommen interrupted.

"Essentially...yes."

"What happens if she doesn't?"

Walter shrugged. "Many of them live. Some die naturally. According to her, a body can still be Harvested within half an hour of death. Given her work, I expect most of her Harvesting is done in such a way."

"Is this knowledge or a hope?" Tommen wondered.

Walter could only look guilty. "What she does is legal by the Laws of Time. I can't enforce a Law that does not exist, nor impose my own personal feelings and morality onto it, especially given the vastness of the Time industry. The same way I can't take in a stupid teenage graffiti artist if the property owner doesn't want to press charges. Until someone's actual life is in danger, legally there is nothing I can do. And it's even worse when dealing with the Laws of Time and the Hands who make them."

Tommen sighed. "Fine. What do Harvesting colors have to do with tonight's murder?"

"I've only witnessed half a dozen Harvests in my time as a Timekeeper. It doesn't take long, only about fifteen seconds. I expect you saw the grid pattern on the face and the pierced hands?"

"Yeah."

"Harvesting marks are invisible to those not exposed to Time, the same way our Bands are invisible. Only the effects are visible. In the case of a Harvest, death. And a Time Capsule." Walter leaned forward in his recliner and held one hand out in front of him, palm down. "The Harvester places her hand on the face of the victim. Scientifically, I think it has to do with the electrical activity in the brain being the actual 'potential energy' or 'Potential Time.' And for lack of better term, she sucks the Time out of the victim, relaying it through her own body to the other hand." He held his other hand out, palm up. "The Time Capsule essentially grows out of the other hand, never any bigger or smaller than a salt shaker, encoded in Universal Base Time how much Time is contained. When it's full, it simply 'breaks off' as it were, with no apparent injury to the Harvester."

"So the Time Capsules are automatically a part of them?" Tommen pressed.

"Oh no, not at all. The Time Capsules are not automatic, it is an effort of will. It would be nothing for Lily to simply put both hands on a victim and take all the years for herself. But that is called stealing, and she would be prosecuted for it, especially since we're talking entire lifetimes. According to her, second-theft or minute-theft is about as common as stealing pens or sticky notes from work. Day-theft is likened to stealing a candy bar from the gas station."

"And...lifetime-theft?"

"Like not only stealing a Lamborghini, but totaling it."

"But there have to be side effects from having all that coursing through your body."

"There are. For every decade that passes through, Lily estimates that about three to six months rubs off on her. Whether that's honest exposure or if she's figured out a way to get her cut without it looking like stealing, I can't say."

Tommen nodded thoughtfully. "So the grid lines on the face are for the Harvesting, and the pierced Hands are for the Harvester. So we're looking at someone who is part of the Time industry."

"Knows of the Time industry. More likely it's a Runner, but the last time I heard about Runners getting this violent on Earth was back in the sixties and seventies."

"What reason would a Runner have to turn violent?"

"I don't know." Walter got out of his recliner, back and knees popping. "But that's what I intend to find out."

Tommen followed him to the kitchen. "Do you know the identity of the woman who was killed?"

Walter poured himself a glass of root beer. "No ID on her."

"Doesn't mean you don't know who it is."

"Doesn't mean I'm permitted to release the name."

"I'm still in trouble, aren't I?"

"Oh yes."

"Well, the bakery's closed and we got all the small work done. All that's left is for the contractors."

Walter smiled. "That's all right."

Tommen eyed him warily. "What am I going to be doing this weekend, then, since I suspect I won't be going anywhere?"

"Winter is coming, and I'm tired of going out to a cold car every morning. Don't break anything and only throw away trash, but get the garage cleared enough so I can get my car in at night. Do that tomorrow before I get home. Then, Sunday, I'll have a better idea of what I do and don't want and need. Clean and organize the garage as best you can—and I'll know if you got lazy and are holding out on me—and come Monday, I might just conveniently forget your little illegal escapades this evening."

It was not a task that Tommen wanted to do ever, but if it got him out of trouble, he figured he could grit his teeth, square his shoulders, suck it up and do it. Tommen couldn't remember a time when the garage was clean and clear enough to park a car in there, though Walter maintained it had been cleaned for a year or two after he'd arrived. It wasn't really trashy and moldy or anything with rats scuttling in the darkness; mostly it was just cluttered with tools and machines and half-done, long-forgotten projects. New doors on the cabinets. New cabinets. New trim around the windows. All of them abandoned and left to die in their own sawdust.

"Okay," Tommen agreed reluctantly.

"Remember, I want to do this on an honor system. I already have enough bad guys that need more watching than you do. At least I hope so. Got it?"

Tommen nodded and headed off to bed. It was still early, but he had a headache and the excitement and the adrenaline had left him feeling like an empty tank. Still, he lay in bed for a while, staring at the ceiling. He heard Walter go to bed after a while. He'd be up early, off to work, punched in, have a cup of coffee and a pastry—well, maybe not the pastry since the bakery was closed—and probably following his first leads before Tommen was even conscious.

And yet, for all that had happened in just the last few hours, Tommen remembered drifting off to sleep wishing he had stayed at the dance with Varad and Eric. Because...damn, he'd wanted to get laid.

Chapter Six
A Matter of Time

Walter fumbled for his alarm clock and grouchily punched it off. Some days, he couldn't wait for Tommen to become an Apprentice so he might be able to "test" his ability to create an Outside Band by letting Walter get a full, natural, restful night's sleep. Other days, he dreaded the thought of Tommen becoming an Apprentice because that meant a whole extra workload being thrust upon him. Why, oh why, hadn't he left the mentoring to the twins? They saw Tommen more than he did, much to his shame and discredit as a father, a single father at that.

Still, he pulled himself out of bed, showered and shaved, marveled that even for the way the Bands slowed their aging, his beard and mustache still grew at fairly normal rates. Or were they simply running on their own Times in their own Bands? He didn't want to think about it.

He went and started the coffeemaker before returning to his bedroom to pull out a fresh uniform. The one from the night before had been a frumpy, wrinkled one out of the dirty laundry, but in the dark, no one seemed to notice. In the frenzy that was a murder scene, they didn't care much either. And yet, it was in those random moments of the little things that he wondered what Paige would say. Then he realized he didn't know, because that was in a time before washing machines, before people gave much of a damn about whether clothes were wrinkled or pressed.

He was halfway through his coffee and some article about someone receiving some award when it occurred to him that the bakery was closed and he wasn't going to get his pastry. He should have remembered that, but something about it being four a.m. just made his mind fuzzy. Still, he managed to scrape together some peanut butter toast—Tommen's staple breakfast...and lunch...and sometimes dinner—and scarf it down with the rest of the coffee.

As always, the last thing he did before leaving the house was check on Tommen, pushing the door open just a crack. He'd kicked his blankets almost completely off the bed and was sprawled out like, well, a teenage boy. He hadn't worn pajamas since he was eleven, and his clothes—his borrowed tux, less the jacket which was hung lazily on one bedpost—were about as frumpy and wrinkled as Walter's uniform had been the previous evening.

Despite all their abilities and prowess, Walter was keenly aware that they were still only mortal. He could easily Band Time in order to dodge a bullet from the front, but be completely susceptible to the one coming from the back. And for however Fast or Slow they went, Time still only moved forward. There was no reversing it and coming back, no redos.

He shivered as he stepped out into the chilly morning air, blew on his hands as he started the car and backed out of the driveway. He'd been meaning to clean the garage for years but never got around to it. He either put it off and chalked it up to being too tired, or, when he did have the motivation, decided he never had the time. Perhaps what was worse was that he felt no guilt whatsoever about essentially conning Tommen into doing it for him. Well, he had a punishment to work off, so that was the chosen chore. Unfortunately, if he needed to come up with another chore in the future, he wouldn't have that one to fall back on.

He pulled into the parking lot at the station, grumbling because the heater had just gotten up to temp. Oh well, the station was warm enough. District Captain of Timekeepers he might be, but here he was just another guy. Homicide Detective Walter Forbes, his position earning him a cubicle, and that only because he needed someplace to pin pictures, notes, and little strings connecting them. Some things were just like the movies. And sometimes, if he was really good and he asked really nice, there was a little open office room down the hall he and his partner could use to put little pieces together to make big pieces and hopefully solve a case.

"Morning, Cynthia," Walter greeted as he walked in past the reception desk, the net into which the fish swam and got redirected to the appropriate department.

"Got a big one this time," Cynthia said.

"Oh, I know it."

The five a.m. crew was just getting in, pouring coffee, passing around donuts and assorted goodies, and making small talk before starting another rousing day of everything from speeding tickets and graffiti to domestic violence and rape. Walter headed for his little cubicle, a paper sign telling everyone who lived there. He might have been offended by the paper sign except Tommen had drawn it when he was nine, right after Walter moved from Missing Persons to Homicide.

"Walter Forbes, Homiside Detektive. He kaches bad guys that kill peple so lissen to him."

Below it, there was a child's drawing of Walter arresting a bad guy who killed someone.

Next to the sign, however, Jim Standish leaned against the fragile fabric wall of the cubicle, swirling cream and sugar in his coffee, bushy red-blond beard as impeccably groomed as ever.

"Morning, Jim. You're my partner on this one?" Walter asked.

"Yup." He took a drink of coffee. "You get anything more from Tommen last night? I could smell it on his breath."

"I've got him cleaning out the garage this weekend—"

"Holy shit."

"—so it's been taken care of. This time." Walter moved around Standish to get into his cubicle. "Next time, I won't be so lenient. But right now, we've got bigger fish to fry because I have a feeling this isn't a one-time deal."

"You and me both."

His cubicle was sparse, comparatively speaking, and the large chair was as close to his recliner as he could get. He sat in it and leaned back. "So, identity first."

"Already got a tip on that one," Standish said. He took another drink of coffee. "Sam Pietrowicz, nurse at NICU at the children's hospital."

"NICU?"

"Got called in about an hour ago to missing persons by her roommate when she didn't get home from work."

"Playing devil's advocate, maybe she stopped to get coffee or...I don't know, do some early shopping."

"According to her roommate, Sam has come straight home from work every single day for the last three years that they've been rooming together, so this is entirely out of character."

Walter nodded. "All right. What's the 'availability' of the roommate?"

"Works retail during the day, sets her alarm by Sam coming home. She overslept; that's how she knew Sam was gone. But she says she's willing to answer questions anytime."

"Great. If you want to talk to the roommate, I'll check out NICU. What did evidence turn up?"

Standish handed him a puny stack of files and paperwork. "Not much. Stomping around by the boys destroyed any evidence of footprints. Otherwise, it's as if she just suddenly appeared there, like your boy said."

"He does stupid stuff, but he's not a liar." Walter tapped a pen on the desk. "Were there any other witnesses around? Someone who saw the suspect pull into the little dirt lot there on the other side of the trees? I can't believe our guy could have carried her effortlessly, especially without being seen."

"Someone said they thought they might have seen a beige van, but they were pretty sure that it was just pulling in and turning around. No make, model, year, or any distinguishing features. Other than that, no go."

"Cameras? I know Layman's kind of a stickler about graffiti, or someone across the street?"

"Nada. The best camera is positioned on the flood lights overlooking the soccer field, but it only catches the trees."

Walter checked his watch. "School's not open yet; that'll have to wait until after interviews. Do we have an ETA on an autopsy?"

"Sean said he'd get it done as quickly as possible, could be tomorrow or the day after for the preliminary forensics."

Walter nodded. In big cities where murders came down the pipe by the dozen, autopsies were backed up a week or more. Thankfully, Charleston was not so crime-ridden. Murder actually made the news. And the infrequency of it allowed Walter to spend more time on each case than might be afforded in big cities. It also allowed him to get his autopsy answers that much faster, though if he was right, everything would look entirely normal to a normal human's eyes.

"Wonderful." Walter pushed himself up out of his chair. "But for right now, it looks like we have our day's work cut out for us."

Most times, it was better to conduct interviews together, but as Walter headed to one car and Standish to another, Walter knew it had to be done this way this time. And it wasn't entirely unusual for him to want to do it this way. Do strange things occasionally on normal cases, so that when weird cases like this came up involving Time and Runners, his need for secrecy wasn't a surprise because it was just Walter being Walter.

So it was that he pulled into the parking lot of the children's hospital and sat for just a second, gathering his thoughts. It wasn't that he didn't like Lily, it was more that he found Harvesters about as attractive as a slimy slug or worm. Radioactive worm. Regular NICU nurses, elderly patient caretakers, those who cared for all the sick and dying in between, there was a Romantic bravery and heroism about them, that they sacrificed their lives to make other people comfortable in death.

There was nothing brave or courageous about Harvesting, waiting for something that was ill and dying to get to that optimal moment when they could leech the remaining Time and then sell it—for a pittance, for a fortune, didn't matter. It was sickening.

He managed to wipe the scowl off his face by the time he reached the receptionist who looked up with stunned surprise.

"Can I help you?" she wondered.

"Looking for NICU," he told her, hoping he came across as genial and non-threatening.

The woman's breath caught and she nodded slowly. "Of course."

The way her attitude changed sent up red flags everywhere for Walter. There was no way news of the murder could have gotten out already. But then, if she'd gone missing last night and then maybe her roommate called the hospital to ask where she was, and then people started commenting that they hadn't seen her, now the police show up...it was logical to think that something terrible had happened.

Of course, as Walter got on the elevator, there was the other option, too: social media. Despite the scene safety officers trying to block cameras and phones and politely requesting they be turned off, someone in that crowd would have gotten pictures, and then the Internet would explode, and word would get around pretty quick. Someone would identify her, and then all hell would break loose. As if it already hadn't. People wanted sensation, they got it. People wanted to be helpful and spread the word faster than the news could report it, well...word spread faster at least. How helpful it was would remain a mystery. And even if it didn't go straight to the Internet, because that could be more easily tracked, people would simply text the photos around. Same process, except then the police department couldn't see it, couldn't track it. And it just made everything that much harder.

The elevator stopped once to let more people on, most of them children. Walter tried to keep his expression neutral, if not amiable. He didn't need to scare the kids because his inner thoughts leaked out to his face.

He looked down as a small hand tugged on his pants. It was a little girl, dressed in a white shirt and pink tutu. She couldn't have been much older than six or seven.

"I'm this many!" she said, holding up seven little fingers.

"Really?" he said with mock interest. "That's a lot. What are you going to do when you run out of fingers to count on?"

"Then I use my toes, silly!"

"Ah. And what about when you run out of toes?"

"Then I become a police officer like you!"

Walter's gaze darted to a woman he assumed was her mother. She offered a shy smile and a small shrug, like, "That's this week's obsession. Who knows what she'll pick next week?"

"And how does counting fingers and toes help you become a police officer?" Walter wondered.

"Because Mommy says that you have to count all your fingers and toes, because if they're not all there, then they're probably up your ass and that doesn't make a very nice police officer."

Once the woman realized what the girl was saying, she made to put a hand over her daughter's mouth, but it was too late. Rather than be offended, Walter burst into laughter. Even others on the elevator tried to stifle snickers. He was pretty sure Mommy had said something a little different than that, but it was the comic relief he needed, and probably the best one he'd heard in a while.

"I am so sorry," the woman said, her face and neck bright red. "I don't know where...or how..."

"It's all right," he assured her as the elevator came to a stop. "Believe me, since my kid grew up, I don't get that kind of humor anymore."

He got off the elevator, momentarily forgetting why he was there, but remembering as soon as he saw a little neonate in a glass box being rolled from one area to another.

"Can I help you?" a nurse inquired.

"I'm looking for Lily Guile," he told her simply.

"Sure, she's in her office. Right this way."

Walter actually knew very well where Lily's office was as he'd been there on multiple occasions, most often as liaison between her and the twins on the rare occasion that they needed to converse. She was the head of NICU, set up in a rather expensive office, furnished in part by the hospital and partly by her own money, and not always from the legal tender as recognized by the United States of America Department of Treasury.

She sat behind her desk going through some files and having the posture of someone who needed to find something and leave quickly.

"Lily?" the nurse said, knocking softly on the door.

Lily looked up and grinned hugely. "Walter. How kind of you to seek me out today. Thank you, Sarah."

Sarah, the nurse, nodded once and bowed out, closing the door behind her as Walter strode forward.

"All in uniform, purposeful stride. Either you're here to arrest me, Time-arrest me, deliver some serious news from Dumb and Dumber, or you have news on my missing tech."

"So news does reach you in this cave of yours," Walter said, rummaging for a photo and showing her. "She was murdered last night."

"Shit," Lily hissed. "And she had a good forty years left in her."

He pocketed the picture. "What do you know about her disappearance? How did she go from here to the soccer fields of South Charleston High School?"

"Where, judging by your general demeanor, your upstanding son just happened innocently upon her body. Entirely a coincidence."

"What do you know?"

Lily folded her arms. "I know that she punched in at three yesterday afternoon, same as always. Normally she punches out at three in the morning. Obviously, she didn't."

"Do you have any clue when she was last seen?"

She indicated the files before her. "These are charts from all the units. Every tech has to sign off on everything they do. Name, treatment, time, date, the whole shebang. The last signature of hers that I've found is at six-fourteen."

"Is there anything significant about that time or where she was?"

"Nothing."

"Has anyone made threats against her that you know of?"

"Sam wasn't a social person. She never went out, never did anything fun. She works NICU because she's as isolated as much as the neonates. She doesn't have any enemies. She doesn't even have any friends. And she hardly strikes me as the secret alter ego kind of girl. But, let me see that picture again." Walter handed it over to her and she flipped it around to show him. "These are Harvesting marks made visible. This murder isn't about Sam."

"Maybe not, but I'll play along. How do you figure?"

"Because I was supposed to be on the floor last night, doing exactly what Sam did. She came to me the day before, on Thursday, and asked if she could just add a shift, said she needed the extra hours for the extra pay and so she could retain her benefits." Lily rolled her eyes and waved her hand dismissively. "As if I care. But, whatever. Take a Friday night off? Sure. So I just gave her the shift."

"And where were you?"

"I went out. Jen, Martha, and Yuri can all attest to it. We went out drinking for a while, went to a club. Got laid."

It was far more than Walter needed to know, but he knew Lily was doing it just to spite him. "If there's anything else you can think of that would be relevant—"

"Oh, there is." Lily grinned like she'd won some mischievous battle. "See, all employee entrances require these special little swipey key card doo-dads to get in and out." She fished out a card with her picture, information, and a magnetic strip. "Everything's logged with tech support. If she went out a main entrance, either someone would have seen her or she would at least be on camera, which would also be logged with tech support."

"And where do I find tech support?"

Lily gave him directions and spitefully wished him a good day and happy investigating. He wasn't sure how to feel about tech support being on the same floor as the morgue. Thankfully, it was less like some nerd living in his mom's basement, and more like a professional, organized team.

"What can I do for you, Detective?" Roger, the head of tech support, wondered, leading him through the small lab of computers to his office.

"I need the log of Sam Pietrowicz's key card yesterday as well as all NICU cameras starting at six p.m."

"Well, fortunately for you, I already have a printout of her log. I was just about to send it up to her boss, Lily Guile; have you spoken to her yet?"

"I have," Walter said stiffly, taking the papers. "According to this log, her last swipe-out time was at six-twenty-four at door E2. Where is that?"

Roger shrugged casually as he worked on his computer to bring up camera footage. "It's a smoking area; lots of people go there on their breaks."

"Can I get the camera at that time?"

"Here's your NICU cameras," Roger said, finding one of Sam. "Six p.m."

They watched the cameras in double-time up until her last signature at six-fourteen when they slowed it to real-time. She talked to another nurse for a minute, went to the vending machine, took a quick break to eat a bag of chips and pop a stick of gum in her mouth. Then she went to the bathroom. And then she was gone. No matter how far forward they went or which camera they checked, Sam never emerged from the bathroom.

"No," Roger said, almost panicking. "No, that is not possible. No, these cameras cannot malfunction like this!"

"How about door E2?" Walter wondered.

But there was no activity there, neither inside, nor outside.

"Could the key card log have been lying?" Walter wondered.

"It doesn't misread. The only way to change the log is to physically get into the program, and even then, it's set up so that each unit is separate. Essentially, someone would have to hack into that specific unit. But it just doesn't make sense why anyone would do that." Roger looked at Walter with an expression of wild terror. "You know where Sam is. You just need to know how she got there. Where is she?"

Walter sighed. "She's dead."

Roger looked ready to speak, but Walter simply thanked him, told him to have a good day, focus on his work, and call if he was able to find anything. Maybe the unit had been hacked and she'd gone out a different door instead. When he got back to his car, he called Standish.

"Jim Standish," came the answer.

"It's Walt. You talked to the roommate yet?"

"Just finished, why?"

"Meet me back at the station."

"Roger."

Within fifteen minutes, they met back in Walter's cubicle, each with a fresh cup of coffee and a new story to tell.

"According to the roommate, everything was perfectly normal," Standish reported. "No boyfriends, no girlfriends, no kids, no family problems. Essentially, she was socially invisible. Her biggest concern of, well, the year, was getting enough hours in to keep her benefits at work. She has to work so many hours in a year and blah, blah, blah."

Walter nodded. "That's what Lily said. She said Sam came to her Thursday and asked to trade shifts with her Friday night in order to get the hours. Lily agreed, gave her the shift, and ended up going to a club."

Standish took a drink of coffee and sucked some of it from his beard. Walter felt his stomach do a backflip. "So. Question becomes, was the killer after Sam and stalked her from her apartment to the hospital? Or was he after Lily and got the wrong person because she switched shifts?"

Walter leaned back in his chair. "But if he was after Lily — who has black hair and is less than petite — and gets Sam — blond hair and the ideal hourglass figure — that means he was going after her completely blind."

"Hitman?"

"I don't know." Even if Walter did know and wished he could just go screaming forward with the investigation he knew they needed. "Check more into Sam. I'm not buying the cute little shy angel everyone's making her out to be."

"I hear you. I keep hearing about these girls, but I never seem to be able to meet any of them. What are you up to?"

Walter checked his watch. "School's open. I'm going to talk to Layman, see if I can't get the view off his cameras."

Standish chuckled even as he finished off his coffee. "He runs that school like a prison, man. I don't even think the jail is locked down that tight."

"Maybe we ought to hire him here."

Walter turned to head out once more, then stopped. "You said the roommate works retail?"

"Yeah," Standish replied, heading for the coffeemaker.

"What store around here opens so early that she has to get up as early as I do?"

Standish scoffed and smiled somewhere beneath his beard. "She goes to the gym before work. Because sleep just isn't as important to some people."

"Those people need to be beaten. Just sayin'."

"Whatever, man. I'll call you if I find anything good on our girl."

Walter did an imaginary tip of the hat as he headed out once more, this time to South Charleston High School where the entire staff, from the day care and elementary school all the way up to the high school, including all coaches and PTA members, was in a special, private conference. Although, when he walked in the school, he got a special ticket. Immediately when he walked in the door of the conference room, he was barraged with questions.

"What actually happened?"

"Who was it?"

"Where did it happen?"

Teachers and parents up tight and fearful that somehow their school was the target of a sick wacko and not just a convenient dumping ground because of poor gardening choices.

"Please, I am not qualified nor permitted to speak about the case at this time," Walter told them formally. "I just need to speak to Orville."

Layman nodded and excused himself from the room.

"I need a look at your cameras," Walter said. "I'm told you have one placed on the soccer fields pointed toward the tree line."

Layman nodded and they headed toward the main office, turning off to a locked side room where a number of cameras resided. "It's all yours, Detective. And how is Tommen this morning? I seem to recall he'd gotten in another fight?"

"He's cleaning the garage today," Walter told him levelly as he sat down at the desk. "Tell me what I'm looking at."

Walter was not particularly tech savvy, enough to use a smart phone and get around on the computer, but anything beside the basics was well beyond him. Layman eventually got him about where he needed to be.

"What time did the dance start?" Walter wondered.

"Dance started at seven, but the game started at six," Layman told him.

"Is there any reason anyone would have gone to the soccer fields beforehand? I know you've got a lot of storage buildings around there."

Layman shook his head. "No, not really. Most of the decorations came down from the auditorium; the theme was Alice in Wonderland, the same as this year's school play."

"Makes sense, then."

By now they'd gotten to the part where Tommen and his friends were making laps of the field, coming in range of the cameras for only a minute or two each time. As angry as Walter had been about him sneaking off to go smoking and drinking, there really didn't appear to be anything sinister going on. They had, just like Tommen said, just simply made laps of the field.

"There!" Layman said suddenly, pointing to the trees.

The cameras were hardly the stuff of Hollywood legend, but just after the boys passed out of view of the camera, there was movement behind the trees. Like one witness said, it was only enough time for a van to simply turn around and head the opposite direction in traffic, and yet, in the next moment, just the edge of the woman's body appeared where it had been found. A few minutes later, the boys came back. Tommen approached, Eric got sick, Varad tried to run. All according to story.

"Is there any way to send this footage as an email attachment?" Walter asked.

"No problem," Layman told him. "Where should I send it?"

Walter gave him his business card and the footage parameters before leaving. He'd just pulled out of the school parking lot when he got a call.

"Walter Forbes," he answered.

"Walt, it's Greg." Greg Steggmann, the Chief of Police. "Sam Pietrowicz's parents are here; they'd like to talk to you and Jim if that's all right."

No, because he had nothing to give them. "Sure, I'm just on my way back."

He wished he could buy time by getting a pastry—and theoretically, he could have; the twins weren't the only bakers in Charleston, just the only ones he could stand—but it would only delay the inevitable. For a grieving family, it was rude to keep them waiting.

He met them in Steggmann's office. Mr. Pietrowicz wasn't quite six foot, balding, overweight, the typical middle-aged man. Mrs.

Pietrowicz was as blond as her daughter, though if she'd ever had such a slender figure, it had long since deserted her.

"Mr. and Mrs. Pietrowicz, I am Detective Walter Forbes. I am so sorry for your loss," Walter told them.

"Who would do this to our little girl?" Mrs. Pietrowicz whimpered.

"She only ever wanted to be a doctor," Mr. Pietrowicz said. "She worked with such tiny babies to bring them life. She did so much good."

"I know, and everyone I've spoken to has only had admiration for her. Is there anything you can tell me that might shed light on who could have done this? Jealous exes, enemies in college?"

The parents shook their heads. "No. She got along with everyone. If she ever socialized. She was never a very outgoing person. She got anxious around people; that's the reason she wanted to work with neonates. It was either that or a veterinarian."

"When can we bury her?" Mrs. Pietrowicz asked.

"Once the autopsy is done and we have collected all the evidence we can."

That didn't actually happen until late the next evening just as Walter was going to punch out. He grabbed Standish, and they headed to the morgue where the medical examiner waited for them.

"So, Sean, talk to us," Walter said. "What killed her?"

"In simple terms, her throat was cut," Sean answered from the opposite side of the table where Sam lay, cold and blue. "But what's interesting is that she suffered no blood loss."

"That's not possible, she should have been gushing like a garden hose," Standish said.

Sean shook his head. "Nope. As crazy as this sounds, her artery was cut, however, both ends ultimately clotted and essentially healed themselves shut. Blood backup caused congestive heart failure. Same with the cuts on her face and the pierced hands. No blood loss because they're all clotted. Which also means that the face and hands were done first while she was alive."

"How long would this have had to take?" Walter wondered.

"CHF like this? God, a matter of...minutes, at most. Maybe even seconds. Whoever did this knew what he was doing and was ready for it. But the advanced stage of clotting would have taken quite a while to perfect, and probably had to be done artificially once the body could no longer form platelets to combat the blood flow."

"How does that happen?"

"These days, especially in the military, there are two types of artificial blood clotters. Straight synthetic platelets, and synthetic blood clotting agents to aid the body's natural ability to produce platelets. But either way, I haven't been able to find any injection sites, unless he dropped it directly into the artery. I'll know more once the blood cultures come back."

"What made the cuts?" Standish asked.

"Something really sharp, something precise. Like, scalpel kind of precise."

"Any signs of struggle?"

"Not a thing. No bruising from restraints, no defensive wounds, no skin under the fingernails, no fibers. It's like she just stood there and let him do this to her."

"One hell of a fantasy," Walter commented and slapped Standish on the back. "Guess she wasn't the angel you'd hoped she'd be." He looked back at Sean. "Any evidence of rape?"

"None. No fluids, no penetration."

"Got an idea on time of death?"

"When the coroner got to her, he estimated time of death to be about half an hour prior. *Rigor mortis* was just starting to take hold."

"Damn," Walter whispered. "Is there anything else you can tell us?"

Sean frowned. "Not until some of the tests start coming back. That's all I got for you right now."

The detectives thanked him and headed back out to the car where they sat for a minute in silence, each with his own cup of coffee.

"Hospital records put her last definite movements at six-fourteen," Walter stated. "Camera footage of her ends at six-twenty-four."

"She wasn't found until after eight o'clock," Standish continued. "Coroner's estimation puts time of death around seven-thirty. So what the hell was he doing with her for an hour?"

"I don't even want to know the answer to that." Walter started the car. "I think we need to do some snooping into that beige van."

They returned to the station and got into the little office just down the hall from Walter's cubicle. One wall of the office was dedicated to a very detailed map of the city, laminated so those working with it could draw on it as they needed to. Walter found a marker and started marking locations. School soccer fields and the hospital for starters. Standish also grabbed a marker, but to no one's surprise, it was dry. The man just had that effect on things.

"So, dirt lot here, witness says she saw a beige van pull in and turn around," Walter said, drawing a line in the dirt lot to reflect his line of thought.

"From the hospital to the school, though, is only like a ten minute drive," Standish pointed out. "He had to have camped out somewhere."

"Yes, but there could be traffic cams that caught him crossing the expressway, or at least the river."

"I'll talk to the guys."

Walter nodded approvingly. "I'll check around some of the other businesses, too, see if anyone has cameras pointed in a very convenient direction."

His first stop was a small string of gas stations. The first one didn't have any conveniently-directed cameras. The second didn't either. The third said the outside cameras were primarily just for show, and half of them didn't work anyway. The fourth did have a camera with a fair view of the road and managed to catch a beige van driving by at approximately the correct time. Unfortunately, it didn't give Walter a plate or a view of the driver.

The van disappeared once it got to the bridge, reappeared

briefly in the poor camera footage at a pharmacy, and then vanished again, leaving Walter with only a timeline of events from hospital to school. He was thinking about trying to backtrace and go from the hospital back in time, when he made a pass by Bakery na hÉireann. He might not have stopped because of the contracting vehicles taking up most of the room in the parking lot, but he also spotted Micaiah's car, so he pulled in.

Micaiah met him at the door. "Got nothing for ya, Walt," he said, shrugging. "Hopefully we'll be reopened by the end of the week."

"That fast?" Walter wondered.

"Well, you know how it is with these hard-working guys pulling long hours."

Walter could see that the entire store was ensconced in a Fast Band. The poor guys were probably doing twenty-four hour shifts in a ten-hour span. The huge rolls of plastic and paper covering all the windows and doors probably didn't help them any. "You're a dick. You know that, don't you?"

Micaiah shrugged again. "What can I do for you, Walt?"

"We need to start a Time-side investigation, and I need you to head it," Walter started.

"No problem. What's the word? Is it that girl?"

Walter immediately threw up a Fast Band. He took out Sam's picture. "The best we've been able to gather is that she was abducted around six-thirty Friday evening and murdered around seven-thirty. The only thing we've got here is that the perp drives a beige van. We have no plates or description of the suspect."

"Those marks on her face, those are Harvesting marks," Micaiah said, taking the picture.

"Exactly."

"So, he cuts her throat, and—"

"Here's the messed up part. She didn't bleed out. Didn't lose any blood at all."

Micaiah handed the photo back to Walter. "You're joking. A

throat cut like that and it *doesn't* rain Egyptian plague?"

"It was clotted. Her face and hands, too. ME says it might have been an experimental artificial clotting injection."

"You're thinking it was Banded."

"Right."

Micaiah let out a breath. "Walt, we both know that most Runners don't have Banding skills worth peanuts. That level of skill and control...Walt, I don't know if I could do that."

"I don't know if I could do that either, which is why we need to hit the ground running."

"Great, give me something to run with."

Walter hesitated. "I know you're not going to like this, and Micah may not care at all, but I think Lily was the guy's actual target. She was supposed to be working instead of the girl, Sam, but they traded shifts."

Micaiah frowned. "Lily can't be intimidated by someone trying to 'send a message' by killing her underlings, so what you're saying makes sense. And given how different they look, we're talking a hired hitman, someone who doesn't know what she looks like, just knew that she'd be working Friday night."

"Or they might not have known what she looks like now. Maybe it is a personal grudge, but the perp hasn't seen her since her hair change."

"True." Micaiah nodded. "So we're looking at a Runner who is targeting Lily and has insane Banding prowess. But if this was a Time murder, why make the Harvesting marks visible? Doesn't that only set him up as a potential serial killer or something, just making him more visible to the public eye."

"That could be what he wants, a way to flaunt that he can commit murder and get away with it. But I think the Harvesting marks are meant as a message for us, the Timekeepers. We uphold an order, the laws of a way of life in which the Powers That Be are corrupt. Lily is a huge buyer of votes. Runners are rarely so sophisticated, but if I had to hazard a guess, she's only the first.

Unless we catch him."

"Can I see that picture again?"

Walter handed it over, and Micaiah studied it for a minute or two. "I'll put the word out." Immediately, the Band over the store was released, and Walter dropped his Band. "Micah and I will get right on this."

"Good man."

Walter turned to leave, but Micaiah called after him. "Walt." He stopped. "If this is a message for us, then it's likely that he or she or they or whoever has already figured out that you, me, and Micah are Timekeepers. What are the chances that they'll go after Tommen, too?"

The thought made Walter's stomach churn and he tried to walk coolly back to the cruiser. As soon as he was out of visual range, he called Tommen.

"The garage is almost clean," he said. "When are you coming home?"

"I'm on my way now. Listen, have you seen or heard from or had any unusual contact with anyone today?"

"You're the only person I've had contact with all weekend. Why?"

"Just stay put; I'll be home soon."

"Soon" was a relative term as Walter and Standish regrouped to compare notes, but Walter was happy any time he got home before Tommen went to bed. In fact, he was just sweeping out the last bit of dirt and stepped aside so Walter could pull the Cadillac into the garage for the first time in probably five years or more.

"You did a good job," Walter commented as they walked in the house.

"So...am I off the hook?" Tommen wondered.

"You're off the hook. Just don't give me a reason to put you back on."

Spaghetti was a staple in the Forbes household, right up there with pizza, and they ended up making both, choosing to chow down in the living room while watching late night programming.

"So, what was up with the cryptic phone call?" Tommen wondered.

Walter hesitated. Sometimes he wished Tommen was still a little boy, so that he could shut down his questions with a few well-placed but probably untrue scare phrases, followed by some well-placed and entirely sincere reassurance phrases. But he wasn't that little boy anymore. He was almost an adult, capable—most of the time—of making his own decisions, coming to his own conclusions, and learning to fend for himself. He was almost an Apprentice Timekeeper and would not only learn about the dangers of his secret trade, but how to master and control those dangers.

"The person who killed Sam is a Runner," Walter began diplomatically.

"Yeah, you said that," Tommen told him. "And that was why he cut up her face and stuff."

"From the ME's report and my own knowledge, and talking to Micaiah, whoever it is, isn't the average Runner who has no more ability than you. Chances are, this person has abilities even greater than I do."

"What? But that's, like, impossible!"

Walter shook his head. "I wish it were. And a Runner who is that powerful likely has a greater vendetta than just trying to scare us."

"What do you mean?"

"I mean that if he knows that I'm a Timekeeper, and a Captain at that, he may come after you. And this isn't like your run-of-the-mill average criminal who you can defend against by sheer ability to Band. He killed Sam with zero resistance, I suspect, because it happened just that fast."

"Do you have any idea who it is or anything? Are there any leads?"

"A beige van that has managed to successfully elude all security cameras that matter, during such time as it would make a difference if we picked out a beige van in traffic. No descriptions or leads whatsoever yet." Walter finished off his spaghetti and stood. "But that's nothing a good night's sleep won't help, I'm sure. And you should get some sleep, too, since you spent all day in backbreaking labor and have school tomorrow."

Tommen nodded reluctantly, but Walter could see the fatigue. Eventually he dragged himself to bed, again sprawling out in his clothes from the day. Walter closed his door, leaving just a sliver of light, and headed off to his own bedroom for another night of lying awake and staring into the darkness that was broken only by a small night light.

He'd dealt with Runners before who had some semblance of control over their abilities, most of them barely begun in their Apprentice training before they turned. But the man they were dealing with now, if Walter's suspicions were correct, was more powerful than anything he'd ever had to deal with. This was like walking into a room, expecting a gun fight, and being confronted with grenades, land mines, and a nuclear bomb.

And if the Runner would eventually turn and go after Walter, Micaiah, Micah, all the Timekeepers, what was there to stop him from getting to Tommen? Against such a powerful foe, what could Walter possibly do to protect his son from that? Could he dare hope that the Runner would see Tommen as just a non-threat and leave him alone? Or did he view him as simply an easy target in order to draw Walter deeper into the fight, knowing that his abilities were inferior? Was it really possible for a knife to win a gun fight?

He lay awake for a long time, staring into the darkness. He wasn't sure how long he lay there or if he slept at all, as the next thing he knew, his alarm clock was screaming at him.

Chapter Seven
Popularity

Tommen always seemed to be the kid that everyone talked about for one thing or another. If it wasn't the fighting, it was because Walter was investigating a super-juicy case, and everyone seemed to assume that the two of them had some kind of late-night, super-secret confidential discussions where they shared secret knowledge and cracked cases using only a single strand of hair found by chance during a second view of the crime scene.

Suffice to say, such things did not happen, at least, not the way his classmates thought. The most Tommen had been told about the case beyond what the police had deliberately released to the public, as far as the normal public was concerned, was that Sam and Lily had traded shifts that night, and it was possible that the killer had been after Lily instead. The reasons why went more into the realm of an investigation that the public didn't know about.

Tommen was not invited to help Micaiah and Micah with their Time-side investigation, though reportedly it was having about as much success as the Earth-side investigation. Any of them might have thought that a Runner with such abilities would help to narrow down the pool of suspects. But as Micaiah pointed out, if a Runner that powerful didn't want to be found, he'd find a way to make it happen, even managing to hide from the Timekeepers.

Teachers were a little more subtle about their curiosity. They never asked him outright if he knew anything or if Walter had some bit of case-cracking evidence, but when, on Tommen's first day of driving for his driver's ed class, the instructor asked him to casually pull around the school and turn around in the dirt lot on the other side of the soccer fields, it wasn't hard to guess why. Especially when the instructor made him get out and demonstrate how to properly inspect a vehicle before driving, and then spent an extra five minutes just looking around the lot. What did the man hope to find, anyway? Did he think that he was going to be some kind of TV hero who catches some microscopic piece of evidence in his peripheral vision, turns it in, and suddenly it's the piece the entire police force has been looking for, and once again, the day is saved?

Generally, work was the only respite he got once the bakery reopened, and the twins were more than happy to discuss something other than the Time-side investigation. The oven alcove had been repaired, rebuilt, and reinforced, the electrical brought back up to code and beyond so it could handle all the ovens which were back to working overtime. The new ovens, those that had replaced the ovens that had been completely destroyed, were actually very nice and made for better baking. Plus, as an added bonus for the insurance, they were more energy efficient and less taxing on the electrical. The insurance company greatly encouraged the twins to look into replacing the rest of the ovens.

Tommen might have hoped that time and silence would have made the conversation and the whispers die, but as usual, it never did, and the telephone game erupted from it instead. First, Tommen was just the kid who found the bodies. Then, he helped the killer unload the body from the van and move it to where it was found. Then, he was the driver of the van, the getaway vehicle of a heinous crime. And, of course, Eric and Varad were his accomplices, this only fueled by Eric suddenly disappearing for a week or more with zero explanation.

The hype finally peaked in History class one day as a note that was being passed around finally got intercepted by Mr. Morris. It was on its way to Tommen, but who wrote the note was anybody's guess. Morris unfolded the piece of paper and sighed, like even he was hoping for some bit of juicy gossip to spread around the teachers' lunch table. For as much as the teachers discouraged gossip, Tommen knew they gossiped just as much.

" 'Know anything?' " Mr. Morris read aloud.

He let that linger for a minute or two before crumpling up the paper into a little ball, then slowly walking over to the trash can and making a dramatic display of throwing away the note. Then he turned on his heel in true military fashion and walked back to the center of his little stage. He watched the class for a minute more until they squirmed. Were they supposed to give up who wrote the note? Were they supposed to apologize? Finally, he spoke.

"Something tragic happened a couple weeks ago here," he stated. "Tommen Forbes, our Chivalrous Welshman, and a couple of his friends found a body that had been dumped on the soccer fields."

"Actually, according to witness reports, the body was in an upright position with her hands on her lap, suggesting a caring pose, which suggests the murderer felt guilty," Olivia interrupted. "Or at least, that's what *Criminal Minds* says."

"Nothing else happened that concerns us," Morris went on. "This school was not targeted in any way except as a convenient location." He went on before someone else could interrupt him again with some TV crime show logic. "It's news, and we will discuss it as such if we must discuss it at all. We will not concoct our own theories or pretend to know something special and secret. Anyone who may know something relevant ought to turn it over to the police and let them do their job without interference.

"Furthermore, it is not a secret that Tommen's dad is the lead investigator on the case. However, he is still a sworn police officer, and I do not expect that he would share any more information with his son than he would you or I. This not only puts Tommen at risk of knowing too much, but it is a breach of the security and confidentiality of the case.

"That said, I am putting an end to this discussion. Not just in this classroom, but in this school and on these grounds. We are going to return to our lesson, and there will be no more talk about what happened, nor wild theories that serve only to embarrass and belittle your classmates. And when you leave this classroom to go to third period, I expect the same. This conversation is over."

And just like that, the whispering stopped as Morris turned his back to them and continued writing something about the Industrial Revolution.

Tommen pretended to take notes. Really he just kept writing his little stories. He wrote about a time when Teo came home from the mine when he was but sixteen. Once all the soot got washed off his face, he was whiter'n a ghost. It was the first time he'd seen a dead man. Oh, they'd both butchered goats and calves and chickens, and they'd been to half a dozen funerals. But it was the first time he'd actually watched a man die, as the mine collapsed and some of the other miners didn't make it. For some, only a hand was visible. For others, their hips and legs had been crushed. But the one that haunted Teo the most was the man who he'd turned and was reaching to help, when a rock came down and crushed his skull, splattering blood and brains all down the front of him. Teo might have been the next man to die if another miner hadn't pulled him along.

How fitting then that Tommen should see his first dead body when he was also sixteen. He wondered if it was some cruel trick of the universe to have that in common with his older brother. Of all things, it had to be the sight of a dead body.

Spanish was a similar if slightly more sadistic story, as Mrs. Perez gave them a similar speech in Spanish, except she turned it into a pop quiz by making them write down both the Spanish transcript and the English translation. Furthermore, for every day that she had to repeat that speech, it would not only get harder, but it would be moved from a pop quiz to a very heavily weighted test grade.

"Are you all right, Tommen?" Mrs. Perez asked as the bell rang for lunch. "You're not as cheeky as normal."

Since being revealed that she enjoyed their banter, she'd been a little more relaxed about it.

Tommen sighed and shrugged. "I'm just ready to go home is all."

She nodded sympathetically. "I imagine it's been a very trying couple of weeks. Hopefully things will get back to normal soon for you and you can move on."

Tommen was more ready to just move on to lunch: ham on rye with a generous helping of mustard. Varad sat silently next to him, some sort of Asian noodle dish for lunch.

"My mom's been cooking us nothing but traditional Indian food lately," he said to no one in particular. "For a while, I just packed my own lunch. Then my dad found out and basically unpacks my lunch so my mom can pack it. I'm either going to have to start buying my lunch here or stashing a second lunch in my backpack."

"You don't like Indian food?" Tommen wondered.

Varad shrugged. "I wouldn't mind it so bad if just for the reason we're all being made to eat it."

"Well, at least you guys haven't joined the popular crowd in my absence."

They looked up as Eric sat across from them. He looked a wreck. His face was gaunt, eyes sunken, skin pale as death. His hair was messy and greasy, and he looked like he hadn't showered the entire time he'd been gone. His lunch bag contained only a peanut butter and jelly sandwich; as he ate, he looked like he wanted to both scarf it down and throw it up. For a minute, Tommen and Varad could only stare at him.

"Dude, what happened?" Tommen finally dared ask.

He might have expected any kind of response except bursting into tears. He'd seen Eric laugh, get angry, even seen him grieve silently when he lost his dog, his best friend for as long as he could remember. But never had Tommen known Eric to cry. Instinctively, Varad moved to sit beside him and Tommen turned his body to shield the emotional outburst from the vultures who would come picking for meat as they smelled weakness.

Eric cried for probably five full minutes, and Tommen couldn't figure out what could have possibly happened to make him feel so powerfully. Maybe his mother died. It would explain the outburst and the time off. Maybe they were going to lose the house or something. But he wouldn't cry over that; he'd just grit his teeth and work to find a way to make a way.

"My life is fucking over," he said finally, sucking in gasping breaths. "It's over. I'm done. I'm fucking done."

"What happened?" Tommen asked again, now severely concerned for his friend.

Eric sniffed hard. "I've spent the last week and a half in jail."

"Wait, what?" Did Walter know about this? How come he hadn't said anything? "For what?"

"Saturday afternoon, Michelle's dad came over to our house. I was the only one home. He accused me of raping her and said I could either marry her when she turned eighteen, or I could spend the next forty years in prison for statutory rape."

"Shit," Tommen hissed.

"I told him I didn't know what he was talking about. We exchanged words. Monday after school, the cops show up and arrest me for raping Michelle and threatening to murder her dad."

"They can't just hold you for that long without formally indicting you."

"Yeah, well, no one was coming to bail me out of jail, and Mr. Olson did end up pressing charges on Michelle's behalf."

"You didn't rape her, though," Varad said. "She practically begged you to fuck her."

Eric spit a humorless laugh. "Not according to the State of West Virginia. And then, this morning, word comes down that she's pregnant."

"It's been, like, ten days," Tommen said. "They couldn't know that fast."

Eric shrugged. "I don't know how they determined that. In my defense, my lawyer ordered a paternity test, saying the same thing. Then he got me out of jail basically by stating that if the kid was mine, then statistically it was better for me to have graduated high school and start college in order to better financially support them. And if it's not mine, then the last ten days have ruined me more than is considered ethical." He sighed and wiped his nose with a napkin. "I literally woke up in jail, got released, and was home just long enough to change into some clean clothes."

Could have fooled Tommen, but he didn't say anything.

"So what happens now?" Varad wondered.

"If the paternity test comes back saying it's mine, I'm basically going to be forced to marry Michelle when she turns eighteen or else spend the better part of my adult life in prison. And if the test says it's not mine, then I'm off the hook. That's the deal we made."

"Could be worse," Tommen mentioned unhelpfully.

Eric nodded and shrugged. "Yeah. I mean, at least I have the option of not going to prison. But still...my life is fucking over either way. Even if the test says it's not mine, I'm fucking ruined. She's probably already started a ton of rumors around here."

Tommen hadn't heard any, but that didn't mean much. He didn't pay much attention to girl gossip, and even if it had made its way around into the general gossip rings, he still probably wouldn't have believed it. For goodness' sake, look at the rumors circulating about him right now. Even Mr. Morris, for all his preaching about not adding fuel to the fire, still referred to him as the Chivalrous Welshman.

"So how are things around here with you two?" Eric asked, coming back to his senses enough to try and finish his sandwich. "Obviously neither of you have been arrested for killing that woman."

"No, but apparently I was the driver of the getaway vehicle," Tommen said, hoping to inject some humor into the situation. It had little effect.

"Has anything happened with it?"

Tommen sighed and shook his head. "Just that the vehicle in question is a beige van, possibly an older one." He shrugged. "It's all I know, which is what everyone else knows. I don't get any special information from my dad."

Eric set down the last bite of his sandwich and rubbed his eyes.

"God, I don't know what I'm going to do if the kid really is mine. I'm supposed to go to college, not prison."

"Then go to college," Tommen told him. "And take Michelle and the kid with you."

Eric scoffed and shook his head. "Easy for you to say. You're the fucking Chivalrous Welshman! Everything is easy for you, even if it means you get the shit beat out of you every fucking week."

Tommen bristled. "Easy? You think my life is easy?"

"Sure. You get in trouble and Detective Daddy is always right there to defend you."

"And what's that supposed to mean?" Tommen stood. "You think I get away with shit because my dad's a cop? I get away with nothing. It only looks like I get away with shit." Out of the corner of his eye, he saw one of the lunch ladies step away, likely to go get Layman. Perfect.

"Guys, calm down," Varad said peacefully, apparently seeing or sensing the same thing. "Eric, we know you're stressed right now. It's not fun and it's not fair. But there's nothing that the three of us can do about it, and getting mad at us and insulting Tommen won't fix anything. If we all remain calm and civil, and if we can all still be friends, then we can support each other."

"The fuck is this, group therapy?" Eric snapped.

Tommen wasn't sure what happened next except all three of them were sitting in Layman's office. He remembered a fight, but he was fairly certain that he hadn't actually been involved. For once. Layman sat on his desk, facing them.

"Well, Tommen, for once you weren't involved except to pull Eric off Varad. Let's hear your side of the story first."

Tommen racked his brain, trying to remember. "Um, Eric was having a hard time, and he was telling us about it. Then he started getting mad at me. So Varad tried to calm him down. Then Eric went after him, and I guess I just reacted and tried to pull them apart."

Layman sighed. "I understand the gist of what happened to you this last week or so, Mr. Brown. But it's no reason to start a fight, especially with your friends. And if what I hear is true about what could potentially happen, you're going to need all the friends you can get here soon." He folded his arms. "So, this is what I'm going to do." He paused. "Nothing."

The boys glanced at each other.

"I am going to do nothing," Layman repeated. "Tommen, Varad, you both did the right thing trying to help calm things down. Eric, I understand things are not going your way and in no way will a suspension help your cause. However, this is a one-time offer only. You either make up with your friends here or find new friends, but there will be no more fighting. Understood?"

"Yes, sir," they all said in turn.

Tommen left the office feeling rather elated, if for no other reason than he wasn't in trouble this time. Actually, Layman had commended him for stepping in and doing the right thing. He paused for just a second and shook his head. It must be a full moon. Everything about it was just too weird.

"Ah, Tommen, there you are. Do you have a minute?"

He turned to see Mr. Gillingham walked toward him, lunchbox over one shoulder. Tommen was surprised to find it was decorated with superheroes of the Marvel variety.

"Yeah, um, sure," Tommen said awkwardly.

"I got the analysis of your test back from the maker," Gillingham informed him. "By general academic standards, you passed. Some day soon, me, you, your dad, and Mrs. Wendell should have a sit down and discuss your class arrangements and career options. How does that sound?"

"That sounds awesome. Yeah, I mean, actually he has today off. I can call work and let them know I'll be a little late. Otherwise I'm pretty much stuck between work and driver's ed."

"Great. We'll meet in Mrs. Wendell's office after school, then."

Tommen watched Gillingham leave, unable to contain a stupid grin. He called Walter.

"Hello?" Walter wondered cautiously, probably silently

praying that Tommen wasn't about to tell him that he'd gotten into another fight and needed to be picked up.

"Hey, so, you need to come to the school after school gets out," Tommen told him, trying to keep a level voice even if he couldn't manage a straight face.

"Why?" Translation: Was there another fight? Are you being suspended or expelled?

"Just, please? It won't take very long."

"Tommen, you are going to tell me why I'm coming."

"It's just about a test I took."

Walter sighed, a mix of relief that it wasn't a fight and resignation that he wasn't going to get the full story over the phone. Not to mention that Tommen did, sometimes, get into trouble for sarcastic remarks he made on tests instead of writing down the answer the teacher was looking for.

After hanging up with Walter, Tommen called the bakery to let them know he was going to be late. The twins were less than enthused. Judging by background noise, they were busy and probably assumed he was staying after school for detention. Still, they thanked him for letting them know and promptly returned to work.

The last two classes seemed to fly by as Tommen reflected that it had been a pretty good day, actually. Well, except for the part where his best friend was being accused of rape that resulted in a pregnancy, and said best friend tried to beat the shit out of another best friend. But he hadn't gotten in trouble for the fight, been commended, then told that he was able to move up in his science classes.

Walter was far less enthused when he showed up after school. His presence by itself seemed to generate rumors as he met Tommen and Gillingham in the office.

"So what's it about this time?" Walter asked, his demeanor pretty deadened to Tommen being in the office for something.

"When Mrs. Wendell returns, we'll step into her office to

discuss this with her," Gillingham began.

"You're not going to try and move him to special ed classes," Walter told them sternly. "He's a smart kid if he cares to apply himself."

Gillingham blinked. "He didn't tell you?"

Walter raised a brow.

Mrs. Wendell returned then, and as they moved into her office, Gllingham explained. "Tommen is being moved into Advanced Placement classes, specifically those concerning science. A couple weeks ago, I allowed him to take a test which would help place him in those AP classes in high school, and then map out some potential career paths."

The look on Walter's face when he learned that Tommen was being praised and not sentenced pretty much summed up how Tommen felt about the entire day. Proud, excited, bewildered, confused, and a little suspicious.

But because Tommen hadn't mentioned the test—most likely because of the events of later that night had pushed that to the back burner and then out of mind completely—Mr. Gillingham had to take the time to briefly go over the test with Walter, explaining how it was administered and graded and analyzed.

"Your strongest point was Physics," Gillingham told Tommen. "No surprise there. But a close runner-up, and by close I'm talking within five points, was Medicine. Since it would be ideal to move you into AP classes as soon as possible, which means next semester, I would recommend moving you into AP Physics. Any objections?"

Tommen and Walter shook their heads.

"It would have to go in place of your Government class, and the only other viable option to fill the spot is an elective." Mrs. Wendell handed Tommen a schedule sheet. "I placed you in Drawing and Painting IA because it was the only one open, unless you're interested in Weight Lifting?" Tommen shook his head. "It'll give you another elective this year, but virtually none the next two years."

"So what are we looking at the next couple years?" Walter

wondered. "Is there a dual-enrollment option?"

"Not until senior year," Gillingham told him. He looked at Tommen. "Your junior year is essentially going to be all required credit courses in order to make sure you get all your credits you need to graduate high school. That way, you can dual-enroll your senior year and not have to worry."

"What are my options for dual-enrollment?" Tommen inquired.

"Well, that depends on what you want to do, where you want to go. The field of Physics can be a little more school-exclusive, depending on your chosen profession. Medicine is not only ubiquitous, but in desperate demand."

"What about the other sections of the test?"

Gillingham looked through some of his papers. "Astronomy was nearly tied with Medicine. Geology was a polite fourth place. And Chemistry was a lonely fifth place."

Tommen ran his tongue over his teeth. "I want to do the AP Physics. Didn't we have an astronomy class last year?"

"We did," Mrs. Wendell answered, "but it was discontinued for lack of interest. We're working with the library and one of the universities to set up an online class, but that won't be ready until next year at the soonest."

"When does he need to have this...career plan turned in?" Walter asked, looking through some of the papers Gillingham gave him.

"Any time, really. The most we can do at this point is get him in AP Physics next semester. I would encourage you both to sit down together and decide what you want to do, Tommen. Figure out your goals, your plans, and your means. Dual-enrollment in college is cheaper, but not free. Obviously, the sooner we have a plan, the easier it will be to both follow and make necessary adjustments."

"If you want to have a leg up in claiming your classes for next year, try to have it turned in around spring break," Mrs. Wendell told him. "After that is when everyone starts filling out their course request sheets. Hopefully I can have you done and preplanned and set before it gets lost in the scheduling overload."

"How much harder is the AP workload?" Walter asked.

"Not harder than this test," Gillingham assured him. "I'm confident in his abilities to learn the material as long as he takes the time to diligently study and learn it from the inside out, which it seems he's already done to some degree."

"So if he takes the AP Physics this year and dual-enrolls his senior year, what happens next year? Would it be better to do the AP Physics next year instead of skipping a year and losing all that?"

"No!" Tommen protested. "I want to do it this year! I can't sit in those average classes anymore!"

"What if he switched the AP Physics with, I don't know, Anatomy? Still science, still in with his strong points, but it keeps the hard classes closer together," Walter suggested.

"But what about the online astronomy class?"

Gillingham grinned. "Tommen, you seem to be thinking only in terms of high school classes. There will be more of these classes in college that you can take, and they'll be far more in-depth."

"And they'll be far more expensive."

"Very true. And this is what we call prioritizing." Gillingham leaned back in his chair. "For now we'll keep you were you are in the AP Physics for next semester. If you change your mind by Thanksgiving—right, Thanksgiving?" Mrs. Wendell nodded. "Then we can do a little last-minute shuffling. Until then, sit down, think about what you want, and come up with a plan to get there. Then we can talk again."

Walter shook hands with Gillingham and Mrs. Wendell and then he and Tommen headed out to the car.

"So why didn't you tell me you'd taken such a high-level test?" Walter wondered, his tone more curious than accusing.

Tommen shrugged. "I don't know. It was the night of the murder, so I just didn't think about it later on. Then either you're not home or it just didn't seem important. I didn't even think about it much until today when Gillingham told me I passed and then I called you."

"Well, I'm proud of you."

"You are?"

"Why not? You're taking initiative, Tommen. And you're going after something you enjoy."

"I thought you always wanted me to be a cop like you."

Walter chuckled. "What father doesn't want his son to follow in his footsteps? Tommen, as long as you are willing to pursue your goals and work for them, I'll support them. Within reason, of course."

Tommen grinned. "There's always a catch, isn't there?"

"At the same time, you do understand that AP courses are going to be harder and will require more work and more studying, right?"

Tommen sighed and rolled his eyes. "I know."

"You're lucky because you can pretty much just create more time in the day to do your homework and study. And as beneficial as that is, I don't want you relying on it. Don't forget to function on a twenty-four hour day, otherwise you'll only mess yourself up more."

"I know."

"All right. Now then, you have to work today, right?"

Tommen nodded. "I didn't interrupt your nap, did I?"

Walter shrugged. "I didn't get called in for a fight, so I'm not too mad. I'll just go home and pick up where I left off."

They arrived at the bakery. Tommen left his backpack in the car, and Walter followed him in so he could get a pastry.

"Dia daoibh," Tommen greeted as he hurried in.

The store wasn't actually busy. A couple people sat on barstools looking out the big front windows, but otherwise, Micaiah was in the office and Micah was in the kitchen, everything as normal as it should be.

"Walter's out there," Tommen said as he punched in and grabbed an apron.

"So serve him," Micah told him coldly, not looking at him.

Tommen flushed red as he returned to the front counter. "And how can I help you today, sir?"

"I'll take one of those," Walter said, pointing to the last chocolate-filled pastry. As soon as he paid, he said, "I'll see you later," and headed out.

When he was gone, Tommen turned and almost bumped into Micah who jerked his thumb toward the office. "Office."

It had been way too good of a day for there not to be some catastrophe waiting at the end of the tunnel. It was like Wile E. Coyote looking for the light at the end of the tunnel only to have it be a train ready to squash him flatter than a pancake. That was how Tommen felt as he slunk into the office.

"Shut the door," Micaiah commanded, not looking at him. "And sit down."

Tommen felt his stomach roll and his throat tighten as he wordlessly did as he was bid. For a long moment, Micaiah simply went about his business like Tommen wasn't there. Then suddenly, he turned toward him.

"Tommen, we are not pleased with your attendance record," he said very matter-of-fact. "It's gotten to the point where you're late an average of once a week."

"But today was good! I got moved to AP Physics!" Tommen blurted.

"Great. We'll add that to the list of excuses." He went on before Tommen could protest further. "Whatever the reason, we expect you here at a certain time, and you seem unable to manage even that. When you're here, you're a good worker. It's getting you here that's the problem."

"Am I being fired?"

Micaiah looked like he had a few choice words but elected not to say them aloud. Instead, he leaned back in his chair and put an ankle up on his knee. "Not yet, but you're this close to it. We've decided to give you one more chance. Unless the school bus goes round and round off the road for some reason, we expect you here on time, whenever you're scheduled. Otherwise, we're going to be looking for a new Baker's Assistant. Got it?"

Tommen couldn't deny his words; he was often late to work. Not only did it look bad on him, but between losing hours from that and losing days because of driver's ed, his paycheck was suffering. He sighed. There was nothing to say except, "Yes, sir."

"Dismissed."

And Micaiah went back to his work without so much as a "How was your day?"

Tommen returned to the kitchen where Micah was busy decorating a cake, squeezing out blue icing and making little flowers. It looked like one of their pre-made generic cakes. Tommen elected to start on mixing ingredients for some loaves of bread.

"I got moved up into AP Physics for next semester," he began conversationally.

Micah nodded. "Cool."

"My senior year I should be able to dual-enroll."

"Good for you."

"I had to take a placement test. According to the results, my strongest area of science is Physics. No surprise there. But my second-strongest area was actually Medicine. But I guess Astronomy was a really close third. The Geology and Chemistry I'm really not too worried about."

"I expect you'd have some insight into the physics."

Micah's tone was still cold, but Tommen couldn't help but grin. "Yeah, no kidding."

They worked in silence for a while, trading off as needed to help customers, both of them going up front when it got too busy. Tommen was the first to break the silence after they'd more or less recovered from the evening rush.

"I know I'm late a lot. My excuses are usually pretty lame. And I'm sorry. It's not fair to you, and you would have been justified in firing me. Instead you gave me another chance. But it would be really nice if you gave me another chance to still be you guys' friend."

Micah stopped in his work, scraping the last of the day's cookies onto a tray to go in the display case. For a moment, Tommen was afraid he would just keep working in silence. Finally he shook his head and turned, a coy grin on his face. "Tommen, you never stopped being our friend." The grin vanished. "But don't forget that we are above you in a lot of other ways. We are your bosses. We have a business to run, and you being late makes it very hard, even with all this." He indicated the Bands running to and fro. "If you still work here when you're an Apprentice, you can be damn sure we're going to have you practicing your skills and helping with this to ease up on our strain. We just want you to be reliable about it. Because if we have to try and do this with someone who isn't a Timekeeper—which is pretty much everyone else—it's only going to make it harder."

"I know," Tommen admitted.

"Being reliable is important, Tommen. Telling someone you'll do something and then doing it shows character and integrity. And that's important in all aspects of life, from school to work to your social life. One day, you won't have a nice set schedule from school to plan your day by. You won't have Walter there to remind you of things. And if you aren't reliable and responsible and self-disciplined, then the ones who do remind you of things—like your bills, your rent, your job—aren't going to be as nice as we are about it. If you don't discipline yourself, someone else will."

His words were serious and the conversation lingered in the air, but it helped to ease the tension between them. Still, Micah pressed on. "At the same time, courage is another aspect of character and integrity. Technically, both me and Cai are your bosses and we made the decision together to not fire you. I appreciate the apology, but I'm not going to just go to Micaiah and tell him that you apologized and we're all good. You owe him an apology, too, from your own mouth."

That thought was more daunting than voluntarily walking into a pit of vipers. It wasn't even like Micaiah was a bad guy or a mean boss or a terrible person. Actually, it was more that he was a nice guy, too nice for his own good sometimes, but able to conjure up some righteous anger when the situation called. Today, Tommen had been on the receiving end of that righteous anger. And it scared him. It changed Micaiah, at least his perception of him. He was above Tommen. They both were. They were friends, but not in the same way that he, Eric, and Varad were friends. Here, in the bakery, and within the sense of Time, there was hierarchy. And Tommen was beneath them. He cast a longing glance at Micah who simply nodded once toward the office.

Taking a breath and swallowing his pride, Tommen went and knocked on the office door.

"*Tar isteach,*" came the reply. (Come in.)

Tommen slunk into the office and closed the door quietly behind him. He didn't dare sit. He wasn't even sure Micaiah was aware of him until he cut him off.

"I heard you out there," Micaiah said. His tone was impossible to judge. He looked up. "I understand, and I accept your apology. But Micah was right. We're friends. Outside the bakery, and outside Time. In here, or when we are discussing Time, we are your bosses, your Lieutenants, your mentors. We can laugh and joke and have a good time, make fun of customers and play pranks, but you still do as we tell you. And you do as you promise. Your schedule is a promise, telling us that you will be here on certain days at a certain time. And we hold you to that. If there is a problem, let's work it out. Don't go pulling stupid stuff and trying to cover it up. All right?"

Tommen nodded.

"Good. Now then, when is your next day of work?"

"Thursday."

"What time?"

"Three."

"We'll hold you to it. We're not your dad, Tommen. And like Micah said, if you don't discipline yourself, someone else will. Dismissed."

Tommen left the office, not sure how he was supposed to feel. Embarrassed. Guilty. Put in his place. Those were all very good descriptions. He finished out the night, running through the chore list fairly easily since it was a quiet night. He had just come back in from taking out the last trash bag when he saw Walter pull into the parking lot. After a few more small clean-ups, he punched out, said a meager "Good night" to the twins, and headed out, trying to hold his head high and act like anything but a whipped puppy.

"How was work?" Walter asked as they pulled away and headed for home.

Tommen shrugged. "It was work. People come, people order pastries, people go. How was your nap?"

"Couldn't get back to sleep, so I did a little yard work."

"Why? The snow's just going to cover it up anyway."

"Maybe, but it gave me something to do. Figured I'd been lazy about it for long enough. Discipline and all that."

Right. Discipline.

Chapter Eight
The Cold Facts

Every case started off the same in Walter's mind, a mystery brimming with possibilities as names gave way to leads, and any bit of information or shred of evidence lent itself to a bigger picture. It was like trying to solve an enormous jigsaw puzzle where the box did not show the picture that was supposed to be created.

The case had started off on the rocky side as Sam had apparently been that cute shy angel who had no enemies or jealous exes, or anyone at all in her life beyond her parents and roommate.

But once the working class got back into the swing of things on Monday, tips started coming in. The culmination of these ended up being a black man between thirty and forty wearing a light brown leather jacket, jeans, and heavy work boots. He may have also worn glasses. This came from a description of a beige van pulling into a gas station/car wash to use the vacuums. The anonymous tipper just happened to casually walk by as if to check the prices on the vacuums when he noticed that the back of the van had a case full of surgical tools and a white coat that was, by witness estimations, far too small to be the driver's. The van had no plate on it and nothing particularly outstanding about it. The cameras at the gas station were crude at best and did little to give a better suspect or vehicle description, but it was put out for the public to search and identify.

At first, there were a number of sightings of the van, albeit all with plates. The police tried to move as swiftly as the calls, hoping to trap the guy before he caught wind and slipped away. Walter went out a number of times, trying to pick up on the wake of a Band. If the guy was a Runner who could Band, he'd get away from most average cops.

"You're sure it was the van were looking for?" Walter asked as he chased a tip to a small grocery store. Supposedly the cart boy had seen the van and called it in. Not surprisingly, no one inside the store remembered him. He'd probably Banded too fast for them to perceive him as he stole whatever it was he needed.

"Oh yeah, it was him." The kid couldn't have been older than Tommen, with heavy acne, greasy hair, braces, and no apparent concept of deodorant or regular bathing. "It was parked right over there. The guy was sitting on the back bumper, door open, eating one of the rotisserie chickens from the deli. I told him he had some kind of leak. When he got off the bumper to go look, I saw a clear plastic container of, I don't know, gauze, tape, scalpels, blue surgical gloves. And there was a white coat lying on the floor."

"And when he saw the van had no leak?" Walter wondered.

"Oh, it did. I work with my dad in the garage sometimes. He was leaking something. I wasn't close enough to say what, though."

"Okay. So what did the guy look like?"

"Black. I saw that right away." He stopped as if that solved everything, like there was only one black guy in the entire state of West Virginia. He paused, then appeared to realize that Walter was looking for more than just skin color. "He had short hair, kind of a fuzzy mustache, goatee. He was wearing a black turtleneck, like the old school kind your grandma used to knit, you know? Tan coat, leather maybe. Jeans. He had worn out the stupid little napkins from the deli and was wiping his fingers on his jeans. And he had big construction boots, like, steel toe, steel shank, steel covered in leather basically. Except they didn't really look worn. They looked like they just came out of the box. Everything he wore did, except his jeans, obviously."

"Could you estimate how tall he was?"

The kid pursed his lip and looked around at the cars in the lot. He walked over to a white work van, company logo on the side and back doors. He put a hand about midway on the windows. "When he got off the bumper to check his leak, he stood like this tall."

In all reality, that was probably the safest way to measure a suspect's height.   Rather than relying on someone being able to accurately measure feet from a distance, simply mark an invisible line on a relative object, then measure that.   As it was, Walter guessed it was about six-foot-one or so once he factored in an inch or two for the boots.

"Do you know which way he went?" Walter asked severely.

"No, man. I was kind of hoping he'd leave quickly so I could tell you, but once he, you know, caught me staring, he got really scary."

"What do you mean?"

"I...can't really explain it. I guess the only thing I can think of is, like, a couple years ago I went hiking with my dad. And we saw this bear. From a distance, you know. So we take a few pictures, and we're trying to back away. Well, then it sees us. And it was like, 'Holy shit, are we about to die?' That's kind of what it was like, the vibes I was getting off him. I finished up my rack, and by the time I got back out, he was gone."

Walter nodded and finished up his notes. "What's your name, kid?"

"Aaron."

"Aaron, how confident are you in your description of the guy?"

"I know what I saw, man."

"Do you think you could give a more detailed description to a sketch artist? That means nose shape, the set of the eyes, mouth, ears, everything?"

Aaron hesitated. "I want to say yes, but I don't want to get it wrong. I mean, I wanna help, but..."

Walter didn't want to push the kid for the same reasons, but he still fished out a business card. "If you see him again, remember anything else, or want to give that sketch, give me a call."

The kid assured him he would, and Walter returned to the

station to stare at the case sprawled out over a giant map and whiteboard. Standish was there, staring at the same map. Walter picked a marker and put a big X on the grocery store.

"He's not trying to run," Walter said, going to stand beside Standish. "He's staying in the city."

"So why aren't more people seeing him?" Standish wondered aloud. "He's got to have a hiding spot somewhere." He shifted his stance and took a drink of coffee. "What's his end game? If he was just after Sam, he could have high-tailed it out of here and been all the way to the west coast by now. If he is after Lily Guile, why hasn't he tried to kill her again? What's he waiting for?"

Walter sighed and folded his arms. "He's toying with us. He's trying to rub it in that he hasn't gone anywhere, and we still can't catch him. That's why he hasn't tried again. Once he gets bored with that game, I expect that's when he'll make another hit."

"So what happens if he's successful the second time? Does he disappear?"

"With any luck, there won't be a second time."

Walter left the office, and Standish followed. "Where are you going?"

"Out," Walter said.

"Walt, it's been a long day. Go back and study the map a little more, study the notes. Get a good night's sleep. Maybe it'll come to you then."

It was good advice, really, and Walter wanted nothing more than to go home more or less on time and be able to spend a few hours by himself, spend a few hours with Tommen, before having to go to sleep, only to wake up to more of the chaos.

In the end, he did as Standish suggested, returning to the office to memorize the map and the notes on the board before reluctantly punching out and heading home. That was the problem with these mysteries sometimes. All the puzzle pieces spoke of endless possibilities as he worked to find pieces that fit together and bring the big picture into focus, until he realized that the big picture needed a thousand pieces, and there are only five hundred in the box. Even worse, of those five hundred, only about two hundred of them were even relevant to the puzzle at hand. The rest meant nothing at all and were placed there only to confuse.

That was how it happened as Walter chased his mystery suspect, whom he ironically dubbed the Runner. Over the next week, he followed lead after lead as the van or the suspect was spotted. But the sightings became less frequent and less certain. Once, he got a tip that the man had actually gone into a gas station and paid for a bag of chips.

Walter's first clue that it was the wrong guy should have been that he was able to catch up to the guy as he walked down the street. The guy didn't Band or show any Time tendencies, didn't even try to run. The most he did was roll his eyes and stomp a little bit as he stopped and folded his arms.

In all reality, he might have been honestly mistaken for the Runner as he was a black man about thirty-two years old, maybe six feet tall, with short hair and a beard. Glasses perched on his nose. He wore a brown suede jacket and jeans.

"I knew it was only a matter of time before y'all came bangin' after me," he shouted, despite Walter being close enough to have a civil conversation. "I dint kill nobody. But I know, all black men look the same to you white boys, an' we all criminals."

"Sir, my name is Detective Walter Forbes. We're looking for a murderer and we have to follow every viable tip that we're given. Would you mind telling me your name?"

"Chris Temper," the man replied, like a toddler frustrated that his tantrum hadn't won him any supporters. "And I didn't kill nobody."

"Mr. Temper, do you mind if I ask where you were two weeks ago Friday evening between six and eight p.m.?"

"I was at the homecoming game in South Charleston. I would've kept my ticket on me, but I never expected to be accused of murder."

"I'm not accusing you of anything, sir."

"I don't even have a fucking car! I'm poor! And still my tax dollars go to pad the pockets on your fat ass!"

"Sir, I'm only doing my job."

"Yeah, and making pretty good money off my tax dollars, I'm sure."

Walter gave him a cheeky grin. "Not if you saw my house." He became a little more serious and handed the gentleman a business card. "If you do know or see anything, give us a call."

The man grumbled some more and hurried off, accidentally "dropping" the business card and shoving his hands deeper in his pockets. Walter headed back to his car and rubbed his face.

There was no good way to do this. Well, there was always the right way, but the right way and the politically correct way were often two different things. He had to investigate a murder, and in this case, that meant the possibility of the suspect being black, but God forbid he talk to any black men and ask them if they'd killed someone.

But it wasn't all bad, really. They'd gotten a handful of such tips and only Mr. Temper here had copped such an attitude. But each time, the man didn't fit the description even with the benefit of the doubt, or he had a rock solid alibi, or he had zero motive.

As the week wore on, the sightings of the man or the van became less frequent to nonexistent, and people moved on to the next big crime story. It felt a cruel and heartless thing, but the public was only interested as long as something exciting was happening with it. Reluctantly, Walter returned to the station.

"Anything good?" he asked Standish who was sorting through his notepad papers.

Standish sighed. "Beige van on William Street belonged to a cleaning company. The van on Patrick Street Bridge is from out of state, has a plate, and the driver is white. Suspicious person on Oak Street suffered a car breakdown and was waiting for a ride. Other suspicious person on Monroe Street was a crackhead who was so high he only knew three colors: psychedelic, paisley, and wishes. You?"

"Pretty much the same. Got time for a coffee?"

"Believe me, I'm not going anywhere else right now. Captain's talking about shelving the case."

"Damn."

"I know, man, but...the guy's gone ghost. It was hard enough when it looked like he wanted to be found, just enough to keep our noses in the air, a carrot to chase after. Now the carrot's been yanked and we're still spinning in the wheel."

Walter paused. "What did you say?"

"A carrot. You know, like a hamster running—"

"No, before that. About the guy going ghost."

"Yeah. For a while, it looked like he wanted to be found, just enough to toy with us. Now that he's gone underground, he could strike again if your theory is right about Lily."

Walter shook his head. "Shit."

He turned and headed out of the room, Standish following. "Shit, shit, shit. I am an idiot!"

"Whoa, wait, what happened? Walter!"

Walter headed to his computer. "I found him. I found the guy. I talked to him to his face and never even knew it. He wanted to be found, changed his behavior, said look at me, and I passed him right on by."

"Did you get a name?" Standish wondered.

"He called himself Chris Temper. I doubt that's his real name, but it might give us a clue as to where he's hiding, or at least where he's been."

"Or maybe he picked the name out of thin air."

Still, Walter ran the name through every database he had access to, the only true hit coming from the state obituaries.

"Chris Temper died eight years ago," Walter read, feeling his excitement deflate into rejection. "He was an electrician for forty years. His estate passed to his only child, a daughter."

Standish let out a breath. "Yup." He patted Walter on the shoulder. "I'm sorry, man. You had me going for a minute there, too.

But this guy is just too smart for us right now. He'll slip up, though."

"So you're giving up?"

"We don't have anything. Captain's already drafting the paperwork to put it in cold storage."

Walter leaned back in his chair and let out a breath. "That's not going to be a fun thing to tell the family."

Standish shook his head. "No, it's not. Thankfully, we don't have to be the ones to tell them."

It wasn't much comfort as Walter tried to move into cold case mode. It wasn't a fun place to be, coming to the realization that he'd been outsmarted, that a killer had gotten away. It was only made worse when he considered all the extra resources he had access to. Worse than that was the knowledge that there was every chance that the killer was going to strike again, and it was just as likely that he would get away with that one, too. Even as he thought it, Steggmann approached, folder in hand.

"I think you know why I'm here," he said, handing Walter the folder.

Walter sighed. "We're shelving the Pietrowicz case."

He nodded solemnly. "It's not a fun thing to do, but we have to admit that we have nothing to go on. Tips are becoming more sporadic and less accurate, and we have other cases coming in that need attention. Unless you found something while you were out today?"

Walter hesitated. "I encountered the suspect."

"Excuse me?"

"I followed a tip that led me to him. But he slipped right through my fingers. He changed his appearance, his clothing, his attitude. But it was him. And I feel a fool for not seeing it when I had him right in front of me. Unfortunately, I got nothing of substance and we're right back where we started."

"You're sure about that, about seeing our guy?" Steggmann asked.

"Positive, sir. But it's no more helpful than the gas station attendant, or the cart boy at the grocery store. On that, I am certain. Because no doubt he knows that I realized my mistake. And now that he's had his little bit of fun, showing that he can walk right up to us and still walk away, he's going to disappear completely."

"Do you agree, Jim?"

Standish nodded as he took a drink of coffee. "Yes, sir, I do. We've just been sucker punched and now he's going to walk away laughing."

Steggmann sighed. "All right. Well, there's the paperwork. I expect the office to be cleaned up by the end of your shift. Otherwise, go home. I'll have something for you in the morning."

Reluctantly, Walter and Standish went through the paperwork, logging everything and committing everything to cold storage before heading to the office. They gathered papers and notes, erased the whiteboard and washed the giant map.

"So, what do you think?" Standish asked as the last of the marks were washed away and the map was clean once more.

"About what?" Walter wondered, looking at him as he wiped down the tables.

"You think our guy will strike again?"

"I expect so." They headed out of the office, turned off the light, and Walter shut the door behind them. "And I expect that we'll be right back on the case when he does."

They paused out in the hallway before moving to the small break area, a small cart of coffee and various snacks as they arrived throughout the day. Standish refilled his coffee cup. "Well, Captain told us to go home, clear our heads, and be ready in the morning. Where you off to?"

"Home, I expect, get in some time to myself before Tommen gets off work."

Standish nodded. "Well, I'll see you in the morning then."

Of course, there was always that little trip to the bakery that Walter had to make. He pulled into the parking lot and hurried across a light dusting of snow into a warm bakery.

"You're here early," Micah observed, pausing as he swept behind the counter. "Everything all right?"

"Micaiah in the office?" Walter wondered.

"When is he not?" Micah went and rapped on the door. "*A Chai, tá Walter anseo a fheiceann tú.*" (Cai, Walter's here to see you.)

Walter slipped behind the counter and into the office where Micaiah sat at the desk, working on some invoices. He spun around.

"*Dia duit, a Walter,*" Micaiah greeted.

"*S'mae,*" Walter retorted as he pulled up a chair and sat down.

"Now, now, none of that foreign stuff in here. We get enough of that from your son."

"I bet you do. How's he been doing?"

"Better since we had our little chat. Honestly, I don't envy you having to raise and train him."

"I can't imagine it's much easier on him."

Micaiah leaned back in his seat. "But I don't think you came here to check up on Tommen, especially since he's not even here yet. So, what's the news?"

"Well, Captain shelved the case today, put it in cold storage," Walter admitted. "We have nothing to go on."

"Your look tells me something happened and not the way you wanted it to."

Walter explained the incident about running into the suspect, having a less than civil chat with him, and ultimately completely letting him walk away. It wasn't something he liked to admit, but if nothing else, it put him in contact with the suspect. But still.

"I should have known, Micaiah. Somehow, I should have seen it."

Micaiah let out a breath. "Walt, you've been hanging onto the image that other people have described, so much so that one little change and he completely threw you off."

"Thank you, Captain Obvious," Walter said sarcastically. "I know. I messed up. But does any of it mean anything to you? Has a 'Chris Temper' been mentioned at all in your investigations?"

"No," Micaiah admitted. "We did some digging into the hitman theory, trying to find out who would want Lily dead."

"And?"

"God, the list is too long to effectively narrow down. There are a number of Auctioneers who resent how much of a cut she gets from her sales. Other Harvesters hate her because of her rare and expensive stock. And among the Runners, I guess they have a betting pool of who's going to kill her first."

Walter shifted in his seat. "That ought to be interesting. Anyone stand out?"

Micaiah shook his head. "Every group of Runners has a different pool. Essentially, it's like trying to take a poll of three random workplaces for March Madness brackets. There's nothing to go on there." He frowned. "The only ones interested in keeping Lily alive are the Hands, at least a select few."

"Because she bought their seats," Walter sighed. "What about those who lost to those Hands?"

"Oh, they want her dead, sure enough. But none of them are human and don't have enough of an understanding of humans to effectively pull it off."

"All it takes is enough money."

"Walt, I'm only giving you the quick version of our investigation."

"All right, fair enough. What about his abilities? What does that take?"

Micaiah hesitated and Walter didn't like his expression. "Walt, we're talking either a Gatekeeper or a Warden, at the least."

"Shit," Walter whispered, leaning back in his chair until he almost fell back. "Shit."

"That's what we said."

"Cai, that's like me trying to go after the deputy chief for murder. The only ones above a Warden are Dominion Timekeepers and the Hands." He shook his head. "Shit."

"The good news is that it should narrow down the list of who the killer could be. We may not get the one who ordered the hit, but we'll get the hitman."

"Okay. So how many human Gatekeepers and above are there?"

"That are currently accounted for?"

"Accounted for?"

Micaiah nodded. "You must have forgotten some of your history. You remember the Dispersal of '63?"

"Right. The elections that year were the most contested in over four centuries, and the Hands almost went into civil war. The only reason they didn't was because they were all too selfish to form alliances and potentially give up their power. It was never declared a war, but secret assassinations were carried out over a period of twelve years until the number of Hands equaled the number of seats."

"Exactly. And afterwards, the Hands made some changes to the Timekeeping system to better protect themselves and their rigged elections. Which basically meant that those who were in power went after those who had supported their rivals. Some were killed and some went into hiding."

Walter folded his arms. "What do we know about those that we know about?"

"Only Mi Chin is active. She caught a lucky break by being good friends with the Hand of the Timekeepers and was appointed by said Hand to rule as the Gatekeeper for Earth. She's out of China as you might imagine."

"Any others?"

"Laying low, trying to fly under the radar of the Hands. The Hands know where they are, but as long as they largely keep their abilities to themselves and don't cause any trouble in the Wheel, well, they can go about their daily lives. We looked into them, but there aren't any in North America right now that we know of. Basically, all eleven Gatekeepers are accounted-for."

"All right, what about the Wardens?"

"Only two humans, neither of them in power. One is an older man looking to retire. He suffered from the accelerated aging process. The other hasn't been seen or heard from since the Dispersal, presumed dead."

Walter groaned. "God help us, what about a Dominion?"

Micaiah shook his head. "No human has attained Dominion ranking since Roman times."

"So what you're saying is, we could be looking at a grudge match that goes back to the Dispersal of '63?"

"Potentially, yes."

"Is it possible to get a list of everyone involved in that civil war?"

Micaiah raised a brow and looked uncertain. "The Hands don't like people digging into their stuff. They want Lily alive to buy their seats, but they want to hold onto their secrets even more. Micah and I can ask, but we may be treading into dangerous waters. And, quite frankly, Walter, I'm not going to risk my life for a corrupt system. Lily is the big buyer of seats today. Tomorrow, who knows?"

Walter sighed but nodded sympathetically. "I understand where you're coming from, and I would be lying if I said I didn't share your sentiment, at least in part. But we have a job to do. All I want is a list of names, focusing on those who are human. At this point, I'm not too concerned about who was on whose side in the war."

Micaiah dipped his head. "We'll see what we can do." He glanced at the clock. "Tommen ought to be here in about ten minutes. Do we want to bring him in on it?"

"No. The higher above his head this is, I hope the safer he'll be. Go now to the Wheel. Get me those names. I'm going to do a little investigating of my own."

The elder Durvin twin nodded and poked his head out the door to call his brother.

Opening a portal to the Wheel was not a terribly difficult thing to do, but it was very disorienting given the nature of the place. But the strangest part was that no matter how much time was spent in the Wheel, upon returning, it was like no time had passed at all, as long as the same portal stayed open. The twins could have spent ten minutes, ten hours, or ten days in the Wheel, and yet to Walter, it was like simply watching them walk in front of him. He had the spots in front of his eyes where he'd seen the portal open and close, but ultimately, nothing appeared to have happened.

They didn't look like they'd been beaten and imprisoned for any length of time, but they had the uptight look of having to fend off a pack of hungry dogs.

"Trouble?" Walter asked severely.

"Hands don't like talk about the Dispersal," Micaiah said, handing over a stack of papers. It had a list of names, ranks, posts, and last known locations. "They didn't like us asking questions about it."

"What did you do?"

"We had to tell them that some of those who had gotten away might be planning something similar in their upcoming elections, starting with the murder of their biggest seat buyer," Micah told him. "Not exactly a lie, at least I hope not."

Walter let out a breath. "Believe me, Micah, I wish it was a lie."

He left the bakery before Tommen got off the bus, and headed home. He'd only glanced briefly at the list, and now it sat in the passenger seat, begging him to pick it up. He refrained until he had finally pulled in the garage.

Notes from Micaiah said that there were over five hundred thousand involved, Hands, Timekeepers, Harvesters, Merchants, everyone from the Time industry, plus another five thousand if Runners were included, though those names were harder to come by. The list was narrowed down to all humans of all ranks in all disciplines. That brought the total to exactly six hundred seventy-three, and most of them were Timekeepers, most often bribed or contracted to protect one Hand or another, regardless of their sworn job. But humans played a very small role in the Time industry.

He went in the house and made a pot of coffee and an egg salad sandwich before sitting down at the computer. He might not be able to track down every single name and might have to use his work computer for some of it, but he could probably narrow down the list quite a bit anyway.

He started with the human Timekeepers, figuring to start at Warden and work his way down. But as he looked through the list, he found that one human was listed as Dominion. A quick Google search brought up a number of articles on the man called Daniele Ivolo, an Italian professor straight from Rome. According to his bio, he was gifted in languages, history, culture, and antiquities. According to his obituary, he'd been murdered in '67 when he tried to apprehend some thieves after they'd stolen some priceless items from a museum. He was listed as being only forty-two years old at the time; Walter had his doubts. He'd been married twice and had three children between them. In his will, his estate reportedly bypassed both ex-wives to be split equally amongst the children. His debts, however, had gone on to be split just as equally by both ex-wives. A sort of poetic justice.

Walter crossed Daniele's name off the list.

Of the Wardens, Walter found little to make him suspect either of them. Igor Baryana was the Russian Timekeeper who'd been the unfortunate victim of an accelerated aging process. He was a kindly clockmaker in St. Petersburg who, as near as Walter could tell, hadn't been engaged in much Timekeeping since the Dispersal. His counterpart, Rifun Ndolo, showed up only in a little blurb in a Madagascar newspaper in 1970, first that he'd disappeared, and then that a body was found in a river, presumed to be his but the state of decay made it impossible to say for sure.

Two more names, off the list.

The Gatekeepers showed a little more promise as they seemed to be the bulk of the "rebels" as the Hands had called them, depending on which Hands were asked. Unfortunately, none of them turned up anything more than any of the others. Some were dead in tragic accidents. A few were upstanding citizens of their respective countries or cities. Still some were as average as Micah and Micaiah.

Problem was, the only one in North America was of Arab descent. But still...

Walter leaned back in his chair as he listened to the phone ring and ring and ring and...

"Hello?" an accented voice inquired.

"Captain Walter Forbes, Quadrant One, Parsec Eleven, Sector Five, System Four, Planet Thirty-Eight, Region Four, District Four," Walter began formally.

The man hesitated for just a second. "Gatekeeper Assim Foyez, Region Four, District One." That put him in Alaska or Western Canada. "How can I help you, Captain?"

"I'm from Charleston, West Virginia, and I'm investigating a murder."

"I have never been to West Virginia."

He was way too jumpy. Walter went on, hoping to come off as genial. "My leads have taken me on a wild ride, but I think you might be the key to the name of the man I am looking for."

"I do not know how that can be, but I will help however I can."

"I need to ask you about the Dispersal of '63."

The man caught his breath. "I am sorry, Captain Forbes, I don't know anything about that."

"If I give you a description of a man, can you give me a name?"

"I am sorry, sir, but I am very busy. I have to go." Click.

Walter sighed and resisted the urge to throw the phone across the room. It was like walking into Vietnam and asking directions to the local church. If he didn't tread carefully, he'd be singing in the choir for the big church in the sky.

He glanced at the clock and figured getting to the bakery a little early wouldn't be a bad thing, especially since the roads were starting to get a little slick.

As he drove, he pondered. Most of the Gatekeepers, Wardens, and the Dominion who had been involved in the Dispersal had been killed within ten years of the Dispersal, with some exceptions here and there. Would Assim really be afraid of that over forty years later? What was his part in the Dispersal? Why was he so reluctant to give up a name? More to the point, what had he been doing recently that might prompt such odd behavior?

He parked in the lot and saw Tommen look up from where he was sweeping. He waved and Walter waved back, though he wasn't sure Tommen could see. He really did appear to be doing better. He'd been staying out of fights, doing well in his driver's ed class, and wouldn't shut up about all the things he could do with his AP and college classes. Walter was proud of him. The boy seemed to finally have some direction, some drive in his life.

Walter saw the Band a split-second before Micaiah helped himself to the passenger seat.

"Find anything?" he asked.

"The only human Dominion was murdered in '67," Walter replied. "Same story for most Wardens and Gatekeepers. Those who are still alive are living very low profile. Of the ones who could feasibly be in the area...none are."

"Damn."

"Instead, I tried calling the only remaining Gatekeeper from that time period who is, in fact, in North America. Name is Assim Foyez, District One. He got real on edge when I mentioned the Dispersal. When I asked if I could describe the suspect and he give me a name, he hung up."

"You think he could be our guy?"

"Our murderer? Not likely, not unless he can cop a pretty convincing Middle Eastern accent."

"You never know. With as much time as we have in our lives, there's no excuse why we couldn't learn any number of things."

Walter nodded. "I'll keep digging. You two take time to cool off; we don't need the Hands sniffing around us when there's a bigger threat around."

Micaiah scoffed. "The only threat the Hands perceive is a threat to their power, and they treat it all equally."

"How's Tommen doing?"

"You'll have to ask him, but I thought he had a good shift. We had a surprise order for a giant cookie, which he handled well. He took an order over the phone for a retirement party cake. He's a good worker, Walt, when he's here. You should be proud of him."

And Walter was proud of Tommen, even if he wished the boy would talk about something other than his science classes. They returned home and made a quick chicken dinner before settling down to watch a little TV. Then Walter finally badgered Tommen into doing his homework, after which he went straight to bed.

Walter checked on him a little later when he finally decided sleep was an important aspect of life. Tommen's room was arguably the coldest in the house during the winter, but only one blanket was still on him; the rest had been kicked and pushed and pulled to the floor. Oh well, he'd pick them up tomorrow. His backpack was packed but not zipped shut, sitting at the end of the bed, a couple pencils spilled out beside it.

Once, Tommen had wanted a puppy. He'd promised to take good care of it and keep it in his room. Sometimes Walter wondered if he shouldn't have allowed him to get that puppy. Maybe it would bring companionship to Tommen when Walter worked long hours and didn't get home until late. Maybe it would bring comfort to Walter on nights when he knew a killer was walking free somewhere in the city.

Chapter Nine
Thanksgiving

O nce upon a time, in a land not too far away geographically but quite distantly removed from present day, Tommen had lived on a tiny farm. His parents had built that farm from the ground up when they emigrated from Wales. His pa had gone to work cutting down trees, sawing logs, and building not just a cabin but a barn as well. His ma had tended the animals, which included everything from chickens, goats, and a cow, to three year old Teo who always swore he could vaguely remember the old home in Wales and the journey over.

The little plot of land the Forbes family called their own was enough to support and shelter them. They lived miles from any neighbor and yet visited and were visited often to exchange news and pleasantries, make marriage matches for the children, and generally socialize.

Those who lived in the mountains lived and died by the fruits of their labor, and they knew it. They knew that every winter, there would always be death from sickness. They knew that every spring, there was a chance that snowmelt could flood rivers, ponds, and wash away houses if they weren't carefully built. They knew that every summer, there was a chance that drought could kill their crops and leave them with nothing. They knew that every fall, there was a chance that game would be too scrawny and small to provide enough meat to last them the winter.

Perhaps living that close to death was what fed the drive to celebrate life in all sorts of ways. There were the celebrations and the gifts for a newborn child, every woman pitching in her sewing and knitting to be sure the babe could survive the winter, or at least have a chance. There were the solemn celebrations of a funeral as the entire valley gathered to remember, mourn, and reflect on the life of a loved one.

And then there was Thanksgiving. It wasn't called Thanksgiving, not to them, but merely a harvest festival. It was a celebration that spanned most of autumn as neighbors traveled to and fro to help each other get in the crops before the birds and beasts got to them or they went to rot. Tommen could tentatively recall following dutifully behind his pa and Teo as they trekked up and down the mountain and valley, taking shovels, hoes, hitching up horses, riding in wagons, and making mischief when the adults weren't looking.

Thanksgiving was where Tommen had actually first kissed a girl, though it was more of an accident. He didn't remember her name and the only thing he could recall about her was that her lips had been as pink as her cheeks from cold and she wore a little yellow dress, faded and resewn a number of times. He couldn't say why he'd kissed her exactly, only that it had to do with showing his pa something or answering his pa's question in a cheeky way. His pa had wanted to switch him for disrespecting a girl, but his ma intervened, citing the festivities and simply the innocence of children.

That was also where Tommen had first learned about sex, although he didn't know it at the time. His pa had sent him to look for Teo to help hitch some horses. Tommen had found Teo with the neighbor's daughter—both of them about fifteen at the time—in a very compromising position. But to his young mind, all he saw was Teo and the neighbor's daughter doing exactly what the goats did during the fall. The thought that what the goats did in the fall was what brought the kids in the spring hadn't quite made made it through his mind, and he'd been completely unphased to stand there where Teo was still inside the girl, both of them very embarrassed. He didn't know what exactly he thought they were doing, but he still told Teo that their pa was looking for him and needed him right away. Teo, in a very strained voice, told him to tell their pa that he was on his way in a few minutes.

Tommen had pretended to run back to their pa and tell him Teo was coming, but actually he'd just circled back and found a bush to hide in. He didn't have some kind of sick animal tendency, but he was honestly, innocently curious if people did it the same way goats did it. It took a little longer, and Teo and the girl made more noise, but yes, it was generally the same.

Later, when Teo asked Tommen if he'd told their pa about what he'd found, Tommen said no, because his pa knew what the goats did and he didn't care.

Oh, the days of innocent youth.

But for all the neighborly comradery and the harvesting and the festivities and celebrations, the one thing that had always acutely stuck with Tommen beyond the shadow of a doubt, was the hunger. The people of the valley were not rich in anything that really mattered. Love was good, but it didn't put a rabbit in a snare or make the corn grow. The harvest festivals of the valley were instead loving labor. They did gather for one day to share a great meal with all the folk of the valley and all contributed something, but it wasn't a grand feast like many historians might have painted.

Tommen remembered the neighborly Thanksgiving dinner being one of the few days out of the year when he actually got to eat until he was full, where no one took his plate away and said he'd already eaten his share. It was the one day out of the year when he could have homemade sweetmeats. One year, he could recall someone had gone to the dingy little town that was Charleston and brought real sugar candy back for all the children. That was probably the year Tommen was convinced that there was probably a place called heaven and it was filled with candy. It made him sicker than he'd ever been in his entire life up until then, but it had been more than worth it.

When Tommen had emerged from the cave into modern day, he'd been hit by a car on the road and taken to the hospital. Later on, one of the nurses asked what he wanted to eat. They couldn't bring him goat liver, like he wanted, but they brought him some chicken nuggets and macaroni and cheese.

The sight of all that food on one plate all for him made him cry even if he tried to hide it, and he refused to eat it because he couldn't, not with his brother and ma and pa still hungry. The nurses assured him that when they found his family, they would all get just as much food. There was plenty to go around, and he should eat to get big and strong. So he did. It tasted odd and foreign to him, his natural tongue unaccustomed to the fake foods. He ended up getting sick on it, and most foods for about the first, oh, couple years, until his system readjusted to the fillers and preservatives. At that time, everything was a new sensation, a new experience. Walter had been the first to bring him ice cream, a little chocolate sundae, and Tommen had been pretty convinced that he'd died and gone to heaven.

When Tommen had first gone home with Walter and discovered the fridge and freezer, a cellar inside the house just stuffed with food—well, that might be an overstatement—he had again broken down in tears. There was no way that such bounty was possible. He hadn't seen any gardens or planted fields, though one of the neighbors had a buck goat that could be smelled a half mile down the road. And when he'd been introduced to the grocery store, Tommen had literally had a seizure. He'd spent two years taking anti-anxiety medication until he could finally cope with everything that had transpired that only he and Walter could appreciate.

But despite his apparent reliance on pizza, spaghetti, and ham on rye, and working at a bakery, Tommen never got over how much food was readily available in the modern day. It boiled his blood when he saw people wasting food, throwing it away like it was diseased or contaminated. He wished he could take them back in time and show them the hunger of their forefathers who had to hunt and trap and grow their food, and pray it was enough to make it through another year, all the while being extremely conscious of not just themselves to feed, but a wife and children, some of whom were completely helpless and at the mercy of their actions or inactions.

So it came as no surprise that as soon as he was old enough to be trusted with the oven, Tommen was the one in charge of the Thanksgiving turkey. Time and again, he tried to remember how his mother used to prepare fowl, but could never bring it to mind. He'd always been out with his pa and Teo, doing men things, while his ma and sisters had been doing women things. His pa had taught them how to snare, skin, and dress a rabbit for survival, but his mother had been the cooking and spices guru, able to revive even the oldest pot of stew and make it palatable.

Still, Tommen didn't think his birds came out half bad, and his audience often told him so. He figured it had better turn out halfway decent at least. Because the Forbes house was too small to host Thanksgiving, Tommen and Walter headed over to the twins' house a little farther out in the country. This meant that Tommen had to spend pretty much the entire evening prior preparing the turkey and the stuffing and letting it slow-cook overnight so that it would be ready by morning, and they could just go over and start eating.

Tommen figured that if he wasn't such a science buff, he might have become a professional chef. Or, maybe he could do both and become a food scientist. He wasn't sure how, though, since most modern food science clashed with his more deeply rooted beliefs that food shouldn't be messed with. He figured that if someone wanted bigger cows, they ought to learn to breed bigger cows. Of course, mentioning this out loud would mean agreeing with Eric in a sense, and he wasn't ready to concede that fight yet, even if it had lost its fun in recent weeks.

He pondered this as he drove to the twins' house, Walter in the passenger seat holding the pan with the turkey, the smell permeating every fiber in the car and making them both salivate.

"So how's your friend Eric doing lately?" Walter wondered, as if reading his mind.

Tommen shrugged. "Better. He's been okay since the paternity test said the kid wasn't his, but his reputation at school is ruined. Michelle made sure of that. Next semester he's switching to all online classes."

Walter shook his head. "That's too bad. He still going to college?"

"Yes. It just might be a few states farther away than expected."

"Well, it'll be good for him anyway. Go to a place where he isn't known and start a new life for himself. Maybe in a few years, it will all blow over."

Tommen had his doubts, but he didn't say anything. He didn't tell Walter about the "Go kill yourself" notes that regularly showed up on Eric's locker, or the "Rapist" that had been spray painted on his car. Even when it finally came out that the father was a graduate from last year, Eric still endured intense bullying and scrutiny. It was the only reason that Tommen had managed to stay out of fights lately, because Eric was the bigger target. He really wouldn't have been surprised if they all got back from Thanksgiving break to find that Eric had transferred to another school or something.

In a way, it made Tommen think about transferring, too. It was nice to not be bullied (as much) and to not be constantly getting into fights. He didn't disillusion himself by thinking that there was any school out there where he wouldn't be bullied, but getting Tyler off his back would be a step in the right direction. And if Eric and Varad were both leaving, which was looking more likely every day, there was no reason for Tommen to stay.

He pulled into the driveway at the twins' house and turned off the car. He hated the Cadillac. He was definitely saving for his own car.

The twins lived in a neighborhood that was like a new construction suburb from the nineties that had been left to rot for a decade, then tried to be revived by some well-meaning, overly-enthusiastic, somewhat-unrealistic community organizers. Their house was originally brick, but covered over with vinyl. It was well-kept, and yet just kind of sad. There was no good way to describe the general feel of the place other than sad, like a fine piece of art in a museum that puts the viewer in mind of a somber walk through a cemetery on a cloudy day, not really looking for any particular grave, but simply reflecting on mortality and all those who had gone before.

Inside the house, though, was another story, as the twins' wealth made itself known. Granite countertops, stone tile, hardwood floors, anything that one might expect to find on the showroom floor at some homebuilders' expo could be found in their house. Supposedly, that's exactly what it had once been, when the neighborhood was slated for total rich-snob renovation. But the plans fell through, and the showroom houses sold for dirt cheap.

"Hey, you arrived just in time," Micaiah said as he pulled a casserole out of the over. "Breakfast is served."

"Good, because I have to be punched in by lunch," Walter said, slipping his boots off and taking the turkey over to the table.

"I saw you driving out there, Tommen," Micah told him, arranging a dish of cranberry sauce and trying to fit it next to a plate of rolls. "Good job, not crashing into our garage."

"That would have been the car, not me," Tommen informed him.

"Driving isn't just about you behind the wheel," Micaiah told him philosophically. "It's about understanding the car you're driving, all its little quirks and nuances. It's not just the Cadillac either; that's true for all vehicles."

"Well, I can tell you that I won't be driving that thing. I'm saving up and buying my own car."

"He thinks he is," Walter corrected as he headed down to the bathroom.

"I am," Tommen said confidently. "I have it all saved up for my next driver's ed segment, my testing, and I've got quite a bit saved for my own car."

"Good for you," Micah said sincerely. "But remember that the car is only one part of the equation. You also have to figure on insurance, which is more expensive the newer you get. And you have to figure plates and plate renewal, license renewal. It's all part of the package, and the government doesn't care about your excuses. They'll repo your stuff just as fast as you can say, 'rip-off.' "

"I'm, like, a year away from actually getting the car. I think in that time I can come up with that kind of cash."

Micaiah chuckled. "No one cares about cash anymore, Tommen. But you have the right idea. Don't buy what you can't afford. Some bills you will always be paying, like insurance. But insurance can be changed. You get a car with a payment on it, but if you total the car, you're still paying for that car. Best advice, get a car you know you could pay off today, and space it out. It'll help you out later when you go in for bigger purchases like an apartment or a house or even college."

Tommen let out a breath and shifted his stance. "Here I thought I came over to eat until I got sick, not get an economics lesson."

Micah grinned as he fished in a drawer for assorted spoons, forks, and ladles to put in the various dishes. "Some things you'll only learn with time. But if you want, grab some pot holders and bring these baked beans over to the table."

Tommen found some pot holders and carefully carried the enormous batch of baked beans from the oven to the table. They weren't baked beans out of a can either, but real homemade baked beans made by Micah himself. The beans had been soaked for two days before being marinated in molasses for another day, then poured into a pot with brown sugar and a variety of spices that Micah just liked to call "his secret formula." Like Tommen's turkey, they had to be slow cooked all night in order to come out to utter perfection. It made for a wonderful concoction, and it even held over well to be reheated.

"All right, I hope you haven't all started without me because it smells pretty dang good, even all the way down there," Walter said, coming back down the hallway. "So, take a set and let's bless the food."

They all settled around the table.

"Lord, we thank you for this bountiful food before us..." Walter began.

Tommen bowed his head obediently, but he hadn't really cared to participate for some years now. He couldn't understand how Walter and the twins could keep any sense of religion, even after all they had been through and all they knew and all they could do.

"We thank you for the gift of friends and the joy we derive from each other..."

The first year that Tommen hadn't participated and refused to go along with the prayer over the meal, Walter had scolded him and told him that even if he didn't believe anymore, he could either be respectful of a tradition or at the very least, respectful of those who still held such a tradition.

"We ask that you keep us safe as we go our separate ways and bring us all home safely..."

But Tommen knew that Walter was still loosely religious. He didn't blame him, really. In a profession where any day could be his last, Tommen would take help wherever he could get it, too. But still...God?

"Just because you can fly doesn't mean you stop believing in gravity," Walter had once told him.

And that was great, as far as physics was concerned. If Timekeeping was limited to just the human race, he might have even bought into that argument. But there was the Wheel. Wasn't that like a kind of Tower of Babel, creating an artificial dimension outside of Time? And that wasn't even going into all the alien races. Was God the god of all of them, or only humans? Where was the line drawn? And then there was all the aspects of Time. For Timekeepers, there was the slowed aging process. Wasn't it appointed for all men to die once? For Harvesters, it was the taking of Time. Was that considered stealing or murder? And selling it to the Merchants, didn't God hold every moment in His hands? Or did He get a cut of the profits, too?

"In Thy Name, Amen," Walter finished at last, picking up the knives and slicing into a tender, juicy turkey.

For Tommen, there were simply too many basic questions that couldn't be answered by Walter's simple faith. But, sometimes he envied him for it, that no matter what the day brought either Earth-side or Time-side, Walter still had his little faith. Other times, like Thanksgiving, it was almost nauseating.

But to that end, Tommen almost felt guilty. He remembered sitting at his ma's foot while she knitted. Teo sat next to their pa, shaving a block of wood in slow, methodical motions. And their pa would read to them out of an old family Bible. He would read the tales everyone knew—David and Goliath, Daniel and the Lion's Den. He would read the Levitical commands and then the Messianic commandments. He would read about the daring deeds of the Apostles and their heroic martyrdom.

Tommen's pa was not a particularly lettered man. He read as much from memory as the actual words on the page. Still, he knew the sounds of each letter and could sound out what he didn't know. Teo could read better, but the Bible reading was always their pa. He had a deep, firm voice that always put Tommen to sleep, and he would wake up all upset that he didn't get to hear the end of the story, even if his ma assured him he had heard it.

On Sundays, after the necessary chores were done and they took their commanded day of rest, the whole family would gather together again. Tommen's pa would pick one of the Ten Commandments or one of Jesus' parables, and he would ask each of the children—who were old enough to have half a mind what it was about—what that commandment or parable meant to them and how they could apply it in their lives. He wasn't a man of the cloth, had only ever been in a true church half a dozen times in his life, but Tommen was still sure that he was better than any pastor who'd spent ten years locked away in seminary school.

Tommen had never been to a church before meeting Walter, and the idea of going to God's House had terrified him. They didn't go often, and Tommen figured they had done it to try and give him some kind of rooted familiarity, that despite all the changes he was experiencing, some things hadn't changed. It had been nice and somewhat comforting, true, but he'd always had a hard time finding God amid all the bright lights, distracting movies, and loud music. And while the child wranglers had meant well, he always felt lost in the mix of children.

He couldn't really point to a time and say that was when he'd probably lost his religion, but it must have been around twelve or thirteen years old. Maybe it was just him hitting puberty and starting his rebellious teenage years. Maybe he was corrupted by evil science classes. Maybe he really just didn't care.

And he couldn't really say, either, why it bothered him so much that Walter prayed at Thanksgiving and Christmas. After all, it was only two meals a year, and normally he couldn't care less about his religious classmates who prayed over their lunches everyday.

But they were important meals, traditional meals that signified family, generosity, community, plenty, all the good things in life. Maybe it was just that Tommen didn't feel like he had those things in his life and he resented those who did. He was sure there was some sort of psychological explanation behind it, but the only thing worse than thinking he was crazy was having someone else not only confirm it, but charge him for that confirmation, then offer to help manage or treat his craziness—and charge him for that, too.

He tried not to scowl as the dishes were passed around. He felt like he could have eaten everything laid out before him, but knew he felt like that every year, and every year, without fail, he could not, in fact, eat everything laid out before him. Whatever poverty a person went through, their stomach is still only so big. However morbidly obese a person was, their stomach was still only so big.

So Tommen refrained from slopping huge portions of food onto his place, instead trying to follow a "two-bite" rule. Two bites of everything adds up a stomach full of everything. And if not, he could always take more. Even though it was only ever the four of them, they still managed to cook enough for ten people, and they would be eating the leftovers for the next week or so.

Except the cranberry sauce, or so it first appeared. Micaiah had just set the dish down and was reaching for another when his elbow bumped the little wiggly dish. Tommen was almost sure it was going to splat on the floor and stain it and make it look like the twins were secretly crazy ax murderers, but then his vision lit up as Micaiah dove into a Fast Band and managed to save every last drop of the sauce, arranging the dishes so it could be placed in a location safer than the edge of the table.

"Good catch," Walter said around a bite of mashed potatoes.

"Damn it," Micah grumbled. "I was hoping to finally get new floors around here."

"Why can't you get new floors?" Tommen wondered.

"Because I won't let him," Micaiah said. "Not until we move."

"You're moving?"

"No, not any time soon. But I'm not paying for new floors now, wearing it out in five years, and then having to buy new flooring again when we do decide to move."

"Why not do hardwood floors?" Walter inquired. "It looks nice now."

"In this neighborhood? The return on investment wouldn't be as great. We bought this house for dirt cheap and that's probably how we're going to sell it."

Because the twins were really strapped for cash, Tommen thought sarcastically. Between what they made from the bakery and their salaries for being Lieutenant Timekeepers, he knew that they had a good stash of cash hidden somewhere. And whether or not they exchanged their Timekeeping salaries for Earth-side money, it could buy a lot of exotic knick-knacks and doodads and, probably, carpets and wall-hangings of some form. They could easily redecorate their house. Tommen had tried to convince Walter to do the same with their house, even just a little bit, but Walter refused. He didn't have the energy to pull off a redecorating job. Strictly speaking, he did have the time, but there were only so many hours he could add into a day before it became overwhelming.

"So, speaking of returns on investments," Micah was saying, "are you ready for your review, Tommen? Have the Hands officially set a date?"

"Earth-side, it would be January 2nd," Walter replied.

"Hey, at least it's while you're on Christmas vacation, right?" Micaiah said. "So, do you think you're ready for it?"

Tommen knew where this was going. They wanted to quiz him and test his knowledge. The review was done live in front of the Hands. As soon as he walked into the Coliseum, his review was begun, and his entire Timekeeping career was on the line. Walter would not be with him; he would be made to wait outside.

The review was done in three parts. The first part of the review was a basic knowledge and history test. It was all oral. He would have no foreknowledge of the exact questions they would ask—not even Walter would know—but he had a basic idea of what it would be about. He would have to know the history of Time as it related to the human race. He would have to know important events, important figures. It was about like any average history test. Names, dates, places, things that really didn't matter in everyday life but were good to know. He would have to be able to list all functions of Time. He would have to list all the various Time Agents and all the associated ranks, listing Timekeepers from Probationary to Dominion, Harvesters from Probationary to Triage, and so it went. He would have to understand the role of the Hands and the basic premise of their election cycle, of which voting day would take place the week after his test.

The second part was a test of skill, and it was as much about demonstrating his skills as explaining that he understood how they worked. He would have to demonstrate the extremes of his abilities as a Fast Band and a Slow Band. He would have to be able to create a Band with parameters specified by the Hands. If a Hand told him to create a ten-minute:one-hour Band, he would have to do just that. Likely he would also have to hold it as long as he could, until a migraine threatened to tear his brain apart. And the whole time, he would have to explain the properties of a Band, the parameters and perimeter, how to identify a Band, how to find the strength of a Band and how to find its wake. The whole time, he would be monitored by a Dominion Timekeeper who would intervene and pull Tommen out of a Band if he became trapped.

The third part of the test was a psychological evaluation, and it wasn't as fun and cheery as Earth-side doctor-patient cry-session therapy. It in itself was done in two parts. The first was a simple question-and-answer, and the second was like a simulation to put ethics to the test. According to Walter, it was different for everyone, but the ethics test was always made to be reflexive. If he had the ethics that supported the Timekeeper's Oath and defended the Laws of Time, everything he did would simply be a natural reaction. If he lacked such ethics, essentially, he would do nothing. Supposedly, it took more effort to do nothing than something.

The whole review lasted about twelve hours and ran continuously. With exception of the psychological test, if he got hungry or thirsty, food and drink would be brought for him, and he would just have to eat while doing his review. Bathroom breaks were non-existent, according to the twins, and it was advised that he make every effort to go beforehand. Also according to the twins, some parts of the psychological test were so realistic and scary that he'd probably wet himself anyway. Tommen wasn't sure if they were just trying to scare him or if it could be true. In the Wheel, anything was possible.

"I guess I'm as ready as I'll ever be," Tommen said, shrugging and taking another bite of food. "The only thing I'm really not sure about is the electing of Hands and appointing of Timekeepers."

"Okay," Micaiah said. "What don't you understand?"

"Why are there six Lieutenant-level Timekeepers in District Four, but you two are the only officer Lieutenants?"

Micaiah wiped his mouth. "Okay, fair question. When a Timekeeper gets to be a Journeyman, he gains the power to arrest Runners. When he becomes a Master, he can take on an Apprentice to train. However, that's not where Timekeeper abilities necessarily end.

If that Timekeeper wants to learn more abilities, he has to train under someone at least two ranks above him. So if I wanted to learn Captain abilities, I couldn't go to Walter. I would have to find a Manager or above. If you wanted to become a Lieutenant, you'd have to go to a Captain or higher. Then you would be in the running for an appointment."

"But why?" Tommen wondered. "What makes his abilities so special?"

"Those are the rules. The Powers That Be reviewed all abilities available to Timekeepers and determined that after a certain point, if you want to go through higher education, you are going to have to prepare yourself for greater responsibility within the Time industry. If something ever happened to one of us, the Hands—or, more likely, the Gatekeeper of Earth, or the Regional Manager—would review the available candidates and appoint them to take our place. It's possible to appeal the appointment, but generally, you don't have a choice in the matter. There are ranks and hierarchy and the positions must always be filled."

Tommen nodded. "So if something happened where Walter couldn't be the Captain anymore, would one of you be appointed?"

Micah shook his head. "No. We are only Lieutenants. We would have to train under a Manager to get to Captain level in order to be appointed."

"So if you did train and become Captains, would you still remain as the District's Lieutenants?"

"That would be at the discretion of the Manager, depending on how many available replacements there are," Micaiah explained. "Because our District has six Lieutenants, chances are we would not remain in our positions. Essentially we'd be on vacation, but if something happened to Walter, we would again be called to a higher position of responsibility, no chickening out. Basically, if you don't want the position, don't train for the abilities."

"So why not train everyone up to the same abilities? Why the exclusivity?"

"Because there is no need for even the average Master to have such abilities," Walter told him. "Even I rarely use them. But that is largely because Earth is not heavily involved in the Time industry. There are some worlds out there where the Time industry is as normal as the pharmaceutical industry or the food industry. Going to work as a Timekeeper is no more unusual than going to work as a line cook. But because it's so common, that means Runners are also very common and those Timekeepers need the expanded range of abilities."

Tommen shook his head. "Weird."

"Does that help explain it?" Micah wondered.

"I guess."

"Is there anything else you're having trouble with?"

Tommen chewed his lip. "Kind of, but I don't know how much of it you're going to talk about."

Walter raised a brow but motioned for him to continue.

"If the election of the Hands is so corrupt, how does the Time industry move as smoothly as it does?"

Walter and the twins glanced at each other. It was Walter who answered. "That goes back to Earth being a very minor player in the Time industry. In those other worlds where Time is common, it can get as brutal as Earth-side political riots. Think like South America."

"But why?"

"Do you understand the basic premise of the Hands elections?"

"Kind of."

Micaiah took over. "A Time Agent can be a Hand, but a Hand cannot be a Time Agent. Every seventeen years during the elections, all of the Hands are on the chopping block."

"Right, I understand that," Tommen said.

"Except each Hand nominates a replacement. It isn't a guarantee, but there's an unusually high percentage of nominated-to-elected positions. Using Timekeepers as an example, Wardens and Dominions may be nominated, or they may also send in an upset nomination, like a write-in candidate. Do you understand the difference in positions?"

"A representative in the U.S. government represents where he's from," Tommen recited. "A Hand represents a type of culture across the entire industry."

"Precisely. So if, say, Walter became a Hand, he wouldn't be the representative of Earth. He would be the representative of 'Scientifically Advancing and Unengaged Civilizations.' Or he could be appointed to some other representation, but the Hands are at least smart enough to try and match their nominations with the experience level of the nominee."

"Who is allowed to vote in the elections?"

"Posted officers only. The three of us could vote, but Terry, who is only a Lieutenant-trained Master out of Massachusetts, would not be able to vote. Supposedly, this is to keep any one planet from training up their Timekeepers and skewing the votes. As if the buying of seats wasn't obvious enough. Or the rigged tallying of the votes."

"How do you buy a seat?" Tommen wondered.

Micah grinned. "Why, you want one?"

Walter answered a little more seriously. "You know Lily buys seats. She can do this either by bribing a Hand to pick, excuse me, nominate a certain replacement, or by bribing enough voters to nominate and vote for an upset candidate."

"But what does it get her?"

"The influence of a Hand can drive up Time Capsule prices exponentially," Micaiah replied. "Or she can bribe certain Hands to influence certain Timekeepers to let her bend the rules a little more than would normally be allowed."

"She's bribed you?"

"No, but we only have the ability to arrest and turn in. Gatekeepers, Wardens and Dominions are the official 'prosecutors' who take criminals before the Grandfathers. If a Warden won't prosecute, we can't push. Kind of like Walter. He can arrest criminals all day long, but if the prosecutor, judge, and jury are corrupt and will just automatically let them go, his job is basically meaningless."

"Oh." Tommen knew he should have already known and remembered all this. He should have been the one schooling them on the elections and the Hands. Sometimes he thought that maybe he was overthinking it, demanding more complex answers than necessary, and the actual review would be much easier. "But what's her motivation?"

"What motivates most people?" Walter asked rhetorically. "Money. Greed. The lavish lifestyle of the rich and famous."

"Oh. Does she vote?"

"The other Time Agents are set up a little differently than Timekeepers," Micah replied. "They have their ranks like we do, but among Harvesters, only Intervention and Triage Harvesters are considered officers."

"How do the ranks get such funny names?"

"It's all about translation," Walter said. "It's the same way most of the titles are so punny in English. We deal with Time where we have the Wheel of Time, the Hands of Time, the Grandfathers like the clock. English joined the game late. Some of them I'm sure were intentional puns coined by the first English-speaking Timekeepers. Others are just the culminated translation from a thousand other languages."

"It's been a while since you've been to the Wheel," Micaiah said. "I'm sure that once you're there again, a lot of this will come back to you and make a little more sense."

Tommen nodded. He'd visited the Wheel only once, when he was ten years old. It was actually Walter who'd been called before the Hands as word of his training Tommen early had reached their ears. Tommen didn't remember a lot about the hearing, only that Walter had remained perfectly stubborn about the whole thing. In the end, the Hands had relented, saying that when his Apprentice review came up, there was no excuse for him not to pass with flying colors.

Now that his review was actually coming up and had a real,

tangible date attached to it, Tommen felt less prepared than ever. He should know all this already. He should be the ones to answer their questions and correct their mistakes, like he often did when one of them made an incorrect assumption about something he was learning in school but they'd understandably forgotten.

Micaiah sighed and looked forlornly at his empty plate. "Well, I expect we should get this cleaned up and get some leftovers packed for you before you have to go, Walter."

It was a rather displeasing task, but necessary. Tommen gathered the plates and empty dishes while Micah started the sink for water and Micaiah went to rummage for tupperware to put the leftovers in while Walter brought the dishes to the counter. They had a system going.

Walter's phone rang then. When he checked the number, Tommen saw his face go pale. Still, he managed a cool excuse and stepped out to the garage to answer it.

"So, are you ready for a new semester?" Micaiah asked amiably as he dished out leftovers into various containers.

"Yeah," Tommen said, as if he didn't say that every day at work already. "I'll be so happy to get into AP Physics finally."

"Hoping it will help you fine-tune your Banding?" Micah wondered, jabbing him in the ribs.

"Hey, if it did, that would be cool. If I knew not only how to Band, but the science and math behind it, think of how much more I could accomplish."

"And what do you hope to accomplish?" Micaiah asked. "Do you see Banding as a compliment to your AP Physics, or AP Physics as a compliment to your Banding?"

Tommen paused and thought a moment. Actually, he wasn't really sure. He couldn't have both in equal parts? Finally he said, "I don't know. I guess I'll have to see how my Apprenticeship goes to figure that out."

"Good answer," Micah said, grinning as he rinsed off a plate and set it aside to dry.

Walter walked back in then, but it wasn't a friendly walk. It was something just short of a very pissed cop kicking in the door, gun first. He sat down heavily on the little bench seat and fumbled to get his boots on. "Guys, I need you to take Tommen home."

"What's wrong?" Micaiah demanded.

"We've got another body. Washed up on the riverbank, same markings as the girl from the soccer fields."

"Shit." Micaiah shook his head. "Yeah, we'll take Tommen home. You need us for anything?"

"I don't know yet, but stay alert and bring out everything you had from the last case. We may need it. Tommen?" Tommen looked at him. "Sit tight, and stay safe."

Chapter Ten
Face-Down

Walter left the twins' house and drove straight to the scene, trying to decide if it was deliberate that the body had washed up only a couple miles from his house. Steggmann hadn't been too specific on the condition of the body, but if they were able to still tell the fine cut marks on her face, Walter guessed it couldn't have been in the water for very long.

Steggmann also hadn't said if they had an ID of the woman, only that he should come as quickly as possible. This wouldn't have bothered Walter too much except for how cryptically he'd said it. For a moment, he was afraid that whoever their killer was, he'd gotten it right this time and finally killed Lily.

For as difficult as she could be, Walter had no desire to see her hurt. Well, rephrase. He had no desire to see her killed or driven to such a point. There were a number of times he would have liked to punch her, have someone else punch her, or randomly get hit by a car when she snootily walked away like she'd just won some incredible victory and was expecting palm branches laid out before her. Yes, sometimes he wanted to see her put in her place. No, he didn't want to see her dead.

He ran through a list of those who might, trying to remember anything from his conversations with her, anything at all. Even if it hadn't been from the first murder, had she ever indicated that she was afraid of anyone? Had she ever mentioned any frustrating rivals, grudge-holding Auctioneers? She would never admit to being afraid, of course, but just a mention that someone was upsetting her auctions might be a clue.

He ran over his many conversations with the twins. Had they found something from the first investigation that they'd dismissed as unimportant that was worth a second look? They had said something about a disgruntled Auctioneer, hadn't they?

Walter ran his tongue over his teeth. Timekeepers had long lives, so Timekeeping grudges could go back a long way, especially if their killer was still upset about the Dispersal of '63. He racked his brain, trying to remember the list of names, if any of them had ever sounded familiar, but none did.

And, God help him, he thought about the time when Micah and Lily had dated. He didn't suspect Micah of doing it—for one, he knew exactly what Lily looked like. But in the beginning stages of puppy love, and even once they'd gotten serious, he couldn't talk about anything or anyone else. And Walter was no idiot; he knew they'd been sleeping together pretty much the entire time. Had Lily ever divulged anything to him during some sappy pillow talk about rivals or enemies?

Of course, there was always the point that Lily had no shortage of enemies. Some of it had to do with her winning personality, but most of it had to do with her great success. She was only a Master-level Harvester, not even an Assistant- or Physician-level, which were almost the same position but only the Physician-level had a chance to become an officer. Assistants basically wanted the training and prestige without the responsibility.

But being a Master-level Harvester and easily making seven or eight figures a week at the auctions was akin to a med school dropout working experimental procedures alongside doctors who had spent twenty-plus years in med school, and being just as good as those doctors at the experimental procedures. It was ludicrous.

It was actually almost more surprising that there hadn't been any attempts on her life before now. Lily had been buying seats for the last four or five election cycles it seemed like. Not everyone was happy, understandably. Not only that, but her many millions and her many high-end Time Capsules bought her nothing if not veritable immunity from prosecution for anything. Unless she murdered a Hand, Walter and the others really couldn't touch her. And even then, it all had to do with the likability of the Hand.

An idea occurred then, and Walter could have kicked himself for not thinking of it earlier. He fished out his cell phone and punched in a number.

"Hello?" a grating, snooty female voice answered.

"Lily, thank God," Walter said, letting out a sigh of relief, something he never imagined doing when Lily was concerned.

"First time anyone's ever said that to me, at least outside of NICU. Is there something you needed, Walter? Shouldn't you be enjoying Thanksgiving with Hairless and the Tweedles?"

Walter ground his teeth, and he could practically feel her smirk of satisfaction. "Just calling to make sure you're all right."

"Oh, has something come up on my mysterious stalker killer who has yet to actually kill me? Is there new evidence or a new body?"

"When are you off work?"

"Four, theoretically. I expect some people are going to play hooky today and call in so-called 'sick' so they can gorge on food they wouldn't normally eat with people they wouldn't normally willingly associate with."

Walter sighed. "I'll probably be by your apartment later today. Just call me if you're not going to be off at four. Can you do that?"

"I expect I could, but only if you do me one little favor."

"I'm trying to save your life, Lily. Isn't that good enough for you?"

"My life is only worth as much as people are willing to pay at the auctions, and I'm losing Potential Time every day."

"Fine. Tell me your favor but know that I am only taking it under consideration and I don't guarantee anything."

She tsked. "Oh, Walter, always so noble. As chivalrous as your son."

"What's your favor?"

"I want to talk to you about a seat in the Hands."

"That's it? You want to talk?"

"No, but I expect it will sweeten the deal and motivate you a little more when you come over to my apartment. The favor we'll discuss then. Until tonight, then, Captain."

She hung up, and Walter tried to collect his scattered nerves. He hated dealing with Lily.

He released his Band as he finally pulled into a roadside park rest area lit up like Fourth of July with red, white, and blue lights and criss-crossed every which way with police tape. The deciduous trees had long since shed their summer coats, and the few leaves that remained were curled, brown, and dead. Now the coniferous trees reigned, branches and needles spread out, interlocking like a canopy, protecting all that roamed beneath it. A squirrel chittered as it ran from branch to branch high above.

Walter got out of the car. The roadside park was big enough for a couple overnight camping spots for people on their way to anywhere else, or truckers looking for something more scenic than the average rest area. The little building just off the pavement contained restrooms with showers, a little tourism room with a number of maps of West Virginia, Charleston, the innumerable trails in the area, and of course the Appalachian trail itself, as well as various places of interest in the area. The brochure display graced the middle of the room like a cherry buried in a sea of whipped cream. Around the other side of the building was another little room filled wall to wall with vending machines of all varieties: junk food, healthy food, gum, water, sports drinks, energy drinks, soda pop, and so on.

And through it all, graffiti was architecture's constant companion. Mostly it was names, profanity, a few obscene pictures. On one corner, someone had made an effort to spray paint something decent—a mural, or the beginnings of one—only to have it destroyed by a picture of a giant yellow penis.

It was at this building where scene command had been set up. Steggmann looked up as Walter approached.

"Detective Forbes, good to see you," he greeted formally. "Not so good to see our latest catch."

"Who found her this time?" Walter asked.

Steggmann pointed to a family of five standing a good distance away, being interviewed by a couple other detectives, Standish among them. Walter felt bad for the family, actually. This would haunt their family vacations forever. They looked like the average American family. Dad probably went to work, did the nine to five, brought home bacon, complained about his job a little bit over dinner even as he probably flirted with other girls in the office. Mom might stay at home or work part-time, probably retail in some fashion, starting her shift after taking the older kids to school and day care, getting off work when she picked them up. And she probably spent each night packing cute little brown paper bags for the kids to take for lunch, each with a little hand-written note.

The children would probably get out of this unscathed, and that was all that mattered in Walter's mind. The youngest looked hardly a day over two or three while the oldest probably still thought boys had cooties and made little paper cootie-catchers to ward them off. The middle child might still be in day care or just started school. But at any rate, they would have virtually no memory of whatever happened here.

"Playing Frisbee," Steggmann said. "Dad throws it into the bushes, oldest kid goes to get it, Mom goes with her. And what should they find in the water but a body?"

"How are they?" Walter wondered.

"Freaked, but they're okay. The kids really don't know what's going on, and I figure that's all that matters."

"Good."

"They're from Pennsylvania heading to Texas and we're trying to encourage them to keep moving and have a fun family vacation."

"Because 'memorable' opens up too many possibilities," Walter said, chuckling dryly.

Even as he said it, the detectives finished up with the family and returned to the command post. The parents of the family tried to pack up quickly, but there was no hurrying with children. Walter could hear one complaining that she had to go to the bathroom, another that she wanted the purple snacks from the vending machine. He shifted his gaze to Standish who approached him.

"Glad you could make it," he said. "How was Thanksgiving before this?"

"Dull," Walter answered. "They all right?" He nodded toward the family.

"Oh yeah, they're good. They will be departing posthaste and attempting to reach Texas by tomorrow evening."

"What'd they have to say?"

"Not much. Playing Frisbee, lose the Frisbee, mom finds body in the river." Standish started to move off. "I'll show you what we got."

The family that found the body wasn't the only one in the park and Walter looked around as officers scoured the banks up and down, as much telling people to get out of the water and leave the area as looking for evidence. One officer said it was *E. coli*. Another said it was swimmer's itch. One by one, cars and campers packed up, and disgruntled vacationers left the park.

"How long ago was it called in?" Walter wondered.

"About half an hour ago. Originally, it was just a body in the water. Well, Percy took the call, came out to investigate. When he saw the body, he called Steggmann. I was already at the precinct, so I hitched a ride with him. When we got here and confirmed it was the same MO, Greg called you. You got here pretty quick."

"I wasn't too far away."

The path down to the river was not as well-kept as the rest of the park. Originally, the steps had been wood, but as was to be expected, those rotted within just a few years of installment. Only when they'd gotten so bad that someone had gotten hurt and sued the city were they replaced with concrete steps. But years of people, kids, and pets, as well as weather, the river itself, and a number of tree roots burrowing under and through the stone had crumbled the concrete until it had simply been chewed up and spit out as gravel. These days, the wear and tear of people laboriously climbing up and down the embankment had pushed the gravel mostly into the water so all that was left was hard-packed soil in some places and soft quicksand in others.

Once they got to the bottom, the story wasn't much better. Only a small part of the embankment was sandy beach, enough for a couple towels, but overgrown bushes and low-hanging tree branches prevented an umbrella from being erected. In the city, the river was kept at bay with levies and concrete sea walls. Out this way, the concrete walls gave way to huge boulder sea walls, like the kind used to build man-made marinas and harbors. That was on one side of the tiny beach. On the other side, the sea wall ended and gave way to the natural embankment which was sorely overgrown with spindly bushes and willow trees whose low branches made any shoreline trekking virtually impossible, and whose roots jutted out into the river, tripping up any shallow water trekking.

"Hope you brought your water shoes," Standish said, smirking as he and Walter waded out into the shallows and headed toward the low willow branches and tricky tree roots.

The water was freezing. Literally, it was freezing. This close to the city, the heat kept the water warmer than upriver or downriver where, even though the current was too strong to allow much ice formation yet, the water was still literally freezing. Walter sucked in a breath at the shock but followed Standish down the river a short distance to a spot that was inaccessible from the shore except for a mom looking for a lost Frisbee.

"This is where she was found," Standish said. "Face-down, caught on some of those bushes there. Had to drag her back upriver to the path to get her out. Basically frozen, stiff as a board, almost didn't fit in the bag. Coroner wasn't able to give us a time of death."

"So we're going to have to get an identity and trace her last-known movements," Walter mused.

"Right."

"Where is she now?"

"EMS already took her to the morgue. Coroner got excited at the condition of the body and wanted to get it to the ME as soon as possible in order to be able to pull as much evidence as he could."

Walter shook his head. "Coroner gets excited about the condition of a dead body. It's dead."

Standish gave him a coy smile. "Yeah, well, hopefully he can pull more evidence off this one than the last one, or at least some different evidence so we have more to go on this time."

"Did he give an estimation for the forensic analysis?"

"Nah. Same as always. Maybe tomorrow, maybe the day after."

Walter shivered. "Come on, let's get out of here."

But it wasn't like there was anywhere to go specifically. Unlike Sam, no one called in a missing woman at a time convenient to the investigation. It wasn't until the next morning that they got a call from the woman's sister. Walter and Standish went to talk to her. Telling someone a loved one has died was the worst part of the job, especially when it was under such gruesome circumstances.

"We're sorry for your loss," Walter finished.

He watched the woman sink to her knees before her husband helped her to the sofa. Her name was Marissa, the sister to the victim, Cassidy Wilhall.

"We just had Thanksgiving dinner Wednesday. She had to work on Thanksgiving because of all those greedy people who want to go shopping," Marissa whispered. "She brought the pie. God, she always made the best pies. It was cranberry pie, that way no one had to suffer through that godawful store-bought cranberry sauce out of a can."

"What time did she leave here?" Standish asked.

"Um..." Marissa wiped her eyes. "Must have been after two. Maybe closer to three. Our other sister has kids and they had some program that they wanted to watch at three. She left, and then the kids went to watch TV not long after that."

"Do you know where she went?"

"Not immediately. She was supposed to have dinner with her boyfriend that night."

"Why didn't her boyfriend come here?"

"He had to work. He works at the gas station there just off the expressway; he's the day manager. They were supposed to have dinner Wednesday night. And then he called me this morning asking if I'd seen her. I thought she was staying with him. We both made a few calls around to other friends and her work, but...when we couldn't find anything, I called the police." She let out a breath and choked out a sob. "And now she's dead."

Marissa's husband held her to him so she could cry.

"Do you know where they had dinner Wednesday night?" Walter wondered.

"Uh, the really fancy restaurant there on Second Avenue, the Italian place," the husband answered. "She wouldn't stop talking about how romantic it would be. I guess she expected her boyfriend to pop the question."

"And what's her boyfriend's name?" Standish asked.

"Michael," Marissa answered. "Here, I can get you addresses and stuff. Just...give me a second."

She got up and went to rummage in a kitchen drawer for an address book. *People still use those?*

"How do you feel about the boyfriend?" Standish asked. "He a good guy, not so good guy, kinda questionable?"

"Well, there are more prestigious careers than a gas station manager, but it could be worse," Marissa said, desperately trying to find some humor. "He's not a bad guy. He has his faults. But I never got any bad vibes from him, if you know what I'm saying."

She handed Walter a list of addresses for Cassidy's apartment, her boyfriend's apartment, her workplace, the whole deal.

Their first stop, however, was the Italian restaurant that apparently didn't believe in taking Thanksgiving Day off of work.

"It's a volunteer-only schedule," the manager said as Walter and Standish met with him. "Some people celebrate Thanksgiving earlier or later or not at all. Why relegate people to a single day? We just try to make it convenient and flexible for everyone. Now what's this really about, gentlemen?"

Standish showed the manager a picture of Cassidy that her sister had given them. "You remember this woman from Wednesday night? She was here—"

"With her boyfriend now fiancé," the manager finished. "Yes, I remember. I've seen a lot of proposals here but somehow he managed to hit every corny cliche and make it almost romantic. It was cute. And she said yes."

"What happened after that?"

"They had dessert, and then they left. I stopped paying attention after the proposal. Maybe you should talk to Will; he was their waiter."

The manager flagged down Will who approached skittishly. Guilty of something, but probably not the crime they were investigating.

"That couple that got engaged Wednesday night," Standish said, showing him the picture of Cassidy until recognition dawned on the poor man's face. "What happened after she said yes?"

Will swallowed. "Ah, they ordered dessert. Chocolate cake *á la mode* with a bottle of champagne. I brought them the bill—they tipped really well. Then when I brought them those little after dinner mint things, they were just getting their coats on, and she said something about having to go home and pack. He offered to drive her, but she refused. He kept asking her all the way out the door."

"Did they leave together?" Walter asked.

"Well, they walked out together. They sat at that table—" Will pointed to a window seat overlooking the parking lot. "—and when I was clearing the table, he got into a car alone and drove off."

"Do you know what he was driving?"

The waiter shrugged. "It was dark, man. The headlights were

like new LED headlights so I guess it was a newer car."

Walter and Standish glanced at each other. "Thanks a lot."

Will headed off to a table, and Walter and Standish left.

"If they both drove, why would he be offering to give her a ride and leave her car here?" Standish wondered.

Walter looked at him. "How does the day manager of a gas station afford a brand new car?"

Once they were sitting in the cruiser in the parking lot, Walter took another look at the list of addresses. "Maybe Cassidy didn't drive here. Her apartment building is less than a mile from here. Maybe she walked."

They drove the short distance to the apartment building where a crew they'd called in was busily scouring Cassidy's apartment. Walter took aside the team leader.

"Cassidy may have walked home last night from the Italian place just up the road. Take a team and check out the street, any alleyways, you know. I have a feeling this place is going to be clean."

"I expect so," the team leader confirmed. "I'd say that unless she's an impeccable housekeeper, her bed hasn't been slept in recently. And she likes to cross out her days on the calendar, but yesterday and Wednesday are still unmarked."

Walter patted him on the shoulder. "Keep me posted."

As he was finishing up, Standish approached him, fresh off the phone. "That was the ME."

"That was fast," Walter observed.

"Said he couldn't sleep. Either way, he's got the forensics."

Or lack thereof as, once again, Sean presented them with a victim who had basically completely accepted her punishment.

By a general description, Cassidy bore a close resemblance to Lily. Only about five-foot-five, topping out around a hundred and sixty pounds with more curves than was considered pretty. She had black hair and, Walter could safely assume, brown eyes. Her face wasn't quite the same—she bore more familial resemblance to Marissa than Lily—but to someone who didn't know, she could easily have been his target.

"No defensive wounds or marks of any kind beyond what you can obviously see," Sean told them. "Everything here is as precise as it was before, and just as puzzling."

"Did the water make any difference on the clotting?" Walter wondered.

"Not much, given the temperature. Nothing that would present anything forensically significant. If it's the same as last time, I would say that the face and hands had been done while she was alive, just like the last one, but exposure to the elements makes that difficult to determine."

"So we're not going to get a more accurate time of death, are we?"

Sean shrugged helplessly. "Afraid not."

"Is there anything particularly significant about the trachea being removed?"

"Psychologically, I don't know. Like everything else on both bodies, it was surgically precise. And the missing piece was also never recovered if I recall correctly."

The detectives thanked him and headed out, slowly, each in their own thoughts until they hit the door, when a blast of cold winter air hit them. Then they hurried to the cruiser and jacked up the heat.

"Why would our killer not only cut out the trachea, but keep it?" Walter wondered aloud.

"And if your theory is true, and this guy's after the Director of NICU, even if he's been hired by someone else, why is he only going on vague descriptions? Black hair, brown eyes, that kind of thing? Why doesn't he just find a picture of her on the Internet, like on the hospital's website? Is he trying to scare her?"

Walter shook his head. "You want to scare someone, you send threatening letters and go after friends and family, not random strangers who get mistaken for you." He put the car in gear and started backing out of the parking space. "But it might be a good idea to check out our girl's boyfriend."

Of course it was too much to hope that her boyfriend might be "Chris Temper" under another alias. The guy they were presented with in a dingy little apartment building couldn't have been old enough to even drink, never mind be the manager of anything or drive anything newer than a 2000 Chevy S10. Covered in rust.

"Michael Bailey?" Walter asked, holding up his badge.

"Um, c-can I help you?" he asked shyly through the crack in the door.

"Your future sister-in-law call you yet?" Standish asked.

"Yeah, um...hold on."

He shut the door and undid the locks.

Walter couldn't believe Cassidy wanted to move in with this guy. His apartment was a mess of stained carpet littered with beer cans, the walls covered in plaster patches and comic book superhero posters. The furniture was too awful to be called second-hand, maybe third- or fourth-hand as they were old, sagging, stained, and smelled of urine, probably from the little mutt curled up in an old recliner looking guilty. Good God, he should be moving in with her. What kind of game did he talk that she saw anything in him?

"In mourning, are we?" Standish asked, looking around, just as disgusted as Walter.

"I just proposed to her just last night!" Michael shouted. "Or...Wednesday...I don't know. I just...we were going to get married."

"And she was going to move...here?"

Michael sniffed and shifted his stance self-righteously. "It's only right that the woman move in with her man."

"Right...what time did you leave the restaurant Wednesday night?"

"Around eight-thirty. She lives just down the road from the restaurant. She walked there while it was still pretty nice. By the time we left, it had gotten really cold, so I offered to drive her. She said no, and we went our separate ways."

Standish raised a brow. "You didn't make her take a ride with you anywhere?"

"What?" Michael glared at him. "No."

"Mr. Bailey, what kind of car do you drive?" Walter asked.

"A '96 Subaru."

"Well, that's funny, because the waiter at the restaurant says he remembered you got into a nearly brand-new Lincoln MKZ."

Michael rolled his eyes. "That's my dad's car. I borrow it to kind of show off sometimes. I was hoping she'd take the ride so I could take her somewhere special. Since she didn't, I took the car back to my dad, grabbed my little car, and then I came straight home."

"Sounds like you do a lot for her," Standish observed. "Maybe someone got a little jealous of the attention she was giving you? Ex-boyfriends, anyone like that want to hurt her?"

"She had a girlfriend once, years ago. She got really jealous when she found out Cassidy was dating a man, but it wasn't anything really threatening."

"Uh-huh." Standish fished out a card. "If you think of anything else, let us know."

Michael took the card emotionlessly. "I will."

Again, Walter and Standish went to sit out in the cruiser.

"The waiter didn't say it was an MKZ," Standish said.

"He's an asshole future wife-beater who's lying through his teeth," Walter confirmed, "but I don't think he killed her."

"No motive. You don't kill the woman who just agreed to sign her life away to you. Not when he could get more fun out of thirty years of abuse. And he doesn't strike me as the intelligent type to use reverse psychology on us."

"Agreed."

Standish shifted in his seat, took a drink of coffee, and looked at him. "So, you still think this is your so-called 'Chris Temper' guy?"

Walter nodded. "I do."

"And you still think he's after Lily Guile?"

"Most certainly. And if our guy is smart enough to go from Sam to Cassidy, once he realizes he got the wrong girl again, I have a feeling that he won't make a third similar mistake."

"So, what do we do, boss?"

Truthfully, there wasn't much that normal people could do. Alias Chris Temper could easily just Band, go anywhere Lily was, kill her like she'd asked for it and stood there to let him do it, and get out. Still, Walter had to do something, even if it was just for show.

They headed back to the precinct and dropped off their notepads in Walter's cubicle. As they headed for the coffeemaker and a very enticing plate of cookies, Walter flagged down a couple of road patrol officers.

"What's it take to get an extended stake on someone?" he asked.

"How long are we talking?" one of them, his tag reading F. Reynolds, wondered.

"I don't know. Could be anywhere from a day to a month."

The officers glanced at each other. The other one, her tag reading L. Nathaniels, replied, "Well, obviously it'll have to be done in shifts, and it'll take probably two or three shifts and a lot of coffee. You'd probably have to talk to Greg for the specifics."

Steggmann was a nice enough guy, good at his job, but Walter just hated talking to him. Maybe it was because he was a Captain of Timekeeping. He was someone. And here he had to report to another captain. For whatever reason, it just grated on his nerves.

"Walter, come in," Steggmann said from his desk. "How's the investigation coming?"

"To a head, I hope," Walter replied. "I need to ask for something."

"As long as it's not a foot massage or a vacation."

"I need to put a stake on Lily Guile."

Steggmann glanced up from his papers. "A stake or a tail?"

"Either will do, but I'd like to get eyes on her at all times."

"You still think your cutthroat is after her?"

"He went after where he thought she'd be, at work, but she traded shifts. Now he's killed someone who, by a basic description, does look like her. If she is his target, I don't think he'll make the same mistake a third time."

"You have a point, but it took over a month for him to make his second mistake. That's a long time to put a stake on someone. Have you had any more leads or get any evidence that you didn't have before to pursue the guy, your—what was his name?"

"Chris Temper. And, no, sir, I haven't. Not yet. There are evidence teams out at probable crime scene locations, and Jim and I are tracking down several leads, trying to link the victims, or the victims and Lil—Miss Guile. I don't think he's going to wait a month to strike again."

Steggmann sighed and leaned back in his seat. He was about six-foot-four, roughly two-fifty. His haircut put Walter in mind of Frankenstein. His mustache was more well-groomed than Walter's but less flattering given the mole on one cheek that made the whole thing look off-balance.

"Walt," he said, like a father about to impart some very basic advice to his young son, "I like your theory. It fits. But it only fits because there are no other parameters with which to bind it." He went on before Walter could protest. "I'll give you your stake. It'll be set on Lily's apartment building, and they'll have the description of your Chris Temper. If they see him, they may detain him. But this is only going to go for one week. You have one week to get a lead, get some evidence, or find something to further the investigation and make me believe that doing a longer stake will be worth the time and money. Are there any questions?"

Walter sighed. It was the best he was going to get, and more than he would normally get. "No, sir. Thank you."

"Very good. Anything else I can do for you?"

"No. I have some calls to make."

Walter left Steggmann's office and headed outside where he could get decent cell reception. He called the bakery. No surprise, they were obscenely busy, and phones were as difficult to Band as the Internet.

"Make it quick, Walt," Micaiah said. "We've got a line out the door."

"I need you to reopen the case," Walter told him. "But I think I know a way you can get around the Hands and their secrecy about the Dispersal."

"I'm listening."

"Tell them you want to investigate the Runners involved in the Dispersal. Human Runners only. Ask around and see if any of them had a particular fascination with throats."

"Throats?"

"Yes. As in, ripping them out."

"Sounds...gruesome. I expect we'll be brought up to speed on this later?"

"I'm planning on it."

"Right. Talk later."

Walter didn't get to say goodbye before Micaiah hung up. Tommen was working today. Walter had given him a ride in at four-thirty, proper baker's hours. He would grumble and moan and hate on the shift, but Walter bet he wouldn't be arguing with the paycheck that followed.

Walter returned to his cubicle and was just about to sit down when Standish interrupted him.

"Hey, we got a hit from one of the evidence teams," he said, knocking on the wall of the cubicle and moving away.

"What is it?" Walter whirled and grabbed his coat. He was still fumbling with the zipper as he followed Standish out the door to the cruiser.

"Just like you thought, between the restaurant and Cassidy's apartment, in an alley. Found some jewelry the sister confirms was hers, and apparently a piece of evidence that the team thinks was meant for us. And by us...I think he means you."

"What makes you say that?" Walter's stomach twisted at the thought of what that could mean.

"Just the way he said it. He didn't tell me what it was, said we just had to see for ourselves."

It was not a comforting thought, and Walter's mind ran through a thousand different unpleasant scenarios between the station and the alley. At the very least, he knew Tommen was safe, and both Durvins were with him. They hadn't received any calls about Lily being dead. Still Walter felt uneasy about what message could have been left. And if it was meant only for him, there could be another thousand double-meanings and hidden messages incorporated, too.

Like the park and every crime scene from recent ages past, the alley was criss-crossed with police tape and lit up like the Fourth of July. Or maybe less so, since it was only the evidence team and photographer. As Walter and Standish approached, the team leader, the same one from Cassidy's apartment, approached them.

"This where she was killed?" Walter asked.

"Except for the jewelry, you'd never know it," the officer replied dishearteningly. His nametag read J. Vincent. "Something happened here, but we're not sure what."

"Our guy's gotten sloppy," Standish said hopefully.

"So she dropped a necklace," Walter said, shrugging. "Doesn't matter unless it's got his fingerprints, her blood, and the address of his secret lair."

"True," Vincent said. "But, we may have gotten the next best thing." He went to a little table set up a short distance from the scene and picked up an evidence bag. "This was found with the jewelry. Sister says it's not our victim's."

"So it's our guy's."

"Could be."

Walter took the bag. Inside was a little silver pocket watch, straight out of the 1800's. It was a little tarnished, but otherwise in remarkable shape. One side was the original engraving of a mountainous landscape. But the other side had a brand new etching as the silver had been polished.

Tick Tock, it read.

"Jim said that you said that you thought this was meant for

me," Walter said. "What makes you say that?"

"This." Vincent opened up the bag and took the watch out. He clicked the button and it snapped open, just as crisp as the day it was first wound. Inside, the watch hands ticked in time, even set correctly according to Walter's phone. But it was the opposite face of the clock that caught his attention. Tucked inside the watch was an old picture, brown and faded, but there was no mistaking that face, the deep-set eyes and bushy mustache.

"Looks kind of like you," Vincent observed. "Actually, it looks almost exactly like you. My guess is that our guy found a picture of you and doctored it to make it look older and fit the watch—in both size and era. But what do I know?"

A chill breeze buffeted them, making them pull their heads into their coats like turtles.

"Oh, and one more thing." Vincent took a pair of tweezers and carefully lifted the photo from its spot. More fresh engraving, this time reading, *Beaumaris Gaol, 1847.*

"Shit," Walter hissed.

"Mean something to you, Walt?" Standish asked.

"More than I'd like." He shifted his stance. "Keep it with the rest of the evidence. I might look at it later."

"Any idea what happened here?" Standish indicated the alley.

"So far, everything is coming up clean."

"Think maybe our guy planted the evidence for us to find?" Walter wondered.

"It's possible. I would have a hard time believing that a necklace and earrings like these would go unnoticed for a day or two. I'm no expert, but they'd be worth a pretty penny at a pawn shop."

"So this was all about us."

"He's taunting us again," Standish concluded.

"And you found nothing else?" Walter asked. "What about tire tracks? He couldn't just drag or carry a body from here to the river without someone noticing." Except he could, if he was moving too fast for any witnesses to perceive it.

"Nothing," Vincent said. "But we're still giving it a good look-through. I'll call you if we find anything else of particular interest."

Walter and Standish turned away and headed back toward the car.

"Damn," Walter hissed.

"So, what's the watch mean to you?" Standish wondered. "Your grandpappy's watch you thought you lost years ago?"

"No, not quite. But I do need to find a list of names I was working on earlier in the first case." He started the car. "When we get back to the precinct, you set up the board in the office. I'm going to try to find that list, and I'm going to have a chat with Miss Guile."

"Whatever you say, boss."

But Walter's search inevitably took him to the bakery which had calmed down some from the mad rush earlier.

"How's the long day?" Walter asked Tommen as he bought a pastry.

"Long," Tommen said, stifling a yawn.

"It'll be over in no time."

Since there were witnesses around, he casually left the bakery and went back to the car. As soon as he was in, he Banded and walked right back into the bakery, past the next person in line, around the end of the counter, and into the office where Micaiah was waiting for him.

"So what's the good news?" Micaiah asked.

"Whoever our killer is, he knows who I am," Walter said, explaining the pocket watch planted at the crime scene, as well as the photo and the engraving.

"Well, that doesn't sound too good." Micaiah leaned back in the chair and folded his arms. "First question, does Tommen know?"

"No. I promised myself that I'd never tell him. It's not something he needs to know, and I don't want his opinion of me to change because of it."

"Catch this guy, and you may get to keep your promise. Good news is, we may have a hit on the guy." He reached behind him, picked a paper off the printer, and handed it to Walter. "The Archives didn't have much, but I think this is all we really need. Name is Calis. He's called Calis Cutthroat in the Runner circles. Not really politically aligned, he's more of an opportunist, an anarchist. During the Dispersal, he was hired by Time Agents on all sides to assassinate one Hand or another, one Agent or another. It's believed that he is responsible for more than half of the deaths during the Dispersal."

"Well, it certainly looks like him," Walter said, feeling as though Calis' black eyes were staring at him through the printed image. "What about his history?"

Micaiah shook his head. "No one really knows. His last official record was his Apprenticeship, and that was back in the 1800's. And that's not just his last record, it's his only record. Someone went through some painstaking effort to erase him from the Archives."

"But if he was only an Apprentice, there's no way he could pull off half the stuff he's doing to the bodies. What was his exact work during the Dispersal? His MO?"

"It depended on who he was assassinating. Merchants, he would cut off their hands and cut open their bellies. Timekeepers would have their hearts carved out. Harvesters would have their faces sliced open like graph paper and their hands pierced through. But for all of them, he always cut the throat and removed the windpipe. That's how he got his name."

Walter let out a breath. "So we could be looking at two killers. Calis does his job the way he likes it, and someone with greater Time talents than you or I cleans it up to zero mess."

"Looks like it, but who would ally themselves with a man like Calis?"

"Someone with more to gain than they have to lose. Someone who's desperate, and quite possibly stupid."

"But we've already determined that the only ones with that kind of power are Wardens and Dominion Timekeepers. They've got a lot to lose. Especially with the elections coming up."

"So maybe it's time we took a second look at our glorious candidates."

"Will do."

"While you're doing that, I'm going to talk to Lily." Walter held up a hand when Micaiah started to speak. "I know. But it's my job, and as much as we all loathe her, she might actually have some insight as to who is trying to kill her." He went to the door. "Wish me luck."

"I don't wish you luck, Walter," Micaiah said. "I wish you sense."

Chapter Eleven
A Chat with Lily

With all her millions, Lily had homes, condos, and villas in more than two dozen countries, and the furniture to make each one feel like it belonged to a bazillionaire, which essentially she was. Walter wouldn't have been surprised if she had homes on other worlds as well; God knew there were some beautiful ones out there. Her condo in little old Charleston, West Virginia, was perhaps as modest as she was ever going to get.

From the ground, it didn't look like much, just a three-story condo building with a penthouse at the top which, of course, belonged to Lily. She spared no expense to make sure everyone knew a rich person lived there, assuming anyone could see the furniture. Exotic plants—some from Earth, some from foreign worlds—graced the balcony, branching out to conceal the richness which it was simultaneously meant to put on display, flowering richly, with creepers and vines looping lazily down the railing to tickle noses of her neighbors below. Having been up there only once before, Walter figured she still had enough fur rugs and furniture—some from Earth, some from foreign worlds—to make PETA have a heart attack. Supposedly, since his last visit, she'd also acquired a very rare and exotic snake which she kept up there as a pet.

"How's it looking?" Walter asked the stake shift sitting an unremarkable distance away from the front door.

"No sign of our guy," one officer said. "But we've only been here ten minutes."

Right. Banding. Made Time feel longer.

"You know who you're looking for, right?" Walter wondered.

"Black guy, mid-thirties, short hair, maybe a beard, maybe not, probably going to use the name Chris Temper."

"Right. Here's another name to watch out for. Calis. Supposedly his street name is Calis Cutthroat."

The other officer nodded. "After hearing about what he did to those girls, I wouldn't doubt his name. We'll be on the lookout, Detective."

"Great, thanks. I'm going to go up and chat with her for a few minutes. Do you guys need anything?"

"We're good for now, but thanks for offering."

Walter thanked them again and crossed the street. Taking a breath, he walked up to the front door and hit the buzzer. For a minute or two, there was no answer. Was she home? Had Calis already gotten to her? Trying to remain calm, he buzzed again.

"Who is it?" a female voice asked testily after a moment.

"Detective Forbes," Walter said.

"You're late."

"I know. I got busy."

"This is not how you impress a woman, Walter."

He had no desire to impress her, but everything that came to mind to retort was far less than appropriate for him to say while in uniform. He figured she must have taken it as a victory, for the lock clicked, and Walter went inside.

The condo building itself was rather posh for Charleston, but nothing compared to the multi-million dollar condos of places like New York City. The walls in the shared hallway and staircase were a tasteful off-white, the wood floors waxed and polished more than a 1970's disco dance floor and probably more expensive than Walter's car. The fixtures were slightly dated, old brass, but with the charm that only posh snobbery can bring. The elevator was designed to look like an old-time hotel elevator, and Walter almost expected an elevator boy to ask which floor he'd like to go to. But all these fixtures were modern and he simply punched a button that took him to the penthouse.

The door to Lily's condo was ajar and Walter cautiously poked his head in.

"Lily?" he asked, knocking lightly on the door.

"Come in, but stay in the living room," she ordered from somewhere inside.

He did so, keenly aware that his shoes were probably muddy. He looked behind him to make sure he didn't track. It didn't appear so, but he couldn't be sure since her rugs were thicker than his ancient 60's shag carpet, though with far more elegance and style. The general color scheme seemed to range from pink and red, to orange and yellow, with splashes of white to break it up, and blue and green to accent.

He stood in the living room, looking around and hearing her banging about in the bathroom. He made no noise at all. His footsteps were completely muffled by the pink, white, and orange rugs. He bet that any sound would be muffled, and no noise passed between Lily and her downstairs neighbor.

Large tapestries adorned either side of a huge bay window that opened up to greater Charleston, the centerpiece of the view being the capitol building. One might have dismissed the tapestries as being depictions of knights battling dragons, but Walter knew they were not of Earth origin. He couldn't remember which world Lily said they had come from or what the history and significance of them was, but he did remember that when she told him how much she paid for them, his jaw hit the floor.

That was the story of most everything in the apartment, from the tiny hollow glass marbles filled with sand from a thousand different worlds, to the rugs, to the tapestries, to just about everything she owned. Walter was fairly certain that the only thing that had come from Earth-side manufacturing was her kitchenware, and even then he wasn't completely sure.

The kitchen was tiled with glass tiles blown from sand from a dozen different worlds, each tile only about one inch by six inches, colors varying from clear, to white, to aquamarine, to black. The final pattern was psychedelic, but in a way that won home and garden awards. The countertops were some kind of black stone, cabinets a light-colored wood. Stainless steel appliances tied the whole room together, leading effortlessly to an open dining room. The table was an exotic wood, though it wasn't made traditionally, by fitting pieces together, but carved perfectly from a single block of wood. The chairs were also done this way.

He looked up as the bathroom door opened and Lily stepped out, wearing only a light T-shirt, underwear, and a towel to wrap her hair. She caught him looking and winked. Infuriating.

"I'll be right out, Walt," she said, as if he'd walked in and said, "Honey, I'm home."

The bathroom was the same story of sickening indulgence. She told anyone who cared to listen that it was some kind of rare granite found only in a small part of Africa, when it was really some kind of polished stone from somewhere across the universe. She'd paid for the stone and then paid for a mason experienced in that kind of stone to cut it into tiles so she could just hand it to some contractors and have them tile her bathroom for her. The floor, the bathtub, the countertop, and partway up the walls were all that stone. And, really, it was a beautiful stone once it was polished, as if sand had been taken from the beach and pressed between a couple of thin glass panes, preserved exactly the way it was, and dyed various shades of red and brown.

The bedroom door opened and Lily stepped out, this time wearing at least jeans and a long-sleeve shirt.

"I'll just be a minute more," she said, heading back to the bathroom. A moment later, he could hear a hair dryer.

Her bedroom was similar to the living room except the rugs were less shag and more woven, and the walls were a deep chocolate brown, making the whole room look as dark as her greedy heart. From his vantage point, it looked like her bed was similar to the dining table, the frame carved from a single block of wood. He could also see a wooden chest with a very obvious and very heavy-looking padlock on it. Maybe that was where she kept her billions.

The bathroom door opened again and she stepped out, hair as fresh as a model ready for her close-up.

"Sorry, Walt, you caught me at a bad time," she said. "I was in the middle of a shower."

"So I gathered," he replied diplomatically. "Is now a better time?"

"If you don't mind sitting out on the balcony."

It really didn't matter to him either way. She would flaunt her wealth, and she did, leading him out to the covered balcony which was overrun by a tiny jungle of exotic plants that he had seen from the ground. Underneath a few fur rugs, the balcony was tiled, but the light-colored stone had a wood pattern to it. Lily went and stretched out on a padded bench, seemingly unaffected by the chill wind. Behind the bench, a stone table had been erected and a sixteen-foot glass aquarium rested on it. Inside it, the biggest snake Walter had ever seen lay motionless but for the flick of its tongue and the nearly imperceptible movements of its beady little eyes.

"Don't mind Hades," Lily purred. "He won't bite unless I tell him to. Now, even though I can already guess, why did you decide to pay me a visit today?"

"Or, we can cut to the chase and get right into your little games. I'll go first. Why do you think I'm here right now?"

"Officially, I expect you're here to tell me about some break in the case. Like I said over the phone, either new evidence or a new body. So which is it?"

"And unofficially?" Walter pressed.

Lily grinned and for a second, Walter thought the snake the more honest of the two. "You're curious to know about the favor I want to ask."

"The thought had crossed my mind. Are you going to tell me the favor or shall we continue with the games?"

"Oh, let's continue with the games. They're such fun and you are the only one I really get to play with anymore."

Walter sighed and pinched the bridge of his nose. "So where'd you get the snake?"

"Not a snake, a Juerillian water beast." She grinned. "Yes, it's a snake, at least by our standards."

"Did you get an exotic pet permit for him?"

She shrugged. "No, but what Animal Control doesn't know won't hurt them. Besides, the dogcatcher's son is one of my patients. Poor dear was born three months too early. He has so much to worry about that I wouldn't bother him with such trivial matters like a snake that, as you can see, is very well-contained and well-cared-for. Be a shame if something happened to little Samuel because he tried to take away my pet that isn't doing anyone any harm."

Walter did not wish for Lily to die, but there were days when he wanted to throttle her. "You realize that your revenge exists only in your mind? Quinlan would never grasp the depth of the connection."

"Maybe, but it's my revenge and my mind, and as long as I am satisfied, that's all that matters."

"You're despicable, has anyone ever told you that?"

"Dear Micah used that word a lot after we broke up, along with a few other choice words. How is Tweedle Dumb anyway? Has he found himself a new girl to fawn after yet? It's been, what, ten years? Or does he do like his brother Tweedle Dee and just go out for one-night stands?"

"I'm sure I don't know." Actually, Walter did know. Micah had spent a year refusing to look at any girls, which was, in Walter's opinion, a smart move. Then he spent three years kind of shadowing Micaiah and attempting one-night stands if for no other reason than bestial sexual release, which was, in Walter's opinion, a stupid move. Then Micah finally grew a conscience, found the scattered pieces of his moral compass, and while he hadn't dated anyone lately, he wasn't opposed to the idea. The problem was either finding a woman who was already a Time Agent, or else finding a woman so special that he would deliberately expose her and hope that she would be okay with it and remain special.

"Too bad," Lily said, picking at her nails. "Maybe you ought to join them. In all the time I've known you, I have never seen you even look at a woman. Wouldn't dear Tommen have benefited from having a mother?"

"A mother, yes. Maybe not dating and potentially finding a wife before adopting him was my error. But a revolving door of women, no. He needed, and still needs, stability and a role model. Regardless if it's 1855 or 2013, he is still a teenage boy and needs guidance. He doesn't need to see me as hopeless as his high school friends."

"Oh, come now, Walter. It doesn't always have to be a human woman. There are a few decent races in the universe. Some of them even have viable, if not compatible, parts that you could utilize from time to time. Step into the Wheel, find a closet, you come back, and he never knew you went anywhere."

Walter shook his head. "No. You call me old-fashioned, Tommen calls it ancient superstition of morality, but I still hold onto it."

"Hm. Suit yourself. What are you going to do when he goes off to college, hm? Will you find a woman then? Or have you embraced twenty-first century ideals?"

"God help me if I ever do."

Lily chuckled darkly. "God cannot help you here, Walter. There is only you, me, and Hades."

Walter studied her. "How intelligent are Jarallian water beasts?"

"That's Juerillian, and they are nearly as intelligent as chimpanzees, just with fewer thumbs and communication abilities, at least to us humans. To the Juerillians, they're almost like dogs."

"I see." Walter leaned forward and rested his elbows on his knees. He just wanted to get out of there as fast as he possibly could. Damn it but he wanted to throttle her. He tried not to sound exasperated, tried not to give her the satisfaction of seeing how weary she was making him, even if it was as obvious as the snake in the glass box. "Are we done playing games yet?"

Lily shifted and stretched out on the bench. "The game never ends, Walter. It just gets put on hold."

"Fine. Can we put it on hold? I'm on the clock and I have work to do. So let's start with your favor. You said it has to do with the Hands and the election."

"Oh, naturally. What doesn't these days, hm? Another seventeen years has gone by and here we are again. Although, technically, it is only eleven years. Those 564-day Wheel years get me so confused."

"But I'm sure you make it to all your auctions on time. What's the favor?"

Lily grinned. "Why, Walter, I'm surprised that you couldn't guess. What am I known for but buying seats and other political favors? All I want is to buy your vote."

Walter sighed. He might have guessed as much. He rubbed his eyes. "Okay, I'll bite. Who and why?"

"He's an upset candidate for the Hand of Scientifically Advanced and Engaged Civilizations." Those who were scientifically advanced—go figure—an actively and openly engaged in the Time industry. "His—or 'its' name is Uqataqololonita, or something like that. He's Araxi. His chances are good, but I need to secure him."

"What do you get out of it?"

"It's not what I gain, but what I don't lose. The nominated replacement wants to change the profit percentages to favor his representation."

Walter leaned back in his chair. "That Hand is always threatening to do that. Even when it does happen, it's never more than half a percent, and by the next election cycle, it's usually been repealed because it—"

"Except this time, Walter, the vote might actually go through and stay that way because the nominee is going to bargain a percentage match to go directly into the pockets of the Hands. So that means I go from a twenty percent cut to a fifteen percent cut because

Earth is not part of that representation, and then down to ten percent because of the cut that goes to the Hands."

"Yeah, I can see you're hurting for funds."

She glared at him. "Maybe you ought to see what else the nominee wants to do. Some of those changes affect the Timekeepers, too."

He had no doubt that what she said was true, but probably not to the degree that she was implying. "Lily, you've never been good at threatening other Time Agents, me least of all. You prefer to speak the language of Cha-Ching. What are you offering?"

She went from moody to mischievous as he stroked her ego. "A hundred thousand."

"That's not much coming from you. It's like dropping a quarter in a homeless man's tin cup. And I don't do much shopping in the Wheel."

"Interesting analogy, but I wasn't talking about turns. I'm talking cold—hard—cash. U.S. dollars. Or whatever currency you prefer. Twenty-five in good faith, the rest once I see that you voted my way."

That was a good way to get Walter's attention, and only then did he fully understand how it was that she was so damn influential. She didn't just speak Cha-Ching; she spoke every dialect, getting to know each of her targets and exactly how to motivate them. He couldn't be swayed by a pocket full of turns, but real U.S. tender, that he could use.

"How would you get it to me? A hundred grand landing in my bank account is a good way to get the federal government sniffing around my turf."

Lily shrugged, unconcerned. "Like you said, I'm not hurting. I simply make a donation to CPD. Half a mill to the precinct itself to update computers or cars or whatever they need, a quarter mill for the higher ups, and a hundred grand for each sworn officer—and maybe fifty grand for the office staff—to do with and spend however they see fit. No strings, no loopholes, and completely tax free."

Shit.

"And you get a pretty plaque posted for everyone to see for all time," Walter said, trying to sound scornful, but his resolve was severely wavering.

"If someone just dumped a hundred million dollars of tax-free income in your lap, what wouldn't you do to thank the donor? I expect they're going to want to do a lot more than some meager plaque."

She was right.

Shit.

She grinned, sensing victory. "Elections are January 14th. I'll give you until the 10th to decide. Oh, and if you get the Tweedles to go in on it, I might make another donation. Two hundred to the bakery itself and twenty-five for each of them."

Walter suddenly came back to himself. "I promise nothing, especially on those two."

"Fair enough." She crossed one leg over the other. "Now then, I've said my piece. I expect we can be completely honest with each other now as I've just admitted to conspiracy and bribery of a public official and a host of other felonies."

Right. Case. Murder.

"How much do you know about the Dispersal of '63?" Walter asked.

Lily's expression turned thoughtful. "The Dispersal? It was a massacre. For the Harvesters and the Merchants, it might as well have been the Great Depression, assuming you lived long enough to care about your money. What does that have to do with the case?"

"What role did you play in the Dispersal? What seats did you buy?"

Lily tsked. "Walt, you assume that I've been buying seats since Julianna tried to Harvest me prematurely and I stepped into the magical world of the Time industry. I was barely an Apprentice during the Dispersal. I was no more significant to those elections than Tommen is to the current upcoming one."

"When did you start buying seats?"

"By the time the 1980 election rolled around, I was just about to graduate into Master status; my review was set to be a month after the new Hands took power. I only bought one seat that year. The Zero Hour. It nearly put me into bankruptcy, but I passed my review and have since learned better money management. I practically own the elections."

"So you had nothing to do with the Dispersal? Lily, for your sake if nothing else, I need you to be totally honest with me."

"No. But it taught me an important lesson."

"What's that?"

"Democracy is fleeting. Monarchy is absolute. What I do openly in the Hand elections is no different than what a number of corporations and interested parties do secretly in our precious United States elections."

"And look where that's brought us."

"Ah, but here there are innumerable parties all vying for breadcrumbs. In our elections, I am the one doling out the bread."

Walter gave her a long look. "So you have basically admitted to being, for lack of better term, queen of the Time industry, and you are entirely unconcerned about there being two apparent assassination attempts? Given the leap the killer took from the first woman to the second, I doubt he's going to make a third mistake."

Lily smiled and stood. She stretched a little longer than necessary in a pose that Walter guessed she hadn't learned from some modest meditative yoga class. Then she walked over to him and walked her fingers up his shoulder. "Walter, how much do you know about Harvester abilities?"

"Enough," he said curtly.

"Did you know that Intervention and Triage Harvesters have the ability to Harvest regardless of sickness or death? They can literally walk up to anyone on the street and suck the Potential Time right out of them."

Walter didn't know that. But he gave no indication of his

dread as he looked up. "And did you know that Wardens and Dominion Timekeepers are able to cut someone's throat, and stop and clot the bleeding before a single drop leaks out? I'm sure I don't need to tell you that the backup of blood to the heart can kill a person in mere minutes. Best part is, they can slip into a Band so fast, it's like time literally stands still. The victim can't fight back because they have no idea what's going on. It's like they're just walking down the street and suddenly they drop dead, their throat cut, heart burst."

Finally, he saw Lily flinch. Her hand jerked away and she took a step back.

"Where were you Wednesday night?" Walter asked, finally finding his opportunity. "Between eight and nine?"

She regained her composure and returned to her seat, her expression struggling to remain as cold and calculating as ever. "I went to dinner."

He cut her off. "Let me guess, little Italian restaurant."

"Yeah."

"You saw the couple get engaged?"

"I was sitting two tables away from them. God, it was disgusting to watch." She rolled her eyes.

"She was murdered on her way home."

"Better a quick death now than a slow one over fifty miserable years, I suppose."

"Based on a basic description, she looked a lot like you."

"Once again, right place, wrong person. Has this guy never heard of the Internet?"

"It really could be that simple. The name Calis mean anything to you? Specifically Calis Cutthroat?"

Her facade was as dodgy as Tommen answering a question about a girl he liked. "I know the name."

"How much do you know?"

"He was responsible for a number of murders during the Dispersal. My mentor did her best to both train me and keep me as far away from that drama as possible."

"He's our killer."

"And you want to know if I know where to find him?"

"I'm warning you, too, that he was only an Apprentice when he turned Runner. That means the only thing he is doing is killing. So he has to be working with someone else who is or was a Warden or Dominion Timekeeper who can prep the bodies in such a precise and clean manner. What Hands do you know of were once one of those two things? Probably the closer to the Dispersal you get, the more likely it is that's who he's working with."

Lily let out a breath and seemed to go through a mental list. "In the last few elections, I can only remember twenty-four being one of those. If you're looking for records from the Dispersal, you'll have to go to the Archives."

"I sent Micah and Micaiah," Walter told her. "The Hands didn't like them sniffing around the Dispersal, and the information we got was limited."

She leaned back in her chair and looked behind her at the snake—ahem, Juerillian water beast, as it slithered around and adjusted position in its cage, moving to catch the most sunlight. "What makes you think this has to do with the Dispersal anyway? Maybe Calis is in league with someone who's either in office or about to be out of office."

"Because all Wardens and Dominions in the present-day are accounted-for. Not all of them from the Dispersal are. And after that massacre, probably not everyone was thrilled to see someone like you buying up the elections."

"I keep the peace!" Lily snapped. "Without me to buy the votes, what's to keep another Dispersal from happening? Nothing!"

Walter met her icy glare as he stood. "It's like you said. Democracy is fleeting. You aren't sustaining democracy; you've put it on life support to keep it from dying so you can suck the life blood out of it for your own gain. But once the blood is gone, it's gone. And you're dried up."

"And what happens when there is a revolt in Time, huh,

Walter? What happens when the Hands are deposed and a true Time King or Queen is installed? Will you be their heroic knight to bend the knee and pledge his sword?"

"I don't know. I'll make that decision when the time comes. Until then, I have a murder to investigate."

She stood and followed him back inside the condo. "Walter, wait."

He stopped halfway across the living room and turned. He did not say anything, simply raised a brow.

"You're...not going to not stop Calis or his employer if they do find me, are you?"

"My job is to protect and serve, Lily. Earth-side, that is all I do, or all I try to do. But you are guilty of a number of violations of the Laws of Time, and I will not stop justice from happening when it does indeed happen."

Her expression turned pouty. "Let me give you a piece of advice, Walter. Your boy has got his review coming up. Well, not all the Hands like that he started his training early. Most of them don't like you much either. Be a shame if they failed him intentionally to spite you. I could fix that, make sure he passes with flying colors and glowing reviews."

"Tommen is an excellent student and my son besides, going to prepare for a test of knowledge and skill, not a product on Amazon to be reviewed and then bought."

With that, he did an imaginary tip of the hat and headed out, again half-expecting a lift boy to ask him which floor he wanted to go to.

Perhaps the most unnerving thing about the whole interview had been that she was afraid. Lily was not a person to withhold knowledge if it made her look smarter than everyone, anyone else. She had a golden opportunity to brag about how much she knew about the Hands and their dealings, about Calis even when she said she knew the name. Instead she'd clammed up like there had been a sniper's laser sight pointed right at her, threatening to shoot if she said anything about it.

At the same time, he also knew that what she said about Tommen's review was true. There were not a few Hands who would gladly fail him just to spite Walter. It might not have been so bad except for the punishment that they would bestow upon Tommen in order to ensure that he could never use his Banding abilities ever again. It was a bit like martial arts. He couldn't unlearn his skills, but he could be crippled beyond repair.

Walter stepped off the elevator and headed out the door, crossing the street to the two officers.

"You know, we're supposed to be incognito, but you just keep coming up to us," the man said, half-seriously.

"You guys sure you don't need anything? Last chance," Walter said.

"Thanks, but no thanks. We're good."

Walter shrugged and returned to his cruiser. Shivering in the crisp air, he called Micaiah.

"Yeah, Walt," the elder twin answered. "What did our snow queen have to say?"

"Not a lot that was helpful, unless you consider a hundred million dollars helpful."

"I'm sorry?"

Walter briefly explained Lily's bribe, including the offer to the twins and the bakery. For a long moment after he was done, Micaiah was silent. Then came the whistle. "That kind of cash is nothing to sneeze at, Walt."

"I can see how she became so successful at buying seats."

"Are you going to do it?"

"Of course not, but I needed to hear her out in order to get anything out of her. I fear it was a wasted effort."

"Well, no surprise there."

"Any luck reviewing the current Hand nominees and candidates?"

"As always, of the most-likely-to-win, most of them are

Harvesters and Merchants. Only two are Timekeepers. The Hands treat Timekeepers wanting to become Hands like we might treat a chicken that thinks it's a duck. You might humor them a little but secretly hope they drown when they get in the kiddie pool."

"Interesting analogy."

"It sounded better in my head. Anyway, I'll let you know what we turn up."

Walter thanked him and hung up. He tapped his phone on the cruiser absently before climbing in and heading back to the station. He dropped off his coat in his cubicle and went to meet Standish in the office. Once again, the map was marked with all the locations relevant to the case, and the whiteboard was a chaotic mess of notes and scribbles. The little trash can in the room had half a dozen markers in it. Standish was not actually in the office, but showed up a short time later, a couple papers in hand.

"Hey, glad you're back," he said. "So, I took the liberty of researching that pocket watch and the engravings—"

"No one told you to do that," Walter cut in, alarms going off in his head.

Standish looked like he'd been slapped. "That's why I said I took the liberty of doing it. I figured we'd get to it eventually, and since it seems to be a message from our killer to you—a detective on the case—I figured it was pretty important. Don't you?"

Walter sighed, closed his eyes, took a breath. "What'd you find?"

"According to an antique dealer, the watch itself is genuine, early 1800's, pure silver, probably cost a fortune. The mountain engraving is original, but the other engraving is brand new. But without a signature on it, it's impossible to tell who did it. I figured we could check out laser engravers once we check out of here."

Because that made more sense than hiding it in a deep, dark corner of the evidence room. Got it. Walter was not thinking clearly, obviously.

"The dealer couldn't tell me much about what was inside, so I went to the university, met with a European history buff." Standish flipped to another paper. "Beaumaris Gaol was a Welsh prison built in the early 1800's, expanded in 1867, and closed in 1878. It would appall us in modern society, but back then it was considered the most humane prison. Supposedly it was cursed by its last hung inmate, but that's not relevant. What is relevant is that according to what records that have survived, there was a prisoner named Walter Forbes who was in prison for murder. He escaped in 1847. He was captured briefly about two months after his escape, but never made it back to the prison before he escaped again. Now, no one can say for sure, but there are immigration records for a Walter Forbes entering the United States in 1848 who may or may not have been the same person."

"What about the picture?" Walter asked.

"I showed the antique dealer the picture as well as a picture of you. I told him we thought the photo was doctored, but he says that if it was doctored, it's the most convincing doctored photo he's ever seen. He explained the details, but for all intents and purposes, he swears that it is a real 1800's photograph. He also found some imprinted marks on the back that he thinks were 184-something, so taken in the 1840's was his guess."

"So what was his explanation for the uncanny resemblance?"

" 'An unusually high occurrence of a lot of dominant genetic traits,' " Standish mimicked. He shrugged. "I asked the same thing of the European historian and even one of the science teachers and got pretty much the same answer, as well as a plea to encourage you to research your family and build a family tree in order to 'preserve the heritage of your ancestors.' "

"Uh...huh." Walter nodded slowly. "Right. Okay then."

"That's what I said."

"I think we need to talk to some silversmiths and laser engravers."

There was only one true silversmith in town, and he simply scoffed at the sight of the watch. "If you want it cleaned up, do the whole thing, and do it right. Picking and choosing spots to shine up, it'll only destroy it faster."

"So why did you do it?" Walter asked.

The man gave them a nasty leer. "I didn't." He waved a dismissive hand. "Even an apprentice could see that's a shoddy job. Amateur work. Worse, it's like someone watched too many of those commercials for the magic cleaners you can buy at the store that are supposed to shine up old pennies and stuff. Antiques like that deserve better."

The detectives thanked him and went back to the car to consult the list of engravers.

"So, our guy isn't too rich," Standish said.

Walter nodded. "Let's start at the bottom of the coin purse and work our way up then."

It took four tries, but they eventually found the guy who remembered the watch. He owned a little nondescript engraving shop tucked away in an insignificant part of town. More importantly, he remembered the person who brought the watch in, but when they showed him a sketch of Calis, he shook his head.

"No, not like him at all," the man said, his dark eyes squinting in certainty. "White guy, 'bout six foot give or take, solid build. Not bodybuilder, but athletic. Long brown hair, kept it tied back and it still went down to his waist, like he was trying to be Native or something. Longish face, kind of a big nose. Freckles on his cheeks; I remember that because my little granddaughter's got freckles and it reminded me of her."

"Did he say anything?" Standish asked.

"No, nothing beyond business and the weather. I found it a little odd because people love bragging about why they're doing the engraving—wedding, anniversary, birthday. I learn more about a person's life story than most bartenders. But not him. Oh, he did have an accent. I didn't recognize it, and I've heard quite a few in my day."

Standish leaned expectantly on the counter. "Could you give us a ballpark estimate, a region? Middle Eastern, Eastern European, anything like that?"

The man thought for a moment. "Not Middle Eastern, like not Egypt or Saudi or anything, but close to that geographically. African."

"Geographical closeness doesn't mean linguistic closeness," Walter pointed out. "How do you figure that's what it was?"

"Well, back in the day, I did safaris and big game hunting in eastern Africa. I can't explain why, but that's what came to mind when I heard it."

"Can you describe what he was wearing?" Standish wondered.

The man shrugged. "Nothing special, really. Blue jeans, black boots, gray sweatshirt. I'm sorry, I notice jewelry more than clothing."

"Was he wearing jewelry?"

"A little gold chain around his neck, square masculine links because there's supposed to be some sort of difference between men's and women's gold chain jewelry." He shrugged again. "I don't know."

"How long does the engraving take?"

The man leaned back against the wall. "Well, the face of the watch, that's nothing. Computers these days, that kind of thing doesn't take more than twenty minutes. The inside face is a little more tricky to set up, but the engraving itself is..." He snapped his fingers.

"How did he pay for the engraving?" Walter wondered.

"Cash. Had one of those little slim clip kind of wallets. Only had cash that I saw, no IDs or anything."

"Is there anything else you can tell us about him? Anything at all?"

"Sorry, guys, but I'm tapped."

Walter fished out a card. "If you think of anything, or if he comes back, give us a call."

"Oh, no problem, happy to help."

They thanked him and headed outside. The shorter days cast long shadows over the city and made the temperature plummet. Standish took a drink of coffee. "I don't like this."

"I don't either," Walter agreed. "Basically we've got two

suspects now." As if he didn't know that before.

"And they're getting bolder. Walking around in public as long as they can, showing themselves but not enough to give us anything to go by. They're ramping up to something. How was your chat with Miss Guile?"

Full of secrets, bribery, and political intrigue. "More unhelpful than it was worth. She confirmed she was at the restaurant Wednesday night, sat within view of the couple who got engaged. Our guy just picked the wrong girl again."

"But if there are two of them, wouldn't you think one of them would be smart enough to, I don't know, check Facebook and get a more recent photo?"

"I don't know. Right now, I'm all for having technologically-impaired criminals."

Standish nodded and took another drink. "I'm right there with you, man. We need more of them. Where to next? You find the list you were looking for?"

"Yeah, and I might be able to narrow it down even more thanks to the description we just got."

Region One, which was Africa, only had three Districts. How difficult could it be to find one little Timekeeper from Africa in the 1960's?

Chapter Twelve
Rumors

Tommen rolled over and smacked his alarm clock silent. Was one day of sleeping in too much to ask? Thanksgiving vacation had been Thanksgiving awakation. Friday, Saturday, and Sunday he'd pulled double shifts, from prep to close, five in the morning to nine at night at least. He was pretty sure there was some child labor law prohibiting such things, to say nothing of how many extra hours they were able to squeeze into the day via Banding. At the very least, he could sleep until six on school days. It didn't make him feel much better, and a shower did little to wake him up further.

Not that he wanted to be very awake today, or needed to be. For one, it was the start of a new semester. Okay, technically they ran on a trimester schedule in order to be able to fit in more classes in a year so students wouldn't cut so close on their credits; it was just easier to call them semesters as it was a familiar term with less-damning consequences and jokes associated with it. But the first day of the new semester was like any other. The first ten minutes of class would be just making sure the students were in the right class. Then it would be basically a full hour of class overview and "get to know your classmates" games, as if they didn't spend enough time with each other to already basically know each other. Tommen figured if he knew someone's name, he knew them well enough. Of the few people he'd cared to get to know better, Eric was spending the rest of the year doing online classes; Varad was lost in his own world as he contemplated his impending doom of moving back to India with his family; Emily was still dating Luke, and still purporting the "cute" story of how Tommen chivalrously tried to save her from the big bad dragon Tyler, whom Tommen knew better than he ever wanted to.

All this and it didn't even scratch the surface of how big the double murder story was going to be. It was exciting and terrifying to think that Charleston might have its very own serial killer whom the news had dubbed The Cutthroat Killer because he ripped the throats out of his victims. In a helpful way, the news asked everyone to be on guard, but especially women as both victims thus far had been women. Unhelpfully, the news also said that both suspects were of foreign origin and to be on the lookout for any such persons. Needless to say, this only added fuel to Varad's father's fire when Tommen talked to Varad when he'd come into the bakery the previous afternoon. And even though the news had a picture of one suspect and description of the other, Tommen had seen the looks that other customers had given Varad. Paranoid suspicion that, if not for the media hype, would never have manifested itself.

So it was almost a relief when the first thing that Tommen heard on the bus had nothing to do with the murder. Of course, the chosen topic wasn't much better.

"I heard they found out who the father of Michelle's baby is," one freshman girl whispered to another. "Guess it's one of the seniors from last year."

The other girl scoffed, and Tommen could imagine her rolling her eyes. "How much of a slut is she that they have to guess and narrow it down? If you don't know who you've been sleeping with in the last three months, you've got issues."

"Is that how far along she is? Jeez."

"No, it's more like two months. She'll be taking that kid up on the stage with her, assuming she shows her face at all at graduation."

Tommen remained silent, pretended to be half-asleep, which he was, and uncaring, which he wasn't. He didn't like Michelle for what she'd done to Eric, didn't like her at all, figured she deserved everything she was getting, and yet she didn't deserve to be treated like that. He wasn't going to stand up for her or anything, but he wasn't going to spread gossip. And yet, part of him had to wonder what made her pick Eric as the supposed rapist. He didn't take what the girls behind him said to heart necessarily, but they had a point that if she was sleeping with so many guys she didn't know off-hand who the father could be, she probably had some issues.

He figured he must have dozed off because the next thing he knew, the bus jolted to a stop and the high schoolers were getting off. Tommen followed them inside and hurried to his locker. He wasn't sure why. He didn't have any homework to catch up on, wasn't like some of the students who spent all their time talking and socializing. He didn't even smoke in the boys' room like a few did. Now that he thought about it, he hadn't smoked or drank at all since the soccer fields.

"Hey, Tommen."

He looked up as Varad approached.

"You look as bad as I feel," Varad observed.

Tommen raised a brow. "Yeah? How's that?"

"Your hair is all tangled, your coat's all frumpy..."

"No, idiot, what's up with you? Something happen since yesterday?"

Varad sighed. "My dad has decided that if it's possible, we're moving over Christmas break."

Tommen felt like he'd been punched in the gut. "What? Why? You're almost done with school!"

"He's all paranoid and afraid that we're going to be arrested and detained by evil cops, or that my mom and sisters are going to be kidnapped and raped, or that him or me or my brothers are going to be jumped while walking down the street. He's basically gone entirely insane. The problem is, it's not something he's likely to come out of, you know, calm down, think about it, give it time. He's ready to act and he sees no reason why we should stay any longer."

"But...they're really close to catching these guys," Tommen said helplessly.

Varad shook his head. "Tommen, the media does no one any favors. This is a sensational story. Charleston has its own claim to fame, The Cutthroat Killer. That will never leave this place, but in the end, all that will remain is that it was foreigners who committed the crimes."

"But—"

"It's a vicious cycle, Tommen. Yes, minorities may commit more crimes, but the more the media perpetuates it, the more children hear it, the more it becomes a self-fulfilling prophecy. And we have problems like my family is having now, and you're going to face once it's over. You're lucky; no one knows you're foreign-born until you open your mouth. Me? You can spot this skin across the room."

"So what? Means you suck at hide-and-seek. You're still my friend."

Varad grinned. "And you will always be my friend."

"Does this mean you won't come back when you turn eighteen?"

"Oh, I expect I will. If nothing too terrible happens between when I leave and when I come back."

"I think you overestimate the shangri-la of the rest of the world that society promotes. The rest of the world has problems, too."

"I know. I guess I just want what everyone else wants, a place to fit in."

Tommen closed his locker. "I hear you there."

Varad shifted his stance. "Would you ever go back to Wales to find your family? When you turn eighteen I mean?"

Tommen shook his head. "My parents are dead. My brother, too. That much I know. Unlike you, there's nothing for me to go back to."

"I'm sorry to hear that. I feel for you. Well, I guess all that's left for you is to build your own family. Your dad seems like a good start."

Tommen nodded absently. "Yeah. And I guess Micah and Micaiah are kind of like the crazy uncles."

"Yeah, it was pretty funny when they threw that flour ball and it hit you square in the back of the head and just went *poof* all over your clothes."

"So what's your first class?"

Varad dug in his pocket and brought out a crumpled piece of paper. "Drawing II followed by World History and English 12B before lunch. You?"

Tommen's paper schedule was neatly folded and tucked safely in his coat. "English 10B, Economics, and AP Physics B before lunch."

"Hey, good for you, doing what you finally want to do. Good luck fending off those seniors; you're invading their turf, you know."

"Oh, I'm planning on it."

Of course, in order to make it to AP Physics, he first had to suffer through his first two classes. He no longer had Reisig for English and Mrs. Righting—ha ha, Righting, English class—was less friendly to non-traditional students. She was incredibly buddy-buddy with the popular crowd, more willing to forgive her favorites and penalize the rest, or so Tommen had been warned by those who had gone before.

She stood only five-foot-one and had bright red hair unaffected by her advancing age. Her glasses had red frames and were on her head as much as they were on her little hooked nose that reminded Tommen more of a hawk's beak. The sun had not been kind to her, and where her skin was probably once the envy of all, it was now a walking advertisement for sunscreen and tanning bed boycotts. She was especially proud of a tiny tattoo on her ankle which she swore was The Three Stooges, but Tommen thought they looked more like furry potatoes.

Teambuilding games amounted to three rousing rounds of Two Truths and a Lie. The first was a standard round where everyone read his own card and the class had to guess the lie. The second was done in groups of four where one person read a card, different from the first, and the group had to guess who it described and then the lie. The third round was like the second round except it was the whole class.

As usual, Tommen decided to be a smart ass, so in the third

round, he wrote his card in Welsh. He knew exactly when Righting got to it because she stopped and then sighed.

"Tommen?" she asked flatly, turning over the card and showing off the Welsh writing.

"That's not fair," he said in mock offense. "You're supposed to read it and then we all guess."

A few people in class snickered. Righting simply gave him a look and set his card aside to move on to the next one. Tommen smirked. He had to get in his fun somewhere. He didn't have Spanish again until third semester, so he had to have one teacher to banter with, or at least make fun of. He guessed Righting would be that teacher.

After all, if Mr. Morris was that teacher, Tommen would have been bantering with him from the very start. It was kind of awful to have the same teacher at the same time, even if the class was slightly different. Perhaps the best part of it was getting a new seat assignment.

"I know you are all expecting class bonding games on this first day," Mr. Morris said, "but we're actually going to be starting on one of three class projects, all of which will be incorporated into your final exam in some fashion."

Now Tommen was interested.

"Throughout the semester, we are going to be doing an investment project." He grabbed a stack of papers and began passing them out. "If we can get through the rubric fairly quickly, we can probably go down to the computer lab and get started looking around, otherwise we're starting tomorrow. Now, we are not going to be investing actual money. We are going to be doing everything but that. However, that means that we will be doing all the calculations by hand. Not to worry, though, I will have all the equations you need so you don't get too hung up."

When the papers had gotten into everyone's hands, he returned to the front and center. "We will be working on this every Tuesday in class, but there will be homework assigned for it over the weekend when the stock market is closed so you can better analyze what's happened. Obviously, this will be a very small-scale project as many investments take years to produce desired results.

"What you will do is pick ten stocks. I am not going to tell you which stocks to pick. You have a hundred thousand dollars in 'money—' " He used air quotes. "—to spend on whatever you want. Pick stocks you have heard about on the news recently. Ask your parents what they're investing in. Take a chance and pick something you don't know a lot about. Any ten stocks you want. Every Tuesday, we'll go and check on them as a class, and there are some analyses that I will have you do that we'll get to once we begin.

"This will be very confusing at first for some of you, and I want you to know that's okay. In fact, that's good, because over the course of this class, it will become clearer to you, and I want to hear about how your understanding changed as we learn about terms and concepts that right now mean nothing to you."

Tommen wasn't as interested in economics as he was science, but he was always glad to have a real-world, hands-on project that actually taught them something practical. No, he wasn't likely to become a stock broker on Wall Street, but there was something to be said for retirement savings. Even if he wasn't going to retire, knowing how it worked and what his paycheck taxes went to was somewhat important to him.

He left second period feeling almost excited for the class. Maybe it was just as well that English was his first class so he could get the awfulness out of the way first before heading to a better day. Did he dare hope things at school were finally, honestly turning around?

Tommen had intended to walk into AP Physics like a bad ass, take his seat like a bad ass, and not give a damn about what the seniors thought of him. Like a bad ass. So he was a little thrown off when none of the seniors or the sole junior jeered at or mocked him. Of the fourteen of them in the room, most didn't really pay attention to him, and those who did notice him offered a smile or a hand and welcomed him to the class, congratulating him on being in the class and being on track to dual-enrollment.

His table partner was a senior named Ollie. Five-foot-ten, all skin and bone with blond hair in a bad hair cut and a blond goatee making him look like some creepy stalker, he was probably the friendliest senior Tommen had met besides Eric and Varad.

"Glad you could make it, dude," he said as the teacher prepared her notes and shuffled papers.

"You're not going to make fun of me?" Tommen questioned, wanting to just get that out of the way.

"Nah, dude, we've heard about you. I mean, yeah, everyone knows about your fighting because of your girl chivalry or whatever, but we also know you've been singled out for being a whiz kid. It's great that you finally put that behind you and just...stepped out, you know? No fear." Ollie held out a fist.

Tommen offered a shy smile and fist bumped him. "No fear."

He desperately hoped that the whole class was going to be as awesome. Less about the classmates, but just the class in general. He hoped that his whole semester was going to be as awesome. Finally able to move on and...grow up, and do something that mattered.

The teacher took roll first thing. Her name was Mrs. White, and there were more than a few *Breaking Bad* jokes, especially since she also taught the AP Chemistry class. She took the jokes in stride, but her smile left much to be desired as smoking or chewing had rotted away several of her teeth. Her long brown hair was rapidly turning gray and she admitted that she'd finally caved and gotten a glasses string so she wouldn't lose her glasses around her neck. Her chest was scrawny and withered, but everything below that was pudgy and just plain old fat from having six kids—three sets of twins. She waddled more than she walked, but during the course of the introductory class, Tommen could see that unflattering appearances hid a wickedly sharp tongue and an even sharper mind. He ended up leaving the class feeling higher than he ever had been smoking weed. He hoped it would last.

"Hey, Tommen!" Ollie jogged up to him in the hallway. "Hey, so, you're friends with Eric, right?"

"Yeah," Tommen answered cautiously.

"How's he doin'? I mean, not everyone was okay with what happened, and I'm sorry he left. I mean, I know he's taking online courses, but still..."

"He's all right," Tommen said. Actually he hadn't talked to Eric in a couple weeks. His mom had simply said he needed some alone time and once school was back in swing, he'd probably come around.

"Okay. That's good. Since he's gone, you got anywhere to sit at lunch?"

"Yeah. I do."

Ollie stepped in front of him and gave him a thumbs up. "Awesome. See you in class tomorrow."

It was the first time Tommen could remember anyone complimenting him on his intelligence, congratulating him for some kind of perceived courage, offering to save him a seat at lunch, and saying they couldn't wait to see him in class. Had he finally stepped out of the realm of losers and into the realm of normal people, or was Ollie gay? After a minute, Tommen figured it didn't really matter. For the first time, he actually felt like somebody, felt normal. He wasn't just the weird loner with the funny accent who got in fights but was secretly super smart.

Through all of this, though, he also realized that he hadn't been incessantly pestered for details about the double-murder or The Cutthroat Killer. At first he couldn't figure it out, since having a serial killer in their midst, with his dad being the lead detective on the case, was way bigger than just a single murder, even if he had been the one to find the body. Then he realized that the only people who'd really pried were the same ones who had beaten him down and taken the time to make sure he stayed a loser.

But he'd graduated from that run of people. He'd moved up, moved beyond them. He was on his way to the Nobel Prize, and they were going to be delivering the pizza to his acceptance party. He wasn't going to be bothered for details of the murders because the people around him now respected his dad's position as the leader and that he wasn't going to just spill secrets to his son. They had more respect for the criminal justice system. They wanted to see justice, not vengeance. They wanted information, not entertainment.

Of course, Tommen could have easily been fooling himself into thinking life was any different than it was before as he grabbed his lunch and headed for the cafeteria. It was only the first day of the semester after all. Once things settled down, everything would likely be back to normal. But still...he could hope, right?

It was strange to arrive at lunch and see only Varad sitting in the usual spot, and it wasn't until that moment that Tommen realized that Eric wasn't going to join them at the table ever again. Still, he tried to keep a cheery attitude as he sat down and pulled out his sandwich. Ham on rye with a generous helping of mustard.

"How was your morning?" he asked Varad who simply stared at the food his mother had packed. He couldn't say what it was, rice and beans with something-or-other. And curry.

"This will be my most miserable semester ever," Varad sighed. "I hate my classes."

"Drawing and English, maybe, but...dude, history is your thing. What happened?"

"World History means...World History. History of the world. The world is bigger than Europe!"

Tommen frowned. "Sorry, I don't know what to say."

Varad shook his head. "There is nothing you can do."

"See, I don't understand something about this whole thing, you moving and all. I thought you loved history, and your dream was to go back to India to the little remote villages and record the oral histories before they were lost. Why do you have such a problem with this?"

"Because I only wanted to visit. I don't want to actually live there. I'm no missionary."

"Maybe not, but how long do you think you'll be there at a time? You think it'll only take a week to gather all the stories from a village, stories that go back centuries and might need more stories and research to fully appreciate their meaning?"

Varad sulked and looked guilty. "I know you're right."

Tommen took a drink of his water. "Having second thoughts about going? Without all this stuff going on?"

"Kind of. I thought maybe it was just jitters because that time is coming up fast. You know, once I get going, I won't be able to stop? Except now everything in that timeline has moved up super quick and I don't want to go at all."

"That's because someone is forcing you. There's a difference between trying to force a stubborn ass to move, and letting him get where he wants to go on his own."

Varad finally grinned and shook his head. "You're an idiot."

"You're a stubborn ass."

"Aw, such cute pillow talk."

Tommen closed his eyes and let out a breath. He knew the day had been too good to be true. Way too much had gone inexplicably right for it not to have some sort of evil to balance it out and potentially destroy it. And why did it always have to be the same evil? Why couldn't there be, just once, some other bully? Or failing a test? Or...having to walk home in the snow? Anything at all, just something other than Tyler Freeman goading him into a fight.

It was then that Tommen decided that he wasn't going to let Tyler goad him into a fight. Not this time. It was a new semester and he was running with a different crowd now, one that appreciated him and didn't see a need to constantly berate him and try to make him a loser. Let Tyler blow all the hot air he wanted, Tommen would—

He found himself spinning around as Tyler grabbed his shoulder, hauled him from his seat, and forced him to face him.

"I'm talking to you," Tyler growled.

"Well I'm not," Tommen told him, trying to hide both the rage burning through him telling him to get in the first punch, and the fear twisting his stomach telling him to run before he landed in the hospital.

"Oh, so a new semester comes around and so you don another layer of chivalry. Trying to be the bigger man—"

"I am the bigger man," Tommen said smartly, doing a quick obscene motion.

His smirk was cut short as Tyler's fist buried itself in Tommen's stomach. He coughed, tried to catch his breath, tried to curl up and protect the wounded area without going down and seeming defeated. Tyler threw him back in his seat. "You think you're the bigger man? Think you're such a hotshot? Think that because you get moved into special classes that it makes you some kind of hero?" Tyler grinned smugly. "I guess out of the three of you, one had to turn out semi-decent. Hanging out with a rapist and a murderer and all."

When Tommen was twelve years old, Walter decided to foster another son, as much to give Tommen a brother and friend as a babysitter. Ryan was fourteen years old and had been in and out of foster care most of his life. Needless to say, he didn't much appreciate Walter being a cop and did everything in his power to get out of the Forbes household. When he wasn't calling and filing complaints with Protective Services about perceived slights, illegalities or abuses, he was literally trying to get into juvie. If he wasn't stealing cigarettes from the corner gas station, he was breaking into homes or stealing cars.

Ryan ran with a tougher crowd than Tyler. For as street thuggish as Tyler was, Ryan had made friends and allies with the real breed of street gang, like the kind that terrorized the darker neighborhoods of Chicago. Perhaps worse than that was his penchant for breaking a number of track and field records, and holding several state and national titles in Brazilian jiu jitsu. So when he went out with his gangbanging buddies, he always took joy in not only committing the crime, but being able to run from authorities and dispense Brazilian jiu justice on whomever he deemed liable to snitch.

Tommen was not immune to Ryan's personality either. At

first, Ryan had thought to win a convert to the gang, the ultimate slight to Walter. Tommen went with Ryan on a couple small break-ins and vandalism runs, but snapped back to sainthood when they got caught one evening. After that, Ryan only saw Tommen as an obstacle and a punching bag. At the time, his Banding abilities were still crude and just starting to finally pull together and properly develop, and the more Ryan tried to hurt him, the more he used his Banding and fine-tuned it in order to escape the wrath of his big brother from hell.

This was after all the business with Tyler started, back when Tommen was ten. And with Walter's agreement to teach him to Band early, he had to promise not to use it in order to beat Tyler bloody. He could defend himself, but ultimately he had to run and get help.

Walter was finally forced to admit defeat eight months after Ryan came to stay with them. The night before he was supposed to leave, Ryan tricked Tommen into going outside to the back yard. At the time, they didn't have many neighbors, and in the dark, no one could see what was happening.

In a nutshell, Ryan tried to kill Tommen, or at least severely wound him and send him to the hospital as a farewell gift to Walter. But it was in that moment that Tommen got tired of running. He was tired of running and tired of feeling weak when he knew he had the ability to gain the upper hand.

So it wasn't the first time that Tommen threw the first punch in a fight; it was just the first time that anyone at school knew about. Given his history of fighting and general predictability, his move was enough to stun Tyler as Tommen all but bulled him into the wall, snapping his head back against the stone. Tyler tried to get his knee up for a quick ball-crusher, but Tommen slipped into a Band and let the kick miss, instead grappling for a pressure point.

But Tyler would not be manipulated so easily. He snaked his arms around Tommen's arms, around his elbows, trying to gain leverage, trying to pinion him. Tommen let him have the move, but in a Fast Band, he was able to get his body up enough to kick back and his feet made contact with Tyler's thighs and hips. Surprised, Tyler let go. Tommen hit the ground ungracefully but managed to roll away to a somewhat safer distance as Tyler picked himself up.

Tyler's expression was almost worth whatever punishment Layman would have in store for him. He was in absolute shock. This kid that he'd bullied since the fourth grade, who'd never thrown the first punch, always got his ass kicked, and usually went crying to the principal or daddy, had not only thrown the first punch, but the only mark he really had on him was from the floor. It suddenly set a whole new stage for the fight.

Tommen didn't really know a whole lot about fighting. He'd taken only, like, a year of karate classes, but rehearsing forms and strength training didn't do a whole lot for real-world fighting. He remembered some of it, enough to gain the element of surprise which was quickly waning, but he knew his tricks were wearing thin; the only thing he had left was his Banding.

Around them, students were whispering and pointing. A few exchanged money, making bets. Tommen saw Varad at the edge of the circle that had formed, eyes wide. He managed to pick out Ollie's bad hair cut as he strained to see over the crowd. The lunch ladies were hiding behind the salad bar as if the fighters might suddenly whip out guns and start shooting people. And where the hell was Layman? Usually that man was in the middle of the fight by now.

In his moment of observation, Tommen was caught off-guard by Tyler who made to full-on body-slam him. Tommen Banded enough that he could twist in his grasp and land safely and not on his face, but he wasn't like Micah or Micaiah or Walter who could throw up extremely focused, extremely narrow Bands at a mere thought. For him it took a couple thoughts.

His head hit the floor, and color burst in front of his eyes. He blinked to clear his vision and tried to Band again to wiggle out from under Tyler, but the thug had pinned his hips just by sheer weight. Tommen managed to dodge the blows, but he also noticed that as they were coming, he could almost see their projected path, even without much Banding ability. He hoped that it would be enough to simply dodge and wait until help arrived. Of all days for Layman to take his sweet time. Or had his summoning been delayed since Tommen had thrown the first punch and everyone wanted to see how this would turn out?

Tommen didn't want to find out. If he could end the fight on his own, he would. No more crying to the principal or daddy. Tyler would respect him.

Tyler sat up from his useless punches, his weight still holding Tommen tight to the floor. He took a breath like he might actually stand up and walk away. Tommen didn't know what his next planned move was, but he wasn't going to just play defensive and find out. Instead, as Tyler came down, Tommen Banded and brought his head up, cracking Tyler square in the forehead.

A moment of surprise and hesitation was all Tommen needed to Band again and wiggle out from under Tyler who stood and stumbled back, hand to his forehead. It was then that Tommen realized how much his head was aching, too, and he flopped down into a chair.

For a minute, the whole cafeteria stood in an awkward silence. Were they going to fight more? What had changed? This was exciting. Who won? What did all this mean?

Tyler brought his hand down and Tommen saw he had a cut across his forehead which bled down into his eyes, but it wasn't deep. Tyler looked at the blood, looked at Tommen, and looked ready to kill.

"I'm not fighting you, Tyler!" Tommen said forcefully, grabbing a napkin and pressing it to a slightly smaller wound above his right eye. He thought about trying to stand and make himself tall and give some sort of heroic speech worthy of Hollywood, but figured that if he tried, he would probably fall drunkenly, and his speech would mean nothing. Better to stay put. "I'm done!"

"You're damn right you're fucking done!" Tyler snarled.

"And so are you, Tyler," Layman said, his mere presence

parting the crowd of onlookers. "You're both done. My office. Now."

Tommen grabbed a couple more napkins and followed Layman to his office. They passed one of the lunch ladies and a couple other students, probably those who had gone and told on them. For once, Tommen wasn't bitter. He was done with the fighting. Of course, he'd said as much when Tyler had started this fight, but then, he'd been insulting his friends in the most heinous way. Had he only been insulting Tommen, he probably could have stayed out of the fight. Of course, that was only a theory. Did Marty McFly ever get over being called chicken? Tommen racked his brain but couldn't remember.

Layman's office always looked like it walked out of a magazine, or several magazines. One for cleaning products as everything was always spic and span and smelled like it. Another magazine for candles as he tried to rid the office of those chemical smells. A third magazine promoting organization and efficiency. A fourth magazine warning of the signs of Obsessive Compulsive Disorder. And a fifth magazine advertising the United States Marine Corps. Somewhere in all the sickening organization and military pride, Tommen was told, was a poster about motivating children and molding young minds for the future.

Tommen knew the drill and took a seat. It was remarkably comfortable; clearly there hadn't been time for Layman to swap out the comfortable seats with the old, rusty, metal fold-up chairs, or else he'd just been in a meeting. Tyler leaned on the door with his arms folded until Layman ordered him, with all the force of a drill sergeant, to sit down. He couldn't touch Tyler, but he knew how to motivate, and probably not in the way that the cute little poster was referencing.

Layman knew how to control a situation. He never let his guard down, never allowed himself to be rushed, and he never let them see how exhausted he was from dealing with their constant fighting. He sat down calmly, and only when he was ready.

"So, first day of a new semester, and we seem to have forgotten our truce," Layman said calmly. "Witnesses tell me this was a different sort of fight. Tommen, would you care to explain?"

"I wasn't going to fight him," Tommen replied honestly, "I tried to ignore him, but Tyler pulled me out of my chair and punched me. Then he called my friends rapists and murderers and...I really...I just couldn't let him get away with that. I wasn't going to let him insult them like that, especially when Eric isn't even here to defend himself."

"Tyler, did you say that about Eric and Varad?"

Tyler scoffed. "Well they are. It's not like I said anything that wasn't true. If I said Varad was Indian, would you still be mad?"

"Innocent until proven guilty, Tyler. And guilty you are looking." Layman looked back at Tommen. "So you did start the fight?"

Tommen shrugged. "Technically, he did throw the first punch, but yeah, I guess I did. I kind of threw him into a wall and when he tried to pinion me, I kicked him in the stomach. Then he got me to the ground and sat on me and tried to punch me. I dodged them and then cracked my head into his to make him get off me. Then you came in."

"Anything to add, Tyler?"

Tyler scoffed. "Would it matter?"

"In my office, no. In a court of law, it might."

"Sir?" Tommen wondered.

Layman leaned back in his chair. "I think I've been very generous with you two in that the only thing I've done is hand out a couple of detentions and suspensions. Tommen, you've always done well to defend others and make sure Tyler throws the first punch, but while there are times where it is noble, I think that it is simply becoming a smoke screen to hide behind to stay out of trouble. No more. If you are truly The Chivalrous Welshman, then you ought to learn what chivalry means and its code of conduct; it may surprise you. That said, I will hold you to your word that you did not intend to fight Tyler and, as you said in the cafeteria, you're done. And so you are. The next time you get into such a fight, you will be suspended. And that's not just for the rest of the semester, but for the rest of the year.

"To that end, you will be working on a project especially for me, a report on traditional chivalry. I don't care what format it's in, as long as you tell me what traditional chivalry is, how it applies to today, and how you will apply it in your life. Properly. You have until the end of the year, so no excuses for why it can't get done. Am I clear?"

Tommen went through a myriad of emotions during Layman's little speech, but it was pretty well summed up in the words fear, relief, fear again, dread, horror, and revulsion. He took a measured breath. "Yes, sir."

"Tyler, I have been more than generous with you. Any number of these fights I could easily call the cops for assault, but perhaps I am a fool for thinking that you might come to your senses. Only because this case would not hold weight on the assault given that he got the upper hand here, I am simply giving you your final warning. For good. If you get into any more fights on school property — I don't care who it's with — you will not only be expelled from this school, but you will be removed from the premises in handcuffs and you will stand for assault. And I have every report of every fight you've been in since you set foot in this school. You're an adult now, Tyler, and I'm done playing Mr. Nice Guy. If you want to know what happens in the real world, I will gladly show it to you. Do I make myself clear?"

Tyler's expression hadn't changed, but Tommen watched his body language and knew enough to know that he was sweating a little. Layman had finally gotten to him. Of course, Tommen highly doubted that the adult justice system would do much to correct his behavior when the student justice system had failed on every occasion thus far, but for now, the fear appeared to be enough.

"Very clear," Tyler said at last.

"Good. Now then, as I said, I will not send either of you to detention, nor am I doing anything more than issuing you both a severe warning. Tommen, suspension. Tyler, expulsion. Keep that in mind not only whenever you want to fight, but whenever you look at each other in class or in the hallway or anywhere at all." He looked at the clock. "You still have ten minutes left for lunch. I expect you to sit on opposite sides of the cafeteria."

Tommen left Layman's office wondering how he should feel about what just happened. Relieved, he wasn't being suspended or anything, just warned. Afraid, would Tyler simply say fuck it and take an expulsion for the opportunity to beat him one last time? Revulsion, he wanted little and less to do a project for Layman, but at least if it was only due at the end of the year, he could work on it here and there with no real need to rush.

Thankfully, Varad was still sitting at the lunch table, apparently guarding Tommen's lunch.

"You could have just taken it back to my locker," Tommen said, taking his lunch and finishing his sandwich in three bites.

Varad shrugged. "Seemed safer just to stay here."

"Why? Someone try to hurt you?"

He shrugged again. "People say that Tyler's an idiot, say that he's a hateful son of a neo-Nazi, say that he doesn't know what he's talking about. But it's easier to dismiss a word than it is the idea behind it. Sure, they know I'm not a murderer, but the idea that I could be prone to unpredictable violence will stay with them until they can't remember why they don't like me, only that they do and I am not safe to be around."

Tommen raised a brow. "Don't you think maybe you're overreacting?"

Varad stood, collected his lunch box and utensils, and Tommen followed suit. "Believe me, Tommen. I am not much of a praying person, but I pray desperately to Vishnu that I can still prove my father wrong."

It was not a comforting thing to think about as the bell rang and they parted ways to head to class. Tyler was not exactly shy about being the son of a neo-Nazi—and pretty much one himself—but everyone knew it, and that was why few people put stock in what he said. Sure, not everyone at school was buddy-buddy and sat around singing kum-ba-yah, but most of the time it was simply for lack of mutual interests and personalities. Just because Nate wasn't good friends with Varad didn't mean he wouldn't stand up for him if something happened.

Except he hadn't. Nate and Tom and Erika and Kate and everyone else in that lunchroom simply stood and watched while Tommen took on Tyler alone. To be called a murderer—and Eric a rapist—and still Tommen went against him alone. Were they simply too afraid of Tyler because of the example he often made of Tommen? Or were they simply too enthralled by the spectacle to care much?

Tommen sighed and tried to tell himself that the morning had started off very well, and there was no reason the afternoon couldn't be similar. Fourth period was Web Programming after all. It was all up in the air whether it was considered a math credit, science credit, or elective credit, so Mrs. Wendell assigned it according to each student's needs. For Tommen, it was an elective credit.

Mrs. Floyd was the teacher of the class. A woman of about thirty years and three-kids-and-counting pounds, Tommen thought she would probably do better teaching middle school. She knew her stuff, but her attitude and the way she spoke to the students was more appropriate for sixth and seventh graders. She kept her blond hair swept up in a bun like a proper business lady, but her general T-shirt and jeans approach to fashion spoke more of a mom who just couldn't be made to give a damn anymore about looking prim and proper for a class full of teenagers who didn't care too much about fashion, in the same way her three kids under seven didn't care.

The biggest problem with the class, though, Tommen thought, was that there was no possible way for them to always be current with web programming, especially as web programming became more and more obsolete as everyone moved into apps. That wasn't to say that websites weren't important, but when Tommen opened his textbook and saw the copyright was 2005, he knew the entire semester was probably doomed to a chorus of, "Your textbook does it wrong, but that's what it teaches so do it anyway." Never considering the fact that advancements in web browsers probably wouldn't even render those codes properly anymore anyway. As he flipped through the pages, there were more pen marks crossing out old code and writing in new than there was standard printed text.

Yes, this class was pretty much doomed.

Drawing and Painting IA was something Tommen hoped he could get into, by interest anyway. He was never much of a drawer, and could never understand why art teachers always pushed so hard for one painting technique or another and handed out grades on student work, when he'd seen some pretty shitty artwork in museums. Why couldn't his painting be considered an abstract expression of self, and not a failure to follow criteria? Weren't some of the most celebrated artists those who didn't follow the crowd?

At the same time, for a beginner's art class, there was something to be said for learning the basics. What a paintbrush was, for example. That was very important for those who had been entirely deprived as a child and couldn't figure out what to do with the stick with bristles on one end. Same with a palette and an easel and the canvas. Oh, for goodness' sake, it was like being in kindergarten again. Not that Tommen had ever been in kindergarten.

Of course, this might have been easily explained just by the teacher, Mr. Robinson. He was about fifty years old though he looked only about thirty, stood just under six feet, and stayed in decent shape. But his most prominent feature, one which everyone noticed on the first day of school, was the afro wig he insisted on wearing everywhere, in and out of school. The guy wasn't anywhere near black. He was whiter than Tommen.

The reason for this, as anyone who knew art, or at least watched public programming, was his admiration for Bob Ross. Mr. Robinson had a number of posters, portrait paintings, and replica paintings hung all around in the little corner of the room that constituted his office. He even had one real Bob Ross painting, signed by the man himself in person. Two entire shelves of his bookcase were dedicated to holding his nearly-complete collection of The Joy of Painting. And he promised the class that when they did move into their painting portion of the class, they would have all the classic colors, especially Titanium White. Because Tommen was really worried about having to use regular old White.

Even his mannerisms were reminisce of the dead artist, the way he made everything "happy," and the way he tried to smooth out his smoker's voice to sound calm and caressing. Tommen was glad he couldn't get his voice that soft, though, because it probably would have put half the class to sleep.

Still, he didn't complain when Robinson simply gave them some paper, a pen, a pencil, and some assorted coloring materials to share. It was simply a time to free draw — with suggested styles on the whiteboard — so that he could get a basic feel for the drawing abilities of the class. Well, Tommen figured, if anyone in the class had any drawing abilities, they probably would have skipped over the kiddie coloring course and gone straight into his independent study course.

At the same time, the drawing was relaxing and helped Tommen to forget about the fight earlier. There were worse classes to end a school day with, so overall, he guessed he could suffer through it.

And he'd had worse semesters overall, too. Starting off the day with English wasn't his idea of fun, but there really weren't any bad classes that he dreaded going to, and his mood as he got on the bus to head to work was neutral, calm even. He wasn't riled up or anxious, wasn't dreading going to work to get a lecture from the twins, wasn't already hating the next day of school. It was one of those rare good days.

But then, it was still only the first day of the semester. None of his classes had really done much. Once the work started pouring upon them and everyone got their favorite group partners and stuff had to get turned in and tests started coming, it probably wouldn't be any different than any other semester.

Tommen got off the bus and headed into the bakery which was modestly busy. Neither twin seemed to notice him, and he simply punched in and slipped right into his work routine. But instead of taking Micah's place at the counter so he could go back and get things baking, he found himself working alongside him, Micah on register with Tommen running back and forth in the display case, going after brownies and cookies and goodies; the front cooler, retrieving pre-ordered cakes; the little fridge that contained milk, juice, and other assorted cold beverages; and the coffee pots, feeling like he worked at Starbucks for the decaf with two creams, a sugar, and a shot of the seasonal creamer.

Micah didn't say much, simply concentrated on his job, and Tommen noticed the door to the office was open, very unusual for Micaiah who generally didn't like a bunch of noise when he was trying to do paperwork.

"Is everything okay?" Tommen asked once the last customer had been served and they were allowed two minutes of breathing time. "I mean, the ovens aren't down, are they?"

"No, no," Micah said. "Tommen, come here."

Fear immediately hit him as he followed Micah into the office. "I haven't been late and I haven't tried to make you guys mad. Did I do something wrong?"

"No, you haven't done anything wrong," Micaiah assured him, though his tone was still serious. "Tommen, what we are about to ask you is of the utmost importance, and we want you to take it with all seriousness."

"Um...okay?"

"Walter wants us to do some more investigating in the Wheel for our murderer. Normally, we would just go and so what. But Walter is concerned for you. Threats have been made."

"Threats?" Tommen echoed. "What's going on?"

"Right now, Tommen, we're asking you if you want to come with us to the Wheel to...watch and shadow us in our investigation," Micah went on. "You do nothing we do not ask, but the way it's going, there could be some serious consequences in it for all of us. But Walter feels that such consequences are little compared to what could happen."

"So you're asking me if I want to help you, and that by helping you, we could all be in trouble?"

"You are not even an Apprentice; you should not have to get involved at all. We're in murky water as it is. We're only asking if you want to come with us."

"Sure, but...what's the danger? I mean, going to the Wheel and coming back, it's like no time passes at all, isn't it?"

Micaiah sighed. "There are ways. But if you're coming, tell us now."

"Yeah, I'm coming." Sounded like a neat adventure before coming back to work.

He stood. "Good. Come on, then. Time's wasting."

Then Micah and Micaiah opened a portal to the Wheel, stepped through, and Tommen followed.

Chapter Thirteen
The Wheel of Time

Opening a portal to the Wheel was not something Tommen would learn officially until he was a Journeyman, but even he knew it was a Herculean task. The Wheel was not a planet, not an asteroid or other celestial body; it was not a space station or other man-made celestial element. For lack of better word, the Wheel of Time was a man-made self-sustaining dimension that acted as the hub of the Time industry from all corners of the universe. Essentially, every time a Timekeeper, or someone who was trained, opened a portal to the Wheel, they were literally ripping open a door between dimensions and stepping through it. This was no small feat, hence why Tommen would not learn it until he was Journeyman, although he'd been told that he would not truly master it by himself until he was a Master Timekeeper.

Micah and Micaiah, by opening the portal together and both shouldering the burden, it was less of a strain on them. Still, as they stepped through, they both dropped to a knee and tried to catch their breath. Appropriately, there were sick bags within easy reach, and Micah utilized one of these.

"If the Wheel is supposed to be so advanced, why can't they make the portal and the journey easier?" Tommen wondered. Even just stepping through the portal, though he'd had no part in creating or shouldering it, was a dizzying experience and he stumbled drunkenly for a moment before deciding it was best to just sit down and wait until the vertigo passed.

"It's better than it used to be, if you can believe it," Micaiah told him, shifting around until he was sitting with his knees drawn up. "Back in the day, humans used to completely pass out when they came through. And way before our time, only Wardens and above could make the portals and survive. Sometimes, humans would make portals, but halfway through them, they would pass out and they'd never be heard from again. They wouldn't cross through to the Wheel, but they wouldn't fall back out to Earth. Just *poof!* Gone."

"Where did they go?"

Micaiah shrugged. "No one knows. Legends say that there's some sort of 'Land in Between' from which no one has ever returned. That's why Journeymen are taught how to open the portals, but they can't do it by themselves until they become Masters. Reduces the number of fatalities."

"Oh."

Micaiah patted Micah on the back where he still lay curled up, sick bag in hand. "You okay, brother?"

Micah held up a finger for a moment before finally nodding and sitting up. "Yeah, I think I'll be okay now."

"Sure?"

"Yeah."

"If you say so."

Gradually, the three of them stood.

The portal room was the only part of the Wheel that had any kind of sci-fi look to it, at least as dictated by the standards of twenty-first century Earth. It was an enormous room, one Tommen did not care to measure, but its metal panel floor extended as far as the eye could see and could accommodate literally hundreds of thousands of portals. The portals did not actually close once they'd been opened, not until either the original opener went back through or it was forcefully closed, but that took as much effort as opening it. So theoretically, Tommen could walk through any open portal into any world and then walk back into the Wheel.

Of course, this presented a number of problems, not the least of which being that of a questionable atmosphere. He could walk through a portal into a world and be perfectly fine, or he could drop dead instantly because of toxic gas. It was easy to think that creatures often passed through one another's portals—after all, where did Sasquatch come from, and why was he so rarely seen except that he was usually just an alien passing through—but about ninety percent of the time, alien species rarely wanted anything to do with each other. Cultures were far removed from each other, languages were a major obstacle despite the translators, and typically, there was very little interest. Other than haggling in the marketplaces and occasionally sharing warnings and information about Runners, alien species did not speak to each other often.

That didn't mean that Tommen couldn't wonder and be in awe of the different worlds as they passed by them. One portal led into total darkness, and Tommen created a thousand stories of what lay in that darkness. A fugitive Runner who had to keep his activities secret. A bat-like creature of darkness who lived in some sort of cave. Maybe an entire world that was big and bright and beautiful but could not be seen through the narrow eyes of humans.

Another portal led to a huge, bustling city with streets ten cars wide but with no cars, only creatures that might have been the end result of a pig having incest with a naked mole rat and then getting it on in a threesome with a vampire bat. The buildings, if they were buildings, were tall and spindly, twisting like cheese that wanted to stay on the pizza as the slice was lifted farther and farther up, just stretching thinner and thinner but still not breaking.

Still a third portal led to some kind of jungle, leaves appearing a bluish color until being hit by sunlight when they turned silver. Tommen spotted a small creature creeping under a large leaf that almost looked like a cat got it on with a cockroach. Oh, the strange specimens of the universe.

The portals were set up in rows, like infinitely long corridors of nothing but doors, except the portals could be entered through either side. No one quite knew exactly how many rows there were or how many doors in each row, but estimates put the number of rows at about a thousand and the counter had stopped counting portal positions at another thousand.

So it was quite a walk from their specific portal just to the door to the rest of the Wheel. Tommen looked around at the walls. They, too, were proper sci-fi walls, metal panels with tubes and wires and other miscellaneous gizmos, gadgets, and blinking lights, all snaking their way up toward a ceiling that was black, hidden from view so it was impossible to tell just how high the room was. Supposedly, the make-up of the room and all the equipment helped to focus the spatial and temporal energy needed to create the portals, narrowing the fields and sending the energy through the rods of each row until an empty spot was found and a portal could be opened.

Perhaps the strangest thing about the walls was the way they almost seemed relative to the floor. Tommen could focus on a single panel of a certain arrangement of flashing lights, and forty doors later, that panel would still be in the same spot, as if the walls didn't move, and the floor was either some type of treadmill, or was completely detached from the walls and merely suspended.

Despite the walk, they reached the front portion of the room in good time, and no worse for wear. Micah and Micaiah seemed readily recovered as they headed to a wall with a panel and a hole, Tommen trailing like an eager puppy.

There were no written signs in the Wheel. No universal language had been created for the simple fact that there were too few sounds that even half of the species involved in Time could make within reason of understandability. Instead, anything that needed to be marked was done so with pictures and symbols. Generally speaking, an eye was an eye. There were also common symbols for "ear", "tongue", "Time", and numbers up to a billion.

The panel they approached was marked with the symbols for "mouth" and "ear," the translator dispenser.

The Hands had no shortage of secretaries, and an entire legion of them was dedicated solely to the translation program, like Google Translate, except it actually worked. Of course, the translators were not perfect. The army of translation secretaries worked tirelessly to keep the linguistic software up-to-date, but there were always regional and familial slangs that would never get through, even with explanation. The translators were different for each species and a small sample of flesh was all the dispenser needed in order to recognize the species and spit out the appropriate device, like a diabetic pricking his finger to get a blood sample.

For humans, the translator was designed as a soft fabric collar that went around the neck to hold it in place on the vocal chords, and an attached earpiece which would receive any spoken language and translate it for the wearer. The two parts combined resulted in, among Earth-side languages, about a ninety-nine percent accuracy rate. Two speaking parties typically had to be within a few feet of each other in order to be picked up; it helped to cut down on background noise being translated, but the sensitivity could be adjusted. A few small buttons on the collar let the wearer choose his spoken and receiving language. To no one's surprise, the twins chose Irish and Tommen chose Welsh.

"All right, is everyone set up where and how they want to be?" Micaiah asked.

Tommen found it amusing that he could see Micaiah speaking Irish, could even hear him to an extent, and yet the earpiece of his translator still rendered it in Welsh.

"So, what are we here to do?" Tommen wondered.

"We're here to...*research* the candidates for the upcoming election," Micah said diplomatically. "You are here in order to better familiarize yourself with the election process because of your upcoming review. Most importantly, you are here to keep an ear out and see things that we don't see. Because we're officers, people will sweet-talk us and tell a lot of lies and try a lot of bribes and tricks. Your job is to see what they say behind our backs and what other deals they're making. As a probie, you are practically invisible. Use it to your advantage."

Walter had taught Tommen a number of things about code-talking, key words or phrases to pick up on and how to respond appropriately. It was one way in which Walter had also become a very good hostage negotiator, able to talk to a victim and get information that couldn't be said explicitly.

"I know I'm not too familiar with the elections, but I have to ask," Tommen said, "are there any humans in the running? I know I can't vote, but if I could, I mean, I'd be partial to them."

Micaiah smiled. He knew what Tommen was doing. "I think there is, but I can't say which position he's running for. Probably the Scientifically Advancing and Unengaged Civilizations rep, but you never know. His name is Calis, or that's what we think his name is. He's a Timekeeper like us."

"If I find him, do you want me to see if he'll come so I can introduce him to you? Us minor races have to stick together, you know."

Micah nodded. "Yeah, if you can convince him. But just be careful. Politicians are the same anywhere you go."

And with that, they exited the portal room, Tommen feeling very much like James Bond out on a super secret world-saving mission.

The rest of the Wheel was not appropriate to twenty-first century Earth science fiction standards. Actually, it seemed more like the sloppy paintings of a child who would one day grow up to be a scientist and make those sloppy paintings become something wonderful and useful and wholly unnecessary.

The majority of the Wheel was dedicated to the buying and selling of Time, but it also had to cater to thousands of alien species, each with different needs. Tommen was told that the translator had some sort of dual-capability to generate a tiny personal atmosphere around him, but the atmosphere was the least of alien needs.

For the most part, the Wheel was a mix of translucent colors, all the walls translucent gray, the floor translucent blue, and the ceiling translucent silver. There were swirls and designs mixed in, and while everything looked and felt like glass, it was as hard as diamond, if not harder. And the translucency was mostly just for show or to let light in; from where it came, Tommen did not know, as there was always just a constant light in the Wheel. No light bulbs, light bars, light beams, or anything. It's like light simply was.

And it wasn't like the translucency let him see rooms above or below or beside them, because it didn't. There were no rooms above or below or beside them. Portals took them wherever they needed to go, but the set-up was a serious mind-fuck. Portals stood open in the middle of the floor. Walking through one way went to one room, walking through the other side led to another room.

That wasn't even considering that there were stairs that led up into the wall where, by walking up to the top, gravity literally changed, and Tommen could walk on the walls or ceiling just as easily as being on the floor, no dizziness or head rush. And there were portals open on the walls and ceiling with the same configuration as the ones on the floor. If it could be considered the floor. A few times around the room going from floor to wall to ceiling and back to wall to floor, and the words started to lose meaning. Like trying to view the painting *Relativity* and have it make sense.

"Where should we start?" Tommen wondered, trying to catch up to the twins.

"You keep an ear out in the lower marketplaces," Micah told him. "We're going to make some formal appearances so we can be formally bribed."

There was no shortage of marketplaces in the Wheel, as could be expected, and they were largely divided by the amount of Time to sell. The marketplaces themselves were probably the most normal thing about the Wheel. Any civilization that was able to use Time, whether openly or not, had some idea of commerce and economy. Replace Time with cocoa beans, cows, precious gems, or anything at all, and the laws of supply and demand were pretty universal, Tommen thought. Different species had different ways of setting up their allotted sales locations, but money transcended all interstellar barriers.

Time Capsules containing less than one Base Second to one

Base Minute were so worthless as to be given away, dumped in baskets at each merchant's table like free samples of candy or hot sauce. Supposedly, there were actually different grades of purity to the Time Capsules, but Tommen figured that was more in the realm of the Harvesters. He didn't need to buy Time, not when his use of Banding would keep him young. Well, there was the super-aging possibility of it, in which case he probably should stock up.

There was also the marketplace for one Base Minute to one Base Hour, the marketplaces of one Base Hour to half a Base Day, half a Day to a whole Day, and so on until the traditional markets reached the one Base Year to ten Base Years. Once the Time Capsules got that high, they went to auction, and even the auctions were divided into classes, from ten Years to fifty Years or more. Tommen had once heard that Lily held the human record for auction pricing, a One Hundred Year Capsule going for a billion turns. But the all-time record was for a One Thousand One Hundred Seventy-Two Year Time Capsule that topped out at almost a trillion turns. That record had been standing for over seventy years now. Tommen wondered what species that Capsule had come from and what the Harvester had done to get it, and what he had done with all his riches.

Harvesters and Merchants got a cut of the profits from their Time Capsules, and their riches were entirely dependent on how well the Capsules did at auction. Lily had no problem amassing a fortune. Other Harvesters were on the verge of starvation. Timekeepers and Scouts were paid on salary. Tommen wouldn't start getting paid until he started his Apprenticeship, and even then, it wasn't like working for the bakery. He didn't get paid by the hour for being a Timekeeper. He got a hundred-turn advance just for making it to his Apprenticeship, then ten turns every month after that plus another five for every skill he learned.

"What are you doing here?"

Tommen blinked back to reality as an alien—which he honestly initially mistook for a giant pile of poop—stood in front of the portal to the High Auctionhouse.

"Do you have an invitation?" the thing asked.

"Um, no," Tommen said, already slinking away even as the giant poop pile started yelling at him to get lost. He looked back just in time to see that the giant poop pile was actually more resembling some sort of intergalactic slug. Then it was gone through the portal into the Auctionhouse. The portal closed behind it; the auction was about to begin.

So maybe his assumption about the alien races wanting little to do with each other had been a little presumptive. There was still the fact that he was merely a probie, and he was a Timekeeper probie at that. That basically meant that he was an idiot about Time-related things, in training to become about as useless a police officer as the industry needed because they were corrupt anyway, and not rich enough to merit an invitation to any of the auctions. Hell, he didn't even have any money to spend at the non-Time marketplaces.

There were fewer of them, but there were a few marketplaces where intergalactic wares were sold. It wasn't as exciting as spaceship parts, blasters, or teleportation devices, but it was interesting to see the craftsmanship of other worlds as different species utilized their basic biological capabilities and talents.

One species were like Loch Ness Polar Bears with hands that could bend back and forth. Supposedly they had different perceptions in their eyes, something other than rods and cones, and they wrote stories in ice by sculpting them. Somehow, the shaping of the ice molded different characters and worlds and plots, and by viewing the sculptures from different angles, different parts of the stories were revealed. Some contained songs, and the most skilled of sculptors could even carve music into the ice.

None of this could be seen or heard by Tommen, but that wasn't to say that the standing sculptures alone weren't interesting. They weren't of swans or hearts or anything recognizable really, but he thought that just maybe he could pick up on a faint trace of the stories kept within them.

After a short time, Tommen grew depressed at seeing the

wares but having no money. Turns could be exchanged into any local currency, but not the other way around. Eventually he decided he should probably do as he said and help the twins. But where to start? How did one approach a literal alien and strike up a conversation?

In Earth-side science fiction, there were generally two types of aliens: the ones from *Star Trek* which, being humans in costume, were pretty much all humanoid, so that even the poorest Trekkie fan could dress up for ComiCon with minimal effort; and then there were the aliens from *Star Wars*—new *Star Wars*, that is—which were eighty percent CGI so as to look like actual aliens. Well, there was also a third type, if it could be considered as such, and they were the "fantasy" aliens, like the Ents of Middle Earth, the Elderlings of the Six Duchies, and dragons from every fantasy story known to man.

The aliens found in the Wheel were a mixture of all of them, leaning heavily on the *Star Wars*. They came in all shapes and sizes, with any number of arms, legs, and other assorted appendages. Some had ten eyes that saw all around, others had no eyes and appeared to get by with feelers all around the body. Some gave him a hard, threatening regard like he was some kind of enemy, and others paid him no regard at all.

So what did he do? Walk up to the alien that was thirty feet tall, looking a spider had sex with a jellyfish, tap it on one of its shoulders and ask if it had seen a murderer walking around? Maybe he could start with a humanoid alien, just so he could shake off the jitters. Tommen was never very good at public speaking when he was in front of his own kind. There was no way he was going to be able to strike up a conversation with an alien.

He zeroed in on an alien that put him in mind of a Cardassian. The Cardassians weren't "friends" per se of the Federation, but they weren't really enemies, were they? Could he apply that logic here?

"Excuse me," he began, trying to sound friendly. "Excuse me, can I ask you a question?"

The alien looked at him and Tommen had to force himself to keep walking as if he were simply walking up to the service counter at

Kmart. This was not like any alien on TV. The alien had no lips that he could see, and all its teeth were bared, sharp, pointed teeth, ringed with tan and black. As he got closer, Tommen could see that the alien's tan skin was actually more like hard armor, like a turtle's shell.

"What is it?" the alien snapped.

"Um," Tommen said, momentarily forgetting why he was there. "I'm looking for a candidate. For the Hands. His name is Calis. He's human. I think he's running for the—"

"Get away from me, white thing!" The alien took a menacing step toward him. "And do not speak to me again."

Tommen's heart skipped a beat as he took a step back, turned on his heel, and hurried away. Had he said something wrong? Was there any way to tell? Trash and treasure and all that, what was a common pleasantry to one species was a grave offense to another. One of the first lessons learned in the Time industry was to not take offense at everything for that very reason. Maybe that guy had missed that day of class.

He tried making conversation with non-humanoid species, trying to tell himself it was like confiding in a dog or cat or other animal, but when that animal started talking back, it freaked him out a little. Not that it really mattered much since most species wanted little to do with him or the elections anyway. The best answer he got actually did come from the spider-jellyfish thing, and she had simply and politely replied that, no, she hadn't seen a human named Calis because she did not know of a politician by that name.

So Tommen was left to sulk and wonder where to go and how to break the language-culture-species barrier and get them to talk to him.

Except one thing had already broken that barrier, and it was the reason they were all there right now. Money.

Tommen returned to the main hub of the marketplaces, which was really just a large room with portals set up strategically on various walls and the ceiling to denote the class of marketplace. On the floor, again if it was actually the floor, were eight portals for the lowest classes of marketplace, from one Base Minute to one Base Hour. On another wall, nine portals leading to yet a slightly higher class. And so on it went. Thirty-one marketplaces in all, and these were only the lower markets. The intermediate or modest markets were far more numerous and that much more expensive.

Micah and Micaiah had really only asked him to keep an ear out, not necessarily to start interrogating anyone. What was he, a cop? Assuming Timekeepers could even be compared to Earth-side police, Walter was a Captain, and Tommen was basically not even entering the police academy. Like, he was still working on the paperwork to get accepted into police academy. He had no business even trying to pretend to be a cop. His best bet would be to just walk through the marketplaces unsuspectingly and see if any interesting bits of gossip popped up.

Reluctantly, Tommen increased the range on his translator and stepped through one of the portals to a marketplace. Immediately, he was bombarded with sound and noise and conversation and sights and colors. It was like stepping into the world's largest flea market except there was only one product.

Vendors and customers bought, sold, haggled, shouted, argued. Time Capsules of all shapes and sizes littered the ground. Tommen picked up an empty one, marked with the universal Time symbols for forty-two Base Seconds. Depending on the species and the average life span and life expectancy, forty-two seconds could be a rip-off or a steal.

Expanding the translator's range let him catch a broader range of conversation, but it also decreased the accuracy of the more distant conversations. Within about fifteen to twenty feet, everything was as true-to-form as the translators would get, but by about a hundred feet, he might only catch one word in twenty, and that was assuming he could pinpoint where that conversation was coming from. It wasn't as if he could on any one particular voice and the translator could read his thoughts and focus on that one, too. He would have to move around and do things the old-fashioned way, like playing Hot and

Cold.

Ninety percent of the conversations he came across were, as expected, related to the selling of Time, and more than once, a Time Capsule was shoved in his face as the Merchant screamed at him to buy, buy, buy now. Good prices, good quality Time, many options to choose from, any price range, good deals. Tommen wondered how he was supposed to sift through the noise and find any specific conversation, never mind one about Calis.

The remaining noise was a mixture of insults traded back and forth between grouchy Merchants and unhappy buyers, conspiracies between two or more parties about how to swindle a Merchant or steal from them outright, and plans for later on in the day.

There was something else to be considered, Tommen thought, as he left that marketplace and returned to the marketplace hub. If the twins had been good enough to say that Calis was in the election, that meant that they figured he was a very powerful Timekeeper. And a Warden or a Dominion Timekeeper wouldn't waste time puttering around in the lower markets. He would be like Micah and Micaiah, making pleasantries with other candidates, making and accepting bribes, fabricating all sorts of stories, buying votes, doing the things that politicians do. So even if Calis wasn't an actual candidate, he would probably be hanging around with them.

Which meant that either Tommen had been sent here to be out of their way out of some sense of "protecting" him — which wouldn't make sense given that they hadn't let him stay behind because they thought it too dangerous — or else they thought he had some kind of accomplice who wasn't important enough to merit an invitation to the high-end auctions or the other snooty events reserved for the elections. It was probably the accomplice's job to cover up Calis' activities and make sure he got into office.

There was another option, though. He could just be overreacting and coming up with wild conspiracies, like he was some lame character in some lame young adult trilogy where dumb teenagers outsmart a corrupt and evil government scheme, proving that wit and dumb luck always win against well-thought-out plans, guns, armored vehicles, and advanced technology. Yeah. Right. Tommen had an ego and he knew it, but he wasn't dumb.

He left the marketplace hub and made his way to another area of the Wheel, a room that bore a resemblance to the portal room except with real doors made of steel or some such thing, and only half as many. This was the Arena, the training grounds for Timekeepers in order to practice their skills in a safer and more controlled environment. Probies were not allowed in, and Apprentices and Journeymen had to be accompanied by a Master or higher.

What if Calis or his accomplice was hiding in there? Tommen would never know.

At the same time, what did he expect to do if he did actually find who he was looking for? Mirandize them? For goodness' sake, Calis was murdering people and they were barely putting up any resistance. There was no way Tommen was going to be able to do anything, and that was assuming he could move at all instead of standing there like a deer in headlights.

He sighed and closed his eyes. He was only here to listen for conversation about the murders. Except there wouldn't be any. Not only for the noise and the confusion, but because Calis would be hiding in the higher places where Tommen couldn't go.

One of the doors opened and a Timekeeper pair stepped out. Humanoid, but uninterested in him. After they'd gone, Tommen walked up to the door. It had no handle that he could see, and no random taps or hits produced any hidden panels. Feeling like an idiot, he turned and walked away, hoping no one had witnessed it.

"There you are."

Tommen had just stepped through the portal from the main training room to some other part of the Wheel when he heard Micah's voice. The twins approached him.

"Everything okay?" Tommen wondered.

"Fine." But Micah's disposition, to say nothing of his hasty answer, said everything was not fine. "We're just heading to get something to eat and take a little break from politics."

To call the Food Court a food court was a gross misrepresentation of what it really was. A food court implied something like a marketplace where vendors set up stalls selling product. The Food Court of the Wheel, however, was far more intricate. For one, the Wheel did not treat food as an industry, simply a basic necessity of life.

Like the marketplaces and the training grounds, the Food Court had a main hub with portals leading to a variety of food dispensaries, most of which were simply various landscapes carefully farmed with an infinite number of food sources. One portal led into an area designed for species who hunted their food and, to an extent, consumed it raw. Another area was for those who fed on rocks, salts, and minerals. A third area was for those who ate waste and carrion. And on and on it went for various disciplines of vegetarianism, veganism, pescatalianism, even cannibalism.

The portal that Tommen and the twins walked through led to what might have been considered a cross between a traditional food court, like one might find in a mall, and a restaurant. The largest salad bar Tommen had ever seen ran in a dozen rows in the center of the place, boasting not just the usual lettuce, spinach, and cheese, but a variety of exotic fruits, vegetables, leaves, nuts, and things Tommen couldn't properly classify. To go down even just one row was to need four or five plates.

Around the court were a number of vendors serving up made-to-order meat-based meals, the kind where the animal was kept in back, butchered on the spot, and prepared right there. Needless to say, sanitary regulation in the Wheel was a little more lax than in Charleston.

The Food Court vendors were like the secretaries, employees of the Wheel and the Hands themselves, coming from a variety of backgrounds and species. Tommen wondered if they worked shifts and went home to their planets, or if they just stayed in the Wheel.

Tommen had to smirk as he followed the twins to a small

section of tables. Here he was in some man-made dimension, sitting among a thousand alien species, and he was still able to get a cheeseburger with all the fixings. Granted, it was a little different than what he might get at a normal backyard barbecue, but it was a cheeseburger nonetheless.

"How did your research go?" Micah asked Tommen casually as he stuck his utensil—which was supposed to be some kind of...fork?—into his salad.

Tommen shook his head. "I really couldn't find anything." He took a bite of his burger.

Oh, if there was a God, this was probably heaven. When Tommen finally learned how to open the portal to the Wheel, he would never have to go hungry. And he would have more variety to choose from than the biggest all-you-can-eat buffet. And he could get gourmet food without paying gourmet prices.

"I do have a question, though," Tommen said. "Why are the lower marketplaces so crowded? I get that not all species live as long as humans, but...three seconds?"

Micaiah frowned as he used chopsticks to eat some kind of Chinese-looking dish. "Time is like a drug, Tommen. It can help, but it can also be addictive, and the thing that feeds a Time-addiction is fear, an awful fear of death."

"But how is, you know, four minutes going to—?"

"It's all psychological," Micah continued. "It's staving off a natural death using the same concept as, say, saving up for your first car. Sure, foregoing dessert at lunch and saving a buck or two every day doesn't sound like much until you realize that by the end of the year, you've pocketed two to three hundred dollars. The whole idea of buying such small Time Capsules is banking those seconds until they become years."

"But it's better to buy in bulk," Tommen pointed out.

"That's where the addiction mentality comes in. As soon as you have enough money to buy a Time Capsule, you buy it. Some might save up to buy an hour or a day, but the worst addicts just go for seconds at a time, not even realizing that in the time it takes to save up and buy the capsule, they've already wasted more than a hundred times what is contained and they could have been doing something else, something real with their lives."

"Why buy it, though, if most in the Time industry already suffer life-prolonging side effects?"

"Only Time Agents experience those," Micaiah went on. "But civilizations who are considered Engaged, their citizens can come and go as they please. The Time Agents of those worlds work like any average 9-5er, and the non-Time Agents buy from the Merchants like it's a normal stop on errand day."

Tommen nodded and took another bite of his burger. "So that explains why I didn't see any humans in the marketplaces."

"Most likely," Micah confirmed. "Timekeepers who end up suffering from the accelerated aging process are usually the only ones who buy Time at all. That and Merchants, but Merchants will 'accidentally' drop a Capsule and lose a sale before they buy one, usually in order to avoid paying taxes on the sales."

So basically, Time was a drug. The Hands were the drug lords, the Harvesters were the growers and the makers, the Merchants were the dealers, and the Timekeepers were the muscle to intimidate and keep order according to the whims of the lords. Wonderful. So what did that make the Scouts and the Grandfathers?

"What does it take to get an invitation to the auctions?" Tommen wondered.

Micah shrugged. "Rank, usually, unless you are somehow a very wealthy underling. The higher your rank, the more prestigious auctions you can get into. There are some auctions we can't get into that Walter can, and some are closed even to him."

Tommen nodded. For a time they sat and people-watched. This court was one of the least busy ones, and they even spotted a couple humans across the room. After a minute, they managed to flag them down.

"Master Johan Ljós and Journeyman Petyr Móse, Region Six,

District Two," the elder of the two men said as they approached. He was an older man, maybe fifty years old in appearance with blond hair and blue eyes, built like a grizzly bear. His counterpart was a younger man no older than thirty, also blond hair and blue eyes, but as lanky and awkward as Tommen.

Region Six, the UK and Scandinavia. District Two, Scandinavia. That explained it, then. There were not a lot of Time Agents in that District and Tommen knew there had been arguments for years over whether they should have their own District. To hear Walter tell it, Scandinavia only kept their District because of general undisguised animosity for the UK, or at least their Time Agents, and threats of dissent if they were ever forced to share a District. Because...drama?

"Lieutenants Micaiah and Micah Durvin, Probationary Tommen Forbes, Region Four, District Four," Micaiah replied smoothly.

"What brings you to the Wheel, Lieutenants?" Johan asked amiably.

"Nothing good. The elections." That earned a chuckle. "Do you know anyone by the name of Calis? Specifically Calis Cutthroat? Dark skin, bad temper?"

The two men glanced at each other and shook their heads in honest ignorance. "No, but the name does not sound friendly."

"He's murdered two people, and we think he's hiding around here."

"That is most unfortunate. You think he is one of the Hand candidates?"

"Hard to be certain. We hope not."

"As do we. It's bad enough that money changes hands in these elections. The last thing we need is an exchange of blood as well. We will keep an eye out for him."

"That's all we can ask. But what brings you here, Master?"

Johan beamed. "Petyr, my young Journeyman friend. We are here training. His review is coming up very soon. I will be sad to let him go, but he has learned all I can teach."

"Well, good luck on your review," Micah told him, shifting in his seat. "We will let you get back to training then."

It was a dismissal. The Scandinavians bid them good day and moved off, their conversation turning back into their native tongue as they moved out of range of the translators.

"So, it's time to discuss your review, too," Micaiah said, turning back to Tommen who was just finishing the last of his burger.

"Huh?" Tommen wondered dumbly and swallowing hard. "Didn't we just go over this like a couple days ago?"

"We went over the material you're expected to know, but there is more to the review than just knowing your stuff."

Tommen leaned back in his seat. "Okay...so, what am I looking at?"

"When your review date is finally set—which I believe Walter said was in January—it is expected that you will refrain from using any of your abilities for the week leading up to it. It isn't required, but it demonstrates another crucial ability. Self-control. You will be marked up or down based on how well you handle that week, less extenuating circumstances."

"What kind of extenuating circumstances?" Tommen wondered.

"The kind you're not likely to face," Micah told him. "It's more for the benefit of higher-ranked Timekeepers. Same principle for our review, but extenuating circumstances for us would be like having to catch our murderous Runner."

Tommen shrugged. "Whatever. What else do I have to do?"

"It is also expected that you present yourself as the best representation of your species as possible. That means a shower, a shave, clean clothes, and your best behavior. Think of it like your dad going to meet the president, and he has to present himself as an ambassador of Charleston PD."

Funny thing was, Walter actually had met the president. Well, a president. And to hear him tell it, Nixon wasn't much to behold.

Might have been a nice guy to go and have a drink with, might have had some good ideas at one time as a bright-eyed new politician, but in the end, he was just like everyone else.

"Will I be marked down for this kind of stuff?"

"It's not a grade. This is pass or fail. Fifty-one Hands and you have to convince thirty-seven of them that you have what it takes to be a Timekeeper."

Tommen raised a brow. "Thirty-seven? That's, like, way more than a majority. Majority would be twenty-six."

"It's not about a majority, Tommen," Micaiah told him severely. "These are the rules we play by. You either play by them, take your chances as a Runner, or walk away. Now is the time to choose, because it only gets harder from here."

"I'm not walking away."

Micaiah grinned. "Good answer."

"What else do I have to do?"

"You will be taken to the Coliseum where you will be made to wait. The Coliseum is like the Judgment Wing; all Time abilities are suspended. It's not a matter of willpower that you won't use them, but some kind of dampening field technology that makes it so you can't use them."

Tommen had to admit that thought kind of unnerved him. He'd grown so used to having Time at his beck and call. As if not being allowed to Band for a week was bad enough, now he wouldn't even be able to Band? Another thought crossed his mind. Did that make him as much of a Time-addict as those in the cheap marketplaces?

"When you are finally called," Micah went on, "Walter will stay and you will be escorted to stand alone before the Seat of the Hands. What happens there is unique to everyone and is not to be discussed. The Hands will send their final report to Walter with either a pass or a fail. Assuming you pass, you can begin your Apprentice training just as soon as you recover."

"Wait, recover?"

Micah smirked, but Micaiah maintained a serious, even grim, expression. "Not to be discussed."

Tommen let out a breath. "Okay. But I do have a question."

"Fire away." Micaiah shifted in his seat.

"I...kinda got in another fight with Tyler the other day. But this was a little different." In more ways than one, but there was no need for them to think it was anything other than the usual fight. No need to worry them by mentioning he'd thrown the first punch this time. "When he was trying to hit me, I...I don't know, I could, like, see where he was going to hit, where he was aiming. And I could avoid it."

The twins nodded; it was Micaiah who answered. "That's a little trick we like to call Predict. If it has to be taught, it's normally reserved for Apprentices, one of the first things they learn. But it's not uncommon for some probies to make that breakthrough on their own."

"What does it do?"

"It just lets you see the current projected path of a moving object," Micah told him.

"Will I see everything that way now, or can I turn it on and off?"

"Generally it takes either focus or a heightened emotional response. Watching something from a distance, probably focus. Fighting for your life, emotional response." He shrugged. "Really, there's nothing to it. Essentially, your mind is taking basic physics and constructing a visual model for you to act on."

"Oh." Tommen mulled that over for a minute. So basically, he could now see where Tyler was going to throw his punches. Or where, say, the basketball was likely to rebound to, or any of a thousand things. "So, even though it's already set, how is my review scheduled?"

Micaiah shrugged. "The only ones who know that are the Hands, and by the Hands I mean their secretaries, and Walter when they finally schedule you."

"So he can't, like, set it up like a dentist appointment?"

"He can file a request for a range of dates and times," Micah continued, "but ultimately it's up to the secretaries, and they're not always good about reconciling the Wheel's calendar with Earth's calendar."

"So they could literally schedule me at three in the morning? Or right in the middle of a school day?"

"Yup. But don't worry; they're not usually that off. And if I remember right, you won't even be in school that day anyway."

Tommen sighed. "How can the Hands and the secretaries be so precise when they need to be—with the translators and the scheduling and everything else—but it seems like there is no help to be found when there's a murderer running loose?"

"A lot of it has to do with non-interference," Micaiah explained. "Because Earth is not openly engaged in the Time industry, the only time the Hands will truly step in is if Calis were to break a Law of Time or commit a crime against another species, or commit a crime on a world that is engaged, and even that depends on the crime committed."

"But...if he's a candidate...?"

Micah sighed. "The problem is, Calis himself isn't the candidate. He's only the killer."

It was like hitting Tommen in the face with a shovel. "Whoa, wait, so there's two guys in on this?"

Micaiah nodded gravely, his expression more frightening than when Tommen had been called into the office to discuss his bad attendance record. "Yes. Calis is only the instrument. His employer is the higher rank, possibly a candidate or high enough to get close to them. But the Hands don't recognize accomplices or conspiracy or any of that the same way we do on Earth. Part of it is non-interference, and part of it is this." He rubbed his thumb and forefinger together. Money. "Non-interference in their elections."

"So the Hands don't care at all that one of them has a hired hitman to do his dirty work?" Tommen wondered.

"He wouldn't be the first," Micah said, shrugging in resignation, "and he's not the only."

"Then why are we here? If the Hands can—"

"We are here to protect the Laws of Time," Micaiah cut in. "The Hands will do as they do. Our job is only to ensure the legal Harvesting, selling, and buying of Time."

Tommen blinked and shook his head. "So you don't care either."

Micaiah gave him a "Really?" look and leaned back in his chair. "You're right. It's not right. It's not fair. But there is nothing we can do about it. If we don't do our job, the Hands will send in someone who will, and that's how we get those like Calis and his employer. Difference is, they'll go completely unchecked."

Tommen folded his arms. "I heard Walter say that he thought Calis was actually targeting Lily from the children's hospital. Is that true?"

"It's one theory, yes."

"If Lily is the richest Harvester, like, ever, why wouldn't the Hands be rushing to protect her?"

Micah smirked, but it lasted for only a moment before it lapsed into a sigh. "Because there will always be others. Lily fancies herself someone important, someone the Hands and Time could never live without. But corruption and votes change hands more often than you change your socks. The Wheel would survive without her, and I doubt it would look very much different."

It was no secret that Micah disdained Lily, but the voice in which he said such things was not one of a man looking to spite or belittle an ex-lover. Rather, it was a simple stating of facts.

"So then, what keeps the Wheel running? Why doesn't it, you know, implode? Great Time Depression or something?"

"It has," Micaiah answered. "Many times, when the corruption gets too bad. But the only requirements for the government of Time are one person to fill each of the fifty-one Hands, and a change of power every seventeen years. There are no Laws stating in what manner this must occur, only that it must. Whether through honesty or corruption, election or revolution."

"What would it take for Earth to get out of Time?"

Micah shook his head. "Never happen. It would require the elimination of everyone connected to Time. That could be done, but it would only take one Runner to deliberately expose someone. Once that Runner is recruited, there has to be accountability for it; because Earth is not engaged, it must be one of our own kind. Therefore, someone must be deliberately exposed to be a Timekeeper for them. Eventually, it just spirals into where we are now."

"And what would happen if Earth became fully engaged?"

"Assuming we survived another global war and probably some kind of ensuing intergalactic war, we would probably have a time of peace, followed by as much corruption as you see here as Earth tries its damnedest to do what we do best: conquer."

Tommen let out a breath. "At this point, why should I continue with my training? Why do I want to get involved in this?"

Micaiah smiled. "Because you're a good kid, a smart kid. Despite your flaws and whatever else, you still maintain your inner sense of right and wrong. Whatever evils happen with the Hands, you are still willing to pursue justice for the regular people, those who have no clue of the secret life you lead. You're willing to take a stand and get your ass kicked, but your conscience is clear."

Tommen wasn't sure to feel encouraged or insulted by Micaiah's evaluation. He had flaws; he knew that. And yes, he was willing to stand up for people, but did he have to make such a point of the getting his ass kicked part? He'd been taught Banding early in order to avoid that as much as possible, and still it happened.

"So...is my fighting likely to count against me?" he asked, following the twins' lead as they stood and prepared to leave the Food Court.

Micaiah raised a brow and Micah grinned though he tried to hide it. "The Hands don't give half a shit about a murderer running loose. What are they going to care that a probationary Timekeeper is getting his ass kicked in school?"

It was a fair answer, but still, why did they feel the need to emphasize the ass-kicking?

"What are we doing now?" Tommen wondered as they stepped through a series of portals back to the main hub of the Wheel.

"Now we're going home," Micah told him. "We found the information we needed, and snooping isn't exactly encouraged around here."

"Oh. So you have to report to Walter now?"

"Yup."

"Is there anything you want me to do?"

Micaiah gave him a brief glance. "Just lay low and try not to get involved. Your primary focus should be studying for your review. If you learned anything—even if you think it's unimportant—tell us when we get back to the bakery. Otherwise, anything you heard...you didn't hear."

"Why did you bring me, then? I mean, it's not like you would have been gone for very long; I could have handled the counter by myself for a while." Tommen smirked, hoping to inject some humor.

Instead, all he got was a severe look from Micah. "Because for the infinitesimal moment that passes between entering and exiting the Wheel, it is possible for someone to make a move. And given the status that we believe Calis' 'employer' is, he could very well take you. Or he could forcibly collapse the portal and potentially kill both of us. It was a gamble to bring you or not bring you, and until we're actually back standing in the office, it still is a gamble."

"Oh."

Tommen had often wondered what more power there was to obtain beyond Banding and opening portals to the Wheel, but if Predict was one of the first things an Apprentice learned, and collapsing someone else's portal and potentially killing them or sending them into some unknown oblivion was an ability reserved for the highest order of Timekeepers, what else was there in the space in between?

They returned to the portal room and removed the translators before heading back toward their portal. It was like the worst case ever of finding one's parking spot, but somehow Micah and Micaiah knew exactly where they parked. The twins paused for a moment as they prepared to enter through it and shoulder the weight long enough for all three of them to pass through before closing it behind them.

Tommen envied their strength as they stepped through—the air being forcibly pulled from their lungs, and all their strength and their strength reserves being sapped. Stars exploded behind Tommen's eyes and a migraine followed.

Then they were through, stumbling to find one chair or another. The atmosphere felt different here, unfamiliar, and yet exactly what they needed. The artificial atmosphere generated by the translators just couldn't compare. Tommen rubbed his eyes as everything realigned itself and the world was upright once more.

Outside the office, the service bell dinged.

"Think you can man the counter?" Micah asked, looking very pale.

Tommen hauled himself to his feet and tried to make himself seem presentable as he exited the office.

He almost swore and returned to the office when he saw who it was. He recognized the crabby lady from the day the ovens caught fire. Miss "I-Have-Special-Dietary-Needs-So-I-Need-Everything-Done-My-Way" and such. Before, he'd been taking the trashes out and she'd flipped. Now he probably looked like he had the flu or something, the way he was feeling. She'd probably chew him out for showing up to work sick or some such thing.

He spent a good twenty minutes dealing with the lady, from assuring her that, no, he wasn't sick, he just had a headache, to washing his hands twice, once in bleach water and then once in warm soapy water because...bleach. Then, he had to basically divulge the recipes of everything in the display case—because asking if something contained nuts or Red 40 or anything at all was much less convenient than having him list not only the ingredients in the products, but the ingredients of the ingredients. And using chocolate frosting that used cocoa beans processed in the same plant as peanuts was entirely unacceptable, even if the cocoa bean plant and the frosting plant were literally thousands of miles and an ocean apart.

So he was more than delighted to sell her a plain old sugar cookie and see her on her way. And she didn't even tip, not even the loose change she got back.

"How's it going?" Micah asked when he finally came out of the office, looking about as sick as Tommen felt.

"I'm just ready for the day to be over," Tommen told him honestly.

Unfortunately, he didn't even get to leave at his regular time because, as expected, the twins had important business to discuss with Walter regarding whatever information they found. Tommen had learned long ago that it was impossible to eavesdrop on them, so instead he waited by the front door, always glad in the wintertime to work in a bakery where it was always nice and warm.

"Ready?" Walter asked as he emerged from the office.

"Been ready," Tommen replied, following him out to the car. He sighed as he went to the driver's door, but Walter stopped him and shook his head, saying, "You're too tired from the portals."

"So, is there a break in the case?" Tommen asked as they pulled out of the parking lot.

Walter let out a measured breath. "Depends on if I can get my Time-side ducks to play nice with my Earth-side ducks before this case gets shelved, too."

"Is there anything I can do to help? I mean, I might have been able to help a little more today if I had known what I was looking for a little better."

"No. They explained what you did, and you did all you could. Sometimes it pays more to be the underdog than the alpha dog."

"Do you know the name of Calis' employer?"

"I don't know. The name that came up doesn't make sense.

Which is where the Time-side and Earth-side ducks come in."

"Oh. Okay."

"We'll know soon enough, I expect."

Tommen didn't expect Walter to unload the entire case on him, but sometimes he wished Walter trusted him a little more, enough to give him something to go on. True, being the underdog might be better than being the alpha dog, but only if the underdog was smart enough to do what he needed to do in order to be an effective surprise weapon.

Still, he accepted the fact that he was barely the underdog. He was a probationary underdog. And right now, he needed to focus on his review so he could start learning some real shit and actually be of help to someone.

Chapter Fourteen
The Man With No Face

Wednesday night, woman gets killed. Thursday morning, woman's body is found. Friday afternoon, evidence is found planted at the suspected murder scene meant to send a message to Walter. Obviously, Walter already knew the perpetrator was in some way involved with Time. And, obviously, Walter himself was involved with Time and oversaw the investigation on both sides of the crime. Because Earth was not engaged in the Time industry, there was no conspiracy to bust open. None of the guys would ever believe the Walter Forbes from Beaumaris Gaol was the same one who led the murder investigation today. Calis gained nothing by communicating with Walter.

Walter circled the meeting table again, trying not to stare at the whiteboard or the map or anything else, but just be alone in his mind.

Calis Cutthroat, bloodiest mercenary from the Dispersal of '63, carries out a series of murders and then vanishes. With all the technology available for creating new identities, he could have gone anywhere, but Walter had found no mention anywhere of similar murders carried out between the Dispersal and present day.

One day, Calis is approached by Unknown Warden who contracts him to kill Lily Guile without giving him any kind of photograph or anything to go on beyond a vague description, which leads to the deaths of two more women who have little and less to do with anything.

Walter plopped down in one of the chairs and turned away from the whiteboard, determined not to look at it lest the red scribbles muddle his mind even more.

According to the twins, the only name that had been subtly passed around in the Wheel at some candidate/bribery soiree was Rifun Ndolo. Except, by all accounts, Rifun was dead. And even if, somehow, he wasn't dead, he was probably the only person truly "Wanted" by the Hands, and when the Hands got something in their collective heads, especially if it involved killing a rival, the Hands got what the Hands wanted.

He stood again and made another pass, rubbing his eyes. Dead men may not tell tales, but the speculation itself was murderous. He couldn't pander to every "what if" and "maybe." He had to work with what he knew. Except he knew he was missing something.

Eventually, he returned to his little cubicle, only to stare at the computer screen for a full five minutes. Calis or Rifun or someone else, they were baiting him. And he knew it. They knew it, too. They were probably watching from the metaphorical bushes like metaphorical hunters, rubbing their hands together and salivating as their metaphorical prey inches closer to the not-so-metaphorical snare they so ingeniously laid for him. Finally, he took a breath and opened a web browser.

"Beaumaris Gaol," he typed.

His search brought up everything from history of the prison, to tours of the now-museum, to conspiracy theories surrounding the curse supposedly bestowed upon it by its final execution. After several refinements, he finally got to the more accurate historical records — that is, the handwritten records and accounts.

For the most part, everything was exactly as it should have been. Appalling by modern standards as grievously inhumane. Appalling by ye olde standards as too comfortable. But whether it was a collection of slimy stone boxes or a luxury resort, prison was prison.

"Hey, Jim," Walter said, flagging down his partner as he walked by on some errand. "How'd you find those records for Beaumaris? The personnel records and stuff?"

"Oh, yeah, the guys at the university showed me how. Here, you have to refine your search," Standish said, stepping into the cubicle and basically doing the work for him until a few clicks of the keyboard brought up scanned-in images of the records.

"It hasn't been, I don't know, indexed yet?" Walter asked in disbelief. "It's not searchable?"

Standish shrugged. "Guess it's just not high on the indexing priority list."

"All right. Thanks, Jim."

"What are you looking for, anyway?"

"If someone with my name was in Beaumaris Gaol, maybe someone with our guy's name was also there."

"How are you going to know when you find it?"

Good question. "I don't know. Maybe it'll just hit me."

But first it would bore him to death. Beaumaris hadn't been open very long, and it wasn't particularly big, and the records weren't exactly complete, but still they were thorough. Or maybe it just seemed that way as he kept going back to the page with his name on it.

Forbes, Walter; Cell 12; Murder; February 21, 1843

He sighed and fiddled a bit with his mustache. Names weren't ringing any bells. Maybe the date was significant somehow, except that was February and this was December. Maybe Cell 12 was important, but he couldn't for the life of him figure out why. It wasn't important to him, and he didn't know enough about Calis or his employer to say if it was important to them.

After a while, he stood and stretched, refilled his coffee mug, went back to the office, decided the notes weren't helpful, and returned to his computer.

"Okay, Walter, think logically," he told himself. "Calis likes to use aliases, but they're not particularly clever and don't deviate too far from his name. Calis, Chris. Temper...Templeton? Temple? Temporal?"

It wasn't much of a hope, but it was something. God, he

wished this thing was searchable. He didn't know computers too well, but he knew how to use Ctrl+F. He didn't get too excited over one name or another, simply compiled a list which he set off to the side until he'd gone through the almost innumerable pages.

"Got anything?" Standish wondered, dropping by and leaning on the wall of the cubicle.

"A list of possible names. I was going to run through them unless you have something that will spare me hours of tedious research?"

"I wish I did. I was hoping you would have something for me so I'd be able to get a break from answering bullshit calls."

Walter shook his head. "Nothing yet. I'll let you know."

"Damn." Standish shook his head and walked away, leaving Walter with a list of almost sixty names.

He managed to match a couple names to photos or stories which eliminated them, but most of it was just tedious and slow. And really, it wasn't too terribly slow. His biggest help was elimination by skin color. After that was age. By the time he got done with all that, he had only seventeen names.

Cai Orlon, killed in an attempted escape.

Christopher Farwell, suicide.

Cal Wur, killed in a bar fight the night of his release.

Kobin Den, considered lost at sea while on passage to France. So he was a possibility at least. Walter put a star by his name.

Then he came across the next name, one he hadn't really paid attention to but suddenly grabbed his attention. He went back and, after ten painstaking minutes of trying to find the right page and get it to load on obnoxiously slow Internet, found the man again.

Hand, Cassius; Gaoler

Walter leaned back in his chair. Gaoler? How could he have been a gaoler? Just the time period, black men wouldn't have been prison guards, would they? And why would he have been a guard? Just his personality would peg him more as a prisoner. Maybe the name being so odd was just a coincidence and this wasn't Calis.

By the time he got through his list, he had only four possibilities: Kobin Den, Cassius Hand, Chris Tanner, and Cai Uwin. Problem was, like most genealogical research, once the research got so far back, names started disappearing because the common folk were forgotten. Churches kept meticulous records, but, barring fire, theft, or other catastrophe, that was assuming the family had a religious affiliation. In the case of family members being prisoners, they might also blot out names in order to preserve the family tree. Because black sheep were a taint on the white sheep, after all.

"Shit."

Walter practically dove for the phone even if it was unnecessary and punched in the numbers violently, even though that was unnecessary, too.

"Come on...pick up pick up pick up."

"Thank you for calling Bakery na hÉireann," the recording said. "We're busy baking all the fresh goodies you love, but we'll call you back as soon as possible."

Walter hung up. "Shit." He tapped his finger on the desk. He could just drive over there. After a minute or two, he called Micaiah's cell phone.

"This better be important, Walt," Micaiah said testily.

"Are you busy?" Walter asked.

To answer the question, Micaiah growled and hung up.

Walter took the opportunity to go to the bathroom and take a quick coffee break before attempting to call the bakery again. This time it was Micah who answered.

"Are you guys still busy?" Walter asked, hoping he sounded both apologetic and urgent.

"Walter, if it's so urgent, you can always come over and we can chat privately," Micah told him.

"Is that a yes?"

"Depends. Is your end of the conversation going to make you sound like a lunatic to those standing around you?"

"Good point. I'll be over."

He hated it when his enthusiasm outran his logic, but he was soon pulling into the bakery parking lot. They were less busy now, but Walter still Banded and went inside, passing Tommen at the counter, and grabbing Micah in the kitchen and taking him into the office where Micaiah scowled over some paperwork.

"I think I know why we haven't been able to find anything on Calis either in the Archives or as a Timekeeper," Walter said.

"So spit it out," Micaiah said curtly.

"I don't think he was a Timekeeper. I think those records were planted to throw us off. I think he's a Harvester."

Micah folded his arms. "How do you figure?"

Walter briefly explained his exploits to find the records of Beaumaris Gaol. "I did some digging to see if I could find any suspicious names in the prison records and the only one that really, truly stood out was Cassius Hand who was one of the guards. Back then, a black man would not be able to be a guard. But a white man would."

Micah glanced at Micaiah. "Guarding a prison...back then, conditions were less than ideal. Starvation, exposure, sickness, he would have had lots of opportunities to Harvest, and no one would bat an eye because no one cared what happened to prisoners."

Micaiah shifted in his seat. "You said that there were two suspects. Calis and a weird white guy. You think he's changing his appearance?" He shook his head. "Walt, I don't know a ton about Harvesting, but I do know that a huge change like that takes a lot of Harvesting of that particular trait and a lot of time. Going from white to black over a period of a hundred years, possible. Going from black to white in a couple weeks? I don't think so."

"He waited a month between murders," Walter pointed out. "If he's working with a Warden or a Dominion Timekeeper, how much time do you think he's had to acquire those traits?"

Micah sighed. "A lot."

"Still doesn't explain why he can't seem to get the right girl," Micaiah said. "It also doesn't tell us who his partner is."

"No," Walter admitted, "but I think I know someone who can shed some light on this."

"Lily?" Micah scoffed. "Good luck with that one. You'd have better luck sharing a steak with a lion."

"Why would she talk now when you said your first interview was less than helpful?" Micaiah asked.

"Because the first time, Lily was afraid. She knew what was coming, but she wasn't going to put a name on it. I'm going to see what happens when I put a name on it."

"How do you know Cassius Hand is his real name?"

"I don't need his real name, just the one he was using at the time."

"Lily wasn't even alive back then."

"Maybe not. But her mentor was."

Walter did not voice his suspicions that Lily was not as young and innocent as they all thought. She might profess to being young and "hardly an Apprentice" during the Dispersal, but she was not immune to lying, especially when it suited her. And if by lying she could save her skin, lie she would.

"You're sure about this?" Micaiah asked.

Walter looked at him. "No, I'm not. I'm not even sure it will be helpful or stop Calis or Cassius or whoever he is from killing again. But I have to follow all the leads. Wish me luck."

Micaiah sighed. "I don't wish you luck, Walter. I wish you sense."

Still, Walter headed purposefully out of the building to his car where he released his Band and walked casually back inside.

"So, what'd you talk about?" Tommen asked as he retrieved a pastry and a couple cookies for him.

Walter took the little white paper bag. "Sit tight, stay safe."

With that, he was on his way back toward Lily's condo. He stopped by the officers currently on stake-out duty.

"Hopefully this will make your day better," he began, handing them both a cookie which they accepted gratefully. "Anything interesting so far?"

"Nada," one said. "We did get the memo about the mystery white guy, but so far, of the six white guys with long brown hair who have passed by, they've all just...passed by."

And any one of them could have Banded, slipped upstairs, killed Lily, and you would never have known. "All right. She home?"

"Hasn't left since she got here."

"I'm going up to talk to her. Hopefully, by the time I'm done, you both can go home to your warm beds."

The other officer grinned and chuckled nervously. "Believe us, we'd like that very much."

With a short, chattering breath, Walter turned away from the car, wishing some of that sense that Micaiah wished on him would hit him before he made it to the front door to ring the buzzer. The older Durvin twin was right; he didn't need luck. He needed sense. He also needed a foot massage and a vacation, but Steggmann had explicitly excluded those things from the list of things he could ask for. He rubbed his hands together, reminded himself that it was going to get a lot worse in the coming months anyway, then finally mustered the courage and rung the buzzer.

"Who is it?" Lily asked over the intercom.

"Detective Forbes," Walter answered.

There was a pause, then the door unlocked. He tried not to hurry, didn't want to give the impression that he was kicking down the door and running up there on some urgent mission. But every step to the elevator and every second of elevator music felt like an eternity before he finally reached the penthouse and Lily opened the door to meet him.

"Well, Walter, this is very unexpected," she said pleasantly as she welcomed him into her condo. "To what do I owe the pleasure of your company?"

Walter had had enough of her bullshit and games. "Cassius Hand. Know the name?"

Her charming smile wavered, just a little, but enough that

Walter caught it. "Excuse me?"

"Cassius. Hand."

She blinked and shrugged. "I'm afraid not."

"I think you do. He was a Harvester, a guard at Beaumaris Gaol in 1847."

"Fascinating bit of history."

"Don't play games with me, Lily. You suck at it, now more than ever. You know something about him. He has something over you. What is it, secret lover? Secret child?"

"How dare you!" She slapped him then, and he knew he deserved it. Maybe he'd gone a little overboard, gotten a little too into the TV-drama cop, but he was done playing cat and mouse. Instead of pursuing that line of thought, however, he remained silent and just waited.

Finally, she sighed and nodded. "I know him. He wasn't after me, at first. He was after my mentor, Julianna. I don't know the whole story, but the way she told it, her husband was there too, in Beaumaris, locked up with you. As his guard, Cassius could leverage her to do anything."

"Sexual favors," Walter stated.

Surprisingly, Lily shook her head. "No. Cassius' only appetite is for torture and death. He was already a Runner by the time he was a gaoler, but the Hands were unwilling to pursue him because of how dangerous he was. And anyway, he Harvested the prisoners' Time only for himself."

"What did he want from her?"

"Julianna's husband was a Scout. Supposedly he had some kind of journal or diary that interested Cassius."

"Why? What was in this journal?"

Lily shrugged. "I don't know. Not even Julianna knew. But as long as her husband was in prison, she was obligated to search for that journal. If she found it, the deal was that he would be freed. She never believed Cassius would honor the agreement by himself, but it gave her hope.

"Eventually, she did find the journal. But when she turned it over to Cassius, instead of being freed, her husband was sentenced to death."

"So what did she do?"

"She broke into the prison, stole the journal back, ran, hopped the first ship to America she could find. But Cassius followed her." Lily folded her arms and went to sit in a recliner, her feet on a fuzzy footstool. "She ended up following in your footsteps, Walter. Yours...and your boy's."

A knot twisted in Walter's stomach. "What do you mean?"

"Everyone knew about the salt cave, Walter, how it was essentially a time machine to the future. Tommen stumbled into it accidentally, and you followed. Julianna ran into it, hoping to escape Cassius, but he pursued her even there. She hid the journal in some old miner's bones before going deeper into the cave. Somehow, Cassius got to her. He pierced her hands and cut her face, but in the end, she got away, landing in 1943."

"So where do you come in?" Walter wondered.

Lily ran her tongue over her teeth. "Julianna was back then what I am now—extremely rich, extremely influential. Jumping a hundred years into the future had made her empire crumble. Seeing what had happened, she volunteered to be a nurse in World War II, get as close to the chaos as possible, hope to ride out both storms. That is how I came to be introduced to the Time industry."

"Something tells me Cassius didn't give up."

She shook her head. "Not by a long shot. He still thought she had the journal or had stashed it away somewhere, maybe given it to someone. Between World War II and the Dispersal, he had every excuse to kill as much as possible, as many as possible, looking for the damn thing. Being hired by one Hand or another just brought in a little spare change. He finally succeeded in killing her in Vietnam. But..." Lily shrugged again. "She didn't have the journal."

Walter let out a breath and sat down in another chair. "If he knew she had taken it into the salt cave, he might have thought she stashed it there. So when he killed her and she didn't have it, he went back to look for it. He comes out, and it's present day. That would explain how he knew about you, knew roughly what you looked like, but why he has zero clue about how to use the Internet to find an actual photo."

"It would," Lily confirmed.

"You said you were barely an Apprentice during the Dispersal of '63, but you just told me Julianna Harvested you during World War II. What were you doing for twenty years?"

Now her expression turned thoughtful, even sad, something Walter didn't think her capable of feeling. "Living in denial, mostly. I lost my husband overseas, and I spent twenty years watching my friends and family grow old and die while I stayed more or less youthful. I didn't return to Julianna until 1962."

"Why wait to tell me this?"

"For what purpose? It's nice exposition, but how does it help you solve your case?"

"Because it tells me who I'm looking for and why he's acting the way he does. But I do have to ask something. Is it possible, in your Harvesting, how you sometimes acquire traits of the victims you Harvest, for someone to change skin color, from stark white to stark black and back again?"

Lily looked thoughtful. "You're talking about Cassius?"

"Yes."

"Cassius always had dark skin, or so Julianna claimed. I mean, yes, it is possible, but only from years of exposure and only Harvesting black or white people. Or any trait, eye color, hair color, face shape. But between a hundred-year jump and a forty-year jump, and considering that I don't think he went on a whole lot of humanitarian missions to Africa, I really don't think that, even if he was white, that he would have turned black so quickly."

"Damn. So that puts turning black to white out of the picture, too. In, say, a month?"

"Absolutely. And, as much as I know you espouse the

greatness of the Timekeepers and all, Walter, but, not even a Dominion Timekeeper could generate enough Time for that to happen, not the way it would have to happen."

"Damn. So I'm still looking for two guys."

"Two guys?"

Walter gave her the description of the second guy. He found himself not liking the frown on Lily's face.

"The only Warden I know of with a description like that was Rifun Ndolo. I met him once before the Dispersal."

"His name has come up several times, but he was killed. His body was found in a river in Madagascar in the seventies."

Lily took a measured breath. "What I am about to tell you is a secret of the highest order of Harvesters. Even I'm not supposed to know about it. It is possible, for a Harvester of high enough rank to not only acquire traits from his victims, but to give traits away as well. For Intervention Harvesters, we're talking from self to someone else. For Triage Harvesters, we're talking any two compatible species."

"Wait a minute. So you're saying that someone could have transferred Rifun's face onto a body and dumped it in the river to pass him off as dead?"

Lily nodded gravely. "And it's not so much a transfer as it is...copy and paste. A bad one at that. Body in a river with features vaguely resembling Rifun...the Hands get the body they need, and Rifun goes free."

"You only said Cassius was a Runner by the time he was a guard. What rank was he?"

"I don't know. But like I said, too, for all his crimes and bloodlust, none of the Hands would touch him because they feared him that much. Whoever it is who's gotten in league with him—whether it's Rifun or anybody else—they're not your average class of criminal. They don't fear death, Walter. They are death. And the fact that I'm still breathing says they're ramping up to something huge, something where they're not going to care if the whole world is exposed to Time, as long as they get what they want."

Walter tried to be calm as he let out a breath he hadn't realized he'd been holding.

"So under the grim assumption that this could be our last meeting, is there anything you'd like to add?" he asked levelly.

"It's all I know," Lily told him, and for once he honestly believed her.

"You know how to reach me."

And with that, he left the condo, getting into the elevator and calling the twins.

"What'd you find, Walter?" Micaiah asked, like a bloodhound ready to get on the trail.

"Rifun Ndolo is alive," he told him. "He's Cassius' employer. Worse, Cassius is a Triage Harvester."

"Shit. Are you sure? That's what Lily told you?"

"It is."

"And you believe her?"

"Like I've never believed anything she's ever said before."

"Shit. Do you at least know their end game?"

"Aside from killing her, they're after a journal."

"A journal?"

"They're after the journal Tommen discovered in the salt cave and brought out with him. Supposedly it's some super-secret high-level journal kept by Lily's mentor."

"Is Tommen in danger?" Walter could hear some background noise like some activity had just stopped.

"For safety, I'm going to say he is. Rifun and Cassius are becoming more sophisticated with twenty-first century technology. They might find an old newspaper article when Tommen first appeared with that journal. I have that article hanging on my wall; I remember they mention that journal. If they don't follow up on it and find that the journal got donated to the museum, they could go straight for him."

"What do you want us to do?"

"Keep an eye out and stay safe. If it does come to a

confrontation, do not engage. I repeat, do not engage. Run. Find anywhere safe."

"Yes, sir. What are you going to do?"

That was the problem, wasn't it? What was he going to do? Nothing he'd learned would help his murder investigation. Nothing he'd learned was admissable outside of an asylum. This was all purely in the realm of Time. And if the Hands wouldn't touch Cassius then, they sure as hell wouldn't touch him now, especially if he was also in league with Rifun Ndolo. Two of the highest ranking Time Agents in league together as murderous Runners. As he was a Timekeeper Captain who was going to do...what, exactly?

"I don't know," Walter admitted. "This is falling more and more outside of the Earth-side justice system, and according to Lily, the Hands are too afraid of them to go anywhere near them."

Micaiah sighed. "I might be able to pull in a few favors, but it might mean accepting some bribes for the elections."

Walter laughed because it was the only logically insane thing to do. "Micaiah, the elections are shit and we both know it. Right now, we've got two terrorists running free because no one wants to do anything about it. Go stroke some egos and win some self-righteous hearts to our cause."

He could almost hear him grin over the phone. "Will do, boss."

Chapter Fifteen
Break-In

Tommen did his best to tell himself that he ought to be focusing on his review and leave the case to those who knew how to handle it, but there was just something so enticing about trying to listen in on conversations, figure out backstory, needle out information like some kind of savvy Casanova detective. Not that he possessed a silver tongue or sleuthing skills of any kind. If the conversation Micaiah had with Walter was any indication, Walter had managed to dig up more in half an hour than he had in some unknown length of time in the Wheel.

"What's up?" Tommen asked, trying to sound casual as Micaiah got off the phone.

"I'm going to give you a ride home tonight," Micaiah replied.

"Oh. But...I was going to walk. Really, it's no big deal."

"It will be if you don't make it and Walter has my ass."

"Why? I mean, what would Calis want with me?"

But even as he said it, he knew the answer. It wouldn't even be about him. Ultimately, he would just be the hostage used to get to Walter for who knew what reason. Tommen couldn't fathom what Calis would have against Walter except he was both a detective investigating the murders he'd committed, as well as a Timekeeper Captain. That wasn't even accounting for the reasons for the murders in the first place. He hated not having all the information, hated knowing that he probably wouldn't get all the information, so he was left in the dark like the rest of the public eye with only a faceless evil stalking the streets of Charleston.

But Micaiah actually had a surprising answer to his question.

"He doesn't want you; he wants the journal you brought out of the old mine eight years ago. And if his information about that is as good as his information about Lily so far, he might think you still have it."

"Oh. Wow. But what's in that journal that he could want? I mean, it was just a bunch of scribbles and stuff."

"Just because we didn't understand it doesn't mean it wasn't important. Whatever is in that journal, Calis is willing to kill for it."

"So if he's after the journal, why go after Lily, too? Did she have it before I did? I thought she wasn't that old?"

"I think you're too smart for your own good," Micah said, butting in. "Counter."

Tommen went up to the front counter. He was ready to be done for the day. Working double shifts over holidays was murder, especially on the weekends; he didn't know how they pulled it off day in and day out except they probably Banded, went out for a walk or something, got something to eat, and then came back. Or maybe they really did just bull their way through each day, sixteen hours at a time.

The day was winding down, but Thanksgiving and Chrismas, especially the time in between, was always the busiest time of year for the bakery. A good day was when they punched out within an hour of the posted closing time. Only child labor laws let Tommen go home early, even as the twins stayed up until eight or nine or later before even being able to think about closing chores.

Those same chores were what Tommen tackled once he finished up serving the line that had formed. Sweeping was easy; trash was harder but necessary; wiping down tables wasn't bad except when there came in a party of small children who didn't understand the concept of napkins and inevitably spilled glaze, icing, frosting, and whatever candy toppings all over the floor. This was only to the embarrassment of the inattentive parents, who had also apparently never heard of the concept of cleaning up. Of course, they did that all day at home; why should they also clean up after their kids in public when there was some loser sixteen-year-old able and willing behind the counter? Never mind that he had a line of a dozen people also waiting for his undivided and sacred attention.

Tommen couldn't decide if his little mental speeches helped his mood overall, but they did wonders for his attitude in the short-term.   Throughout the day, he came up with a dozen witty and sarcastic remarks to silently think at the customers who said all manner of dumb things and expected him to care that they had an important date, as if they thought he actually cared that they were cheating on their diet. More likely they were cheating on their spouse, but who was he to say for sure?

Micah took care of the kitchen end of the clean-up, retrieving trays as Tommen reported them empty, changing rag water, and filling the mop buckets. One nice thing about it, as long as they were busy and Tommen was on the counter, he didn't have to clean the bathrooms.

Instead, he shuffled and rearranged trays in the display case, turning off lights as he emptied sections until only a few trays were left. With no one to currently wait on, he stuck the "25% off" tag on the front of the case and took a small armload of empty trays back to the sinks where Micah was busy washing dishes, up to his elbows in soapy water, nose streaming from the strong odor of bleach. Even Tommen's eyes burned from the strong smell, and he wondered if Micah had accidentally dropped the bucket in the water again. Micah looked up at him, sniffed hard, wiped his face on his sleeve and nodded to the empty sink at the end where all the waiting dishes sat.

"How's the front?"

"Pretty quiet now," Tommen reported. "I put the 25% off tag on the case; you think I should just pitch the stuff and bring the trays back?"

Micah looked at the clock, almost nine. "Wait until nine. Then I can get these done. And maybe they'll sell. If nothing happens, yeah, pitch them and we'll close up."

Tommen nodded. *"An bhfuil an t-uisce an mhapa glan?"* He pointed to the yellow bucket. (Mop water clean?)

Micah stared the bucket for a moment, probably trying to

decide how long ago it had actually been since he had filled and used it, and if he'd cleaned it. Finally he nodded. *"Tá sé glan."* (It's clean.)

Tommen was interrupted only once as he put up chairs, and swept and mopped the front of the store, but otherwise the sea of people had ebbed. He turned the sign from *"Oscailte"* to *"Dúnta"* at exactly nine o'clock, grabbing the last few pieces from the display case and reluctantly tossing them before taking the trays back to Micah and the last trash out to the dumpster.

"What does Micaiah do all day in that office anyway?" Tommen wondered.

"The same thing a whole team of people does for any ordinary business," Micah replied. "Promotions and marketing, advertising, billing, catering, purchasing, complaint department, maintenance, all of that rolled into one person. Most days it's him on the counter and me back here until you get here, so this holiday with you being willing to take so many hours means he's able to catch up on a lot of stuff."

"Too bad the Internet and phone don't Band well."

"Well, they don't, so we do what we can. Besides, it's not all bad having to work Base Time. I could have gotten these dishes done in one Base Minute, but then I'd still have to wait. Which reminds me, you got everything you need?"

"Oh, um, yeah. I don't have my backpack, so I don't have much."

"True. Well, once I'm done with these dishes, I'll holler at Cai and we'll head out. Are the front lights off?"

"I'll get them."

Tommen went to a small panel and flipped the switches for the front of the store, casting shadows over most of the area but leaving just enough light for Micah to still work. Then he returned to the kitchen where Micah was just drying off his arms and wiping his nose. Tommen punched out and turned as if to leave.

"I'll get Micaiah," Micah told him.

"Hey, fine, I'm just going to hit the bathroom before we go," Tommen said.

He went to the bathroom and closed the door, listening for the telltale squeak of the office door. There it was, as Micah went in to grab his brother. Then Tommen simply Banded and stepped out of the bathroom. Despite being in a Fast Band, he didn't want to alert the twins and he glanced toward the office only briefly, breathing a sigh of relief that the blinds were down. He hurried to the back entry, shrugged on his coat and hat, slipped on a pair of mittens, and stepped out into the snow, pulling the door quietly shut behind him.

He couldn't say exactly why he disobeyed Micah and Micaiah, why he essentially went under their noses to walk home in the cold and snow late at night, when there was nothing really wrong with just getting a ride home in a nice, warm vehicle. He certainly wasn't the emo, depressed, walk-home-alone-in-the-cold-and-snow-and-think-about-life-and-your-feelings kind of person; his notebook was a book of stories and memories, not a diary.

Besides, it was almost more dangerous to Band-walk home in the cold. He Banded so the twins wouldn't catch up to him—at least, not immediately. But being in the Band created a false sense of security. Air was not affected by Bands, so it was just as cold inside the Band as it was outside, meaning that there was virtually no difference whether or not he Banded while he walked. He could still feel the cold creeping in to bite his toes through a small hole in his tennis shoes, and his long hair as much as his hat protected his ears. Walter still nagged him about getting a hair cut, as if getting to the point where he could almost make a ponytail was some great sin or something.

As he walked, Tommen's mind wandered around to others on the street which he wove around. As far as they were concerned, they had simply been walking, and a trail of footprints suddenly appeared in the snow. It was comical to think about, the things he could do and the tricks he could play. Maybe he should write a mysterious message and just leave it for someone to find, see what happened, see what conspiracy theories came out about it. Pranksters, aliens, government cover-ups?

But, like everything he thought of during such times, it never came to pass. Well, almost never. He did do something like that once in fifth grade. The class had just handed in a math test, and then they had some free time so the teacher could correct them. Tommen Banded every time he flipped to the next person's test. When he got to Tyler Freeman's test, Tommen Banded, grabbed a crayon, and wrote nasty messages all over the front of it—because "poopyhead" is still a nasty message for a fifth-grader. He got away with it in school but Walter managed to needle it out of him later that day. Tommen ended up spending Halloween doing nothing but stare at a wall.

Truthfully, that had never bothered him too much. Like Thanksgiving, or even more so, Halloween was a total mystery to him. Dress up as goblins and demons and who knew what else, then go up to strangers and beg for candy? When Walter told him time and again not to take candy from strangers? And, generally speaking, Tommen didn't particularly enjoy modern candy anyway.

Christmas was perhaps the least confusing holiday for him to reconcile, at least in principle. Birth of Baby Jesus. Hooray. Tommen didn't have anything against the man, just believed he was a little delusional. But there was nothing wrong about peace on Earth, good will toward men, no matter who it came from. And seeing a cute little light-up Nativity wasn't too annoying. Those enormous air-up life-size ones? Yeah, those grated his nerves.

More often than not, Tommen just enjoyed seeing all the decorations as Charleston geared up for Christmas. Some store owners or managers were out stringing up lights, since it was easier to see them and place them in the dark. Others hung up garland or put up small trees, all decorated with ribbon and tinsel and glass ornaments. More modest stores opted for plastic window clings or seasonal open/closed signs. The Santa hats hadn't come out yet, but they were on the way. Tommen silently dreaded the day he walked into work and Micah handed him the box of Irish Christmas decorations. It got him out of work, true, but sometimes he would rather deal with an annoying customer than have to sift through a box of junk, picking out good decorations, and discarding anything that got broken or damaged.

Perhaps that was what still mystified Tommen about modern Christmas. He didn't mind the Baby Jesus part, but he didn't understand the part about just buying junk because it's on sale. As if there weren't sales on anything the whole rest of the year. Getting gifts for others was great in the spirit of family and love and kindness, but for the love of all that was good and loving and kind, why did Christmas shopping feel more like grand larceny under duress? In years past, Tommen had gotten small gifts for Walter and Micaiah and Micah, what he could afford out of his paltry paychecks, and they'd always been grateful. But when he went back to school and listened to stories of not only what his classmates and teachers got for Christmas, but what they got for their loved ones, he always ended up feeling guilty and inadequate. Even knowing that it was all psychological didn't help.

He tried to think back and remember if his family had ever celebrated Christmas. Certainly it wouldn't have been anything as extravagant as all this, but anything at all. His best recollection brought to mind a vague memory of a dinner that was larger than normal and everyone wearing their best clothes. He remembered candles and story-telling and singing. And, if he really thought about it, he supposed he could remember some gift-giving: his mother giving him a brand new pair of wool socks, fresh-spun off the sheep from earlier that spring and dyed red-brown from tree bark; his father giving him some wooden toy to play with while they waited out another blizzard; his brother giving him a hard time in a wrestling match because he was the older brother.

This year, there was every chance Walter would get him a music gift card so he could download some new music. Probably get him a new coat or a new pair of shoes, things he needed that he wasn't normally willing to get himself, instead waiting for his birthday or Christmas to come around so Walter would buy them for him. And there might be a book in there, too. If it wasn't a blatant hint sort of book—"The Guide to Leaving Home and Living on Your Own" and "Surviving College Without Mom and Dad" had been the books of choice for this year's birthday—then it would probably be a novel translated in Welsh. One year, Walter had managed to find an original Welsh novel which actually hadn't been too bad.

Tommen startled as he rounded a corner into an alley cut-across and almost ran into a homeless person, tucked down next to a dumpster. He let out a breath, collected his frayed nerves, and moved on. Walter wasn't trying to kick him out, just trying to remind him that one day he would have to leave home.

And where would he go? With his current course in school, he could go anywhere, do anything. But there had always been another option, to be a Time Scout. It was hard work to the nth degree, and extremely dangerous. Most Scouts were told to treat every home visit like it was their last. But becoming a Scout would take him to places completely untouched—not only by man, but by Time itself. He could go anywhere and do anything.

He emerged from the alley and continued on his way, crossing the street with no concern for the green light or the huge truck that loomed beside him. His abilities were a curse some days, but other days they were a blessing. Today, they were simply a tool for amusement as he passed by a brightly-lit smiling snowman in the middle of a wave to passersby.

He looked at the bridge, excellence in engineering itself, spanning the Kinahwa River, also preparing for Christmas as extra strings of light were run here and there in a giant net with a large green wreath of lights on either side. He saw the cars crossing the bridge, most of them heading the same direction as him, toward the outer hills, toward home. Drivers squinting their eyes against the lights, eyes tired, would be no more relieved when the lights suddenly disappeared and they were left in the warm darkness of their vehicle. Walter had been on many an accident where the driver was too tired and got too comfortable in their car, never realizing they drifted off until they simply...drifted off. Most often into a ditch, but sometimes a tree, a sign, another car, or someone's garage.

Tommen might have felt the same way if he were in a cozy car right now, exhausted from a string of long work days, listening to the hum of an engine and the whir of a heater fan, driving a mechanical, familiar route. He was pretty sure the only thing keeping him awake now was the cold.

He paused and looked around. He couldn't feel his feet. One shoe had come untied, but he didn't feel like kneeling in the snow for fear of not wanting to get back up. Maybe he should drop his Band and let the twins find him. He could take a verbal tongue lashing from them, and later from Walter. How stupid was he to think he could walk home? Sure he'd done it before, but usually only in the summer into late fall. But fall was long gone; winter wasn't just coming, it was here. And he was dumb enough to be stuck in it.

He knelt in the snow to tie his shoe. He was in front of the West Virginia State Museum, a big, beautiful brick building housing the history and culture of West Virginia and the Appalachian Mountains, everything from the Native Americans to the miners and loggers, right up until present day. Tommen had been on more field trips to that museum than he cared to count, which now stood as a shadowy, ghostly apparition. It was also, ironically, part of a government complex which the police department shared. Maybe he ought to see if Walter was in. Just a friendly visit, right? Would Walter really fault him for that? Most of the guys knew him anyway—for one reason or another. Some would be glad to see him, others would probably roll their eyes, shake their head, and return to their newspaper.

A sudden twitch of his sixth sense interrupted Tommen's line of thought, and for a moment, he could have sworn he was being watched. But that wasn't possible; he was safely in a Band and, basically, Time around him was stopped.

Then, there was a flicker of movement. Yes, there it was. Carefully, so as not to disturb or spook the other person, Tommen shifted his head just barely, just enough to look up from his shoe with a decent view. At first, there was only the museum, the snow, and the people in it, motionless, oblivious.

Several thoughts were running through Tommen's mind as he tried to pick out which person was not as motionless as they appeared. The first was that this was the work of the twins, a clever prank trying to spook him a little, get a little payback for not listening to them and riding home with them. That would be just perfect. But it would be preferable to the second, more sinister thought, that it was Calis or his employer, and they were finally going to make their move on him.

Was this how they did it with the other two women? Did they play these sick games, scoping out the women, following them, stalking them in absolute silence and anonymity despite being in plain sight of everyone? Had they, just before killing them, released the Band just long enough for the women to see their faces so they would forever know the faces of their killers?

If they were here for him, would they press into a Band so Fast that it would render Tommen motionless to them, so they could kill him and he would look like he walked right up to them and asked to be murdered in such a brutal fashion? Would they beat him senseless and leave him as a warning for Walter and the twins? Would they kidnap him and then ransom him to Walter? Tommen knew there was nothing Walter wouldn't give, especially if he knew he was sorely outgunned and had no hope of force.

Fear snaked its way through Tommen's brain and reached his spine. He was still kneeling in the snow, laces in hand. A new thought occurred to him then, that even though he was physically motionless, he was still in a Band. Motionless or not, he would be lit up like a Christmas tree, a giant neon sign with an arrow saying, "Here I am! Come and get it!"

Taking a breath and with only a split second to weigh his options, Tommen dropped his Band. Immediately, Charleston came to life around him. Lights sparkled, people talked and laughed, dogs barked, cars honked, brakes locked up on ice and cars went sliding out of control, snowmen and santas waved, angels proclaimed peace on Earth, somewhere music was trumpeting out a rendition of "We Three Kings," children begged parents for a toy or a candy, teenagers and young lovers walked hand-in-hand down the sidewalk or stole precious moments together in a side alley, and old lovers walked shoulder-to-shoulder down the memory lane of Christmases past.

Most importantly, however, was the fact that Tommen wasn't dead. In the four seconds in took for him to notice all of that, he knew he could have been killed, if indeed the other person was Calis or his employer. If it had been Micah or Micaiah, he expected they would also drop out of their Band, laugh at him, humiliate him, call him a few names, then proceed to scold him and lecture him and all manner of tongue lashing things.

Except Tommen knew that would not happen. Because he knew the twins were not the ones responsible. Even as the music blared and the people talked and the cars honked and the lights sparkled, there was something else not immediately noticeable, and that was the alarm system of the museum, an ear-piercing wail that was almost too high-pitched to be heard on a normal day, now almost completely drowned out in all the festivity. The lights themselves could not be seen flashing except when viewed directly, but they were invisible in the not-quite-dark.

More than that, invisible to the normal eye, was the wake of a Band leading away from the museum doors. It was a Fast Band, woven so tightly and so narrow in its field so as to be blinding and yet almost invisible in itself, like trying to focus on a laser with the brightness of the sun. All Bands left a wake. Generally speaking, the greater the distortion of the Band—that is, the farther removed the Band was from Base Time—the greater the wake it left behind. Keeping a Band tight and narrow helped to cut down on the wake, but it was still there.

Tommen stood, frozen, staring at the wake. Most likely, almost guaranteed, this was Calis. He really ought to call the police, report the robbery—assuming the museum didn't already have an automatic burglar system that linked directly to dispatch, in which case the cops would be on their way in just a minute from around the corner—and then call Walter to report the Band.

At the same time, he had an opportunity to follow Calis. Maybe not to a secret lair or anything, but even just to some kind of getaway car. Get a make and model, a plate. He was no hero, and if Walter was wary of the guy, Tommen knew he didn't stand a chance. But average people could be heroes any day as long as they tried and did what was right, broke out of their fear and stood up for justice and all that other TV propaganda crap.

Tommen Banded, a Fast Band so the rate of decay on the wake slowed. Cautiously, he moved toward it. He'd never broken into a Band before. He'd been broken in on, knew that it was like being wrapped in shrink wrap and having it pushed and pulled until the other person got sucked in. If he did it that way, guaranteed they would know their Band had been broken into. They'd left Tommen alone when he was in his own Band and lit up for them to find and kill if they chose. If he broke in on their Band deliberately, they might not be so forgiving.

He walked right up to the edge of the wake. Maybe there was another way to break in. Maybe he could do it like any kind of running or racing; maybe he could essentially draft into the wake, draft into the Band, and increase the strength of his own Band until he slipped effortlessly into their Band, and they would never know the difference. Was that possible? Could he do it? Should he do it?

Images of the dead woman under the bleachers at the soccer field flickered through his mind. and dread pulsed through him with every beat of his heart. He could end up like her. He took a few more steps toward the wake as it faded, feeling the Band like feeling water on the edge of the tide on a sandy beach. The same sandy beach where the second woman had been found. He could end up like her, too.

The wake was receding quickly. Probably they'd already exited the Band, and it was decaying. Who knew where they'd ended up? How far would he chase them? Gingerly, he pushed into the wake far enough that his Band matched the decay rate. So far, so good. They hadn't come back to kill him. Trying to push aside the migraine, he pushed deeper into the wake, feeling like he was being pulled underwater to a depth that was starting to crush his lungs. Gasping for air, most unnecessarily, Tommen pushed harder into the wake until the pressure released and he was almost swept away in what he could only describe as a Band-current. Now it was like the air was being pulled out of his lungs. He fought to keep some measure of control, but the harder he fought, the worse the feeling became and he felt dizzy. Nausea started creeping in.

At the last second, he dropped his own Band, hardly realizing he'd been holding onto it like a lead weight in deep water. Once it was gone, suddenly he was afloat, free to move within the Band. But it was fast-decaying. If he wanted to gain any distance on Calis, he would have to get moving.

Telling himself that he would only go as far as the city limits or until he found some kind of getaway car or secret lair or other such thing, Tommen pressed forward through the Band, feeling it grow stronger as he walked. Fear had lodged itself in his gut, but he just kept telling himself that average people did heroic things all the time. Of course, they also did stupid things in the name of heroics all the time, too.

For the most part, though, "chasing" Calis was little different than walking home. Tommen ran a bit, trying to keep warm, but he never felt like he was ever catching up. More than once he considered just dropping out of the Band — which couldn't be much different than how he got in, right? — and heading home. More than once, he doubted his resolve. What exactly was he going to do if he did catch up to Calis, anyway? The plan was to simply hide and collect some kind of damning information, but what if things didn't go according to plan as was almost guaranteed in this sort of thing? He couldn't fight, couldn't run.

He passed a police car en route to the museum, lights flashing but the driver in the middle of a drink of coffee. Tommen couldn't tell who it was, only that it wasn't Walter. Maybe he could go get Walter, bring him into the Band and then they could go after Calis together. Surely Walter would know what to do better than Tommen, if and when they confronted him. At least Walter might have some kind of cool Captain-y abilities to unleash.

For all his consideration, however, Tommen passed the station by, remaining stoicly inside the Band and following it as it meandered its way through town and eventually headed toward the bridge. Now where could Calis be going across the bridge? The city was where everything was at, more places to hide. Unless he was going back to the school for some reason. Or maybe he was heading to Tommen's home. Maybe he was looking for Tommen. Or Walter.

A thousand different worst-case scenarios flashed through Tommen's mind. Everything from murder, to life-altering bodily harm, to a number of unpleasantries involving his backside. He forced himself not to think about such things and instead concentrate on just following the Band. Be a bloodhound. Just follow the trail and alert the hunters.

The Band grew stronger as he followed it to a small wharf just west of the bridge. This was the place for honest fishing charters and where the police dropped their boat for water ops. Well, who needed a getaway car when a getaway boat worked just as well? Head downstream, ditch the boat, and get lost in the mountains. Assuming that was what they were doing.

But a nagging suspicion told Tommen that was not what Calis had in mind. It was too predictable, too perfect. And the Band was kept in tact the entire way. They'd known Tommen had seen them, might have guessed that he would follow. If they didn't want to be followed, they could simply slip out of the Band and meander their way here, cloaked among the crowds. There was only one reason that a Band would be left so strongly in tact that led straight to a perfect getaway spot.

"Good God, you're right. He is stupid."

Tommen did not believe in God. He had a hard time buying into any version of Fate either.   But there were times when a coincidence was a little too coincidental to completely ignore. How was it, that on a night when Tommen just happened to disobey the twins, not get a ride home, and walk home late at night, that he would witness a theft right in front of him committed by the two most wanted men in Charleston whom his father was avidly hunting? Either it was just one weird coincidence, or they'd been watching him and it was all planned out.

The men who confronted him now were just as described on the news. Calis Cutthroat, about six-foot, dark skin, short hair, thin beard and mustache, and hands big enough for killing. And a white guy, also about six-foot, but he had long hair, tied back, that fell to his waist, and freckles that were less than flattering.   Tommen remembered the description, but no name had ever been given.

"Now, Cassius, we mustn't be rude," the white man said. He had an accent, one Tommen couldn't place. "After all, he is only a probationary Timekeeper, and he has done well to follow us here."

"Because you wanted me to follow you." *Shut up, Tommen. Just close your mouth.* "My dad is a Captain and he'll be here."

The white guy put a hand to his chest in a mocking precious gesture and even Calis, or Cassius, grinned, though it made Tommen want to throw up. "Oh, how cute. Daddy to the rescue." He sighed. "Well, I suppose we should thank you after all."

"Thank me?" *Don't get distracted, Tommen.*

He held up a leather-bound book Tommen almost didn't recognize until he realized it was the same journal he'd brought with him out of the salt cave. Tommen raised a brow and pointed uselessly at it. "That? You killed two women...for that?"

"A simple case of mistaken identity. One mistake we will not be making again, I can assure you."

"And who are you?"

"Ah, so the good captain has not released my name because many would find such things impossible. But for you, I will introduce myself. My name is Rifun Ndolo." He did a sweeping bow, making sure to shift his body so Tommen saw the revolver at his hip.

"So what's in the journal?" Tommen wondered. "And why haven't you killed me?"

Rifun grinned, a meager improvement over the ugliness of his freckles. "Ah, dear child. What did you expect from me? That I would lure you here, divulge my evil plans by way of a Shakespearean monologue, then leave you to my henchman to be killed, only for you to weasel your way out of danger and report my activities to the police where this all comes to a dramatic climactic Western-style shootout, and everyone goes home safe and sound, and I am led off stage in chains?"

Tommen blinked. "Well, that would be helpful."

Rifun laughed, perhaps the only charming thing about him, something that could win girls right and left. And he used it for his evil supervillain laugh. How appropriate. "Ah, dear child. How naive you are. The only plan I shall divulge to you tonight will be the one where I do not tell you my master scheme, and instead leave you here to be killed and Harvested by my henchman, while I make an escape to you know not where."

With that, he walked down toward the dock. "You know where to meet me, Cassius."

Cassius merely grunted.

Tommen had been in a few fights in his day. Most often they got him nowhere, but he always learned something from them. Perhaps the best thing he had learned, especially in his last fight with Tyler, was to be unpredictable. And the best way to be unpredictable was to set a pattern and then suddenly break it.

If not for a few words from Rifun, Tommen might have engaged Cassius. But that, too, was a pattern. Focus on the threat at hand while the mastermind got away. Except Rifun had said Tommen would be killed and then Harvested. But that meant that Cassius was not a Timekeeper. He was a Harvester. That meant that Rifun had to be the Timekeeper.

Tommen only had one shot at the element of surprise as Cassius grinned and advanced toward him. He took a breath and got in an uncertain stance. Cassius smelled his weakness and uncertainty. Out of the corner of his eye, Tommen saw Rifun pick a boat, a small thing, unsuspecting, something that would go completely unnoticed in the dark.

Then he sprang. But he didn't launch himself at Cassius. Instead, he jumped away from Cassius, bringing all his strength and focus to bear and pushing into a Band, streaming toward the boat as Rifun was just shoving off.

He was caught by surprise as Rifun effortlessly broke into Tommen's Band and seemed to physically use it against him, slamming him into the bottom of the boat and then releasing the Band with such force as to drive the air from his lungs. Still, he lashed out with his fists. He grunted as Rifun not only blocked the blow, but grabbed his arm and twisted it around, maneuvering him carefully down until his face was pressed against the bottom of the boat.

"You've got spirit, kid," Rifun observed, putting his boot on Tommen's back. "A real fighter. I like that. I could use you. See, that's another good thing about me not telling you my master plans. No skin off my back if I decided to let you go right now. You run to daddy, train really hard to be the best Timekeeper you can be. But you'll always remember this night, and you'll always want your revenge for how I defeated you. Maybe then we'll talk, hm?" Still holding Tommen's arm and his boot on his back, he knelt down. "What's your name, kid?"

"T-tommen."

"Tommen. Nice name. Well, Tommen, can you swim?"

"Huh?"

Then suddenly he was wet. And cold. The frigid water hit him like a thousand knives, and all his muscles contracted at once. Instinctively, he tried to suck in a breath but found only water. He flailed until he got upright and his head broke the water's surface. Rifun's boat wasn't far away.

Rifun was right. He was pissed, and he wanted revenge for that one. Coughing and sputtering but still sucking in as much air as possible, Tommen slipped underwater, hoping it looked like he was struggling.

Instead, he swam right back to the boat, Banding the Fastest Band he'd ever tried to build. He pulled himself into the boat and went for Rifun, went for his gun. Though surprised, the large man was still ready for him, bringing his arms up in a total block that made Tommen stumble back and nearly fall out of the boat again.

"You're persistent," Rifun said, his tone bringing to mind a man who put up with a child's antics only once, but now they were annoying him. He stood over Tommen who still lay on the bottom of the boat. "But we're done here."

He drew his gun then and fired. Maybe he thought Tommen couldn't Band Fast enough to escape the bullet, but with the help of an emotionally-charged Predict, Tommen managed to dodge, covering his ears as he scrambled for the edge of the boat which was already taking on water. Rifun cursed, but there was nothing he could do. He'd only planned for a short trip with no hassles and had nothing with which to plug the leak.

Rifun leapt over the side of the boat. As he hit the water, Tommen Banded and swam over to meet him. Fortunately for Tommen, Rifun was momentarily confused and blinded by his long hair swirling about his face. But it was all the time Tommen needed to rescue the journal from his jacket and head back to shore.

When he hauled himself onto the snowy beach, he counted it a victory that he'd made it at all. Spitting water, he looked out over the river, but Rifun was nowhere to be seen.

His problems weren't over, however, as he was hauled to his feet by Cassius and sucker punched twice in the gut before being dropped into the slushy sand, again gasping for breath.

"Your daddy ever tell you he and I know each other?" Cassius said, pacing in front of Tommen.

"What?" It wasn't a particularly "stunned" sort of question, more like a gasp of air as Tommen tried to recover from the last twenty minutes of walking in the cold, getting in a fight, getting thrown into cold water, getting in a fight in cold water, and then having to swim through that same cold water to shore only to have what little air was in his lungs punched out again.

"Oh yeah, we go way back." Cassius kicked Tommen in the gut and he rolled over, groaning, trying to keep the journal hidden in his coat. "Maybe you should ask him about it." Then he kicked him in the face. "But then, maybe you won't get a chance."

"Tommen!"

Cassius looked up, startled. Then he took off. Tommen coughed once and tried to sit up as a couple flashlight beams swept the beach and the docks and settled on him. In a moment, Micah and Micaiah were beside him, peeling off his jacket and draping theirs around his soaking wet shoulders.

"Tommen, are you all right?" Micaiah demanded. "Can you understand me?"

Tommen waved them away. "I can understand you fine. How did you find me?"

"We followed your tracks to the museum where there was a break-in. When we saw the Band wake, we knew it was too strong for you to have made it, so we called Walter. He's on his way. We followed the Band here. What happened?"

"Calis, er, Cassius. He called him Cassius."

"Who did?" Micah asked.

"The white guy from the news. He called himself Rifun Ndolo." Tommen spit out some blood. "I was an idiot. I thought I could follow the Band and, I don't know, get a plate on a getaway car or...getaway boat. But it was a trap the whole time. Rifun left Cassius to finish me off, but I jumped in the water after him. We fought."

"He shot you," Micaiah interrupted, pulling down Tommen's shirt to expose a new hole in his shoulder just above the collarbone on the right side. It wasn't bad, more of a graze, taking off a few layers of skin.

Tommen shrugged, noting a stinging in that shoulder, but the cold had numbed him pretty well. "We fought. We went in the water. I swam back to shore. Rifun was gone. Cassius was still going to beat me up, but he ran when you guys came."

"Okay." Micaiah nodded, perhaps more vigorously than necessary. "Walter is on his way, but I'll call 9-1-1 and get more cops and an ambulance down here."

"Whatever, man." Tommen sniffed and shivered. He turned stiffly and rummaged through his coat which was beginning to freeze solid. The journal tumbled out. "I did manage to get that back."

The twins seemed stunned, and Micah reached out with a tentative hand, as if he might burst into flames upon touching it. He picked it up and looked it over a bit. Finally, he put the journal in one hand and with the other, helped Micaiah help Tommen to his feet.

"Let's get you warmed up," Micah said, and together they slowly got back to Micaiah's car parked at the top of the hill overlooking the river.

Tommen sat in the backseat of the running vehicle, feeling the chill of the water melt away as the heater blasted hot air for all it was worth. Outside, once Micaiah got off the phone, presumably with dispatch, the twins were arguing, though Tommen could not make out their words. Micah had set the journal on the hood of the car and both of them gestured to it frequently, coming out of it only when flashing lights lit up the entire wharf. Three police cruisers and an ambulance filled the tiny space. Micaiah went to speak to one of the officers while Micah directed the medics to the car. Reluctantly, Tommen got out of the car and was hit with a blast of cold air, nearly making him stumble and fall. Like vultures they were on him, and he followed them back to the ambulance where he was made to strip down to his undershirt and boxers.

With the back doors closed, the heat cranked, and a heat-reflecting blanket around his shoulders, Tommen figured he warmed up fairly quickly.

"Breathe for me," one medic ordered, holding a stethoscope to his chest while another taped dressings on either side of the gunshot wound. Tommen obeyed and breathed. "Lungs sound clear. How do your sinuses feel?"

Tommen chuckled. "It's not my first fight, believe me."

The medic with the stethoscope was a middle-aged woman, not quite forty, blond hair, rimless glasses. Tommen could see the bulge of a wedding ring under her glove. Her nametag read Stephanie.

The other medic was a man of roughly forty or fifty years, sorely overweight so he had a hard time moving around in the back. He might have been better off if he was going straight bald, but the thin, patchy spots did him no favors. His nametag read Larry.

"How are you feeling? Warmer?"

"Yeah." He shifted position and pulled the blanket tighter around him. "I hope they told my dad to bring an extra change of clothes."

"Well, he can bring them to the hospital."

"Hospital?"

Stephanie nodded gravely. "Gunshot wounds are nothing to sneeze at, and they are a mandatory transport."

Tommen started sputtering protests. "But I feel fine. I mean, it's not even that bad. A few stitches at most, but Micah or Micaiah can take me."

Now she shook her head. "No can do."

Tommen sighed. "What if I refuse? Sign a waiver?"

"How old are you?"

"Sixteen."

"Not valid. Under eighteen, parent or legal guardian has to sign."

He rolled his eyes. "Whatever. But I am telling you, I'm just fine."

Even as he spoke, the doors opened and Walter looked in. If Tommen was any judge of expression, Walter was terrified and yet relieved when he saw him. He let out an audible sigh.

"Tommen, thank God." He looked helplessly at the medic. "How is he?"

"Fine," Tommen answered, even as Stephanie replied, "He's getting there. He was hypothermic, but that's being managed pretty well now. Took a few socks to the gut, one to the face. His nose might be broken. And he did take a gunshot wound here." She pulled the blanket back enough to show Walter the dressing. "It's nothing big, but it is a mandatory transport."

Walter's face and body went through so many expressions during her short speech that by the end he just looked exhausted. He nodded. "Mandatory transport, I know." He sighed. "Take him. I'll catch up."

Stephanie nodded, but Tommen thought he saw a smirk as Walter closed the back doors. While she got Tommen strapped in to the cot, Larry went out a side door and around the ambulance to the driver's seat.

"I've worked with your dad before," Stephanie said conversationally as she fished for a run form. "He's a good guy, good at what he does, and he cares."

"You don't have to convince me," Tommen told her. "I know he's good at what he does."

The hospital wasn't far away, and soon Tommen was sitting alone in a little room in the emergency wing with ugly beige walls, paintings that made little and less sense, and sheets that had been washed so often they couldn't even be bothered to be scratchy anymore. Heating pads had been slipped between the two blankets they laid over him and now he was almost overheating. He flipped lazily through the channels on the TV, eventually settling on some movie that was more commercials than programming, but that's the way it was with most shows these days.

The stitches hadn't actually taken that long, but now that the cold had worn off, he was starting to feel the burn and the ache. He'd been told multiple times that he'd gotten lucky, that he should have been going in for some serious surgery. As it was, he'd only sustained a minor flesh wound. Well, that and the broken nose which was also feeling pretty tender. But he'd sustained worse in his fights with Tyler Freeman, so this had to count for something, right? At least this time he wasn't being sent to the principal's office and being threatened with suspension or some stupid shit. If word of this got around, who knew, maybe he'd stop being challenged. Hey, there goes the kid who got in a fight with a hardened criminal, got shot, and came out on top. Don't wanna mess with him, dude, who knows what he might do?

It was a fantasy of course. This would only add to his reputation for being a fighter, and getting in a scrap with a hardened criminal did nothing for his image as The Chivalrous Welshman who refused to sink to the level of the common street criminal. But what did they know about chivalry anyway?

It was almost midnight before the door opened. So far it had only been nurses ducking in and out to check on him, finally removing the heating pads once his temperature swung to the other end of the pendulum. But if Tommen was expecting Walter, he was sorely disappointed. It was only Standish.

"Had a bit of an exciting night, eh, Tommen?" Standish said, scribbling all the pens in his pocket, looking for one that worked.

Tommen shrugged, wincing at the pain in his shoulder. "I guess." He muted his movie. "I've done worse in fights at school."

Standish seemed uncertain how to respond to that and instead moved on. "Well, I'm just here for your official statement of what happened. I need only the facts and none of the fluff. Where did it start?"

Tommen ran his tongue over his teeth, feeling the slight swelling of his upper lip. "I was walking home from work. I stopped in front of the museum to tie my shoe, and suddenly the museum alarm system is going off, like totally insane. And I see two guys running away from it, so I chase them to the docks where they're untying a boat like they're going to get away. They see me and..." Tommen shrugged again. "One of them takes off; the other stays behind and decides he's going to, I don't know, beat me up, kill me, whatever. I get past him, jump in the boat. That guy tries to shoot me, and he does." He indicated his shoulder. "But he puts a hole in the bottom of the boat. Boat sinks, we go in the water. He gets away, and I swim back to shore where the second guy is still there. He starts whaling on me but he runs away when Micah and Micaiah find me."

"And do you know who the two men were?" Standish wondered, still cycling through pens.

"Yeah, they were the guys from the news. The one on shore was Calis, but he called himself Cassius. And the other one, the white guy, he introduced himself as Rifun Ndolo."

"Your friends, Micah and Micaiah, they said you recovered some stolen property from these two."

"Yeah, a journal. I grabbed it when the boat sank and Rifun and I were underwater."

Standish nodded, clicked his pen purposefully like he'd done a very satisfying job taking notes, and pocketed his notepad. "Very good, Tommen. I expect you'll be called in very soon to conduct a more thorough interview. But for now, your dad is here to see you. Off the record." Standish winked like they shared some great secret.

He left then, and hardly two minutes later, Walter walked in. He looked absolutely ragged, like he'd run a marathon and then walked another marathon just pacing. The first thing he did when he walked in was hug Tommen as best he could, minding his shoulder. When he withdrew, tears were streaming down his cheeks into his mustache.

"You are in so much trouble for not taking a ride home," he said though his voice carried no malice or threat.

Tommen felt his cheeks turn red. "I know. I'm sorry."

"I'm just glad you're safe. What happened, really?"

Tommen let out a breath. "I guess I just wanted to walk home. I Banded to get out of the bakery. I stopped in front of the museum to tie my shoe, but then I saw movement. Like someone was moving Faster than I was and I could see them moving. And when I released my Band, the museum security system was going off. But the other person's Band was just blinding, like it was super tight and narrow and Fast."

"Why did you follow them? How did you?"

"I just...I don't know why. I guess I just wanted to see if I could follow them to a getaway car or a secret lair or something. I just wanted to be helpful." He flinched at Walter's exasperated sigh. "So I drafted my way into the wake of the Band and just kept moving Faster and Faster until I was in the Band itself, and I followed them to the wharf."

"You pushed into their Band?" Walter asked. "All on your own?"

"Yeah. Anyway, I got to the docks and..." He shook his head. "I should have known it was a trap."

"Yes, you should have." Walter said the words reluctantly. "Rifun's Bands are extremely tight; he's a Warden Timekeeper. There's no way you should have been able to overpower it. But continue."

"At first, Rifun said he was going to have Calis, or Cassius or whatever his name is, kill me. But I got by Cassius and jumped into the boat with Rifun. Then he said that he admired my persistence. He said he would let me go and we would talk in a few years. Then he dumped me over the side of the boat." Walter seemed to age before him, but Tommen pressed on. "I got back in the boat. Then Rifun said he was getting bored of me. He shot me but he put a hole in the boat, too." It sounded so ridiculous and hilarious now. "When the boat sank, he dove in the water. I swam over to him and stole the journal while he was confused. Then I swam to shore. Cassius was waiting for me and kicked me around a little, but he ran off when he heard Micah and Micaiah."

Walter nodded, more to himself than anyone. "Okay."

"I do have one question. I thought Cassius was a Timekeeper? But Rifun said he was going to have Cassius kill me and Harvest me?"

"Yes, Cassius is a Harvester of the most dangerous sort. He is a Triage Harvester, and he has the ability to Harvest anyone point-blank if he so chose. And Rifun is a Warden Timekeeper. They've been working together."

"Oh. I assume there's more to this you're not telling me?"

"Of course, only inasmuch that we don't have a lot to go on either."

Tommen nodded. "One other thing. Cassius said he knew you, that you and him went way back. What did he mean?"

Walter's expression changed then, almost imperceptibly except that Tommen knew what cues to look for. The slight widening of the eyes, the shallow breathing, a slight slump of the shoulders. Then he was recovered. "He knew me a long time ago. Up until recently, I did not know him, at least not in the same sense."

"Is it anything bad?"

"Only as a tool to try to get under my skin, the psychology of the man who I hunt, knowing me when I did not know he knew me. You understand?"

"I guess."

"Good. Now I—"

"Will I ever get to hear that story?"

"It's better if you didn't. Now —"

Tommen studied him. "What about your story, about how you became a Timekeeper? You've never actually told me that."

Walter sighed. "I knew you were going to ask me these questions one day."

"And are you going to answer them? One day?"

After a moment of hesitation, Walter nodded. "I will. One day, hopefully soon, when all this is over, and Cassius and Rifun have been brought to justice."

"So you do have a plan to catch them?"

"It's in its preliminary stages. Micaiah's working on garnering some support. But you don't need to worry about that."

"But—"

"Tommen." Tommen shut up. "Right now, you just rest. I just talked to the doctor and he wants you overnight for observation of your shoulder there. Tomorrow is Sunday, and I imagine Micah and Micaiah will be nice enough to allow you the day off of work. If you want, I'll pinpoint Band you so you can heal and be ready for school on Monday. Unless of course you'd rather have some wounds and scars to show off."

Tommen grinned. "I haven't decided on that one yet. But I'll let you know."

Walter nodded sadly as he embraced Tommen again. "You know I love you, right, Tommen?"

"I know. I never doubted it."

Walter broke off and took a step back, his expression relieved. "Good. Yeah. You're all right, then? To stay overnight?"

"Yeah, I'm fine."

"Okay." He opened the door and took an awkward step, not quite in the room, not quite out. "I'll see you in the morning."

"Don't forget a change of clothes!" Tommen called after him.

Then he was left alone in the room with ugly beige walls, ugly paintings, and tired and worn sheets. He stared at the remote in his hand for a second, then looked at the movie, still muted and playing on the TV. He glanced at the door, shut and silent. His shoulder throbbed. His nose felt huge. After a minute of consideration, he turned off the TV, turned off all but the mandatory lights, shifted and wiggled until he found a semi-comfortable position, and waited for sleep to claim him.

Chapter Sixteen
Reputation

Thanks to the magic of social media, Tommen was again a star at school. Walter had Banded him enough to heal his nose and take the edge off the pain of his gunshot wound, but he was still forced to bear the brunt of that burden and wear his arm in a sling for a few days, which he felt entirely unnecessary. But hey, whatever got them talking, right?

Actually, he wasn't that big of a star. Hot girls weren't exactly crowding around his locker waiting to admire his battle scars. The only ones who gave him any sort of greeting were Layman, who again seemed to blame Tommen for whatever scrap he'd been in, and Varad, who seemed particularly troubled.

"I got shot and you're the one who looks like your dog just died," Tommen said, trying to find some kind of humor to brighten his friend's dark mood. When it didn't work, he asked, "What happened?"

"We're moving over Christmas break," Varad said.

"Wait, what?"

Varad nodded. "My father has all the papers and passports and everything we need. He's already contacted his family in India. We leave December 31st on the last flight of the year. 'All the better to greet the new year with our new lives,' he says."

"Dude, I don't even know what to say." Tommen let out a breath. "I don't know if I should congratulate you or offer to smuggle you into the next state in witness protection."

That finally got Varad to smile a bit. "If you had the means, I would gladly do that, but it would only end badly for both of us."

"Listen, man, we've got to do something before you leave. We'll grab Eric, and let's go skiing or something. How does that sound?"

Varad nodded. "I would like that. And I think Eric would like that, too."

They didn't get to say any more as the bell rang for first period. Juggling his books in one arm, Tommen set off for English class. Righting stared at him as much as the rest of the class, but she did not ask any questions. Nor did she see it as a viable excuse for why he hadn't completed the reading assignment. Because reading the next chapter of *Of Mice and Men* trumped all other little excursions over the weekend.

At least Economics wasn't a horrible class to go to. He would have rathered it be Tuesday where they could work on their investment projects, but muddling through basic supply and demand wasn't all bad. Maybe it would help him figure out the Time industry a little better, though a gut feeling told him that Government class would be more beneficial there.

AP Physics was probably the best class of the day, if not of all time, as Mrs. White announced that it was lab day. Tommen cheered the loudest out of everyone in the class and eagerly snatched up the assignment sheet as it was handed out. Even better was the assignment itself. They would be crashing cars together. Not real cars, obviously, but any combination of little die cast cars Mrs. White had brought in, unbeknownst to her young grandsons. They were the kind that were set on a base and launched forward at the pull of the zip strip.

"There is another sheet up here for you to grab when you get your cars," Mrs. White told them. "It gives you some weights and other variables that can't be gained from little die cast cars. These cars are for demonstration only, so you can see how everything works. The paper with your equations is what I will be grading you on."

As could be expected, those instructions more or less went in one ear and out the other as each table went straight for the cars and found a place on the floor. The first five minutes were spent just crashing cars together, racing them, and stomping around other groups and Godzilla-ing their crashes and races. But after a minute of sheer childhood fun and a few threatening words from White, work ensued.

"Dude, this is what we need more of," Tommen said as he and Ollie launched the cars into each other and went to work on the math. "More hands-on stuff."

"No kidding," Ollie agreed. "You'd never do this kind of thing in a regular class."

"I know, and I don't understand why. When did the fun hands-on stuff go away? I mean, everyone remembers kindergarten fun and stuff from elementary school, but when did the education lords decide to take all that away and just put us in front of books and powerpoints?"

"Dude, I don't even know, but it needs to stop. Seriously, all it is, really, is brainwashing. Make something dull so people don't care, so that if something does change fundamentally, no one cares because they only remember it was dull."

Tommen liked Ollie well enough, but he was forced to wonder if his political views were as much brainwashing as the brainwashing he was describing. Tommen didn't particularly like the establishment, but just because an idea went against it, didn't mean it was good.

The two of them had chosen a spot close to Mrs. White's desk to do their high-speed vehicle collisions, and Tommen looked up briefly as the phone on the desk rang.

"Sharon White's Dungeon of Doom," she answered. "Yeah, he is. Okay, I will. Uh-huh. Bye."

She hung up the phone and looked around the room until her gaze settled on Tommen. His stomach twisted uneasily. "Tommen, Mr. Layman would like to see you before you head to lunch. He said it shouldn't take long, so you can go five minutes early if you want."

"Okay," Tommen said, hoping he was able to hide the dread.

"What are you in for now?" Ollie asked.

Tommen shook his head. "I have no idea. The guy's got it out for me."

"No kidding. I mean, yeah, fighting is one thing. But the guy practically stalks you, day after day."

It was not a comforting thought as Tommen finished up his math work and turned it in to Mrs. White before taking his books and heading to Mr. Layman's office. To his surprise, he found not only Layman, but Mrs. Wendell there as well.

"Hello, Tommen," Layman greeted, almost amiably. "Have a seat."

Tommen sat down slowly and in such a way as to keep both of them in his sight at all times. "What is this about?"

"Quite frankly, Tommen, we're concerned."

"About what?"

"About you," Mrs. Wendell replied. "We're concerned that you're under too much stress and don't have a good outlet for it."

"What do you mean?"

"First, it was the fighting," Layman said. "Then there was your...*discovery* out on the soccer fields. And there is the ongoing case that your dad is in charge of; I know the other students bother you, wanting to know the details. You have your AP class, plus a job. We all know what happened with Eric, and I know Varad is leaving, which can be hard on you since you three have been close friends for a long time. Then there was the incident this weekend."

"You don't even know what happened," Tommen told him.

"You were shot," Mrs. Wendell pointed out. "That's all we need to know."

Well, yeah, she might have a point there. Getting shot was kind of a big deal, especially since it could have been a lot worse.

"We want to help you, Tommen," Mr. Layman said, cutting into his thoughts.

"Help me?!" Tommen blurted. "Everything I do is wrong to you. You're always stalking me and treating me like I'm always at fault for whatever happens. I fight Tyler, it's my fault. I don't fight

Tyler, it's my fault."

"It's the fighting that concerns us."

"Because you think it's my fault. I try to be a nice guy, stand up for what's right, and I get the shit beaten out of me. And it's my fault. I decide I'm not going to fight, I get the shit beaten out of me anyway. But it's still my fault. I throw the first punch in a fight. That's the only situation here I see where it's actually my fault. What do you want me to do, run away? 'Just walk away' and 'just ignore him' don't work here, so I would literally have to run away. What am I then but a coward?"

"Fighting does not make you a martyr, Tommen," Mrs. Wendell said quietly.

"You're right, because martyrs die. Fighters survive."

The bell rang for lunch.

"Which leads us to some suggestions we have in order to help you relieve some of the stress without the need to fight," Layman went on, as if Tommen hadn't said a word. "We're not going to ask you to quit your job. A job is a good thing to have. Make money, save up for a car, whatever you want. But maybe if you dropped your AP class—"

"What? No!" Tommen protested hotly. "That's the best part of my day! That is the least stressful part of my day."

"All right, but what about your other classes? It's the twenty-first century; we can get you into online classes if it would help, and you can move at your own pace."

The idea was actually appealing, at least in the English department. If he could get out from under Righting's eye, he might actually make it through that class. Layman and Wendell apparently saw his silence as a victory for them as Layman continued to speak.

"There are also some before-school activities you might take part in. Art Therapy meets in the art room. The Dead Poets of South Charleston High School meets in the auditorium. There are a few religious groups of students who meet around the building, depending on your preferred affiliation." Tommen rolled his eyes.

"Drama Club will be holding auditions soon for the school play in the spring if you are interested and can arrange your schedule."

"Can we get on with it?" Tommen cut in.

"There is also the option of standard counseling," Mrs. Wendell suggested. "Whenever, wherever, and however you feel comfortable, you and I can meet, or you and Mr. Layman."

"Why, so I can talk about my feelings?"

Layman shifted in his seat. "The thing about chivalry, Tommen, is that it so forces you to put others so far ahead of yourself that eventually you forget that the number one person who needs protecting is yourself. There's nothing wrong with being a nice guy and standing up for what's right, but if you're going to put up a wall, make sure it has the backing to withstand attack."

Tommen sighed and stood. "I'm done here."

"Sit down."

"So I can be lectured and ignored?" Tommen shook his head. "Next you're probably going to tell me you'll be calling my dad. Well, that's fine. Because at least he understands me, and he listens. Unlike you."

With that, Tommen picked up his books again and left the office. There was a wall there, all right. Layman might have said talking to him was like talking to a wall. Well, Tommen felt like that wall as he was just completely ignored, brushed off as having nothing of importance to say. Okay, the analogy sounded better in his head, but whatever. Mrs. Wendell probably meant well; after all, she was the one who was scheduling him to get him into AP classes and dual-enrollment. But Layman? No, he had it out for Tommen; of that he was certain.

He never understood why, either. Ever since the first day of high school, it always seemed like Layman was a hawk, watching Tommen who was a mouse, deciding if he wanted to swoop down and snatch him up for dinner. There were any number of theories explaining this that he'd concocted. First, he'd heard of Tommen's fighting and was keeping an eye on him from day one. Plausible.

Second, he just hated freshmen and staying silent was the best way to deal with them. Somewhat unlikely as Layman was actually pretty partial to freshmen in other areas. And Tommen was a sophomore now. Third, he was secretly a pedophile sifting through the students to find his next batch of victims — both female and male. The jury was still out on the plausibility of that one. Fourth, he had something against Walter and was taking it out on Tommen. Unlikely since Layman was always more than happy to help the cops and make a good name for himself. Fifth, he had some sort of childhood trauma that made him an asshole to whoever reminded him of that trauma, and Tommen just happened to fit the bill. Plausible, if life was a TV show where that shit actually happened. Sixth, he really did care but his time as a soldier had worn away at his outward empathy and now he was incapable of expressing such emotions. The jury was still out on that one, too.

Ultimately, Tommen figured it really didn't matter. Layman was an uncaring asshole, and they still had to put up with each other for another two and a half school years. Maybe less since Tyler was graduating and, hopefully, there wouldn't be anymore fighting once he was gone. Wouldn't that be lovely? Tommen couldn't even imagine life without having to constantly look over his shoulder, or cringing at every interrupted conversation. Was there really such a thing as just going to school and going home, without the fear of having to fight his way out? Was there a chance that he would one day be able to have a conversation with a girl that didn't end in violence?

Tommen made it to his locker with rage in his heart and wonder in his mind. He dropped his books off and considered removing the sling; it was more hindrance than help. He decided against it in the end, figuring it was still good for a rumor or two by the end of the day. Maybe he would get rid of it tomorrow if he could convince his dad. Or maybe he would forego the Banding and keep it until the doctor cleared him, like a good little patient.

Sighing, he gathered his books one by one for the next class, then grabbed his lunch and headed for the cafeteria. Ham on rye with a good dose of mustard, sitting in the company of the only friend he had left, and even that would be taken from him when the new year rolled around.

"You look as enthusiastic as I feel," Varad said as Tommen sat down. "What happened?"

"Layman tried to pull me out of AP Physics," Tommen grumbled, fishing out his sandwich.

"What? Why? Physics is, like, your thing, dude. It's what you're good at."

"Well, he and Mrs. Wendell seem to think I'm under too much stress, so they decided to take it upon themselves to relieve me of some of that stress."

"By taking away one of the good things that's happened to you recently?"

"That's what I said. Then they wanted me to do counseling, or at the very least join some group like the Art Therapy group or Dead Poets' Society or whatever."

"Well, you do have your writing," Varad pointed out.

Tommen gave him a look. "Yes, I have my writing. My writing. By me, for me, only. I don't have to read it in front of a bunch of emo scene kids in order to somehow validate it and make myself feel better."

"Hey, don't take it out on me, dude. Or you'll start stressing me out."

Tommen shook his head and grinned. "Yeah." He took a bite of his sandwich. "Because you don't have enough of that in your own life."

He looked around the cafeteria. Tyler was nowhere to be seen, but that didn't mean he wasn't skulking around, waiting for him. Tommen hated being afraid. Even if he didn't admit it aloud, he was afraid of Tyler. He had a sneaking suspicion that his graduation wouldn't solve the problem either, not since his brother was also a sophomore.

Varad shifted in his seat and tried to put on a more optimistic face. "So I was texting Eric in second period, and he's totally game for going skiing over Christmas break. When were you thinking?"

"Uh, I was going to leave that up to you since you're the one moving, and I figured you have a pretty busy schedule."

Varad shook his head. "Nah, I'd just sneak out anyway. Anything to get out of the chaos that's become my home. But hey, got free skiing Christmas Day at Snowshoe."

"That's when everyone goes skiing," Tommen complained. "Besides, I was figuring some night skiing, get some dinner at the lodge, then head out back for a binge one last time. My treat this time."

Varad grinned. "My dad was right; you are a terrible influence."

"Yeah, so sue me. What do you say?"

"Hey, man, I'm totally down for that. How about the Monday before? Mondays are usually pretty slow at ski resorts."

"It's Christmas break," Tommen pointed out. "Text Eric, see what he thinks."

Varad shook his head as he was already on his phone, clicking away. "Already on it, dude."

They didn't have to wait long before Eric replied. Varad read the text aloud. " 'Sounds good. Anything to get me out of the house that doesn't involve the kids.' "

"I'd call that a set date," Tommen said.

Varad nodded. "I'll drive."

Lunch felt shorter than normal, or maybe that was just from losing time because of Layman's little heart-to-heart chat. Either way, Tommen was less than thrilled to head to Web Programming. They'd finally made it out of the introductory chapter in the textbook—titled, "What is the Internet?"—and gotten into the basics of programming, doing some real work on the computers at least. But as if the outdated textbooks weren't bad enough, the computers in the lab they were assigned to were outdated themselves, running outdated software.

They were programming like it was 2005 or something.

Still, Tommen did the work dutifully, reflecting that in 2005 he'd never heard of the Internet or computers or cell phones or anything at all. This outdated stuff might as well have been magic. Even Walter who'd been around for the advent of this technology still couldn't do much more than get online, his expertise limited to Google, Facebook, and an assortment of police databases and technologies. But, like all children, Tommen had absorbed things quickly. First it was Walter's ancient flip-phone, then an ancient desktop computer from 1999. Then the age of the tablets arrived, and he was as much a tech junkie as the rest of them. Now here he was, complaining the same as everyone else about the quality of work they were being forced to produce.

Eventually the bell rang, and Tommen slogged off to his last class. Drawing and Painting wasn't a bad class, really, and Tommen figured his drawing was improving somewhat with some of the techniques Robinson showed them. Assuming those techniques could be seen around the massive afro wig. They were still in pencil drawing, and that was hard enough to see against the glare of the light on the paper.

Personally, Tommen was more excited for the charcoal or the pastels or chalk, but those wouldn't be until the very end of the class, after the painting unit, once they'd mastered some of the techniques on cheap pencils. Once or twice he'd gone back to add little drawings to his stories, but decided that they would just look better in charcoal or pastel or chalk. Maybe he had some delusion that using charcoal automatically made him a master artist, like Mr. Ross-Robinson. At any rate, it wasn't a bad way to end the day. Maybe it wasn't a bad way to begin it either.

Tommen looked around the room at his classmates. No one ever admitted to being in Art Therapy — it was kind of like Fight Club, he supposed — but there were always telltale signs of who might be part of it. Paint or chalk on hands and arms when they weren't doing paint or chalk in class. He only spotted one person who had dried paint spots up to her elbows. A senior. And one who loosely associated with Tyler. Tommen sighed and returned to his meager pencil scribbles. The last thing he needed was word getting back to Tyler that he was in Art Therapy. He could hear the taunting now.

The end of the day couldn't come sooner. Tommen made sure he'd cleaned up his area just a little early—and not without a little help from Time—so he could be the first one to bolt out the door. He wasn't sure why he was bolting anywhere, least of all his locker. There was nothing exciting in there except a thousand subtle reminders of all the homework that was due the next day. Papers sticking out of books and folders, *Of Mice and Men* in the bottom of his backpack where he'd tossed it haphazardly after class. The remains of the day sitting in his backpack like a sack of old bones.

He was just about ready to grab his backpack when he spotted Varad. Tommen flagged him down.

"Need some help there, gimpy?" Varad asked, grinning.

"You're sure about the 23rd for skiing?" Tommen asked seriously. "I need to know when and where and how I'm going to get the stuff."

"Yeah, dude. I was texting Eric a little during last class, and he's totally up for it. He's going no matter what and so am I. Screw packing; I'm going to have some kind of fun before I go."

"Just making sure. I'll see you tomorrow."

Varad turned as if to leave, then stopped and whistled. "Oh, dude, you did it this time."

"What?" Tommen grabbed his backpack, slung it over his shoulder, slammed his locker shut, and turned to see what Varad was looking at.

Not a few people stopped and stared—or at least stared on their way out the door—as two men in blue entered the school and strode purposefully toward the office. Tommen might not have been too worried except he knew that bushy blond mustache anywhere.

"What'd you do this time?" Varad asked, elbowing Tommen in the ribs. They walked cautiously toward the door, hoping, maybe, to slip by and get out to the bus without being noticed.

"I didn't do anything," Tommen said quietly.

It hit him half a second later that this could be his escort to go downtown and give a more thorough report of what had happened Saturday night, like Standish had promised him. Indeed, even as he and Varad tried to blend in with the crowd and make it out the door, Layman exited the office with Walter and Standish following. Almost immediately, Walter spotted Tommen and motioned him over with just a look.

"I gotta go," Tommen told Varad.

"See ya, dude," Varad replied, clapping him on the shoulder. He pointed at him severely. "Don't die, okay?"

"Yeah, I'll make a point of that."

Tommen tried not to slink over to the waiting men like a puppy about to get whipped, but that was honestly how it felt. Layman was the asshole who was threatening to take away his AP Physics class. Walter was his dad, but at the moment he was a uniformed police officer who undoubtedly meant business. And Standish...well, he was Standish, the poor guy who could never get a pen to work right.

"Glad we caught you before you got on the bus," Layman said amiably, as if they hadn't had an argument just a couple hours previous. "Shall we step into my office where it's quieter?"

The bulk of the student body had already left, and the halls were pretty quiet as it was, but Tommen saw no real reason to argue. Instead, he nodded and meekly followed them back into the office, into Layman's office, and shut the door behind him.

"I don't think this was quite necessary," Walter said, voicing Tommen's thoughts. "All we needed to do was just take him down to the station to answer a few questions about something that happened over the weekend."

"Yes," Layman acknowledged, his tone immediately alerting Tommen to his real intentions, "and I respect that your time is valuable." He sat behind his desk. "However, since you are here, I was wondering if you had just five minutes to discuss something."

Walter raised a brow. "Was there another fight?"

"No, but we—Mrs. Wendell and myself—are concerned that Tommen may be under too much stress and has no way to constructively express it."

"That sounds like more than a five minute conversation. And your right, my time is valuable and will be better spent down at the station doing my job. I would, however, be more than interested in carrying on this talk at a later date."

"Excellent. I expect you will call to make arrangements?"

"I will. But not today."

There was something in the tone of Walter's voice that set off red flags in Tommen's mind. Walter was on edge. His words were friendly enough, but they were sharp, dismissive. He was a man on a mission. Sure, he had every imperative reason to want to catch Cassius and Rifun, but this sounded like he was on a hot trail and Layman was like a stumbling block that was tripping him up, like water that was messing with the nose of a bloodhound.

"Very good. As always, a pleasure to see you, Mr. Forbes," Layman said. His words were kind, but Tommen could tell the friendliness was wavering. He did not like being dismissed. He might take it in stride in public, and he might like to put his glowing face out there as a good citizen to help CPD, but here in his own office, he was the boss. Right now, Walter was not letting him be the boss, and it was grating on him. Tommen felt immense satisfaction at that realization.

"Got your stuff?" Walter asked as they left the office.

"Yeah. Does Micaiah know?" Tommen wondered.

"He knows; I called him. We'll head down to the station, talk for a few minutes, then I'll take you to work. Sound good?"

Tommen shrugged. "No arguments from me."

Chapter Seventeen
Witness Testimony

Walter led the way to the cruiser, noting the points and stares from students and parents alike. Dutifully, he opened the backseat door for Tommen who tossed his backpack in first before wiggling in with only one good shoulder. Standish took shotgun, and Walter headed for the driver's seat. He navigated the treacherous maze of buses, cars, and people, almost getting clipped once by a lunatic senior who shaped up immediately once he realized he almost hit a cop car. Walter considered a ticket, then figured intimidation worked well enough, pulling up close to the kid's rear bumper, feeling immense satisfaction as the kid kept checking his mirrors to see if he was still there as the cars crept out one by one into the main flow of traffic. Only once they were out of the parking lot did Walter Fast Band and turn to look at Tommen.

"So what's up?" Tommen asked. "You weren't yourself in there. What happened, another body?"

"Steggmann is threatening to take me off the case, assign it to another detective," Walter told him. "He says it's become too personal."

"Is it because of me?"

"Well, partially. Part of it does have to do with your actions Saturday night. The other part of it is my relationship to Lily, or what he perceives as relationship. Obviously Steggmann doesn't know the true extent of it, but he thinks it's clouding my judgment. And Saturday sure didn't help." He went on before Tommen could speak. "I don't blame you for it. I know you. And, to an extent, I think Cassius and Rifun planned the robbery that way. Maybe they staked out the bakery or the museum, waited for you to walk home one night so they could pull it off and drag you out alone into their territory. I don't know, but it's not your fault. Not entirely."

"So what do we do?"

Walter let out a breath. "Well, I managed to convince Steggmann to let me carry on normally. He was ready to shelve it again when the robbery happened. Basically, I have until end of shift tomorrow to find some sort of lead or break. After that, the case gets shelved, and if and when it gets reopened, it goes to another detective."

"I gave you a name, though. Rifun. Isn't he a good enough lead?"

"As invisible as Cassius, probably living under a dozen different aliases, a dozen different identities and lives. They're not stupid, and they have access to the resources to pull it off. Believe me, I'm looking, but I'm not going to find anything in the time I have. Lily was helpful up until the point that her information was made null and void by Rifun revealing himself."

Tommen shifted in his seat. "Why not let the case get shelved? Get Earth-side eyes off of it so you can go full-tilt on the Time-side investigation."

Walter shook his head. "Because they want to be seen. They want to make a show of it and snub their noses at Earth-side justice."

"Why? I mean, first they're after Lily, and then they rob a museum for a journal...what's it all for?"

"Lily seems to think the journal is their endgame. Right now, you are the only person linking them to both the murders and the robbery. Otherwise, I got nothing."

"You got the journal."

"Yes. And what I need you to do is give the most accurate, most detailed account you can of what happened Saturday night. Everything you did, saw, smelled, heard. Everything they did, said. Every little detail."

"How will that help?"

"In ways that you can't yet imagine, but only if you tell us everything."

Tommen sighed, and Walter shook his head. "Aw, no. Don't go doubting yourself now. Don't think, just remember. Once you start talking, the rest will start coming. You remember what I've taught you about giving statements and describing what happened?"

"Yeah. I'll try."

It was probably the best he was going to get from him. Walter turned back around, put his hands on the steering wheel, and released the Band. It was a lot to expect from the boy, and Walter hated putting the pressure on like that, but he was the only well of information they had. Walter just hoped that well wasn't dry.

His thoughts drifted back to the school office. Sure, he'd been a little short with Orville, but he heard the principal's words and understood them. Tommen was under incredible stress, and he knew that. Walter wasn't home as much as he'd like, plus Tommen had work and his AP classes and his friends and everything else a teenage boy has. And then there was that whole Timekeeper business. It was probably pulling him in so many directions, it was tearing him apart.

Walter let out a breath. He wanted to help him. But everything he knew to help him either involved taking away things he liked—such as his AP class—or pushing him deeper into Timekeeping. Walter knew Tommen was eying becoming a Scout. Truthfully, Walter had nothing against Scouts. For Tommen, it would be like the ultimate studying abroad experience, to get out and see, not just the world, but the galaxy, the entire universe. But, would it really kill him to stay home for another year or two to get in some college and a real Earth-side degree, something that might help him if he ever did decide to return to Earth and stick around a while?

"So...that journal..." Tommen began.

Walter Banded and looked back. Tommen was slumped a bit in the seat, looking guilty. "Something private?"

Tommen shrugged. "No, not really."

He dropped the Band. "What about it?"

"Did I ruin it when I made Rifun go in the water?"

"I don't know; I didn't see it." Walter glanced at Standish who shrugged. "Don't know. But it is possible, given how old it was."

There was every possibility that the journal had been ruined, and, privately, Walter hoped it had been. A quick drop in a puddle was one thing, but total submersion and a swim to shore couldn't have been kind to it. And if it had been reduced to a soggy lump of old leather and parchment paper with none of the entries left readable, it would be the ultimate way to thwart Rifun's plan, whatever it was. Whatever had been written in that journal would be lost, and maybe rightly so. Just because there was knowledge to be gained didn't mean that it should be, or that it wasn't hidden for a reason.

At the same time, perhaps the journal had also housed secrets to preserving paper and ink, long before modern times invented laminating. If it was some sort of Time journal with Time secrets, why wouldn't there be some small footnote indicating a way to preserve such things from as simple a thing as water? Maybe it wasn't even paper and ink from Earth. If Julianna's husband had been a Scout, who knew where that stuff came from or what it really was?

Walter racked his memory, trying to bring to mind either Cassius as a guard or Julianna's husband, but nothing was coming up. Not that it was terribly surprising; they could have been in a completely different wing. Still, the coincidence and how they were all related through time and space was remarkable. Cassius and Julianna? The root of the story. Walter being in the same prison as her husband? A small stretch but not impossible. Tommen being the one to find the journal, being Walter's son, and Walter being the detective on the case? Was it really a coincidence? Or was it like Einstein said, God being anonymous? And for what purpose?

Walter knew Tommen had given up on God years ago. In a way, it saddened him, but there was nothing he could do about it. Personally, Walter had seen too much and been through too much to not believe in God, but those were the same reasons Tommen had for being a rather staunch, prickly atheist. Sometimes Walter wondered what went through Tommen's mind while all this was going on. Did he just blame the awfulness of human nature itself, or was it a case of him believing in God and just not liking Him very much, blaming Him for the awfulness of human nature? What did he see when he went to the Wheel and looked out across a secret industry that Earth, in all its proud glory, was blissfully ignorant of? Did he see a conglomeration of accidents, or the beauty of Creation? Maybe one day they would have that discussion, about Time and faith, but that discussion was not for today.

Walter pulled into the station parking lot and opened the door for Tommen who still struggled a bit with having only one arm.

"Can I please take this thing off?" he whined, slinging his backpack onto his good shoulder.

"Not until the doctor says," Walter told him.

Standish smirked but said nothing as he led the way into the station. Most greeted them on friendly terms; a few gave disapproving looks toward Tommen or rolled their eyes. So he got into a few fights; he was still a good kid. Actually, Walter was generally very proud of his son for holding to the old ways. It wasn't the fault of these guys who didn't seem to understand how things used to work. Sure, meeting in court was the more neat and tidy way of settling things, but it often led to boiling resentment and retaliation. Fist fights were a little bloodier, but the settlements were reached within a matter of minutes and were, more often than not, more absolute.

Not that Walter encouraged the fighting—he'd broken up more than one bar brawl in his day—but he fully believed that there was a time and place for it, when only sheer bravado would settle a matter. For instance, the day Walter got the call that Tommen had finally thrown the first punch against Tyler Freeman, and the details of that fight. Maybe it was the threat of punishment, maybe it was the fight itself and Tommen finally demonstrating his skill, either way, there hadn't been a fight or even a nasty look between them since. The issue was settled.

They ended up in the little office where notes of the case were sprawled out across the whiteboard and the map. Walter arranged some chairs so Tommen was facing away from the notes, so he wasn't influenced by them. Standish went and retrieved Steggmann as well as Hannah Garner, the sketch artist.

"How are you, Tommen?" Steggmann asked, walking in and taking a comfortable seat closest to Tommen.

"Been better," Tommen replied warily.

"If it's all right with you, we'd like to start with a sketch artist to get a drawing of this Rifun Ndolo. Miss Garner here will walk you through it. Sound okay?"

"I guess."

"Good." Steggmann stood and Hannah took his seat.

"Hi, Tommen, my name is Hannah. I want to start with you telling me everything you remember just off the top of your head."

Stegmann glanced at Walter and Standish and made a small gesture. They followed him outside, and Walter shut the door behind him.

"Curator of the museum was able to pull security footage of the robbery," Steggmann said. "Problem is, it looks like it was hacked."

"What do you mean?" Standish asked.

"The recording looks like it was scrambled. The times are wrong and it cuts out at points, leaving us with virtually no usable images of the robbery. Thankfully, we already have a photo of Calis or Cassius or Chris or whatever the hell his name is, but we're relying on your boy there—" He pointed to Tommen through the glass. "—for a description of Rifun."

"He'll do his best," Walter promised, a little offended that Steggmann would suggest anything to the contrary.

"Did the curator do an inventory, see what all was taken?" Standish wondered.

"The only thing that was missing was the journal Tommen recovered."

"How badly was it damaged?" Walter asked cautiously.

Steggmann folded his arms. "Oddly enough, not bad at all, considering it was submerged for quite a while. The leather was more or less undamaged and some of the papers are discolored, but the ink was pristine. Curator couldn't tell me why, but that's not important."

And so Walter's hopes for an incidental destruction of the journal and thwarting of Rifun's plans went down the drain. Briefly, he entertained ideas of how to "accidentally" set it on fire. And if the journal survived fire, well, there was always the shredder.

"We've got these guys' faces and descriptions plastered everywhere in Charleston, but we still have nothing," Steggmann was saying. "No viable vehicles, no address, no history, no motive, not even a secret underground lair. For God's sake, we don't even know their real names. I hope your boy gives us something to go on, Walter. Otherwise these guys are just going to keep killing and getting away with it."

It was not a comforting thought as Walter returned to his cubicle. Tommen would be in with the sketch artist for a while, so he might as well get some work done. What work that was, he wasn't entirely sure since, as Steggmann said, they had the guys, knew what they looked like, but had no way to track or catch them.

He wasn't sure if he did get anything accomplished, but pretty soon, Hannah was knocking at the wall of his cubicle.

"All yours, Walt," she said.

"You get a sketch?" he asked.

She opened her pad and showed Walter the sketch. Wasn't half bad, really, but Walter hadn't seen the guy in person to actually know what he looked like and how it compared.

"Paint the town with him," Walter told her, and headed down to the office where Standish was already sitting, notepad open, fumbling for a working pen.

"I hope that isn't contagious, Jim," Walter said, handing Standish a pen which he knew worked, but, when the man tried it, mysteriously dried up. "Or we might have to go back to chiseling on stone."

"My luck, the chisel or the stone would break," Standish said, sighing, but finally finding something that worked—a pencil. Two strokes in, the lead broke.

"Is this the part where I tell you what happened?" Tommen asked.

"Now it is," Walter said, sitting in another chair and producing his own notepad and working pen. "How about we start with why you didn't go home with Micaiah?"

Tommen shrugged. "I don't know. I guess I just wanted to walk."

Walter wanted to Band and ask him more about that, but he didn't need to cause anymore anxiety and potentially ruin the rest of the testimony. "What route did you take?"

So Tommen outlined his route, one that he always took when he walked home, with a few shortcuts through alleys just because of the cold.

"What happened when you got to the museum?" Standish wondered.

"I tripped over my shoelaces, so I stopped to tie them. Then, suddenly, like, the museum starts freaking out. There were lights flashing and some high-pitched alarm that I almost couldn't hear because the street itself was just loud with people and Christmas music and stuff. Then I saw two guys running out of the museum. So...I chased after them."

"Why?"

Tommen shrugged again. "I don't know. Just...instinct I guess. Saw a crime being committed, saw where they went, wanted to stop them."

"Did you know who the men were when you started after them?"

"No, I didn't."

Standish nodded. "Continue."

"I thought they were going to have some getaway car, you

know, get a description and a plate? But I ended up following them down to the launch. I lost them there, but..." He squirmed a little. "It was a trap."

"Tommen, this is very important," Walter said severely. "We need every word, every detail about what happened next."

Tommen nodded. "Well, first they—Cassius, I mean—called me stupid for following them. I didn't know it was him until he got out in the open. Then the other guy told him not to be so mean, that he admired my persistence. He introduced himself as Rifun Ndolo." He let out a breath. "He taunted me for kind of being like a wannabe vigilante, but said he wasn't going to tell me anything because that made me a liability, and in the event that I did somehow escape, then I wouldn't have anything to give to the police."

"Damn," Standish hissed. "Sorry, go on."

"Rifun got into a boat and told Cassius to kill me, then said to meet him at the rendezvous. He didn't say where that was."

"Did you fight Cassius?" Walter asked.

Tommen shook his head. "Not immediately. I waited until Rifun had untied his boat and was shoving off. Then I kind of faked out Cassius and made for the boat. I jumped in and confronted Rifun. I tried to get the journal or his gun or something, but he basically kicked my ass. He said he admired my determination and said he was going to let me live, and in a couple years we'd talk again."

"Do you know what he was talking about, talking in a couple years?" Standish asked.

"No, but it didn't sound good. He threw me over the side of the boat after that."

"Why did you go after him a second time instead of returning to shore?"

He let out a breath. "Because I don't like to be bullied, and I don't like to lose so easily."

Walter nodded slowly. "Okay. So what did you do next?"

"I went underwater and swam up to the boat. I hauled myself in, but I was really slow, and Rifun was waiting for me with his gun pointed at me. I managed to move fast enough that it didn't kill me, but still..." He indicated his shoulder. "It put a hole in the bottom of the boat, though, so it sank. I jumped over the side and waited for Rifun to jump in, too. When he did, I just took the journal and swam away as fast as I could."

"What happened when you got to shore?" Standish wondered, fishing for another writing utensil.

"Cassius was waiting for me. We fought. Then Micah and Micaiah found me and he ran off. They called 9-1-1 and put me in the car to warm up."

"Tommen, do you know what kind of gun Rifun was carrying?"

"Um, revolver. Seven-shot, I think, because I remember thinking it was unusual in some way. Wood grips, shined up like they were brand new or it was his pride and joy. Couldn't tell you the caliber, though. Bigger than a .22. Just by the sound, I might guess a .45."

"All right, Tommen, is there anything you want to add or change, anything you might have forgotten? Anything at all; no detail is too small at this point."

Tommen thought for a second and rubbed his eyes. "I don't think so. I mean, if I do think of anything, it's not like I have to go far to find someone who's working on the case." He smirked and even Walter had to smile a bit and shake his head. "I think that's it."

Walter and Standish finished scribbling their notes.

"I'm not going to make it to work," Tommen sighed, looking at the clock.

"I'm afraid not," Walter said, pocketing his notepad. "I didn't know Steggmann wanted a sketch artist, so that ate up a lot of time. Either way, Micaiah and Micah already know; I'll vouch for you on that. In the meantime, go hang out in my cubicle for a bit. Work on your homework, and we'll get going as soon as I'm done here. Fair?"

Tommen shrugged. "No choice."

"Good answer."

Tommen grabbed his backpack and left the room, heading down to Walter's cubicle, leaving Walter and Standish alone in the office.

"Well, that was less than helpful," Standish sighed. "Not that he wasn't thorough with his story, but...Rifun was right. By not telling Tommen anything, he couldn't tell us anything."

"True," Walter said. "But I'm more curious about the timing of the whole thing. What are the odds that they would rob the museum on the same night that Tommen just happened to walk home? He was supposed to have gotten a ride."

"Think they planned it that way? How?"

"I don't know." Walter stood and went to the whiteboard. "I couldn't even tell you why except to get to me."

"Steggmann is threatening to pull you from the case because it's getting too personal," Standish said, standing. He put his hands up when Walter started to protest. "Not say I agree with him, but that's the reason. Maybe that's what they want. Maybe you're getting too close to home on something, and they want you out of the way."

"So the question then becomes, what did I find that I didn't know I found?"

Walter didn't buy that excuse, but he elected to play along. If Rifun wanted him out of the way, he could very easily kill or maim him. More likely, Rifun wanted to draw Walter deeper into the game, first by showing him that he knew who he was and how he was connected to the case historically, even if he'd been unaware of it for decades, and then by threatening his son. But to what end?

Or maybe it really was as simple as sadistic pleasure. Steggmann and a court of law wouldn't buy it, and the general public wouldn't like it. In every TV show, there always had to be a reason, usually stemming from some childhood trauma that set a person irrevocably on a path of crime. People didn't like it when the only reason was evil for its own sake, a twisted mind game for its own pleasure. There was no reconciling that kind of behavior, nothing to point to and say, "That's where it started, and this is the reason." Evil simply was, and people didn't like it. That's why Rifun and Cassius would get away with it. At least on the Earth-side of things.

"What if we're looking at it backwards?" Walter wondered aloud. "Every time the case gets shelved or is threatened to be shelved, something else happens, and it gets closer and closer to me."

Standish ran his tongue over his teeth. "First murder happens, you're assigned to the case. Case gets shelved. Next murder happens, they leave a pocketwatch specifically for you to see. Case is threatened with the shelf again, they rob a museum and try to kill your kid." He folded his arms and shifted his stance. "Why the shift, though? Murder is their style, but why go from women, who you thought would lead to Lily Guile, to your son? And robbing a museum?"

Walter sighed. "Earlier Saturday afternoon, I met with Lily again. She said the journal used to belong in her family but was lost two centuries ago in that mine until Tommen found it. She said that Cassius and Rifun might have thought she had the journal and that's why they were trying to kill her. When they realize it was in a museum instead, they skip killing her and go rob a museum."

"And Tommen?"

"Maybe they did stake it out and wait for a night when Tommen would be walking by."

"Well, sketchy family history aside, what exactly is in that journal?"

"I don't know, but I want to find out."

They headed downstairs to the evidence room where a tired middle-aged man sat, reading through an inventory list.

"Evening, Brian," Walter greeted. "We're looking for evidence."

"Never heard that one before," Brian grumbled and straightened. "What kind of evidence?"

"A journal. Leather-bound and probably still a little water-logged."

Brian nodded. "Yup, I know the one." He retrieved it and

waited as Walter signed for it. "Steggmann says the museum curator's been chomping at the bit to get this thing back. Probably when this case gets shelved again, it'll be returned."

"Then it's a good thing we got it when we did. Thanks, Brian."

The first thing they did when they got back upstairs was make photocopies of all the pages. Rather, Standish stood and made the copies while Walter checked on Tommen who was not doing his homework, instead playing some game on his phone.

"Homework done?" Walter asked.

"Yeah, it's done," Tommen replied, not looking up from his phone. "We leaving yet?"

"Not yet. Making some copies and then doing a preliminary perusal."

"Of the journal."

"Yeah."

"So nothing I said made any difference."

Walter frowned. "Nothing you said. But your actions may prove to be louder than your words." He Banded. "And if Cassius and Rifun follow the pattern we think they're following, they're not going to wait a month or a week to try something else. The journal is intact. We can expect they'll come for it again."

"What's in the journal anyway?"

"That's why we're making copies of it, so we can find out."

"Okay."

Walter dropped the Band. "You sure you're okay here? I think there's some cookies in the break room."

"I'm fine." Tommen still didn't look up.

"Okay. It won't be much longer."

He hoped. The journal was 3/4 full, but that was still a hundred and fifty sheets of paper, written on both sides, which meant three hundred separate pages spitting out of the machine.

"Man, this stuff is gibberish," Standish said forlornly, flipping through the pages already copied. "Whatever miner wrote this spent one too many nights breathing that asbestos."

"Let me see," Walter said, taking a couple pages.

It was, as Standish said, gibberish. It didn't even look like a proper language, just scribbles. Truth be told, Walter had actually seen the journal briefly when Tommen first brought it with him, before it was turned over, but he'd forgotten how ridiculous it all looked. At first glance, it might have looked like Braille. Another person might have said some archaic form of Arabic. None of the history or linguistic experts at the university had been able to decipher it, so it was simply turned over to the museum as a novelty, the diary of a miner, gone mad from darkness, being trapped in a collapsed mine. The mine was not actually collapsed, but who would know the difference, right?

"So, before I waste another two hundred perfectly clean sheets of paper, what do we want to do with it?" Standish asked. "I haven't found any evidence of English or other viable language."

"Well, that's the problem, isn't it?" Walter said, looking through the pages. "It's a viable language to someone." He looked around. "We can wait on copying the rest, but I'll take the pages you have so far. Tomorrow I might know of someone who would be willing to take a crack at decoding it."

Standish handed over the papers. "I still think it's gibberish, but if it's something these guys are willing to kill for, go right ahead."

Walter took a few minutes to sort the pages and used a marker to write numbers at the bottom. When he was finished, he straightened and did a quick stretch. "I don't know about you, but I've had enough fun for one day on this. What do you say?"

Standish was already pulling on his jacket. "I'm right there with you, buddy." He refilled his coffee mug. "I'll see you in the morning. Tell your kid I said thanks, and I don't want to see him here again."

Walter rolled his eyes but bid him farewell as he returned to his cubicle.

"We leaving?" Tommen asked, still playing some game on his

phone and not looking at Walter.

"Yeah, we're leaving."

"We going home?"

Walter let out a breath. "Not immediately, but don't worry; I'll make it quick."

"Whatever." Tommen put his phone away, grabbed his backpack, and followed Walter out to the car.

"So is there something you want to tell me?" Walter asked as he pulled out into traffic.

"About what?" Tommen wondered.

"I'm giving you the chance to speak your bit before I go talk to Layman."

Tommen slumped a little. "So, you're actually going to do that?"

"Like I said, I'm giving you the chance to say your piece so I have an idea of what's going on before I walk in. He just said that he and Mrs. Wendell think you're too stressed."

"Yeah, and their ideas for un-stressing me involve taking away my AP Physics class or sending me to Art Therapy or some stupid thing."

"Why is Art Therapy a bad thing?"

"I'm not some emo kid who, you know, needs to paint and throw things at the canvas to express my feelings and shit. I'm not depressed or anything. I don't need to show my work to the world and have them feel bad for me and my woeful sorrows in order to feel validated."

Walter raised a brow and gave him a sideways glance. "Tommen, Art Therapy isn't about emo kids and depression. It's designed for you to be able to just do. Without being graded, or fear of judgment. And if you make friends, that's a good bonus."

"Yeah, until word gets back to Tyler Freeman."

"I also believe AT is meant to be anonymous?"

"Yeah, except when his friends are in it, too. Word will get back around."

"And there are no other groups that you might enjoy?"

"I'm not an actor. Drama Club isn't for me."

"There's more to theater than acting. There are more people behind the scenes than on stage."

"Layman also tried to suggest one of the religious groups. As if talking about feelings wasn't bad enough, now I have God or Allah or Vishnu judging me, too."

Walter could only sigh at that one. One day they would have that talk. "What about your writing? We both know what it's about, but the rest of the world will just see it as historical fiction."

Tommen looked out the window. "I know."

He said no more after that, and Walter judged it best not to pursue that line of thought. Tommen just wanted to be normal, to have friends who weren't being accused of being rapists, or moving halfway around the world; to be able to talk to a girl without being bullied; to be allowed to excel at his chosen career path without having to choose between it and everything else; to write stories he knew to be true without sounding like a lunatic. He needed help of some form. Walter knew it, and he suspected Tommen knew it, too. But Tommen would not go if pushed; he had to go of his own volition. Walter just wasn't sure what that tipping point would be, or the consequences.

Eventually they made it to the bakery. It wasn't too busy, but Walter had promised Tommen he would be quick. To make a point of it, he left the car running and walked in casually.

"Evening, Walter," Micah greeted from the counter as he took his place in line. "Everything okay with Tommen?"

"Yeah." He Banded. "I really did plan on bringing him in, but Steggmann decided he wanted him to recount to a sketch artist, so that ate up quite a bit of time. After that, there just wasn't any point. It's all on me this time."

"No worries; we haven't been busy. You need something?"

"I do."

"Step into our office." Micah went to the office door and

opened it, extending the Band to Micaiah. "Cai. Captain's got something for us."

Micaiah never seemed too pleased to be interrupted in his work, but he managed to keep his grouchiness under control as Walter entered the office, closed the door, and laid the journal pages out on what little open space there was on the desk.

"What's this?" Micaiah wondered, picking them up. "Are these...?"

"Pages from the journal, yes," Walter said.

"It survived?" Micah wondered incredulously.

"Almost perfectly." Walter leaned against one wall. "No one at the university has been able to decipher it—cryptographically, linguistically, nothing."

"So you want us to take these to the Wheel and see if we get a hit," Micaiah finished.

"When it's convenient, but I need these back preferably by noon tomorrow before this case gets shelved again and I lose it."

"Lose it?"

"Steggmann's taking me off the case, says it's gotten too personal, my judgment is too cloudy. Unless I can crack this case before it gets shelved again, which is end of shift tomorrow."

"Shit." Micaiah took the papers in hand. He frowned. "You know I'll do it for you, Walter, but I don't like it. If what you said is true, and Julianna's husband was a Scout, well, Scouts exist kind of in that hazy gray area between Timekeeping and Running. And if Rifun is willing to kill for it, the information in these pages may not be safe, and we might end up being implicated as Runners. Just the accusation, with this stuff as proof, would not likely end well for us, especially as Lieutenants. It may not go well for you, either, since you gave it to us."

"I know," Walter sighed. "But the way I see it, the information is incredibly valuable to Rifun. Translating it may bring him out of the shadows. And we'll either be seen as trying to apprehend a dangerous criminal and commended for it, or we'll be seen in association with him. But if the Hands won't touch Rifun and Cassius, I'm hoping they'll be too cautious about coming after us."

"Yes, but as we all know, image is everything," Micah pointed out. "We either need to catch him with this, or else our image is tarnished forever. And we can say good-bye to any future help we might get."

"Were you able to get a few candidates to help us?"

"Only one. She's willing to help, but she'll take no charge and no heat. Everything is on us. Assuming...we have a plan?"

"Not yet. Not until this gets translated and something helpful comes out of it."

"Well, that's a gamble in itself, but we'll see what we can do." Micaiah gathered the papers and set them in an otherwise empty file folder. "Noon tomorrow, you said? Stop by for your usual pastry and we'll have it for you. Or we'll have something for you."

"That's all I can ask."

Walter ended up buying a couple brownies before heading out to the car where Tommen was again on his phone.

"You know, for complaining about never having enough battery life, you sure seem to be on your phone a lot," Walter observed handing him one of the brownies.

"It's almost dead," Tommen said mildly. "Didn't use it almost all day at school, and then there was that little vacation to the police station and all."

"What do you kids look at on those things all day, anyway?"

"Funny videos, blog posts. Sometimes schoolwork gets posted online or on the school's app."

"The school has an app?"

"Yeah, you didn't know that? Jeez, give me your phone and I'll put it on for you."

"What does the app do?"

"For teachers, they can post homework and class updates and stuff. Students can view homework and stuff. I don't know about parents but I think it's like a calendar of events and speed dials to the office and stuff."

"Sounds like a lot of stuff."

Tommen shrugged. "Not really; it's going nowhere faster."

"Why do you say that?"

"Because most of the teachers are as old as you and don't always understand how to use it, so half the time it's useless anyway."

"Most of your teachers are two hundred years old?"

"You know what I mean."

They rode in silence for a while after that. Tommen finally broke it when they were almost home. "So what are the twins up to?"

"They're going to take some pages I copied out of the journal and show them around the Wheel, hope they get a hit on what it says."

"Before you get taken off the case," Tommen stated.

Walter sighed. "Yeah."

He pulled into the garage, and they went inside. "You're sure your homework is done?"

"Yes," Tommen repeated lamely as he headed to his room. "Can I take this sling off now?"

"For tonight. Back on tomorrow."

"If you crack the case can I leave it on?"

Walter was about to answer when he realized what the question was. "Trick questions aren't fair. And I don't appreciate the lack of faith in me."

"It wasn't about lack of faith in you," Tommen said, reappearing and gingerly stretching his arm and shoulder as much as he could. "It was about you getting two birds with one stone."

Chapter Eighteen
Left Out

Despite Tommen's unusual, sideways attempt at encouragement, Walter did not crack the case. Tuesday night, the case was shelved and, were it to reopen with another murder or other related incident, Walter was officially off the case anyway. Micah and Micaiah had taken the pages to the Wheel as promised and gotten a little more than they bargained for. They came up empty on a language match, but some of the Hands were uncomfortable enough with their inquiries to have them apprehended and turned over to the Grandfathers for a short time, until Walter could be summoned and clear the whole thing up. The Time-side version of bailing them out of jail.

Ultimately, the Time-side investigation was shelved, too. The Hands claimed that the inquiries into potential Runner activity encouraged further Runner activity which could disrupt the elections. At least, that was the official statement. Unofficially, Micah mentioned something about some threats being made against all four of them if the investigation persisted. Something about having their clocks broken, which Tommen assumed to be a very bad thing, given that it put all three officers quite a bit on edge, and they essentially retreated like a pack of whipped puppies. Tommen was not present for this of course, instead getting the short story from Micah at work Wednesday after school.

"Tommen, when did you say your Winter Wonderland Christmas Dance Hoo-Hah was?" Micaiah shouted from the office. "Was that this Friday?"

"No, it's the 20th," Tommen replied.

He heard the elder twin's audible sigh. "Okay. Well, you have this Friday off, too, then. You wanna work a double Saturday or you good?"

"I'm good for this weekend, thanks."

"I don't blame you," Micah told him. "Doubles are murder. Take the hours and get the cash, but kill yourself in the process."

That was basically how Tommen felt about it. Yeah, the money was decent, but what good was it if he was still stuck at the store and unable to do anything with it? Not to mention that he was just plain sick of dealing with customers. The people who came in and got a pastry or a loaf of bread were fine. It was dealing with all the holiday customers that was tiring. If they weren't being contracted to cater a bazillion different company Christmas parties, they had to deal with a bazillion individual customers who wanted special Christmas cookies or New Year's cakes. Those on top of the standard birthday and anniversary orders they had to deal with. So, yes, Christmas season, great for hours and a good paycheck. But Tommen wasn't fooled; he was more than happy to take a couple Fridays off. He might work a double on the 21st to help out with the rush of last-minute orders, but taking a three-day weekend this week was just what the doctor ordered.

To say nothing of the conference between Walter, Layman, and Mrs. Wendell about his stress issues. Walter had managed to convince them not to pull him from AP Physics, and since he was already in an art class, they wouldn't force him to attend Art Therapy. But his English class had been modified to be a hybrid class. Three days a week he would do online coursework, and the other two days he would sit in with the rest of the class. Problem was, that schedule wasn't consistent from week to week; he would have to get that from Mrs. Righting every week. And Tommen had been greatly encouraged to check out the Drama Club and was given a list of all available positions, both on stage and behind the scenes.

He still wasn't particularly interested in Drama Club, but at least if he was forced to choose a group, it might be his most likely option. Actor he was not. Costume designer and makeup artist he was not. But he could paint a tree or something, he supposed. Or he could do lighting or sound or something. That was, if he was forced to. The drama of Drama Club was not limited to the stage, and the last thing Tommen wanted to get involved in was a fight between a couple petty wannabe actors and actresses who thought their petty fights were going to end up on the cover of *People* magazine and trend on Twitter.

Really, he just kept telling himself that Christmas break would be just what he needed. A break from schoolwork and his classmates and the drama, a day at the ski lodge with his best friends, and everything would be put to rights.

Of course, he still had to get the ski passes, plus he still had to hit up one of the seniors for the weed and booze, but in his mind, the plan was already set, and the day was already awesome, even if it was still about three weeks away. Just a couple more weeks of slogging through school, then two weeks off. After that, there was spring break to look forward to, and then summer vacation.

He was pulled from his thoughts by the service bell dinging. He wiped his hands and went to the front counter where a prim and proper lady of about sixty years stood, dressed like it was Sunday morning and darn it all but she was going to meet with the Lord.

"I got a call my stuff was ready. Two dozen cookies and two dozen cupcakes," she said, like hers was the only order they had waiting to be claimed and Tommen ought to automatically know which order she was talking about just by a vague description.

"What's the name on it?" he asked, going to the cooler.

"Carver. It should already be paid."

He found the trays with the specified items, a taped note with "Carver - Paid in Full" marked on it. Carefully, he removed the trays and began bagging them up in larger brown paper bags, not like the ones in the grocery store, but the fancier ones like from a department store. She watched him like a hawk, as if these cookies and cupcakes meant the salvation of all mankind. If he had to hazard a guess, she was going to some churchy thing, a bake sale or Christmas party, and she either didn't have the skills to bake simple cookies, or she wanted to be remembered as the one who brought the cookies, the ones with elaborate little Christmas trees, little shepherds, little snowflakes, little mangers, and other assorted pictures that would get eaten just as readily as plain old frosting. And if he had to further his guess, she would probably claim she baked them herself and spent hours slaving away over a hot oven and an icing tip that just wouldn't cooperate.

But that was just his guess. Still, she tipped well, wished him a Merry CHRISTmas, and left without another word.

Thursday wasn't much different, really, just more people picking up special orders or placing special orders. Even Micaiah in the office was swamped on the phone with calls for special orders, and it wasn't unusual for Tommen to get a moment to go to the back and find a new stack of order papers waiting to be categorized and subsequently baked.

"Does anyone ever question how two guys can do all this?" Tommen wondered as he sorted a new stack of special order slips. Large cookie orders, small cookie orders, cakes, cupcakes, mixed orders, urgent, soon, later, all the little piles stacked neatly on the counter before getting filed away.

"Sometimes," Micah said, working on putting the finishing touches on a large sheet cake. "But no one has ever been able to explain how we do it." He looked up and smirked. "But, since we've proven that we're not just buying out the Betty Crocker aisle, and we have our handcrafted masterpieces like this one, people just kind of stopped questioning." He paused then chuckled. "I think the best conspiracy theory I've heard is that we outsource to other bakeries — specifically ones in China or some shit like that. But again, we've proven all of the theories wrong. So we let people believe what they will. How are those slips coming along?"

"All sorted," Tommen said, putting the last slip in its place.

"Good. Get started on closing duties."

Tommen did so, eager to start his three-day vacation,

chomping at the proverbial bit as he swept, helped customers, mopped, helped customers, wiped down tables, took out trash, helped customers, cleaned the bathroom, and, in the middle of it all, helped customers.

"Ready to get out of here?" Walter asked, walking up to the door as Tommen was heading out.

"Heck yeah," Tommen told him excitedly, practically skipping out to the car. "Three-day vacation is calling my name."

His vacation started out even better as he was able to skip first period for a trip to the doctor where his sling finally came off. As if he hadn't already not been wearing it when he wasn't at school. Walter had been gently nudging the healing process along here and there, so it was ruled more of a speedy recovery than inexplicably miraculous.

"Your arm will probably be sore for a few more days, so take it easy," the doctor told him. "Your lucky it was only a flesh wound, otherwise you'd be going through some intense physical therapy."

"That's what they keep telling me," Tommen said. "Being lucky, that is."

That wasn't to say he wasn't wary of his luck. Getting the sling off, three-day vacation. It was almost like the beginning of the new semester. What sort of ill fate was about to happen to him? Was he doomed to get into another fight with Tyler? Was Layman going to yank him from AP Physics anyway?

But school passed uneventfully except for a few observations about his sling being off, and Varad was absent so he had to sit alone at lunch. He didn't get in a fight with Tyler; he didn't even see Tyler. Layman left him alone. He got a solid 100% on his Web Programming test. And the school bus didn't flip over when it took him home.

"Today is way too good to be true," Tommen said to no one in particular when he entered the house.

But still, he had the evening and house all to himself, which meant he could have his music as loud as he wanted, and he could catch up on some TV shows he'd been missing out on. It also meant he could cook a decent meal if he so chose and play around on the

Internet without Walter looking over his shoulder.

So it was, that within an hour of being home alone, Tommen was on the couch, eating some canned ravioli, watching TV but also watching videos on his phone. He almost jumped out of his skin as his phone suddenly started ringing. He muted the video and the TV, forced down his bite of ravioli, and answered.

"Hello?"

"Tommen? It's Mrs. Brown." Eric's mom. Among the three of them—Tommen, Eric, and Varad—all the parents wanted not only each other's phone numbers but the phone numbers of the other kids as well. Old school parenting and stuff.

"Hi, Mrs. Brown," Tommen said, not a little confused. "Is everything okay?"

"Well, I was looking for Eric. He's not answering his phone, he's not at work, and I don't know where he'd be. Did he say anything to you?"

"No, I'd just as soon assume he was at work or home."

"So, he's not with you? You're not hanging out at all?" She sounded genuinely distressed which set off a number of alarms in Tommen's mind. Eric didn't just disappear. Yeah, he might bang girls, smoke a little weed, and swipe a little booze, but he was always where he said he'd be. And with his family's generally precarious financial situation, he wouldn't just ignore a call from his mom, especially since she'd likely called multiple times.

"No. I haven't seen him. Listen, I'll give him a call and let him know you're looking for him. Maybe he's just somewhere he can't hear his phone, or maybe it died."

"Yeah, maybe. I'll try Varad. Thanks, Tommen."

"No problem."

Tommen hung up and tried not to hurry through his phone to find Eric's phone number.

"The number you are trying to reach is unavailable at this time," the automatic voicemail told him. "At the tone, please record your message." *Beep*.

"Hey, Eric, it's Tommen. Your mom is looking for you. She's called you multiple times. She just called me. She's calling Varad next. Hope your phone is just dead or you're at the movies or something because she's super worried. Bye."

He hung up and waited a few minutes before sending a similar text. He waited again, but when Eric didn't answer, he figured he could only hope that he'd gotten one of the half dozen messages and finally called his mom. Cautiously, he unmuted the TV and returned to the video on his phone.

Still, it was hard to concentrate knowing that Eric wasn't responding to anyone. Fear lodged itself in his gut that maybe the berating and the insults and the bullying had finally gotten to Eric, and he wouldn't be responding to any calls or texts. He tried not to think about that, tried to focus on maybe an excursion to the movies, but his thoughts were torn between the possibilities.

So when his phone rang again, he answered without looking at the number.

"Eric?" he asked.

"No, but we seem to be on the same page." It was Walter.

"What do you mean?"

"I just got a call from Eric's mom asking if I knew where he was, and the station just got a call to report that Varad is missing, too. You guys aren't hanging out, are you?"

"No."

"Tommen, at this point, I don't care if it's illegal. Just tell me the truth. Are you guys hanging out?"

"No, we're not. I'm sitting at home eating ravioli and watching TV, I promise. Eric's mom called me too. I called Eric, but it went to voicemail, and he never answered my text."

"When is the last time you saw them?"

"I don't see Eric too much, but he was on Facebook yesterday after school. Varad I saw yesterday at school, but he was absent today."

"Do you guys have any, I don't know, secret hideouts, hangout places where you go on your binges or egg houses or something?"

"Mm...none that you haven't already found," Tommen admitted. "But even if they were there, I mean...Eric wouldn't just ignore his mom. And we did have plans for Christmas break, so I don't think it's likely that we'd suddenly be ignoring each other either."

"What plans were those?"

"We were going to go skiing before Varad leaves, the Monday before Christmas."

"Where?"

"Snowshoe."

"Is there anything else you can think of, where they might be, why they're not answering their phones or anything?"

"The only thing I can think of is...I don't know, maybe the bullying finally got to Eric. Or maybe Varad got scared of moving."

"You're talking suicide?"

"I don't know. It's the only thing I can think of. I know it's not helpful and it definitely won't help their moms, but that's all I got. Honestly."

"All right. Call me or their moms if you see or hear from them."

"I will."

Tommen hung up and slumped in his seat. Both Eric and Varad were missing. Varad he might believe would slip away for a few hours to himself, maybe try to find a way out of having to move, but Eric just wouldn't ignore everyone. And both of them going together was way out of character. Running away and suicide aside, there was another possibility that Tommen didn't want to consider, but it bulldozed its way into his thoughts and demanded to be attended to.

What if Rifun and Cassius had taken them? What if Tommen was going to stumble upon their bodies over the weekend? Oh, he'd known the day was just too good to be true. It was like his curse or something. Every action, equal and opposite reaction. It was a curse of physics. The very universe was against him, it seemed.

Tommen soon found himself pacing the living room, racking his brain, trying to figure out if there was something he could do. The last time he'd taken matters into his own hands, he'd risked death by gunshot, drowning, and a physical beating. Taking Eric and Varad might not be about murder, but ransom. Tommen was just fine if he was only risking his life, but put Eric and Varad in the middle of an invisible war, and he was completely frozen. He felt his heart rate jump and a cold sweat break out on his palms. He again didn't even bother to check the number on his phone when it rang. What was the worst that could happen?

"P'nawn da, Tommen." Rifun's accent was hard to mistake. "I hope I didn't catch you at a bad time."

Tommen swallowed hard and tried to be cool as he answered, *"S'mae, Rifun.* No, just sitting at home eating ravioli and watching TV."

"Oh, good. I know your schedule is so busy." The sarcasm oozed over the phone. "So, I'm going to cut to the chase. There is a tap on your phone to record this call, because I know the cops and your dear daddy are going to want to hear what I have to say. So rather than play the telephone game, we're just going to give it to them straight from the horse's mouth as it were.

"I have your friends, Eric and Varad. Actually, we have your friends. And you have something of ours, something small, bound in leather, and containing quite a bit of information that I am betting you have as yet been unable to decipher. So, here is how it's going to work. Tomorrow afternoon at exactly two-thirty, myself, Cassius, and your two friends will be at Yeager Airport. Now before they go and get their britches all in a bunch and bring in Homeland Security, we have no interest whatsoever in any planes. We just want the noise. We will be in Hangar Four.

"Now, I'm going to assume that Walter is going to have his little partner and probably his little chief listening to this, and that's okay. Bring them, too. But make sure you bring the journal. We'll do a little trade, and then we'll go our separate ways. No one has to get hurt."

"You've killed two women!" Tommen blurted.

"Ah, yes, an unfortunate misunderstanding. But fear not, for this is the closing act. And if we all do as we're told, no one need be harmed."

"How do we know you'll keep your word?"

Rifun laughed. "You don't, dear child. You don't know that I will. But wouldn't you rather gamble my word that I will let your friends go unharmed if you bring the journal, than my word that I will kill them if you have not shown up by two-thirty-five?" He let that sink in. "Now then, Hangar Four at two-thirty. Bring the journal itself, not the copies I'm sure they've made of the pages. And if anything about that is unclear, well, we'll have plenty of time to chat about semantics later."

"Walter has been taken off the case, though."

"Hm, so maybe I wasn't clear enough."

There was some static and rustling and then a whimpery, "Hello?"

"Eric?" Tommen asked.

"What the fuck is going on, man? They've drugged us or doped us up with some fucked up shrooms or something. Oh my God...ah, the fuck? The things I'm seeing...I swear, dude, I am never doing weed again. I promise you. Forget that shit when we go skiing."

"Is Varad with you?"

"Yeah, he's here."

"Where are you?"

But the phone was pulled away and Rifun was back on. "Now then, one more time. Hangar Four at two-thirty. You and your daddy at a minimum, but I'm not opposed to a party. But don't bring out the big guns just yet. This is the closing act, but we haven't even made it to the finale."

And with that, he hung up.

Tommen suddenly felt very cold and very alone in a big, empty house. The TV was still on, advertising some magic cleaner that promised to send a second item free if you just call now. His empty bowl sat on the counter, waiting to be washed, a single fly buzzing around the rim, looking for the goods. His phone buzzed, signaling a low battery.

Suddenly panicking, Tommen rushed to his room and threw the phone on the charger, Banding for all he was worth so it would charge completely in just a few seconds. Then he felt very weary and just wanted to lie down and take a nap. His muscles turned to jelly and he lay back on the bed. Thousands of incoherent thoughts and fragments of thoughts and images rushed through his head in such a blur he couldn't pick out any single idea. Fatigue swept over him but he willed himself not to sleep.

Can't sleep now, there's work to do.

Eventually, some semblance of order returned to his mind and his body obeyed even if he wasn't fully conscious. He glanced at the clock. Five minutes had passed since Rifun had ended the call, and yet it felt like an eternity. Tommen sighed, pulled himself to his feet, and went to get a drink of water to clear his head.

Standing at the bathroom sink, he looked in the mirror and took a measured breath. Rifun and Cassius had Eric and Varad, and they wanted to trade them for the journal. They wanted the police there, especially Walter. This was probably another way for them to snub their noses and show off that they could do whatever they wanted, and there was nothing that either the Earth-side or Time-side cops could do about it.

Tommen pulled down the collar of his shirt where the bullet hole had been stitched up to nothing but a tiny scar. But it was a scar that he would always remember. And Rifun was right. He would want revenge. He did want revenge. He didn't like bullies, and he didn't like getting his ass kicked. So if Rifun wanted a fight, he was going to get a fight.

Half-expecting some kind of dramatic theme music to start

playing, Tommen whirled around and stalked toward his bedroom, pulling on an extra pair of socks, a heavier coat to go over the first, and bringing out his hat and mittens. He went to the kitchen and stood in front of the door, wondering if there was anything he really needed to take with him. Ultimately, he just needed his phone.

Curiosity striking him, he pulled off one of his mittens and dug his phone out of his pocket. Rifun had said there was a tap on his phone, except, as he pulled off the back plate, he couldn't find any evidence of new hardware. Unlocking his phone, he went into his apps and found one he didn't recognize. Opening it up, he found it was indeed a phone call recording app with three new messages on it: one from Eric's mom, one from Walter, and one from Rifun, whose number came up as Restricted. Tommen couldn't recall ever losing track of his phone, so the only thing he could guess was a remote hack. Damn, he needed to befriend a nerd and protect his stuff.

Shaking his head, Tommen headed out the door, taking care to lock it behind him. A chill wind buffeted his face with all the comfort of a bucket of needles, and his first step into the snow that had accumulated on the front walk immediately alerted him to the presence of a hole in his boot. He got out to the sidewalk and paused. Maybe he should just call. Maybe he should get a ride. Maybe he could wait the last half hour or so until Walter got off.

No, this couldn't wait. Better to do it now while there were still cops manning the station and the chief was still there so they could come up with a plan as soon as possible. Better to gamble that Rifun would let them go if he received the journal, than he would kill them if he didn't. And if they were going to take that gamble, they needed a plan.

Tommen Banded and set off down the sidewalk at a brisk walk. They were shoveled, but not at night, and the gently falling snow was laid out in a pure, pristine, one-inch blanket. Tommen immediately appreciated the extra layer of socks, but as the bridge came in sight, he wondered how smart it was. Being wet and cold was not a good thing, whether it was sweat or melted snow. He wondered if he ought to break out at a run and hope the saved time would be worth the sweat and melted snow that would inevitably coat him in wet which would freeze in the cold, causing hypothermia. Or did he stick it out with the wet in his shoes and hope to stay warm everywhere else on his body?

A slip, a fall, a scrape, and a tear in his mitten made his decision for him as he fought for balance on a hidden patch of ice just as he started crossing the bridge. He brushed off the snow, but small snowballs wedged their way into his boots and down his coat and shirt. Shaking out his hat did nothing and he ended up with a wet spot behind his ears and down the back of his neck.

"Fuck this," he whispered to himself. Finding a more stable patch of road, he took off across the bridge in the middle of the road at a dead sprint.

Tommen was not an athlete. He didn't have the bulk to play football, the height for basketball, the coordination for tennis, the speed for track, or the endurance for cross country. His ragged gasps for air came in short puffs in the frigid air, and by the time he was halfway across the bridge, he was done for, coming to a wild and ungraceful stop, hands on his knees, already feeling the sweat freezing on his body.

He looked at the car beside him. A soccer mom in a minivan, talking on her phone. Well, that was one idea. Still breathing heavily, Tommen went around to the passenger side and got in.

It was nice and warm, and Tommen leaned back the seat for a minute. He shouldn't do this. He was going to get too comfortable. If he didn't fall asleep, the snow and ice on his body would just melt, and he would walk back out there in fresh wet, and he didn't have time to wait for his clothes to dry.

He glanced at the cupholder. A cup of coffee or some hot liquid was steaming. Well, even if Walter did somehow find out, what was he going to do, really? So Tommen took a drink, pleasantly surprised to find it was hot chocolate with an abundance of tiny marshmallows. Then he took a breath and got out of the minivan.

It was like diving right back into the river, the way the cold hit him again, and he had to force himself to keep moving, trying not to let his pace slow to less than a hurried walk, running whenever he could, counting it a victory that he made it across the bridge in one piece without dying.

The government complex where the police station was housed wasn't far from the bridge, but it still felt like an eternity before Tommen got within a comfortable enough distance to release his Band and walk in normally, stomping his boots and shaking his coat like a dog.

"Well, good evening, Tommen," the receptionist on shift, Lisa, greeted. "Out for a bit of a chilly stroll, aren't you?"

"Where's my dad?" Tommen asked, hoping he was able to convey urgency without the panic that was starting to creep into his head.

"I'm not sure exactly, but I think he went out on a call. Is there something I can—?"

"What about Chief Steggmann?"

Lisa frowned and turned around in her chair to look back toward the offices. "I know he was going home soon, but he might still be here." She picked up the phone and dialed an extension. "Let me see if I can grab him."

"Just tell him it's urgent."

She gave him an uncertain look but turned her attention to the phone when it picked up. "Chief? Tommen Forbes is here to see you; he says it's urgent." She paused a moment, then looked at Tommen.

"How urgent?"

"It has to do with the double murder and museum robbery."

Her expression was enough to tell Tommen he'd at least gotten through to her as she went back to the phone conversation. "Imperative." Pause. "I will."

She hung up and looked back at Tommen. "He says to come on back. You know where his office is?"

"I do," Tommen said, already lugging open the heavy bullet-proof glass door to the offices.

Chief Steggmann's office was the second one on the right, and Tommen nearly collided with him as he stepped out of the door. He did not seem particularly pleased about being sought just as he was leaving, but still he put on a good face and said, "Evening, Tommen. How can I help you?"

Tommen took a breath. "Sir, Rifun Ndolo contacted me."

That turned Steggmann's surly attitude right around, putting him into full police mode, ushering Tommen into his office and closing the door.

"Ndolo contacted you?" he echoed, putting just enough stress on *you* to make Tommen think he didn't believe him. And why not? Why would a criminal contact some kid—even if his dad was the investigating detective—and not the Chief of Police himself?

"Yes, sir. He called me. I don't know, but somehow he put an app on my phone to record the call. He said to play it for you and my dad."

Steggmann still seemed skeptical, but as Tommen brought out his phone to bring up the call, he went to the phone on his desk and dialed a number. It wasn't long before there was a pick up. "Walt? It's Greg. Tommen is here, says he's been contacted by Ndolo. Uh-huh. Says Ndolo gave him a message for me and you. Yeah. Yeah. All right." He hung up and looked at Tommen. "He's on his way back. Now, what is this about?"

Tommen swallowed nervously. "Rifun kidnapped my friends, and he says he's going to kill them unless we give him the journal."

It was difficult to judge Steggmann's thought process as he told Tommen to stay put and left the office. He wasn't gone but a few minutes, and even after he returned, it was only a couple minutes more before Walter knocked and entered the tiny office.

"Walt," Steggmann greeted.

"Sir," Walter acknowledged, then looked at Tommen. "Rifun contacted you? When?"

"Like, I don't know, twenty minutes ago? Half hour?"

Tommen offered.

"And somehow he put an app on your phone to record the call," Steggmann said skeptically.

Tommen nodded. "Yeah. I mean, it's got three messages on it, so it's been on there since at least this afternoon. I checked the hardware; it doesn't seem to be tampered with."

"We'll see about that. First, play the message for us."

Tommen got into his phone and brought up the call. He set it up against Steggmann's nameplate on his desk and hit Play.

"P'nawn da, Tommen." Rifun's voice was crystal clear. "I hope I didn't catch you at a bad time."

"S'mae, Rifun," Tommen answered, his voice shaky. "No, just sitting at home eating ravioli and watching TV."

"Oh, good. I know your schedule is so busy. So, I'm going to cut to the chase. There is a tap on your phone to record this call, because I know the cops and your dear daddy are going to want to hear what I have to say. So rather than play the telephone game, we're just going to give it to them straight from the horse's mouth as it were.

"I have your friends, Eric and Varad. Actually, we have your friends. And you have something of ours, something small, bound in leather, and containing quite a bit of information that I am betting you have as yet been unable to decipher. So, here is how it's going to work. Tomorrow afternoon at exactly two-thirty, myself, Cassius, and your two friends will be at Yeager Airport. Now, before they go and get their britches all in a bunch and bring in Homeland Security, we have no interest whatsoever in any planes. We just want the noise. We will be in Hangar Four.

"Now, I'm going to assume that Walter is going to have his little partner and probably his little chief listening to this, and that's okay. Bring them, too. But make sure you bring the journal. We'll do a little trade, and then we'll go our separate ways. No one has to get hurt."

"You've killed two women!" Tommen cut in. In the office,

Tommen felt his cheeks burn bright red.

"Ah, yes, an unfortunate misunderstanding. But fear not, for this is the closing act. And if we all do as we're told, no one need be harmed." Steggmann folded his arms and grunted.

"How do we know you'll keep your word?"

Rifun laughed. "You don't, dear child. You don't know that I will. But wouldn't you rather gamble my word that I will let your friends go unharmed if you bring the journal, than my word that I will kill them if you have not shown up by two-thirty-five?" Walter shifted his stance. "Now then, Hangar Four at two-thirty. Bring the journal itself, not the copies I'm sure they've made of the pages. And if anything about that is unclear, well, we'll have plenty of time to chat about semantics later."

"Walter has been taken off the case, though."

"Hm, so maybe I wasn't clear enough."

There was some static and rustling and then a whimpery, "Hello?"

"Eric?" Tommen asked.

"What the fuck is going on, man? They've drugged us or doped us up with some fucked up shrooms or something. Oh my God...ah, the fuck? The things I'm seeing...I swear, dude, I am never doing weed again. I promise you. Forget that shit when we go skiing." Tommen could see Walter's curious gaze out of the corner of his eye, and he elected to remain silent, intent on the call.

"Is Varad with you?"

"Yeah, he's here."

"Where are you?"

But the phone was pulled away and Rifun was back on. "Now then, one more time. Hangar Four at two-thirty. You and your daddy at a minimum, but I'm not opposed to a party. But don't bring out the big guns just yet. This is the closing act, but we haven't even made it to the finale."

The call ended. For a moment, the entire office was silent. Steggmann was the first to speak. "I want that taken to the nerd herd upstairs, see if they can get anything from that. Where it came from, how they got the app on his phone, everything."

"And the meeting tomorrow at Hangar Four?" Walter questioned.

"Right now, Rifun is calling the shots. But you're a damn good hostage negotiator, Walter. What do you need?"

Walter let out a breath, thinking. "He's right; we don't know he'll keep his word to let them go. But I don't think we should bring in the big guns since all we're trading, hopefully, is just a journal. However, I would like a reserve team, just in case things get ugly."

"Done."

"What do I do?" Tommen asked.

"You stay close to me and do nothing I don't ask you to," Walter replied severely. He Banded. "And if things do turn bad, you Band and run. Don't worry about who sees you or any of that. Get yourself to safety."

"What about you?"

"Don't worry about me. I have more than one trick up my sleeve. Just get out. Got it?"

Tommen sighed. "Yeah."

Walter released the Band. "If Rifun wants us there at two-thirty, I want us there at two-twenty-five which means leaving here no later than two."

Steggmann nodded. "First thing in the morning, I'll call the airport and let them know. We'll have Homeland Security ready, but out of sight, just in case he decides to try something."

"Fair enough."

"Go home and get some sleep if you can. I'll rally the troops."

Walt nodded gratefully. He glanced at Tommen. "Wait for me in the lobby."

Tommen did so. Thankfully he was not kept waiting long, and he followed Walter out to the car, wet socks squelching in his shoes.

"Did you walk here?" Walter asked.

"Well, I didn't drive," Tommen told him.

"Okay, good point. Listen, tomorrow, I want you to stay close to me."

"Yeah, you said that."

"Tommen, I'm serious. Why would Rifun and Cassius go through the trouble of kidnapping your friends when he could have just walked right into the station and stolen the journal out of evidence? He's putting on a show. He wants the journal, but he wants to make a point. And the fact that he wants you there worries me. I'm going to call Micaiah and see if he can be there as a backup, but like I said, if anything happens, run, and keep yourself safe. Is that clear?"

Tommen let out a breath. He didn't like the way Walter was making so much sense. In the end, he could only nod. "Yes, sir."

Chapter Nineteen
Fair Trade

To say that neither Tommen nor Walter got any sleep that night was a gross understatement. Tommen figured he wandered out to the living room sometime around two in the morning, only to find Walter was already up, sitting in his recliner, trying to sleep but having little success. Eventually, they turned on the TV and watched some old 80's B-movie about an alien invasion or some such thing. Fatigue muddled Tommen's memory. Either that or he did finally get a little sleep because the next thing he knew, Walter was shaking him awake.

"What time is it?" Tommen mumbled.

"A little after eight," Walter told him. "Come on. I made breakfast, then we have to go."

"I'm going with you to the station? Why so early?"

"Because I have to meet with a whole bunch of people and plan this out, and I'm not going to make a special trip home just to get you. So you get to come with me today."

As a kid, Tommen was always excited to go with Walter to the station. Mostly it had to do with the cookies in the break room and the way everyone thought he was just adorable and gave him attention like some wounded puppy. Now that he was older, he dreaded the thought of spending five or six hours there, not that it happened often, if ever anymore. Still, he understood the importance of the situation and did not argue, just sat at the table dutifully to scarf down some scrambled eggs and bacon before taking a minute to make himself look somewhat presentable. No need to show up to a hostage negotiation looking like a billboard that said, "Yup, you made us real nervous and we lost some serious sleep over it."

"Should I bring anything?" Tommen asked as he pulled on his boots, still wet from the night before.

"No," Walter answered. "Anything you need, if you need anything, we'll provide. For now, pack light but warm. We don't know how long this is going to take. Hopefully, this will be just a simple exchange."

"Why would Rifun want the original journal and not the copies?"

"Because that's what he asked for. And at this point, that's what he's going to get."

Walter's stride was long and purposeful, and Tommen had to hurry to keep up with him, even just out to the garage. As they were backing out of the driveway, Walter was on his phone.

"Micaiah? Walt. I need a favor. Today. And it is of the utmost importance. Rifun's taken a couple of Tommen's friends and is ransoming them for the journal. Yeah. Yeah. He contacted Tommen yesterday and has arranged a meeting today at the airport. Hangar Four. Yeah, we're supposed to trade the journal for his friends. Right. Believe me, I know. Listen, what worries me the most is that he wants Tommen there. I don't know, but I don't like it. Right. Can you get out there and be a backup for us? I've got a reserve team coming in, but we both know they won't do much good against Rifun and Cassius. Okay. Yeah. Right, Hangar Four. Yup. Uh-huh. Thanks, Cai. I owe you one."

"He'll do it?" Tommen asked as Walter hung up.

"He'll be there. Same as the reserves, out of sight unless things turn bad."

"You expect things to turn bad, huh?"

"Always expect that things will go horribly, horribly wrong. That way you're pleasantly surprised when they don't."

When they arrived at the police station, Tommen noted that there was a quiet hum of activity, an urgency that wasn't there most days, and the smell of coffee was stronger than ever as all the burners on every machine were being utilized. As Walter walked through the station, a few broke off from the crowd and made their way to a room down the hall. Tommen headed for the break room where a box of donuts lay, completely unguarded.

"Stay here and be good," Walter ordered as he walked in, opened the box, and took half a dozen donuts. "And above all, no blabbing. We'll be out of here by two at the latest."

Tommen simply nodded. Wasn't like he could get online if he wanted to, anyway, since his phone had been confiscated by the "nerd herd" as Steggmann called them. His biggest fear was actually his Internet history being discovered, but there was nothing he could do about it now.

So he sat. He ate a donut which might have been delicious if fresh, but cold, it was just a chewy ring of dough. He walked around the room. He sifted through a pile of magazines whose genres ranged from sports, to hunting, to police and first responder, to catalogs, to half a dozen swimsuit model editions of *Sports Illustrated* at the very bottom.

In the end, he read through probably every one of the magazines—the *Sports Illustrated* ones two or three times—before Walter returned. He held up Tommen's phone, but Tommen knew his expression.

"Nerd herd finished with your phone," Walter said obviously. "Said they couldn't figure out where the app came from, where it had been hacked from. They did, however, find a very peculiar Internet history. Is there anything you'd like to tell me?"

"Are we playing good cop, bad cop?" Tommen asked, his stomach twisting.

"No, we're playing good dad, bad dad, the latter of which I have apparently been. So, instead of giving this back to you, I'm just going to be confiscating it for myself for a while."

"You can't do that!" Tommen protested, standing and almost losing his balance as his feet got tangled in the legs of the chair.

Walter dropped the phone in a pocket. "I just did. Sue me.

The only reason I'm not currently punishing you further is that I haven't come up with anything good yet, and we have bigger things to worry about."

Tommen snorted and looked away. "Are we leaving?"

"Not yet, just taking a short break before our eyeballs bleed. But you, come with me."

He did so reluctantly, following Walter down the hall, out the door, and to a small pole barn warehouse out back. It was lit and heated and apparently officiated by a man who Tommen guessed would have been retired if not for the position, whatever the position was.

"Well, Walter, to what do I owe the pleasure of your visit?" the man asked.

"Hey, Ernie." Of course his name would be Ernie. "Need a vest for my kid here."

"He's going with you?" Ernie's eyes got huge.

"That's what the guy demanded. But I'm not taking him in unprotected."

"And right you shouldn't." The man stood and Tommen saw he had two prosthetic legs at the knee. His gait was awkward, but it worked for him. Walter moved past the desk and Tommen followed both of them through the storehouse.

It was a tactical storehouse, Tommen saw, furbished from floor to ceiling and wall to wall with enough gear for the U.S. Army to be jealous. The outer sheet metal of the building was extra thick, probably bullet-proof, and everything inside was either locked up in solid steel chests with big ass locks, or else behind more bullet-proof glass with more big ass locks. They headed to a section loaded with vests, helmets, shields, and all manner of protective clothing and gear.

"How tall are ya, son?" Ernie asked.

"Five-ten," Tommen admitted meekly.

Ernie rummaged around a bit and brought out a vest. He tossed it to Tommen. "Try that on."

"How is it supposed to feel?" Tommen asked as Walter helped

him into it.

"It's a bit snug," Walter said. "And a little small. Try a little bigger."

So maybe he had finally hit six feet, Tommen thought, willing it to be true. He exchanged the small vest for a new one and slipped that on, Walter helping.

"How's that?" Ernie wondered.

Walter stepped back to admire his handiwork. "Just right. Hopefully it's an unnecessary precaution." He nodded. "All right, now we just need the rest of the guys. Thanks, Ernie."

"Anytime, Walter, you know that."

They headed out of the warehouse back toward the precinct.

"So what's Ernie's story?" Tommen asked.

"You mean how did he come to have two prosthetic legs?" Walter wondered. "He's retired U.S. Army. Got out, became a cop. Bomb squad, naturally. He got sent to defuse a bomb that showed up in a bank one day. He couldn't defuse it, so he did what a good solider does. He threw himself over it. Saved the bank. Lucky he made it out of there alive. His lower legs were the only things unprotected. Since then, he's been our tactical administrator. He understands protection, and I would gladly put my life in his hands, which is why I took you to him."

Tommen nodded and followed in silence. They headed to a room where the reserve team waited expectantly.

"Welcome back," Walter said wistfully as he walked to the front of the room, motioning Tommen along. He gestured toward him at the front of the room. "This is my son, Tommen. He will be going with us, per Rifun's demands. However, he is still a civilian. Even though we are trading the journal for the release of Eric and Varad, we must assume that Rifun holds no fond feelings for Tommen either, and he may be a target."

Maybe for the first time that day, Tommen finally understood what could potentially happen. Yeah, journal for friends, blah, blah, blah, but if Rifun wanted him there, it was possible that Tommen was a target as well, and something could actually go horribly, horribly wrong. For a second, he thought he might be sick. Thankfully, Walter dismissed him to sit, which he did gratefully, finding a seat in a back corner so he could think and process everything.

Rifun had already tried and failed to kill him. Cassius had failed to kill him. The journal might be only a decoy. After all, why *wouldn't* Rifun just Band, walk in, and steal the journal with none the wiser? But if he brought everyone out into the open, he could finish Tommen off, like Walter said, put on a grand show, and snub his nose at the police that he could get away with murder, even in front of a SWAT Team of cops.

Suddenly the meeting was over, and they were on their way to the airport. No lights, no sirens, and only Walter's vehicle was marked. No need to get the public's attention any more than necessary, and no need to alert Rifun and give him the satisfaction of hearing just how many people were coming. He had great powers, true, but he wasn't God. He couldn't see and know everything.

"You understand your part in this?" Walter asked.

"Stay close to you," Tommen said levelly, still feeling woozy from the whole idea that this could be about him.

"Just making sure. I just...I don't want to see you get hurt. Okay?"

Tommen sighed. "I know. I don't want you to get hurt either."

Walter put a hand on his shoulder. "I love you, Tommen. No matter what. And we're both walking away from this."

"Everyone goes home."

"Exactly. Everyone goes home."

At first glance, there was nothing particularly sinister about the airport. It was just...an airport. There were cars in the various parking lots for short visits and longer stays. People milled about, hauling luggage out of vehicles or packing it into shiny rentals, kissing loved ones good-bye, hugging friends not seen in years. Children ran around, excited to be going on a trip. A seeing eye dog halted at the crosswalk, alerting its owner to the presence of an oncoming vehicle.

None of these people had any clue about the life-and-death situation taking place in Hangar Four.

Walter checked his watch. "Two-twenty. Right on time. Come on."

Tommen followed, not saying a word, sticking as close to Walter as he could without treading on his heels. Surprisingly, they did not attract too many stares. One child tugged at her mom's sleeve and pointed, but mom just brushed her off. A dog in a car barked wildly. A few people gave them no more than a cursory glance, as if cops and civilians in bullet-proof vests walked into the airport every day.

"Detective Forbes," Walter said, walking up to a TSA supervisor. "I believe you are aware of the situation in Hangar Four?"

"Oh, you mean the plane that was suddenly and mysteriously grounded for mechanical problems?" the supervisor said in the cheesiest voice Tommen had ever heard. "Yes, of course. The mechanics are on their way around the west side of the airport, but you can come with me."

Tommen figured the bit about the mechanics was meant for the rest of the team as they followed the supervisor first into a tiny room, like the ones they used to pat down old ladies in wheelchairs who they deemed suspicious. Then it was through a heavy metal door and down an unsuspecting hallway where only half the lights worked and the other half flickered menacingly. Another metal door saw them into a service hallway, and the farther they walked, the louder it became with fans and engines and power tools and assorted golf cart craft zipping this way and that.

Then they were on the tarmac, almost first run over by a baggage train, then by some other small vehicle. The runway was heated from beneath, so snow did not accumulate, and the worst it got was extremely wet. They got into a small golf cart, and the TSA agent scooted them down the open runway to a large building marked with a big, faded, red 4. Inside, a jet sat dormant, one of the engines torn to pieces, parts and wires and various tools strewn about the floor haphazardly.

"Hangar Four," the agent said, stopping the cart.

"Thanks," Walter said absently, climbing off. "I expect the mechanics will arrive soon, then?"

"I expect so. Until then."

And the man zipped away.

That left Walter and Tommen standing there in the hangar, alone. It was cold, Tommen reflected, and not just because of the air temperature. The hair on the back of his neck prickled like the feeling of prey being hunted. His hackles rose. He did not like feeling like prey. At the same time, he knew that fisticuffs would not solve things this time. This time, the fight was about cunning and wit. If you can't beat them, confuse them, then run away laughing. Except Tommen highly doubted Rifun would take too kindly to being confused and then having his prey run away laughing at him. If that happened, it was more than likely that he would give chase, his mission to seek and destroy. So what options did they have to defeat him? If street fighting was out, and cunning was out, what else did they have?

In front of him, Walter had one hand on his gun. Carefully, he took his eyes off the empty hangar and checked his watch. "Two-twenty-six. Technically, we've got four minutes."

Of course, when you had the ability to control Time itself, why would you really need to be anywhere early? In all reality, they could be hiding out at some hotel, nice and warm, watching a movie or eating sandwiches, and then just Band their way to be at the hangar at two-thirty. Well, the movie and sandwiches were probably a stretch given the whole hostage situation, but the point was there.

Tommen wondered where the team was. Were they still moving down the west side of the building toward the hangar? Were they already waiting outside, watching for a signal? He didn't know. Even if they were meant to stay out of sight, Tommen might have felt a little better if he just knew where they were so he didn't feel so fucking alone.

"Two-thirty," Walter said quietly, looking at his watch.

"And you never fail to disappoint, Walter."

The voice came from everywhere and nowhere. Walter's hand went to his gun and Tommen could see it was a severe effort of will to keep him from pulling and shooting outright. No need for anyone to get hurt. No need for this to go horribly, horribly wrong.

Then there was a short wake of a Band and Rifun appeared from behind the jet's rear wheel. Just as Tommen had suspected, he hadn't been waiting for them in the hangar, but somewhere safe and sound and warm.

He was just as Tommen remembered him: tall, athletic, hair to his waist in a neat ponytail, high cheekbones and more freckles than would be considered handsome. His sweatshirt and winter jacket might have made him look pudgy and overweight if Tommen didn't know what lay beneath them: solid muscle that could lift him and throw him over the side of a boat.

"I'm disappointed, Walter," Rifun said. "You seem to lack faith in me. The gun, the Kevlar, the team waiting outside, why, I might have thought that you didn't trust me. But here I am at two-thirty, true to my word. Now then, prove that you are also a man of your word and show me that you brought what I asked for."

"Not before you show us Eric and Varad are safe," Walter told him, meeting his gaze.

"Ah, proof of life, is that it? But let us consider who holds the cards, Walter. I could kill them if—"

"And I could burn that journal right here in front of you. It may have survived water, but it cannot survive fire."

Rifun grinned. "Now we're negotiating. But your words imply that you do have the journal with you. I like that, I really do. A man of your word with words to spare. Even if the threat is empty, it just makes things that much more exciting. So instead of pushing the issue, I shall simply take you at your implied word and implied threat, and thus I will make good on my end of the bargain. I will show you the boys, and you will see that we have not harmed a single hair on their chinny chin chins."

Tommen didn't like the way he was speaking. The man was apparently given to theatrics and Shakespearean monologues—when they didn't reveal his evil schemes—but the way he spoke, his choice of words and the way he said them, it sent chills down Tommen's spine. He shifted his stance, hoping it looked natural when really he was just trying to calm his anxiety, hide the shiver and pass it off as a reaction to the cold wind blasting into the hangar. He glanced at Walter. The man was physically stoic, but the sweat dropping down the back of his neck showed Tommen that he was just as nervous and fearful and uncertain about any of the things that could happen next.

"And here we are," Rifun said.

Tommen had completely expected Cassius to show up with Eric and Varad. But he was quite unprepared for the rest of the gang.

A woman with neon yellow skin and brown hair, dressed like some sort of steampunk anime chick, except the part about the ram's horns that sprouted from her hairline above her ears and curled around under her jaw. A beast that appeared made of solid rock, moving as swiftly as an avalanche but with the certainty of a rock slide. Another man who appeared human, Oriental, chewing gum and listening to a music player, hardly paying any attention.

"Shit," Walter hissed.

Neon Yellow Steampunk held Varad and Rock Monster had Eric. Both of them looked like they hadn't slept in days and possibly escaped from a mental hospital. They both had a bit of stubble and their hair was unbrushed. Their clothes were rumpled and stained with sweat. It was hard to guess their mental state as they did not struggle, and they looked only at the floor.

"Eric! Varad!" Tommen called.

The two of them looked up. As promised, they did not appear to have been harmed. They did not have any cuts or bruises, no black eyes or missing teeth or swollen jaws. When they looked at Tommen, they seemed startled.

"Tommen! What the fucking fuck in hell?!" Eric cried, looking for more extreme words than "fuck" to describe the confusing situation, but coming up with nothing except an awkward combination of curses. "I don't know what the fuck they did, but they fucked with us somehow. Gotta be fucking shrooms, dude. Shrooms or some shit."

"Have they hurt you otherwise?" Walter asked.

"No. No, they haven't touched us. Except they gave us water, which I'm pretty sure was laced with something."

"How do you feel? Out of control?"

"No, but these fucking hallucinations are weirding me the fuck out. But they only happen after blackouts."

Tommen watched Walter's expression change. Then he Banded. Only himself, and only for a moment. Right after he began, Eric squeezed his eyes shut and screamed. Varad just looked away and groaned. Then Walter released the Band and watched their reaction.

"He's exposed them," Walter scoffed.

He Banded again, this time the entire hangar so they could all speak freely.

"You exposed them to Time," Walter stated incredulously.

Rifun shrugged. "Yes, I did. I only said I did not harm them. And I did not."

"How much exposure?"

"Oh, a Band here, a Band there."

Eric and Varad were crying now as they probably saw the red of the Fast Band covering the entire hangar and everyone in it. Tommen closed his eyes and could only feel sympathy for them. He remembered the first time he finally saw a Band. Walter had been putting the last finishing touches on his new room so he could move in. At first, he thought the color was cool and thought it was some kind of magical illusion. Then, once Walter explained what it was and, eventually, began teaching him how to make his own cool magical colors, the magic went away. Tommen didn't even think twice when he saw a Band, except when it came unexpectedly.

But for Eric and Varad now, it had to be a horrifying

experience. The fear probably didn't even come from the colors or the Bands themselves, but from wherever they'd been kept and whatever psychological torture Rifun and his goons had inflicted on them, made them think they'd been drugged. That was an okay explanation for now, but how about when those "hallucinations" didn't go away? What did they—Tommen and Walter—do with them now? Could they hope to explain what had happened, explain the Time industry? Would Eric and Varad have to be trained? Or would they just have to step away quietly and make sure that they spent as little time together as possible? With Eric gone already and heading to college, and Varad moving to India, that wasn't much of a problem. But what if they did have a run-in with another Time Agent and the "hallucinations" started again? What did they do then?

"How much exposure?" Walter demanded.

"Not as much as your boy. Not as much as you. Not as much as anyone here," Rifun answered. "Just enough to make them think they've been drugged."

Which meant they were only able to see a temporal distortion, but didn't have enough ability to create one.

"What do you mean?" Eric demanded.

"We haven't been drugged?" Varad said. "Then what is this?"

"This is called Time, boys." Rifun gave a villainous grin toward Walter. "What you are seeing is the base fabric of reality. Your friend Tommen over there has the ability to control Time. So does Walter. So do I. There are other elements to the Time industry, but you'll have to ask about them later." His expression turned into the same one he'd had when he leveled the gun at Tommen in the boat. "But, I'm on a timetable. Places to be, things to do. The journal."

"Let the boys go, Rifun," Walter said, releasing the Band. "You've proven you're a man of your word and you haven't harmed them. Now let them go."

But Rifun was done playing games, and he wasn't budging to Walter trying to pander to his ego. "You know, Walter, I like you. I really do. Always admired you and what you did for your brother and your kid here. So, we've established that we're both men of our words. That's lovely. I have the boys, you have the journal. So I suggest you cooperate and hand over the journal, let's say…now."

"The journal is an object. You have two lives resting in your hands. Release the boys first."

Rifun did not reply to that immediately, simply closed his mouth, shifted his jaw, studied them like a cat might study a mouse, and just breathed. Tommen found that he was holding his breath and tried to let it out slowly, as if making it audible might spook them and cause some kind of catastrophe. Finally, Rifun spoke.

"See, the problem is, Walter, you're right. The journal is just an object. And your number one priority is human life." He started walking forward, just one slow step at a time. Walter moved in front of Tommen, hand on his gun. Out of the corner of his eye, Tommen saw the reserve team just around the corner of the hangar.

"You seem to have deduced that Tommen is very important in this situation also," Rifun went on, "or you would not have given the journal to him for safekeeping. But love and hate seem to be your two greatest weaknesses, Walter." Now he was only a couple feet away. "So I will ask again. Hand over the journal."

Now it was Walter's turn to be quiet and consider. Rifun could have Banded and walked into the police station and just stolen the journal. Instead, he kidnapped Eric and Varad and demanded a hostage exchange. Even while they were standing there, Rifun could have just Banded, walked up to Tommen, and stolen the journal. He could have even killed him with the same ruthless efficiency he and Cassius had pulled off the last two murders. But he didn't. He needed Tommen alive and unharmed, but for what?

"I propose a compromise," Walter said at last. He Banded. "We meet in the Wheel. Me and Tommen and the journal. You and one of your cronies. We give you the journal, then we all leave the Wheel. Then you and your little pals here leave, and leave Eric and Varad behind."

Rifun frowned. "That's a very interesting proposal, Walter.

But I have to wonder, why do we need to go to the Wheel to do this?"

"Neutral Time territory so no one need be harmed," Walter replied firmly.

Rifun chuckled. "Ah, but I think it is so your little Lieutenants can rally their forces and be waiting for us. Oh, yes, I knew you would call in your own little secret weapons. I don't blame you. After all, going up against a Warden and a Triage Harvester is bad enough. But all this?" He gestured to his gang who was looking rather bored with the whole exchange.

There must have been some gesture or signal Tommen didn't catch because the next thing he knew, Oriental was standing next to Rifun. In front of him, Micaiah was on his knees, shaking, spitting blood, arms protecting his midsection. Oriental had a gun to the back of his head.

"He's a fighter," Oriental said. "Just didn't fight hard enough."

Oriental looked like he hadn't even gotten a scratch.

"Now I have three lives before me," Rifun said. "Where is the other one?"

Walter was fighting to maintain composure. "He didn't come."

Oriental chambered a round.

Micaiah spat some blood. "He didn't come." His voice was shaking.

"Call him," Rifun ordered. "Call off your dogs. Then we'll go to the Wheel."

Walter glared at Rifun for a moment, tried to read his face, his body language. Oriental pressed the gun harder against Micaiah's head. Tommen thought he might be sick. Finally Walter fished out his phone and dialed Micah.

"Micah," Walter said. "It's Walt."

"Speakerphone, please," Rifun said pleasantly.

Walter did so. "You're on speakerphone."

"What's going on? Did you get Eric and Varad back?" Micah asked.

"Here's the deal, Micah," Rifun said. "I have your brother here, and he's not doing so well.   But as it is, he can still make a full recovery."

"Is that Rifun?"

"Now then, I know you have allies in the Wheel who are more than happy to try and arrest me if I set foot there—"

"I swear, if you harm a single hair on his head, I'm going to—"

Oriental rolled his eyes, lifted the gun, and fired it into the air.

"Micaiah!" Micah screamed.

"I'm f-fine," Micaiah said. "He shot in the air."

Oriental put the gun back where it was at Micaiah's head. Rifun huffed irritably and continued. "As I was saying, I know you have allies.   Walter here is proposing that we meet in the Wheel in order to do our little exchange.   So, here is what is not going to happen.   You, Micah, are not going to go into the Wheel to forewarn your allies and so have a rallying force waiting for me.   And if you don't want the next bullet to end up buried in your brother's brain, you are going to agree to it in the next te—"

"All right!" Micah interrupted. "All right.   I won't go." He sighed. "Sorry, Walt."

"I don't blame you," Walter told him, though Tommen could hear the disappointment.   They were Timekeeping officers, trained to be ready to give their lives.   But they were not soldiers.   They did not have that instinct ingrained in them.   They were not like Ernie.   They were still just common humans, and Micah was doing what every common human would do in a similar situation, putting the life of his loved one, his twin brother, over the lives of two kids who, yeah, might be the best friends of his best friend's kid, but kids he still didn't know.   Truthfully, Tommen didn't blame him either.

Walter glanced at Rifun who grinned. "I am holding your brother to your word, Lieutenant." Then he nodded and Walter hung up, slowly putting the phone back in his pocket. "Now then, what were you saying about that little trip to the Wheel?"

Walter glared at him. "Me and Tommen and the journal.   You and one of your friends, and the boys.   We go in, do the exchange, and get out. No one need be harmed."

Rifun raised a brow and glanced at Micaiah. "A little late for that, wouldn't you say?"

Still, he motioned for the rest of his goons. Neon Yellow Steampunk dragged Varad forward and Rock Monster all but carried Eric. Cassius stalked up alone.

"I will go. As a show of good faith, I'll even go alone," Rifun said. He looked at Oriental. "If I am not the first one back through the portal, kill him." Oriental nodded. "Captain?"

Walter let out a breath and took a step back. It was hard enough for the twins to shoulder the strength it took to open a portal to the Wheel, but to watch Walter do it alone was like watching Hercules lift a mountain. Rifun went toward the portal and then paused. He gave Walter a stunned look. "Why, Walter, I just realized. Taking dear Eric and Varad into the Wheel will all but guarantee sufficient Time exposure that they will have to be trained. Are you up for taking on two more Apprentices?"

Walter just grunted with effort. Until someone actually stepped through the portal and locked it in place in the portal room, he was shouldering all the power and energy needed to keep it open.

"After you, Tommen," Rifun said, gesturing.

Tommen took a breath and stepped through the portal. It was like being pulled in a thousand different directions at once as his muscles turned to jelly and the air was forcibly sucked from his lungs. He fell more than stepped into the portal room, gasping for air like a fish out of water. He rolled away just in time before Eric and Varad landed on him. They almost appeared to be unconscious, and Tommen had to drag them out of the way as Rifun and finally Walter stepped through.

Walter collapsed upon arrival. Rifun merely watched, his expression annoyed, as Tommen slid beside him. He was breathing and had a good pulse. After a moment, he sighed and opened his eyes, pupils wildly struggling to adjust and he groaned.

"I made it," he stated groggily, trying to sit up.

"Yeah, you avoided the Land In Between," Tommen said, helping him first to sit, then to stand.

"Okay." Walter worked to put on a good face and appear strong despite his obvious display of weakness, even if fleeting and understandable. "Now then, the boys?"

Rifun gestured to Eric and Varad who were just starting to sit up. Eric looked around, wide-eyed. "Oh God, where the fuck are we? What happened? What was that light?"

"That light was your death and this is the end of the tunnel," Rifun told them. "Welcome to Hell. Not quite as hot as the old boys predicted, but close enough."

"What?" Eric looked like he was close to a nervous breakdown.

"Please, guys, I'll explain it all later," Tommen said helplessly.

"There they are," Rifun said. "Now then, Tommen, the journal?"

Tommen glanced at Walter who looked at Rifun. "Just hand him the journal and step away."

Rifun grinned mischievously, and Tommen swallowed a lump in his throat. He fished the journal out of his coat, having a hard time of it because of the vest. Finally, he produced the item in question and could have sworn Rifun started to literally drool at the sight of it. Gingerly, he took a step toward Rifun and held out the journal. Rifun snatched it from him and ripped it open like a kid tearing into a long-awaited candy bar.

"So then, I trust all is in order and we can all walk away?" Walter questioned. "And Micaiah is free to go as well?"

For a long moment, Tommen wondered if Rifun had even heard him. Finally he looked up. "Oh, yes, all is very much in order here. Take the kids and go. You have a lot of explaining to do."

Walter still kept one eye on Rifun as he and Tommen went to help Eric and Varad to their feet.

"You said you wanted to be the first one back," Walter reminded him.

Rifun closed the journal and tied it shut. "So I did. Although I am disappointed in you, Walter. You never asked the one question that I'm sure has been bugging you this whole time."

"What's in the journal?"

"No, longer than that. Since this whole fiasco began. Why go after Lily Guile?"

"She's a buyer of seats, the epitome of the corruption of the Hands. You thought she had the journal."

"Yes, but now that I have the journal, what else is on your mind?"

Walter sighed, and Tommen could see the fatigue. He was too stressed for his own good, both from the portal and the negotiations. "Are you still going to go after Lily?"

"Why shouldn't I? As you just stated, she is the epitome of the corruption of the Hands. And you are unable to do anything about it."

"Vigilanteism will solve nothing. And regardless of my distaste for her, I have a duty to protect her."

Rifun nodded, frowning. "Perhaps. How far would you go to protect her, Walter? Earth-side?"

"I am duty-bound to give my life for her if necessary, if it would protect her."

"Sounds like a serious relationship. But tell me this, too, Walter. What wouldn't you give to ensure your son's safety? He is your son, isn't he?"

"There is nothing I wouldn't give," Walter told him sternly.

"Excellent. I expect you will hear from me again soon, then."

And with that, Rifun Banded, grabbed Tommen by his vest, and jumped back through the portal.

Chapter Twenty
From Bad to Worse

Walter had a brief revelation in that billionth or trillionth of a second that it took for Rifun to move, grab Tommen, and run out of the Wheel. It was simply a realization of just how dangerous and how powerful Rifun was. He suddenly understood just what it took for him and Cassius to pull off both murders, and what it took to plan the robbery of the museum in such a way to get Tommen to follow them to the deserted launch. It was all so effortless and well-planned and extremely well-executed. Walter was forced to wonder how long they'd been planning to kidnap Tommen. Had this been part of their endgame from the beginning?

By the time his revelation ended, hardly half a second had passed, but Rifun and Tommen were gone. He might have jumped back through the portal after them except at the last moment he remembered Eric and Varad were there with him, completely confused and extremely afraid.

Trying to keep his nerves calm, Walter gave them both a hand up. They took it and a step away from him.

"What the ever-loving *fuck* is going on here?" Eric demanded. "Just tell me honestly; are we dead?"

"You're not dead," Walter told him. "But you're not drugged either. This is a real place; it's called the Wheel of Time."

"That's a fucking metaphor, not a literal place," Varad said.

"No, it is a real place. It's where the metaphor comes from. But I don't have time to explain everything to you now. We have to go. I have to get Tommen back."

The boys were wary of the portal, but they went through after a moment of consideration. Walter followed, dropping to one knee but determined not to pass out again. The portal closed behind them.

They were alone in the hangar as far as Walter could see. Rifun and his gang were gone, and the reserve team was nowhere to be seen.

"Walt?"

Walter turned to see Micaiah lying on the floor, one arm across his face, the other still protecting his stomach. He went to him.

"Micaiah, what happened? How are you feeling?"

Micaiah waved him off. "I'll be fine. Rifun came back through with Tommen. He started shouting at his minions. They ran out, started a small shooting match with the reserve team. It's been quiet for about a minute."

Walter let out a breath. "Okay. You need to see a doctor."

"I'm fine. Nothing a little—Ah!" He started to sit up and winced in pain. Walter came under him from one side, then looked at Eric and Varad, staring, eyes huge.

"Help me with him," Walter said, hoping to convey calmness and a sense of order.

Eric moved first and together they got Micaiah to a standing position. As they were doing that, the reserve team returned, Steggmann at the head.

"Shit, Walter, what happened?" he demanded. He turned to one of the team. "Call an ambulance, and someone bring us a chair."

"It was an ambush, sir," Walter said. "I tried to just have Rifun take the journal and walk away, but..." He let out a breath. "It got out of hand before it could be contained. And they took Tommen. I think it was planned."

"Shit. He got another one of your friends, too, apparently."

"Yes, sir." Best to just leave it at that, Walter figured.

Steggmann sighed. "Go with your friend, collect yourself. I want you back in my office by four o'clock."

"Yes, sir."

The ambulance came and took Walter, Micaiah, Eric, and

Varad to the emergency room. Eric's and Varad's parents were already there, waiting, and ran to embrace their children. Both mothers gave Walter enormous, heart-felt thank yous, but Walter wished he could be doing the same thing with his son. Instead, he'd let his guard down, and now who knew what Rifun was doing to his boy? He had about half an hour to ponder this before being allowed to visit Micaiah.

"So, how bad is it?" Walter asked.

"Nothing terrible," Micaiah told him. "Couple broken ribs is all, but they want to keep me overnight for observation for possible internal damage. You call Micah at all?"

"Yeah. He said he'll close up early and be over."

"Okay. Give me time for a nap, then." He sighed. "Fuck." He shook his head. "I should have been better prepared. How could I have let him get to me like that?"

"It's not your fault. He's got more power and experience than we do."

"Doesn't make you feel any better about losing Tommen, though, does it?"

Walter looked away. "No, it doesn't."

"Listen, man. I want to get revenge on that asshole, too. Believe me, I do. But first we have to clear our heads and think about this for a little bit. If Rifun went through all that trouble and scheming to get Tommen, he probably isn't going to hurt him. Much. But it also means that you're going to have to start thinking about exactly what you're going to have to do or give in order to get him back."

Problem was, Walter was pretty sure he knew what Rifun would ask for. He would probably demand that Walter turn over Lily in exchange for Tommen. If he did, Rifun would kill Lily on the spot. If he didn't, Rifun would kill Tommen on the spot. Walter would gladly take Tommen over Lily any day, but it would still be giving in to the demands of a terrorist, especially when he knew that Rifun would kill whoever he had in his possession. Was there any way for them both to come out alive? Was there any way to really beat Rifun at his own game?

Walter left the hospital and walked into the precinct feeling very much like a dark thundercloud of despair. He glanced at the clock. Almost four, but still enough time to grab a cup of coffee.

The station was abuzz with activity as news flew from person to person, changing, twisting, exaggerating, and lying. Some were laughing, some ranting, others telling heroic tales of grandeur. Walter closed his eyes and wished they would all just be quiet, stop the noise and let him think for ten seconds without having to listen to them and their version of events.

He made it to the break room. Thankfully, it was empty. Overwhelmed, Walter sank into a chair, Banded, and wept. He was exhausted. From the murder cases, from the incident at the launch, from the negotiations, from holding open a portal for so long, from losing Tommen and not being able to stop or prevent it in any way. He was tired, he was confused, he was sad. God Almighty, but he felt like a little boy and just wanted to curl up in his mother's arms while she rocked him to sleep. Dead for over a century and he still missed her dearly.

Fortunately, he did not fall asleep and avoided losing the Band, thus avoiding anyone walking in to find him both asleep and having wept. Finally, he sat up, rubbed his eyes, grabbed his coffee, and went to the bathroom to try to make himself presentable before heading to Steggmann's office.

"Walter," Steggmann acknowledged. "Sit, please."

He did so, gratefully, hardly caring about the motives for the gesture or even what this meeting was about. He took a drink of coffee to try and quell the fear and sadness threatening to break his composure.

"How's your friend?" Steggmann asked calmly.

"He'll be fine," Walter replied levelly. "Nothing serious."

"And how are you?"

"I'll be better once I get my son back."

"Good. So tell me, what the hell happened in there?"

Walter tried to explain it in a way that made sense, without mentioning such crazy concepts as Time and Banding and portals to the Wheel and all that. Oh, and without going into great detail how one of Rifun's minions was a giant rock monster and the other was dyed hot pink and seemed to have a thing for something the kids were calling "steampunk," whatever that was. He tried to tell a story of Rifun being a hard-ass negotiator, turning what was supposed to be a simple exchange into something far worse with the introduction of a third hostage, who was already beaten and had a gun to his head, and the threat of taking Lily as a fourth. He tried to tell a story of an almost Western-like showdown, where Tommen was just supposed to hold out the journal for Rifun to take, except Rifun took him along with it and then made a break for it, his cronies starting a shootout in the process in order to cover his escape.

Steggmann listened patiently, not interrupting, just simply listening, gaze appearing attentive and not darting around, hands folded politely and not fiddling with pens or other knick-knacks on his desk. When Walter finished his tale, it was a moment before Steggmann spoke.

"Go home, Walter," he said.

"What?"

"Go home. You need to rest. You need to grieve and think and collect yourself." He went on before Walter could protest. "Believe me, I've already got guys combing through it with a fine-tooth comb and canvassing the city. We'll interview Eric and Varad, see if they can give us any clues as to where they might have taken Tommen. But we can't do much until Rifun contacts us, and most likely he's going to contact you. Take the time to rest and plot your revenge. Then come in tomorrow, and tell us your ideas. Okay?" When Walter hesitated, he pressed harder. "Don't make me make this an order."

Walter sighed. "Yes, sir."

But he did not go home right away. He returned to the

hospital, first visiting Micaiah who complained about Walter interrupting his nap. Then he went to see Eric and Varad. Varad had already gone home, and Eric was getting ready to leave.

"Detective Forbes, thank you so much for bringing my boy home," Eric's mom said as he walked in the door. "I don't know how to thank you."

"That's not necessary, Mrs. Brown," Walter told her. "Actually, I was hoping I could ask Eric a few questions."

"Well, sure, but the doctor said it might be better if he got some rest first, in order to avoid retraumatizing him."

"It's okay, Mom," Eric said. "Will you start the car and warm it up?"

Mrs. Brown still seemed uncertain, but finally nodded. "Not too long."

After she left, it was a minute or two before Eric spoke. "All that shit you were saying about Time...was that all true?"

Walter hesitated. "Eric, look at that clock." He pointed to the clock a short distance from the TV.   It was a digital clock, the colon in the middle blinking with the seconds. "Watch that clock. Or if you like, watch the nurses outside here."

Eric started with the clock. Walter Slow Banded. The blinks on the clock got faster, and the minutes went by quicker. Outside Eric's room, in the nurse's station, nurses scuttled to and fro like the sped up images of traffic in a big city. Then he Fast Banded, and everything seemed to stop. Eric looked around, mouth hanging open.

"How...? What...?"

"It's Time, Eric," Walter told him. "All I'm doing is a simple manipulation of physics."

"Simple manipulation, fucking shit...fuck. What the *fuck*? You can do that? And Tommen can do that?"

"Yes. There is far more to it than what you see here, what we call Banding. Your exposure to Time has also gifted you with similar abilities."

"Wait. I can control Time, too?"

"At first, it will be uncoordinated, crude, hardly sophisticated. At your age, you might be able to bring it under some control on your own. Most often, though, Timekeepers need training." He hesitated. "Ideally, you ought to be trained to at least control the Banding. If you are interested, I could arrange for a couple mentors to help you advance. But it requires a lot of work, and a lot is expected of you."

Eric gave him a wide-eyed look like Walter had just kicked his puppy. "No," he said, shaking his head. He stood and backed toward the door. "I can't...fuck, shit...fuck no. This can't...this cannot be real. This...I can't...no. I'm going home." He opened the door. "Don't come after me. And tell Tommen to stay the fucking...fuck *shit* away from me."

Walter did not say anything more, did not immediately leave the room. Instead, he gave the kid a few minutes headstart before going out himself and leaving the hospital, heading home and ruefully thinking about how Tommen would react when he learned his best friend from high school wanted nothing to do with him anymore. On the other hand, Eric might come around eventually, if he started Banding on his own and couldn't control it.

It was strange for Walter to be home so early. Instinctively, as if it were late at night, he went to Tommen's room and pushed open the door. His backpack was still flopped open on the floor next to the bed which was still not made. A couple socks and a pair of boxers were scattered around on the floor, and his laundry hamper was full. Walter closed his eyes and tried to tell himself it was only temporary. He wouldn't be gone forever. Whatever it took, Walter would find a way to bring him home. Letting out a breath, he went and picked up the hamper, taking it to the laundry and trying to feel normal, even if doing Tommen's laundry for him hadn't been a normal thing since he was thirteen years old.

Eventually, Walter figured he must have dozed off because he woke up in his recliner. The TV was off, and the clock said it was midnight. The light on the washing machine said it was done. Carefully, Walter stood and transferred the clothes to the dryer before heading off to bed. He changed slowly as new aches from a hard day's work made themselves known. Then he got under his blankets, turned out the lights, and again cried. But this time he did not Band, and he cried himself to sleep, wondering where Rifun had taken his only son.

He did not dream, which was more welcome than a barrage of nightmares, but Walter still woke up feeling like he hadn't slept at all. Grudgingly, he slapped his alarm clock off and rolled over, wishing he could just go back to sleep. But he had work to do. He had to plan on how to catch Rifun, and how to get Tommen back without sacrificing Lily.

But deep down, he knew that was unrealistic. Assuming Steggmann let him in on the case beyond a mere bystander, unless Eric and Varad were able to provide clues of Rifun's potential whereabouts, it was all going to be a waiting game. Waiting for Rifun to contact them. Waiting until the arranged meeting time and place. Waiting to see how it all turned out in the end.

Distracted, Walter almost didn't get out of the house in time to make it to the station. Briefly, he wondered if he'd shut the coffee maker off. A habitual thought told him Tommen would catch it when he got up. Reality slapped him in the face to say that no, Tommen would not be catching that.

"Morning, Walter," Standish greeted somberly. "Get any sleep last night?"

"Doesn't feel like it," Walter said, refilling his mug.

"Well, Greg's got the boys coming in to interview today. Maybe they can tell us where Rifun held them and we can start checking for clues."

"What, like Scooby-Doo?" Walter shook his head and took a drink. "Rifun's too smart for that. He knows that's the first thing we'll do."

Actually, Walter's bigger fear was that Rifun hadn't been keeping them on Earth at all. Portals to the Wheel weren't the only way to travel from place to place, and someone like Rifun probably knew a thing or two about back doors, if his companions were any indication. They didn't just traipse around willy-nilly through the Wheel to get from one planet to another.

"We still have to try," Standish said patiently. "Listen, Greg's got a whole team canvassing everything police-style. He wants me and you to investigate this on a more personal level. Since Rifun seems to be fixated on you, we ought to figure out what it is he's tapping into and see if we can't wring some clues from that."

It made sense except for the part where Walter spent time in a Welsh prison, only, you know, a hundred and sixty years ago. How did Walter explain that one? And then there was the part where Cassius was supposedly a guard there at the same time.

They returned to the familiar little office. At a motion, Walter took a seat while Standish spent a full three minutes just trying to get a marker to work, which he eventually did.

"So, first woman is murdered," Standish said, drawing out a squiggly timeline and marking one end with a large "1st Murder" under it. "Tommen is the one to find her. Theory is, he was after Lily Guile, a friend of yours." *Loose term*. "Second murder. At the suspected murder scene, Cassius or Rifun leaves a pocketwatch with an altered photo of you or one of your ancestors in it. You remember what was written in it, exactly?"

" 'Tick Tock' and 'Beaumaris Gaol, 1847,' " Walter recited.

"Right. Then the robbery happens, where they steal a journal that your boy happened to have found, and they lure him to a deserted wharf where they try to kill him. He steals back the journal and gets away. After that, they kidnap his friends and hold them hostage for the journal, end up taking both the journal and Tommen."

"So then the question becomes, is this about me or about Tommen?" Walter wondered.

"Well, there is that, too. But if it's about Tommen, why? I mean, we're cops. People come after us all day long. And they might try to use loved ones against us. But if they wanted Tommen specifically...what makes him special to them?"

Walter stared at the whiteboard for a minute or two before a small revelation sparked in his mind. "He's not."

"Who's not what?"

"Tommen isn't special to them. Neither am I. We're wondering what makes me special, what makes Tommen special. Jim, what if this whole thing hasn't been about focusing on *us* per se, but about *not* focusing on Rifun and Cassius? First murder, Sam wasn't anything special either, so we went straight for the murderer. Second murder, suddenly they leave some kind of bombshell evidence, and then everything turns on me and Tommen."

"Okay, so then what about Rifun and Cassius? I mean, we can't find anything on them. Nothing. Nada. Ka-put."

"Because we haven't been looking in the right places." Walter stood. "What time were Eric and Varad coming in?"

Standish let out a breath. "Ten, I think."

Walter started out of the room. "Call me when they get here. I want to ask them something."

"Okay, but...where are you going?"

"To get a pastry."

Micah was just unlocking the bakery doors when Walter pulled into the parking lot. The younger twin held the door for him and wordlessly followed him into the office where he Banded.

"Did you find Tommen?" Micah asked.

"We were right the first time," Walter said, "but not all the way right. One of them isn't just a candidate for the elections; one of them is a Hand. Cassius Hand."

"Walt...it's been centuries since Cassius—Calis used that name. And he was a Runner by the time he was a gaoler."

"In the same way he was an Apprentice Timekeeper? Micah, you remember the story of the Missing Hour?"

"Yeah, the Zero Hour that was elected in 1838 suddenly went missing..." The light came on. "He went missing in 1848 before his term was up, and a stand-in had to be named for the remainder of the term."

"Cassius jumped just as many decades as Julianna, more even, to get to this time period. Who had you apprehended when you and Micaiah went snooping?"

"Um, one of the Hands, why?" The realization came a moment after he said it. "The Hands are always shrouded to try and prevent favoritism. Cassius is a Hand, which means that his DNA is still in the system as such, and he gets shrouded whenever he goes in. He also has access to the Archives where he tries to prevent us from finding out certain information by changing it."

"His position would also get him access to the Hands, like Rifun Ndolo, during the Dispersal of '63," Walter said. "They meet there, use the chaos to advance their cause, and hatch their evil scheme. During that time, they could have input Cassius' DNA back into the system to 'extend' his term. The term only lasts eleven years, but the Dispersal lasted twelve, so they could have re-input it again at the end of the Dispersal to give him another eleven years. Cassius follows Julianna looking for the journal and kills her, but she doesn't have it. He goes back to Forbes Cave looking for it, still can't find it, and when he comes out again, it's present day. Rifun probably accompanied him, seeing how they were both clueless as to modern technology. And, depending on the year they departed, Cassius likely still has time banked in the Wheel, meaning he's still a Hand."

"Except...if Cassius is masquerading as a Hand because his term is not technically over, that means we have more Hands than we should. Which means..."

"Which means that Lily probably stumbled onto him by chance in her quest to buy seats."

"Okay, so posing as a Hand allows Cassius access into the Wheel where he wouldn't normally get in because of his reputation. He gains access to funds, research, and resources that are practically unlimited. Lily comes along, buying up seats, finds that there is a miscount in the number of Hands, also revealing herself to Cassius who spent decades and a number of time portal jumps looking for her, thinking she has the journal which is important to him. He and

Rifun try to kill her, but because of the time difference and his illiteracy regarding technology, they botch it up. They discover the whereabouts of the journal, steal it, but they can't just leave Lily unattended. But because Tommen interfered, they need some kind of revenge, so they kidnap his friends to teach him a lesson. Then, in order to attempt to secure Lily to themselves, they kidnap him and now they're going to ransom Tommen for Lily." Micah nodded. "Impressive theory. Makes sense. But if Cassius was the Hand who had us arrested, why did he release us? Why not break our clocks or kill us outright?"

"For the same reason that, if you spread this story around the Wheel, I'm betting he won't show up to the hostage negotiations for Tommen. It would look bad on the seat he's trying to claim."

"And what seat is that?"

"The Zero Hour."

"Zer- are you sure?"

"How else would Cassius have had so much power over Julianna to get her to search for that journal? Why else would Calis Cutthroat and Rifun be considered so dangerous that not even the Hands would touch them, except that an order came down from the Zero Hour not to touch them? And why, when they were so confident about being up against an entire SWAT Team of cops, would they order you and Micaiah to stand down with all — what, one or two of your allies? — when we went into the Wheel? Except that if they were subdued, suddenly the Zero Hour would be missing?"

"So Cassius is pretending to be the Zero Hour...or he is the Zero Hour?"

"Both. He starts out as a Hand, and he jumps through a time portal a hundred years or so. By technicality, his term is not yet up, but the Wheel needed a Zero Hour in order for the Hands to function. So, he bides his time until the Dispersal when there were upwards of a thousand so-called Hands running around. During that time, he keeps reinserting his DNA into the system in order to keep power, and makes another jump into present day before his term is up.

Because the system wasn't purged after the Dispersal, seeing how all but the final fifty-one Hands were supposedly 'disposed of,' his DNA is still in there, which means he is still in power. He's a rogue Hand, Micah."

Micah ran his tongue over his teeth. "Okay, I'm following you so far. I think. So what happens this election, then? Okay, Lily's got all her seats set, voting day comes around, ballots are turned in. What happens?"

"If Cassius succeeds in killing Lily, all her bribes mean nothing, and he can kill and maim and create another Dispersal so he can get his Council of Hands set however he wants. Then all he has to do is simply walk in and take back the Zero Hour seat. If she lives, she exposes him and his reign of terror, and his orders not to touch him are null and void because they were given *pro per.*"

"Why not kill everyone and take the seat anyway?"

Walter sighed. "I don't know, except that it's part of an even grander scheme which we are blind to. Point is, we need to keep Lily alive."

Micah frowned. "The way you phrase it, I'm inclined to agree. But does that mean we are literally promoting bribery and the buying of seats?"

"I told you to try and buy help, didn't I?"

Micah shrugged. "Fair enough. But then the real question becomes, how does this help you find Tommen?"

"I'll be talking to Eric and Varad today. If you're willing and Micaiah is feeling up to it, I need you to do some serious rumor-spreading."

"Anything in particular?"

Walter paused. "Take Lily. Explain to her what's going on. Tell her that she's offering a million turns to anyone who votes for not-Cassius for Zero Hour. And remember, he may not be going by the name Cassius."

Micah did not seem thrilled at the idea of taking Lily anywhere, but still he straightened his back and nodded stiffly. "And what do we hope to accomplish?"

"If he's worried about losing his campaign, it may draw him out of the shadows. At the very least, it will keep him occupied and away from my son."

Micah nodded in understanding. "We'll do our best." He shifted his stance. "When did it become law that all Hands and candidates had to be shrouded 'to prevent favoritism' and whatever else?"

Walter sighed. "Long before you or I, but it seems to be backfiring now."

With that, Walter bought his pastry and left the bakery, doing a quick city patrol before returning to the precinct, acutely aware that he still had several hours before Eric and Varad appeared. Standish was still in the office, looking over some papers. He looked up as Walter entered.

"So what's the word, boss?"

"I think I found a way to draw Cassius out of the shadows," Walter said.

"Care to share?"

"I haven't quite worked out the details." He said it as a dismissal.

Standish gave him a hard stare. "Now isn't the time to be going freelance on us, Walt. We all want to see your kid back, believe me. But don't go doing nothing stupid or rash, you hear me?"

"Not planning on it. What are you reading?"

"Report from the nerd herd, their analysis of the recorded call from Rifun to Tommen."

"Anything interesting or helpful?"

"Well, they noted what sounded like rocks or moving earth in the background, and there might have been an echo, which suggests some kind of cave."

Walter let out a breath. "These mountains have more holes than Swiss cheese."

Standish grunted in agreement. "Background noise that might

have been laughter suggests multiple persons present. Well, Rifun set his goons on the team yesterday, so that's not particularly insightful." He shook his head. "Nothing of real usefulness."

Walter sat down in one of the chairs in a heap, rubbing his eyes. "There has to be something. We just have to find it."

"And we will. Take a lap around the building, Walt. Clear your head. Then come back, and let's sit down and think about this like rational cops."

But it was all Walter could do to focus until Eric and Varad walked in and were escorted to another office. Before another officer could go in, Walter put a hand on his shoulder. "You mind if I talk to them for a few minutes?"

"Be my guest."

As Walter walked in, both boys gave him leery looks, like they weren't sure quite what he was going to do. Ultimately, all he did was Band, that way they could speak privately. Varad seemed ready to freak out, but Eric just met his gaze with cold determination. Walter spoke before either could say anything. "I'm not here about Time or the Banding or any of that. I'm here because I need to know what, if anything, Rifun or Cassius or any of his goons said to you. And I'm talking about all that insane crackpot stuff that convinced you that they were lunatics."

"They said a lot of stuff like that," Eric told him. "They kept telling us that we didn't have a lot of time, but soon we would have all the time in the world or in the universe and what did we think about adding more time to our day, and blah, blah, whatever."

"Did any of them mention Tommen?"

Eric shrugged. "He might have come up, I mean—"

"Eric, stop bullshitting me. I know you're a good kid. I know you're a decent guy who likes to help people. I know you didn't rape Michelle, and you're being put through hell, and you are scared out of your mind, trying to act the tough guy to cope. But my son, your best friend, is missing and in the hands of the same lunatics who took you. And I need to find him. Now I am asking, I am begging for your help.

No one outside knows what we're saying here. So please, just...what did they tell you?"

Eric sighed, his gaze still stone cold, but finally he spoke, his attitude a tad more cooperative. "They didn't tell us anything. Everything we heard was second-hand, little conversations going on around us. Rifun always wanted to make sure that they didn't say anything to us or around us so that way we wouldn't have anything to give to the police."

"But you must have heard something. Where were you kept?"

"In some cave. I don't know where it was or how we got there, just that they would grab us, and Rifun would do something, and suddenly we were in a cave. Or at the airport. Or wherever."

"Who guarded you?"

"The pink chick and the rock dude mostly. The Japanese guy came and went sometimes."

"And Rifun and Cassius?"

"I don't know."

"I do," Varad squeaked. "It was at night. They thought we were asleep, but I was awake. The pink girl and the rock guy were complaining. I couldn't really understand what they were saying, but the Japanese guy walked up to the fire, dumped an armload of wood, and sat down and he said something about hands and some elections or something. And something about grandfathers."

"Can you be more specific?" Walter asked, trying not to get angry or excited.

Varad let out a breath and seemed to come around to some semblance of normalcy. "Not really. Well, there was something else mentioned. I don't know, maybe it was just a Japanese word the guy didn't know the English word for. 'Akari' or something like it. Does that mean anything?"

"I don't speak Japanese," Walter told him, which was true, except the word wasn't Japanese, not the way he understood it to be used. Except the Akari fell into the realm of the Holy Grail: something everyone loved to gossip about as if it might be true, but most just passed off as a legend, while some spent their whole lives searching for it. What was it doing in a conversation about the Hands and the elections? Was Cassius really that far off his rocker?

"That's all I heard. I was trying to pretend to be asleep," Varad said.

Walter looked at Eric who shook his head. "I got nothing else. They made it a point not to talk around us, that way we wouldn't have anything to say to you."

Walter let out a breath. "That's what I was afraid of." He stood. "If you think of anything else, you know where to find me."

He went to the door and released the Band. "Forgot something," he told the interrogating officer. "Go ahead; I'll be back afterwards."

But he had no intention of going back.

Chapter Twenty-One
Fog

Tommen wasn't sure exactly what happened after Rifun grabbed him and pulled him back through the portal to Earth. He felt the weakness and the air-sucking force, but he also felt Rifun dragging him painfully across slick tarmac. After a moment, Rock Monster scooped him up and started running, enormous, stony feet thumping mightily on the ground.

Oriental, who had been passive thus far, suddenly reached into his backpack, turned around, brought out two AR-15's, and started firing at the reserve team on either side of the hangar. Rock Monster made an impressive leap over a baggage train, the car abandoned by its fearful driver. He huddled there until the others joined them, pulling something against the train to use as a barricade. Oriental had his AR's, Rifun his revolver. Cassius had a shotgun and Neon Yellow Steampunk had a couple 1911's. Only Rock Monster did not have a weapon, but his sole job appeared to be protecting Tommen, which his apparently impenetrable body did a good job of.

"Oh, I always love a good shootout," Rifun said, twisting and standing just long enough to get in a couple haphazard shots. He sat back down to reload. "But, we are on a schedule. Donojok, stay here and help Tadashi and Cassius. Isthim, get Tommen to a safe place and wait for me there."

Tommen had recovered from the portal, but all the action and sudden movements, and a number of thoughts telling him this was not supposed to happen, kept him from putting up much of a fight as Neon Yellow Steampunk grabbed him and started running again, their movements covered by Donojok standing, picking up the baggage train like it was a Tonka train, and throwing it at the cops.

Another thought hit him just before they reached the main airport building. Rifun had told her to get him to a safe place and wait for him there. But "a safe place" was an ambiguous phrase and could mean any place that was safe, presumably from the hail of bullets raining outside as well as the manhunt that would no doubt ensue. But that he'd also said to wait for him, meant that this ambiguous locative phrase was actually some kind of code phrase, and he had a specific place in mind for her to take him to wait.

A third thing occurred to him then, and that was he was thinking stupid shit like a half-drunk idiot. He was putting up no resistance to being dragged along by someone who was not easily mistaken, and who would be identified easily as being part of the shootout. If he wasn't fighting, that meant that he was cooperating. And if it looked like he was cooperating and part of them, he was just as likely to get shot as she was. It took a minute for his body to catch up with his brain before he stopped running and dug his heels in, the heel of his shoe catching on the lip of some peeling carpet.

Neon Yellow Steampunk, or Isthim, if he heard correctly, did not jerk to a stop or waste any motion as she came to the end of her reach, then wheeled back, turning motion into momentum into power, and clubbing him across the head with the butt of her pistol. Tommen stumbled, almost went to a knee, lost his heel-brake on the carpet, and was soon being dragged along again. Except this time, it was not at a pace he could keep up with if he wanted to do anything but run. Isthim never slowed down, instead increasing her speed, and she never tired as she dragged Tommen along behind her. Well, at the very least, no one would mistake Tommen for cooperating now. Small comfort as one of his pant legs rode up, his sock came down, and the carpet chewed hungrily away at his skin.

By the time they made it to the main airport lobby, security was scattered, trying to figure out what was going on without causing a panic among the people. All the flight times on the monitor were changed to "Delayed," and customer service had a growing line of angry people demanding to know what the holdup was, why every single flight at the airport was suddenly thrown off-kilter.

Still Isthim went, dragging Tommen behind her, never once attracting a stare or a question. The one time Tommen tried to call out for help, she clubbed him again, dazing him and sending his vision spinning. Thankfully, he did not taste blood, though he figured his cheek would be at least a little swollen.

He was hit a third time, this time by the cold air of the automatic doors giving way to a chill winter wind. His leg, burned to hamburger from the carpet, was momentarily relieved by the comfort of new-fallen snow, only to be eaten alive again when they hit the parking lot asphalt, which used the same snow-melting technology as the runway tarmac. By the time they reached a rather familiar beige van, Tommen could hardly put weight on his left leg. Not that it mattered since Isthim dead-lifted him like a boss and simply rolled him in like a sack of flour. Then she got in with him and slammed the door shut.

Tommen rolled over and groaned. "That hurt."

Isthim said nothing.

"Do you have like some gauze or a bandaid or even just a fucking napkin I can put on this?" he asked as he sat up to inspect his leg in the dim light filtering in from the windshield.

Isthim rolled her eyes but retrieved a fast food napkin from the front seat. Tommen took it, wanting to snatch it from her to make a point, but not wanting to get clubbed again. He sighed. "Since I know you're not going to let me get out to do it, can you get me like a cup of snow or something to wash this and cool it down? Clean snow. White snow."

She gave him a look. "I know snow," she said, her voice sounding like it might have belonged to a hot girl, except that hot girl was talking through some spinning fan blades, making it sound all choppy and like it might have been used as a background track to an 80's song.

Still, she went out and retrieved a handful of fresh snow,

which Tommen pressed against his leg. He gritted his teeth, not sure if the pain came from the wound itself, from the wound being clean, or from the tiny ice shards tearing into tender, exposed flesh. Eventually, the snow turned red and melted, and he wiped up the wound with the napkin, holding it until it was soaked, but starting to clot.

He just peeled the napkin back to look at the wound when the doors of the van opened. In front, Oriental Tadashi was driving, with Cassius in the passenger seat. Rifun and Rock Monster, Donojok or some such thing, joined them in the back.

"Well, I was about to say we all got away without a scratch," Rifun said, looking at Tommen.

"It was a wound of his own doing," Isthim informed him.

Rifun grabbed Tommen's hand and peeled back the napkin to see for himself, inspecting it like a wino snob might inspect a bottle of fine vintage. "Well, it's not deep, and it's not bad. Good news is, I think you're going to live."

"Where's my dad?" Tommen asked, intending to sound strong and defiant, but figuring he came across as little more than a scared little boy.

Rifun waved a hand dismissively. "Oh, he'll be fine. He has no idea what's just occurred, I reckon."

"What happens now?"

"Rifun, we should go before Captain Forbes finds us here," Tadashi said from the driver's seat.

"Excellent," Rifun said.

The van started up, and Tadashi carefully maneuvered them through the maze that was the airport parking lot. Rifun continued to speak. "Now, dear child, we take you to what you might refer to as our secret lair. It's all sorts of fun. It's kind of like summer camp, except you're our prisoner. Then we let your dad sweat for a few days before contacting him and making our demands."

"To trade me for Lily," Tommen stated.

"Oh, you are a clever boy, aren't you? Must run in the family.

Now then, there are some precautions we have to take in order to ensure that you don't accidentally blab about how to get to our secret lair. But don't worry. It wears off quickly."

Tommen was about to ask him what he meant, but then Rifun gestured, and the last thing Tommen remembered was a sack over the head followed by a club.

What was it with Isthim and clubbing people? Was it just something her species did, or was it just something she enjoyed doing to prisoners? And when did it suddenly go from Cassius—as Calis—to Cassius and Rifun, and now to Cassius, Rifun, and a band of freaks? More to the point, how were they able to just waltz around and not attract attention? Okay, so Donojok might not have been able to get away with it, but how could Isthim have just walked right through the airport, dragging Tommen, and not gotten stopped? Was it because of her looks alone, or because she was dragging Tommen against his will?

It took a while before Tommen realized that he was able to think, and yet he couldn't really make out his body. It was kind of like dreaming, except...maybe lucid dreaming? He tried to envision the concept and claim some kind of movement, bring together some sort of setting or landscape, but it was like hitting a mental wall. He tried to feel his way around it, but to no avail. He was like a consciousness trapped in his own body.

He reflected on this for a moment. Eric and Varad had been screaming that they'd been drugged. Tommen had assumed that meant that they'd been exposed to the Time. But what if it wasn't just Time they had been experiencing? What if they truly had been drugged? Tommen tried to recall when he might have been drugged, except he hadn't been given food or water, obviously. Maybe it was a naturally occurring drug given off by Donojok or Isthim. If it was Donojok, then it would have been while he was carrying him, and then, maybe proximity alone.

On the other hand, maybe it was Isthim, able to give off some sort of agent that not only made Tommen compliant, but was able to turn away the heads of security, cause them to think that she was somehow insignificant. Maybe the clubbing wasn't just a physical clubbing, but a double dose of this naturally-occurring drug.

This was all speculation of course, as Tommen had zero knowledge of her species or Donojok's species, had never even seen them before. Well, not entirely true. He had seen something like Donojok once, but whether it was the same species was hard for him to discern.

So instead, Tommen lay somewhere in his consciousness, mulling things over, trying to figure out what happened, why it happened, and how to escape. There were several obstacles in his line of thought, however. The first was that he had no idea where they were going. In theory, Rifun could simply Band, and they could literally drive anywhere without being stopped. The second problem, probably the bigger of the two, was that Tommen didn't know if Rifun had any more goons stashed away somewhere. Tommen had been able to take Rifun and Cassius alone—well, more or less anyway—but throw in a trigger-happy Japanese kid, a rock monster that moved a lot faster than he probably should have been able to, and a hot chick who gave off depressant hallucinogens, and Tommen knew he wasn't going to fight his way out. No fisticuffs, only cunning. And even then, he felt his wit was in short supply here.

Wherever "here" was. Slowly, his body came back to him, unfurling from his brain like a comfortable pair of socks fresh from the dryer. First, he became aware of breathing, which he was glad to still be doing. He couldn't smell anything or feel his face or sinuses, just his lungs as they expanded and deflated. Then, as he gained awareness of his shoulders and arms, he felt his face begin to tingle like pins and needles, like a limb that had fallen asleep was coming back alive. He became aware of the burlap sack still over his head and how it pressed uncomfortably against one ear, despite the long hair that mildly cushioned it. He really ought to cut his hair at some point.

He drifted out again, probably to sleep. When he came around again, he found he had regained limited spatial orientation, and that he was lying down, which was why the burlap sack was uncomfortable against his ear. But he also had general awareness of the rest of his body, his arms and legs, his abdomen and hips. Later on, as temporal orientation returned, he found his feet and hands.

Pain sensation came rushing back all of a sudden, and if he could have, he might have gasped as he could suddenly feel his leg wound in all its burning glory. But he could also feel that someone had put a gauze pad over it and taped it around his leg.

The last thing to return to him was his greater spatial orientation and the greater senses. He felt his eyes, closed, eyelashes pressed against the burlap sack. He could feel the dirt on his eyelashes, too, from the sack, and did not attempt to open his eyes. He could smell again, the musty, moldy smell of the bag, but also a fresh, earthy smell of whatever lay beyond. He felt dirt on his lips and could almost taste the dust and mold from the bag. His tongue felt swollen from lack of water.

But he could also hear, and in his current predicament, Tommen knew that as long as he stayed still and just listened, he just might hear something useful.

For a short time, he could hear the crackling of a fire, the popping of sticks. Judging by the slight reverberation, he might have guessed he was in a cave. Adding the earthy smell and the well-contained warmth, it was plausible. Judging from the fact that he felt no chill winter wind, they were either someplace where it wasn't winter, in which case there ought to be some sort of birdsong or sounds of life, or else they were well and deep into the cave beyond the reach of the outside world.

It wasn't long before he heard several sets of footsteps. One dropped an armload of wood against one wall of the cave and began feeding sticks into the fire. Tommen could see light dancing against his eyelids. Another person set to rustling and fussing with something or other and it wasn't long before the smell of spit-roasted fresh game hit Tommen's nose through the mold and dirt, and an overwhelming sense of fear and homesickness washed over him, making him long deeply for his pa and Teo and the hunting trips they used to go on. His stomach rumbled.

"Think we ought to save some for him?" Tadashi asked. "Think the drug's worn off by now?"

There was a pause. Then Isthim spoke. "If he moves, I will save some for him."

Tommen wanted desperately to sink his teeth into a fresh rabbit leg or a squirrel or anything at all, really, but he forced himself to remain still and quiet, simply breathing. Walter had taught him a thing or two, and he wasn't about to let a little thing like hunger erase his best chance for getting some useful intel.

"Still don't understand why we had to go through all this trouble," Tadashi went on. "He doesn't look like any Akari-bearer I've ever seen."

"Because he is not yet a bearer," Isthim scolded him. "But he will be. In time. All we do is guide him on the path."

Tommen almost groaned, but the best he figured he could safely do was roll his eyes. Okay, so they were a little crazy as it was, being murderous bandits and all, and kidnapping his friends, and then kidnapping him and so on and so forth. But this was really pushing the limits of whackjob as they spoke of some Akari-thing and having to lead him on a path, as if citing some religious text where he was the Chosen One or some godawful thing. He didn't condone terrorism or political upheaval like they were apparently attempting, but this basically just crossed the line into religious nutcase whackos following some obscenely misguided, made up—or, more likely hallucinated—prophecy. Maybe it was just him overreacting, but he knew crazy, and these guys just reeked of it.

"Yeah, well, as long as I get paid," Tadashi said, sounding as skeptical as Tommen about the whole thing. "As long as Cassius fulfills his end of the bargain on these elections, I'll take this kid wherever the fuck Rifun tells me to."

All right, so maybe he did overreact a little. Tommen calmed his racing thoughts and tried to think logically. Maybe an akari was an actual object. But what role he played in it, he didn't know, considering he had no idea what an akari was.

His heart leapt into his throat as he heard another set of footsteps enter the cave.

"Is he awake yet?" Rifun asked.

"Still out," Tadashi replied.

"Is he? Well, let's see about that."

Tommen kept his eyes closed and made his body as still as possible without tightening his muscles. In fact, he went as limp as he possibly could, letting his head go with the motion of the sack being ripped off, settling in gently back in the dirt. He could practically feel Rifun's scrutinizing gaze burning a hole through his eyelids to see that he was awake.

"All right, then," Rifun said breathily. "Test number two."

Tommen cried out in sheer agony as Rifun ripped the tape off his leg, taking neatly-defined strips of hair with it. Tommen pulled his leg up to his chest and whimpered, touching the reddening skin and examining the larger wound which had more or less clotted closed and was beginning to heal. He tried to gauge how much time had passed by the healing of the wound, but couldn't come up with more than a day or two.

"That's how you do that," Rifun said, standing and going to sit on a rock seat close to the fire.

Tadashi simply gave him a dark look and went back to shaving sticks, the curls of wood landing in the fire. Isthim seemed unaffected as she continued turning a rabbit on the spit.

"How was I drugged?" Tommen asked, his voice scratchy.

Rifun looked back at him, then back into the fire, poking a stick around in the coals. "Did you know that in the Amazon rainforest, the most brightly-colored frogs are the most poisonous? A single, accidental touch will stop your heart in ten seconds flat." He pulled his stick out and admired the burning end. "Isthim, her entire species is, essentially, that poisonous frog, though to a lesser degree. Sheer proximity, touching something that she has touched, without the mental fortitude to withstand the drug as it were, will make anyone reasonably compliant. Brief skin-to-skin contact will knock you out for a time, as you have experienced. Prolonged skin-to-skin contact will kill you. And I am told it is a slow, painful death."

Tommen sat up and leaned against the cave wall. "Where are we?"

"In a cave," Tadashi said, like Tommen was an idiot child, and Tommen glared at him.

"Now, now, no need to be rude," Rifun purred. "He is merely curious. At the very least, he isn't getting anxious and excited like his friends." He rolled his eyes.

"Why did you take Eric and Varad? Why not just Band and walk into the evidence room to steal journal, like you did at the museum?"

"It's all about sending a message, dear boy."

"And what message is that?"

"One that I am certain a clever son of a cop like you could figure out if he really tried. See, people seem to think that by not talking, we give out no information, when in fact we're practically screaming our plans. The only thing is, we like to make things a challenge. After all, if we simply told you our master plan, you would have a ton of questions and doubts, and you'd be so skeptical it would break my heart. But by giving you pieces and bits of information, you can work things out for yourself. Then not only are you less skeptical, but I love the moment of 'Aha!' that lights up people's faces when they finally get it. It's like reading a good mystery novel, wouldn't you say?"

"Are you from, like, 1600's London or something?" Tommen wondered. "Because I'm getting a serious Shakespearean vibe off of you."

Rifun grinned. "I am not, but I am flattered by the compliment. I do enjoy theater, when done properly. It may be difficult to believe, but I was once quite the actor, renowned for my skill for monologuing."

"You ought to do more of it."

"Ah, so his sense of humor returns as well, a little late, but never missing an opportunity to present itself. Lovely."

"So where are you from? I don't recognize your accent."

Rifun hesitated, studied him, seemed to weigh his options. Tommen wondered what terrible, damning knowledge could be gained just by asking where he was from, what awful secrets might be used against him. But eventually he did answer. "Madagascar, actually. My father was a French soldier during the Imperial age, when the continent of Africa was ripe for the taking by the 'more civilized' Europeans. My mother was a humble Malasay homemaker, raped by the more civilized European men and left to raise me by herself, shamed and scorned by her own people."

He paused and met Tommen's gaze. "You don't believe me. You don't think a man such as myself could have humble beginnings?" He shrugged. "Well, you're right. My mother was not shunned by her village, but I was, as if I somehow had a choice in my parentage. When I became a man, I went over to my father's world, to the French. It was there that I was exposed to Time and so set on this path that we all invariably trod alone."

"You look like you've made friends," Tommen observed casually as Rifun brought out a flask and drank from it.

"Friends? Friends have nothing to do with it. Friends come after."

"After what?"

Rifun held the flask out to Tommen. He eyed it suspiciously, but figured there would be nothing gained by killing him, especially if Rifun wanted to ransom him for Lily. But even as he took a huge swig, he was instantly aware that it was not water in the flask. He spit out what he could and choked on the rest while Rifun and Tadashi looked on and laughed. Tommen was on his hands and knees coughing and gasping for air, spitting out as much as he could. Rifun fished the flask from his hand and took another drink for himself.

"For all your binges with your friends, I might have thought you had a little more sense than that, or at least a palette a little more steeled to the strong stuff," Rifun said.

"I don't drink that much," Tommen informed him hoarsely.

Still, the man fished out a second flask and handed it to him. This time Tommen sniffed it first and took only a small sip before deciding it was actually water this time. He took a long drink. He handed it back to Rifun with a weak and grudging, "Thank you."

"No worries, kid," Rifun said, still smiling as he stood. "Get yourself something to eat, too, while you're at it."

"Thought you said that if I touched what she touched, it's like a drug?"

"Well, there are two ways to look at it. First, it's only a drug if you aren't aware of it. At least the proximity and second-hand touch part of it is. Second, you're not going anywhere faster right now, so you could just as well enjoy yourself a little bit while you're here."

Tommen figured he could do that just as easily with a Slow Band, but he wasn't about to pursue an argument, just grunted and tried to find a comfortable position to sit. Rifun was just turning as if to leave, when Donojok entered the room like a rockslide moving slowly through a tunnel.

"Thought I told you to wait outside and stand guard," Rifun said irritably.

"A message arrived from Cassius," the rock monster told him, his voice deep and rumbling like an earthquake. "There is trouble in the Wheel." He stole a glance at Tommen through eyes that were little more than holes bored into rock. "The twin Lieutenants are attempting to sabotage the elections."

Now Rifun got an expression of stoic determination, as if a fly had been bothering him and now he was actually going to do something about it. He sighed, shifted his jaw, turned to look around the cave, letting his gaze rest on each person—lingering an extra five seconds or so on Tommen—before turning back to Donojok.

"Stand guard. No one enters the tunnels." He turned his head only a fraction to look behind him. "Isthim, your expertise is needed."

Immediately, Isthim got to her feet. "Tadashi, stay here. Make sure the boy doesn't leave. And if somehow our location is compromised, kill everything, and head to one of the other hideouts. Any questions?"

No one said anything. Donojok turned around with more flexibility than Tommen thought natural for a rock, and then slid back the way he'd come, Rifun and Isthim following purposefully, leaving Tadashi alone in the cave with Tommen.

"So if Rifun and Cassius are anarchists, what is their interest in the elections?" Tommen wondered. "What do they care who wins and who loses?"

Tadashi scoffed, rolled his eyes, and tossed his little whittled stick into the fire. "Are you really that dense? They're not anarchists." He paused, as if considering his next words. Finally, his expression turned into the epitome of "fuck it," and he shifted on his rock seat to face Tommen, saying, "Cassius is the fucking Zero Hour."

It was like Tommen had been clubbed over the head again. "What?"

"Duh. How else would an order come down not to touch him or Rifun? The Hands are mandatory shrouded to try and prevent favoritism and bribery. No one would know."

"But...how did he botch up two murders? I mean, the Hands have access to basically unlimited resources and records and histories and everything else about Time and all the Time Agents."

"Because Cassius went through a Time Portal that launched him over fifty years. He was unfamiliar with twenty-first century technology, and Lily had changed in that time. But you may have noticed, he's gotten a little better at it."

"So why go through all this? Why not just Band, go to Lily's apartment, and kill her?"

Tadashi shrugged. "Fuck if I know. That's what I thought, but no, they have to go through all this horse and pony nonsense."

"I think you mean dog and pony."

"Do I look like I care?" He rolled his eyes. "Anyway, I really don't care much as long as I get paid."

"So how did you get mixed up in this? What are you, like Gatekeeper or what?"

"I was a Journeyman Timekeeper when I turned Runner. I got sick of serving the sick, corrupt, twisted ideology of the Hands." He shook his head. "And somehow, I'm still serving that sick ideology. I figure that once this is over with and I get paid and my contract is up, I'm just getting out of this completely. No more Banding, no more Time, nothing. I'm going to go back home, find a girl, find a home, and just...live normally."

"Got a girl waiting for you?" Tommen asked, daring to hope that he might be able to win over Tadashi.

"I did," Tadashi answered. "Keiko was her name. She was Korean. Beautiful girl with the most wonderful smile. I asked my parents for her. They consulted their stars and signs and determined that she was a good match for me. So they went to her parents to arrange the match." He sighed. "That is when I was exposed to Time. I thought I could live both lives, but being gone to train for months at a time — when it was but a second here — she said I was changing. I took a little time to myself to be with her. We had a daughter. But my wife was growing up, growing old. And I was not. For a while, we joked about me being blessed with the gift of life. But I knew the truth, and it hurt me."

For a long time, Tadashi was silent, and even Tommen had to reflect on such an experience. He dated girls, true, but while the thought of marriage and a family was naturally frightening, there was always that knowledge hidden in the back recesses of his mind, knowing that unless he married another Time Agent, she would grow old...and he would not. Or if he did find a girl, would he deliberately expose her to Time, teach her, train her? Would they really want to stay married that long? "Til death do us part" was nice and all when the high end of the scale was sixty years or so, but what about a hundred and sixty years? Or six hundred?

More to that point, what about children? Would they want to have any? Would the children already be exposed *in utero*? Would that affect a pregnancy? If the children weren't affected and already exposed, would they want to deliberately expose them in order to all stay together, or would they leave the decision up to the children? And if the children didn't want to be exposed, could they really watch those children grow old and die?

"In the end," Tadashi went on sadly, "my mentor and I faked my death, getting a Harvester who worked in a hospital to declare me dead and smuggle me out of the city." He looked at Tommen. "I have not been home since. It has been thirty years. I do not know what my daughter looks like as a grown woman, or who she married, or if she has any children of her own. I do not know if my Keiko remarried, or if he is good to her."

"When you do go back home, are you going to look her up?" Tommen wondered.

"No, no." Tadashi shook his head. "It would only cause longing and heartbreak. And perhaps anger. Better to stay away and simply start a new life. I am told that if I simply stop Banding, stop getting involved with Time, eventually the effects will wear off, and I may be able to grow old with another woman...together this time."

"That sounds nice."

"You do not have a girl?"

"Well, heh, the last time I tried to get a girl, it kind of ended up as a fistfight and a trip to the principal's office. Ever since then, well, no girls for me."

"Would you?"

Tommen let out a breath. "I don't know. I haven't met any Time Agent girls I like—haven't really met any at all—and so far I haven't found anyone I would willingly expose in hopes of bringing her with me as it were."

Tadashi shook his head again. "If you are a real man who truly loves a girl, do not curse her with this life. Go to her. Time is an evil, demanding mistress. Send her away, and stay close to the real girl you love."

"If I find that kind of girl, that choice might just come naturally."

"No. It won't. Time is also a drug in its own right. And you will want to use it, even for the smallest things. Standing in line at the grocery store—or standing in line anywhere. Sports, you will want to be the fastest or the strongest. Work, you will want to get everything done so you don't have to take anything home. Home, you will want to get everything done, but you will also want to just bypass the screaming arguments, or a sick infant, not have to listen to it cry for hours. Just skip right through it. Once you have the power, the desire to use it will never leave."

"And you think you can beat it?"

"I have not Banded or used any of my abilities in over two years. Rifun Bands whenever we need to move quickly, but I myself have done nothing."

"How long until you know if the effects are really reversing?"

"I don't know. Perhaps when I look in the mirror one day and see lines, wrinkles, gray hair."

Tadashi moved around the fire and lifted the rabbit off the spit. It might have been a little overdone, but it was hard to tell in the firelight. And anyway, Tommen was too hungry to care. Tadashi grabbed a plate from a small sack in one corner of the cave and started ripping the limbs off. Then he broke the ribs off the spine and picked the rest of the meat off in scraps. He returned to the fire and sat facing away from it, toward Tommen, the plate between them.

"Eat," Tadashi said. "It may be a while before you eat again."

"Why?" Tommen wondered, choosing a hind leg. "I mean, I know it's slim pickings during the winter, but still."

It was then that he also considered that, being wanted, they also did not have free access to the Wheel, to just walk into the Food Court and order up any meal they wanted free of charge. All their power, and they had to hunt for scraps in the forest.

He took a bite of the rabbit and was instantly transported to a time a long time ago in an ancient, familiar valley. Tommen and Teo and their pa had been tracking small game through autumn leaves crunchy from fresh frost. They were hoping that small game being out and about might lead them to larger game also out hunting. "Trade a rabbit for a mountain lion," as his pa would say.

Tommen had been excited to go. It was one of their long hunting trips where they would be gone for several days, and it was the first one he'd been allowed to go on. They'd planned for a four day journey, just the three of them. They set up some snares the first day on their way out for ma and the girls to check, so even if the longer trip was a bust, at least they might catch something. Then they set out, heading farther up into the mountains where men did not live, only hunted.

They found a rabbit warren the second day, and they waited and watched until mama rabbit came out in search of food. They tracked her for a short distance before something startled her away. At first, Teo had blamed Tommen, but as he went to berate him for it, there came the mountain lion. Except the lion didn't care much for a scrawny winter rabbit; he was more interested in the three big men standing there arguing.

They got the cougar. On the way back to the camp, they also got a rabbit. They saved the cougar for the winter meat stores but ate the rabbit there in camp as celebration for a good day of hunting.

"Hey, Tommen."

Tommen blinked back to the present with Tadashi hardly two inches from his face. He jerked back and hit his head on the cave wall.

"What?" Tommen asked.

"Are you okay? You zoned out, and then you started crying."

"Huh?" Tommen wiped his face, immediately ashamed of the tears he found. Fuck, he was already a captive; he didn't need to look like some sniveling coward homesick for his mommy, too. Even if he felt like it. "Shit."

"Thinking of another time and place?" Tadashi wondered, sitting back. "It happens. Little things you didn't know you remembered, things you didn't realize you wanted and missed until you saw them again years later."

Tommen took an embarrassed bite of meat and chewed hurriedly. "Cassius said he knew my dad—that is, Walter, my adopted dad—from way back. Do you know what he meant?"

Tadashi shrugged and shook his head. "I don't know nothing about nobody here. Well, not entirely true as you've noticed, but I don't care to know anyone's life story."

"Then why tell me yours?"

"Maybe I wanted someone to know. Maybe I wanted to see how you would react."

"So it was a lie."

"Our lives are only stories, Tommen. How true they are is only up to us. And we have more time and ability to craft our stories than most. So whether it is true or false does not matter. Just make sure that your story is a good one."

Tommen studied him for a moment, finishing off the hind leg. Finally he leaned back and said, "You were telling the truth."

Tadashi raised a brow. "How do you know?"

"I don't know. Something in the way you told the story, maybe, the way you described her or the events. I can't say for sure, but I'm ninety-five percent positive you were telling the truth."

Tadashi looked at the ground. "Well, as I said before, does it really matter? Does it change the here and now? Does it matter if I was a rich boy or a poor boy, or if you had four brothers or none at all? No, because we are still here in this cave, eating rabbit roasted on a spit. So as I said, the truth does not matter, only the story. So make it a good one."

Tommen wasn't sure how to take his words, and he mulled them over for a while as he picked up one of the racks of ribs and started gnawing on them. Would things have turned out differently if even minor things had been different in his previous life? What if he'd had three or four brothers? What if he'd had only sisters? How would his life have been different? Would he have spent his ninth birthday in a tiny cabin in the mountains, or at Bakery na hÉireann in the bustling city of Charleston?

They'd just about finished off the last scraps of meat when Rifun returned to the cave, looking none too pleased and saying little as he unrolled a mat and adjusted it to his liking before taking a seat at the fire.

"Take care of the twits?" Tadashi asked, all business once more, and Tommen was forced to wonder which was the real Tadashi — the one who worked for Rifun, or the one who'd left behind a wife and daughter?

"For a short time," Rifun said wistfully. "But it seems as though we may be on a slightly longer stakeout than originally planned."

"What do you mean?" Tommen dared ask.

Rifun turned on him, any mask of friendliness or amiability gone. "It means that dear Walter did discover some of the clues we left for him to find."

"If you left them for him to find, isn't that a good thing for you?"

"Yes, but he also managed to figure out a lot more, and now he's on a full frontal assault. So I suggest you get comfortable, because you won't be seeing the outside of this cave for some time."

With that, he stormed out. Tommen glanced at Tadashi who shrugged. "There's no night and day in here, so sleep when you can, and Band through the rest of it if you want."

Tommen let out a breath before grabbing a mat, hoping it wasn't already claimed, then uncomfortably settling in on the hard ground. He tossed and turned for a while, then figured he must have slept some because he found himself running after two men long since dead as they tracked small game through autumn leaves, crunchy with fresh frost.

Chapter Twenty-Two
Wind

Walter figured he should have felt proud and determined when Micah and Micaiah reported a pretty severe political shake-up as they spread and propagated rumors of a False Hand and a False Zero Hour, of Calis Cutthroat, a.k.a Cassius, or Rifun Ndolo being alive, of them manipulating the system to bring about another Dispersal after which they would crown themselves Kings of Time. The last part was purely speculation, but it made for a good story, enough to make the candidates and eligible voters nervous. Supposedly there were even reports of sightings of Cassius and Rifun, or one of the goons who worked for them, but nothing could be confirmed. For once, mass hysteria worked in their favor.

Lily, who had been reluctant to take part and have her money spoken for, was suddenly making a killing, ten times her normal profits, as a nervous market brought buyers afraid that the supply of Time Capsules would dry up if there was another Dispersal. She and other Harvesters and Merchants capitalized on this somewhat, propagating that message by restricting Time sales and hoarding their stores, driving prices sky high.

But Walter did not feel proud, and his determination was waning. Christmas was fast-approaching, and still there had been no word of Tommen, nor had Rifun contacted him. They both knew the terms, so Walter could only conclude Rifun was trying to break him, demoralize him, make him fear for Tommen so much that he would willingly hand over Lily in order to get him back. Problem was, his strategy was working. If not for his oath as a police officer to protect Lily, if it was just a gamble between him, Rifun, Tommen, and Lily,

Walter honestly believed he would have pushed Lily over the cliff himself if Rifun had told him to in order to save Tommen.

It was only made worse when Steggmann effectively suspended operations regarding the kidnapping and probable ensuing negotiations, and began assigning other tasks. Normal tasks. Noisy neighbors, domestic disputes, a mysterious trailer fire. They were things that needed to be dealt with. Steggmann assured Walter than they would not hesitate to jump in if word of Tommen's whereabouts came down, but until then, the public still needed them.

Walter tried to keep a good face and high spirits, tried to get into the Christmas spirit as little advent calendars counted down the days with little gingerbread houses or snowmen or santas or angels. He tried to keep to a normal routine at home, when he was home, but the house just felt empty. He wasn't getting after Tommen to clean his room or turn down his music or do his homework. Instead, he found himself sitting in his recliner, TV dinner in hand, and not quite sure what to do with it. He wasn't really hungry, but he knew he should eat something. They say that stress makes a man gain weight, but Walter found himself finally losing that last ten pounds just for the fact that he rarely ate. He basically existed on coffee, a pastry in the morning, and a tuna sandwich at night. He didn't even stress eat from the cookies and donuts in the break room.

"So, you taking any time off for Christmas?" Standish wondered. It was less than a week before Christmas, the Friday that all the schools let out for vacation. Walter had reported Tommen as being on an extended absence and so had collected his homework, desperately hoping he could satisfactorily thump it down in front of him and tell him to work on it.

"No," Walter told him, taking a drink of coffee and leaning back in his chair in his cubicle. "As of now, I have no reason to."

"How long are you going to keep on like this, man? It's not good for you."

"We know the trade terms, but Rifun still hasn't contacted us."

"He's trying to break you, trying to discourage you. Best way to kick him in his arrogant balls is to keep fighting, keep going, and not give up, no matter how long it takes."

Walter supposed that the best encouragement he had was that it was unlikely Rifun would keep Tommen longer than the elections, so, theoretically, he only had to keep going until January 14th. At the same time, that was still a month away, which was forever when speaking in terms of captivity. His biggest fear was that Rifun would keep him through the elections. And what would happen if they didn't go his way?

"I guess. When are you taking off?"

"I'm taking the 28th through the 30th off, then the second week of January. Kim and I are going to Hawaii for five days."

"Sounds nice."

"It is much-needed and, I think, well-deserved. Five days as far away from here as I can possibly be, at least in the United States."

Walter found it mildly amusing that for as much power as he had, the ability to access the hub of Time and travel to any of thousands of different worlds, he didn't do more traveling. He could go places where literally no human had gone before, and his greatest claim to fame was a few national parks, and even that had been some years, since Tommen was young.

"I'm sure I'll see all kinds of pictures," Walter told him.

Standish grinned. "Nope. Not this time. We're keeping this one a secret, all to ourselves. No pictures, no posts, no nothing."

"Going unplugged, are we?"

"No, we'll still have our phones in case, you know...in case. But this is our vacation and no one else's."

Walter frowned. "Is everything all right? Between you and her?"

"Huh? Oh, yeah. We just don't want to be social media monsters. Any pictures we take are going to be on her old Polaroid from, like, 1970. Still works, man, I'm serious."

"I don't doubt it."

Walter was happy for him, really. But it was just hard to see everyone else having such a good time, when his joy had been taken from him, virtually at gunpoint. Everyone else was due for mini-vacations between holidays in order to keep their sanity intact, or else longer vacations before or afterwards. Stacy was taking her kids to Tennessee for a couple days between Christmas and New Year's. Jordan was just coming off a short vacation from his hunting cabin in Michigan. Pete was probably the luckiest son of a bitch out of all of them since his wife was due Christmas Eve, their first, so naturally he would get Christmas Eve, Christmas Day, and probably the day after off. Walter was due some vacation time as well, but he had no idea what he would do with it. All he could think about was getting Tommen back.

He drove to the bakery after he got off shift, trying to feel festive amid the lights and the music, the electric waving snowmen and santas, the snow falling gently down like something out of a romance movie, the bell ringers standing out in the cold and dark next to their little red buckets. But it all felt terribly empty, hollow, fake, like a puppet show, and not a very good one at that.

"Don't you know it's Christmas outside?" Micaiah asked as he walked in the door and stomped off his snowy boots.

"Yeah?" Walter said.

"So why do you look like you just walked through a war zone?"

"Has there been word?"

Micaiah sighed. "Nothing. And our campaign is losing its effectiveness. Mass hysteria only works for so long until nothing comes from it. Time and Hand elections are not like American elections. The hysteria doesn't stay long before the black market, business-minded folk come out of the woodwork. They take advantage of the situation, bring some illegal order to the chaos, make a killing, and then disappear once the threat is over."

Walter let out a breath. "Is there any news to share?"

"Well, there may be something of interest." But he seemed loathe to share it as he walked out from behind the counter. "One of

Rifun's goons, the girl all in pink with the horns? She's a Borelian."

"Shit. I was afraid of that."

"That's what I said, too."

"Probably how Rifun was able to just walk out without much of a fight."

"Yeah." Walter sighed. "So if it does come back to a fight, which it will if we want to keep both Tommen and Lily alive, we have to make sure to cover as much skin as possible."

"And take her out first, if possible. The good news is that she's only a pink one, and not a green one. Maybe I'm being cynical, but I would rather take death than being broken."

"I won't blame you for that one, but I have heard of some Borelians being able to change. And if Rifun is as much of an evil, conniving bastard as I think he is, we ought to assume the worst. Even more, we should assume that he has a lot more minions that just what we saw."

"True." Micaiah folded his arms. "So what's the next step, boss?"

Walter sighed and rubbed his face. "The same step we've been waiting for the last, what, ten days? We just wait for Rifun to contact us."

"How do you suppose he'll do that?"

"I don't know. But if I had to hazard a guess...I still have Tommen's phone; he might call on that. So I always keep it with me."

"Oh." Micaiah nodded. Then he raised a brow and grinned. "You messed with his phone yet? Changed backgrounds, moved stuff around, any of that?"

"No. I want to leave everything as it was so I can ask him about some stuff that was found on it."

"Like, stuff that Rifun put on it? I know you said he, what, hacked it and put an app on there?"

"No, like, stuff that Tommen's been looking at online. Videos and whatnot."

"You mean...?"

"Yes."

"I see. Well, spending time in captivity without his phone to look at that stuff might help to break him of the habit."

"We can hope."

Micaiah went back behind the counter. "So, what can I get for you, Walt? I can tell you've lost weight, and in such a short amount of time, it's not good for you. Pastry? Donut? This one's on the house."

Walter was set to refuse, but he finally gave in and went with a chocolate and peanut butter brownie cookie with hot fudge drizzled over the top. He thought about going back out to his car and going home, then figured there was nothing waiting for him at home, so he chose a seat by a window.

"So, what are you doing for Christmas?" Micaiah wondered. "You know us, we've always got more food than we can handle. You're always welcome to join."

Typically, they spent Thanksgiving socializing, while Christmas tended to be a more private meal, just father and son. Walter shifted in his seat. "I don't know. Guess it depends."

"Well, if you don't show up to our house, we might just show up to yours," Micah said, appearing from the kitchen, his entire front side covered in flour. "We're still looking for Tommen, but we also have to look out for you, our Captain. And for all intents and purposes, you shouldn't be left alone this Christmas. How's that for a deal?"

There was nothing he could say to argue the point, and there was no reason to, either. Finally, he just nodded and took a bite of the cookie. "All right, fine. If I'm not at your house by noon—"

"Eleven," Micaiah told him.

Walter gave him a look. "—by eleven, come on over. I don't know what I'm going to bring."

"Just leave the cooking to us," Micah said. "It's all we ever do anyway."

Walter finished his cookie, thanked the twins, and left the building. He was glad to have friends who cared for him, even better that they were essentially his employees, and they still looked out for him. Once this was all over, he would owe them a huge debt of gratitude.

The house was dark when he got home, pulling in the garage and noting that for as clean as Tommen had gotten it, stuff had begun to accumulate once more. He would have to sort through some things and get rid of stuff once and for all. He climbed out of the car and went in the house, flicking on the kitchen light and noting the light on the dryer was flashing, signaling it was done.

Walter let out a breath. He'd long since washed all of Tommen's clothes, sorted them, gotten rid of holey socks and underwear, stained pants and old shirts, folded the rest, and put them back in his dresser as best he could remember how they had been, but if Tommen had any system of organization, it eluded Walter. He'd also washed the windows, the walls, dusted the furniture, made the bed, and vacuumed the rugs. He'd organized the desk, gotten the backpack and schoolwork off the floor, and discarded a few questionable magazines. It not only gave Walter something to do and a sense of normalcy, but he clung to it in hopes that on a day when he cleaned Tommen's room, it would be the day he returned, and Walter could rue that he'd spent a day cleaning the room when Tommen could have done it himself. But that hadn't happened yet.

Instead, it was another night of reading his newspaper—or rather, looking at the pages and turning them at regular intervals—while occasionally remembering to take a bite of his sandwich—tuna on toast with mustard, mayo, and relish. Once he bored of the paper or finished his sandwich, he took much longer than necessary to wash just a couple dishes before finally taking off his blues and retiring to the recliner to flip through TV channels. He settled on some old crime, murder mystery movie, but he couldn't say who'd been killed or who the detective was. Part of the reason was that he had a hard time focusing on the movie without somehow inserting himself into the scene. The other part of the reason was that he fell asleep.

He knew he'd fallen asleep because there was no way he could have gotten from his recliner — or the middle of winter, for that matter — to the backyard which, in the dream, was just starting to get covered in bright yellow and orange leaves. Tommen was only about nine years old, still pretty new to the house and the twenty-first century, and he was just so excited to show Walter what he'd done. Walter had been expecting a huge pile of leaves to jump into, or maybe some kind of stick structure or rock sculpture that only a child could see the beauty in.

What he had not expected was a perfect leg snare and the rabbit that was caught in it, wriggling and squealing in terror. Tommen was so proud of himself for perfecting his pa's snare and catching meat for dinner, and maybe they could use the fur for new mittens. Oh, and the entrails would be great bait for larger animals.

Walter had admitted that he was very impressed and very proud. In the end, they did eat the meat, and Walter did send the fur to be tanned and made into a hat that Tommen wore until he was eleven. But he'd also taken Tommen, and they'd had a long discussion about how things worked. He couldn't just go trapping rabbits in the backyard; there were rules to it now. Like a game. There were certain seasons for hunting, and lots of people went, each person trying to get the biggest deer, the biggest...whatever.

Tommen was never big on firearm hunting unless it was big game like mountain lions. Prey game he preferred traps and snares, especially traps he could build and set himself. And he was good at it. He was better at not getting caught by the Game Warden. About once a month, Walter came home to find fresh, unidentifiable meat in the freezer, and a five-gallon bucket in the garage, vinegar stinking to high heaven despite the lid on the bucket. Never had he found the traps, and never did he ask questions. It was one of the few things that kept Tommen linked to his boyhood, and Walter wasn't about to take it away from him.

Walter couldn't remember what was happening in the dream except that something about it was off. Slowly he came to realize it was consciousness. Something had woken him. It took another moment to realize Tommen's phone was ringing. He bolted out of the recliner, almost tripping over his own two feet, and got to the phone, sitting on the kitchen counter. He answered just before it went to voicemail.

"Tommen Forbes' phone," he answered formally.

"Oh, good, for a second I wondered if something awful had happened to you, Walter." Rifun. Walter had learned his accent well. Even managed to identify it as a Malasay accent from Madagascar. Not that it did anything for him to know that. Rifun went on. "After all, Christmas season, missing loved ones, it can make things very gloomy and depressing."

"Rifun," Walter acknowledged.

What he really wanted to say was, "You fucking bastard son of a bitch! Where the fuck have you taken my son because I am coming to get him you slimy, worthless, motherfucking worm!" But he refrained. Better to do things slightly diplomatically and not give in to emotion.

"Ah, so he does speak. But not much. Which means he is keeping a tight lid on his words, for vile they are as they race around his mind."

"What do you want, Rifun? Terms, I expect."

"You know, Walter, I have to say I am very impressed by your determination and your resourcefulness. You found every clue we set out for you to find, and even a few we thought were very well-hidden. But your detective brain sleuthed them out. More than that, you managed to do some very serious damage to our political campaign. I am both impressed and very, very annoyed."

"Where is my son?"

"Your son, you call him? I think not."

"Where is he?"

"Safe and sound, I assure you. But where he is, is not—"

"I want to talk to him."

Rifun was silent for a moment and Walter could hear him

breathing, slow and deliberate. He was just as angry as Walter, keeping just as tight a lid on his words. Finally he spoke, his tone sounding like a grudging compromise. "Proof of life you ask for, and so proof of life you shall receive."

There was some rustling, then, "Dad?!"

Walter literally sank to his knees and almost wept. "Tommen?! Oh, thank God. Are you all right?"

"Yeah, I'm fine. I mean, as good as I can be. I don't know where I am. I mean, I'm in a cave. I haven't been outside since, I don't know, a long time it feels like."

"Tommen, listen, just—"

He was cut off as there was more rustling, then Rifun came back on the phone. "There is your proof of life."

"What do you want, Rifun?" Walter asked, struggling to keep his voice calm.

"As you well know, this message is being recorded thanks to an app we had installed on Tommen's phone. So, just like the first time, I expect this message to be played to anyone and everyone you deem necessary for the operation to rescue your dear boy, which I know you are already formulating in your mind.

"Now, this is how it is going to work. Today is Friday. Monday afternoon, at three o'clock, we will be at the shipping docks on the east side of town. One of the ships is going to be conveniently late to pick up its load, but provide us ample time to negotiate." *And more cargo for you to hide behind.* "We already have the journal. Now we just need Lily Guile. Bring her to Warehouse 8 at exactly three p.m. to trade for your precious son. If you are not there by three-oh-five, your son, you, and everyone involved in your little rescue operation will die. And you've already seen Cassius' handiwork."

"If your goal was Lily and the journal, why get me and Tommen involved like you have?"

Rifun chuckled. "Oh, dear Walter, you already know the answer to that question. And one more thing. I expect that Tommen might have a few questions for you once you are reunited. I won't tell you them now, of course, I'll leave that for a father-son discussion. Perhaps Monday night, after all this is over, when you two have dinner together. That is your plan, isn't it, Walter? To have dinner with your son Monday night?"

"That's one plan, yes," Walter answered grudgingly, trying not to let Rifun's words get to him. He was trying to confuse Walter, throw him off by painting a picture of just him and Tommen and make him long for that more than he wanted to protect Lily.

"Excellent. So I will leave the reservations where they stand. Dinner for two, seven o'clock, at a lovely little Italian restaurant. You know the one. Already paid, too, with dessert and gratuity."

"I expect it will be very nice."

He could hear the satisfaction in Rifun's voice. "Wonderful. Then we have come to an understanding. Half the battle is already over, Walter. Now you just need to deliver the goods. Monday at three, Warehouse 8. Oh, and one last little detail I forgot to mention. You are not to mention or play this message for anyone or start rallying your team until Sunday. And believe me, Walter, if you do...we'll know. And the same consequences will ensue as if you are late. Enjoy your weekend."

He hung up, but Walter did not even move the phone from his ear for a full minute. His mind was reeling from the call. On the one hand, he wanted to call the twins and Steggmann immediately and tell them to bring in the National Guard. On the other hand, he had little doubt that Rifun would make good on his threats. It didn't matter how he would know if Walter even mentioned the call, but right now they had to play by his rules. And if Rifun said he would kill Tommen if Walter even mentioned the call, best to take the threat at face value.

Eventually, Walter stood, put Tommen's phone on its charger, and returned to the living room. The first movie had ended and the one that followed looked like it was almost over, too. Mechanically, Walter found the remote and turned off the TV. His feet took him to his bedroom where he set the alarm clock, got under the blankets, and stared at the shadows on the ceiling for well over an hour. He didn't remember what he was thinking except that Tommen was alive and well, even if he was sitting in a cave and hadn't seen the sun in two weeks. Finally, Walter took a breath, fought his blankets to roll over, and eventually cried himself to sleep.

Saturday was a day of torture for Walter, starting from the moment he got up, and he honestly thought he might have understood the awful burden of Christ in the Garden of Gethsemane. Except rather than going to his death—which was still a very real possibility when dealing with Rifun and Cassius—he bore a great secret. He knew his son was alive, knew the terms of his release. He knew where and when to meet Rifun. But as part of the terms, he was not allowed to tell.

Compounding that secret was the one he kept every day from his fellow officers, the one where he was a Captain Timekeeper, where Rifun was a Warden, and Cassius was not only a Triage Harvester, but an impostor Zero Hour Hand, the final authority of the governing body of an industry so vast and so universal, it thought no more of Earth's significance than a human might think of a spider. Useful in its own right, but no terrible, rippling effects if it suddenly got squished under a boot or swatted with a newspaper. Walter guarded that secret daily and had perhaps become accustomed to the things that went with it: having to fudge a report in order to account for the use of Bands, offering bogus theories like hacked security cameras when really a criminal was just moving too fast for the camera to record much more than a brief, fuzzy image. But now he was feeling the weight of that secret burden, now when it was his own son caught in the middle, his life and Tommen's life on the line. When he knew exactly why Rifun wanted to kill Lily, but the rest of the men just thought him an insane maniac, which he was anyway.

People around town thought he was just being lenient and in a little more Christmas-y, festive mood as he let things slip by that he normally wouldn't, or ease up on a ticket or a potential arrest when normally he was ready to lay down the law and take no BS during an already busy season. So, overall, he won some PR points, which he tried to raise as a tiny victory flag, for the precinct if not himself.

He avoided the bakery at all costs, knowing that just a look from either Micah or Micaiah and he would spill everything to them. Better just to sit tight, bury himself in his work, and ride out his shift. Then he could go home, sit in his recliner, and maybe Slow Band his way into Sunday. Once the clock struck midnight, he could call the twins and set them on the hunt. And when he rolled into work, he would hit the ground running so that way the whole day could be spent planning how to ultimately take down Rifun while saving both Tommen and Lily and everyone else.

Unfortunately, his plan didn't quite work out the way he'd hoped. He fell asleep before he could Band and woke up at the time he was supposed to be punching in. Fast Banding got him out the door quickly and saw him at least to the bridge—not before he had to turn around because he forgot Tommen's phone with the message on it—but after that he just had to release the Band and go with the congested flow of traffic, walking in the door half an hour late.

"Morning, Walt," Steggmann greeted in the break room. "I was beginning to think something had happened to you." His expression was a deeper, searching gaze, like he was trying to feel Walter out for any suicidal tendencies or other coping mechanisms—drinking and whatnot.

"I have something. We need to talk," Walter blurted. No time for niceties and pleasantries. It was Sunday. Time to get down to business.

Thankfully, Steggmann seemed to understand his words. He nodded once as he finished filling his coffee mug. "Who should be there?"

"Anyone deemed necessary to the operation."

Steggmann grunted. "Bring it to my office in five minutes. We'll go from there."

Walter nodded and left the room, grabbing a donut on his way out. He went to his cubicle, nearly bulldozing Standish in the process, but not stopping as he ripped off his jacket and logged in to his computer.

"Whoa, big fella, you look like a man on a mission," Standish said, intending it as a joke, though his smile faded when he met Walter's gaze. "You got something?"

"Steggmann's office. Five minutes."

"Roger that, boss."

It was a long five minutes as Walter skimmed through his email, checking the clock every ten seconds, Banding his way through thirty seconds at a time, heel stomping anxiously. That was the thing about Time. He could Band it; he could use it. But Time was still Time. No one actually controlled it.

When the clock finally ticked five minutes, he all but ran to Steggmann's office, and even then, the man wasn't ready yet. First he had to talk to Cynthia, then he had to make a phone call. By the time Walter and Standish actually got into his office and sat down, fifteen minutes had passed.

"Tell me what happened, Walter," Steggmann said calmly.

"Rifun called me Friday night, sir, on Tommen's phone so the message would be recorded." He continued before Steggmann could protest. "Part of his terms was that I would not mention or play the message until today or else he would kill my boy. I have no reason to doubt his word."

Steggmann huffed but nodded. "Agreed. At this time, we ought to take all threats at face value. Do you have the phone with the message?"

It took another five minutes for Walter to figure out where the recording app was and how to use it before setting the phone against Steggmann's nameplate for the recording to play.

Standish turned his head and stared at some spot on the wall while the recording played. He blinked and made facial expressions at certain points, mouthed a few words, took a quiet drink of coffee in consideration, but he never said anything out loud.

Steggmann was harder to read, leaning back in his chair, arms folded, expression as still and as cold as a statue, listening intently and hanging on every word, learning, cataloging, cross-referencing, profiling, thinking. When the message ended, he still did not move for a long time, and Walter could see the wheels turning as his dark eyes glittered with the hope of action and, more importantly, revenge. Hurt one, hurt them all. Taking Walter's son was like taking Steggmann's daughter, or Tammy's son, or the child of any officer there. It demanded retribution.

Standish broke the silence first. "What political campaign is he talking about?"

"I don't know, but I would be terrified to see him in any office," Walter said, only half-lying.

"If he wants to meet at a warehouse because a ship is going to be late, that means there is going to be a lot of freight sitting around. A lot of places to hide and potentially get away."

"I had the same thought, sir."

Steggmann was silent for a moment more. Then he spoke. "We're going to need a few more people."

It took only twenty minutes to assemble a crew of thirty in the large meeting room where Tommen's phone was hooked up to the sound system and the message played for all ears. Most of the team was already in an action-ready mood, but as the message played and ended, every expression turned dead-on determined.

At the end, Steggmann stood and went to the front of the room, turning on the projector as he did so. He was silent for a long moment as he looked over everyone in the room. And they looked at him. An exchange of respect and the silent request for direction, bloodhounds waiting for the word from the hunter. Finally he took a breath and spoke, every word deliberate. "We are not going to make the same mistake we did at the airport. Forget the ship that's supposed to be late. We're shutting down the docks completely; all the warehouses are to be secured, and all personnel are to be evacuated by two o'clock or risk arrest on suspicion of conspiracy. I know he did not specifically request you, Walter, but I have a gut feeling you are the one he wants to deal with. You will lead a full team to meet with Rifun and there will be a back-up team at your command."

He turned to the map on the projector. "This is Warehouse 8. I want snipers here, here, and here. We must assume that he is heavily armed and dangerous, on top of having hostages. Always remember, the hostages are the number one priority, and Lily Guile is as much a hostage as Tommen. That said, I want two officers posted at her condo complex overnight, ready to escort her here by ten a.m. We will leave here no later than one o'clock to shut down the docks whether you are ready or not."

It felt like forever before they were dismissed. Problem was, everything was taking place tomorrow. Not today. Which meant that when Walter returned to his cubicle, his grand feeling of production, like he'd finally accomplished something, was washed away at the first call for a noise complaint. One nosy neighbor bitching about her neighbor a quarter mile up the road doing some target practice.

That call took a lot longer than Walter thought it should have, but the way he saw it, every call took him a little closer to the time he could finally get his boy back. So while the target shooting neighbor was thrilled that Walter wasn't going to fine him—because he wasn't doing anything wrong anyway—the nosy neighbor was irate and went into a screaming rage. She was harmless except for her tongue, but Walter still did his best to calm her down before leaving.

As usual, his daily endeavors took him past the bakery more than once. On his fourth pass, he finally stopped in.

"Walt! Damn it, you had me worried yesterday," Micaiah said.

"Get Micah," Walter ordered.

Micah came in an instant, and Walter Banded. "Rifun contacted me. Shipping docks, Warehouse 8, tomorrow at three o'clock." He brought out Tommen's phone and played the message again. The exchange had only been brief, but Walter still felt a surge of relief and joy when he heard Tommen's voice. Then the call ended.

"So that's why you weren't here yesterday," Micah said.

"I knew I'd spill my guts, and I didn't want to risk it," Walter admitted.

"Fair enough," Micaiah agreed. "So, what do you want us to do?"

"Rifun wants a party. Well, we'll give him a party. I have no reason to expect that this will go smoothly. Those warehouses are stuffed with shipping containers and smaller freight, which means plenty of places to hide. Any humans or humanoids you can get to help, do so, with the understanding that they will have to stay out of sight until all hell breaks loose. Any non-humanoids, keep tucked away in dark corners and covering potential exits. Rifun will blow by the officers easily enough; let's give him a run for his money."

"We'll see what we can do," Micah said uncertainly. "Support comes and goes quickly. It's all about the money and the power."

"What about the ones you promised to vote for if they'd help you catch Cassius?"

"In the hysteria, some dropped out of the race completely, not wanting to be implicated with him. Others have upped their prices where we can't pay. And because Cassius still has the power of the Zero Hour, he still wields considerable influence. Some backed out with no explanation."

"We'll see who we have left," Micaiah promised him. "Though it might be less Cavalry and more Pony Express."

"Well, we're going to need all the help we can get."

"Roger that, Captain, we won't let you down."

It was good to know they had his back, but with everything else he knew, it was small comfort given that even if everything did go more or less according to plan, it could all still go horribly, horribly wrong. Walter chewed on that as much as his pastry as he returned to the precinct. The undercurrent of urgency as Steggmann worked to hash out a plan and get all his ducks in a row was a comfort to Walter, even if he himself was stuck having to deal with a car hitting a deer, a girl getting bit by a neighbor's dog, and a number of domestic disturbances.

By the time Walter punched out and headed home, he found that he had, at some point in the day, come back to life. He had hope again. His son was alive, and now he knew the day and time when they would be reunited. And he had all the fury of the Charleston Police Department, coupled secretly with the power of a dozen Time Agents who were just as powerful as Rifun and Cassius, all coming to bear against those who would murder innocent women, rob a museum, kidnap innocent civilians, and take for ransom the son of a police officer of two worlds. Blood running hot and seeing red, Walter knew then that this could end no other way. Too much blood had been spilled already for blood to not end this. Retribution was coming.

And yet, as he prepared for bed, changed out of his blues, set his alarm, too excited to sleep but needing it anyway, the adrenaline slowly died down, and the familiar, nagging doubts began tugging at him again. Regardless if Cassius had made himself out to be too dangerous to touch, there would always be those rogue cowboys hoping to catch themselves a big fish—win fame, fortune, and maybe the seat or favor of a Hand. And if Cassius had been elected Zero Hour in 1838, and was already deemed terribly dangerous, how many of those cowboys had died trying to reel in that big fish? All the firepower of the Earth-side policemen and all the Time prowess of the Time-side Time Agents, all hitting them at once...that was like a small bomb going off, really, if anyone cared to calculate the physics involved. But even then, what if it still wasn't enough?

Chapter Twenty-Three
Freedom Fighter

Tommen sat against the cave wall, wide awake. He stank. He hadn't had a shower since he was taken. He wasn't exactly out doing laps, but he sweated when the fire got really warm, and it dried to him. His clothes were stained. He smelled quite a bit like smoke, too. At the very least, he was allowed into an adjoining cave to relieve himself, so he didn't stink like shit and piss, too. And his beard had grown, or what he took to be a beard. He didn't have a mirror, but he knew he didn't really have his pa's full, luscious beard that his ma loved to stroke and gush over, and he was capable only of a thin beard on his jawline and a small mustache.

In a way, he was almost terribly ashamed to go before Walter looking and feeling so ragged. He at least wanted some water to wash his face, maybe a razor, or a knife would do. As it was, he barely got enough water each day to slake his thirst. His stomach was usually on empty, and he counted himself lucky to eat once a day.

That was assuming he had correctly judged day and night. He had only vague inclinations of the passage of time. Tadashi going out to hunt. Isthim bringing small supplies like more blankets or bottles of water. He did not see Donojok at all, and Rifun and Cassius were infrequent visitors. He hadn't even seen them since Rifun had finally contacted Walter. If that had been Friday, then it was reasonable to assume that it was at least Saturday, if not Sunday.

At the very least, the call had given him hope of seeing daylight and being reunited with his dad. He had no reason to believe that it would be a simple trade of persons and everyone went their separate ways, but Tommen was holding onto the hope of just seeing Walter one more time. He tried not to be pessimistic about it, instead clinging to the image Rifun had conjured up about going to dinner Monday night, even though he also knew that Rifun had conjured that picture just to get in Walter's head and mess with him, give him a carrot on a string and lead him right over a cliff — that is, let Lily go with no care for the consequences as long as he got Tommen back.

But Walter was smarter than that. He would think of something. Rifun had all but told him to call in the Cavalry, and that he would do. Rifun and Cassius might have been powerful, but unless they were indestructible, they couldn't hope to withstand an assault on all fronts. And if Walter was able to get some Time-side help, then they might be evenly matched against Rifun and Cassius and actually have a fighting chance.

"What day is it?" Tommen found himself asking.

Tadashi sat at the fire, shaving a stick. "Sunday."

Tadashi hadn't said much since their little heart-to-heart chat, and Tommen was left with only his imagination to fill in the gaps. He'd hoped to win him over, maybe get some extra food, extra water, a trip outside just so he could see daylight, anything at all. But the young man remained as impassive as ever, coming to life only when Rifun or Cassius appeared, acting all big and bad and badass-ish, then lapsing into silence upon their departure.

Tommen had nothing but respect for prisoners of war and those who spent even a moment in tortured captivity, being beaten and waterboarded and punished within an inch of their lives, but captivity that was boring as hell was its own kind of torture, wasn't it? It was like being stranded on a deserted island with only a coconut named Charlie for company. Eventually, he would go completely insane. Tommen wondered how long it would take for that to happen. Not too long on a truly deserted island with no hope of rescue, but sitting in a cave with occasional companionship might stave off the insanity for a little while. Unless, of course, the occasional company was also insane, in which case the onset of his insanity would only be expedited. Wouldn't it?

Such were Tommen's musings as he sat alone in the cave. He would have taken Righting's class over this. He would have taken double shifts at the bakery for a week over this. Hell, he would have taken a fistfight with Tyler Freeman over this.

"You know, I was supposed to go skiing tomorrow," Tommen said. "Supposed to be me, Eric, and Varad, down at Snowshoe. Eric is going off to college soon, and Varad is moving back to India with his family, so this was supposed to be our last big hurrah. Originally, the plan was to go up skiing, have a good time, and I was going to score a little booze and a little weed so we could all do it together one last time. Well, then you all had to go and kidnap them and fuck up their minds. Well, fine, so we don't do the booze and the weed, whatever. But now, I am going to miss the skiing altogether because..." He lifted his hands and slapped them on his thighs. "I'm stuck here in a dark fucking cave."

"Everything goes like it's supposed to, you can go skiing after Christmas," Tadashi told him matter-of-factly.

Tommen had nothing to say to that because it was probably true. But still, things would be different between him and his friends. They'd been exposed to Time. They knew things now, things that he knew. And they would know that he'd been holding out on them, that he led a completely different life than just the simple one he presented to the rest of the world.

He rubbed his thighs absently, then pulled one knee up to his chest so he could check his lower leg...again. It wasn't like he didn't look at his wound every hour at least. It was slow to heal because, in his boredom, he'd spent more than ample time picking away at the scabs and flesh, making the burn into a nice deep hole which was still only partially healed, so he now would have a cratered scar about the size of his fist on the side of his calf. Wasn't infected, didn't hurt, so he counted it a small victory. And it would make a really cool story to tell around school, proof of his weeks in tortured captivity.

"So if Donojok is guarding the entrance, why are you here?"

Tommen wondered.

"Donojok is guarding the entrance to the tunnels," Tadashi told him. "There's a whole network of them down here. I'm here to make sure you don't go wandering off."

"Another exit nearby?"

"You're more likely to get yourself lost and die before you find another exit."

As much as Tommen figured there was some truth to that, he also had a few pearls of wisdom from Teo. Tommen had been terrified of losing his older brother, and he remembered asking him one night what happened if a mine collapsed and he was trapped. Teo had just given him a lopsided smile, got down on one knee, looked him in the eye, and said, "The mines may be long and winding and there may be many branches, but smart miners always have a second way out. It may be distant and it may be confusing, but there are always ways to find your way out."

It brought Tommen comfort to hear his brother say that, even more when hardly two months later, that very thing happened. A mine collapsed and would have trapped Teo in there to die, if not for an emergency exit they'd built first-thing before even beginning to go after the ore.

At the same time, that logic only applied to mines. Naturally-occurring caves and tunnels formed most often by underground rivers and the movements of the earth could be long and winding for miles and miles with no convenient second exit, which meant that Tommen could get lost and die before finding a back door to this place. And, really, they were leaving tomorrow, so there was no point in trying to escape now. If he'd wanted to escape, his best bet would have been upon his arrival, and even then he was still cautious about putting weight on his leg. Probably, when he was finally freed and on his way home, Walter would want to have him checked out at the hospital. Assuming Rifun was speaking the truth about dinner and all that, Tommen hoped that a check-up could wait until after said dinner.

He looked up at the sound of footsteps and stone grating on

stone. Cassius entered first, dropping a load of wood on the pile in the corner. Isthim followed, some large bird in hand. Donojok came last, stopping at the entrance to the cave where he, somehow, someway as Tommen suspected only his race could, seemed to dismantle himself stone by stone, and rebuild in the shape of the entrance, effectively blocking them in completely.

Tommen had learned a little bit about his non-human captors as well. Donojok was a Grunjor from Sector Three, System One, Planet Ninety-two, Region Eleven, District Three, a place that was very much engaged in Time. He described himself as being from a mine called Rejar, and Tommen could only assume that a "mine" on his world was like some kind of city. From what he gathered, the Grunjor were great miners and crafters, able to go far deeper into their planet, proportionally, than any other species that did man-venturing expedition mining. They were the sole exporters of a number of metals and stones to several worlds in their system as well as in the Wheel.

And while Tommen did not understand the details, the way he understood it, the Grunjor did not reproduce. Rather, they built more of their own kind. Donojok explained the process, many of the words going untranslated or mistranslated, and the most Tommen could gather was that they were built from a particular kind of rock found on their world, one that was illegal to take from the planet or handle in any way inconsistent with building more Grunjor. There was a special way in which the rocks were put together that, when combined or infused with some kind of plasma or energy or something, brought the formation to life as a fully-functional Grunjor who only had to be named and set to a task.

The Grunjor did not sleep per se, but "melded" with the world around them, like spreading out conscious feelers into the soil and rock around them, retracting those feelers when their rock form body was called upon for something. Tommen looked around the cave and wondered if Donojok was actually able to "see" out of the rock of the cave to watch over them silently, or if it was more of a metaphysical experience.

He did not eat with them either, as the bird finished roasting and Isthim went to work carving it up and setting it on the communal plate.

She probably scared Tommen the most, once he learned the full extent of just her physical powers, never mind that she was an Intervention Harvester. She was a Borelian, the preferred species to recruit to be a Grandfather in the Wheel because they were all incredibly deadly in their own right.

The Borelians were extremely technologically advanced and had mastered space travel within their own solar system and several neighboring systems, but they originated from Sector Nine, System Three, Planet One, Isthim being from Region Five, District One. According to Isthim, a few freelancing vessels—namely those who were considered poor and insignificant—were every bit the kind and curious innocent explorers most humans envisioned themselves as in space travel, to go where no man has gone before. But actually, the Borelians as a whole were extremely dictatorial, clawing their way through advancements in space travel for the purpose of conquering others. Their involvement in Time was unclear, as Isthim described it as being a secret known only to the elite commanders, that they may prolong their reigns, while the average person had no knowledge of it.

It was just as well, given that their talent for dealing death wasn't something Tommen was keen on prolonging any more than necessary. The different colors of Borelians denoted different types of toxins and effects. Pink Borelians like Isthim had a side effect of compliance, while the main weapon generally went straight to death. No muss, no fuss, just dead. Blue Borelians did something to the respiratory system. Isthim explained that a blue Borelian could make him drown without ever needing water, or suffocate him with no allergen to agitate his system. Yellow Borelians affected the circulatory system, able to stop a heart instantly, or boil the blood until the victim burned alive from the inside out. And there were others from a spectrum of colors greater than the human eye could perceive, so she ended up naming colors which Tommen could not even comprehend, and they had abilities and poisons and side effects Tommen would never have even imagined. The ability to change brain patterns so different senses got all switched around, making a person smell a sound or hear a taste. When Tommen tried to describe the phenomenon as synesthesia, Isthim simply shook her head and said this change was far more literal. When affected like this, a person would open their eyes and be able to smell, open their mouth to see, effectively breathe through their ears, and so on.

But it was the green Borelians which the Grandfathers favored, and that was when Tommen finally learned the meaning of having his clock broken.

It was as simple as breaking his internal clock. Not his biological clock, although that was also certainly possible, but his simple sense of temporal orientation, the very ability to perceive the passage of time. In the cave, it was difficult to tell night and day, but if he wanted to, he could count seconds and minutes and hours with varying consistency. But to have his clock broken, to remove all sense of time, two seconds and two years would pass as the same amount of time in his mind. There would be only a vague sense of before and after, day and night, but in the moment, everything simply was. Sunrise and sunset were the same, and one day was the same as any other with nothing to separate one from another. A human with his clock broken would set the microwave for thirty seconds, walk away, and not come back for hours because time had simply left him. He wouldn't be able to say what day it was because one day was the same as the next. He couldn't say what he did yesterday because that word had virtually no meaning, and he had no way of reconciling events into a logical order to even hazard a guess. It was like the ultimate case of short-term memory loss, where the memories flitted away as soon as they were created.

Tommen suddenly understood why Micah and Micaiah had been hesitant to go snooping around in the Wheel and the Archives. It wasn't difficult to imagine that simply dying was preferable to having no concept of time, something even base creatures had.

It was not a comforting thing to think on as he finally drifted off to sleep, and Tommen's dreams were filled with nightmares as his mind went through each of the deadly things different Borelians could do. He felt Isthim's proximity compliance like chains holding him in place while a blue Borelian squeezed the air from his lungs and a yellow one played with his circulatory system, making his blood first flow one way and then the other, like switching the directions of a model train track. He squirmed and tried to fight and get away as a white Borelian approached him, this one capable of unspeakable crimes against his private parts, most notably his balls and his brain which controlled everything. And the white Borelian did toy with him, making him do foolish and embarrassing things to the amusement of a green Borelian who simply watched for a while, then approached. Slowly. And whether it was fear of the green Borelian or the amusement of the blue one, but Tommen found that he couldn't catch his breath. Terror spread through his limbs while the white Borelian worked against the terror, implanting obscene and contradictory pleasures deep in his brain, making him want to fuck something as much as he wanted to run away screaming. Holy hells, but he had a great bit of respect for the Borelians now, and he had little interest in breaking any Time Laws and being sent to the Grandfathers for punishment.

The green Borelian drew closer, reaching a polydactyled hand toward him, always slowly, building the suspense until Tommen thought he might burst into tears at any moment and beg to just die. He didn't want his clock to be broken; just kill him now, please. Then he did start to cry and sob and beg. Let it be swift and merciful, a touch from Isthim, and let him drift peacefully into that long and lonely sleep.

When the green Borelian touched him, Tommen came fully awake though his body was utterly paralyzed with fear. It took him a minute or two to get his muscles to release enough that he could get up and make his way to the adjoining cave. His twisted dream had left him with a confusing sense of needing to piss and needing to fuck. He took a calming breath and closed his eyes. He tried to envision Emily, but she no longer held sway over him. He brought to mind the *Sports Illustrated* swimsuit models. That helped some. His mind moved to his Internet musings.

But the white Borelian from his dreams had chased away all the fantasy. Tommen leaned his head against the cave wall. He felt like an idiot, his sense of pleasure being toyed with. At least with a white Borelian, he had something to blame. This...he had no one to blame but himself. His pa would have been so ashamed to see what had become of him. At the same time, he was straining something awful and had to do something. When he was done, he took a piss and zipped up his pants. When he turned, he startled as he saw Cassius standing in the cave entrance.

"Should have asked Tadashi," he said. "He would have sucked it for you if you needed it."

Tommen wasn't sure what to say to that, so he elected to stay silent and returned to his mat. Tadashi and Isthim were still asleep, and Donojok was doing whatever it was he did for sleeping, melding with the earth or whatever. But Tommen was wide awake now, adrenaline still pumping through him, blood rushing through his ears, fear doing just as much to keep him from falling back asleep. After a short time, Cassius also returned. He tossed a few sticks onto the fire, poked around a bit, and returned to his mat. But he, too, remained awake.

"How do you know my dad?" Tommen asked.

Cassius gave him a sideways glance and grinned. "I was a guard at the prison where he was held."

"Prison?"

An old business acquaintance, an old archrival for a girl, maybe even some story of master and slave from way back, those Tommen might have expected. But Walter being in prison and Cassius being his guard? That was something completely out of left field. And yet, didn't the best arsonists make the best firefighters?

And the best criminals made the best cops? In theory, of course.

"Beaumaris Gaol.   In Wales, no less.   You should ask him about it someday."

That might have been all Tommen was going to get from him about Walter, but there was more he wanted to know. He shifted on his mat and sat up. Cassius was sitting against the cave wall, head back, eyes closed, but Tommen knew he was awake and listening. "How did you kill those women?"

Cassius opened his eyes and looked at Tommen with such eyes that he was honestly afraid he might suddenly drop dead. He grinned fiendishly, and the sight of it made Tommen want to throw up.

"Slowly," he answered, making sure to pronounce each syllable, each letter. He moved toward Tommen. Tommen backed away until he hit a wall. "Rifun kept them in a Band so they could not fight back, but he advanced them so they could see my face and always know it was I who killed them. I cut their faces first." Rifun drew a finger down Tommen's face, slowly, softly, like a lover's caress. "Line by line. Up and down first. With a scalpel so sharp, it cuts the skin and makes you bleed long before the pain hits, like a paper cut." He brought his other hand up and Tommen closed his eyes, but Cassius only lightly touched his eyelids. "Then I cut the eyelids, but I leave the eyes. Eyes are so beautiful, and I do not want to mess them up." He traced a finger across Tommen's forehead. "Then I do the lines left to right. And for each line, I follow the contour of the face, an artist working on a master portrait, wanting to capture all the little curves and grooves." He traced Tommen's cheeks and chin.

Then he took Tommen's hands in his own. "Then I pierce their hands, straight through the palm." He tenderly pushed the end of his thumb into Tommen's palm. "First, I use a knife to make the hole. Then I push bigger things through, a little bigger each time. A pen. A sharpened stick. When I get to the metal rod, I put it through both holes, and then I twist the rod around and around, breaking the bones and making the hole very big."

Cassius put one finger against Tommen's throat and another in the nape of his neck, and Tommen thought he might have wet himself a little. Cassius raised his brows and his expression became very serious, but in a way that reminded Tommen of a scolding a parent might give to a young child. "Then, I go for the throat. I make a small incision here—" He gently indicated his finger in Tommen's nape. "—and I cut up to here. I fold the skin back and then I take the sharp scalpel I used to cut their faces, and I simply cut out their windpipe." He grinned again. "Then, once Rifun has managed to pinpoint Band to stop the bleeding, he releases the Band for just a single moment. And I see the reaction on their faces as their lives have just been cut short. They do not feel the pain in their faces yet, but they feel the rush of wind through their hands. They try to gasp or scream, but they can take no air. They look at me with such fear.

"Then Rifun Bands them again so the wounds do not immediately kill them and I may cut their throats, sever their arteries. Rifun is able to use a Band to heal over the artery. And I watch as the lungs die from lack of oxygen and blood backs up into the heart. And the fear and surprise in their eyes, I cannot explain to you the joy it brings me. And when they are dead, I masturbate to my success, and then we dump the bodies."

Tommen almost wished he felt like throwing up in order to have an excuse just to run into the next cave and get away from the madman, but as it was, he felt both light-headed from hearing such gory, intimate details, some of which were far more than he ever wanted to know, and another round of paralyzing fear just from having Cassius within arm's reach of him, never mind actually touching him. He might have even been able to handle being treated roughly—a slap in the face, a hand around the throat—but the gentle touches and motions were far more terrifying. And Cassius knew it.

Cassius grinned and returned to his spot against the wall. "That is how I killed those women. And that is how I plan to kill Lily Guile as well."

Tommen didn't really feel like throwing up, but he still got up and ran to the adjoining cave. He thought maybe a dry heave or a finger down the throat would produce something, but it didn't; he hadn't eaten enough to get more than a little stomach fluid and spittle. Still, he stayed there for a minute or two longer before returning to his mat. He had no choice. Donojok blocked the only other way out, so he either slept in the cave with a bunch of lunatics, or the piss and shit cave. In all honesty, he seriously considered the piss and shit cave the better option as he felt Cassius' laughing eyes on him the whole time he crossed the cave to his mat and settled down.

"Sleep well, Tommen Forbes," Cassius said, still grinning. "Tomorrow is going to be a day you never forget. See that you are awake to remember it well."

Tommen wasn't sure he was going to be able to sleep. Between his terrible Borelian dream and his terrible Cassius waking nightmare, he was pretty sure he would never sleep again, or at least for the rest of the time he was going to be spending with these whackjobs. But eventually the initial terror died out and the fear deserted him, leaving nothing but an empty well of fatigue. He tried to drum up the terror again, tried to stay awake, but in the end, he did drift off peacefully into that final, murky blackness.

Well, murky blackness anyway. The finality of it was debatable as he felt like he'd hardly closed his eyes before he was being kicked awake. Tommen sat up, immediately feeling the weariness and the fatigue, followed a moment later by all manner of aches and pains.

The cave was busy with activity. Tadashi was the one who had kicked him, and now he was running around, gathering up mats, blankets, plates, utensils, all items and remnants of any occupancy. Isthim was working on putting out the fire while simultaneously offering up leftover food and drink scraps, which Tommen partook of greedily, electing to just stand in one corner and watch the hubbub. Donojok was no longer in the cave entrance, and Cassius was also missing, which was more than fine with Tommen.

Monday, the day he finally went home, when all of this would be over. He would go home tonight and get a shower. He would sleep in his own bed. He would finally be able to get out of these awful, stinking clothes. He would probably burn these clothes just so he would never have to be reminded of what happened here, to say nothing of his leg wound which suddenly didn't seem like such a heroic trophy.

He barely had time to register all of this when Rifun stormed into the cave.

"Let's move it!" he snarled. "Places to be, things to do, people to kill!"

Tommen was forced to wonder, for a Warden Timekeeper, what his obsession was. Why not simply Band the cave? When he had control over the very fabric of Time, why was he so worried about being late and keeping a timetable? Well, such was the mind of a madman, he supposed, and figured that his best course of action would be to stay silent and just go with it. Don't fight it. Let Rifun do his ranting, let Walter do his job, and hopefully everyone would come out of this alive. Except Rifun and Cassius who were the insane instigators who needed to be punished. And even then, Tommen found that he did not wish them dead. Worse, he wished for their clocks to be broken. Take them from the greatest of the Time Agents to lower than a base creature who didn't even understand the very concept of time.

Rifun left the cave, and Tadashi followed soon after, hauling a bag of stuff with him. Isthim went after him with a much smaller bag, and suddenly the cave was almost completely clean except for the ring of stones and the fire ash which they also set to cleaning up. Rifun came and left several more times before being satisfied that they were packed up and ready to go. Whatever bug was up his ass, it swept away any of the genial, smirking, sarcastic facade he still had, and he was all business. He roughly grabbed Tommen by the back of the shirt and dragged him along through the tunnels.

It was not a long trek to the outside, and Donojok waited for them at the entrance. Rifun stopped and dropped Tommen to the ground where he shielded his eyes from the sudden sunlight.

"Seal it off," Rifun ordered.

Tommen blinked and slowly let in more light through his hands until he could look around. They were in the mountains, as expected, but other than a few small farms here and there, hardly recognizable except as bare, square patches of land amidst towering trees, the valley and the mountains as far as the eye could see was largely uninhabited. Once upon a time, he might have been able to say exactly where they were, but it was unfamiliar to him now.

Then he was moving again, this time with Rifun holding his upper arm in a death grip. Tommen looked back just long enough to see Donojok reform himself into a shape near the mouth of the cave. After a moment of no movement, the ground began to shake just a little, and a tiny earthquake caused rock and debris to collapse over the entrance to the tunnels. Then, Donojok was back in his mobile form, and moving with them.

It wasn't a long trek. They stayed high in the mountain, hiking through a narrow pass which overlooked Charleston at a great distance, maybe thirty miles or more down the valley. Thankfully, the van was parked in a small nature trailhead parking lot only about half a mile away. Again, Tadashi was in the driver's seat, Cassius riding shotgun, leaving Tommen in the back with Isthim, Rifun, and Donojok. Rifun opened up his revolver and inspected it thoroughly despite the rocky, rutted, pitted roads that tossed them this way and that.

"So, this is how it's going to work," Rifun was saying, making a point of shining up each bullet before inserting it into the gun, "I'm expecting Walter to bring in every gun he's got. But for the negotiating part, it'll just be me and you, Tommen. And since I know you want this to go over smoothly, I expect you to cooperate fully. Like I told him Friday night, he asked for proof of life, and he got proof of life. He did not specify in which condition this life need be, which gives me the freedom to beat you within an inch of it, if I'm feeling like an honest, decent man. If I'm not, well, I can just kill you outright. Follow so far?"

Tommen nodded absently. He had no disillusions about Rifun being an honest, decent man.

"Good. Now, there are some things I'm going to have you say. And you're going to say them exactly as I tell you to. I'm also going to do a few things which, if you flinch, will kill you. It's in your best interest then—" And suddenly he shot at the floor of the van between Tommen's feet. Tommen jumped and fell out of his seat. "—to not flinch."

Tommen's ears were ringing. Rifun might have said more, but he was hardly paying attention now. Let the man inspect his prized revolver. Seven shots were no match for twenty cops. Except when he had the ability to fire off each round and then reload in a fraction of the time it would take a single bullet to reach him. Tommen tried not to think about that.

He closed his eyes and tried not to be carsick. Think about happy things. He was going to see his dad again finally. Walter would have a plan, one that would get everyone home safely and Rifun and Cassius locked up, whether in an Earth-side prison or turned over to the Grandfathers. He had to believe that, had to hold on to some kind of hope. He was not going to be the kooky old hermit who lived in a cave with only a rock named Rory for companionship.

"We're here," Tadashi said, bringing the van to a rather violent stop. "Cops have got this place locked down, all the warehouses, no personnel."

"Wonderful," Rifun said, grinning, as if it was the best news he'd had all day. "So it will be just us two, like an old Western showdown. What do you think of that?"

Isthim and Donojok had already gotten out of the van. Isthim was checking her 1911's, and Tadashi had come around to inspect his guns. Meanwhile, Donojok just stood there like a huge, lumbering rock formation, and Cassius turned his face toward the sun as if expecting some sort of sign of approval from some sick and demented gods who were about to open up the celestial coliseum for the meager mortals to fight to the death, and he was their champion.

"Are we set?" Rifun asked, looking at his watch.

"Ready," Isthim reported, rolling her neck as best she could with her horns the way they were.

"When you are," Tadashi replied, keeping an AR in either hand, pointed up.

"Ready," Donojok said, his tone difficult to judge if he was enthusiastic or just compliant. Tommen wondered how he'd gotten mixed up in all this.

Rifun looked at Cassius who smiled. "Always ready."

"Excellent. And so the mighty foes entered on stage to meet the great heroes of lore."

Where Tommen might have expected the typical slow motion spread-out epic entrance from every movie ever, it actually turned into all of them basically going their separate ways into the harbor area, with only Rifun and Tommen going together, and even that ended up being Rifun again grabbing the back of Tommen's shirt and dragging him mercilessly along, his leg with its half-healed wound scraping painfully in the icy gravel.

Chapter Twenty-Four
All In

For once, Lily didn't have a snide remark on her tongue the moment she walked in the door, or if she did, she was smart enough to keep her mouth shut, at least until she was deposited with Walter like he was her babysitter or some such thing. He heard a few snickers from some of his fellows, something about acting just like a bickering old couple, maybe they ought to get together. Personality clashes and occupations aside—and not speaking of the Earth-side occupations—Walter looked about in his forties, and Lily in her late twenties at most. That alone was enough of a disqualifier for him.

"I hope you've got a plan, Walt," Lily told him. "I had a lot of things on my to-do list today, and getting my throat cut by a mass-murdering madman was not one of them."

"Not on my list either," Walter told her diplomatically. "With any luck, all you'll have to do is stand around and—"

"Look good?"

"—look appropriately frightened. There will be a time where we have to make Rifun believe he is in control. If you don't act even a little scared, he might think something's up and run away again."

"I've never been any good at hide-and-seek."

"Yeah, well, I don't feel like continuing this game any further. This ends today."

He started to walk away, but Lily spoke again. "Tell me something, Walter. If you were trading me for anyone else, would you really be so determined that this ends today? Or is it only because it's your kid?"

Walter ground his teeth. "We leave at one. Find something to do until then, but stay out of everyone's way."

He walked away after that, determined that even if she did come up with some snappy reply, he would just keep moving. Get out of range, as it were. He ended up heading to the meeting room where Steggmann had papers spread out the length of the table in some odd semblance of organization.

"Something I can do for you, Walt?" he asked, hardly looking up.

"No, just looking at who I've got with me," Walter replied, looking over the papers.

He would have eight with him, six men, two women.

Norm Waters wasn't a new police officer, just new to the station, a transplant from Houston and more than experienced with hostage situations, having handled a number of them, usually involving drug runners from south of the border. Supposedly, he was still legally married, but he and his wife had been separated for nearly three years. She dated and he flirted, but neither could afford to officially file for divorce.

Ian Dorn had ten years in Seattle and ten years in Charleston, a latecomer to the law enforcement world but more physically fit than some of those just coming out of the academy. He was a good cop and a level head, a bit like everybody's grandpa—or maybe the kind, elderly next door neighbor. Walter might have questioned his position on the team except as a calm voice, though he was still unsure of his abilities in a firefight.

Miles O'Connor was the rookie of the team, barely out of his first year, still doing everything by the book, learning how to feel out real-world situations, when to be lenient and when to be a double-dick asshole. Walter severely questioned his place on the team as he'd never dealt with anything worse than a snarling dog in the pen of a well-known house.

Connie Zambowski was as good a cop as any of them, but had a bigger heart than anyone's grandma. She was the first one they called for domestics, rapes, and anything involving children. While

Walter would appreciate her experience and compassion, he was forced to wonder if that wouldn't cloud her judgment, cause her to hesitate for fear of doing the wrong thing—that is, potentially wounding Tommen—and so put lives in danger or give Rifun the chance to escape. Walter didn't want to see Tommen hurt, but he figured he was tough enough to take a small wound for the sake of getting Rifun off the streets. Or maybe he was being illogical.

Sean Tanner was like Walter, single dad of three, all in elementary school. He worked his ass off and devoted his life to his kids. He wasn't opposed to dating; he just never had time. Walter took a level breath. With any luck, his kids would be seeing him at the end of the day and not Steggmann.

Renee Elhart was a good shot, but Walter was sketchy on her judgment. Fifteen years as a cop and she'd wounded as many in friendly fire as intentionally targeting. Only because they used their guns so infrequently was she not outright dismissed, but there was a reason she never had more than five years with any one department.

Finally, Patrick Pence was perhaps the one Walter most trusted in the situation at hand. He was a cop's cop, the good guy as ideally depicted in movies, and the kind of guy that came to mind when anyone mentioned "upstanding citizen." He was solidly built, a good shot, level-headed, able to read a situation and not afraid to get in on the action and get his hands dirty, while also maintaining a sense of when to run. He'd been married almost thirty years, had four grown kids, six grandkids, and Walter was determined that he would spend another Christmas with them, and once again he would be the hero who saved the day.

"Any concerns, tell me now so I can make adjustments," Steggmann said, not looking up from his work.

"Why Renee?" Walter asked. "With all the cargo and freight, if we're running around playing cat and mouse, she's as liable to shoot me as Rifun."

"In that situation, you're as liable to shoot her as Rifun. When you're playing that kind of hide-and-seek, it's a split-second judgment call, and we don't always get it right. But she's a good shot, and that's what's going to make the difference in cat and mouse. I hope you don't have to use her."

"And Miles?"

"He wants to be a cop, he's going to see what it's like to be a cop. Our situations are either terribly mundane, or heart-stopping, pants-pissing action, or at least suspense. There is no good way to ease into that sort of thing. Besides, fresh eyes might see something we're all too old and rutted to consider."

Walter nodded, unable to really disagree. He needed a balance of level-headedness in order to help negotiations go over well, but if things went horribly wrong, he also needed fighting and shooting prowess. More to the point, if things went horribly wrong, he had to hope that Micah and Micaiah were able to drum up a little support to bring along.

"Lily will be riding with you," Steggmann said. "I'm expecting that Rifun will have as many guns as we will, so it may be best to shield her to avoid them taking her out while we're just yammering away."

"Understandable."

"Listen to me, Walter. I included Pat because he's a better cop than you or I. I've also ordered him to keep an eye on you." He went on before Walter could protest. "I want your son back as much as you do, and I don't want to give up Lily to do it. There is no easy choice here, but if Pat believes that you are unstable and incapable of making a wise judgment, he has the authority to step in and take over. Is that clear?"

"How do I make a good judgment when there isn't one?"

"I said there isn't an easy choice, and I only want you to make a wise judgment. If it's wiser to let Rifun escape and buy more time, than sacrifice everyone on the team, I expect you to know that."

Walter sighed. "Yes, sir."

"Good. Now then, lunch should be arriving soon. Get something to eat, and then head out to the barn to get suited up."

Walter left the office without another word and made it to the break room just in time for Cynthia to walk in with a couple enormous sub sandwiches, cut up into a bunch of tiny sandwiches and arranged artfully on a platter. Setting that out, she also pulled out of the bag an assortment of chips and cookies. He grabbed a plate and some food, sat down, and found that his appetite had fled.

"You should eat," Standish said, grabbing some for himself and sitting across from him. "It's going to be a long ass day."

"I didn't see your name on the team list," Walter mentioned.

"Because I won't be on the ground. I'm your eye in the sky."

Made sense. Standish was as good with a long gun as he was with a pistol, his qualifications coming more from hunting than the range, but he was a good man to have watching over things.

"We'll get your boy back," Standish said. "And if I have to put ten bullets through Rifun's head to do it, you know I will."

Personally, Walter would have rathered put ten rounds through Rifun's head himself, but he did not mention it to Standish, instead forcing himself to take a bite of his sandwich, his appetite rushing back to him until he was suddenly staring at an empty plate. He sighed and leaned back in his chair.

"I want more, but I don't want to get too full," he said, suddenly amused at such a tiny crisis in the middle of a much bigger predicament.

"Head out and get geared up," Standish suggested. "Then see how you feel after that."

Walter stood. "Assuming there's anything left to come back to." He indicated the line of hungry cops that had formed, all vying for just one of the tiny sandwiches.

Still, he headed out of the station, through a small wind flurry of icy snow, toward the tactical barn where Ernie sat at his desk in only a long sleeve shirt, the old heater cranking away faithfully. He grinned as Walter opened the door and stomped the snow from his boots, shivering in the last gust of wind.

"Walter, glad you're here!" Ernie greeted. "I know just what you're looking for!"

"Given the hairy canary everyone's been in lately, I would be worried if you didn't know," Walter told him. "You know the situation, I presume?"

"Absolutely. And when you're done, I want to see the girl, Lily." Every woman was a girl to Ernie. "She'll need protection just as much as your boy did. But for you, follow me."

Strictly speaking, Ernie's position was not essential. For him, it was more of an honorary title, something that kept him in the job. Generally, though, it was entirely possible for the entire precinct to share tactical duties — keeping everything clean and organized — whether it was assigning each man his own gear or else forming a specialized tactical team, something the city was loathe to do as they felt it was an unnecessary militarization of the police force, and they didn't want the police department to come off as hostile to the general public.

So instead, they had Ernie, whose sole job was to keep and maintain the tactical gear. Everything from organizing and cataloging to occasionally testing — or more than occasionally, depending on how ambitious he was feeling — to inspecting everything for defects and malfunctions which in turn lead to discarding the old and ordering the new. Everything they got from Ernie, Walter knew he could put as much reasonable faith in as anything else.

"Lucky for you, Santa came a little early this year to the department," Ernie was saying. "We got ten new vests in to replace some old ones where the stitching was coming out." He led Walter to a section dedicated to armor, then to a subsection where all the vests were neatly lined up and organized. He gave Walter a once-over before pulling one out. "The new ones are made of a lighter material and are less bulky to allow for better movement. I also took the liberty of ordering the arm, leg, and neck attachments."

"Attachments?" Walter wondered, removing a plastic bag attached to the hanger.

Ernie took the bag and removed one of the pieces. "They're not plated, but they'll absorb most of the force of a bullet, turning a potentially deadly shot into something of a minor flesh wound. The way I see it, it's better than not having any protection at all." He brought out each piece one at a time and helped Walter into them. "Upper arm, lower arm, thigh, calf, neck. Basically, everything just short of SWAT Team gear and no helmet."

Walter turned his head this way and that, trying to judge the benefit of neck protection against the decreased mobility. It wasn't stiff, but there would be no whiplash maneuvers here. He was less concerned about himself as he could Band if he needed to move faster, and more worried about his team who did not have such advantages. But at the same time, they had zero advantage over Rifun anyway, and their best offense might really be a good defense. They wouldn't be able to outmaneuver Rifun's bullets, but if they could gain some protection from them, all the better.

"What do you think?" Ernie wondered, grinning like a young boy showing off his favorite Christmas gift for all to admire.

"You're too good to us, Ernie," Walter told him. "I just hope we don't need to rely on it."

"Walter, I pray that every time one of you guys walks out of here with this stuff. Now then, send that pretty girl out here. I figure a vest ought to do it for her, unless you think she should have more protection?"

"A vest should do it," Walter agreed. "If things turn bad, she won't be running around with us playing cowboy."

Walter left the barn, unable to hide a smirk. Ernie would be in for one hell of a surprise once Lily got hold of him, and he would see that there was a lot more to her than just being pretty. He found her in his cubicle, looking through any loose papers floating around on his desk, most of them half-written notes or blank forms and reports.

"Ernie wants to see you out in the barn to get you a tactical vest," Walter told her.

She spun around in his chair and looked at him. "Do you really think I'll need it?"

"Better if you have it and don't need it, than getting shot and wishing you had it," he told her bluntly.

"Hm, perhaps. Are they at least fashionable?"

"I don't know; I don't wear the women's vests. Go out there and find out."

She sighed dramatically but got out of his chair and headed for the back door. Walter slumped into his chair and rubbed his eyes, ready for the day to be over already.

He figured Lily must have found something fashionable she liked because he didn't see her again until Steggmann started rallying the troops and sending them out. Walter got in the driver's seat of his vehicle, Standish in the passenger seat, Lily in the back, looking none too pleased about the whole thing. As he pulled out of the parking lot, the second in the procession behind Steggmann, he Banded and turned to speak to Lily.

"Honestly, Walter, don't you know that distractions, especially by other people in the vehicle, are one of the leading causes of car accidents?" Lily said before Walter could even take a breath to speak.

Instead, he forced himself not to react and said, "We've got two teams of nine plus three snipers."

"That sounds like quite a bit of firepower. Manpower, too. Did the city approve that much overtime?"

"You'll be with me in the first team, covering Warehouse 8 and only Warehouse 8. You are to stay behind us; we are your only line of defense against Rifun. Stay behind us and do only as we say. If the shit hits the fan, we'll try to cover you so you can get back to the car where Connie and Ian have orders to stay and defend you."

Lily shifted like an eager little school girl. "Why, Walter, that sounds like a marvelous little plan. Except for the part where Rifun is a Warden and Cassius is a Triage. And I believe I heard something through the grapevine about him having a Borelian with him. Oh, and a Grunjor. No big deal there, just a minor earthquake waiting to happen. With a bunch of cargo stacked high around you."

"Micaiah and Micah have managed to call in a few favors and

drum up a little support. They won't be seen much as they will not be in the fighting, just around to keep Rifun and his gang from escaping."

"Yes, I imagine the sight of a Yukka might be enough to make men not only weep, but turn their sights toward what they perceive as a bigger threat."

"Most likely. Point is, there will be fighting today. That I can almost guarantee. I'm trying to keep you alive as much as get Tommen home safely. The more you know, the better you can protect yourself and help us. Am I making any sense?"

"As a matter of fact, you are." Lily shifted in her seat and brought out her phone. "And I really should mark today on the calendar for it, because it really is a momentous occasion. Most days it's just Timekeeper psycho-Time-babble nonsense."

Walter did not wish for Lily to die, but there were some days when he just wanted to throttle her. Maybe she would get shot today. Not fatally or anything, but bad enough to make her consider her own mortality. She might be able to Harvest Time from people and so lengthen her own years, but she was not indestructible. She was just as susceptible to a bullet as any mortal man walking in with them.

Walter turned back to the wheel and released the Band. Standish looked back at Lily as best he could. "You okay back there?"

"Fine," Lily told him, doing something on her phone.

"We're going to have two teams with us today," Standish explained. "You'll be with us with the first team. We're focusing solely on Warehouse 8 and the negotiations. There will be a second team covering a slightly wider area, ready to jump in and help if things go bad."

"And what is the likelihood of things going bad?"

Standish glanced at Walter who gave him a look that said, "You started it." He looked back at Lily. "Pretty good, actually. If things get ugly, Connie is going to cover you so you can get back to the car where it's safe. Your best bet is to just stay here."

"But until then, what should I do?"

"Stay behind us, and do exactly as we tell you."

"I don't want to die."

"We won't let that happen," Standish told her. "Everyone is going home. Except Rifun and Cassius and all their friends; they're all going to prison for a long, long time."

Well, they were going to go to some sort of prison, Walter figured. It just might not be an Earth-side prison. Really, he would have preferred them to go first to the Grandfathers to have their clocks broken, and then locked up in the deepest, darkest corners of the asylum so they could rot for the rest of their natural lives—or a thousand Base Years, at which time they would simply be executed. Cruel and unusual punishment and all that, something they stole from Earth and used in a more mocking tone than most Earth-side courts.

Walter stole a glance at Lily in the rearview mirror. Apparently using her phone camera as a mirror, she had a tiny coin purse-like bag on her lap, and she was working fervently on her mascara.

"You're going into a hostage situation, and you're doing your makeup?" he wondered disbelievingly.

Lily raised a brow at him over her phone. "I refuse to go before Rifun looking like I've been bawling my eyes out and am about to drop to my knees and beg for mercy. He doesn't care for Tommen. It's me he wants. And if he wants me to beg, well, I am afraid that I will not oblige him. Even if he puts a gun to my head, even if he does manage to kill me, I will not cry for him. And if you have to put some last words in my obituary, those are what I want."

Walter was less inclined to put those last words and instead write something along the lines of, "A pompous, arrogant bitch who finally slept in the bed she made." But he wasn't about to say this out loud, at least not while Standish was there to witness it, and instead managed a level, "There will be no obituaries written today."

"A nice sentiment, Walter," she told him, putting her mascara away and digging for something else in her little purse, "but I think we both know that even if this does go smoothly, Cassius isn't about to leave without somebody dying."

It was not a comforting thought to dwell on, and instead Walter opted to be more interested in the radio traffic as they neared the docks, Steggmann handing out orders about who went where and how they were going to evacuate the entire yard in the fastest and most efficient way possible.

"Walt," Lily said.

Walter sighed but Banded and turned around. "Yes?"

The expression she wore was something Walter did not immediately recognize on her, but he eventually realized it was sympathy. He was momentarily caught off-guard by it, but she did not take the opportunity to make any snide comments. Instead she just nodded once. "For what it's worth, if I do die today, I want you to know I like your kid. He's a good boy. Like his dad. And probably like his pa, too. Stupid and naive, yes, but what teenager isn't? And as much as I loathe you Timekeepers, he'll make a great one someday."

For a moment, Walter was too stunned to speak. Finally he just said, "Thank you. He is a good kid, more like his pa than he realizes." Walter smiled and shook his head. Before he could turn back to the wheel, Lily spoke again.

"And just one more thing, Walt."

He looked back. "Hm?"

"If I do make it, don't tell him I said that. I'm not normally the sappy type, and I don't need it to get around that I do have feelings. All right?"

He grinned and put his hands back on the wheel. "It would never cross my mind, Lily. For one, most would think me a liar for saying so."

Then he dropped the Band, feeling immensely satisfied. Standish gave him an odd look, but he said nothing, instead focusing on regaining his composure and getting his thoughts focused on the task at hand. They were here to confront a psycho murderer and his murderous friends, win his son back, not sacrifice Lily—but if she got wounded in such a way that it made her a better person, Walter wouldn't be against it—and all get home in time for dinner.

"Ready for this?" Walter asked, following Steggmann's car and slowing down as they reached the drive.

Standish raised a brow and gave him a sideways glance. "Hell no."

Walter clapped him on the shoulder. "Good, because neither am I."

The yard was just outside of town on the east side, about as level a spot as could be found for putting up warehouses and building docks to take cargo up and down the river. At the time that the police pulled in, there were two boats currently being loaded and one dead in the water in need of repair.

Steggmann had called a little ahead to warn the dockmaster that they would be coming, and as such, the work crew needed to be going or else be forcibly removed. From what Walter could hear, the dockmaster recalled such a conversation, but was none too pleased that Steggmann had actually been serious about it. There were the usual arguments. They didn't have time; they couldn't afford it; the guys needed work; the shipments had to be on time; they had trucks waiting to take the cargo all over the place or bring new stuff in; one ship was late already; two more were almost set to leave and were as far from Warehouse 8 as could be anyway so those guys should be allowed to stay, or did they really think that his guys were somehow in on it, and on and on it went.

Walter understood his arguments, really he did. He had a stressful job, had to keep the goods flowing as long as possible before the river froze up; on top of that it was nearly Christmas. His men needed work, needed to win bacon and bring home the bread and such. But at the same time, Walter also wanted to look at him and ask if he understood that Walter also wanted to get his son back so he could have as merry a Christmas as any of the men working there right now. They could take half a day if it meant Walter could take his boy home.

In the end, the dockmaster didn't have much of a choice. He issued a general call to all within range. Some were glad to leave, others confused, many of them complaining about the lost work or the late shipments. Steggmann sent out a few teams to round up any stragglers while a few more teams were sent to secure the perimeter. The fence around the yard was not a consistent one. In most places it was chain link fencing with barbed wire wrapped around the top, but there were areas of cast iron bars with hot wire over them, and at least one section that was little more than T-posts with sheet metal scraps finagled together and bolted on, like around a junkyard.

Walter looked around at the surrounding landscape where a huge hill rose up from just the other side of the east fence and eventually made its way into a mountain. Rifun and Cassius could be hiding up there, watching them run around like little frightened ants. Or they could be holed up in any of the innumerable caves in these mountains, waiting until just a minute before the meeting time to Band and race down at their own leisurely pace.

"Perimeter is secure, sir," Ian reported on his return. "No sign of Rifun or any of them."

"Standish, you and your snipers get to your posts," Steggmann ordered.

Standish clapped Walter on the shoulder. "See you on the flipside, Walt. For your kid."

"Thanks, Jim."

Standish left, two more snipers following. They were a sight to behold, like a trio of cowboys clutching their guns and heading off to a showdown at high noon. They disappeared around one building, reappeared elsewhere, then vanished again. Walter expected he would not see them again unless they were doing their job and shooting Rifun.

"Walt, take your team to Warehouse 8," Steggmann said. "Get set up, get settled, and clear your head. For Tommen's sake, you have to think rationally. Borman and his team will be covering a slightly larger area."

Walter nodded. "Yes, sir."

It actually wasn't the hostage situation or the negotiations that had Walter all hyped up, though that was certainly a factor. Actually, he was more anxious about just seeing Tommen again. He'd heard his voice, knew he was alive. Now he wanted to see that he really was okay. He wanted to make sure he hadn't been mistreated or anything; though if he had, it would only fuel Walter's rage and need for revenge.

Walter took a breath as he returned to his car and drove around the yard to Warehouse 8. It was not quite the easternmost warehouse, but the one closest to the water on the east side, which was probably why Rifun had chosen it. If he needed a quick escape, he could jump into the water, Band, get away, and it would be as simple an explanation as...currents. And the hope of a drowning. Of course, he also had the option of the hill to the east, or the warehouses littering the yard.

As promised, one ship had been late, and all its apparent awaiting cargo littered the ground here and there and everywhere.

There was, however, a wide open area in front of Warehouse 8, marked and taped with signs telling workers to keep the area clear for cranes, trucks, forklifts, and so on. No one was to enter on foot. No exceptions. Walter chose to stage outside of this area, directing his team to park in the spaces between the cargo containers in order to effectively create a wall. He ordered them to keep an eye out for any suspicious activity beforehand, but rendezvous at Walter's vehicle at three minutes to three.

"All that stuff you said back there about liking my kid and stuff," Walter said to Lily as he Banded, "how much of that did you mean?"

Lily, who had been riding shotgun, looked at him, but her expression was difficult to guess. "People call me a lot of things, Walter. You call me a lot of things. A liar is one thing I have been accused of, but only when it suits me. I gain nothing by lying and saying I care about your kid when I really don't."

"Sure you do. You know that saying sappy stuff like that will put my mind at ease, make me a better negotiator, increase the likelihood of me being able to keep you alive. Whereas if you had expressed distaste or apathy, you know I might have felt more anxious, less able, and perhaps less concerned for you in the long run, and may have actually turned you over in exchange for Tommen whom you expressed distaste or apathy for."

Lily raised a brow. "Would you turn me over if I said I didn't care about your son?"

"As I've said before, I am required to put you before myself. But if justice finds you, I will not stop it."

"So you protect me only because the law requires you to? Have no you no sense of chivalry like your dashing son?"

Walter glanced at the clock and gave her a look. For a moment, she almost seemed uncertain. "I am required to put you, a civilian, before myself, a police officer." He reached for the door handle. "But in this situation, Tommen is also a civilian. And Rifun is only after one of you."

Just before he released the Band, Lily spoke in a soft but firm voice. "So. This is the real Walter Forbes, the one who was sentenced to death in Beaumaris Gaol for murder but escaped his own justice, not only through distance, but time as well. Who are you to speak of justice finding me, when you also seek to hide from its shadow?"

Walter met her gaze but used the time as an excuse to have to break it and get out of the car, dropping his Band as he did so. There was a difference between the man he had been a hundred years ago and the man he was now. Lily was still an active criminal by all accounts, and she flaunted it. Was there a difference between them? There was no statute of limitations on murder, so technically, he could still be executed for it, assuming anyone believed his story. The only reason Lily got away with it was because she essentially was the justice system, prosecutor, judge, and jury, and she pardoned herself. Was there no mercy on account of Walter's good deeds? Would he ever have done enough to erase that one tragic event that set his life on this course?

He went and leaned on the hood of his car. He sighed. What a time to start pondering his life choices. But then, was there ever any other more appropriate time?

He looked up at the rooftops. He saw a little movement, but if he hadn't known there was a sniper up there, he might have mistaken it for a pigeon or some such thing. He startled as a squirrel ran from one cargo container to another, stopping every three inches to reassess before continuing and finally making it to the safety of the shadows.

Walter studied Warehouse 8. The main door was still open, twice as wide as a semi trailer and probably three times the height. It wasn't stuffed with cargo, just enough to give a criminal good cover to escape. Or ambush. There were catwalks around the inside perimeter and what looked like one spanning the center of the warehouse, ladders in each corner, marked safety spaces for workers to get out of a forklift and climb them. Despite the rule of no one allowed on foot in or around the warehouse, Walter could see at least two man doors, one on their side of the building and one opposite.

This part of the yard was pretty narrow. Warehouse 8 was the only one in its row, while the row behind it could only fit two buildings of similar size together before being pinched between the river and the road. Walter was forced to wonder where and how Rifun planned on getting in. Banding aside, Timekeeping did not make him Superman. He couldn't bend steel bars or leap over the tallest building or outrun a speeding bullet—well, that last one might be relatively debatable.

Walter checked his watch. Three to three. The others on his team were heading his way. He tried to think about which way Rifun would come in as it might give him an idea of...

"Bravo Team from Alpha Team, Borman, status check," he said suddenly over the radio.

"This is Borman, Bravo Team is ready, all appears clear so far," Borman reported.

"Are you sure about that?"

There was a pause. Then, "All accounted for, all clear. Is everything all right up there?"

"Standish, how are things from above?"

"God looked down and saw it was good," Standish replied.

Walter was about to say more, but Standish cut him off. "Hang on, I've got movement. East drive, I've got a beige van."

"Is it our guys?"

"Looks like...we got a Japanese kid in the driver's seat. Someone's in the passenger seat getting out, but can't tell who. Back doors are opening...I've got a visual on Tommen!"

"How is he?"

"Rifun's got him. I've got a visual on Cassius, too. And...the *fuck*?"

"Talk to me, Jim," Walter said, trying not to sound like he was pleading, which he ultimately was.

"They're cracknuts all right. Looks like Rifun is running with the ComiCon crowd lately. Got a guy dressed up like The Thing and some chick dressed up as...I couldn't even tell you. Hot pink with a sheep horn hat. Viking, maybe."

"Maybe he's got some weird fantasies," Connie said. Miles snickered and badly tried to hide it.

"They're splitting up," Standish reported.

"Which way are they going?"

"The Thing and Japanese kid are heading in the main entrance. Japanese kid has got what looks like a couple of AR's. I don't see any obvious weapons on our rock monster. Hot Pink Viking is heading off by herself...ah, I lost her in the cargo. Rifun's kinda dragging Tommen this direction along the fenceline."

"What about Cassius?" Steggmann came on the radio.

There was a pause, and Walter could see binoculars peeking up from Standish's hiding spot. He got back on the radio. "I lost visual on him, sir, and I can't find him with all these containers and buildings."

"Do you still have a visual on Rifun and Tommen?"

"No, sir, they're gone, too. It's a maze out there, chief. A lovely, *fucking* maze."

"Bravo Team, keep an eye out for them. It's one minute to three and they'll have to pass right through your net to get to Warehouse 8."

And Walter knew that anything could happen in those sixty seconds and those hundred yards between the drive and the warehouse, especially if Rifun had a Borelian and a Grunjor with him. After about fifteen seconds, he was on the radio again.

"Bravo Team, report."

"This is Bravo Team," Borman said, starting to sound annoyed. Out of the corner of his eye, Walter could see Patrick scrutinizing him. It wasn't a mean, dark glare like a Catholic school teacher, just an honest assessment, like a father trying to decide if his son was ready to take off the training wheels. "We are all clear down h—"

"Bravo Team, report," Steggmann demanded. "Borman, do you copy?" Pause. "Standish, can you see Bravo Team?"

"Negative, sir," Standish said. "I only have a visual on Alpha Team."

"Oh, don't worry about Bravo Team."

The team snapped to attention as Rifun suddenly appeared in the large door of the warehouse, walking slowly toward them, one arm holding Tommen tight to his chest, the other holding a gun to Tommen's head. Behind him, the Japanese kid waited as nonchalantly as ever, sitting on a small crate, looking through the music on his mp3 player, AR's propped up beside him like regular hunting rifles. The Borelian stood just behind Rifun and to his left, a pistol on each hip, but her real power coming from sheer proximity, if not contact. And the rock monster, as Standish described him but was actually a Grunjor, waited patiently in the shadows in the door of the warehouse, as if he needed to have a running head start to juggernaut his way through any line of defense.

"Ah, so glad you could make it," Rifun said amiably, squinting his eyes against the setting sun as if they were just meeting for coffee at a quaint café. "Now then, I have something of yours, and you have something of mine. Let's talk."

Chapter Twenty-Five
Negotiations

Walter had seen a dozen or so hostage situations in his time at CPD, and it wasn't always the Joker holding up the bank manager and demanding all the money in the vault, or the freaky cult leader holding women hostage for rape and ritual sacrifice. Most often, it happened domestically, drunk and enraged husband, starts beating wife, wife calls 9-1-1, husband holds wife and kids hostage. And even then, it wasn't necessarily holding them at gunpoint, but any situation where the perpetrator refused to grant access to the victims, threatened violence, and made demands. Only once had it ever turned out disastrous for all involved, where the perpetrator, his hostages, and several police officers were killed.

Walter hoped today was not going to be a repeat of that, but he had his doubts.

That being said, he'd also seen the hostages in a variety of conditions. He'd seen them quite nervous and sweaty while wearing a Tommy Hilfiger and brand new shoes. He'd seen them grievously beaten to a bloody, black and blue unconsciousness. Thankfully, Tommen seemed to fall into the former category. He was unspeakably pale and thin, and he looked like he hadn't showered since he'd been taken as his clothes were filthy and stained. His beard had grown in, and, actually, it was starting to look like a real beard rather than just prepubescent fuzz. His hair was longer, covering his ears, but that wasn't anything new. First thing's first, he was getting a damn haircut. But it also looked as though he'd done a little growing, his pant legs coming just to his ankles. After the haircut, new clothes.

"Standish, keep an eye on Pink," Walter said quietly into his

477

radio. "Everyone else, do not let her touch you. She favors contact poisons that will kill you."

"Ah, so you have done your research," Rifun said. "I must say, Walter, you certainly know how to do your homework and pull together bits and pieces of information into some wildly accurate theories. Do you know what I'm thinking right now?"

"You're probably trying to stall for time, give your goons there a chance to size us up and pick their targets so that when this all goes south, all you have to do is give the signal."

"My goons. Why, how very...1980's of you. Please, Walter, if we're going to compare balls, at least let's do so like civilized men. 'Pink' as you called her is Isthim Borelian. My Oriental compadre over there is Tadashi Hajiku. And that's Donojok hiding back there in the shadows." He went on before Walter had a chance to speak more. "No need to introduce your team. I've already researched everyone in the department so I would know who the options were for who you might bring. So I know everyone you brought and everyone you left behind." He grinned. "I even know the names of everyone on your 'Bravo Team.' And my, you should have seen their faces when I whispered their names as they went down."

Out of the corner of his eye, Walter saw everyone in Alpha Team shift stances, finger their guns, roll necks and crack joints, all as taut as rubber bands and ready to fire. Even up above, Walter watched every rifle train itself squarely on Rifun.

"Where is Cassius?" Walter asked, trying to keep things calm.

"He couldn't make it, unfortunately. Meetings to attend and so forth. You know how politics can be. Just me and you, old boy."

"Why me? Why single me out?"

Rifun Banded then, a Band so strong and tight and narrow, it momentarily knocked the breath from Walter's lungs. He stumbled back a step as if he'd stepped into a river expecting a gentle current and instead found rushing rapids. He tried to take it in stride, recover quickly, not show any weakness, but it was too late; Rifun had seen him stumble, seen him falter, and was even now going over a hundred different ways to capitalize on it.

Tommen was not part of the Band, remaining locked in Rifun's arms, his expression somewhere between sheer terror and stoic determination. For the moment, it was only Walter and Rifun speaking.

"At first, it was simply an opportunity," Rifun answered. "It gave me the chance to snub my nose at Earth-side and Time-side cops. Then Cassius told me who you were, both in relation to him and in relation to your so-called son. After that, I thought it would be great fun to see what it would take to get you to tell dear Tommen the truth."

"No," Walter told him solemnly. "There would be no point to telling him now. It would change nothing except the trust we have with each other."

"Perhaps." Rifun shrugged. "Then once we got our hands on the journal, we started doing a little digging, and the last two weeks of observation were especially enlightening as we observed Tommen. Were you ever aware he has the potential to become an Akari-bearer?"

Walter sighed, and even that he tried to do diplomatically. Don't dismiss him as a lunatic—even if he is one—but don't give him cause to think you believe him, which you don't. "The Akari is a myth, Rifun. It's like the Holy Grail, and the so-called Akari-bearers the Knights Templar. Perhaps once it was a real, tangible object, but it has become so steeped in myth and legend that it doesn't exist like you think it does."

It was then that Walter decided that Julianna's husband might have been locked up in Beaumaris Gaol for good reason; if his journal contained writings about the Akari, then his general Earth-side sanity couldn't have been much more promising. There was a difference between writing an Indiana Jones adventure about the Holy Grail, and actually using it as a roadmap to the secret temple and passing through all the tests and booby traps.

Rifun gave Walter a look that was far less than encouraging, and, for a minute, Walter was afraid that he would give some secret signal and everyone on his team would suddenly drop dead.

"The Akari is real, Walter," Rifun told him, with all the seriousness of an impending ultimatum and threat of a shootout. "Richard laid it all out."

So, yes, Richard was insane. And he inspired a cult of insane, zealous worshipers who killed women and kidnapped children in order to find their sacred, holy text.

"Why did you need the original journal and not the copies?" Walter inquired.

"There are abilities even you have not learned yet, dear Walter, things available only to Wardens, Dominion Timekeepers...and Akari-bearers."

"And Richard was...?"

"Warden, naturally. Granted, he lost his mind while he was an Akari-bearer, but the words in his journal ring true, and we have found no cause to doubt him."

Yes, because questioning the martyr of a cult is blasphemy deserving of death, naturally.

"All right," Walter conceded. "You have the original journal. What does that have to do with kidnapping Tommen and murdering Lily?"

Rifun scoffed as if the answer ought to be obvious. "Killing Lily is purely political; I'm sure you and your Lieutenants worked out that much."

"Put Cassius back in power, create a new Dispersal, ensure your reign as some sort of Time Kings."

"Kidnapping Tommen was originally just a clever ploy to get what we wanted. Then when we discovered his potential, we also discovered that this path has always been decided, long before we consciously chose it."

There was no reason that Walter could see not to believe in some version of Fate, but this took it to a whole new level of crazy. Normally the Grandfathers didn't care much for the religions of the various worlds, but what about when Runners like Rifun made Time itself a god, one they obviously felt obligated to kill for, whether by command or manifest coincidence? Would the Grandfathers prosecute Rifun on special charges if he could be found guilty of religious terrorism, the Akari being his god or idol, and the journal his sacred text?

Walter sighed deliberately, shifted his stance, and looked around at the two sides gathered, both appearing frozen in time, trying to take command of the conversation. "We could sit in this Band and chat all day, but there is still a situation going on here, one that does really involve more than just me and you. So then, why don't we get out of this Band and get this show on the road? So, what are you going to tell the normal mortals gathered here about the reason why you singled out me and, by default as evidenced here, my son?"

Rifun released the Band, and again Walter felt like he'd gotten caught in some kind of Time rip current, almost like the feeling of walking through a portal to the Wheel. He tried not to stumble or cough as the air was sucked from his lungs once more and they were back in Base Time. Tommen was still moderately struggling against Rifun; Tadashi was still passively scanning through his music player; beside him, Patrick kept one eye on the situation and one eye on Walter. They were standing in several inches of slush, slowly freezing into rutted ice as the forklifts and machinery were not working to keep it melted and running into the drains; Walter was made aware of a hole in his right boot, right at the seam where heel met sole, and wet and cold began soaking his sock. He tried to shift his stance casually, trying to keep the hole above the water while not slipping on the ice.

Rifun grinned as he answered Walter's question. "Because you are just too interesting of a person, Walter. You and your precious son both."

And there it was. Without the knowledge of Time to aid in the backstory, all it looked like to the rest of the officers was pure and simple evil, the kind they couldn't profile or explain away as "Mommy didn't love him enough" or "Daddy came home drunk every night." Truth be told, even with the Time-side knowledge, Walter still couldn't explain the evil here. What made a Warden turn into a Runner and become obsessed with something that was only a myth? Even if something like the Akari did exist, why couldn't they see it was little more than a simple object? The Holy Grail had no special powers; it was just a cup whose power came from the Man who drank from it, as much as the men who spent their lives and fortunes perpetuating that myth.

But there would be no reasoning with Rifun at this point, not while he was threatening Tommen.

"As I said before, I have something you want, and you have something I want. So, you can obviously see that I've brought dear Tommen here relatively safe and mostly unharmed." Rifun shrugged. "Now then, where is Lily Guile?"

Walter met Rifun's gaze, trying to judge his thoughts and intentions. Would he shoot Lily as soon as the door was opened? No, if he wanted a show, he'd draw this out Western-style. He wanted to make a scene of it, be some kind of superhero, or supervillain, snub his nose and flex his muscles. Killing Bravo Team—if indeed that's what he'd done, which Walter had no reason to doubt—was only the opening act.

Still, Walter nodded once to Connie. She gave him an uncertain look, but went to the cruiser and opened the door. Lily got out of the car slowly, cautiously, standing and trying to walk up with the same arrogant confidence she always portrayed. But there was something new in her walk today, something Walter had never expected he would see from her: fear. She didn't sway her hips like a hooker, didn't try to walk the catwalk, didn't give a pouty lip or look around with an impatient glare. At some point in the last five minutes, she'd come to realize that it was entirely possible that she could die. Maybe it was seeing Tommen held hostage, Walter powerless to help him, or hearing that Bravo Team had been murdered. But something had gotten through to her. The most she managed to do was a straight back and forward stare, taking a position just behind Walter's right shoulder, folding her arms, and somehow managing to make even the bullet-proof vest look like something out of the latest fashion magazine.

"No, no," Rifun said, flicking his gun hand. "Out in front where I can see you."

"She stays here," Walter said.

"How are we supposed to do a hostage exchange then?" Rifun said it in such an innocent, convincing tone that Walter might have honestly thought they were really going to just swap people.

"Lily is not our hostage, nor will she be yours."

"Ah, so you expected that you would leave here today with both of them alive, somehow negotiating their release, put me in jail, and retire to bed as the hero of the day?" Rifun frowned, almost seeming to be disappointed. "I see. Unfortunately, Walter, that is not why I came here."

"I know why you came here, to kill her. And you are using my son to do it. I don't appreciate that."

"Maybe not, but it's working, isn't it? That's what really brought you here today. I can see it in your eyes, Walt, that you would do anything to get your boy back. And why not? But I can see it in your eyes. I can see it. You're wondering if you could get away with turning over Lily. What if the rest of Alpha Team suddenly dropped dead just as mysteriously as Bravo Team? You trade Lily for Tommen, I inflict some wounds on you so it's not too obvious, and you still get to play hero of the day."

If Walter wanted to be entirely honest, that thought actually had crossed his mind, to his shame. But another, slightly adjusted, idea also came to mind then, and he Banded. He wasn't quite as good as Rifun at making it so tight and narrow as to sweep Rifun off his feet, but it was just the two of them.

"Did you actually kill Bravo Team?" Walter asked.

"Why do you question me? Don't you know my handiwork?" Rifun said, but his expression was almost delighted, as if Walter had discovered another little secret.

"Pink Borelians. What can they do?"

"Proximity will make anyone compliant. A brief touch will simply knock them unconscious for a day or two. That's not to say some didn't die, but I needed drama more than I needed blood, much to Cassius' dismay. But as I said, he has more important things to do today."

"Don't kill my team. Knock them out. This fight is between us and us only. Leave them out of it and let's discuss things freely."

"Freely in a Band or in Base Time makes no difference to me, Walter," Rifun told him.

"Then knock them out anyway. Have your gloat."

"I might just do that anyway, except it's more fun when they futilely fight back. And you are still withholding Lily from me."

Walter let out a breath. "You want Lily out of the elections, right?"

Rifun's expression turned dark and slightly crazed, bloodthirsty even. "I want her out of Time completely, and I want to make a severe point of it."

"Knock her out, too. Mock up some blood or moulage or whatever. Take pictures. Make it appear that she's dead. Show your little band of followers. I'll make sure she doesn't interfere ever again."

"Cute, and I admire your creativity at trying to reach a compromise. But there are a couple problems with that plan. First, I didn't promise my 'followers' as you call them, mere pictures. I promised them a body that they would be able to touch and gorge upon if they so chose. Second, we both know Lily too well to think that she'll just go into Time Witness Protection and never come out again. Sure, she might do that for a year or two, but her personality won't allow her to stay down for long. Eventually, she'll rear her ugly head again, and, with her resources and cash lying around, she'll be back and as powerful as ever."

"What about..." Walter closed his eyes and tried not to let his disgust taint his tone. "What about breaking her clock? I know there are degrees of breaking. She doesn't have to be a Time vegetable, just crippled to the point where she can't use her Time abilities, but can still basically function in normal life."

Rifun blinked and sighed, and for just a moment, Walter saw the consideration. And that was when he knew that Rifun was not as bloodthirsty as he first appeared. He did things out of necessity. He thought killing Lily was a necessity, so he would do so. But when presented with another option, he was open to consideration. Problem was, Cassius probably had too great a hold over him, both as a dangerous, bloodthirsty bastard, and the Zero Hour. Finally, Rifun shook his head. Reluctantly, Walter dropped his Band and waited for him to speak.

"I'm sorry, Walter, but there is no other option here for me," he said.

"Why not?" Walter asked diplomatically. "If Cassius isn't here to hold you, why don't we talk? Is he forcing you to do this under some kind of duress? What does he have on you, or what has he promised you?"

He tensed as Rifun bent over slightly to whisper in Tommen's ear.

"Tommen, what is he telling you?" Walter asked cautiously.

Tommen swallowed nervously as Rifun stopped speaking. He took a steadying breath and said finally, "He says that Cassius has promised him great things and that they've extended this offer to me, to rise higher than any other human."

"What does that mean?"

Rifun leaned and started whispering again.

"Send Lily forward two steps, and find out," Tommen repeated.

Walter glanced briefly at Patrick who regarded him with a solemn stare. His gaze flickered once to Rifun, then to Lily, and then he used a single blink and a motion of his eyebrows to nudge Walter forward. Walter took Lily, and together they stepped forward two steps.

"You did not order me to stay back," Walter said before Rifun could protest.

Rifun nodded once. "And so I did not. My mistake."

Then he Banded, but this time he did not include Walter. Instead, he encompassed only himself and Lily. While he was doing that, Walter made a split-second decision to Band himself and Tommen.

"Dad?" Tommen whimpered.

"Are you okay? Did they hurt you?" Walter demanded fearfully.

"Um, I got a burn on my leg from being dragged out of the airport, but it's healing."

"Did they tell you anything at all?"

"No, not really. There was a lot of talk about something called an Akari, but they never said what that was. And they kept calling me an Akari-bearer."

Walter let out a breath. He knew this would not go over well. "The Akari is a myth, sort of like the Holy Grail, but for Time Agents. We can talk about it later if you like."

"Great, so I've been kidnapped by religious zealots."

Walter was more relieved that Tommen's sense of dry and disrespectful sarcasm was still alive and well, than he was annoyed by the fact that he had no respect for any mythology, even Time mythology. But that would be a conversation for another day.

"They also keep telling me to ask you more about my parents and stuff," Tommen went on. "Is there something I don't know?"

"There is," Walter confessed. "I wasn't going to tell you, but this has made it impossible to ignore any longer. When we get home tonight, we'll talk about your parents. Okay?"

There was no real reason they couldn't talk now except that even if they did spend hours inside the Band, there was still a hostage situation at hand in Base Time, one they couldn't ignore and would not be well-served by interjecting years of heartache and selfish sentiment.

Walter's conflict of conscience made him dreadfully unprepared for the sudden breaking of his Band as Rifun barged his way in and ripped it to pieces like a ferocious dog ripping up a pillow or ragged chew toy. He fought to keep balance, to stay strong in front of his team, and to not seem weak in front of Rifun.

Rifun's demeanor had changed completely. Clearly, he did not appreciate the conversation he'd had with Lily. Walter stole a glance at her. She still put on a strong face, but her resolve was quickly wearing thin.

"Obviously, Walter, you care for your son," Rifun said. "But tell me, Lily, do you also care for young Tommen?"

"He's a good kid," Lily replied, her voice straining and almost inaudible. "I don't want to see him hurt."

"But your pride and arrogance and sense of self-preservation just won't quite let you sacrifice yourself for him, now will it? And why should it? Most people need a push, a moment of a split-second decision where they know they can and should be the hero. Average people can be heroes, after all. So then, Lily, what would it take to make you sacrifice yourself? Or, better yet, Walter, what would it take for you to sacrifice Lily for the sake of your child?"

In the next one billionth of a second, several things happened at once.

First, Rifun pulled the trigger on his revolver, which was still pointed directly at Tommen's head, pressed almost up against his temple.

Second, Walter's head exploded in a migraine as he Banded as Fast and as strong and as tight and as narrow as he had never done before in his life. He scratched out Time, feeling Rifun's gun, the cool metal on the outside and the polished wooden grips, slightly slick from a recent cleaning. He felt the hot metal of the barrel, the ignition as the bullet left the chamber at a thousand feet per second, kicking the gun back and automatically chambering another round.

Walter found that bullet in Time and pinpoint Banded it so hard he might as well have been Superman to hold it back, for even as he held a Band in place around it to keep it from advancing any farther than the end of the barrel, it was still an object in motion, straining against the Band with incredible force, like trying to push a finger through the super strong and stretchy trash bags; they were good, but even they could only take so much force before they snapped and tore wide open.

Third, one of the snipers also discharged his weapon. In his own Band, Walter could see the bullet whizzing through the air, one rotation at a time, advancing closer and closer towards Rifun.

But Rifun also saw the bullet heading straight for him. He looked right at it, grinned, and pulled a *Matrix*-style trick, moving back just enough that the most it might have done was singe the hair off the end of his nose, but otherwise he was unharmed. He looked back at Walter with that same sickening grin.

"So, Walter, how long are you going to hold that Band?" he asked menacingly. "How long until the force of the bullet breaks through your shield? How much—?"

His small threat was cut short as a stray bullet suddenly found him, ripping through his hand but going no farther. His shirt split open from the impact, and Walter saw that he'd taken Tommen's bullet-proof vest that he'd worn to the hangar. Rifun cursed as he flinched and struggled to keep control of the gun. Yet in that motion, the barrel moved away from Tommen's head, and Walter got off another shot before releasing the Band on Rifun's gun, letting the bullet fly harmlessly away.

Walter looked around briefly and saw Micah on a cargo container, rifle in hand. He nodded once and slipped away. So then, there was some backup in the area.

Rifun's hand was no more useful to him now than a sack of raw hamburger as blood poured out of it through the artery in the thumb, staining the slush and ice red, bone shards dropping to the icy ground where two of his fingers now lay, white tendons dangling uselessly in mid-air, his thumb hanging on only by a bit of skin and some muscle. He roared in pain and grabbed his injured hand in his good hand, but still keeping Tommen tight to his body.

In a moment of judgment, Walter elected to Fast Band, but not the usual Fast Band where everything else would appear frozen in time. This time he elected for the appearance of quick movements and quicker reflexes, taking advantage of Rifun's distraction as he pushed Lily back toward the other officers, ran forward purposefully, and all but dragged Tommen from Rifun's grasp.

Rifun tried to fight, but he was losing blood quickly and had to choose between keeping his hostage, or Banding and doing a quick tourniquet to stop the bleeding. In the end he chose the tourniquet. Walter might have pushed Tommen back to the line of safety and arrested Rifun then and there, except he didn't like the way his goons were advancing, making a point of brandishing their weapons and rallying behind their leader. Instead, Walter put Tommen directly in front of him, giving him a full body shield, and hurried back to the line of safety.

Once there, the other police officers got in front of them to form a wall while Walter got Lily back in the car and Tommen off to one side just long enough to pull him into an embrace that had been weeks in coming. He didn't even try to stop the tears as they flowed, just made sure to be out of Rifun's line of sight as he cried.

"Oh my God," Walter whispered. "Oh my God, my son, Tommen, are you okay?"

Tommen didn't say anything, just buried his face in Walter's shoulder, his body heaving violently with sobs. He truly was skinny as Walter could feel his ribs and the knobs of his spine. He could feel his beard scratching against his chin, another indication that Tommen had done a little growing while in captivity.

"It's okay," Walter told him, pulling back to look at him. "Micah and Micaiah are here. I expect this is going to come to a fight, but Micah and Micaiah are here. They'll Band and take you home so you can shower and shave and get some clean clothes, then—"

"Huh?" Tommen wondered.

"They'll take you home. You'll be Banded, so—"

"What?" Tommen turned his head.

Walter blinked and took a step back. "Tommen, can you hear me?"

Tommen blinked a few times in confusion. "I...I can tell you're speaking—" He struggled to pitch his voice correctly and at an appropriate volume. "—but it's muffled, and my ears are ringing."

Of course, why wouldn't they be? He'd just had a gun go off as close to his ears as it could possibly get. He took a breath and stepped forward, gently taking Tommen's head in his hands. He spoke first in the right ear. "Can you hear me?"

Tommen simply stayed where he was, head in his hands. Then Walter turned his head and tried the other side. "Can you hear me?"

"Yeah, I can hear you."

"Okay. Change of plans. Micah and Micaiah are here. They'll take you to the hospital. I'm pretty sure they'll let you shower and shave, and they'll check out your ears. Okay?"

"What about my leg?" He hiked up his pant leg to show a cratered wound only partially-healed.

Walter nodded. "That too. Go with Micah." He nodded to Micah who was standing behind him.

Tommen looked at Walter and frowned. "What about you?"

"You and Lily are both alive and on our side. I don't think we're getting out of here without a fight."

"Then I should stay." He still fought for appropriate tone and volume.

"You're no good here," Micah told him, touching his arm. Tommen startled. "We'll wait until the fighting starts and Rifun is distracted, but I'm taking you to the hospital. Walter will catch up later."

"But they won't make it. He's got Isthim and Donojok."

"We know. We brought some help of our own. They're just a little less obvious."

"Go wait in the cruiser, Tommen," Walter ordered.

Tommen seemed reluctant to do as he was told, but eventually he got into the backseat behind Lily.

"You'll look after him?" Walter asked Micah.

Micah nodded, as if there had ever been any doubt. "I always do. Micaiah's ready with the Cavalry whenever you need it, which I suspect will be soon."

"I expect so, too. Take care of Tommen."

Micah vanished again, this time to a more advantageous spot for covering the cruiser where Tommen and Lily waited. Walter took a breath, tried to collect his frayed nerves. Tommen had been rescued. He had him back. He hadn't needed to sacrifice Lily to do it. So far, everything really was going according to plan. They'd gotten the upper hand this time. They were going to win this one, actually. Even if Walter had to fake Rifun getting away from Earth-side justice, Rifun was going to be presented before the Grandfathers before the day was out.

Of course, this was all still speculative, and Walter wouldn't believe it until he was actually handing him over to be prosecuted. But it was hope enough to keep him calm and get him back to the rest of his team. None of them had moved, and they were all facing Rifun with guns drawn, daring him or his friends to make any kind of sudden move. Walter took his place among them.

Tadashi and Isthim stood between Alpha Team and Rifun, guns drawn. Behind them, it appeared as though Rifun had successfully tied a makeshift tourniquet and was working on at least binding his hand, but there was no way it was going to be salvaged. Bones had been blown out of it. His forefinger and middle finger were on the ground. Even the thumb, unless he got some serious pins, braces, and probably some motor implants, his only option would be amputation. The thought was oddly satisfying.

The two teams remained in a cold stalemate while Rifun worked on his hand. Once he stood, Tadashi and Isthim parted to let him through, though they kept their weapons leveled at the officers.

"That," Rifun said, his voice terribly strained, face pale as milk, steps slightly unsteady, "was a very nice trick. I have to say, I am impressed. And you even accomplished what you set out to do today, that is, win your son back and not have to sacrifice dearest Lily to do it."

"You have the right to remain silent," Walter told him. "Anything you say can and will be used against you in a court of law. You have the right to an attorney. If you cannot afford one, one will be provided to you by the courts."

"I'm sorry, did I say I was surrendering?" Rifun interrupted. "Because I don't recall that bit. See, you set out to accomplish a goal, and you did. The problem is, I also set out to accomplish a goal, and I haven't done that yet. And most unfortunately for you, your son, and your entire team—not to mention Lily—I really can't leave until I've also accomplished my goals for the day. So, for as much as I admire your cunning, I'm afraid we're still not done here." He stepped back and Tadashi and Isthim filled the gap. "I'm sorry, Walter, but...I really need to kill Lily." He addressed his goons. "At your leisure."

Chapter Twenty-Six
Into the Maw

Walter knew that with such a threat hanging over his team, Rifun and his crew would have no reservations about using their Time abilities, whatever they were. They would Band, they would Harvest, and they wouldn't care who saw because they were going to kill everyone anyway, or so they thought.

Tadashi was the first to start shooting, scattering the police officers and sending them running for the safety of the cargo containers. Walter was forced to Band Miles so he could get out of dodge of the bullets and just barely take cover with the rest of them.

The Borelian, Isthim, did not advance on the ground officers, instead turning and looking for the snipers on the rooftops. As one sniper raised his head to get off a shot at Tadashi, she fired at him, chipping the rooftop but otherwise missing the man himself.

Donojok the Grunjor did not move right away, instead standing in the door of the warehouse, watching everything go on as if simply fascinated by it. Only when one of the snipers actually managed to wound Isthim, grazing her cheek and drawing heavy blood, did he rise from his position. For a moment, Walter felt Donojok's gaze sweeping around the open area, settling momentarily on each of the cargo containers before fixing his sights on one, which happened to be the one Walter was hiding behind.

The great rock monster gave a roar and started running. Several police officers opened fire but to no avail; Donojok simply bulled through the hail of bullets.

"Scatter!" Walter ordered.

The three of them who had been hiding behind the container

leapt out of the way as Donojok juggernauted his way into the cargo container, crumpling the middle. He stepped back and lifted the container like it was little more than tin foil. He turned and threw it at the officers hiding behind one of the other containers, and they, too, scattered.

While they were scattering, Tadashi again started shooting. In the confusion, Walter Banded as much as he could, slamming into his comrades before the bullets touched them. They would think they'd been shot, but really it was just his weight plowing into them, driving them to the ground.

"We need to get a handle on this situation," Patrick said as he and Walter huddled together behind one of the cruisers. "What do we got?"

"Japanese kid with two AR's, Hot Pink Viking of Death, and Scary Rock Monster. Which do you want?"

"We should draw the rock monster into an open area where he has nothing to grab onto and throw. Perhaps if we could get it to the break, we could push him in the river somehow and effectively sink him like a stone."

That was another thing Walter liked about Patrick. Even when he was confronted by scary rock monsters from distant planets, he didn't take time out of a firefight to ponder such things and potentially put people at risk. He simply took what he had and went with it. Right now, he was prepared to try and sink the bastard.

"How many people you need?" Walter asked.

Patrick puffed out his cheeks and eventually let out a breath. "Me and three ought to do it."

Walter did the calculations. Four for Donojok, two for Tadashi and Isthim each at the least, one sniper per adversary, which left no one to go after Rifun, wherever he'd disappeared to, most likely the Wheel to hide with Cassius.

"Can you do it with two?" Walter wondered.

"I should," Patrick said, though his expression conveyed uncertainty of the highest degree, and Walter didn't blame him. This was the kind of stuff that made men say, "They did not teach this at the Academy!" Because, well, they didn't. There was no chapter in the textbooks about fighting scary rock monsters or hot pink aliens with a death touch.

"Ian and Miles," Walter told him. "I'll cover you. Go!"

Patrick didn't think twice as he left their safe spot and started running for Miles who was cowering behind a container, getting off a shot here and there but otherwise having little progress against Tadashi who was currently being distracted by Norm. They exchanged fire long enough for Patrick and Miles to break cover and head to Ian's aid as he was already engaged with Donojok.

"Ron, eyes in the sky, Patrick's got Ian and Miles; they're going to be trying to sink our rock monster in the river," Walter called over the radio.

"Roger that, Walter," Ron replied. Up above, Walter saw Ron shoulder his rifle as he moved to a more advantageous position on the rooftop, following Patrick as he and his helpers slowly drew Donojok closer to the river, like baiting a rabid attack dog.

"Norm, Sean, see if you can't take out our AR-loving whiz kid," Walter ordered. "Mike, cover them from above. If you get a shot, you take it."

"Affirmative," Mike crackled over the radio.

"Connie, Renee," Walter said.

"Already on the pink bitch," Connie said coarsely. "First, we gotta find her."

Now where could she have gotten off to? Walter surveyed the scene, looking for any evidence of Isthim, fairly certain that she would be pretty easy to spot. Patrick had drawn Donojok well clear of the warehouse and closer to the river, apparently having some sort of plan to sink the rock monster, and Norm and Sean had Tadashi well-engaged, Tadashi looking almost uncertain as he tried to shoot the ground officers, but he was also trying to hide from the sniper.

"Jim, behind you!" Walter barked the words before his mind fully registered Isthim on the rooftop, walking up to him like a walk in the park.

Walter saw the end of Standish's rifle swing around in surprise, but he was already breaking across the yard toward the building, shouting into his radio. "Connie, Renee, south building where Jim's sitting, on the rooftop!"

"On our way," Connie said, and just before Walter disappeared into the building, he saw the two women running his way.

The rooftop door was locked, but it wasn't anything a well-placed kicked couldn't handle since the door was old and rusted anyway, with one hinge barely doing anything to hold the door in place. Once outside, he found Standish with his rifle pointed straight at Isthim, but she was already within range of her proximity influence, where she could just tell him to lower his rifle and he would with no questions asked.

"Freeze!" Walter shouted, leveling his gun at her and hoping that head shots were universal killers.

Isthim stopped as if she meant to, and not because Walter ordered her. She turned slowly and gave him a cat's regard. For a moment then, her ram horns reminded Walter of a couple of pigtails, and her "steampunk" getup—or whatever the kids were calling it—like some cutesy Halloween costume. Well, maybe less of a Halloween costume and more of a soft porn advertisement, but for as much as Walter detested Tommen's Internet history, he himself was still a man and not immune to the effects of a pretty girl, especially when she...turned colors?

By the time Walter realized he had lowered his gun, Isthim was already gone, flinging herself off the roof and landing safely on the ground. Walter glanced at Standish who had also lowered his rifle.

"What the hell was that?" Standish asked, voicing Walter's thoughts. "It's like...I couldn't resist, but I didn't want to either."

"I don't know," Walter said, electing to go the easy route and not try to explain things. He went to the edge of the roof just as

Connie and Renee made it up. "I don't see her."

"Did she jump?" Renee asked, looking around and surveying the scene.

"No, she'd never survive that. We're at least two, if not three stories up," Connie said.

"There!" Standish said suddenly.

Walter followed his finger to see Isthim heading for the cruiser where Tommen and Lily still sat. She paid no attention to Tadashi who appeared to be losing the fight with Norm and Sean. Instead she made straight for the car.

"Come on, Micah," Walter hissed under his breath.

Then he saw Isthim jerk in surprise as Micah's bullet found flesh. It didn't kill her, though, and she whipped around angrily, looking for the shooter. In a moment, she found him.

"We have to help him," Walter said, turning and heading for the door.

"Got it," Connie and Renee said, following him.

"Where do you want me?" Standish inquired.

Walter paused momentarily, then turned back to look at him. "Help Mike cover Norm and Sean. Looks like they've got Tadashi pretty well beat. If he surrenders, fine. Otherwise, if you get a shot, take it."

Standish nodded, shouldered his rifle, and followed them down to the ground where he made for a building with a better view of Norm, Sean, and their present foe.

Meanwhile, Walter, Connie, and Renee made a break for the cruiser. As far as Walter could tell, Tommen and Lily were still safe inside, but Isthim had found Micah and was bearing down hard. There would be no soft compliance mercy for him; her ideas for him went straight to the kill.

Micah had taken several shots at Isthim, and they'd all connected: one to the upper arm, another to the chest, a third through the abdomen, but still she walked like he was merely firing a marshmallow gun or bean shooter. Walter was the first of the reinforcements to shoot, taking her in the side of the lower back, just above the hip. There she stumbled just a bit, her rage momentarily quelled by confusion.

"Stand down," Walter ordered as he and the others surrounded Isthim, all with guns leveled at her.

Isthim looked around at each of them, looking less and less like some kinky Victoria's Secret model, and more and more like the snobby rich girl from high school who was obscenely offended when the hottest guy in school refused to date her. For a moment, Walter wasn't sure what to make of her non-aggression, but always checked and double-checked that he kept his gun up, determined not to fall for the same trick twice.

"What's it going to be, Isthim?" Connie asked sternly. "You can come with us quietly, or die for a lost cause."

Now Isthim smiled, her green teeth almost beautiful in contrast to her skin. "Is the cause lost if you don't even understand who is going with whom quietly?"

For a moment, they looked at each other in confusion. Then something clicked in Walter's mind and he looked around at the cop car. The doors were wide open, and Tommen and Lily were gone.

"Shit," he hissed.

He made to move and go after Rifun whom he saw across the open area heading for the warehouse, but then Isthim was on him, tackling him to the ground and using him as a kind of leap frog to propel herself out of the circle of officers toward Rifun.

Walter sat up, trying to fight the wooziness that he was sure came from either her proximity or a minor skin contact, a graze. He looked around at his team. Connie and Renee were completely out, but when he checked on them, they were merely unconscious. Micah was a little farther away, sitting against a container, rifle in his lap, breathing evenly. When Walter went to check his pulse, his eyes opened.

"I'm okay," he said. "For the most part. She kind of grazed me. Actually, she slapped me. And actually, my first thought was of

Lily. Isn't that strange?"

"You stay here and rest," Walter told him, not feeling much better himself. "I'm going after Rifun before he has a chance to escape."

"Micaiah brought help. Don't worry."

"Sh, rest now. Everything will look better in the morning."

"Go get 'em, Cap."

Then Micah closed his eyes and lapsed into slumber. Walter stood and took off toward Warehouse 8. Off to one side, he saw Norm and Sean corner Tadashi who had all but run out of ammo and weapons, both obvious and secret. Would he surrender, or go down in suicide by cop? On his other side, Patrick and his team were still battling Donojok, Ian and Patrick keeping the rock monster distracted while Miles was fiddling with some mechanical equipment or another, apparently in an attempt to push Donojok the last foot over the wall into the river.

But the warehouse was all that concerned Walter now as he crossed the open yard. It was not as graceful as any kind of chase one might see in the movies. For one, this was the beginning of winter, and almost Christmas, which meant the shortest days of the year, and the mountains on all sides darkened everything even earlier. Walter ran by the light of enormous yard lamps which did a fair job of lighting the yard, except it still left the corners draped in shadow. For another thing, this was the beginning of winter, which meant snow and slush in equal parts, and the fast-approaching darkness brought the cold with it, turning the melted snow and water into rutted ice on which he simultaneously had to fight for balance and try not to trip as he ran.

The concrete pad outside the warehouse had built-in heaters to keep it clear, and Walter was almost surprised when he did finally regain his footing. He skidded to a stop just in time as a short row of enormous icicles came crashing down in front of him. Whether this was done on purpose or sheer coincidence was of little concern, though the thought was a disquieting one. It meant that Rifun was waiting for him, planning for him.

The lights inside the warehouse were giant industrial lamps, but it did little to light the maze of cargo containers within. Walter paused outside, trying to listen and pinpoint Rifun's location. All he heard was the sound of shooting outside and the wind rushing through the warehouse, rattling loose odds and ends and poorly attached sheet metal.

And Walter felt fear. He didn't like going into large, dark, scary places, especially when he was chasing a murderer with abilities far superseding his own. He might have even been content to let Rifun get away and fight another day, except he'd taken Tommen again. Once was a crime worthy of having his clock broken. Twice was more than deserving of having his throat torn out by a vengeful father. So, with ice in his veins, Walter stepped into the warehouse. As soon as he did, all the lights went out, and all the doors came slamming down to the ground, plunging him into total darkness.

For a moment, Walter froze, feeling fear turn into terror but fighting to not let it paralyze him. He closed his eyes, forced his muscles to relax, and tried to breathe. Even as he did, he remembered all the lonely nights in a dark cell, the wails and cries and mad ravings of those who sat in their own cells, waiting to live, waiting to die, waiting for anything at all. It was that same fear that had driven Walter to make a desperate attempt at escape, and why he still slept with a tiny night light in the corner of his room.

But in that moment, he also felt a sort of peace, as well as a sort of silly shame, like how he would shake his head in wonder when Tommen did things that to him seemed so important, but were mundane to the average person. Now he felt that for himself, shaking his head that a grown man over a hundred years old and far removed from those lonely prison nights would still sleep with a night light, like a frightened child afraid of the scary monsters in the closet.

Except those lonely prison nights had caught up to him again. First, it was Cassius, the guard whom Walter did not remember, though that did not mean he hadn't been there. Then there was Rifun, intent on getting Walter confess to something he obviously saw as a crime. And there was the fear again, snaking its way up and down his spine. The fear of a secret being exposed. The fear of losing Tommen's trust because of it. The fear of losing Tommen today before he ever got a chance to explain it. The fear of the dark.

It only took about thirty seconds for these thoughts to pass through Walter's mind, and by that time, his eyes had adjusted to the gloom as oblique light filtered in through filthy windows in the man-door and a single tiny window way up high in one wall of the warehouse. It wasn't much, but he could make out the vague, shadowy shapes of the cargo containers as a whole. Odds and ends lurking around on the floor waiting to catch his foot or his knee, he was screwed, but at least he had some idea of a path through this maze.

Still, he stood and waited another thirty seconds or so, just listening, picking out every sound, analyzing it, categorizing it, and filing it away. The tiny scratches of rat claws on concrete. A draft that stirred up some dust, loose tape and papers, making the overhead catwalk stir and shake just a bit with a metallic clang. The fighting outside that sounded so far away now, as if it existed only in a dream or another life. Then he heard it. The scuff of a shoe, the smack of flesh hitting something hidden in the darkness, a muffled curse. Problem was, it sounded like it came from everywhere at once. With the containers messing with the acoustics of the room, unless a sound was right in front of him, it would be difficult to track.

But no good would come from him just standing there waiting for Isthim to surprise him from behind, and he doubted she would simply stop at leap frog this time. Or the rats would find him. Or Rifun would.

Still listening, Walter fished out his flashlight and let it and his gun lead the way as he started quietly through the maze. He did not move fast, taking the time instead to step carefully. He wasn't entirely sure why he bothered to sneak, really, since the light would give him away long before his footsteps, but he told himself he just had to keep listening. The warehouse was only so big, and if Rifun was hiding in here and hadn't escaped to the Wheel, he couldn't run forever. The only point to dropping the doors and trapping Walter in here with him was so they could "speak" privately.

"You know, Walter, I admire you. I really do."

Walter froze, tried to pinpoint where the sound was coming from. He turned the beam of his flashlight upwards to the catwalk, but the small section visible above him was empty. Trying not to let it get to him, Walter continued on his quiet walk. If he could get to a ladder and get on the catwalk himself, he could shine his light around from above and see more of the warehouse. Even better if the electrical panel was at or near the ladders.

"I have to admit, though, I've never understood why criminals demand that an officer come alone, or maybe a parent or lover come alone with no cops. Believe me when I say this is much more exciting."

"Yeah?" Walter said. "Then why did you run and bring me in here alone?"

Rifun did not answer that one right away, and Walter took it as a small victory. Rifun was off his game. He was accustomed to being the one in control, the one who called the shots, made the plans, and executed them flawlessly with a string of clever, witty statements that needled those he wished to taunt and draw deeper into his games. But now he wasn't in control. He wasn't on the offense. He was on the defense, running away and unsure how to do it gracefully. Or efficiently. Or at all, as evidenced by his lack of actually getting away when he had the chance and ability. Somewhere in his mind, Rifun thought he could still not only win this battle and kill Lily, but somehow attack and cripple Walter, or whatever his goal was for him.

"Three shots," Rifun began again, still not answering Walter's question. "One from a sniper, one from your Lieutenant. But where did the third one come from, I wonder?"

"I had a shot and I took it," Walter answered smugly. He came to an intersection in the cargo units. He tried to picture where he was in the warehouse and get oriented, but the maze had gotten him all kinds of turned around. In the end, he just picked a direction and went with it, heading left down a short path until he hit a wall. As he turned and went the other way, Rifun spoke again.

"Pretty risky to shoot at me while I was still holding your son."

"It was a calculated risk."

"The same one you made when you broke out of Beaumaris Gaol, I presume? You're a very lucky man, Walter. Have you ever thought about what might happen when your luck runs out?"

"Then I expect I'll have to order some more."

"Well, that might be easier than ordering me a new hand."

"Forgive me if I can't muster up enough sympathy to be concerned."

"I should be able to keep my ring and pinkie fingers, my thumb if I'm lucky. But the other two are completely toast. They're gone. Nothing left for them."

"If it keeps you from pointing a gun at my son's head ever again, I don't feel sorry in the least."

"Oh, come now, Walter. Surely you know better than that. Dominant hands only matter in writing and long-distance target shooting. At close range, either hand will do. What is it they say, 'close enough for horseshoes, hand grenades, and nuclear war' ?"

Walter forced himself to keep his steps light even if he did speed up a touch. Problem was, Rifun was right, and Walter didn't relish the idea of him holding Tommen at gunpoint yet again. Briefly he entertained the idea of taking a vacation after this was all over, just getting away, relaxing, and putting as much time and distance between them and this moment as possible. They hadn't been on a real vacation in years, since Tommen started middle school. He needed to make that up to him.

He turned a corner and was rewarded with the sight of a man door. As a bonus prize, there was a ladder not three steps from it. Carefully, he turned his flashlight beam upwards to search the vicinity but saw nothing. Nervous and not wanting to, Walter holstered his gun, turned off his flashlight, and ascended the ladder, still trying to step lightly but unable to stop the clang-clang-clang of his shoes on the rungs and his belt hitting the sides.

As soon as he touched the top, his gun and flashlight were out again, sweeping the catwalk. There were only so many walks, but they were long. And yet, as he navigated his way just far enough to shine his light over the entirety of the walk, he found it all empty.

Confused, frustrated, and not a little afraid, Walter returned to the ladder and slid down the same way he used to do when he was a much younger man, hopping off two feet from the bottom and using the momentum to sweep his light around the area, to say nothing of the jolt it gave his knees.

Only immortal, not indestructible, he reminded himself. *And certainly not a spry young man anymore.*

As he continued his search, he was also forced to wonder where Micaiah and his troupe had gotten off to. Weren't they supposed to be here helping, making sure Rifun didn't escape? He could step into the Wheel at any time, get away, and leave Walter searching this warehouse forever, or at least until...

Relief swept through him as his flashlight found the electrical panel. Given that the lights outside hadn't gone out when the lights inside had gone out and the doors came crashing down, it was an easy bet that he'd only just flipped off the power to the inside of the building. Walter hurried toward the panel and flung it open.

As expected, it was only a flipped switch. The sticker labels had been marked and remarked and covered and marked again, but there was one marked Lights and another marked Big Doors.

He first tried the one marked Big Doors, figuring that it would at least let in some natural moonlight and the light from the yard lamps, even if Rifun had disconnected the indoor lights. He flipped the switch, unsure if the doors were supposed to start opening or just stay closed until they were opened by a button at the doors or manually. Well, only one way to find out.

Walter went to the large door next to the man door and found a smaller panel with three buttons marked Open, Close, and Stop. He pushed the Open button, hoping the door couldn't smell his fear and remain closed. Either it did smell his fear, or it just didn't work, as the button did nothing. He didn't even hear sounds indicating a mechanical failure. There was, quite simply, no power to the doors.

He returned to the electrical panel and, hardly thinking, flipped the switch marked Lights, a lump in his throat threatening to choke him if it didn't work.

It did work, though, and he almost cried with relief anyway. There was light again, and he could see. But at the same time, this also came with the realization that the dark had simply been another ploy to get under his skin, weakening him before a confrontation. The doors had been the real target, a way to cut him off from all outside help. There would be no *ex machina* rescues here tonight. Micah, Micaiah, and whatever help they'd had lined up all meant nothing now. It was just him and Rifun.

"Congratulations, Walter."

The voice was close, and Walter whirled—tried to make it a whirl instead of a frantic, frightened jump—to see Rifun not thirty feet away. He had to have Banded to get there because Walter was sure he'd shined his flashlight down that way just before turning on the lights. Now Rifun stood there, two chairs in front of him. In one, Lily sat, head down, but the blood on her shirt told Walter that she'd been beaten. He couldn't tell if she was alive. In the other chair, Tommen sat, looking weary, like he'd lost all will to fight back. Both were bound and gagged, but Isthim stepped forward to remove the gags.

"We couldn't have them giving away our position all the time," she said silkily. "It would take all the fun out of the game."

"Some game," Walter said grudgingly.

"But isn't everything about this a game?" Rifun said, trying to recover his charisma and control of the situation. "Lily here buys votes like a game of Monopoly. You hunt us down like a game of Clue. And poor Tommen just gets caught up as the Monkey in the Middle."

"Let them go, Rifun," Walter ordered. "There is nowhere to

run."

"Oh, you are referring to your dearest Lieutenants and the Hands and candidates they bribed and manipulated into helping you? Well, Isthim already took care of one and the other couldn't get in here if he tried. And even if he did, he would be in no better situation that you are now, Walter. Because whether it is you or a hundred of you, I still hold the gun." He indicated his revolver, now resting awkwardly in his left hand. But at close range, right or left didn't matter.

"Well, as soon as my guys take care of your goons, they'll be in here, and they'll not only take off your other hand, but they'll take off your head as well. Unless you surrender."

"Ah, so noble of you, Walter. Always offering a way out even for the worst offenders. Is this because you're a nice guy, or because of some sense of guilt that you escaped when no one else did?"

"Not my problem and we're a hundred years removed from it," Walter informed him firmly. "Try again."

Rifun grinned and tilted his head just a little bit as if pleased with himself. "So, you've put the past behind you, have you? Time to move on, start new, turn over a new leaf as it were? So, instead of being a convicted murderer, you've gone to the other side, become a cop. What better way to run from your old life than with a completely new one? And yet, you've still held onto your old life, but he didn't even know it. So, Walter, before your son dies, why not turn over a new leaf with him, huh? Why not tell him who you really are?"

Walter looked at Tommen. He looked so tired and confused, like he'd aged fifty years in just a few minutes. Walter wondered if his hearing had recovered any.

"Tommen..." he began, and trailed off.

"Dad..." Tommen said, his voice pleading.

Walter closed his eyes. He looked at Rifun. "No. I will not let you manipulate me or him with this *bullshit*! He is my son!" He took a step forward. Rifun, still off his game and apparently unprepared for Walter's sudden confidence boost, took a step back. "And you will not take him from me."

Rifun blinked, then appeared to recover. He glared at Walter, but also glanced nervously at his wounded hand, still tightly bound, though the cloth strips were long since soaked with blood. Finally he looked at Isthim and nodded.

Instinctively, Walter jumped back out of Isthim's range, but he could not stop from staring as she advanced and began changing colors. From pink to white to red to green.

"Did you know," Rifun said, "that about forty percent of Borelians are what translates to in English as bitoxic. Not as impressive as bisexual in my opinion, but I digress. They have the ability to change color and so toxicity. Normally these toxicities are closely related, sort of like colors on the color wheel—blue and green, red and orange, and so on.

"But there are other Borelians called *vodrak* Borelians, or, as I call them, Vorelians. Only one in every million Borelians is a *vodrak*, able to change and move through the entire Borelian spectrum of color and toxicity, some colors which we can't even perceive and so don't have names for." He indicated Isthim, who still advanced on Walter, who still tried to keep out of her range. "Isthim is one such Vorelian. She was one of the most feared Borelian Fleet Generals, becoming so feared in fact, that her own people tried to imprison her for fear of what she might do."

Rifun chuckled. "Oh, and get this. She's a Harvester. Only an Intervention Harvester, true, but she'll kill you and then get paid for all the years you had left. And Tommen will be right here watching."

Isthim did not need to hurry as she moved, always in such a way that whatever fight they had would be within Tommen's line of sight. Whatever wounds she'd sustained from the earlier fighting were now either healed or she was able to work through them as she moved from color to color to color.

"Dad," Tommen said weakly.

"It's all right, Tommen, I'll just be a few minutes longer than expected," Walter told him, trying to sound confident, like this was what he did everyday.

"Dad, blue is for the respiratory system, yellow for the circulatory." His voice was still awkward, fighting to speak around apparent hearing loss. "White is for sexual pleasure and red is for the five senses. Green is for your clo—"

Tommen was unable to continue speaking as Rifun forced the gag in his mouth once more. Walter tried to Band, to give Tommen more time to speak, but Rifun not only broke into the Band, but he shredded it to bits like a cat clawing up a roll of toilet paper, leaving Walter momentarily weakened. He was saved from Isthim's first attack only by instinct, putting his arm up and moving, trying to gain leverage and manipulate her arm, but she slithered away like a snake.

Walter danced away, putting some distance between him and her, studying her as she changed colors. Some colors appeared the same to him, but he guessed these were the colors that he could not perceive. There was no telling what those colors meant for her toxicity, but at the same time, did it really matter which color did what if they were all toxic in the end?

She was a Harvester, which meant that she had to touch him anyway. But as long as there was distance between them...

Walter raised his gun at her. Suddenly she was in front of him, Rifun Banding her to give her the speed, her hand around the barrel of the gun. She was silver now, and as she held the gun, it started to get hot, steam, and melt, and her fingers went through the metal like a hot knife through butter. Walter dropped the gun as it got too hot, and he slipped behind her.

Right. Silver for metal. His only choice now was hand-to-hand combat. Thankfully the only thing not covered was his face, but half the point of hand-to-hand was the closeness. If she didn't touch him and kill him, whatever proximal side effects she gave off certainly could.

"Lily is already dead, Walter," Rifun said, like a brother or close friend delivering bad news that he simply hadn't yet accepted. "You gain nothing by fighting Isthim, and you have everything to lose. Why not just tell Tommen the truth?"

"Because you made him deaf, firing your gun at close range like that," Walter spat. "And even so, I'm not giving you the satisfaction."

"Cute excuse when it's a couple of high school girls, but we're grown men with some very high stakes. Can't you set aside your pride just this once?"

"I might ask the same of you." Walter almost missed the last word as he leapt back to avoid a blow from Isthim who was black now. He couldn't say he felt any side effects from the near-hit, but if he had to hazard a guess by her movements, which had become slow and slightly uncoordinated, black did something to put more dead weight into her, like infusing her with lead, making each blow that much more powerful.

He took the opportunity to get in and land a solid kick to her back. Then he realized the side effect of the black. She did not stumble or buckle, but rather absorbed the energy. It made her heavier and slower, but if she did manage to hit Walter, it would be with all the force of that kick plus probably a thousand more just like it. It would send him flying, if not kill him outright.

She did not stay black for long; it was a color of opportunity, not prolonged fighting. Instead, she changed to red. The five senses. As a rule of thumb, she could steal any or all of his senses and so enhance her own. But she would not be absorbing any blows into herself, so when Walter got the chance to trap her arm and wrench her shoulder out of place then kick her away, he took it.

As she went sprawling to the ground, her color changed again, this time to a silvery blue, one that Walter took to mean an imperceivable color. But it gave her incredible flexibility like a snake and, with an incredible twist that would be impossible for any contortionist, she was back on her feet.

"You see why I like her," Rifun commented, like a commentator giving his unwanted opinion for some sports or political news.

"I'm beginning to get an idea," Walter admitted.

"But, we're on a timetable. Wrap it up, darling."

Isthim barely looked at him, but she nodded. Her color changed again, this time back to pink. Walter couldn't say exactly what she did except that it was reminisce of whatever she'd done outside, as if she could expand her influence in short bursts, use a small amount of energy to gain the compliance of a group of people long enough to slap them unconscious and leap frog over Walter.

But this time, Walter was determined to be ready for it. He didn't have his gun, but as long as he stayed ready for anything, any color, any toxicity or side effect she had to throw at him would have no effect. He would be ready for it, and he would fight to the death. Better to die with Tommen thinking he was his father and maybe, just maybe, a hero too, than live and destroy their relationship forever.

Isthim seemed to realize that he'd steeled himself against her attack. She sighed and looked at Rifun. Rifun Banded, but Walter was ready for that too. He wasn't able to destroy Rifun's Band, but he was able to throw up one of his own, fast enough and Fast enough that Isthim just missed him. But Rifun was ready with a double-whammy, and he penetrated Walter's Band like an arrow, dragging his own Band in behind it with Isthim coming through like a leaf caught in a swift current, tumbling toward him out of control.

There was a loud crash, and Walter instinctively squeezed his eyes shut. The whole exchange lasted hardly four seconds, the whole fight barely three minutes. He hadn't felt anything touch him except the concrete coming up to meet his head. Gingerly, he moved his hand to feel the back of his head. Yes, there was blood, but it didn't feel like a terrible wound. A skin wound, and the head always bleeds the worst.

Cautiously, he opened his eyes and tried to sit up, coughing at the dust. When it cleared, he came face-to-face with the business end of Rifun's revolver.

"This has taken entirely too long," he said coldly.

Off to one side, Walter watched Isthim, now an unknowable color, handle each bullet with care, making sure to touch every square millimeter before approaching, opening the revolver while Rifun still held it, and loading them one by one with slow, deliberate care.

"Cassius tells me I'm indecisive," Rifun said. "Says I can't decide whether to do things straight arrow or play games with my targets. Maybe so. He also says that one day it will be the death of me. Again, maybe so."

"Isn't the bad guy's monologue supposed to be where he reveals his overarching evil schemes and tells me how feeble I am?" Walter asked.

Staring up at the blackness of the revolver's barrel, Walter could not say he wasn't afraid, but he was ready, even as he realized his vest had been taken from him. He took the oath to protect and serve and die if necessary. Dying for Tommen was not only necessary, but absolutely worth it. And maybe even a little ironic, in a certain light. Walter could not see Tommen behind Rifun, but he could hear him, fighting the chair and chewing on his gag, trying to speak.

"Maybe," Rifun conceded, answering Walter's question. "Today is certainly a day for possibilities. But like I've told Tommen and the boys and now you, if I tell you my evil schemes and you somehow survive, then I only shoot myself in the foot. The risk isn't worth it."

"Well, like you said, at close range, dominant hand shouldn't matter. Or are you really that bad of a shot? Is that why you got Cassius to do the killing, because you either don't know how or are otherwise unwilling to get your hands dirty for the sake of an evil scheme?"

Rifun chuckled. "I like you, Walter, I really do. And I admire you. Facing death with such cool certainty and still finding it in you to come up with some witty, smart ass remarks. But you're right, what is a monologue without evil schemes but simply the bad guy talking for the sake of hearing his own voice?" He pulled back the hammer. "Goodbye, Walter."

Several things happened then. First, Rifun pulled the trigger, sending a bullet speeding toward Walter's head at a thousand yards a second. Second, Walter fought to build the same Band he'd made when trying to intervene and save Tommen from being shot, feeling the heat of the bullet strain against both his Band and his forehead as he simultaneously tried to move out of the way. Whether it was a roll, jumping to his feet, or flopping like a fish out of the way, he was determined to get out.

But Rifun was faster still, sensing Walter's Band and barreling into it with a temporal body slam. Walter steeled himself against it, gritting his teeth as the hot metal of the bullet brushed his jaw, forcing his Band to stay in place. It was like trying to run from a pack of wolves while a rabid raccoon chomped on his ankles, or ride a horse while someone hung onto one side of the saddle and tried to drag him off. He hopped and jumped and tried to kick him off, but Rifun dug Time Tendrils into him, anchoring him.

Walter released the Band as he felt the pain of the bullet enter his body, ripping apart the skin between ribs, tearing through muscle with white-hot ferocity, and burying itself deep in the tissue and bone just at the bottom of his right scapula, sending more waves of sharp pain through his shoulder and up and down his spine, momentarily dazing him.

But that moment was all Rifun needed, and as soon as he sensed Walter losing his grip on his Band and his concentration, he fired again. Walter feebly tried to Band, but it was like holding up a bed sheet against a machine gun as Rifun tore that Band apart as well, instead encasing Walter in a new Band, one that forced him to feel every moment of the second bullet tearing through his body. This one found his sternum, hitting just the edge before ricocheting off into the intercostal space and ripping through his lung before exiting out his back, taking a chip off his other scapula.

He felt sticky warmth spread through him as blood filled his chest cavity, and he reflexively coughed up blood as if he was just trying to clear phlegm. But this would not clear. He fought for a breath that would not come as he aspirated the blood into his good lung. He was drowning in his own blood, but his body still fought to survive, even though the more it struggled, the worse it became.

Then Tommen was shouting, screaming, and Rifun was laughing. No doubt they were making their escape, leaving Tommen to clean up the mess. Still, blood filled Walter's mouth. Then he was turning on his side, spitting blood. He was rolled back, resting on Tommen's thighs as he knelt down and tried to take his shirt off.

"No, no, no, Dad, no," Tommen sobbed. "Come on, Dad, breathe. You have to make it."

In the movies, the hero always said something encouraging or insightful. Even if they were going to die, they still had some final words of wisdom to impart to their child, spouse, or successor, something that eased their passing.

But Walter had no words. He had no breath. Maybe it was simply that he wasn't the hero in this movie. Or maybe because this was real life, and that's usually how things worked out.

Chapter Twenty-Seven
Out of the Frying Pan

Tommen collapsed more than knelt beside Walter, ripping his sweaty, grungy shirt off and pressing it uselessly against the wound just below the heart. There was not as much blood as he might have expected from a chest wound, and he dared to hope that it had missed the heart. That was to say nothing for the blood Walter was spitting as he glanced once at Tommen before collapsing into unconsciousness.

Tommen jumped as someone slipped down beside him, just as uncoordinated as he was. To his surprise, it was Lily.

"Thought you were dead," he said, hoping he sounded somewhat normal.

He could see she was speaking, but between the cloudy deafness in his right ear and the blood rushing deafeningly through his left, he could not make out her words. He turned his head. "I can't hear you. Left ear."

"I said it's a trick that Harvesters stole from the Timekeepers a long time ago," Lily told him. "I'm more surprised that Isthim didn't realize what had happened, but I'm not complaining."

More selfless than Tommen understood her to be, and as uncaring of modesty as he figured her to be, Lily also took her layered shirts off, pressing one to the other chest wound and another on a thigh wound Tommen hadn't even realized was there. Judging by the blood bubbling up, the bullet had probably found an artery. Lily got up on her knees and removed her belt. She held it out to Tommen.

"Pull this as tight as you can around his thigh above the wound," she commanded sternly, making sure she spoke more to his left ear. "Keep pressure on everything; you'll do him no more harm at this point. I'm going for help."

With that, she stood and ran for the man door, throwing it open and running outside. Tommen fumbled with her belt, tried to slip it around Walter's thigh. He got it wrong two or three times before finally needling it where it needed to go and pulling it as tight as he could, feeling the weakness from his days stuck in the cave.

He had just managed to get the belt tight enough to almost completely constrict blood flow when he heard footsteps, and suddenly someone was sitting opposite him, another police officer. Pat, Tommen thought his name was.

"You're doing good, son," Pat told him. "Medics are on their way."

Tommen looked at Walter's face, pale but not bloodless as dark blood still dripped out from his mouth and bubbled from his nose. He was drowning in his own blood. Desperately, Tommen touched his face, trying to elicit some reaction, trying to feel some kind of life in him, trying to feel anything at all.

Then, suddenly, he did feel. It was like when Predict came to him, a sudden revelation that he felt absurd for not recognizing before. He felt a sense of greater Time. Not just Time itself and how it affected him, but he felt Walter's place in Time. For the moment, they were synchronized, both moving in Base Time. But Tommen could feel the Time around Walter, feel that he could manipulate it. Without hesitation, he threw all his might into Slow Banding him.

By the time the ambulance arrived, Pat was sure Walter was dead as it appeared that he had stopped breathing. But, when one medic brought out the suction unit and began sucking the blood and fluid from Walter's lungs, Tommen bumbled forward into the Slow Band he had created around Walter and released it. He began breathing again, air instead of blood.

"Three entry wounds," the other medic reported. He gently turned Walter on his side. "Two exit wounds. One head wound."

Tommen looked around. The whole yard seemed to be filled

with flashing lights and men and women in one uniform or another. A couple more medics were flagged down, and they began working on cutting away Walter's bloody clothing and having dressings prepared and available as soon as they were needed.

"Hemothorax around the lungs," one medic said. "We need to put a tube in and drain it or he'll never make it to the ER."

So that's exactly what they did, making an incision between Walter's ribs and sticking a tube in. Tommen watched the blood start to drain out. He couldn't help himself; he got sick. He stumbled away from the scene but only ended up in the gloved hands of another medic.

"You okay, son?" he asked. Or rather, that's what his lips appeared to be saying.

"What?" Tommen wondered stupidly. He scolded himself for no good reason. He couldn't hear what they were saying, dammit. He looked back at Walter who had disappeared in a sea of medics. "That's my dad." He choked on the word.

The medic gave him a sympathetic look and nodded, turning and saying something he couldn't quite catch. Then he was being escorted to an ambulance not far away where Micah was speaking to both a medic and an officer who Tommen did not recall as being part of the original rescue team. Micah had a rifle slung over one shoulder.

"He may not be able to hear you," Micah said loudly, walking toward them. Tommen looked and saw the medic who was escorting him had been talking. And walking on his right side. Micah went on, "He had a gun go off right next to him. Hasn't been quite right since."

"What's your better ear, son?" the medic asked, moving to stand in front of him.

"I can hear out of my left ear," Tommen told him. He didn't tell him that both ears were still ringing pretty badly, his left aching like he'd had his music just a little too loud, and his right feeling a bit like the sound of an overinflated balloon trying to be used as a balloon animal. "What about my dad?"

"He's in good hands," the second medic promised as they got

him inside the ambulance on the cot. "Let's talk about you for a minute." Her voice was gentle, and it honestly made him want to cry, but he'd long since run out of tears. "What's your name?"

"Tommen Forbes."

The medics looked at each other. They knew exactly whose kid he was, as if they hadn't already guessed.

"We understand that you've been held captive for a couple weeks," the female medic went on.

"Yeah," Tommen admitted. But just like any vacation, now that it was over, it was like no time had passed at all. Considering how boring it had been, it wasn't exactly a stretch of the imagination.

"Tommen, did they hurt you? Beat you? Anything like that?"

He shook his head. "No. It was just boring. Didn't get a lot to eat or drink."

Somehow, talking about it helping him organize his thoughts. Not that there was a whole lot to organize. They hadn't beaten him or tortured him or done anything bad to him. They all starved together. They all sat in boredom together.

"And what about today?" the male medic asked, moving to the same side as the female medic.

Tommen felt new tears well up. "He put a gun to my head and pulled the trigger." He closed his eyes. "I thought I was going to die. I closed my eyes, and when I couldn't hear anything, I thought it was all over. Then I felt myself being moved, and my dad got me to safety." He took a shuddering breath. "Where is he? I want to see him."

"They're still working on him," the female medic told him, almost guiltily.

He was about to say more when he saw a cot go by, two medics on either side to move and steer it, one working suction, another working a respirator of some form.

"Dad!" Tommen cried, moving to get out of the ambulance.

The two medics were on him in an instant, holding him down almost effortlessly, sensing his weakened state. Tommen went into a blind rage, trying to fight them off, bawling like a child, finally giving up and just sobbing, curling up on his side, never feeling more defeated and alone. The medics left him like that for a minute before the female medic touched his shoulder.

"We're going to take you to the emergency room," she told him. "Your dad is going to have to go into surgery. In the meantime, the doctors will look you over, and you can get cleaned up before going to see him when he wakes up. Sound fair?"

Fair? Nothing was fair about this. But it was a plan, a course of action for the time being, and he didn't have any better ideas. After a second of trying to collect himself, he simply nodded and shifted position in the cot so the belts could go over him properly. Then the male medic hopped up in the driver's seat, released the parking brake, and off they went.

"Whoa, what's that?" Tommen asked as the female medic brought out a bag of clear fluid and a needle.

"If you've been starved for two weeks, we need to get fluids and vitamins into you to combat dehydration and deficiency."

"I got water every day. I mean, it wasn't the whole eight by eight deal, but I did get it."

"It may have been insufficient. Even so, there's no harm in being on the safe side. Now then...this won't hurt, but you'll feel a poke."

Tommen gritted his teeth as she cleaned a spot on his arm and slipped the needle into a vein. He almost jumped out of his skin at the cold rush that initially spread through his body. Then he relaxed and managed to read the medic's nametag. Melissa P.

"They're going to help my dad, right?" he asked.

"They're going to do their best," Melissa told him. "It's not far to the hospital, and if he was alive and breathing when he left, they should be able to get him to trauma in time."

"Should." Tommen looked away.

She tried to distract him then by probing for any other wounds, but the most she found were scars from old fights. It all seemed so silly now, his fighting with Tyler. He tried to think back and recall if any of them had actually been over something substantial, but he couldn't come up with anything. He fought because he thought it meant something, made him appear not weak, like it might bring about some measure of respect. Walter had sacrificed himself for Tommen. Tommen was an amusement, an attraction, like a freak show at a circus. Walter was a real hero.

"Tommen?"

"Hm?" He glanced at Melissa, jerked from his daydreams and lamenting.

"Do you have any type of medical history that the doctors should be aware of? Heart conditions, past surgeries, medications, anything like that?"

He shook his head. "Nothing pertinent. No meds." Though he might need some after all this. He wasn't stupid. There was every chance he'd need anti-anxiety medication, anti-depressants, to say nothing of what he might need for the hearing loss. His heart rate jumped at the thought, and he hoped desperately that his hearing would return with time. If he could have pinpoint Banded, he might have tried to find out for himself, Band his ears for a couple months and see what happened.

Then they were at the hospital. The ambulance that had brought Walter in was already there, devoid of life. Tommen, not considered a priority amid the sudden rush of dead or injured policemen from the shipping yard, plus a myriad of domestic abuse cases straight from the holidays themselves, ended up having to wait in the hallway for a room to open up. Him and three other people.

That was all right, though, Tommen figured. He would have rather people-watched than sat in a small room with nothing but the TV for company. He might be able to distract himself by making up stories about the people as they went by. That old lady just leaving had a heart attack, and the younger woman with her was her daughter, just grateful that it looked like they were still going to have a Merry Christmas. But those people over there, the young couple and baby, they were waiting for news on her father and long-lost uncle who had gotten into an altercation when the long-lost uncle showed up at the door of the brother who hated him the most. And that doctor was approaching that young man to tell him his girlfriend would be fine, that she hadn't been seriously injured in a car accident.

A nurse came by once, giving him the briefest, softest greeting Tommen had ever heard, assuming she had said anything at all and he wasn't completely deaf yet. She read the brief chart that had been scribbled out and checked the fluid bag. It wasn't quite empty and she made some comment about that being good. He wasn't terribly dehydrated, probably wouldn't need a second bag, just a nice bottle of water and a good meal, maybe some vitamin supplements once they did some blood work to actually check his levels. She wrote something down on the chart and then left, and he still wasn't admitted to a room.

A short time later, a room did open up for him, but he still had to wait probably half an hour before a doctor came in to see him. He was a middle-aged gentleman and a prime candidate for Just For Men, having gone prematurely gray. His nametag said Harold McComb, D.O.

"How's my dad?" Tommen asked. "Walter Forbes. He came in before I did, he was—"

"I know," the doctor said gently. "I know your dad; he's been here several times on cases. When they brought him in, he was breathing. The trauma doctors got him stabilized and sent him directly to surgery. I knew you would ask about him when I came in, so I checked on him not five minutes ago. He is still in surgery, but it looks very promising, and he should be admitted to recovery within the hour."

Tommen's vitals on the monitor reflected his relief as he relaxed. Walter was going to be okay. He was going to make it. It might be a day or two, but they would both be home together again. Even if Christmas was late, they would still celebrate it together again. Tommen closed his eyes and breathed, enjoying the relief and suddenly overwhelmed with fatigue. Now that the anxiety and the worst was over, he was ready for a good night's sleep.

"So, let's talk about you for a minute," Dr. McComb said, sensing Tommen's relief and willingness to move on and talk about something else. "If I understand it correctly, you were held in captivity for approximately two weeks with very little food or water, correct?"

So Tommen relayed the story yet again. Captivity only. There was no reason to burden him with the whole bit about one of his captors being a rock monster and another being like a neon yellow Victoria's Secret model. As he spoke, he watched the doctor read his chart and make some notes on it.

"You told the medic that there was a gun fired next to your ear and you reported some hearing loss. Can you compare what it was like then and now?"

Tommen sighed. "When it first happened, I couldn't hear anything at all but the ringing. I mean, my dad had to literally talk into my ear to tell me anything. Now..." He shrugged. "I don't know. My left ear kind of hurts like I had my music player too loud, and my right feels...cloudy. Like cotton or something."

"Okay." McComb nodded, his expression thoughtful. "The fact that hearing has come back to some degree is promising. I'll have one of the guys from audiology come down and take a quick look, make sure there isn't anything serious going on that needs immediate attention. Then you can set up an appointment for a more thorough examination. How does that sound?"

It sounded awful. It sounded like giving up. Where were the TV doctors when you needed them, the ones who proposed outrageous theories and left-field tests and medications and drama, who found an answer and a cure in some obscure disease or medicine from the Pango Pango tribe of central Africa? Why did he have to sit here with this real-world doctor who went straight from easy symptom to easy diagnosis and plan of action, one that involved making Tommen handicapped? Because this was the real world, and sometimes a damaged ear was a damaged ear. No mysterious disease or highly experimental and potentially dangerous medicine needed.

"Okay," Tommen said, not meeting his eyes.

"Very good." McComb sounded relieved. He had a full house and probably had some impatient person in another room who was just irate about not being catered to like a king. "I'll get the audiologist down here as soon as I can. Once he gives you the okay, I see no real reason to keep you here. Go home. Drink a good amount of water and have a wholesome meal. Don't stuff yourself, and nothing rich or sugary. Carbs, protein, lots of fruits and veggies to get your vitamins. If you start to feel a little sick in a day or two, something's not quite right, come back and we'll take another look."

Tommen simply nodded, and the doctor left. Why couldn't he have gotten the cafeteria ladies to his room as soon as possible instead of the audiologist? Food seemed like a much higher priority at the moment, especially if they were worried about him being in captivity for two weeks with little food or water. Exactly what were their priorities here?

Didn't matter, he supposed. His dad was almost out of surgery.

Tommen figured he must have dozed off a little as the next thing he knew, the door was opening and Micah and Micaiah walked in. Micah looked grim and a little sleepy, and Micaiah looked freshly washed though his shirt had bloodstains on it.

"How are you feeling, Tommen?" Micaiah asked.

"You were supposed to help him!" Tommen cried, surprising himself just as much as the twins. "Where were you?!"

"Rifun did something, Tommen. To the whole building. It prevented us from getting in." Micaiah sighed. "I didn't even realize what had been done until it was gone, and Rifun had already escaped."

"What did he do?"

"It's difficult to explain."

"Try me." By now, Tommen didn't care if Micaiah started in a word salad of technical terms, just as long as he knew what had happened and had an idea of how to keep it from happening again. Because if and when Rifun found out that both Walter and Lily had lived, Tommen doubted he would make a second mistake. He would try something much worse and much more permanent. Something more in the realm of Cassius' method of elimination.

So Micaiah did try to explain it, and it was indeed something of a word salad of technical terms relating to Time. But the way Tommen understood it was that Rifun had somehow managed to make the warehouse a quasi-dimension, sort of like the Wheel. It still existed Earth-side and could be seen, but it could not be accessed except by a dimensional tear like the portals to the Wheel. But because it was only a quasi-dimension, caught between the two "realms" as it were, it actually made it harder to get into because of the risk of losing the portal and disappearing into the "Land In Between" from whence no one had ever returned.

"How was Rifun able to do that?" Tommen wondered when he was finished.

"I wish I knew," Micaiah admitted. "It's an ability that has not been heard of since the formation of the Wheel. Yes, some have tried it, foolishly, but they were considered insane, and they always got swallowed up by their creations. That's how we get 'ghosts' and whatnot, as they exist in a quasi-dimensional realm, making random apparitional appearances. Some would say that's how we get demons, those who are more practiced in the dimensions and more stable at controlling it once they've been swallowed up, using hosts in our world to commune with us. But since the two dimensions can't be completely reconciled, the hosts get tossed about in fits of rage and, well, possession." He shrugged. "Up to you if you believe it, but that's the theory."

Made some sense, Tommen figured, but in the moment he didn't really care. He was about to ask more, but the door opened again and another doctor walked in. He was old, short, fat, but his eyes were bright behind a pair of bifocals.

"Are you Tommen Forbes?" he asked, his voice remarkably

strong and youthful sounding.

"Yeah," Tommen replied simply.

"I'm Dr. Howard." He moved forward to stand beside Tommen, small bag in hand, a proper doctor's house call bag from the 1930's. "Dr. McComb asked me to come down and take a look at your ears, said you had a gun go off next to them."

"My right ear. Left hurts, but I can hear out of it just fine, I think."

"Yes, the loss of hearing in one ear is a bit disorienting, and it can be confusing for the person to gauge if anything has been lost in the other ear. I'm just here to make sure everything appears structurally sound and nothing needs immediate attention. Obviously, you will need a more thorough examination."

And he went on and on for what seemed like forever before finally taking a look in Tommen's ears, looking this way and that, touching, pulling, shining a light, asking questions, and generally carrying on for a lot longer than Tommen deemed a quick visit to see if anything seemed to be structurally wrong. And if he was looking for something wrong structurally, wouldn't he need like an MRI or something to actually view his inner ear? Or was he assuming that was fine since Tommen hadn't dropped dead because of some kind of bleed?

"Well, everything looks well enough, structurally speaking," Howard said, putting his bag back together. "But I want to get you in as soon as possible. When you check out, I'll have the receptionist set you up for an appointment with one of us audiologists. It won't be before the end of the year because of the holidays, I can tell you that. Everyone wants to get in before the new year and the new deductible. So until then, stay away from loud noises, and it's not just loud music or loud cars. I don't know what you have planned for Christmas, but if the conversation around the dinner table starts to get loud and people are shouting to be heard, I would recommend removing yourself from the situation. The first twenty-four hours are especially critical, but the first week or two is just as important."

"I understand," Tommen said. Not like Christmas dinner was a rousing experience anyway.

"Excellent. Then we shall see each other again soon. Until then, have a merry Christmas and a happy New Year's."

And he left, which basically meant Tommen was free to go. But before he could do much more than throw the blanket off him, the door to the nurse's station opened and Dr. McComb entered, looking less than enthusiastic.

"I can go, right?" Tommen wondered.

"Are you going to visit your father?" McComb inquired.

The way he said "father" instead of "dad" set off tiny red flags in Tommen's mind, but still he asked, "Can I? I mean, is he out of recovery?"

"He is, but I'm afraid I have some bad news."

Tommen felt his heart race and his stomach twist. "What is it?"

"Your dad did very well for the surgery, but he has since refused to wake up. We tried giving him more time, giving him drugs to bring him around, but an EEG showed that he has lapsed into a coma."

"How is that possible? I mean, I know he hit his head, but...it wasn't bad. He wasn't shot in the head or anything."

"At this time, we don't have an explanation either. We're hoping that simple rest will help, but so far he has been completely unresponsive."

Fear twisted in Tommen's gut, and the only thing he could think of was Isthim handling each and every bullet and loading them into Rifun's gun. He couldn't remember what color she'd been, but she had done something to him.

"Can I see him?" Tommen asked, his voice strained, willing himself not to cry. He was done crying. He was all cried out. He was exhausted.

McComb nodded and gave him directions to Intensive Care.

"You can use my shirt," Micah said, taking off his outer shirt and wordlessly reminding Tommen that his shirt was gone, used to keep pressure on Walter's wounds. As Tommen took the shirt and fumbled into it, Micaiah spoke.

"We'll catch up to you, but we have a few phone calls to make."

"What? Why?" Tommen demanded. "What could be more important right now?"

"Your dad has on record—with the police department, the hospital, I don't know—all the important documents, living will, trust, all that stuff. In the event that something happened to him, he named us your legal guardians. You're only sixteen, Tommen, with no other family. Unless we are granted legal guardian status, you can do nothing for yourself, not even check yourself out of here. Then you go into the custody of the State. Believe us when we say you would rather have us than the State watching out for you. Make sense?"

Tommen sighed. It did make sense, but that didn't mean he had to like it. Just like scheduling an appointment with the audiologist felt like giving up on ever recovering his hearing, having the twins appointed over him as his legal guardians made it feel like they had already given up on Walter and were ready to bury him. Still, he did want to be able to leave and get out of this awful place, so it was a necessary evil, he supposed. In the end, Tommen simply nodded, and he and the twins parted ways.

He found Intensive Care easily enough, and a nurse directed him to Walter's room.

At first, his dad seemed almost invisible amid blankets, bandages, and miscellaneous IVs and tubes. Otherwise, it looked like he was merely sleeping. Tommen's only source of hope came from the fact that he was still breathing on his own, the tubes in his chest there to keep the pressure around his lungs consistent. Gingerly, he approached his dad's bedside.

Bandages were wrapped around both shoulders with thicker gauze covering the sites of the bullet wounds. Tommen glanced at his chart. His left shoulder blade had been chipped by a bullet, the other cracked on the inside where it stopped another bullet. The shot to the thigh had all but severed the artery, but it was otherwise a clean shot. He had some stitches in the back of his head where he'd smacked the concrete, but there was no apparent damage to the skull or the brain, which completely stumped the doctors as to the cause of the coma.

Briefly, Tommen wondered if the poisoned bullets had also affected the doctors who removed them, or if the poison had been pretty well absorbed into Walter by that time. Then he decided it didn't matter.

Tommen pulled up a chair and just sat. His mind was blank. He'd thought too much, cried too much, seen too much. He had nothing left to give. Nurses came and went almost incessantly for one patient or another, and the lights were always on, even as the clock ticked midnight.

"Can you believe all that happened nine hours ago?" Tommen said aloud. Maybe he was trying to do some talk therapy, bring Walter out of his coma. Maybe he was talking to himself and was going insane. "Nine hours ago, we were finally reunited. We missed that dinner reservation, you know. Instead, here we are, finally have time to sit down and talk and..." He didn't even have the energy to sigh anymore. "You're so far away, and no one knows why. Well, I know why, but it's nothing anyone will believe. And even if they did believe it, there's probably no cure for it since it's not a disease found on Earth. But I guess that doesn't matter, does it?" He looked away, looked around the room. "But you'll pull through, won't you? You have to. I don't want to be stuck with Micah and Micaiah for two years." He choked a laugh. "They'll try to send me to bakery school or some shit."

But Walter didn't respond, just lay in his bed, unresponsive, motionless until a nurse came to turn him. When Tommen asked her why she did that, she explained it was to prevent bedsores. Made sense. But Tommen didn't care. He would rather Walter have a thousand bedsores than be in a coma. Would have rathered Walter had anything but be lying there in a coma. Even beating cancer seemed more attainable than beating this coma. Then Tommen chastised himself for belittling cancer patients. Sure, there were always stories of survivors, but there were also stories of those who didn't make it, and it wasn't fair to them.

Tommen wasn't sure what woke him, but he'd apparently slept for a couple hours. It was only about ten minutes later that the twins walked in, looking as haggard as he felt. And he still hadn't showered or shaved or done any of that. He wanted to, still, but he also didn't want to leave Walter's bedside.

"We had to wake a few people up, but the documents came through," Micaiah told him. "We can leave whenever you're ready."

"I'll be ready when he wakes up," Tommen said.

But still he stood. He wanted to do something, anything. A hug, a kiss, a kind word. And maybe Walter would wake up. The most Tommen was able to do, as he got his feet numbly under him, was take Walter's hand, more scarred and leathery than he ever remembered it being, and speak softly to him. "I'll be back, Dad. I promise. And you will get better. You have to."

He sullenly followed Micah and Micaiah out of Intensive Care to Audiology where a receptionist waited for them, more specifically for Tommen.

"So, Dr. Howard said he wanted to get you in as soon as possible," she said. Her tone was more enthusiastic than Tommen's mood, but it was not oblivious. She dealt with this all day, and she was deadened to it. It did her no good to get emotionally involved with all ten thousand cases that walked in and out of the hospital on a daily basis. "So, you won't get in before the end of the year, but we did get a call from one of our patient's families and they canceled an appointment." Translation: one of our old patients kicked the bucket. Would you like to take their place? "It's for January 1st."

"The doctor's in on New Year's Day?" Tommen wondered, almost amused that with all that had just happened, he was bewildered by an audiologist being in on a holiday.

"This doctor is, yes," the receptionist confirmed. "He's Jewish, so his New Year's is a little different than ours." She shrugged.

"Which is great for you if you want the appointment. It's at one-fifteen."

Tommen shrugged. "Sure, might as well. Doing myself no favors by waiting."

"Great. I'll just put you in." She collected his information and wrote him a reminder card. "And we'll see you January 1st at one-fifteen. Happy holidays."

Tommen took the card wordlessly, checked out of the hospital, and he and the twins headed out to the parking lot. The cold hit Tommen like a ton of icy bricks, and he hurried across the lot after Micah and Micaiah to their car which felt like it took forever to heat up. Briefly, he reflected that lately everything seemed to be happening in terms of forever. How quaint.

"We'll take you home so you can shower, shave, change your clothes and whatnot," Micah was saying. "Then you can pack a little bag and stay at our place. At least for tonight."

"So I don't do anything stupid?" Tommen wondered coldly.

"Something like that," Micah admitted after a pause.

The car ride was silent after that, and soon enough they were pulling in the driveway.

Tommen had never wanted to be home more than he did at that moment, and home had never looked so inviting. As if on instinct, he reached for his key in his pocket, but it was gone, so he went fishing under the doormat. Only once he was inside did the twins get out of the car and follow him in.

For a moment, Tommen was overwhelmed just by being home. Everything was exactly as he remembered it as far as placement, but the whole house looked like it had been hit by some kind of maid service. Since Walter was never fond of maids either economically, morally, or ethically, Tommen could only conclude that he had a compulsive cleaning habit when he was stressed. And what was more stressing to him than having his son kidnapped before his very eyes by a deranged lunatic?

"You okay?" Micaiah asked behind him.

"Yeah," Tommen answered blankly.

He headed down to his room, almost reaching for a backpack that wasn't there. He was stunned again when he pushed open the door to his room. It was clean. And not like he'd cleaned it up enough to pass Walter's inspection, but it was clean. Like clean-clean. Like everything had been removed, meticulously washed and cared for, then replaced. There was not a speck of dust on the wood, no carpet fiber out of place, and his bed had been made and clothes folded like the Sargent was going to be by any minute with a ruler and a straight edge.

Tommen almost felt guilty about stripping off his dirty clothes and throwing them in the laundry basket, was almost afraid that someone was going to yell at him for taking a set of clothes off the neatly-stacked pile. But he made it to the bathroom unscathed, never so happy to see the awful 60's paint monster's vomit bathroom.

He turned on the shower, stripped the last of his clothes, and looked in the mirror. If he didn't know he was looking at himself, he wouldn't have recognized the man staring back him. He looked gaunt with greasy hair, dark, puffy eyes, and sharp cheekbones that were covered by a beard. A real beard. Not the little spindly, wiry fuzz of a prepubescent teeny-bopper, but the beard of a man. And never had he looked more like his pa. It was like his pa was staring back at him across time and space. As Tommen got in the shower, he wondered what his pa would think of him right now.

He debated keeping the beard, then decided against it. If he did want to grow it out, it would be because he wanted to on his terms, not because of being kept in a cave for two weeks.

By the time he got out of the bathroom, Micaiah had found food from the depths of rather sparse-looking cupboards, and whipped up something quick. Spaghetti by the looks of it. Pasta made carbs, ground beef the protein, and the sauce counted as a serving of vegetables, right? So, he was technically following the doctor's orders. Right?

"You're looking better," Micah observed.

"I'll give your shirt back after I wash it," Tommen told him.

"I'm not worried about it right now. Get something to eat."

Tommen ate in silence at the tiny table while the twins went into the living room, sitting on the couch and waiting patiently. They spoke. He saw their lips moving, saw their body language, heard a few words if they raised their voices, but otherwise it was lost to him. He looked away when they caught him staring, pretending to be engrossed in the food. He enjoyed spaghetti, had made it countless times himself a thousand different ways, but now it was tasteless. It was simply a nutritional substance to satisfy the demands of his body and replenish potential vitamin deficiency, nothing more.

He couldn't remember much after that. Probably a full stomach and finally being warm again made him sleepy. Probably he just packed a backpack and went with the twins to their house. Probably he fell asleep in the car. He briefly remembered Micah setting him up in the guest bedroom, hurriedly cleaning off the bed and moving a few other things that had collected over time.

Tommen didn't care. He wasn't picky. He simply crawled into the bed and curled up under the blankets. He might have cried. Probably cried. But mostly he slept. He knew he dreamed but he couldn't remember what about. All he remembered was waking up and being sure that someone was watching him. He woke up several times from a fitful sleep, finally surrendering to being awake around nine. He was pretty sure the clock had read three or so when he got his spaghetti, which meant he'd only gotten a few hours of sleep, and bad sleep at that.

Micah looked no better. He was already awake as well, sitting at the dining table, coffee in hand.

"You sleep well?" he asked.

"No," Tommen answered. "You sleep at all?"

Micah sighed and looked in his mug at the steaming brown liquid. "No. You hungry?"

Tommen wanted to say no, but his stomach had different ideas, grumbling in reply. Micah rubbed his eyes and got up. He was saying something, but Tommen couldn't catch it.

"Tommen?" Micah asked.

"Huh?" Tommen looked at him.

"What do you want?"

He hesitated. He was hungry, but he didn't want to be rude to them. And he felt like eating would somehow offend Walter, like he'd written him off and was out enjoying a nice meal. But his dad had entrusted Micah and Micaiah with his care, and they were like his crazy uncles, to say nothing of also being his bosses.

"Tommen?" Micah said again. "Can you hear me?"

"I can hear you," Tommen told him. He shrugged. "I don't know. Something not baked."

In the end, Micah ended up making French toast, the smell bringing Micaiah out of his den, though he looked like he'd also been awake for some time.

"They will call, right?" Tommen asked as they sat down and passed around the syrup. "If something changes?"

"They should," Micaiah said evasively. "If he wakes up." *Or if he dies.* "You have your phone on you?"

"Yeah."

"They'll probably call you first."

"I want to see him."

"Tommen..." Micah began.

"It's Christmas *fucking* Eve!" Tommen shouted. "I want to see him!"

"Okay." Micah put his hands up. "Okay. Let's finish breakfast first. Then we'll get ready, and we'll go. All right?"

It almost felt like a hostage negotiation in itself as Tommen somberly agreed and finished off his French toast, his tongue pleased with the flavor and stomach very pleased with the meal, but his brain unable to make him convey any sort of gratitude. He cleaned his plate and ended up doing the dishes, a feeble attempt at gratitude and a way to distract his mind. Then he retreated to the guest bedroom to change clothes and simply wait.

The conspiracy theorist in him said that the twins were intentionally stalling on going to the hospital. The more rational part of his brain said that there was only one bathroom for three bedrooms, and they had to take turns showering and everything else, plus a lack of sleep made them a little slower than normal. Tommen rubbed his eyes. They were supposed to be open today, the bakery packed with people panicking with last-minute orders for rolls and breads and pies. They weren't supposed to be sitting at a hospital, and certainly not babysitting.

If not for the door being open, Tommen knew he would have missed the phone conversation going on just outside in the living room. It was Micaiah. Tommen turned so his left ear was to the door, but he kept his gaze fixed on his phone.

"Lily, slow down," Micaiah was saying. Lily? What was she calling for? "Just take it easy. Now, what are you saying?" Pause. "You're...you're j—ah, shit. It is. You're sure? How sure? Fuck. Tommen isn't going to want to hear that. Shit. Shit, shit, shit." He sighed. "Okay. Yeah, we're just about ready to come over there anyway. Yeah, we'll meet you there. Uh-huh. Bye."

"Who was that?" Micah asked, his tone more concerned than curious.

"That was Lily," Micaiah told him.

Then their voices disappeared for a moment before Micaiah popped his head in. "You ready?" He tried to hide the fear, but Tommen had been around enough of it and felt enough of it himself lately to know what it sounded like.

"Yeah," he replied, getting out of bed like he hadn't heard a word.

He followed them out to the car and pretty soon, they were on their way. But the traffic on Christmas Eve at ten o'clock was a hell of a lot worse than at three in the morning, and Banding only helped if there was a clear path to drive. When cars became gridlocked, no amount of Time manipulation was going to make them move any faster.

The hospital was the same as Tommen remembered, not like he expected it to change much in just eight hours. People still hurried to and fro, patients, families, doctors, nurses. An ambulance pulled out of the ambulance drive and entered mainstream traffic, another run completed. Just another number to add to the rest of them, a few more hours to log on the time clock and add to the paycheck. The same for every other medical personnel walking around.

They went up to Intensive Care, still as active and as busy as ever with doctors, nurses, and general hospital staff, the janitors and maintenance men. When they entered Walter's room, they found Lily sitting at his bedside, elbows on her knees, looking both contemplative, worried, and pleased with neither. She had two black eyes and a purple bruise covering most of her right cheek, but otherwise she had apparently cleaned up from her ordeal. She looked up as they approached and stood.

"First thing I want to know," Micah said, "is how you lived."

Lily seemed almost offended, not because he'd spoken and cut her off, but because he'd made the conversation about her first and Walter second. Still she answered, more graciously than Tommen would have guessed, "It's a trick the Harvesters borrowed from the Timekeepers a long time ago. Essentially, I Harvest myself, putting all my years into a Time Capsule and storing it within myself. Then I take just a little bit of time and, in some cases that I did, a disease, and I put it to the forefront of my body. So when Isthim went to Harvest me, she found only a couple months left to live because of a very serious tumor she thought was in my brain." She shrugged. "She cursed and said that was probably why I was a greedy bitch who was throwing so much money away on these elections, but she took the bait. So I lost a couple years and a potential disease. No sweat off my back."

The twins just looked astounded.

"Lily, are you feeling all right?" Micah asked. "I mean...you're not..."

"A bitch?" She sighed. "Walter hates me as much as the next

person. But he still not only tried to save me from that madman, but he sacrificed himself for Tommen."

"He's not dead yet," Tommen cut in.

"Not yet. But he will be."

"What can you see?" Micaiah asked, Banding the four of them so they could speak privately.

"As you know, Isthim is a Borelian, which is the preferred Grandfather species. More than that, she has the ability to change into any color and so any toxicity she wants." She glanced at Walter. "Borelians can see a wider spectrum of color than we can, so I can't tell you what color she was. But I know that its abilities, especially its side effects, are a preferred way of getting rid of targets quickly and quietly, especially among races which are not engaged in Time."

"What are its side effects?" Micah wondered. "Why is Walter not waking up?"

"Essentially, it's a neurological poison. His body is functioning fine, but his brain will shut down with no real warning. His only saving grace is that two of the bullets passed through him before the poison could be absorbed, otherwise he would never have made it out of the surgery, if he made it to the hospital."

"But the last bullet did get lodged inside," Micaiah sighed.

"Correct." Lily gave Walter a long regard. "He's got a week. Tops. Five days more likely."

"Wh-what can we do?" Tommen asked, feeling his limbs begin to shake. "I mean, if you know what it is and where it comes from, there has to be some kind of antidote."

Lily shook her head. "Borelians know how poisonous they are, and they do go to great lengths to keep their friends safe. But you don't sick a Borelian on an enemy with the intention of them gaining an antidote. Even if they had developed one, they would never give it to you. Borelians are not keen on helping underdeveloped races."

"But Walter is a Captain Timekeeper."

"Doesn't matter."

"Can it be bought?" Micah asked. "Can they be bought or

bribed in some way to get us an antidote?"

"Assuming there even is one for this particular poison, with all the buying and bribing we've been doing the last few weeks, our money and our word is worthless now. We probably couldn't even get a free Time sample from the lowest marketplace if we tried. And if there wasn't an antidote and we somehow convinced the Borelians to help us develop one, it would take a lot longer than Walter has to make it work."

Tommen rubbed his eyes. "What about Time? The Time Capsules?"

Lily gave him a sympathetic look. "Tommen, Time is only Time. It's not medicine. It's not a cure. Time...Time will not bring back your hearing. If you got Micah or Micaiah to Band your ears and heal them, the only thing they are doing is accelerating Time, accelerating the Base Time needed for your body to repair itself."

"Then what about Slow Banding him? Make our own Time to find an antidote or get the Borelians to help us?"

"Tommen...the reason the Borelians are the preferred species of the Grandfathers...is because their abilities, especially ones like this, transcend Time. We could buy up all the Time in the Wheel and slow Walter to a crawl, but Borelian diseases act outside of them; they are fixed in Base Time. He has one week. No more, no less, and no matter what you try to give him."

Epilogue

Y ou failed. Again."

Rifun stopped his approach and took a breath. "Lily lives, this is true. But her reputation for this election has been tarnished at the very least. And we can always try again."

Cassius blew a puff of smoke from his pipe as he overlooked the valley. He didn't bring his pipe out often, only when he was deep in thought, like a well-practiced, stereotypical bad guy. "I'm tired of trying. Trying leads to failure, as you have demonstrated thoroughly. I want to succeed. What is the status of your friends?"

"Donojok was lured into the river. He may reappear downstream. Tadashi was captured and arrested, but he escaped. I have not heard from him. I sent Isthim out to hunt him down and bring him back."

"Leave him. He was always of questionable loyalty. At least this way we don't have to pay him."

"So then, what's our next move?"

"We wait for the elections. Political upheaval is never fun, but it is often necessary. Create enough fear and panic, and the underlings do all the work for you."

Rifun hesitated and Cassius caught it, giving him a glance from the corner of his eye. "What?"

"I was forced to kill Walter," he admitted.

"Because he wouldn't dance to your little fife?" Cassius was unimpressed. "Your obsession with Walter and making him confess to something so insignificant caused half this mess."

"I know. And I'm sorry."

"Everybody is sorry for something. Difference is, your sorry is entirely insufficient for the crime that has been committed."

Rifun met his gaze with a sullen acceptance. "Are you going to kill me?"

"No. But I am going to punish you." He studied Rifun for a moment. "You liked Walter. I know that. You killed him. And I am sorry that it came to that. So you are going to be, how shall we say, godfather to his newly orphaned son. You will not be seen as obviously as you were in this little adventure, but you will still guide him on the path to being an Akari-bearer."

"What must I do?"

"You will do a series of small tasks and some larger tasks. And they will not make sense to you, but in the end, when you see how everything comes together, it will be glorious."

Rifun had to admit, he was usually a little afraid when Cassius started talking like this, like some kind of nutty prophet. If not for the journal, Rifun might have dismissed him entirely. But he'd seen the power of the journal and the words contained within it. He knew it to be true, and he just had to trust that Cassius not only developed the abilities correctly and strongly, but that he would also lead them along the path of the Akari.

Eventually, Rifun nodded, even getting down on one knee before him. Better to stroke his ego than cause premature strife. "What must I do first?"

Keep reading for a preview of

Tick Tock

the next exciting installment of
The Chivalrous Welshman

Day One: Tuesday

Chapter One
Visiting Hours

Tommen sat silently at Walter's bedside, watching the little blips of the monitors that surrounded him. Hard to believe that just twenty-four hours ago he was alive and well and hugging him, both of them crying after being separated for two weeks when Tommen had been kidnapped by the madman Rifun Ndolo and his equally mad partner in crime Cassius. Both of them were extremely powerful Time Agents—Rifun, a Timekeeper, capable of speeding up and slowing down time and manipulating it in almost perverse ways; Cassius, a Harvester, reaping the Potential Time from dying victims to extend his own years or sell in the industry of Time.

Originally, they'd set out to kill Lily Guile, the richest Harvester in Time, notorious for buying votes in elections, bribing officials, and generally being a bitch. Rifun and Cassius had failed to kill her because of a little magic trick she used, but her demeanor had changed. Most of the credit went to Walter, who had taken three bullets, first to save Tommen. Saving Lily had been a side effect.

But one of Rifun's accomplices was an alien species known as a Borelian. Borelians were different colors and each color had a specific toxic effect on non-Borelians. Isthim was a very special Borelian called a vodrak, capable of changing her color and so having all the abilities of all the Borelians, making her extremely dangerous. She'd dueled with Walter and incapacitated him long enough for Rifun to get a hold of him while she poisoned all the bullets in Rifun's gun.

Walter's only saving grace had been that only one of the bullets had actually stayed in his body long enough for the poison to enter his system. But according to Lily, who knew what had been done, it didn't matter. There was no cure for Borelian poison, and he only had a week to live, maximum. And no amount of Harvesting, Banding, or Time was going to stop it or even slow it down.

So Tommen sat silently at Walter's bedside, watching the little blips of the monitors that surrounded him. He was still breathing on his own, and for all intents and purposes, he was perfectly healthy. Sure, he'd knocked his head on the concrete floor when he was fighting Isthim, but that couldn't account for his comatose state which had been ruled as ideopathic. More like idiot-pathic. There were times when Tommen hated his abilities. He was a Timekeeper also, though only a probationary one. Walter was a Captain. But there were times when he wished he could just tell the doctors exactly what happened, exactly what was wrong. Except that it really wouldn't matter. Lily knew what was wrong; she knew all the backstory. And she was even a doctor. But even she could do nothing for him. Before she'd left, Lily had suggested using what time they had left together to come to terms that Walter was as good as dead.

Tommen wasn't willing to give up, but despair had settled over him. Time was not medicine, simply a tool used to accelerate the healing the body was going to do anyway. Except Walter wasn't going to heal. And Micah and Micaiah Durvin—Walter's Timekeeper Lieutenants, Tommen's bosses at work, as well as now his legal guardians—couldn't come up with any tricks either, whether considered legal, illegal, or somewhat shady. The Borelians were used as Time's executioners. They were sought after because of their various poisons. And as Lily had put it, "No one sends someone to a poisonous execution with the intent of giving them the antidote."

That was even assuming there was an antidote. And if there was, the Borelians were no friend to those they considered a "lesser species." And if they did manage to find someone willing to sell the antidote to them, they would never be able to afford it. It was like seeing a man dying of thirst in the desert and offering to sell him a bottle of water for a million dollars. There was just no point to it. Furthermore, according to Micaiah, the Borelians were very good at the slave trade, and they made slaves of just about anyone, so if they felt insulted by their pleading or a pitiful offer to buy, they would not hesitate to kidnap them and throw them into slavery. So while Walter was, yes, dying as they spoke, without enough foreknowledge of the Borelians or how to approach them and not get thrown into slavery or poisoned themselves and die, it wasn't a worthwhile risk.

So Tommen sat silently at Walter's bedside, watching the little blips of the monitors that surrounded him. He thought about what he was supposed to have been doing today. He was supposed to be working, running around the bakery with the twins like a trio of headless chickens, desperately trying to fill last-minute orders for Christmas rolls, biscuits, bread, pies, whatever people wanted. Because what better time to shop than Christmas Eve, right? Not like they had any plans to celebrate. No, they were more than happy to cater to the stupid and the forgetful and the poor planners.

What better time to have a Western-style showdown at a shipping yard, right? Not like things couldn't have been solved peacefully or avoided all together. No, they just loved a good life and death firefight, especially when one of the hostages was an officer's kid. And Walter wasn't the only one who'd suffered. Five other officers had been killed, eight more severely injured. Rifun and Cassius and all their little friends were easily at the top of Charleston Police Department's Most Wanted list, but there was nothing they could do about it because Cassius had not been present at the yard when it happened, and Rifun and Isthim had just vanished. Reportedly Tadashi had also escaped police custody and was deemed a criminal at large, but Tommen knew he would be long gone by now, run back to his masters like a faithful—or faithless—hound.

"Tommen?"

Tommen looked up to see his two best friends Eric and Varad. Eric was a senior, forced out of the traditional classroom into online classes in order to escape the bullying and even death threats of basically the entire school after he was accused of raping one of his classmates, which he hadn't. Varad was also a senior, an American-born Indian whose parents were now dead set on moving back to India in order to escape what they perceived as belligerent racism, and return to their families. They had also been taken hostage by Rifun, but they had also been exposed to Time to such a degree that they could theoretically become Timekeepers themselves if they so chose. Except Time was a frightening thing to behold, and now they knew that he'd been living a secret double life. So to call them his best friends now seemed a bit presumptive.

"Lost in your own little world?" Eric asked, trying to smile and muster up some old comradery, but it came out as forced.

"What do you mean?" Tommen wondered, but he knew exactly what they meant. They'd probably greeted him halfway across the room, but he hadn't heard them. Rifun had fired a gun next to his head and all but destroyed the hearing in his right ear. His left was a little iffy, too.

"We've said hi, like, four times," Varad told him, having a harder time of not outright sneering at him.
Tommen sighed and looked away. "I lost the hearing in my right ear," he confessed. "I just...I'm sorry. But why are you here?"

"The news had the whole story," Eric said. "About the warehouse and stuff. They said that some officers had been killed or injured. We came down to make sure it wasn't your dad, but...I guess it was."

"Yeah. But why come down at all?"

"Respect. Answers."

Too much had happened the last twenty-four hours for Tommen to continue to put up with evasive answers and bullshit. Grouchily, he Banded. When he'd been beside Walter in the warehouse, he'd broken through part of his next segment of training and begun Banding other people and things he did not have immediately in his hand. Now he Banded the three of them. More specifically, he started out Banding the whole room, then worked to narrow and strengthen the Band, kind of like trying to stuff a giant blanket back into a box knowing that it only gets packed perfectly once but darn it if it will still fit, until it was just the three of them. It was a Fast Band, where they were in a Time faster than Base Time, so it appeared as though everything around them had stopped. It was a perfect Band to use when speaking privately.

"Don't do that!" Varad snapped. "It freaks me out."

"If you have something to say, you might as well say it, because it's only the three of us here now," Tommen told them flatly.

"So that's just what you do," Eric said. "You just will Time to go faster or slower and it does."

"It's not that simple. It's taking Time and...Banding it is what it's called. Bending it around you or something or someone else in order that you move on a faster or slower plane than everything around you."

"And you just do this at your fucking will?"

"Well...yes."

"What about all those fights with Tyler, huh? How many times did he kick your ass?"

"Often enough. I chose not to use it."

"You do, but I don't!" Eric ran a hand through his hair. "Last week, I had to go into school and take a test. Toward the end, I wasn't doing so good, and I remember wishing that I had more time to finish. And somehow I...I saw something. And when I touched it, like with my mind, my will, time fucking stopped. I was so freaked out, I almost couldn't finish the test. I did just to get my mind off it. After that, I had no clue how to stop it, or...make it go. I don't know. Somehow I did, though. I spent my entire weekend at work trying not to look at the clock because I was afraid it was going to, I don't know, spin out of control."

"I had a similar experience," Varad said, "but the opposite direction. It was like my life around me was suddenly sped up like an old VHS tape. I didn't think it lasted very long, but my father said I had been completely still for nearly fourteen hours. He was overjoyed, thought I had finally received a vision from the gods and entered a trance in order to receive it."

"Timekeepers are trained for years to control Banding and learn other abilities," Tommen informed them.

"Timekeepers? Creative name." Eric folded his arms.

Tommen shrugged. "That's just how it got translated into English. There are other roles. Harvester. Merchant. Time is a huge industry in some parts of the universe. Earth is just...not engaged."

"Yeah, and an alien shot your dad, right?"

"Rifun shot my dad, but his bullets were poisoned by an alien, yes. He's..." Tommen took a breath. "He's got about a week to live, tops."

That silenced the two of them for a moment. Eric broke the silence first. "I'm sorry."

Tommen rubbed his face. "Yeah. So am I." He looked at them. "I'm sorry you two got dragged into all of this. It's not fair, and it's not fun."

"You're right, it's not," Varad said, tears streaking down his face though he tried to play tough. "And I'm done. I am moving to India with my head held high."

Even as he turned, Tommen released the Band from around him and he seemed to freeze in place. Eric remained, studying him for a long moment.

"Tommen Forbes," he said.

"Yes?"

"You really are Tommen Forbes. The Tommen Forbes. From Forbes Cave."

"Yes."

Eric shook his head, but Tommen could see the information start to process. "Unreal. I mean, yeah, you read about this sort of shit in books or see it on like Star Trek or something, but you never expect it to actually happen. Just tell me one thing, Tommen."

"What's that?"

"Tell me I'm not crazy."

"Your mind has been expanded to a bigger universe and abilities beyond what the average person could comprehend. Of course you're crazy. But that doesn't mean it isn't true."

"Shit." He let out a breath. "What do I do, Tommen? I have a life. Not much of one since what happened at homecoming, but I have a life, I'm rebuilding. I don't want to deal with all this shit, Rifun and Timekeepers and all that. I just don't want to have this thing sneak up on me and I can't control it."

"I don't blame you. And I might know someone willing to help. Just stay here for a few minutes."

With that, Tommen released the Band. Varad stalked off without a word and without a glance over his shoulder. He left the room. The door didn't even completely close before it opened again and Micah and Micaiah walked in. Micah looked over his shoulder as Varad went past, but otherwise they made for Walter's bedside. Micaiah set a small vase of flowers next to him. It was almost weird to picture Micaiah buying a vase of flowers. He wasn't a bodybuilder, but he worked out. Then, to distinguish himself further from his younger twin, as if he might get mistaken for Micah's thin, lanky frame, he also deigned to keep some tasteful stubble on his chin, cheeks, and neck, straight out of some men's magazine Tommen was sure.

"Eric," Micaiah acknowledged diplomatically. "Didn't expect to see you here."

"The news said some cops were killed or injured. Wanted to pay my own respects since Tommen said his dad wasn't doing too well," Eric told them.

"No," Micah said sadly. "But it's much appreciated."

"And I know this is probably a bad time, but I have something I want to ask of you."

Suddenly the four of them were in a Fast Band created by Micaiah. "Does it have something to do with this?"

Eric shrugged and nodded. "Yes." He unfolded his arms and let them hang at his sides. "I don't want to be a Timekeeper or whatever. I just want to be able to control it."

To Tommen's surprise, they twins nodded. It was Micah who

spoke. "There are those who have been exposed to Time in such a way who don't wish to really do anything with it other than keep it at bay as you describe. It's not a difficult thing to do if all you want to do is keep it from surprising you. But I will caution you one thing: The Hands who govern Time allow only this. However, if you start trying to strengthen it, control it, get better at it, you will be required to either become a Timekeeper or be treated like a Runner."

"A Runner?" Eric looked at Tommen.

"Like a bootlegger," Tommen told him. "Those who use Time illegally."

"Didn't realize you could use time illegally, but okay. No, I just want to get through my day without suddenly being surprised that everyone else is moving faster or slower than me."

"Makes sense," Micaiah acknowledged. "Well, we can either teach you to control it, or we can do something called Suppression. It'll basically take away the conscious ability, but you'll still see Bands and be susceptible to Time-related incidents."

Eric shook his head. "Too much shit going on for me to want to get rid of it completely. I mean, what if that fucker comes back?"

"Fair enough," Micah said. "How much time do you have?"

"I don't know, I have to be up tomorrow so we can travel early, so I was hoping to get home—"

"How bad is it?" Micaiah cut in. "Is it on you all the time, getting you lost and disoriented and everything else?"

"It was at first. My mom almost called the cops or the ambulance on me for a psychotic episode or something. But, I mean, now that I kind of get what's happening, I think I'm figuring out how to make it go away."

"Very good. But even this rudimentary training would take a full day. Go home, go enjoy Christmas with your family. When are you coming back?"

"Oh, we're just gone for a couple days."

"Come by the bakery when you get back and then we'll set something up. Sound fair?"

"But what if I need it during dinner or on the road or something?"

"You're more apt to learn on the fly in high-stress situations," Tommen told him. He looked at the twins. "Which reminds me, I need to talk to you about something."

Micaiah just raised a brow but said nothing. "He's right. Just come by on your way back, and then we'll talk. Fair?"

Eric hesitated but nodded. "Fair." He took a few steps away then turned back. "And I'm sorry to hear about your dad, Tommen. I really am. He was a great guy."

Tommen could only nod.

Then Micaiah dropped the Band around Eric, leaving only three of them. "What did you want to talk about?"

"In the warehouse," Tommen said. "I made another breakthrough on my training. I was able to Band my dad. Like, I Banded him in order to essentially stall the bleeding until the ambulance arrived. Since then, I can Band other things, other people. I did it with Eric and Varad. Well, I started off with the whole room and then I narrowed it down, but I did it."

"Congratulations," Micah told him. "It's not an easy thing to learn, but it's the next logical step. Now you simply work at it like you did your normal Banding on yourself."

"That's it?"

"For all intents and purposes here today, yes. After your review, once you get into the Arena, then..."

He trailed off as they all began to realize what that meant. Yes, it meant that Tommen would be promoted to a full Apprentice, but it also meant that Walter would be dead. He wouldn't be able to take Tommen to his review, would not see him become an Apprentice, would not be his mentor.

Quietly, Micaiah let the Band drop. "I'm sorry. I didn't mean—"

"I know," Tommen interrupted him. "I know what you meant."

The twins pulled up chairs for themselves.

"Is there anything you want to say or want to talk about?" Micaiah wondered.

Forget the crazy uncles, the twins were like Tommen's second and third fathers. They were just as responsible for him as Walter ever was. Now they were taking him into their home while Walter was out. And in a week, they would probably start the process of taking him in permanently.

"It's not fair," Tommen said. "Maybe I shouldn't have provoked Rifun by following them from the museum or...maybe he should have just told me whatever secret Rifun thought he had so he wouldn't have been made to fight Isthim." He sighed, tried not to cry. "What secret does he have that is so important he would rather die than tell me?"

Micah and Micaiah glanced at each other. Tommen blinked. "You know it." When they only looked guilty, he continued, "Tell me. Obviously he's not going to."

"If your dad was willing to die for it, then we are obligated to keep it also," Micaiah told him sagely. "And I will not be the one to tarnish your opinion of him by telling you. Think of him only as the man you know him to be, not who he once was."

It was that sort of shit that spawned books and movies that usually had catastrophic outcomes for everyone involved. The secrets around a man everyone thought they knew. The secret life of the man a family once called father and husband. Why did the twins not see that? Maybe because this was the real world, and in the real world, catastrophic outcomes were pretty limited to emotional turmoil and broken trust and relationships. No horrendous world-ending schemes here.

"So. What do we do now?" Tommen asked after a few minutes of silence. "We know he's going to die. Should probably stop pretending otherwise."

"That's not fair and you know it," Micah told him, struggling to put an edge to his voice. "He's still breathing on his own, and I count that as a good thing."

"Why? Because his directive states that if he ever becomes dependent on machines with no viable hope to terminate treatment? He's got a week. Max. I'm not going to pretend like there's hope and wait for some miracle to happen, because it won't. It never does. There are no such things as miracles. Only science. And the science we have available and the science that could be available won't help him in time."

The only thing he got from the twins was a sympathetic look. Micaiah stood slowly, his knees cracking as he did. "Well then, if that's how you feel about it, I guess we're going to lunch. Care to join us?"

Not accepting the invitation would make him appear to be a whiny child throwing a temper tantrum in the corner and refusing to eat until he got his way. Accepting the invitation and going to lunch, however, would make Tommen feel even more like he was giving up on his dad, just leaving him and going about normal life while Walter labored away, the seconds and minutes counting down until the Grim Reaper swung his scythe.

In the end, Tommen did follow them out of Intensive Care. There was no way he was going to last a week without food, no matter how strongly he felt and how much he was determined to boycott everything but Walter's bedside. Wasn't like he would notice anyway.

They headed to a restaurant not far from the hospital and ended up waiting almost an hour to get a table. A few people recognized the twins as the owners of Bakery na hÉireann.

"I thought you guys were supposed to be open today?" their hostess wondered as she seated them. "I was looking forward to a cookie or something after work to treat myself."

Oh, she treated herself often enough, and the cookie had nothing to do with it. Tommen recognized her as a regular customer, but the only regular order she had was to see Micaiah and talk to him if she could. Micaiah was polite enough, but given that Time essentially made them ageless, he saw little point in dating. If he wanted to do something special for someone, he would, with no pretense. And if he wanted to get in bed with someone, he was more apt to check out bars, clubs, and other one night stand possibilities.

"We thought we would be open today too," Micaiah sighed, not having to fake his exhaustion as he rubbed his eyes. "And what I wouldn't give for it right now."

She gave them an odd look but said nothing except to mention that their server would be right with them.

"Are you ever going to tell her to stop flirting with you and move on?" Tommen wondered.

Micaiah shrugged. "Probably not. Better she flirts with me than some asshole, I guess."

"And you're not an asshole for leading her on?" Micah asked.

"Micah, what ever happened between you and Lily?" Tommen cut in. When both twins fell silent and looked at him, he went on. "I mean, I never actually heard the whole story."

"Why would you want to?" Micah wondered nervously.

"I don't know, because you avoid it. Because it impacted you. Because she's changed in the last couple days?"

"Well, you're right in that anyway; she has changed. I just don't think it will last."

Before Tommen could ask what he meant, their server came and took their drink orders. Only when he returned with the drinks and left the table to give them a few more minutes with the menu did Micah Band the three of them so they could speak.

"Why don't you think it will last?" Tommen asked.

"Because it never does," Micah told him. "Maybe this time will last longer because her life was at stake, but she always goes back to the same old Lily."

"What happened?"

"Lily was exposed to Time during World War II. Her mentor, Julianna, tried to Harvest her prematurely. Initially, Lily ran away from her, tried to get to her husband who'd gone missing overseas."

"Lily was married?"

Micah nodded. "She was. Her husband turned up dead, in the end. She spent almost two decades in Europe, trying to help them rebuild. She came back to America in 1962, just before the Dispersal. During the Dispersal, Julianna tried to hide her, keep her safe during the slaughters. That's how we ended up meeting. Julianna asked our mentors to keep her safe for a time since we were hiding out as well. After the Dispersal, we went our separate ways, but she and I always kept in close contact."

"Oh, come on, Micah, he's a big boy," Micaiah said. "Tell him the truth. You were fucking."

Micah rolled his eyes. "Fine, yes, we were sleeping together. But we did keep in touch after the Dispersal was over and things had returned to normal. Some years later, she wrote to me and said she'd gotten a job here in Charleston in NICU. Well, the District was short a couple Lieutenants, and we just happened to have completed our training around the same time. So we moved here and opened the bakery as a pretext. That's when we met your dad and we became his Lieutenants. And I met up with Lily and we started dating."

He paused and sighed. "Our letters were not frequent, but often enough. She had long periods of self-righteousness, the bitch she usually is, as she developed her Harvesting abilities, got rich, got her college degrees, dated rich men and so forth. Then she would have short periods of humility, most often after the rich men turned out to be abusive or after periods of economic instability where her wealth Earth-side or Time-side was threatened greatly."

"So why date her at all?" Tommen wondered.

"I don't know. I guess I thought that if she dated someone who, yeah wasn't rich, but was moderately successful and not an abusive asshole, it would help her find some stability. In the beginning it did, but she is a slave to greed and lust. She had her millions, but she always insisted on me buying everything. We were sleeping together, but apparently not often enough for her taste because after she got done with me, she would go out to a club and get laid with three more guys, and sometimes other women."

Tommen raised a brow. "I'm not expert, but that sounds like a sex addiction."

"Maybe," Micah admitted, "but love is blind. And I thought marriage would fix it. Probably the best thing that ever happened was her pouring that wine on my head and storming out of the restaurant. It took me a while to get over it, but I see now that she never cared anything for our relationship, only its benefits. And when that well ran dry, she just went looking for a new one."

"Oh."

"Take some advice from me, Tommen: If you want to date a girl, be friends with her first. If you want to sleep with a girl, date her for a little while first. Never jump headlong into a relationship with someone you know in your gut is unstable."

Tick Tock
Book Two of The Chivalrous Welshman

Early 2018

Author's Note

In the summer before my twenty-second birthday, I had the opportunity to work at a Native American children's camp for two weeks as the camp nurse. The camp was fantastic, lots of activities and learning and a wonderful preservation of heritage and culture—and the people were just wonderful. To my shame, I went home after the second day.

Most people, when they look at a calendar or a clock or something of the sort, see a calendar or a clock or something of the sort, and most events are sorted into neat little piles of cause, duration, and effect; before, during, after; yesterday, today, tomorrow.

But when I look at a calendar or a clock or think about time at all, I don't just see a calendar or a clock, I not only perceive it, but I physically feel time. It's difficult to describe, but the best I can come up with is like a river, winding its way here and there. Different events are like rocks or reeds. Fixed points, like work, are rocks, either big or small depending on how much time it takes. The drive into work, or from work, or the time between close events are like reeds, flexible but still there, brushing the river. And I have been known to lose my mind when something that is planned or something regular suddenly gets tossed out or becomes irregular.

I applied, interviewed, and got accepted for the nurse position months in advance, and I was honestly, truly excited. But as the time got closer for me to go to camp, I suddenly went blind to those two weeks. I couldn't see it, I couldn't feel it. It was exactly as if I had lost my vision or my hearing or any other sense; it was just gone, like a black hole had opened up over those two weeks. I could feel before and after, but not during.

That black hole never went away, even once we got a rough

schedule of events for the camp, and it was probably one of the few times in my life when I felt sheer, unadultered terror. I was going to be stuck in a camp with a bunch of children with no way to see or feel or perceive or predict anything. I told myself to tough it out, but it was like going deaf the day before band camp, and I left.

For those two days, I wished I could see Time again. I wanted to be able to feel it. And over time, my fears and wishes and experiences began to conglomerate into the beginnings of a fictional story about people who could control Time, make it move faster or slower and do all sorts of things with it. The result is what you hold in your hands now.